The Legacy Chronicle:
The Sword

By TH Paul

Lori,

   Thanks to you and the whole
Metevier clan for being supportive
of this project and helping my
first book get published. I hope
you enjoy the story!

Cover Art by Sarah Fensore
Map and Formatting by Shane Thurston

This book is dedicated to Ross Markonish, who taught me to love writing.

Teth-Tenir
After the War of the Lion

Thank You

To those who contributed their time, energy, money, or love to this book and were instrumental in its publication.

Hannah Amiet
John Amiet
William Bloch
Samuel Coale
Wes Covey
Ed Crockett
Mattie Crockett
Martha Crockett
Seth Crockett
Teddy Crockett
Jeff Crimmin
Isaac "Will it Work" Dansicker
Michael D.C. Drout
O.C. Dudley
Dain Eaton
Randy Ellefson
Kim Emms
Sarah Fensore
Jake Foley
Sam Gipstein
Dustin Grinnell
Lexi Helming
Deborah A. Hjort
Victoria Hughes
Ellie Hurd
Kelsey Jordan
Anna Kristie
Andy Lindberg
Janine Lipsky
Eliot List
Duncan McCreery
Jennifer Cope Metevier
Lori LaBerge Metevier
Mary Metevier
Gavin Newton-Tanzer

Nick Ostrofsky
Daniel M. Paul
Erica Paul
Molly Elizabeth Paul
Riley Paul
Teresa M. Paul
Seth Perkins
Beverly Peterson
Steve Peterson
David Quist
Sam Richardson
Scott Richardson
Paul Russo
Scott Scheeringa
Steve Seto
Paul D. Shapiro
Ankur Sharma
Christopher Shubert
Lauren Shumeyko
Bjarki Dalsgaard Sigurthorsson
Koby Soon
Cameron Stewart
Nick Stravous
TJ Struhs
Shane Thurston
Sean Valiente
Ian Vaughan
Peter Vose
Nick Walsh
Makoto Watanabe
Cameron Westerback
Ashley Williams
Freda Williams
Robert Williams

Prologue

It is an inn with a well-worn floor of solid oak and a hearty, welcoming fire blazing steadily in one corner. On a cold winter night such as this, a fire is an essential luxury. The patrons are spread about the building at various tables and benches, sipping on mugs of ale and picking at bowls of stew and roast chicken with an air of relaxation and calm. Outside, the wind bellows and blusters against the walls of the establishment, but does not pierce the cracks that have been well sealed by her many generations of caretakers. Unlike city taverns, this is not a boisterous or raucous crowd of customers, but a calmly familiar one. Accustomed to coming regularly for a drink and a bite to eat, they sit with a patience their long days of work require. Nothing at the Inn of the Four Winds happens suddenly, or at least nothing had for quite some time.

The bartender and innkeeper, a young man whose years suggested he should instead have been a stable hand or cook's assistant, rubbed down the long bar with a clean cloth. He wore away at the same spot with a casual boredom, as though some stain only he could see was refusing to come off the wood. His father, and his father's father, and most likely his father before him, had maintained the inn since its construction. The young man had, sadly, recently inherited his family's legacy by unhappy circumstance. His experience came from watching his recently passed father and, on nights like this, he had seen him massage this same spot methodically. Having learned from observation, he followed the example precisely.

There was no need to be ever-vigilant. Waitresses moved languidly about the floor, casually exchanging conversation with the customers and delivering food and drink at a steady but unhurried pace. The crowd, though the term would seem too unruly for such a passive group of people, was comfortable allowing this lethargic pace of life to continue about them. A few children moved around the floor at a slightly faster pace, playing at adventures with one another against invisible foes. To a one, their parents were grateful for the lack of true danger in their lives. On many nights there might be a minstrel or traveling bard in the inn weaving tales, but this evening the raised stages sat empty, though an outside observer would probably have thought this was preferable to the introspective men and women seated about the inn.

The door to the common area flew open and a large, but not especially tall, hooded figure swept in with a burst of cold air and

1

snow that stirred the sedentary patrons within. His cloak, for it was a he, swirled in the wind and swung behind him as he thrust the door closed and stamped his heavy boots free of the white slush upon them. Shaking himself like a dog he reached up and pulled his hood back, revealing a long mane of straight though disheveled grey hair. As he turned the crowd of curious onlookers relaxed at seeing a visitor they knew. A traveler he was, yes, but a frequent patron of the inn as well. Moreover, the man was an appreciated guest. There was an air of quiet respect from the patrons as he turned and took in the scene, a subtle hint of sadness on his face as he scanned those about him.

The innkeeper may have been young, but he knew the latest arrival on sight. He strode earnestly forward and bowed slightly, even as the older man dismissed the honor with a wave of one gloved hand. They spoke in quiet tones and the younger man led his new guest to the bar and a high seat at its curving corner, which hooked back at a right angle to the least popular seats furthest from the fire. The older gentleman, for surely with his fine cloak he was a gentleman even if his armor, scabbard, and other apparel was well-worn and weather beaten, settled with familiarity into his seat, taking a long look at the empty one to his left. Having skittered around the bar the innkeeper placed a mug and some bread rolls before him. The older man glanced at the brew in his mug and grunted, motioning the barkeep closer. "I would prefer the autumn ale."

The younger man looked at him, confused, saying, "But it's mid-winter, my lord."

"Do not call me that." The older man spoke sharply, then with a more civil tone added, "Your father always kept a spare barrel in the kitchen, opposite and sheltered from the ovens. I am sure it's still there."

Before he could elaborate further the owner had swiped the mug from the bar and sprinted for the back, downing half the contents as he went. Whether this was to save the already poured drink or because he was aiming to calm his nerves was not clear, but his newest guest chuckled softly to himself as he unhooked his sword and cloak and settled them against the bar and back of his chair respectively. As he did one of the children, a young girl in a faint blue dress of heavy wool, approached him and stood quietly by his stool. At first the older man glanced at her with a friendly smile and turned back to his bowl, taking a small roll and tearing a hearty bite from it. But, as he chewed slowly, he noticed she had not moved and, struggling to swallow his overly large first taste, asked cordially, "Can I help you, young lady?"

A few other boys and girls stood a short distance back, watching the exchange with anxious excitement and the man realized he had unwittingly acquired an audience. The young girl, her large eyes taking in his worn gear said, "Can you tell us a story?"

The man could not suppress a laugh at the impetuous question, both inquiring and demanding at the same time. He noted some adults by the fire, probably parents who had not expected to fill that role for at least a few precious minutes, realizing to their horror what was afoot and trying to determine how best to interfere. At that same moment the now-pleased innkeeper had returned with a frothing mug, stopping dead in his tracks, color draining from his face, at the sight of the daringly insistent girl whose hands had emphatically found their way to her hips. The entire scene caused the newcomer to laugh all the harder as he bent lower to meet his interrogator's eyes, "Well I think my old mind still holds a tale or two. Would you let me have a drink and then I could share one? Perhaps the legend of Bull the Warrior? Or the tales of the Sun People of the south? Or even the mysterious histories of the distant elven kingdoms?"

The girl did an odd thing then. She glanced back at her companions, who made desperate motions with their hands, urging her on. The brash approach that had marked her first inquiry suddenly evaporated and she struggled to meet the eyes of the man she had just addressed so directly a moment before. "We were wondering," she said quietly as she looked at her wood shoes rubbing uncomfortably against one another, "if you would tell us your story... we heard..." she looked once again at her friends, who now stood stock still in anticipation, "we heard you were a great hero, a king even!"

The excitement in her voice at the last proclamation was audible, but the silence of the unmoving and now very aware crowd of customers was far louder. The grey-haired man sat there and to all about him he seemed to have aged still further, his shoulders and head bent under a great weight none of them understood. He sat there for what seemed an eternity, before letting out a great sigh and saying, softly, "My story." He paused for some time as though pondering, "That is a very long, very sad tale, my child. However, if you and your friends truly wish to hear it then I will tell you."

The distant followers rushed forward earnestly, shouting and crying, "Yes! Yes! Please tell us!"

As they did frightened and embarrassed parents rushed forward, joined by the now terrified innkeeper, to protest emphatically that they were eternally sorry for the behavior of their offspring and swearing to do anything from grooming the man's horse to showering him with the few coins they had if only he would forgive them. He raised his hands to quiet them and eventually succeeded. As the roar died down to a dull hum he said, just loudly enough for all to hear, "The lovely young lady has asked for my story and I have agreed to give it to her." He paused and looked at the girl now blushing at the attention she had attracted and winked broadly. "But first I will wet my throat from the dust... er... snow of the road and then you may have your tale. And be warned," his face now took on a terribly serious look, "I will not abbreviate nor rush the telling. This may require many nights of dull prattling on my part. I will likely need a room..."

Before he could finish the sentence the innkeeper was assuring him his usual space could be provided at a hefty discount, free even, for as long as the traveler wished. Waving away invitations to seat himself on the stage and settling more comfortably into his stool, the man waited briefly for the attention of all. True to his word, he took a long pull from his mug as the already captive audience of adults and children, even the formerly panicked owner of the establishment, pulled stools, chairs, and barrels about him. Setting his mug down, and taking the initial requesting child upon his knee, he breathed deeply and began. "It was long ago, and I was then a very young man on a simple journey, and having no understanding of the hardest realities of the world or the great miseries and joys I was to experience."

As he continued, the eager listeners pulled their seats closer, and this is the story he told...

In the middle of a deep, indescript valley there sits a large meeting hall. Surrounded on all sides by open fields, small streams, and high mountains, it is an unusual sight as it rises up from the grass around its white marble steps. A smooth slate roof covers the top, supported on all sides by high archways of the same polished, simple stone as the base. From the outside the hall looks like nothing more than a nondescript temple to a long forgotten deity, its only curiosity being that it is the sole structure occupying the lands about it. Alone in the valley, the shadows of the roof creating a darkness so deep one cannot see beyond the arches within, the meeting hall waits, seemingly for no one.

Within the hall it is a very different matter. If anyone were to step beyond the pillars, braving the darkness, they would learn the truth behind this temple. Inside, three large hanging braziers of ever-burning flame dangle from the eaves. The archways, simple and uniform on the outside, bear strange and intricate designs to be seen by anyone setting foot within. On one, branches and leaves twist and intertwine to form the arch. Another is formed of broken blades and battered shields. Still another is made from the very bones of men. Just as one cannot see into the hall from its exterior they cannot look outward. Darkness shrouds the world beyond the arches and any attempt to leave through them would yield only frustration and failure.

The room itself holds only one item of interest: a massive table that extends the full length of the hall and houses spaces for fourteen chairs that are not there. At one end, the table is white glistening marble specked with golden stone, extending to a solid but pleasantly glossed oaken center strip, and finally ending in a blackened stretch that looks charred to the point of collapse. Despite the appearance of singed wood and rot, the blasted end is smooth to the touch and colder than a deep frost. That side of the table gives off darkness like a heavy blanket, just as the white marble end emits a pleasant light and warmth. Between them both, the simple wooden center holds a careful balance of the two, as though it consciously strives to temper the auras about it. This is where, long ago, the fourteen First Gods of Teth-tenir were swept into a great torrent of events that would forever change the Godly Realms and the mortal world they had once made and cultivated together. To those fourteen immortals and their lesser kindred, this sacred structure is known simply as the Archway Temple.

On this particular day the oddly isolated building had an even odder occupant. An old man lay sprawled on the floor, snoring uproariously. He was bizarre looking, with pale bluish skin and long snow-white hair with tiny horns protruding up and back from his forehead. His face was fair and smooth, but his fine red coat was rumpled, stained, and dusty despite there being no evidence of grime in the room. Suddenly, he shook his head and cocked it to one side as though straining to hear a distant sound. He blinked his eyes several times, at first from sleepiness and then in surprise. Standing, he ineffectively tried to smooth over his coat and baggy black breeches before he stamped his feet and emitted a massive yawn. Stretching his arms, he lethargically walked toward the table, muttering to himself in a strange voice interrupted by rhythmic grunts and groans, "So, it must come to this again. Hrrm, there will be a meeting, another fruitless argument. Will there ever be an end to this bickering? Hmm hum ho, as much an end as can be made hmm."

Reaching the table's center he held his hand over it and began mumbling to himself again, "What was the word hum ho, old word hmm, old." He suddenly brightened and smiled. "Ah, right! *Calivorsa, alopa calivorsa.*"

The table shimmered and from inexplicable depths within it came a small gong and mallet of shining silvery metal. The old man nodded satisfactorily and picked up the mallet, sizing up the gong hovering above the center of the table with an unhappy eye. "Endless, all of it. Pointless besides, hum hoom, whatever made my ancestors take up this position?" Grimacing he raised the mallet and sighed, "Let us begin then."

The shimmering gong made a clear note that hung in the air with a shine of its own, as though the polish on the metal lent itself to the sound. It subsided shortly and the man walked toward the wall behind him, the mallet still in his hand as the gong remained hovering over the table. Turning to face the expansive hall, he sat on a small, cushioned wooden stool that suddenly appeared beneath him. Placing the mallet on his knees he waited, albeit briefly.

The first to arrive was Terenas, the War God. All who were coming to the meeting would be the First Gods, the greatest of all the immortals, here to discuss matters of consequence to the sphere of Teth-tenir, which they had as one created. Though they had all once made that mortal world together, as a cooperative product of balancing powers, the First Gods are the purest forms of their ideals and ideals often conflict. As mortal beings began to emerge and spread across the home gifted to them, their interactions and evolution gave birth to more, lesser gods. In time, the mortals' passions also changed the more powerful fourteen First Gods in drastic ways. The gods had created mortals, but their relationship was complexly intertwined and in short order it had become mutually dependent. The gods needed the mortals and their faith as much as the mortals needed the gods and their blessings, perhaps even more so. That interdependence had spawned great contention over the responsibility of godly immortals to the residents of their greatest work: the world of Teth-tenir.

All this and more was well known to Terenas as the god stepped determinedly from his arch. His form was that of a bodiless suit of burnished armor that protruded spikes and sharp edges from all angles. His chair appeared before the table's center, opposite and to the left of the strange old man with the mallet. It was a titanic thing of metal and iron that fairly breathed danger. Terenas stood behind his seat, armored gauntlets on its back. He surveyed the table silently with glowing golden eyes from behind his fearsome helm. The old man spoke, "There is going to be more killing perhaps, hmm hum?" Terenas said nothing. "Ho hum, I thought you would be pleased that some new, hmm ho, warriors might be sent to you soon."

Terenas's eyes drifted to the blood red leather on his seat back and his voice rumbled like an avalanche, "There is no honor in these petty feuds."

The old man regarded him quizzically. "Hmm, I thought it was Paladinis who dealt in honor."

Terenas' eyes flared as he turned toward the elderly figure briefly, and then he swept around to seat himself, ignoring the other occupant pointedly. As he fell into his seat, two more shapes appeared from the arches near the blackened end of the table. The two eyed each other as if considering how closely their allegiance held them, and then together stared at Terenas with obvious contempt. Terenas glared right back through the new arrivals, and they shifted slightly under his challenging gaze. These two were not used to being treated with such open fearlessness. They were Balthazain and Xanoroth, Gods of Betrayal and Hatred respectively. A white-hot anger constantly raged behind Xanoroth's dark eyes as he surveyed the table, failing to conceal his fierce personality behind his stiff stance. He wore only a slim black robe with light silver trim and carried a black staff that he gripped with white knuckles, divulging his true emotions. Xanoroth strode to the table from his arch and sat in his chair of thorns, holding Terenas's gaze as though daring him to speak.

Balthazain was far subtler than his volatile brother. A handsome and cutting figure, he was dressed finely in a silk coat of forest green and matching pants with gold trim and well oiled leather boots. His hair was a light brown with gray fringe and he had a disconcerting smile that almost distracted you from his cruel blue eyes. He was utter confidence now as he studied Terenas from his archway, his hands folded carefully in front of his chest while he smiled sardonically. "Terenas, my good warmonger," he said smoothly, "I had expected a friendlier greeting than this."

Terenas' eyes blazed. "I do not associate with spies and cowards, and since you represent both I shall not waste my words on you."

Balthazain's smile never wavered, but his eyes grew tighter. "If you had truly studied the art you supposedly command you would know that spies are as much a part of war as those who shed blood on the field."

Terenas made no move to reply, and Xanoroth jumped at his opening. "You are the coward Terenas! Once you fought beside our father against the danger beyond our realms, now you hide in your pocket of the immortal world and wither away! Only the violence of mortal hearts keeps you fueled with their faith. Violence," Xanoroth grinned devilishly, "and hatred."

The War God refused to rise to the bait from Xanoroth, who fumed at his failure as Balthazain laughed. "You see brother? Even the hot-blooded Terenas may hold his anger when it suits him. That should come in handy today, I doubt this meeting has been called to form some kind of lasting peace." Balthazain's smile disappeared briefly, and a doubtful glaze overcame his eyes before he restored his outward aloofness and sat in his finely carved and leathered chair. "What could she possibly have to say that warrants this meeting? Is she going to again pretend to take the punishment she so rightly deserves? Even I find her past betrayals impossible to forgive."

Terenas lept up suddenly, his massive frame of metal and edges seemed to fill the hall. His eyes flared red and his hand strayed to his side. "You will not speak of her in that tone! Whatever her actions, she is one of the first of us, and you would not be here if not for her!"

Balthazain waved his bejeweled fingers disarmingly and a delicate file appeared, which he began rubbing calmly against his nails. "So I see not all threats can be ignored Terenas, but you know better than any the rules of our realm. You cannot harm me here, nor I you. We are on safe ground. However," Balthazain stopped his preening and pointed the file at the irate god, "if you are interested then I would be happy to welcome you into my home. I have several toys you might find invigorating."

Terenas managed to contain himself, his blazing eyes dimmed and he slowly lowered himself into his seat, ignoring the snickering of Xanoroth and the triumphant smile of Balthazain. The War God chastised himself for his foolishness; he had revealed a hot temper at a most inopportune moment. A calm and relaxed approach would be necessary at this meeting. As he cooled his simmering rage another of the sitters arrived.

Lorima, Goddess of Nature, appeared from her arch unaware of what had just transpired and sat gracefully on her living oaken chair next to Terenas without a word to anyone. Terenas eyed her and inclined his head in greeting, surprised to note that she nodded back. Such an exchange was rare between two who disagreed so often, but now they were clearly allied in trepidation of what was to come. Lorima had bark skin of the same roughness and color as a live pine and hair of moss that hung to her waist. She wore no clothing and her body had a shape vaguely humanoid and feminine, but at the same time indistinct in race or age. Her eyes were large golden orbs, imposing and with a powerful inner light that brooked no argument. She laid a calming hand on Terenas's own as though she could sense his mood and he relaxed visibly. Her eyes shot a sharp look at Balthazain who grinned back innocently and held up his hands in mock surrender.

At that moment a man and woman, both clad in white robes with gold belts and jet-black hair, appeared at the pearly white end of the table holding hands and speaking softly to one another. Delvidia, Goddess of Joy and her twin brother Reas, God of Hope, glided into the room, apparently unaware of the presence of the others. Reas looked to be consoling his sister, something he frequently did for everyone who came to him with a problem. Xanoroth's eyes grew still fiercer at his arrival and the raging god spat out sharply, "I see you still haven't decided whether to counsel your sister or sleep with her, Reas. Perhaps it is because you would not know what to do in bed with a woman?"

Reas calmly held back a furious Delvidia as he met Xanoroth's fierce glare and smiled gently, as though he were dealing with a child in the midst of an especially irrational temper tantrum. Carefully seating his sister at her glowing, soft-cushioned wooden chair he walked around to his own seat of beautifully carved stone depicting many birds in flight. Running his hands over the etchings he studied its intricacies before replying in a soft, lecturing tone, "Xanoroth, you continually seem to think that pleasure can come only from the flesh when you completely miss the greater joy that may be found in the soul."

"Spare me your filthy preaching, coward. Joy is nothing compared to the elation that comes from pain and rage."

Reas smiled and sat slowly, shaking his head. "To think that once you were the greatest advocate of peace among us. How much change has come with time."

Xanoroth's fury seemed to explode and he leapt up, hurling his chair to the floor and thrusting towards Reas a sword that suddenly appeared in his hand. "Damn your blinded eyes! That was never to be spoken of again! I will carve you into shreds and leave the rest to weep in the fires of our realm for all eternity!"

"No, Xanoroth, I think that shall wait."

All the seated gods turned in tense silence from Xanoroth's violent outburst to the woman who now stood behind a high golden throne depicting a sun shedding rays of bright light over the world. She was wearing a golden tiara that matched the silver one on Delvidia's head, though where Delvidia's stood out in her raven-black hair this woman's brilliant tresses by far outshone her own crown. She was Alinormir, the Goddess of Life and Guardian of Mortals, and an imposing presence to say the least. Blue eyes of hard flint stood out in her face, forcing Xanoroth slowly back and into his suddenly righted seat as his blade vanished. Gradually he averted his gaze and tried to hide the fear that washed over him as she continued to stare, reminding him of the one thing so many at the table had tried to forget. The silence was suffocating.

Her glowing presence overawed the other, lesser gods, as Alinormir sat regally in her seat, eyeing the far end of the table. She motioned for those who had come with her to sit also. Virinil, a plump but pleasant middle-aged woman with strawberry red hair smiled, if slightly forced, at her companion and calmly seated herself in a simple rocking chair next to Alinormir's position at the table's head. Virinil was the Goddess of Birth and Fertility and a loving, caring woman who enjoyed the simple things in life. Anything involving dying or the deceased appalled her, and thus she avoided looking down the other end of the table. Instead she knitted away at a small wool shirt to distract herself.

The second arrival still stood, however, his stance an open challenge to the opposing sitters, of whom only Balthazain returned his hard look. With a grimace unbecoming to his fine facial features, Paladinis, the God of Honor, gripped his sword hilt and looked poised to strike. His armor was brilliant burnished steel with intricate gold script in lavish design over it, almost outshining his golden cloak that flowed over his shoulders. Youthful in appearance, the well-groomed dark hair and carefully trimmed moustache belied his righteous fury. The god was often given to fighting before talking, though he was always well intentioned in his actions.

"Paladinis," Alinormir gently placed her hand on her son's, causing his deathgrip on his sword to loosen, "this is not the time to be rash, please sit."

Bowing with the utmost deference, Paladinis released his sword and his aggression, causing hilt and belt to evaporate as he sat next to Virinil with a respectful nod for all at his end of the table. He settled into his smoothly carved maple seat and calmly positioned his hands on the arms with such obvious effort it defeated his attempt to

9

appear relaxed. Terenas caught his eye from the left and he turned as the mass of armor inclined his head, hand over heart. Paladinis smiled, for it was a salute one of his Paladins might use before entering battle. It meant that Terenas would fight with him if it came to that. The two had much in common, but often did not think alike.

As soon as Paladinis had settled back again another sitter arrived, bathed in a blood red cloak that covered him to his ankles. Croarl was a terrifying sight, with his shaven head, blood-flushed eyes, darkly tanned skin, and pointed ears to match his ever-visible pointed teeth. In all his existence, Croarl had never stopped smiling with that horrifying grin. His chair was an instrument of torture, with large spikes protruding from its seat and back, yet he sat in it as though it were padded with the softest of feathers. Croarl did not speak, as he had no tongue, but he really did not need to. His appearance shook everyone, including those at his own side of the table. Croarl was the God of Murder and was known for savagery beyond any bounds. It would be safe to say that his brethren tolerated rather than truly trusted him.

Coming to the table at almost the same time was Galiron, the God of Magic. A middle aged man with an extremely calm exterior he looked perplexed at the staring match going on between the opposing sides. He looked at Croarl almost as calmly as Alinormir did, but with a shake of his head as though seeing a misbehaving child. Nothing ever seemed to startle him, no matter how bizarre or twisted. Galiron was often mistaken for an emotionless god, but he was quite the opposite, as he merely hid his feelings better than his brethren. His chair was of plain wood with stars and moons on the leather cushions. He seated himself calmly, propping his staff against his shoulder as he sat across from Lorima. The two often had spats, as nature and magic tended to conflict with one another, but in the formation of Teth-tenir they had discovered they were also very good at working together. Despite the deep connection between the two, Galiron did not even glance at her, but leaned back in his chair. He stared at the tabletop and traced patterns across it with his finger, saying nothing and looking unusually pensive.

Lorima, rather than being peeved at his dismissal of her, gently extended an arm to him. Resignedly, Galiron leaned in and the two exchanged an unusual, quiet conversation for their ears alone. Galiron looked at her with dark concern and whispered, "This is a mistake."

"I know," Lorima said softly, "nothing good can come of this. No matter what it is."

Galiron sighed. "I wish I never gave it to them, it is too much of a burden for anyone to bear."

Lorima cocked her head in obvious confusion, the faint sound of shaking leaves accompanying the motion. "Gave what, Galiron?"

But the God of Magic did not answer. Instead he turned back to the table and began tracing again. As he did, the room noticeably

10

darkened and the next two sitters arrived. They moved slowly, with deliberate calm, from the black end of the hall. The first, Lovart, God of Change, was a kindly looking man with long thin hair streaked with gray, always seemingly lost in his own thoughts. Lovart was the most confusing of the gods, having given much of his power in the growth and flourishing of the mortal world and, it seemed, having lost some of himself in the process. He came with his father, Neroth, God of Death and Shepherd of Souls. Lovart had been the first of Alinormir and Neroth's "children," born from their love for one another in the earliest days of the gods, a love that no longer persisted.

Neroth and Lovart came forward. The God of Change appeared, as always, to be adrift in his own mind and utterly unaware of any tension in the room. He sat quite calmly in a chair that cannot be described effectively, its every facet shifting and twisting at a speed rending to the eyes, occasionally displaying something so impossible that it drove a close watcher to head pains. No one looked directly at it and Lovart appeared not to take notice.

Neroth had come behind him and stood in his archway, calm and reserved. His drawn face lent him the look of a corpse, but full of an intense and impassioned belief that gave him life. Seemingly larger than any figure in the room, save Alinormir, he stood resolutely before the table. His pale skin was like that of new-fallen snow, standing out against the night black of his dark robes and dark hair that hung past his jaw, held in down by a crown of shining metal with black thorns. Lined with a bleached bone-white cloth the robes settled around a body that filled them despite the wanness of his face. Where Neroth's visage was that of a dead man his body seemed in the prime of youth. He walked softly on heavy black boots, his eyes as deep as an abyss. Without a word to anyone he sat in his obsidian chair, carved in a tapestry of death and depictions of somber funerals. Settling his elbows on the table with his hands in a steeple, he eyed the others calmly over his groomed fingers, preparing to speak. Only when he saw the table was still short one sitter did he do so however, his voice carrying a soft yet unquestionable tone of command, "Where is Kurven?"

There was a pause as the sitters each looked at one another, then at the place where the God of Time should have been. It was rare for anyone to arrive after Neroth. The God of Death used his late entrance to display his authority and intimidate the other First Gods. Kurven was showing a rare bit of defiance by arriving later than usual. The table remained quiet, each god contemplating this new development. It seemed the most benign of their number had found his own passive way of resisting whatever was about to happen. Despite himself, Neroth was impressed, though he was careful not to show it.

A faint blue glow appeared in the last archway and all the seated deities turned to watch the arrival of their final member. Kurven had no semblance of a corporeal body. He, if he could be considered a he, was a strange blue cloud that hovered just off the floor. Kurven's only humanoid characteristic was his bright glowing eyes, a sharper blue than the many hues that made up the shimmering mass of his form. Without a word of explanation he moved to his place at the table and seemed to settle, not actually sitting on anything, but somehow appearing to have set himself down.

Choosing to ignore the strange actions of his fellow, Neroth attempted to assert his control over the meeting. Though he had not called it, he saw this gathering as an opportunity to take command of such a rare moment among his kin. "Well, does anyone know why we have been called here?"

Reas spoke quietly from his seat. "To negotiate a peace, perhaps?"

Xanoroth rose, ready to renew his fight with the pacifist god, but a look from Neroth seated him again. The towering God of Death turned to Reas with a mirthless smile. "I suspect, Reas, that you may be a bit off the mark." Neroth looked pointedly at Alinormir, the first time he had acknowledged her presence thus far, "Would you like to explain why you had the mortal representative summon us?"

Alinormir spoke softly from her seat, "I thought it more likely you would all come if the invitation came from him and not from myself. Though I was not deceptive, you did tell them you were summoning them on my behalf, Fellandros?"

The odd, wiry elder stirred slightly and muttered, "Ho hrmm, yes of course."

Halting briefly as he seated himself, Neroth was stung, as always, by the words of his former wife. He took a moment to gather himself before pressing further. "Well then, we are all here. Now I wish to know to what end?"

"Yes," Galiron echoed, still tracing the table nervously, "what is the meaning of calling this meeting? We have not come together in a very long time. Not since..." He trailed off and a great silence descended like a dark cloud over the Archway Temple.

Alinormir cleared her throat as calmly as she could manage, "For some time, our ability to directly engage in the lives of mortals has been severely limited. This has given them time to make something of their own way in the world, but avenues for interference remain.

"I have long been opposed to our direct involvement in the world of the mortal creatures we helped bring to life and have watched over for eons, but that has not prevented it from occurring. I do not believe the current state of distance between we immortal gods and those mortal races on Teth-tenir will last."

Neroth's eyes narrowed as he watched his former love speak calmly and clearly to the assembled gods. Outwardly he was attentive and thoughtful, but inwardly he was full of fear. How much did she know? Neroth and Alinormir unintentionally exchanged a look that was quickly broken. The others did not observe the uncomfortable moment, lost in their own thoughts and shame. Neroth spoke softly,

"What was given to the mortals came from us, the world of Teth-tenir is ours and so are they. They must remember where they came from. They must remain loyal to their creators. Each day we allow them to go further astray from our guidance the danger to both our realms grows."

"As you say," Alinormir murmured her eyes down, "The world was a gift. We have no right to dictate what is done with it and its people, or to enlist them in our personal crusades."

It was an ancient argument and one that had remained for ages unresolved. The silence following that exchange was the most smothering, as it seemed every sitter waited for the eruption of the old feud that now been brought forth once again. But it did not come. Alinormir waited for what seemed an eternity, then she rose slowly and faced Neroth, forcing herself to hold his gaze. "With the severing of our bridge to the mortal world we can only speak to those on Teth-tenir who are of the strongest faith or enter the temples built in our honor. Others we might find in dreams, should we stumble across them on those myriad half-conscious roads crisscrossing the borders of their world and our own. However, the fact remains that there is a barrier between us and Teth-tenir we cannot cross."

Still Neroth said nothing, now intensely curious as to what Alinormir was up to. He had truly no idea why she had summoned the First Gods to the Archway Temple when the call had reached him, but this meeting was even more unusual and its purpose more beyond his reckoning than he had expected. Unconsciously he leaned forward, rising slightly from his chair, trying to pull some clue from Alinormir's face as she continued. Briefly, the Goddess of Life looked up, but she swiftly broke eye contact with him as she said, "The rift between us and them is one we cannot repair. But we all know that grave dangers lurk beyond our world and theirs. Once, the power of a god was given to one mortal man so that he might face down a great threat and defeat it. Many of us disagreed with this, but it has been done, the precedent was set."

Alinormir took a great breath as she finally came to the reason for calling the meeting. "I propose that we permit such gifts of power be offered again to those mortals who would, in total faith and stringent belief, ask for them."

Lorima was the first to react and did so with relative calm, though the entire room simmered with grumblings of disbelief and confusion. "We already give the priests, the faithful, powers to work feats beyond the constraints of any mortal. Why bring this additional boon forth as a possibility?"

"To say nothing of the fact that you, Alinormir, most ardently called for the condemning of that same aforementioned action when it happened," Reas said with a tone more in line with the near total disbelief of the other immortals. "How can you, of all of us, suddenly have changed your opinion so drastically?"

"I wonder the same," Neroth said with a hard voice, "are you beginning to soften your view on our duty to the mortals of Teth-tenir?"

"The duty you describe," Paladinis grated, "is more in line with their enslavement than our bestowing of blessings."

Neroth shot the lesser god a look that could have set him aflame had it been manisfest as a torch. Paladinis did his best to remain stoic under the authority of Neroth's stare, but his power was palpable even in that house of neutrality. Alinormir interrupted the seething tension, "I am not abandoning my position. The mortals should be allowed to make their own way in the world, with our aid coming only upon request. This is why the bridge was broken. All I am suggesting is that we agree to provide them with more power to defend themselves if they truly seek and deserve it."

"It sounds to me," Balthazain said incredulously, "that you are retroactively admitting you were wrong when you condemned the tactics enacted to destroy the God-Sorceror."

An audible intake of breath came from most of the sitters at the mentioning of the name. Even Lovart, who had appeared almost unaware of the proceedings before him, shot a look of disapproval at the God of Betrayal. Alinormir shook her head defiantly. "No, I am not admitting that. Tristain Azurius was deceived, his request for the ability to save his homeland was not the same as a man or woman of true conviction asking their trusted deity to aid them in a time of greatest need."

"And how are we to determine who is truly in need? Truly faithful?" The irritation in his voice was clear as Neroth at last moved to seat himself once again, believing the meeting was about to dissolve into a stalemate as so many before it had.

The determination is not ours to make.

The "voice," if it could be called that, echoed pleasantly in the minds of the gods about the table. They turned their eyes on Kurven, who remained settled in his place projecting his thoughts out towards them all. *When the bridge between the Godly Realms and Teth-tenir was destroyed it eliminated our ability to reach out to the mortals. We can observe them. We can answer their prayers. But we cannot bestow power upon those who are not strong enough to request it. In the simplest of terms, the road between gods and mortals is now of a singular direction. Even if one of us wished to grant a part of ourselves to a mortal, they would need to be mighty enough to reach out to us, and durable enough to handle the merging of their lifeforce with even the smallest fraction of our own.*

There was silence about the table as the First Gods considered Kurven's words. Neroth leaned back slowly in his chair, understanding beginning to dawn upon him. Alinormir had played this very well he realized. Her proposal was reasonable and in line with his own very vocal belief that the gods had to take an active role in commanding and controlling the mortal races. It would be completely inexplicable for him to oppose this suggestion, and worse still it would reveal the real work he had been doing behind the scenes. Neroth realized what this meant. Alinormir had learned something of his plan and was taking steps to counter it. He was not sure how she believed this would prevent him achieving his goal, but he now knew he needed to find out.

"The proposal is on the table. I brought it here, against the council of some, because I still believe that even with all the violations of order and unspoken law we have seen in our existence there must be some attempt at unity." Alinormir spread her hands beseechingly. "What I ask is already possible. Many terrible things have been done in the name of conflicting ideology, including passing a piece of a god to a mortal. I simply wish us to once again deliberate our actions instead of selfishly taking them in hand."

There was a long silence of consideration. It was, surprisingly, Virinil that finally broke it. The quiet, motherly goddess set her sewing work down on the table and knit her fingers together, leaning forward. "As you say, this giving of power is something we all know to be possible regardless of our consent. Any one of us could do it."

"But not," Reas added thoughtfully, "unless requested by a mortal."

"And," Neroth finished, "one strong enough to accept a piece of a god."

"Then," Virinil said, "I believe this proposal is acceptable. The constraints in place lead me to believe we will not see hundreds of god-blessed mortals running amok on Teth-tenir, unless I am missing something, Kurven?"

The God of Time responded impassively, *Truthfully there are likely less than a dozen mortals in all of history who could ever hope to accept this gift.*

Virinil nodded as though that settled the matter. "Then I support the proposal."

The Goddess of Birth placed her hand, palm down, on the table before her, signaling assent. A few of the other gods followed suit in short order: Paladinis, Reas, and Delvidia. With some hesitation, Lorima glanced at Alinormir. "There is something more to this that we who have been called here cannot see. The bearer of the message, and one so seemingly simple, makes me distrust it. I will not support this."

Lorima kept her hand clear of the table. To her shock, Galiron placed his forward, palm down. He did not meet the questioning glare of the Goddess of Nature, keeping his own eyes down. Terenas and Kurven remained opposed, but said nothing to explain their reasoning. Finally, Neroth broke the stalemate, placing his hand palm down on the table and looking pointedly at Alinormir, "It would make little sense for me to oppose an action I have supported in the past, would it not?"

There was no response, but with Neroth's vote came those of Balthazain, Xanoroth, and Croarl. The proposal passed with only

Terenas, Lorima, Kurven, and Lovart in opposition, though perhaps the God of Change had simply not realized what was happening. As the voters pulled back hands from the table the meeting began to dissolve. Alinormir stood and drew up her chin with faltering regalness, whispering a nearly inaudible thank you to the attendees. Realizing that was all that would occur that day, most of the other gods left swiftly. Lorima tried to corner Galiron, but the God of Magic swept from the table first and disappeared through his archway. Turning to stare at Alinormir once more, still probing with her eyes to understand the hidden game the Goddess of Life was playing, Lorima finally left exasperated. In time, only Neroth, Kurven, and Alinormir remained, with the odd little man, Fellandros, reclining on his rickety stool in seeming obliviousness to the tension about him.

Neroth opened his mouth several times, searching for the correct words, but finally closed it and shook his head. He turned from Alinormir and nodded curtly at Kurven before striding proudly through his arch. Alinormir, who had kept her back to him to ensure her face gave away nothing more of her thoughts, whispered, "Is he gone, Kurven?"

Yes, The God of Time turned his brilliant eyes on the Goddess of Life, his thoughts ringing clear and cool in her mind. *I had truly considered avoiding this meeting altogether.*

"I know."

We spoke of this before, you and I. I still believe it was unnecessary to keep up the pretense of following some misplaced code of conduct among your kin.

Alinormir turned and eyed the god before her. "Our kin, Kurven, or have you forgotten you are one of us?"

I apologize, Kurven shifted slightly, *sometimes it is... difficult to feel the same connection to the others that you do.*

"It was necessary," Alinormir said, seeming to ignore or not have heard Kurven's response to her question. "I needed to do it to remind myself there is morality, right and wrong, among us still."

Kurven did not respond. Alinormir continued. "It means very little. You said yourself that there is a fleeting chance such mortals even exist, and who is to know the character of such men and women? They are as likely to be faithful adherents to Neroth as to any other god."

Kurven considered not answering, but he felt compelled to do so. When he did, the fluid thoughts through Alinormir's mind carried hints of doubt and nervousness. *There is one mortal who has already reached out.*

Alinormir straightened sharply and, despite herself, moved towards Kurven in intense interest. "Truly? Who are they? From which of us do they seek the gift of our power?" Kurven's silence accompanied the slow understanding of the goddess, "It's you, the mortal is a follower of you. How else would you know one had been found already?"

Yes, Kurven replied and Alinormir could sense weariness in the words, *and that is why I thought to avoid this meeting. Not because I believed your honesty foolish and unnecessary, though I still hold it shows your hand to Neroth and gives him an advantage he does not need. No, I wanted to avoid this meeting because I have not decided whether I should grant this request and I know what you would wish of me.*

"You telling me of this is evidence enough you have already decided." Alinormir's face became desperately earnest. "You know this is one chance, and a slim one, to oppose Neroth and give mortals a hand in deciding their own fate!"

Fate, Kurven rose from his settled position, *a strange choice of words, especially for you.* Alinormir did not answer, but her face could not restrain the tic of pain Kurven's insight had caused her. *I have examined the threads of time and the outcomes before us. Even this may change nothing. The end of our world and theirs may be irreversible.*

"But there is a chance," Alinormir insisted, "and even the smallest chance would make it worth doing."

"Hrrmm ho, excuse me." The two gods turned to Fellandros, who had risen from his seat and was once again attempting to smooth his irreversibly wrinkled clothing. "I know it is not my place, but speaking as one of the mortals, a chance to avoid the destruction of our world would be, hum ho, appreciated."

Alinormir smiled slightly, despite herself, and Kurven seemed to have received the reasoning he had been trying to pry from his fellow god through the simple expression of the mortal. *Very well. It will be done.*

Kurven made to leave when Alinormir spoke quietly, "Kurven, who is the mortal?"

Kurven paused at his archway and remained still for a time, long enough that Alinormir thought he had forgotten her question. Then his voice flitted through her mind, *An unborn child.*

Even though she possessed none of his gifts for communication, Kurven could feel the shock emanating off of Alinormir. "How is that possible? How could they request...."

They did not, the mother did. She is not strong enough. A piece of my power would kill her outright or worse. But within her I could sense it, a mortal of incredible depths of resolve and strength. She asked, but not for her.

Before Alinormir could respond, Kurven was gone. Fellandros remained, equally stunned, standing before the table. Without a word, Alinormir left swiftly, her hand on her chin as she pondered this new development. For his part, the Revenant remained in silent contemplation before tapping the brooch on his disheveled tunic and slowly fading from view, returning at last to his home on Teth-tenir.

Xanoroth raged to no one in particular, "How did she know? This was our plan! We have crafted it, and yet somehow she calls all our kind together to reveal everything?"

The black clad god smashed his fist upon the iron table by which he stood. They were in Neroth's home, his realm within the greater plane of the gods, in the main chamber. It was bedecked with weapons from countless ages and the walls lined with tomes of every tongue on Teth-tenir. A massive map, hovering freely above the cool black stone floor, was in the center. Xanoroth was to the left of the steel-spiked double doors of the entrance, a mere aesthetic formality as in their own plane the gods could move freely without a need for conventional portals. No one paid him any mind. Balthazain sat calmly in a fine wooden chair stroking his perfectly oiled goatee and drumming his free fingers on another iron table. Croarl, grin still affixed to his face, stood arms folded off to one side, seemingly unconcerned with the current turn of events. Indifferent, or perhaps just beyond involvement, Lovart ran a finger over the backs of the many books, searching for something only he could want. Xanoroth snarled, as he realized no one was paying any attention to him. He turned from the table and stomped across the hall to the map, still speaking, if only to himself, "And what should I care? My involvement in our little plot has been minimal! At least I can not be blamed for its collapse."

Balthazain did not even look at his brother. "You were kept out because you have nothing to offer a situation that requires tact."

Xanoroth spun on him and pointed sharply at Croarl. "And yet that damned fiend does?"

Balthazain smiled disarmingly. "Croarl excels at murder and mayhem, two of my favorite pastimes, and efficient ways to accomplish certain goals. If anything, his talents are all the more necessary now. I suspect soon we will have a mortal to track and dispose of."

Xanoroth seemed ready to continue the argument, but the room darkened noticeably as Neroth entered. The taut skin over his bloodless face was contorted into a look of puzzled rage. He gestured to Balthazain as he strode determinedly towards the map in the center. "Get that damned fool here, now!"

Balthazain disappeared immediately; leaving an empty chair behind and Neroth motioned for Croarl to fetch him a glass from the table in his corner. Lovart pulled a book from the shelf with a sigh of contentment and began reading where he stood. As Croarl handed Neroth the glass he addressed his son Xanoroth. "Fear not, you will have a chance to partake in the efforts I have begun. It seems our plan has been forcibly altered."

Balthazain materialized by the doorway with a nervous-looking Galiron beside him. The God of Magic adjusted his robes and avoided making eye contact with Neroth. The embattled God of Death drank his glass dry and passed it back to Croarl before addressing the new arrival, "How did you not know?"

Galiron managed to meet his glare. "I am only privy to some of the business of the neutrals. We each mind our own spheres of power. It seems your wife discovered some part of our bargain and moved to stay in front of it."

"She is no longer my wife." Neroth whispered softly and dangerously. He then took a second glass of strangely red liquid from Croarl and turned it slowly in his hand. "It matters not if she knows of our agreement. No offense intended, brother, but it is secondary to the other efforts I have undertaken on Teth-tenir. What alarms me is that she seems to know of more than just our plan to find a loyal servant to imbue with godly power, and that someone in this room gave her that information."

There was a dark quiet as Neroth's last words hung in the air. Though he was openly calm, his anger was clearly just below the surface. Galiron shook his head in disbelief. "You cannot be suggesting that this is my doing! What advantage is there in my exposing our effort? We've laboured on this together for so long, it undermines that work entirely if it is revealed before we are ready to act."

Neroth studied Galiron thoughtfully. "You have been known to retreat from more drastic action in the past."

"I stood next to you against the Forgotten long ago, fought as fiercely as any of us. This is as much my plan as yours." Galiron straightened himself proudly and pointed an accusing finger at Neroth. "I silently accepted her proposal, keeping our pact a secret. Clearly she knew you are continuing to pursue dominion over the mortal world. If nothing else, I did all I could to keep your larger scheme hidden."

Neroth grimaced and took a sip from his glass before setting it down on one of the tables. He knew Galiron was correct, but it did not make the realization that Alinormir was onto him any easier to swallow. "There is only one solution to this little problem that will give me what I asked for in the first place. We go ahead with our original plan, but now we must add a new wrinkle to it."

Galiron shook his head. "I cannot do anything until we have a mortal who seeks me out. You said you could find one, but Kurven made it clear...."

Neroth dismissed his concerns with a wave of his hand. "Kurven's explanation opearated within the limitations of Alinormir's proposal. We are examining other ways for you to empower a mortal."

Galiron glanced about the room, realizing all the other gods were now quietly watching him. "What other ways would those be?"

Neroth stepped forward and placed a hand on his fellow god's shoulder. "Gifting power is possible to a willing and strong enough vessel. Kurven is correct that the collapse of our bridge to physical entry in the world of mortals greatly impairs both our ability to find those strong enough to accept such a gift and to bring it to them without being called."

"I thought this was a difficulty you were working to resolve."

Neroth removed his hand from Galiron's shoulder and turned back to the map. "It is, but I need our agreement to go into action before. To reenter the world of mortals in my true and unrestrained form is essential to saving our world and theirs, but it will take time. If we were to give a mortal a piece of a god, particularly of one that was especially gifted in the arcane, it would both speed the process and strengthen our hold on the world before I can return to it."

"Yes," Galiron sighed, "but that still does not solve the problem of finding a willing servant hardy enough to absorb such a gift."

"Not a gift."

The others, excepting Neroth, turned in surprise to Lovart, who was holding the book he had selected from the shelf open in one thin hand, gesturing expressively with the other as he spoke, "I have discovered a way to extract a part of a fallen god and give it to a mortal, willing or not. This of course, would require the god was already on Teth-tenir since, as you correctly pointed out, there is no avenue for any of us to return there.

"Once the mortal is infused with this piece of a weakened immortal it would improve them in every way, including granting them the strength to absorb a true god's power. In essence, were we to find and extract a part of the lingering immortal essence from a god that had descended to mortality we could give it to any mortal we chose and then you could pass your own gift onto them, knowing it would be within their ability to command it."

"We also believe," Neroth continued, his eyes meeting Galiron's with a great fervor, "that this may remove the need for the mortal to seek out the blessing of the immortal. In short, we could choose who to give your might to and mold them into the perfect servant of our cause."

Galiron's eyes had grown progressively wider as they spoke. "But you said you need a fallen god, a descended immortal, to extract their lifeforce from? I am sorry brother, such an act would be an abomination."

"An abomination?" Neroth's voice rose in anger. "You call that an abomination? The Immorbellum was mere centuries ago, resulting in the demise of two of our own and the departure of still more from the Godly Realms, and yet this is a bridge too far?"

"I had no part in those deaths!"

"No?" Neroth strode resolutely towards Galiron. "Didn't we all play some part in them? We allowed them to happen. I am talking about taking a piece of a god who has given up their immortality so that we can unite the world against the real dangers threatening it."

"You mean conquer the world."

Neroth scowled and swept his arm wide in frustration. "What does the terminology matter? The mortals can help us, but we must command and direct them! Look at their history of wars, feuds, and continual hatred. They must be brought under control and given purpose." Neroth stepped still closer to Galiron, his tone imploring, "Taking the lingering essence of immortality from one of our own who chose to descend will not kill them, Galiron. It will be painful, but it will not destroy who and what they are. And think of the greater good it serves. This must be done."

Galiron did not answer, turning from the beseeching eyes of the God of Death. He scanned the room, looking at the faces of those he had thrown his lot in with: a madman, a murderous beast, a traitor, and the embodiment of rage. What Neroth said sounded like wisdom, but it was hiding a terrible process that Galiron could feel crawling beneath his skin. To grant a part of himself to a mortal so that they might speed Neroth's return to Teth-tenir and his conquest of the world was one thing, but to turn on his own kind to do so was beyond reason, "No, I am sorry brother. I will not do this."

Neroth sighed audibly, turning from the God of Magic he gestured for Croarl to give him another glass. "I was afraid you would make this difficult."

"I do not mean to," Galiron said calmly, "I simply cannot justify harming my own kind."

Neroth sipped his fresh drink and nodded. "A noble ideal Galiron, which I respect," suddenly, Xanoroth and Croarl grabbed the God of Magic's arms and held him fast. "But I fear that I can justify it and I already have."

Galiron struggled, but felt the hold of his captors impossibly strong. He reached out to his own realm within the godly planes to return there, and found nothing. In horror he cried, "What is this treachery?"

Neroth placed his goblet on one of the heavy metal tables and crossed his arms within the folds of his robes; "We have already found the former immortal and made ready to extract his godly essence. All of our plans are in place. All we needed was your cooperation. I knew you trusted me, and I knew you would come here when called. Trust is dangerous, Galiron."

"Let me go Neroth," Galiron tried to sound fierce, but his tone was fearful, "you cannot do this, you are no different than...."

"Silence!" Neroth cut him off. "You will leave when you do what I need of you. We had an agreement, and you will fulfill your part of the bargain." He motioned sharply with one hand and Galiron was gone, whisked away to some far corner of Neroth's home to await further debate. The God of Death turned back to his goblet and stared downward at the still liquid within, deep in thought. Finally he snatched the glass from the table and swallowed it in one long pull, spattering red across his face and robes. Wiping his mouth with the back of his hand he walked to the rear of the chamber. "Leave me. Return once things are ready to begin on Teth-tenir and not before."

Without discussion, the others departed as one. Neroth was alone in his grand hall, the dark metal and somber trappings mirroring his mood. He clenched his fists as he wrestled internally with his decisions, assuring himself again and again that he was doing what must be done. He remained that way for a long time, and at no point did he ever feel he was truly able to convince himself of his own lies.

Along the western coast of Legocia, the Sirrion Sea laps gently against the rocky beaches of her shores. The coast extends from the thick trees of Silverleaf Forest all the way to the most harsh and frozen lands of the Great Northern Waste. Beyond the trees of Silverleaf, several scores of miles north of the homeland of the Silverleaf Elves, commonly called the Foresters, sits the old and stubborn rock of Aves. The fortress is a pinnacle of human defiance against nature. This sturdy castle of stone is a simple structure with a massive curtain wall and domineering keep. It is home to the renowned Eagle Knights and defender to the lands around it. The powerful fortress surveys and protects most of the southern lands of western Legocia, the region known as Dragon's Watch. From here the order defends the bustling seaport of Halden Bay and the surrounding farmlands, historically fighting with the hated elven forces of Silverleaf for domination of the region.

Within the keep, atop a titanic and sturdy throne of thick wood, sat the massive frame of Bullwyf Margrave, known more commonly as Bull the Warrior. He was considered by some to be the most powerful Commander of Aves in recorded history, a legend, even to those from the fabled kingdom of Angladais. Bull was the master of his people and a brilliant military strategist. And yet, at this moment, his huge muscled frame sunk into his cushioned throne as though the weight of his significant years had been tripled. Bull was faced with an invader from across that same sea which marked the western edge of his domain, an invader boasting an army five times his own in size and extremely well trained. Age had crept up on him not with dignity, but in sleepless nights and fear as Bull watched the home he had built so carefully collapse before his eyes.

About him the high hall of his throne room was abuzz with conversation. His advisors, scores of them from many lands and walks of life, were in every corner of the hall arguing and frantically debating how to save the great fortress of Aves, now under siege for several months. Bull stayed clear of their disputes, watching the sun shine through the stained glass windows that dominated the hall. These windows, crafted by the most ingenious dwarven designers around the time of the Arcane Wars, were his favorite feature of his home. They depicted the struggles and trials of the Eagle Knights from their formation under the wise guidance of the first commander, Richard Margrave I, to the noble sacrifice of Orson Jarn. Bull had spent many days in his youth staring at these images from his place below the throne, but he had never imagined he would see the day when they offered him no inspiration.

One of his advisors, a foreigner called Vactan el Vac, strode determinedly through the crowd from the central doors and up the massive blue-carpeted stairs of the throne's dais. The other advisors gave him a wide berth. He was a justifiably feared soldier and cut an intimidating figure. Bull turned his gaze away from his musings to judge the man before him. The most noticeable of Vactan's features, particularly in Aves, was that he was decidedly not human. His sharply pointed ears and entirely green eyes, with no visible pupils or whites, marked him as some strange being from a far off land. Vactan had come to Bull from Ozmandias, the city of wizards and arcane magic to the northeast, but the Commander of Aves knew his kind had originated from far more distant lands. Vactan's elven features and strange eyes and hair were the hallmarks of lost elves, one of the oldest people on Teth-tenir.

Why he had come was never clear. Vactan had claimed to have felt compelled to offer his counsel and services to a man he considered a great warrior. The code of Aves declared that only males of pure human lineage could join the order, but Vactan's ability as a tactician and leader had earned him the role of Bull's second in command. To avoid causing too much of an internal spat over appointing such an obvious outsider, Bull had never officially given Vactan any sort of title. It had mattered little, between Bull's obviously high regard for the lost elf and Vactan's skill as a fighter none would openly question his authority.

But even with his vast knowledge of combat and the silent endorsement of Bullwyf Margrave, Vactan was shunned by most of the men in Aves. Even the few outsiders of other nations gave him a wide berth. Vactan did not help by making no effort to appease anyone around him, even the lord of the fortress himself. In better times Bull would likely have dismissed him outright for bordering on insolent behavior. Unfortunately for Bull, he was incredibly short on soldiers and Vactan was too useful to reprimand for most of his transgressions.

"Report," the king's deep, booming voice caused a wave of silence to wash over the room. "What do our scouts say?"

Vactan el Vac reached the foot of the throne and offered his benefactor a barely noticeable bow. He was decked in silvery metal scale mail and matching gauntlets with a flowing black cloak and boots with armored black leather pants to match. His hair was the purest white, as was common among his people, like new fallen snow and his eyes seemed to glow from within his head. He was a strong man, tall and muscular with a flourish to his movements that demanded attention. Vactan was known for his deadly swordsmanship and a tendency to seriously injure soldiers he deemed incompetent when training them. Many found his severity unnecessary, but Vactan argued it was essential to weeding out the weaker men.

"The northern scouts report at least ten thousand men moving towards the eastern gate of the fortress." Vactan said calmly, "They burn and kill anything that they come across. Most of the survivors were badly mutilated and any of the women we found had been ravaged at least once by the soldiers."

"To the east?"

Vactan shrugged, his oddly musical voice reverberating in the hall. "Another ten thousand men doing much the same thing. They appear to be in no hurry to meet us here, but it is clear that this fortress is their final destination. I have units stationed a mile from the fortress in a crescent shape to defend us from the east and northeast."

Bull ran a hand through his shoulder length graying hair. "How many?"

"Approximately four hundred knights and a few hundred archers. I will try to slow the enemy and then pull them back before we are flanked, but it will not be easy."

Bull furrowed his brow in thought. "The more you can pull into the fortress the better, but do not give ground easily, make them fight for every inch you can."

Vactan offered another slight bow. "As you say my liege."

"And the scouts to the south?"

Vactan grimaced, "I fear they were ambushed, we believe the entire regiment was killed...."

"No."

The two turned in shock to see a young figure, slight yet strong, appear through the entrance of the hall. He was clad in torn and tattered leather armor and wore a battered bow over his shoulder with an empty quiver at his side. His ears protruded back slightly from his head and came to points, showing a definitive presence of elven blood, and yet he was not a pure elf, for his body was too thick and muscular. His eyes were a sharp grey, like stone, and his hair was a curling, cascading dirty blonde that was matted to his face with sweat, mud, and blood. Over his shoulders, slouched by the weight, was the body of a man clad in the livery of an Eagle Knight. The wounded man's blue tunic was stained heavily with blood and his face was pale, but he appeared alive. The youth carrying him, who had interrupted Vactan, fell to one knee and set his burden gently on the ground. He opened his mouth to speak again, but a veteran knight guarding the hall's entrance rushed forward and backhanded him viciously across the face, sending him sprawling. "You have no right to talk to the commander, half-breed!"

Bull roared from his throne, rising in sudden wrath to his monstrous full height, "Leave him!"

The knight stepped back with a low bow as Bull straightened his great frame and strode on his massive legs forward to meet the young man. Even as he was approaching old age, Bull cut an impressive and intimidating figure. He wore a huge breastplate with the image of an eagle, wings outstretched in flight, on its front. He was well over six feet in height and enormous without being cumbersomely so. He knelt by the injured knight, pushing his long, graying black hair back from his face as he gently lifted the man's head from the carpet. Vactan stood beside him, placing a boot on the stunned half-elf's chest with a stern smile. "I would not move just yet if I were you, boy."

The young soldier wiped blood from his mouth and met the lost elf's look with hard eyes, but he stayed where he was. Bull spoke quietly to the wounded man, "Tell me Knight, what happened to your regiment?"

The veteran coughed and reached out to prop himself up with one hand, "My lord, we were attacked near the woodlands. A large group of soldiers had crossbows and caught us between them. We did not stand a chance. My men... most went down in the first volley. Twenty knights dead. I was shot in the chest, but this scout he carried me away from there."

Bull glanced at the young, half-elven form still leaning on his elbows the stone floor then looked back at the wounded knight. "You are the only ones left, how many were there?"

"Not many just enough to ambush us."

Bull turned his head to catch Vactan's eye. "Someone told them we were coming. I smell a rat in my fortress. Bring this man to the temple, have him healed, and get these damned advisors out of my hall. I want to talk to the scout alone."

Vactan motioned for the others to leave and they did so quickly. A few knights came with a litter and removed the wounded man who paused to thank the youth before being carried out. Bull bent down once they had all departed and helped the young rescuer up. He eyed his battered figure up and down before demanding, "Name and rank young man, and your town of origin."

The youth tried to straighten his armor, but gave up when he noticed how battered it was. "Trem Waterhound, scout, no home."

Bull's eyebrows climbed slightly. "No home?"

"No, my lord."

The king digested this a moment. Vactan, unseen by either Trem or Bull, shot the battered man a sharp look upon hearing his name. Bull glanced at Vactan quizzically, as though sensing his reaction and concern, despite not having seen it. Dismissing his suspicion swiftly, he returned his gaze to the scout. "Is what your commander says true? You rescued him from the enemy ambush?"

"Yes my lord. Well, partially."

"Partially?"

The young man averted his eyes and shifted nervously. "I did not take him away immediately. I fought the attackers for a time before I carried him out."

"Did you now? And how many did you take down?"

Trem shifted nervously once again. "Perhaps twenty, I think that was how many arrows I used."

Bull's eyebrows had now reached their peak, but Vactan was less impressed. He snorted his skepticism and crossed his arms. "Arrows used is not the same thing as targets struck boy. What is this? Some attempt to inflate your own accomplishments in hopes of some form of reward?"

"Vactan!" Bull glowered at the lost elf. "There's no need to be so accusatory. He saved a man's life."

The strange eyes of Vactan el Vac met his master's and he grimaced. "All I am suggesting is that you press for details rather than believe everything the half-elf has to say. I am not questioning the heroic nature of his actions towards one of your knights."

Bull cocked his head in confusion. "What reason do I have to distrust the boy? He is as battered as the man he dragged in here!" Bull helped Trem to his feet and steadied him. "We are in desperate need of capable soldiers. The enemy is only a month or less from my front door! I will not allow foolish fears to prevent us from utilizing what fighters I have at my disposal."

Vactan shot Trem a look that unnerved him greatly, though he could not have said why. "Then give him over to my command and let me train him myself, if that is what you intend to do. After all, none of the other officers will treat him fairly given his lineage."

Bull paused in thought, eyeing both Vactan and the half-elf. "As you say, it would be hard going for him with any of the others." Bull turned to the half-elf. "Trem Waterhound, for your valor I am having you promoted to the rank of Sword. You are now a squire and will begin your training on the path to becoming an Eagle Knight."

Vactan stepped forward, his mouth curled in anger. Trem thought the intimidating foreigner was upset at him, but it seemed Vactan directed his frustration at Bull. "I did not say you should...." The lost elf cut himself off as though he knew he could not say what he wished to. "This is not right, Bullwyf Margrave! You cannot set him on this path!"

Bull shot him a glare. "I am commander of the Eagle Knights, my word here is law." Bull turned back to Trem, sizing up the youth before him. "I think I will even take a hand in training him myself from time to time. After all Vactan, I need you to find out who is leaking information about our movements. I would say that is the greater of your concerns than who I do and do not choose to promote?"

Vactan scowled, still clearly unhappy, but gave no response. Instead, he launched a half-hearted salute and stormed out of the hall. Trem remained, still wiping blood from his mouth and looking confused as Bull put an arm around his shoulders. The commander patted his back gently and steered him towards the door. "Do not let him upset you Trem, I cannot account for his strange behavior. He is a capable leader, but a volatile one as well. Go now and find a healer in the temple to take care of you. Oh, and do not forget this."

Bull strode purposefully to the throne and reached behind it to pull free from a small pile of arms a worn looking longsword. The hilt was battered and the steel notched in a few places, but Bull gave a couple effortless swings and eyed the line of the blade. He grabbed a sheath, equally as beaten, and slid the sword into it. He marched back to Trem and handed him the weapon. "We used to dole out traditional broadened short swords, but we have no smiths here to forge them as they are making arrowheads daily now. This will have to suffice. It is a well-balanced weapon and should serve you faithfully."

Trem accepted the blade without comment and strapped it to his belt. Bull continued, delivering a speech that sounded to Trem to have been long practiced, "Your rescue of your commander was the heroic act that earned you the privilege of becoming a Sword. Should you perform another service that your peers commend you for you will be raised to the rank of Shield. A third act of selfless courage will gain you a mount and the title of Steed. Should you live to see that point, Trem, you will have obtained a sword, shield, and then a horse to call your own. This is the progression of our order: three noble deeds of courage, three gifts from the Commander of Aves. And then, if you are so worthy, you may be named an Eagle Knight."

Trem nodded, examining the scabbard and hilt at his side. Bull smiled sadly as he watched him. "Have you ever used a real weapon, lad?"

Trem shook his head. "I was a hunter. I have never touched such a thing before."

Bull seemed to understand. "A sword is a wondrous weapon, Trem. A truly skilled swordsman can change the tide of a battle through his ability alone. The power and standing that comes with a sword makes you more than a common soldier, you will be listened too and followed by those who do not have such fine weapons.

"But you must also beware. A sword does not the wielder make. You will learn many techniques from Vactan and I that will maim and kill your foes. A sword is not an axe, which could be used for chopping wood for your fire, nor is it a bow, which you might hunt your food with to survive. A sword has but one purpose, and that is to kill. When you hold that blade in your hands you possess power over life and death. With training that influence will only increase. But the blade is never the killer, you are, and you must be able to hold back that final blow when necessary."

Bull patted him on the shoulder. "Compassion is not a lesson I can teach you. You must find it for yourself. Then you will know what kind of man you are. Now, go, I have plans to examine in private."

Trem bowed low and departed through the hall doors. He walked in a daze down the hallway past the personal bodyguards of Bull and through the open doors to the keep. He paused outside, contemplating the sudden turn of events. He had come here to hide, and somehow found himself a place and a cause that seemed worth fighting for, led by a man he thought he could grow to admire. He took a deep breath and began to limp down the stairs of the keep.

"So, the bastard gave you a sword."

Vactan was leaning against the wall of the keep by the doors Trem had passed through. He pushed himself off the stone and swept his black cloak behind his silver shining armor as he stepped in front of the half-elf. Even on the lower step he was eye level with Trem, who now noticed his cloak clasps were in the unnerving shape of skeletal hands. Without asking, Vactan reached out and pulled Trem's new blade free, examining its make carefully. "Well, at least he did not give you some flimsy weapon from a dead bandit. This is a true sword."

Vactan handed the blade back to the half-elf who studied the imposing man before him. As Trem returned the sword to its sheath, Vactan continued in a tone that was not unfriendly, "What did he promise you?"

Trem looked up and debated how much he should say. "He said I was a Sword and in time I could continue to rise in rank."

Vactan nodded, but simultaneously let out a quiet grunt of doubt. "Of course he did. Beware of promises from men you do not know, Trem Waterhound. They are always easier to make than they are to keep."

Vactan spun away and moved swiftly down the remaining steps of the keep. Trem followed him with his eyes as he disappeared in the direction of the barracks. He did not understand the exchange, could not pretend to know what Vactan was implying, and it unnerved him. Everywhere he had gone before Aves, trouble had followed him. Here he might be able to blend in as a common soldier and keep to himself. The threat of death in battle oddly did not disturb him. When he was fighting for his life among the knights that day he had felt strangely at peace, as though combat was something he was made for. All around, and likely within Aves, there was danger, but at least now he knew it was one he could stand and face. Touching the hilt of his new weapon, he slowly descended the steps and headed for the temple of Endoth to see if the priests would tend to his minor injuries.

Above Trem, from a vantage point he could never have imagined, Alinormir watched him atop a magnificent mountain within her realm. She stood at the edge of the cliff and stared downward, a soft breeze in her golden hair brushed it clear from her ageless beauty. The wind was not cold, but she wrapped her shawl about her sparse shoulders anyway. A strange fear overtook her when she had watched Trem had met Vactan, and the lost elf's warning to the young man had done nothing to ease her concern. The goddess turned her piercing eye away from the scene below her and walked from the precipice.

A short time, by Alinormir's eternal standards, had passed since that tense meeting of the First Gods in the Archway Temple. In an effort to keep his creation hidden from the other immortals, or perhaps because some sense of doubt at his decision still gnawed at him, Kurven had remained withdrawn from his kin. Alinormir had attempted to reach out to him several times, hoping to learn more of his disciple, but she had failed. It had taken her many years to even locate Trem Waterhound among the millions of mortals on Teth-tenir. Her observations of the half-elf had left her concerned and afraid, both for him and the future of mortal and immortal alike. Trem could either stand in the way of Neroth's scheme or become a powerful ally to her former husband. As Kurven had said, all his gift had offered was the possibility of averting calamity. Shuddering again, despite the lack of cold, Alinormir turned from her post and began walking back towards her palatial home.

As she did, a figure moved quietly from behind the rocks to her left and joined her, leaning on a walking stick with one hand and attempting to smooth his rumpled clothing with the other. They said nothing to one another as they began to descend the mountain, both lost in their own thoughts and more focused on the steps before them than the swirling clouds and mist about their bodies. The smaller figure rubbed his tousled white hair with a pale blue hand and sighed.

Alinormir looked down at him finally and smiled slightly. "Is there something that troubles you, Fellandros Kal'merion?"

The slight man did not take his eyes off the path before him but shrugged his slim shoulders. "Humm ho, same thing that troubles you I would think, hmm."

The goddess nodded and patted the Revenant's back comfortingly. "I fear I may have made a terrible mistake." Fellandros offered no response. "Still I could see no other solution. At least if there is to be hope for your kind now."

"Hmm, indeed." Fellandros's tone sounded unconvinced.

Alinormir removed her hand and reached into her robes, pulling forth a small pendant. It was a made of slim curves that wound thin streams of glasslike obsidian and shining silver mithril around the hilt and blade of a sword. On one side, the blade was mithril and on the other obsidian. Fellandros took it with widening eyes and looked at her quizzically. Alinormir sighed. "I believe he will come to you and your people. Give him this and take him to Silverwing, he will need his aid."

"My lady, hmm," Fellandros shook his head in doubt, "if he goes to him with this it will not matter. Many mortals have tried to enlist his aid and yet...."

"The pendant is not a gift from him, but from me."

Fellandros looked more confused. "An apology of some sort?"

"An acknowledgment."

Felladros said nothing at first, then chose to change the subject, "You assume he will come to me, but the half-elf needs to stay alive that long. He's in grave enough danger now, and if Neroth finds him...."

"It is an unstoppable eventuality that he will. I have thrown my lot in with Trem, and you, and all other mortals. I have long said you should be free to choose your own destiny, I must put my own axioms to the test."

"Hmm, you always did want to trust us with the fate of our world, humm ho. It seems, hmm, that you will get your wish." Fellandros brushed down his clothes again futilely and sighed. "I must be going home now."

Alinormir nodded and watched as Fellandros's form shimmered and disappeared. Alinormir understood that his doubt lay not in the idea of a giving a mortal such power and responsiblity, but in this particular mortal. Kurven had imbued Trem at his mother's faithful insistence, but Fellandros seemed to question the wisdom of trusting a half-elf to show empathy for his fellows. Fellandros's people had been the first mortals. The Revenants were ancient vestiges of the birth of Teth-tenir, and to Fellandros it must have seemed they should be the ones to take up this task. In response, Alinormir would only have needed to point out no Revenant had sought the aid of any god. The Revenants had hidden themselves away from the world long ago, driven by the trauma of a terrible foe that had nearly consumed them and the immortal gods who came to their aid. Their self-imposed isolation was understandable, but it also meant they had moved themselves to the sidelines in the battle for the fate of Teth-tenir.

Alinormir glanced back up the scrying path to the cliff, tempted to go and watch Trem again, to warn him of her trepidations surrounding Vactan, to do something. And yet, she knew Fellandros was right. Trem had stumbled into a terrible trap in the Fortress of Aves, and it would be his greatest trial of character and conviction. She would remain true to her ideals. Alinormir would not interfere by contacting her one hope. Trem would have to make his own choices and suffer his own consequences. She turned away from the cliff once again and walked down the path, fading into the mist as she went and leaving the world of mortals in the hands of one of their own.

Chapter 1

Silverleaf Forest was older than memory. Kings and queens came and went, castles rose and fell, wars were won and lost, but Silverleaf remained. The great forest spread from the Sirrion Sea in the west to the Farwater in the east, a belt across the southern edge of the continent Legocia. Silverleaf was vast and its trees grew thick, casting great shadows on the forest floor, but permitting enough light for determined saplings and ferns to cling to life. It has aptly been called a living wasteland, the only humanoids populating it being the Foresters, a nomadic, nature worshipping civilization of elves and a few men. The forest was impassable to most, but its secret avenues and trails were well known to the elves of Silverleaf and their allies. Once, before invasions had thrown the continent into a prolonged period of strife and conflict, there had been actual roads south, fueled by prosperous trade with the dwarven city of Glimmerhold. Now, none wandered the ragged remnants of the Old Southron Road, fearing ghosts and ghouls that many swore were more than children's stories.

Even in daylight the canopy of Silverleaf Forest keeps the land beneath its branches dim and gloomy. Many are unnerved by the absence of sunlight, but some are comforted by the dark and take solace in it. The Foresters shield themselves in the nest of leaves and twisting arms of trees. Rarely is an outsider thus comforted. Many purportedly brave men walk the rolling knolls of Silverleaf Forest, but few stay long and fewer still venture in after night has fallen. On this night however, a figure did stir. In the dark he was but a shadow of a shadow, his steps quieter than his breath. He moved with a strange, unnerving grace that spoke of power barely restrained and a deep guilt boiling below the surface.

This man was Trem Waterhound. His years at the Fortress of Aves were long in the past, forcibly forgotten, though his face showed no mark of the passage of such a lengthy time. He had done his best to forget and become one with his new surroundings. Here the night was his friend, and Silverleaf his home. He flitted in and out of the trees, stalking inner enemies along narrow paths. He carried only a long hunting dagger strapped to his knee-high deerskin boots, seemingly his only protection among the beasts of the wood. His movements were quick and decisive, his eyes assessing and committing his body to action in a flash. It was an impressive sight, but also a feat borne from experience. Trem was no stranger to Silverleaf Forest and had not been for some time.

Trem had lived most of his days in the wood and he knew his way among its gnarled roots. Here he was safe at last, for life among the civilized people of Teth-tenir had been fraught with danger for him and those about him. Among the trees of Silverleaf he knew only the animals and plants of the forest, deliberately steering clear of the remaining stretches of abandoned roads in the wood that a curious adventurer or fool might travel.

Tonight however, deep in his thoughts, something intangible drew him along a thin path that he had never traveled. Clad in his cloak and weather-beaten leather jerkin he swept through the trunks of great wood like a breeze. Brushing up against deer and wolves that barely noticed his passing, he flew along his newfound trail, reveling in the illusion of solitude. His body was unchanged, healed perhaps from his time in service to Aves, but still full of strength and agility unmatched by almost any other mortal. Only Trem's eyes betrayed his true age. They spoke of haunting experiences beyond count, but nothing in his past could explain the powerful draw of the invisible road he followed.

Something appeared on the path before him, and he slowed his breakneck pace. The folded mound on the forest floor was something unfamiliar, resembling no animal he had ever encountered here. He came upon it slowly, hearing through his sensitive ears only a faint whisper of breath. Trem knelt down, sensing no threat from the form. He felt cloth, a cloak like his own, and slowly rolled the mass over.

The youth, as Trem assessed him, was horribly ashen in countenance. Even for Trem's sharp ears, his breathing was still barely noticeable from such a distance. Something had happened to this man, and for all his instincts clamoring that he leave and never look back Trem found himself searching for the source of injury. The man wore strange armor, hard dark leather with studded, shined bronze bolts at regular intervals across his chest and torso. There were marks of a sharp metal on some and stitched sections in the leather, but they were small and few. Considering the unconscious figure was dressed for battle, Trem paused in his examination to search for the weapon he might have been carrying. Nothing about his attire fit with any nation or organization Trem knew of, but he was hoping for some clue to his homeland in the arms he carried.

Trem's keen eyes spotted a heavy looking broadsword some ten feet from where the young man had fallen. Walking over, Trem knelt and hefted it, feeling its considerable girth contrasting its excellent balance. It had no insignia and a simple design, with a single deep blood channel runnin nearly the length of the blade's center.

There was nothing to learn from the weapon, but he picked it up anyway. Trem then returned to the prostrate body. Setting the heavy blade down beside the unconscious form, he resumed his inspection of the young man. At last he pulled loose several straps and peeled back his armor, finding a ragged gash deep in his left side. Trem breathed a sigh of relief when he saw there was no immediate suggestion of infection. It seemed the loss of blood was the real reason the boy was in such dire straits. Trem paused as he considered his next move, then, with a shake of his head at his own foolishness, he bent low and hefted the body onto his shoulders, sheathing and taking up the fallen sword as he did.

Perhaps he chose to help the other man because of his lineage. He was also a half-elf, like Trem, though a few years beyond his *nai'valen*, the point at which both the elven and human traits are equally balanced and at their strongest. All the unique physical abilities of both races are at their height during this age, and the individual is hardier and swifter than any purebred human or elf can be. Eventually, often swiftly, this heightened period of bodily superiority passes, the individual's physical makeup trending towards one side of their parentage. This youth was beyond his *nai'valen* and his characteristics had chosen to follow more human lines than elven. He still had the faintly angular and pointed ears of an elf and his sharply contoured cheekbones were striking, but his build was thicker and broader and his hair coarser. Trem regretted, at the moment at least, that his being more human had increased his weight as well.

How this man had managed to drag himself to this part of the woods was beyond Trem's reckoning. He remembered the old road, the one connecting Legocia to her sister continent of Southron, lay through the trees at least three miles east. The man might have come from there, but he would have been virtually blind and without much sense or purpose. He had probably stumbled around aimlessly for some time and would not know which way to go if he survived Trem merely patching his wound and leaving him in the forest. In truth that was what Trem had wanted to do, because while his charge was unconscious now if he did succeed in reviving him then the stranger would be awake and questions were sure to follow.

For now that was forgotten. Trem could see the telltale signs of a fever in the sweat rising on the forehead, bobbing over Trem's right shoulder as he walked through the undergrowth. He could sense the heat coming from the unfortunate man's injury and feared he had been mistaken in his initial assessment of the wound. The man groaned and muttered incoherent words but he did not open his eyes. Trem now felt certain there was a fever and it was worse than he had first expected, likely brought on from too much time lying in on the forest floor and too much blood lost. His concern suddenly increased tenfold. Trem quickened his pace as much as he dared, determined to do something before it was too late.

It took Trem almost an hour to reach his cabin, a ramshackle structure butting up against one of the thick trees of the forest. Once he was inside he removed all of the traveler's armor and his thin pack, resting it outside the door with his sword. Placing these items carefully in the corner of the main room he laid the man on his makeshift bed and reexamined the wound. As Trem perused it he removed his own battered jerkin and green tunic, ripped from his hasty dash in the woods, replacing it with another, more faded, brown one.

There was no obvious infection, but the skin was warm to the touch and the flesh around the injury was reddening. Trem could not stop himself from assessing that the neat slicing gash indicated that the wound was probably sword inflicted. Making the youth as comfortable as possible he departed quickly into the woods to search for what he required. A short time later he was back with some white round berries, shiny cross-shaped leaves, and some large reddish roots. He now had what he needed to battle the fever.

Crushing the few berries he wanted for the first dose he set the rest aside on a rickety, unbalanced table. Slicing one of the roots Trem tossed it into a small wooden bowl with the berries, along with the thick pulpy fluid squeezed from a leaf. While he mixed this with one hand he squeezed more sap from the leaves onto a cloth on his table. He then added some hot water he had boiled outside on his old copper pot to the mixture of root, leaf, and berry. Taking this and a poultice cloth into the bedroom he sat down next to the young man.

Carefully he peeled away the worn leather and eyed the injury. He had cleaned around it as best he could and the clothes and armor had stopped it from bleeding, but the scabbing was incomplete, swollen, and raw. Readying himself, Trem pressed the poultice down hard on the wound. The injured man gasped and howled as he tried to rise, but Trem held him down with one hand and forced him to drink every drop of the mixture he had concocted. This process was repeated twice more that day and once later at night, each time rousing his patient long enough to make him to ingest the medicine before he passed out once again. Trem knew he was doing all he could; it would be a measure of the man's will that would decide if he lived or died.

Trem stayed at his cabin for over a week monitoring the outsider. The hermit slept under the sky so as not to awaken his charge, for he rested at odd hours and when he dreamt it could prove disruptive to those around him. The wounded man seemed to suffer a similar challenge, often screaming in his sleep or talking in desperate tones. Though his rambling was often incoherent, one afternoon Trem finally was able to piece together at least a part of what had led him to collapse alone in the middle of the forest.

Trem was holding down the healing cloth against the injury, but feeling no resistance from the youth's body he feared that his guest had finally succumbed to the fever. He eased the pressure on the now stitched and cleaner gash and leaned in close to check the young man's breathing. Trem almost fell back as the bloodshot eyes wrenched open and a tautly muscled arm ripped forward to grasp his tunic. "No Manik! You are staying with us! We are not going to die here! Not alone!"

Trem managed to remove the man's death grip on his shirt and set him back down gently. The youth continued to ramble however, his terrible story rolling out uninterrupted. Trem remained applying the treatment he had prepared and while he sat he listened intently to the snippets of the story. His guest had an unusual tale to tell, and from his eavesdropping and this sudden reliving of the most traumatic event, Trem was able to piece most of it together.

The stranger had been wandering a road through the forest with some companions. They were on their way to a place called Gi'lakil, a town in the middle of the Dust Plains that Trem knew well. Gi'lakil had a reputation as a traveler's haven, a walled town welcoming to every race of mortal and a good place to hear news and rumor. Trem had spent his fair share of time there in his youth, as it was a welcoming settlement that didn't bat an eye at half-elves wandering around. Perhaps this rarity had been what drove Trem's guest there as well.

The group he was traveling with had come from Dragon's Watch, the fertile western coastal valley north of Silverleaf Forest. They had followed the main road east, a straight shot that should have led them past the southern end of the Dragonscale Mountains and to Gi'lakil. Trouble had struck once they reached the Dust Plains. A motley group the young man called the Broken, a name meaning nothing to Trem, apparently threatened anyone on the road. This marauding band had set upon the man's companions and himself, nearly killing two of them in an ambush. In his fevered ravings the injured youth gave few details. Though he rambled for hours, Trem was unable to put a name to most of the man's company and only through concentration could he reconstruct the events of the stranger's unfortunate journey in the proper order.

Trem's focus rewarded him when the boy finally reached the breaking point of his sickness. In the throes of his fever, the injured youth recalled how he had come to the woods. Following the first attack the party had few options. To retreat would have left them exposed on the open plain, and pushing onward would move them still closer to the Broken-infested lands around Gi'lakil. Instead the group had chosen to head south, a shorter march across the plains and into Silverleaf along the Old Southron Road, which should have later connected to another road leading to Gi'lakil while keeping them far less visible. Their travel was slower however, with one of the wounded having to be carried. The young man repeatedly cried out, "No, we'll carry you Manik, I'm not leaving you for those bastards! You will not slow us down, you just need to hold on!"

They had not counted on Broken following them out of the Plains and into Silverleaf Forest. The enemy displayed an unnerving cunning as well, managing to get ahead of the man and his allies and laying an ambush at one of the forgotten road's turns. There had been too many for the youth and his fellows to handle and a friend had apparently pushed him toward the woods, telling him to run. The youth had refused, and his friend had been killed an instant later, the attacker was also apparently the one responsible for the wound on the stranger's side. The young man had fled deep into the trees without any thought to direction and had by sheer luck evaded his attackers, until dropping where Trem found him.

The story pieced together at last, Trem felt a pang of sorrow at what had happened to this traveler at such a young age. Trem had lived a life of death and danger, trying and failing to find his place amid great conflict, but he had accepted his lot long ago and chosen a new life that spared him the trials of his past. This young man, a half-elf like Trem, did not appear to have any violent intent and had met great suffering nonetheless. Trem had made it his business to keep his distance from other mortals, but he still felt a deep sympathy to this youth, merely a child in his mind. The same day he came to understand the full scope of the man's tale the fever broke and Trem, feeling confident he could leave his charge alone without worry, went to hunt for dinner with his old, worn longbow.

On his return from a fruitless hunt Trem did not enter the cabin, but stayed outside to cook the remaining meat of the deer he had killed days before into a thick stew. In his years amid the solitude of the woods he had learned to care for himself, but now he found he was concerned with another as well. He took his time, knowing that with the fever broken his guest might well be awake and able to speak. While Trem tried to convince himself otherwise, he was nervous about the prospect of talking to another person after so long. Using the excuse to cook the savory venison would save him from the interaction a while longer, but eventually he had to bring it into the cabin to feed his guest. Turning the spoon in the pan over his fire for what seemed to be the thousandth time, Trem sighed in commitance. Picking up the pot carefully with a cloth wrapped hand, Trem finally went inside to meet the man he had gone to such pains to save.

Trem came through the front door holding the battered pan before him as it smoked and spattered. He eased it onto his poorly made table and kept the stand steady with one hand as he spooned a hearty portion of the concoction into two bowls. The would-be chef hefted the bowls carefully, judging whether he had fairly distributed their contents, and moved towards the gap in the wall that divided his entryway from his bedroom. Entering the tiny space, Trem saw his patient sitting up in bed and looking about, dazed and unsure of his new surroundings. Trem's arrival brought a look of confusion that gave way to obvious yearning when the injured man saw the hot stew. Setting his own bowl down on the small nightstand next to the bed, Trem walked over and handed the man his food. Taking it between his legs the youth managed to croak out, "Water."

Trem left immediately and went down to the nearby stream with the mostly cooled old copper kettle. When he came back the eyes of his guest seemed to be burning through the bowl before him. Realizing he could not eat until he had something to drink, Trem helped the man swallow greedily from the kettle until it was emptied. Sitting back against the rough wall, his eyes closed, the youth sighed and spoke, "How long have I been here?"

"You have lain in this place over a week." Trem answered, finally settling into a squat against the living tree that occupied one corner of the room to eat his own meal. He found he hesitated to take that first bite, unsure of how he should act. Trem was a little unnerved to hear the sound of his own voice, but simultaneously pleased to hear that of another. His mind worked on two levels at once, ever cautious. Though he was happy to speak with another person, he could not remember the last time he had talked to anyone and the alien nature of the moment made him wary. There was after all a reason he had holed himself away from the world.

"A week," the man's eyes opened wide and he stared at the wall, a faraway look encompassing his gaze. "You did not find any... anyone else?"

Trem chewed a small bite from his bowl before answering slowly, "No, I am sorry. I do not believe your friends made it."

The injured man locked his eyes on Trem. "How did you know I was not alone?"

"You had a fever. Though you spoke of many things I managed to reason out your fate." Trem let the comment hang, knowing he should express some sympathy or compassion for this unfortunate wastrel, but he could not find the words.

"Yes, I suppose you might." The stranger spared Trem the discomfort of the moment. Having lost interest in his meal the patient stared at the wall again and neither man spoke for some time. Trem kept his eyes down on his bowl, but from beneath his brow he studied his companion more thoroughly. He was strong, despite the ravages of the injury and illness, possessing a square chin and curly, towseled, light-brown hair. His eyes were a deeper brown, and stood out very faintly from his lightly tanned skin. For a Legocian he was a bit darker than most, though not the deeper brown of someone from Westia. More than his complexion, Trem noted other features, such as the lack of scars, a sign of inexperience in battle. Though his build was clearly that of a warrior, hard and weathered, this was not a soldier lying in his bed. For one so young, though he might not bear the physical marks, Trem could tell he had been through much. Against his own better judgment, Trem felt a part of him reach out to the innocence of his guest with an unnervingly strong sense of protectiveness. This was a youth raised to accept hardship, but who did not yet know what hardship was.

Before Trem could finish his thoughts the eyes turned to look at him anew. "You are a little young to be a hermit."

It was a piercing accusation and a wise observation that Trem had not anticipated. Unprepared for this moment the host tried to cover his discomfort with a simple response, "I prefer the solitude. I have lived here most of my life."

"Alone?"

Trem nodded decisively, his brief twinge of fear fading. "Always."

The man said nothing, he merely closed his eyes again, then spoke with a deliberate calm, "If you did not learn it before I would have you know my name is Jovanaleth. I am a frontier warrior, a ranger, from the Order of the Blade."

"Jovanaleth," Trem repeated thoughtfully, "it is not a name whose origin I am familiar with."

"My mother chose it when I was born, but my father always said it was too formal. Most people know me as Jovanaleth of the Blade, but father calls me Jovan instead."

"Of the Blade," Trem said curiously. "That is an odd title."

"It simply means I hail from the Order of the Blade, as I said before," Trem stared blankly, this information clearly not registering with him, "have you not heard of my people?"

"No," Trem replied, "I cannot say I have heard of such a group."

Sitting up slightly Jovanaleth eyed Trem anew. "How long have you lived here in the forest?"

"Longer than you would believe," Trem answered. "Tell me about your home."

Jovanaleth sat up still further, clearly taken with the subject. "It was founded in a caldera, north of Dragon's Watch. My father's surname is Blade, taken from his past as a pirate and brigand on the high seas. He formed the order and founded the city, both of which bear his name. The city is young, but already there are many who have come to live there. It seems we never stop building new homes." Jovanaleth settled into the covers a bit more. "You know the story of the final battle at Aves? In the War of the Lion?"

Trem kept his eyes on his guest. "I do."

"My father was there, an officer among the knights." Jovan seemed not to notice his host's discomfort. "He led the only unit composed of non-humans. They came to Aves as volunteers. The Eagle Knights would never accept them until things became so dire they had no choice. After the traitor, Vactan el Vac, killed Bull the Warrior, there was a great fracturing among the knights. Some blamed the Commander for inviting non-human males to the order, for violating tradition. Others claimed those same people had saved the order. My father had fought with those who would never have been allowed to join under previous regimes and regarded them as brave and valiant men. He would not return to a prejudiced and chauvinistic tradition after that.

"Instead he and those who were disillusioned with the Eagle Knights left Aves in control of Richard Margrave III, a man who had never served in battle but was somehow made the new Commander of Aves. He went north to found Bladehome, a new city for a new order that would welcome any seeking to defend the weak." As Jovanaleth spoke, Trem could see the fervor of belief in his face. "We're a young order, but growing rapidly."

Trying to shift away from the subject of the war without being too obvious, Trem asked, "What became of the Eagle Knights?"

Jovanaleth shrugged. "Many of them stayed and they still hold sway over much of the land they defended before the War of the Lion. Halden Bay still exchanges them goods for protection and they have refilled their ranks somewhat, but they also still harbor their prejudice and distrust of all non-humans. My father certainly does not feel the same way."

Trem nodded in understanding. "Because your mother was an elf."

Jovan was caught offguard by Trem's insight, but then realized the conclusion was quite clear with some simple deduction. "Yes, he hid it from the knights while he was at Aves, but it came out after the war. I think that also motivated him to leave. The most dogmatic members of the knights still consider him a traitor for loving an elf."

They were quiet for a time, and Trem motioned to Jovanaleth to eat his stew. The host took his own bowl from the room and washed it in the rain barrel outside before rejoining his guest. The bowl was empty and Trem took it wordlessly to rejoin the first outside by the washbasin. Jovanaleth shifted in bed and flexed his legs with a grimace. "Could I join you? Outside I mean."

Trem eyed his patient skeptically, but offered him an arm. It took a good deal of time and plenty of support from his host, but Jovanaleth reached the doorway of the cottage at last. There he waved Trem off and leaned against the doorframe, wincing as the skin of his injured side stretched slightly. Trem looked up and saw the pained expression as he scrubbed the wood bowl clean with rough dried moss. "Be careful moving about, I am not much of a seamster and my second effort is unlikely to be better than the first."

Jovan made no reply but turned slightly to use his back and thighs to hold his body upright, avoiding extending his arms above his waist. The pain receded gradually and he studied the clearing in which Trem had built his home. It was a minimalist life from what Jovan could see. There was a roughly arranged stone ring for his firepit, with a small three legged iron stand for holding various cooking implements. An old stump, likely the former residence of one of the logs composing Trem's home, served as a spot for splitting wood.

Aside from those features the exterior was lightly trod earth covered in long fallen needles from the trees about it and many vein-like roots that crisscrossed the ground. It would have taken a mere ten strides from the fire pit or cottage to reach the green undergrowth of the forest and perhaps a few more besides to evaporate among the vast nest of living curtains all around.

Trem had scrubbed Jovanaleth's bowl and was now cleaining the iron vessel he had cooked the meal in, but he passed Jovan another small ration of water in the battered copper pot he had provided before. Jovanaleth drank it deeply and examined the wood about him once again, this time hearing the faint call of birds and the rustle of animals small and large all around. He strained his head upward, and though he could feel and see the fingers of sunlight through the canopy he could not see the mighty orb in the sky. "What time do you suppose it is?"

Trem did not look up. "Perhaps a few hours beyond midday. You should return to bed soon, you'll be needing rest for several more days before you can move about freely again."

Jovan would have liked to protest, but he was tired. With resignation he handed Trem back his pot and took his shoulders as a crutch once more. Trem lowered him as gently as he could to the bed and said, "Tomorrow, I will change the dressing on the wound and you can move about a bit more. If you feel comfortable, perhaps you can sit outside."

Jovan thanked him and, despite himself, began to nod off while Trem was still in the room. The stoic half-elf watched him for a time, then went outside and breathed deeply and steadily, his eyes closed, trying to calm himself. Jovanaleth had a surname Trem knew well, a name from his past, and he had grave suspicions as to who his father was. It would be better if he were gone, and soon. Trem briefly considered the convenience of forcibly ending the youth's life himself, but though it was practical it was beyond him. He had done this much to aid him so far; it was too late to turn hostile now. Accepting that he would have to deal with the consequences of saving this traveler's life, Trem went into the woods in search of food for the next day.

The following morning Jovanaleth awoke earlier, before noon, and Trem was waiting with fried eggs and an assortment of berries and roots for him to eat. The young man was famished and devoured them all with haste, only afterward asking in horror if he had eaten Trem's share as well. This actually caused his host to chuckle audibly before explaining he had fed himself some hours before and Jovan should not be concerned. "After all, you're the one who needs sustenance to heal."

Placated, Jovanaleth began to make preparations to leave the confines of his bed again, but his host did not move to help him. Instead, Trem seemed frozen in thought and uncomfortable with what had taken roost in his mind. At last he seemed to come to a decision and said, "Jovanaleth, in your feverish ramblings you mentioned a group you called the Broken. Who are they?"

Jovan sat back slightly, temporarily abandoning his exodus from the cabin. "That's what they call themselves, but in the beginning I think it was a name given to them. When the Army of the Lion was defeated, many boarded ships and returned to the west, across the Sirrion Sea, but there were not enough boats to take them all. The rest that stayed in Dragon's Watch were routed in short order, but many fled to the Dust Plains and began harassing merchants and other travelers there. Some even grew so bold as to raid farms or villages. They're no longer soldiers, most have mixed with the bandits that already roamed the hills and made bigger raiding parties. They have been a threat to the region since the war ended."

"And these are the men that attacked you?"

"Yes," Jovan's voice was soft, but gained strength as he went on, "it is not the first time I have fought them. Some years ago a chieftain named Shatrix raised a great many of the Broken to his banner and had the audacity to attack Bladehome. Some say he had a gem he believed would give him the strength to bring down the walls of the city. He was apparently a shaman of some power, but it failed. Most of his army died against the stone rising high from the caldera or were driven back to their camps in the Dust Plains. He himself is still a prisoner in Wretches Hole."

"Wretches Hole?"

"A prison my father had built to house criminals. There are some there for crimes within the city, but there are smaller cells and holding places for the minor offenses. Wretches Hole was originally built to find and punish those who had done terrible things to the people of Dragon's Watch while in service to the Army of the Lion. Many of their officers who were left behind are now rotting in there."

Trem did not question further, but helped Jovanaleth to rise and make his way outside. It was easier than it had been the first day and Jovan was able to bear much of the weight on his own. Trem sat him in the doorway and leaned him back onto his elbows while he examined the wound. The cloth was bloodstained, but most of it was dry. The injury was healing and seemed far less inflamed and discolored than before. Jovan winced as Trem did a thorough examination, but the time it took to assess the wound and reapply a bandage was mercifully brief. As he sat up, his hand stealing instinctively to the injured side, Jovanaleth said, "You know, it would be easier to talk if I knew what to call you."

Trem was taken aback, having never considered that he had not mentioned his name to his guest. For a moment he thought it might be better to give him a false one, but he reasoned few had known his name when he was not hiding in Silverleaf and letting the truth out now could do little harm. "My apologies. My name is Trem Waterhound."

Jovanaleth laughed and grimaced at the pain it caused him, but despite himself laughed once again with a bit more control. "Waterhound? You said you could not place the origins of my name, but that one surely defies belief!"

Trem stood still and stern, replying through thin lips, "My parents chose their family name. My father was fond of otters, he considered them similar to dogs and they could always be found in water. We were poor and not given a name of grandeur or repute like some more fortunate people."

Jovanaleth realized his reaction had offended his host and held up his hands in sincere apology. "I'm sorry Trem I meant no offense. It is a fine name." To demonstrate his sincerity, Jovan rose from the stoop with great effort and extended his hand in greeting, trying unsuccessfully to hide the pain it caused him as his face tightened. "A pleasure and great fortune to have met you, Trem Waterhound."

Trem did not smile, but his face relaxed significantly and he accepted the outstretched hand. "Thank you, Jovanaleth of the Blade. The pleasure is mine." Trem then had to catch Jovan as he stumbled forward, and admonishingly he led him towards the great stump he chopped his kindling on and set him down. "Politeness is no excuse to injure yourself further. Rest here."

Jovanaleth would have protested, but he did not have the strength. He sat on the stump for some time, the world swimming before him. Gradually, the dizziness and nausea subsided and he was able to raise his head. He flexed his hands and feet and sighed. He could not see Trem, and suspected he had gone off to pursue any of a number of chores and duties necessary to surviving alone in the forest. Jovan was not able to sit still long, he became antsy and reasoned he was a bit thirsty and he ought to be able to reach the water barrel himself and quench his thirst. He rose gingerly, paused to stabilize himself and test his strength, and began the arduous journey across the small clearing outside Trem's cottage. There were several stumbles and near falls, but he eventually reached the barrel and clutched its wooden top with grateful hands.

He did not hear Trem approach, but he was beside him suddenly, a look of genuine concern mixed with chastisement on his face. "It seems leaving you alone for even a moment is unwise."

Jovan glowered at him from beneath his sweat-coated brow. "I was thirsty."

Despite himself, Trem smiled slightly and then swept away. Jovanaleth saw he was carrying several sizeable rabbits and what looked like some kind of larger rodent he could not identify. Trem sat down by the firepit and set about butchering the animals while Jovan, now truly parched and wanting to savor the victory of his challenging stroll, took a long drink straight from the rain barrel.

He felt refreshed and thrust his head beneath the water, pulling it free and tossing his hair backward he exhaled. The water was colder below the surface than he expected, but it made him feel more alive than he had since he awoke from his fever.

Turning back to the firepit he leaned against the barrel and watched Trem. The hermit's back was to him and he was deftly gutting and arranging the carcasses he had brought with him. His speed with the hunting knife was impressive and precise, and Jovan suspected he could have completed the task with his eyes closed if he'd needed to. As Trem turned to reach for the last rabbit he saw Jovan staring at him and froze. Jovanaleth feared he had offended the hermit again, but Trem asked, "Do you like tea?"

Caught offguard, Jovan replied hesitantly, "Yes, my mother used to serve it to me sometimes."

Trem did not answer but went quickly into his house. Jovan debated hobbling over to the firepit while his host was rummaging about in the cottage then decided against it. The other man appeared a short time later carrying a small wooden box, elegantly carved with the image of two dragons, mouths open, facing off at one another. Trem unlatched the lid and held it open in front of his guest. "Choose one."

Jovanaleth could see the delicate bundles of tea were unmarked and was at first unsure how to proceed. But as Trem held the box a bit closer he understood he was meant to smell them and leaned in. Finding an odor he deemed not too pungent and overwhelming he pointed to his selection, Trem nodded in approval, and the copper pot was put back to its duties in short order. Jovanaleth was waiting again, as Trem examined the small shelf in his cottage for the proper receptacle, and then he came out with a small clay pot and two tiny, handless, cups. Jovan was now thoroughly intrigued and, with grim patience, made his way to the fire pit. He set himself down on a horizontal log and watched as Trem carefully lifted the heated water and poured it into the teapot, placing the lid and watching the water overflow slightly with a look of stern satisfaction.

"I've never seen tea cups like those." Jovan remarked.

"I'm not surprised," Trem said as he watched the slow rise of steam from the clay. "They are more common to the south and some places in the west I hear."

"Where did you get them?"

Trem hesitated slightly before saying, "Many of the items I have here are 'found' on the old roads. Abandoned carts, discarded packs, and sometimes a poor soul's last resting place."

Jovan accepted this with understanding and waited as Trem watched the steam rising from the pot, carefully evaluating when the tea had been brewed properly. Once satisfied he poured out small gulps into the cups and handed Jovanaleth one. "This is a darker tea, as are all the ones in the row you chose from. I prefer them more in the morning, but they are quite invigorating at any time of day."

The two sat sipping the tea quietly for a time. Jovanaleth was pleased at the taste, though he was curious as to the origins of his beverage and mildly annoyed at being unable to confirm where it had come from. Trem seemed to relax a great deal with the cup in his hand and was very forthcoming in offering Jovan more. They sat that way for close to an hour and did not speak; Trem because he simply was not one to talk much, and Jovanaleth out of respect for the serenity of his host.

Trem finally broke the silence with a question, one that had been gnawing at him for some time. "Jovanaleth, you said your father founded this Order of the Blade. If that is true, is he some sort of ruler, a king? And if so doesn't that make you a prince?"

Jovan's face contorted in a look of mild frustration. "Techinically, yes. He hates the term and so do I, but I suppose that is an accurate way of looking at our roles."

"I see," Trem said, "then that raises a further question: what were you doing in Silverleaf Forest, so far from home?"

Jovanaleth had frankly been expecting the question for some time. He sighed and set his cup down. "So, that was one thing my fever dreams apparently did not reveal. My father is missing."

"Missing?"

"I suppose that's not the right way to phrase it. He is not lost or taken, but he has been gone from Bladehome for over a year, closer to two in fact."

"And where did he go?"

Jovan shook his head. "That is the problem, his mission was one of secrecy and so it is impossible to know if he reached his destination safely or if he was waylaid by foes before getting there. Either way, he has been gone longer than he should have been and I have to find him."

Trem chose not to probe further, recognizing that Jovanaleth was unwilling to provide more than the vague details of his quest. Wasn't this, after all, what he wanted? The youth would heal and Trem would lead him to the road once again, and then they would both go back to their old lives. Trem would remain hidden and sheltered from the rest of the world, and everything would move onward without him. Remaining locked in time was not so bad if you did not have to watch it pass by before you on the faces of other mortals. Trem rose and took the tea box and his clay pot inside, saying to Jovanaleth over his shoulder, "You will need to rest again, but feel free to stay by the fire as long as you like. I will have to go hunting soon. My snares have been fruitful of late, but a deer lasts far longer than rabbits."

Jovan did not answer, still unsure of his precise relationship with his host. He watched Trem enter the cottage and come out, now clad in his heavy cloak and carrying a quiver of arrows and a curved bow. Without a word or a glance he strode towards the treeline and disappeared into the forest. Jovanaleth contemplated going back inside, but the fire was warm and comforting so he remained. It was unfair of him to hold back the details of his father's disappearance, but then Trem had held back far more if Jovan's instincts were right. Soon it would not matter and he would be gone, and this strange and sad place would be behind him.

Chapter 2

Trem entered the wood quietly and with a determined step. The tea had invigorated him slightly and his sharp eyes felt a renewed focus, making this a good time to go hunting. He tried to dismiss the idea that it was also a welcome reprieve from conversation with Jovanaleth, but the thought lingered. He liked Jovan, found him sincere and stubborn, qualities Trem liked to believe he possessed as well. But he was still an outsider, even if he was half-elven like Trem. There was no room in Trem's little corner of the world for others, and it would be better once he was gone.

Dressed in rough leather breeches, a dark green tunic and a long strap from shoulder to hip that held a water flask, Trem paused to adjust his outfit an ensure nothing was shifting or moving loosely from his body. His dirty blonde hair, shoulder length and wavy, was tied back with a silk cord so it did not affect his vision. He touched his curved bow, slung over his shoulder, and recounted the quiver of arrows to be certain he had enough. Satisfied, he continued to pace steadily forward, putting distance between himself and his home in hopes of stumbling across a deer trail.

He was not far from the cabin, perhaps half a mile when he came across one. Trem could vividly recall his parent's home from years ago and the hunting expeditions with his father. The trail was fresh, he could see the bent and broken stems of plants from a recent passing. His father's voice echoed in his head, "Look for the hoof prints, find the direction they point, and then follow them. It's not so difficult."

A small, insistent voice in the back of his mind kept trying to intercede with the pragmatic tone. "But he wasn't your father. Not really."

Trem quickened his pace and put his mind to work on the hunt. This place had reminded him of that time when he was young, before he learned his beloved parents were not really his true mother and father. Did it matter? He had been happy then, content to live a life of solitude and hard won prosperity with a quiet and honest pair of herders. Trem had felt he belonged in that place, like he belonged in Silverleaf now, and that was all that mattered. The creeping doubts and anger had to be ignored. They would bring him no solace or peace.

Trem did not know why he chose this particular path, but the trail pulled him onward. He paused briefly to consider his position.

He was certain that he was close to his quarry, but he could hear nothing that verified his suspicions. A deer could be quiet, but they were not invisible. Trem raised his head from the tracks he had knelt to examine. Scanning the trail in front of him he spotted a large buck behind a broad tree trunk, grazing on low plants. For a moment Trem was simply in awe. The animal was magnificent, massive full antlers and a strong sinewy body with a symmetrical and curving pattern of tan and brown fur. For a time Trem just watched it, caught in the incredible splendor of the animal. Then he quietly removed his bow and strung it, notching an arrow as he made ready to aim.

Nothing he had done was loud enough to alert the most on guard of animals, but the deer turned and looked right into his eyes as he touched arrow to string. Then it bounded off through the trees, cutting hard and to the left. Trem swung around the curve hoping to get a quick shot in before it found shelter behind another trunk. He paused in confusion, for the deer was standing just beyond where it had turned, waiting and watching. Again as Trem raised his bow the creature darted ahead of him. Trem chased it onward and the pattern repeated itself over and over. Always the beast was one step ahead of him, but close enough that the hunter would not give up his pursuit.

For hours the game went on. Sweat poured down Trem's face and soaked his body. The bow began to feel heavy in his hands and his pace slowed ever so slightly. The deer was always waiting, always patient. Trem refused to give in and followed it relentlessly. As his exhaustion began to take over he saw the buck leap out from the tree cover to his right and break into a small raised clearing. Calling all his reserves into play Trem raced after it and stopped at the clearing's edge, thinking he could hit the animal easily in such an open space.

But the deer was nowhere in sight.

Trem stood dazed on the edge of the clearing unable to believe his eyes. It was a small hillock that rose sharply but for only a brief distance, he could see the edge of the forest on all sides. Not only was his prize gone, the whole area seemed barren of animal life. Yet from the center of the small rise, stretching high into the air like a tower or pillar, was a massive tree. Trem recognized its black and sinuous curving trunk and silver leaves that resembled steel almost immediately; this was a Soul Tree. The dark, oily roots covered the hill it rested on and Trem suspected their girth was so great they had repelled all other growth and propelled the great tree upward to form the mound it now stood watch over.

Soul Trees were believed to exist only in the Forester homeland. When great elves died, they were buried in the Soul Groves, dedicated plots of land where ancestors were laid to rest. There they sprouted a strange sapling of dark wood, black as night, and grew to their full size in a matter of days. The height and width of a Soul Tree was determined by the power of the deceased and the reverence in which the Foresters and gods held them. For one to have grown so large as this, as those Trem had seen only reached the heights of elves or men, it had to have belonged to a legendary figure. But this place was far from any settlement of the Foresters, east of Drena Outpost by nearly a hundred miles. Who could possibly have fallen and been buried here?

Trem approached the giant curving trunk, his hands caressing the black bark that was smooth as glass to the touch. He thought he could feel the steady swell and recession of breath in the tree, but knew it had to be impossible. The leaves glimmered and shown about him, reflecting the sinking sunlight like a thousand tiny mirrors. Trem strode slowly and carefully, aiming to avoid stepping on root or branch out of respect. He searched for some indication of who might be buried here, longing to know. He had nearly completed his circumvention of the great trunk when a voice, old beyond reckoning and powerful, echoed in his mind, *You are not a god.*

Trem stumbled slightly, nearly falling, but a low branch seemed to swing suddenly behind him and stop his tumble. He recovered quickly and looked around in fear, his bow in his hand without hesitation or thought. Before he could set the arrow, the voice reverbated in his head once again, *Put down your bow huntsman, I am not going to harm you.*

Trem turned and faced the tree, for what else could it be that was speaking to him? The branches wavered lightly, it might have been only the breeze and the air was quiet all around him. Unsure of what else to do, Trem spoke aloud, "No, I am not a god. I am Trem Waterhound, a simple hermit."

Boy, the voice fairly thundered in his brain, *do not try to play games with me. I am far too old to be toyed with. You may not be a god but there is a part of one within you. I can feel it, felt it from far off, and therefore claiming to be a hermit is a foul lie I will not listen to.*

Trem breathed slowly, trying to calm himself. He lowered his bow and ran a hand through his hair. "How can you know these things about me?"

Trem was not certain a tree could chuckle, but that was the sensation he felt come back from the being before him. *How? Why, my child, I've known many mortals. In my life I was a druid of great power, no stranger to the ways of the gods and a loyal servant to the goddess Lorima herself. I can sense the piece of one in you and that is not something I have ever felt before. So faint, but burning so brightly. I wish to know why you have this gift over others.*

Trem's lip curled slightly in a smoldering anger. "I do not think 'gift' is the proper term. I did not ask to be what I am."

Hm. That is no different than most, it is just that your circumstances are far more unusual than others.

Trem attempted to redirect the conversation. "I also would ask something of you. I have seen Soul Trees before, but never one of such majesty. I gave you my name, I would ask for yours in return."

A fair request, in life I was called Gerand Oakheart.

Trem's jaw dropped despite himself. "Grandfather Forest? So this is where you finally fell."

Fell? Yes, I suppose I did. Coldran Berron brought me here and he left me at my insistence. I do not recall falling, or dying, only a great weariness overtaking me and then I was awake, but no longer the same. I could feel the forest all about me; the resonance of Silverleaf and the light of thousands of lives, in plant and animal, swirling in an endless spiral outward. It was wondrous, and it remains so. Though, I must admit, I have missed the conversation one has with others. The squirrels and other rodents are too scatterbrained to talk with, and the other wiser beasts hold me in such reverence it is almost as though they fear to talk in anything but formalities.

Trem listened in fascination to the breezy voice in his mind, pacing slowly about the great roots while looking up at the full stateliness of the tree about him. This was a great discovery he had made, and one he did not feel worthy to have been in the presence of. Gerand's spirit spoke again, *How is it that you, Trem Waterhound who carries a part of a god, found me when others did not? Did your divine spark bring you here?*

"No," Trem answered, "I was hunting a deer. It burst through the wood into this clearing and I followed."

I sensed no such animal. Strange. Trem did not respond, his mind raced with things to ask, but he could not settle on one question. The voice echoed about him once more, *Why do you call yourself a hermit, Trem Waterhound?*

"Because I am. I live alone here in Silverleaf. Or at least, I have been alone until recently."

Oh?

Trem, for lack of anything else to say, explained the discovery and recuperation of Jovanaleth to Gerand Oakheart. The strange and otherworldly voice did not interrupt him, nor could Trem be certain he was still listening, but he told what tale there was anyway. "And so once he is well enough I will lead him back to the road and wish him luck. Then it will be me and me alone once again."

There was a lingering silence, then Grandfather Forest said, *Why leave him? This is a young man of similar lineage, whom you admit reminds you of yourself, in need of aid. I sense you have reason to be alone, Trem Waterhound, but does no part of you retain a love and concern for your fellow mortals? Do you not miss them? Even I, who have died and become something more than I once was, relish the sound of another's voice.*

"He is no one to me," Trem insisted, averting his eyes from the great tree. "He's just a man in distress that I helped. He has told me little and kept much of his quest hidden. I do not believe he wants my help and I am content to see him on his way."

Perhaps he would be more willing to share his tale with you if you were more forthcoming about yourself.

Trem waved his hand in violent dismissal. "There is nothing in my past that would encourage trust. Quite the opposite, and that is why I remain in Silverleaf. I am better off alone and the world gets on quite well without me."

Youth, the voice breathed, *so angry and righteous all at once. I remember it faintly. Do not think I do not detect the lies in your voice. Your words may be true, or you have convinced yourself they are, but behind them lies doubt.* Trem was unsure of how to respond, so he let the comment hang. The spirit of Gerand Oakheart continued, *Do you know my tale, Trem Waterhound?*

"I heard it many times, Grandfather Forest. You are a legend, a great hero to all the people of Legocia and even of Teth-tenir entire."

But you have heard the story then, the recounting of events and actions taken or not taken. You have not heard of the friendship, the love, the sacrifice, and all the sadness that came with it. Those are things few but the greatest bards can relate, and even then they pale in comparison to the experience itself.

"You are right, I have not heard the tale in such depth."

It is too long to recount here and now, and I suspect you would have little patience for it. But there is one part that I believe might be of use to you. Coldran Berron was commander of the Eagle Knights when the Arcane Wars began. He was a reasonable man, a practical one, and had he not been their leader I doubt any other would have accepted my offer of aid or that of the Silverleaf Elves. We fought that war together, a human and an elf side by side, despite the countless feuds and wars our own people had held against one another before. I did not want to help him at first, and I suspect he would have refused my help if he had believed he could, but I was commanded by the goddess Lorima to seek him out in visions of what would come if I did not.

That alliance, formed of necessity, killed me in the end. The terrible forces we contended with infested me with their power and tried for a long time to consume me in their indescribable madness. I knew I was dying, knew it was killing me to not give in, to not succumb to the thing that had taken up residence within my body. Coldran knew it too, and when his own men betrayed him and took back the knights, returning them to an institution of hatred and segregation, he and those loyal to him stayed with me. When I could no longer continue on he and he alone walked with me into Silverleaf and was my sole companion before death. A man who my people would have called their enemy not long before was, at the last, my only friend.

Trem was quiet as the voice swirled about him in tones of sadness tinged with love and longing. He did not speak for a time, then replied carefully, "Your sacrifice is well known, Grandfather Forest, but perhaps not all of us are as brave as you or as willing to risk the hope that others will return our loyalty one day."

You misunderstand me, Trem Waterhound. There was no bravery, not even in the end. There was only the task that needed doing and the determination to see it done. Coldran and I became friends not because we were similar, but because we had walked hand in hand to stand against a foe as one. Why must you and this Jovanaleth be any different?

Trem shook his head fiercely. "It is not the same. I have stood, as you said, 'hand in hand' against a common foe with others different from me, and then when the enemy had fallen we too fell on one another with the same old feuds."

What feud exists between you and Jovanaleth? Trem had no answer, though he feebly sought one. Grandfather Forest continued, *Perhaps you are right, Trem Waterhound. Perhaps you and Jovanaleth will not form a bond, will not rise above mere acquaintance to something better, but you and your life of solitude will not sustain you.*

Trem laughed aloud, "I think you are lacking an important piece of knowledge. The piece of an immortal within me is what sustains me. I carry a part of Kurven, God of Time. I do not grow older, for me time itself stands still," he held his hands outstretched in mock invitation to his own grandeur. "I am the persistence of life itself."

That is not life. That is merely a continuation of existence. The voice was harsh and scornful. *Time is not what measures your life Trem Waterhound, it is what you do with whatever time you have. You could live a thousand years alone here in Silverleaf, and a child of ten might have surpassed you in living many times over.*

Trem was growing frustrated, but he restrained himself from responding out of respect. The voice had stopped and silence reigned for a time, enough so that Trem was able to grow calmer and consider what Gerand Oakheart had told him. At last the half-elf shouldered his bow and bowed slightly. "I will take your wisdom into account, Grandfather Forest. Perhaps I will return soon and inform you of my decision."

Farewell, Trem Waterhound. I have enjoyed speaking to you, though I hope if we do converse again it is after you have dared to leave this place and tried to live once more.

Trem turned sharply and walked out of the clearing. He reached the cover of the trees and realized it was growing quite dark. He had found no food for the next day, and it was beyond the point where hunting would be likely to prove fruitful. He walked slowly through the forest, deep in thought after the strange encounter only moments before. He turned to look back before he was too far into the wood, and could not see the hillock or the opening any longer though he was sure it should have still been visible. Without pausing to consider the bizarre occurrence any longer, he began loping across the forest floor back to the cottage. The snares he had set earlier that day would have to suffice for now and he did not wish to leave Jovanaleth alone for much longer.

The bright, late-morning sunlight came through the thin animal hide window and Jovanaleth woke slowly. He had no recollection of falling asleep or of coming into the cottage. His surroundings were strange to him, and at first he did not remember where he was. Once his memory returned he noted that he was feeling more revived and strong than he had since his injury. Leaning on the edge of the bed, he looked out into the opposite room to see if his companion was present. Seeing nothing, he decided to try and stand. Tossing aside the patched sheets he slowly leaned onto his feet. Testing his legs, Jovan wobbled slightly than steadied. He walked a few shaky steps and then, having found his rhythm, discovered he could walk outside slowly but pain free.

"Well, you are looking better."

Trem had been awake for some time. Jovan turned quickly at the sound of his voice and saw the hermit coming from the woods with three more freshly snared rabbits. He smiled and said, "And feeling much better, thank you."

Trem nodded to indicate he had heard Jovanaleth, but his expression did not change. He sat at the firepit and began to butcher the freshly caught meat. Jovan walked slowly over to his host and eased himself down on the same log he had used the day before. Trem continued with his task mechanically, and neither of them spoke. Trem finished skinning the last rabbit and squatted down to begin selecting a spit from the iron skewers next to the pit. Jovan finally felt compelled to break the silence. "I think I should leave here tomorrow."

Trem did not answer right away, though he paused in his work. "Are you sure you are well enough?"

Jovanaleth shrugged. "As well as I can expect and delays are costly at this point."

"Where exactly to you intend to go next?"

"Gi'lakil," Jovan responded decisively. "It was our destination before and there is no reason to change course from the original plan. It is a place for travelers from across the land and if there is any news or rumor of my father I can think of no better place to begin asking after it."

Trem looked up from the fire. "Your last attempt to cross the Dust Plains landed you, bleeding and feverish, in these woods. It was a miracle I found you before an opportunistic predator, or even found you at all. So now you intend to take up your task, which nearly killed you, without the aid of your friends?"

Jovan's face darkened significantly. "I have no choice. My father is missing and I must find him. I do not expect you to understand."

Surprisingly, Trem's face softened somewhat and he turned back to the fire. "No, I do understand, Jovanaleth. Better than you might expect, in fact. I will take you to the road tomorrow and from there you can make your way to Gi'lakil." He stood, the three rabbits now slowly roasting over the fire. "Watch them while I see what I have left for vegetables."

Jovanaleth was unsure how to respond, so he did not. He kept the spits turning slowly, cooking the meat evenly while Trem scraped together a mixture of carrots and beets he thought were still edible. The two ate shortly afterwards, in silence, and then Trem stood. "If you must leave tomorrow you will need supplies and I have few to spare. I'll attempt hunting once again and I will be gone for much of the day. There is some food left inside and you are welcome to it. If I am fortunate, I will have much more when I return."

Without any further discussion or opportunity for thanks Trem strode to the cottage, retrieved his bow and quiver from the day before, and left. Jovanaleth spent much of the day sitting by the fire or making slow, stiff walks to the rain barrel and other places around the cottage. He ventured a bit further into the treeline once or twice, but wisely chose to go no further. Finally, he settled on trying to heft his broadsword again. He was able to raise it, painfully, but could manage only a few feeble and awkward swings. His strength was back, but the wound in his side was still tender and the muscles around it not yet fully healed. Dejected and slightly bored, he sat down by the fire again with the blade on his lap and waited for Trem to return.

Though he had said he was going hunting, and intended to do so, Trem spent the better part of the morning and early afternoon searching for the deer trail that had led him to Gerand Oakheart's Soul Tree; but there was no trace that he could find anywhere near where he had stalked his quarry the day before. He then attempted to orient himself based on things he had seen the day before, and from memory construct a pathway to where the hillock had been, but it was no use. After several hours of frustration he was no closer to finding his way than he had been when he started. He set himself down in the gap between a great tree's roots and rested for a time, listening to the birds and other small residents of the forest all about him.

The thought of leaving had remained deep in his mind all day, and now sitting here he thought to himself: why should he? Here there was peace and relative quiet. No one bothered him and he bothered no one. He had come here for a reason, a very serious and important reason, many years before, had he not? Surely Jovana-leth's arrival and dire situation did not change anything for Trem. After all, he had already done more than was necessary in healing him and allowing him a safe place to recover. Trem owed Jovanaleth nothing and he was certain the young man would see it that way as well.

But the words of Gerand Oakheart still lingered in his head. That sad, sympathetic tone when he had lamented Trem's bitter isolation and fear of the outside world. *That is not life.* Those had been his words. Trem had dismissed them in earnest before, but now he began to wonder. His search had been in vain and it frustrated him, for in talking to Grandfather Forest once again he had hoped to come to some clear-minded decision instead of the mire of confusion he found himself in now. The simple answer was to do what he had told Jovanaleth he would, nothing more or less. However, another part of Trem, one long suppressed, seemed to be growing in strength and command.

Trem stood and brushed dirt from his clothes. There was an alternative to finding Grandfather Forest here of course, one that he did not relish but felt might be necessary. He sighed audibly and shook his head almost in disbelief at his own conclusions. This would likely not be a pleasant experience. Trem set his mind to hunting for now, and tried to forget the looming challenge he would face later.

Jovanaleth was still awake when Trem returned to the cabin. It was a good sign. It meant Jovan's strength was returning along with his stamina. The journey would still be long and difficult, but it seemed Jovan might be better able to complete it than Trem had expected. The hunter came from the brush with a large doe slung over his shoulder. Jovan stood and made as though to come and help him, but Trem waved him off. Walking past the cabin, he tied a rope around the creatures back legs and strung it up. He looked back at his guest and smiled. "More food than we'll need for a while, but good timing. You can take most of the meat with you once it's been cooked. Can you help me with it? The job goes faster with two pairs of hands."

Jovan was happy to have something to do. Moreover, Trem made him feel useful by giving him actual responsibility in the process. Rather than gutting the creature himself, which Jovanaleth expected would have been swift and efficient, the half-elf showed his guest where to cut and how deeply. Jovanaleth had hunted before, but to his shame the butchering of his kills had always been handled by servants or professionals paid for the service. This was a new experience and Jovan was happy for anything to do other than sit and wait.

It took them a little over an hour to completely skin the deer and remove the organs. Trem set some aside to boil into a soup; a practice Jovanaleth was unfamiliar with and not a little nauseous at the prospect of. Noting his companions discomfort Trem proclaimed they would eat the soup that very evening, ostensibly to prove to Jovanaleth it was a far better meal than the sight of the innards might imply. Jovan was just able to avoid retching at the idea.

They spent the rest of the evening cooking, setting the animal skin to dry, and brewing more tea to enjoy while they worked. Trem chopped more kindling, as they had run low, and Jovanaleth was left to watch the food and rotate various items over the fire. It was an efficient and comfortable system and the two talked more than they had in any of the previous days combined. Trem spoke of various hunting escapades he had been on, most in Silverleaf but some near his family's home, a place he described in such general terms Jovanaleth could not place it. Jovan talked of his home and family a bit, but mostly the city itself and the various places he liked to visit. Trem discovered he had read a great deal more than Jovanaleth, who seemed to take knowledge from people rather than texts. A good-natured argument soon arose over which was the more valuable form of scholarship; a debate that remained happily unresolved when they were done.

Jovanaleth finally went to bed well after the sun had gone down, though he was resolute in stating he wanted to arise early and be on his way as soon as was possible. Trem grew quieter as he prepared to leave, and Jovanaleth was on the verge of thanking him profusely for all he had done when he sensed this was not the time. With a slight nod he turned and made his way gingerly into the cabin and to bed, where he was soon sleeping deeply.

For his part Trem made himself comfortable by the fire and allowed his thoughts to drift slightly, but kept meditating on a singular purpose. He needed to walk a fine line between freely letting his mind wander and priming himself for what lay ahead. As he gradually began to drift into sleep, his heartrate slowing and his breath becoming steady and rhythmic, he reminded himself that he was in control and would remain so. When the calm of true unconsciousness took him it did not have him fully in its power, and Trem was able to slowly peel back the curtain and assume command of his dreams.

It is impossible to know how long one sleeps before they begin to dream, as it can vary depending upon their need for deeper sleep and personal tendencies towards dreams. Regardless, the arrival of a dream always feels sudden to the sleeper, as the time before when we are unconscious passes without any notion of it having done so. As Trem felt the dreamscape forming around him he could not be sure how long he had been sleeping before it took him or how long it would be before he would awaken. Time between the realm of mortals and the realm of dreams does not synchronize, and one can never know how long has passed in the waking world whilst they are asleep. Thus, someone who takes control over their dreaming self never knows how long they have in the dreamscape, making the possibility of completing any task in a single sleeping period a difficult calculation.

Trem knew that those who worshipped one of the lesser immortals, Morphus, God of Dreams, often used various methods both magical and medicinal to extend their sleeping period. These were dangerous and often unpredictable, and he had never dared to try any of them himself. Moreover, he was not a trained dreamwalker, just someone who had slowly developed an understanding that he could take control of himself and his surroundings when dreaming and manipulate them. Trem had read a great deal in his youth and understood that control over one's dreams was something that could be practiced and expanded, but often took many years of active attempts to even become marginally successful at. For him it had been a skill he had from birth, likely an extension of his power from holding a part of a god within him, and one that he detested just as often as he found it useful.

Now with the dreamscape fully formed before him, Trem concentrated on a familiar place: his own cabin. The scene shifted and reformed to replicate it, though of course it was not precisely the same. One of the great difficulties of controlling and traveling through the dreamscape is that everything to the dreamer's mind appears normal, even those things which are impossible in the mortal world. This is believed to be because the dream world exists between the mortal realm and the Godly Realms. In the mortal realm there are physical laws that dictate what is possible, and those limitations build expectations in the minds of mortal people so that anything behaving in defiance of those laws is noteworthy and perhaps frightening. In the Godly Realms there are no such physical laws, at least according to what Trem understood from his studies. The gods can create the illusion of physical space or limitations, form bodies and objects that mimic those on Teth-tenir, but they are unnecessary trappings, audacious lies the gods tell themselves and the rare mortal who might visit them. In the Godly Realms, only the power of the god and the scope of their imagination and wisdom set limits on their world, and the dreamscape is a strange amalgamation of the two. When you see a fish float by you in the air as you stand amid the hot sands of a desert you do not question its possibility in a dream, though were you awake you would believe you had gone insane. This is the wonder and the danger of the dreamscape, for we may accept the normality of things that can harm us in that strange intersection of mortal and immortal planes.

Trem allowed the scene before him to fill out with familiar objects and sights, helping him create more stability and grounding in the dreaming realm. Once he felt he had established his presence there strongly enough, he began to consider how he could reach out to Gerand Oakheart. The dead of Teth-tenir were taken to the Godly Realms by Neroth, as was his duty, and there ensconced in worlds born of their own memory and experience or, if they had been especially pious, placed with the deity to whom they were dedicated. Once dead, a mortal was able to shape their world just like a god did, though awareness of their state and raw power greatly limited the changes they could bring. More importantly, the dead could reach the dream world with relative ease, simply by choosing to, as sleep was not a necessity for the dead.

But Trem was faced with an unusual challenge. Gerand Oakheart had died and his soul had given birth to a great tree, as the sacred rite of the Silverleaf Elves decreed was possible. Was he then dead and able to traverse the dreamscape as easily as those in the Godly Realms? Was he trapped within the Soul Tree and the method of reaching him different? Trem did not know, and it occurred to him that if the latter were true it would soon be evident when he tried to make contact with the spirit of the dead man. In his mind he steeled himself and began to try to form the hillock and clearing where he had previously met Grandfather Forest. As it was a place less familiar to him the images about him shimmered and shifted with some regularity, much less stable than the cabin. Trem pressed onward, attempting to pull from his memory the precise appearance of the place and, in particular, the gnarled roots of the tree and its great trunk rising into the air, believing this part of the image would be most necessary to summoning the entity he sought.

The image was still slipping from one sight to another, but Trem felt the appearance of a presence. He eased his attention on the environment slightly and spoke, "Grandfather Forest, is that you? I am Trem Waterhound, the hunter who stumbled across your tree. I have questions I would ask."

The voice hummed in Trem's mind, as before, but he knew immediately it was not that of Gerand Oakheart. *I can answer your questions, Trem Waterhound.*

The arrival of a being Trem had not sought disturbed him, for it meant the other presence had been seeking him and was strong enough to have not only found him, but also to have brought itself to his location in the dream world. Trem's reply was wary, "You are not Grandfather Forest."

No. I am Kurven, God of Time, and perhaps of more assistance to you than the one you seek. As the voice pulsed steady and unabating in Trem's mind, the form of the speaker emerged before him. Kurven was shapeless, though he seemd to have done Trem the favor of forming shades of blue in the shape and placement of eyes. It was only mildly less unnerving. The god spoke again, *You may ask your questions.*

Trem was unsure why, but he relinquished control of the dreamscape to the other and it lurched, violently, to another place. The world swam around them and reformed swiftly. They floated in space, surrounded on all sides by stars, wonderful and bright. Trem, despite his understanding that it was a dream, looked about himself agape. Kurven did not seem surprised or even fazed by the sudden relocation, instead he waited for Trem to collect himself. Despite his wonder, the half-elf was still cautious. "I am not sure you are the one I wish to ask anything of, God of Time. I have what you gave me, unasked for, and I think you have done enough."

Trem's tone was confrontational, though he tried to keep it level and even. Kurven's reply came in the same strange pulsing rhythm, *That is a matter which cannot be undone. Though if you wish to know more of it I will try to answer you.*

"My questions were for Gerand Oakheart, not you."

But I am here and he is not, nor will you be able to reach him unless he wills it, and he does not. He believes he has told you all you must know, he has gone back to his meditation with the wood, earth, stone, wind, and rain of Silverleaf Forest.

"I see." Trem thought for a moment, after all he could simply abandon the dream world and awaken or go into a black, empty sleep and forgo this exchange. Still, his curiosity got the better of him. "Why did you come in his place?"

Was this what you were to ask Grandfather Forest?

Trem detected a hint of amusement in the respone. "Of course not, but you are here now and the answer interests me."

Very well. You have not attempted to control the dreaming world for some time. As you said, I gave you something long ago when you were born, and that piece of me still holds a connection to my greater self. I sensed you here and the tendrils of need you sent in search of another. I interceded, knowing you would fail in your task, to see if I could be of aid to you.

"Now you choose to see if you can help me? After all the times before...."

Kurven cut him off. *The gods can no longer intervene whenever we please, nor make contact under circumstances of our choosing. You know this, as you also know that you could have sought me in any of my temples or in this realm where we now are having this discussion. Do not blame me for your decision to hide yourself away.*

For that, Trem had no answer. He knew Kurven was correct, had he reached out to him, or quite likely any god, they would have answered him. Still, he refused to be cordial. "You are right, I did not want to speak with you or any of your kind. I have hidden, and would choose to remain so."

But you have doubts. Doubts brought on by your new guest and a surprise conversation with a revered druid long dead.

"How did you know about Jovanaleth?"

I cannot interfere with your life or enter your world, but I can observe and what we share makes it easier to find and watch you.

"How comforting," Trem scowled. "Maybe my first question ought to be how to keep you from looking in on me."

It is not something I do often, only when events pique my interest.

Trem did not answer. He scanned the stars all about them and wondered to himself if there was any reason to continue this conversation, again considering if leaving the dreamscape was the better course of action. He could go back, sleep, awaken, and then see Jovanaleth on his way and return to his former life. But the same internal confusion that had led him to this course of action still lingered. With a sigh he asked, "What truth is there in what Gerand Oakheart said, that by remaining as I am now I am not truly living?"

Kurven was slow in responding. *As I am immortal, I do not know if I understand the meaning of his question.* Trem rolled his eyes in frustration, but Kurven was not done. *Though, I suspect he means living in the sense of experience. What have you not already done and learned from Silverleaf, from a lonely life? What is left for you if you stay there?*

"It is not what is left, but what awaits me if I leave that has kept me where I am for so long," Trem answered. "If you have truly watched me then you understand. Outside of Silverleaf, among the others, I have not had great fortune."

I see, Kurven said. *So your past failures assure your future will bring more of the same?*

"I do not do well among others, as I said."

You seem to have enjoyed the company of Jovanaleth.

"Maybe I am just good with individuals. Add more and...." Trem trailed off, unwilling to elaborate.

Perhaps, I am not so knowledgeable of social matters among your kind.

"Is it not one of your powers to see the future?" Trem asked, "As the God of Time couldn't you tell me what will happen if I go or if I remain?"

Time is not a straight line. Nor does it have singular events that, like rungs on a ladder, lead from one to another in a defined order. There are an immense number of outcomes down either path. Therefore the question is difficult to answer decisively.

"And I suppose the possibilities are so many you could not hope to recite them all here, now."

Correct. Though I can tell you one thing with certainty. Despite himself, Trem looked up in curiosity and waited. *If you remain in Silverleaf, if you never leave, then the world will end with you there, collapsing all around you, and all of it that you have and have not seen will cease to exist, forever.*

Trem seemed unfazed. "The world has to end sometime doesn't it? And I do not appear to be in danger of dying of old age."

The world will end sooner if you remain.

"That sounds like a threat," Trem grated, once again crossing his arms and squaring his shoulders. "I know that you gave me this gift of yours for some misguided reason, because you thought I would stand against evil or some such foolish notion. Well I tried that didn't I? Tried and failed more than once, why should I venture forth and do so again?"

No one is asking you to fight against evil, Trem. Good and evil are childish concepts.

Trem's eyes narrowed as the words echoed in his mind. "You sound like someone else I remember."

That was not my intention.

"Fine, you told me what happens if I stay. You mean if I leave it somehow prevents the end of the world?"

No.

Trem threw up his hands in exasperation. "Then what does it matter? How is any of this helping me or you or anyone?"

Your leaving is not enough. As I said, there are many possible outcomes tied to choices you and any number of others, mortal and immortal, will make. All I have told you is that if you remain, if you stay hidden and withdrawn from the world, it will wilt, wither, and fall to nothing.

"And if I leave, now, it may not happen?"

If you leave at all, the possibility of Teth-tenir continuing on for a great while longer exists, yes. Though it might be wise to leave with someone else and not on your own.

"Coercion," Trem muttered. "For a god lacking in knowledge of mortal social graces, you seem very adept at manipulating behavior."

I am only expressing something that I believe to be true. Your leaving with Jovanaleth will undoubtedly be better for you, with a companion to assist you for at least a portion of your journey. And is there no part of you that is intrigued by his undertaking? It seems the search for a lost parent would be of personal interest to you.

"I gave up that search long ago," Trem said quietly, "and I am almost certain I know his father. I met him before."

Indeed?

"Yes, and the connection does interest me, though not in the way that you might think. It makes me wonder who is pulling the strings, who sent him here to be found by me? Was it you, Kurven, or perhaps Alinormir, or Neroth? It could be any number of minor gods, interfering in my life once again. You say you cannot intervene in my life directly, but you immortals always seem to find an avenue to worm your way into it regardless."

You may be right. One of my kin may have arranged these events, but it was not I and, despite what you are, you are not excluded from the possibility of coincidence. And no matter how or why he came to you it was your choice to help him. I wonder why that sense of duty has such limits that you would see him off, alone and injured, into a land you know is rife with danger?

Trem put his hand to his brow and replied, "Once again, Kurven, you seem far more adept at playing games with my mind than you let on. Enough of this, I will make my choice when I awake. Go, and let me have dreams of my own making."

Kurven did not respond, but faded from view. The universe of stars faded as well, and soon Trem floated only in blackness. The empty space was unnerving and he quickly refocused on the cabin, the woods, and the familiar trappings of his home. Once he had recovered his control and was back in surroundings that soothed him he released the dreamscape and allowed his weary mind to wander

Waking was a gradual process. Trem opened his eyes and slowly stirred, a bit at a time, on the ground outside his home. He felt sleepiness in his limbs and head, a groggy disconnect that lingered even as he tried to rouse himself. He listened, but did not hear Jovanaleth stirring within. Methodically he got to his feet and walked to the rain barrel. Rather than douse his head, he scooped up water into his copper pot and walked to the fire pit. Tea would be the first thing he would need to clear his mind, and the process of brewing it would begin the piecing together of the night's travels.

Like common dreams, those in the dreamscape often evade the awakened. Bits and pieces of them might still flit through the conscious mind, and those must be snatched and studied so that the full scope of their meaning and the completeness of memory can be formed. It is a trying process, and difficult when one is just awake, but also most easily accomplished when the dream is fresh. Trem watched the pot heat and went to get his box of tea. As he sat down with it he turned over in his mind the options before him, recalling his conversation with Kurven in increasing detail.

"What's the selection this morning?"

Trem nearly jumped at Jovanaleth's voice, his thoughts had been so fixated on the task and his nighttime adventures. He looked up and saw the young man standing over his shoulder, smiling full and refreshed, and shrugged. "I had not decided. You can choose if you like."

"Oh no," Jovan sat beside Trem, "I know nothing about tea, you should choose."

Without further discussion Trem selected a hearty, earthy red tea and accepted the clay pot from Jovanaleth, who had carried it out from the cabin with him. As the aroma of the leaves rose into the air Trem breathed deeply and sighed. He felt a bit clearer-headed now and refreshed, despite the strain of the evening's activities. Trem passed Jovan his cup and scanned his appearance. His was dressed for travel, his armor back on over his earthen colored tunic and his boots strapped and ready for marching. Trem knew what he had to ask, but also felt he had to explain himself first.

"Jovan," he said in a soft tone, "I must admit I have not been entirely honest with you."

Jovanaleth did not answer, sipping his tea he watched Trem over the top of his cup and waited. Trem cleared his throat and then out it came, "I knew your father."

Jovan's eyes widened enormously and he straightened, though he managed to refrain from standing. "When? How?"

Trem sighed. "His name is Jonathan Blade, yes?" All it took was one look at Jovan's face to confirm Trem was correct. "He was the captain of the unit I fought for in the War of the Lion, as a volunteer for the Eagle Knights."

Jovanaleth seemed confused. "But that was almost thirteen years ago, and you are maybe twenty-five summers at most. You would have been a child." Trem's face showed he had not considered the mathematics of his past as it related to his appearance and unique condition. Fortunately, Jovan took this as an expression of pain and memory rather than a desperate mind racing to formulate the appropriate lie. "You must have been a page or squire of some kind then."

"Yes," Trem was grateful for the assistance in his deception, "I was named a Sword, but did rather little fighting. I doubt your father would remember me."

Jovanaleth nodded in agreement. "He spoke quite rarely of that time, I think it was very difficult on him."

"Yes, it was difficult for us all."

"But why did you keep this from me Trem?"

Trem sat up and set his cup down before continuing, "I was not sure, at first, that it was the same man, but over time the things you told me made it impossible that it could be anyone else. I never knew he had a wife or son, I left the knights soon after the final battle on the hills outside Aves. It was a bloody, terrible affair and I had no desire to remain. I came here shortly after that, seeking refuge from the brutality of the world I had been a part of.

"Your father was good to me. Good to all of the other non-humans as well. He never showed a fleck of prejudice towards any of us. I saw he trusted his soldiers, regardless of who or what they were. What you have told me of your home and his efforts does not surprise me. It sounds like the same man I knew."

"He has always been a forgiving man," Jovanaleth agreed, "and never quick to judge anyone by their appearance or demeanor. He was once a marauding pirate, now turned king and ruler of a city that strives for equality and understanding. I think that is what made him so willing to believe in the redeeming qualities of others."

"So you plan to continue looking for him?"

"Yes," Jovanaleth's face was determined, "I cannot rest until I learn what has become of him."

"Very well," Trem stood and tried to array himself in a military stance before his guest, examining him, "you seem fit enough to travel." He paused and placed a hand awkwardly on Jovan's shoulder. "If you will have me, I wish to accompany you."

Jovanaleth was taken aback by the offer. "But, why? You have done more than enough for me already and you seem to enjoy your privacy. Simply because you once knew my father when you were young?"

Trem removed his hand and looked back towards his home. "I have lost both of my parents. In truth, I lost them some time ago. I sympathize with your plight, Jovanaleth, and I also fear that if I lead you to the road north I will simply have delayed your death. Wandering into the Dust Plains alone and injured gives you little chance, no matter your bravery or determination."

"I can make it," Jovan said defiantly, "but perhaps it will be more difficult than I expect. Still, I know you are a gifted hunter and survivor Trem, but what of combat? War? How much training could you have received at so young an age, and how much of it has your body forgotten?"

Trem shrugged. "The only way to know is to test myself. Regardless, my eyes and ears will be of great use, perhaps enough to avoid fighting altogether." He turned his eyes back on Jovan. "I ask again, will you have me?"

Jovanaleth paused, hand on his chin, considering. Then he smiled and nodded firmly. "I will, Trem, thank you."

The hermit seemed neither pleased nor unhappy with this answer, but almost consigned to it. "Gather your things then, I have to retrieve my own gear."

Jovan did not argue, he went to the door of the cabin and retrieved his pack and warm wool cloak, tossing it over one shoulder, as it was still rather warm. Beside the doorway he checked the release on his scabbard and strapped the heavy broadsword his father had given him to his back. The additional weight was noticeable, but not overwhelming. Testing his feet once again, he found he felt able to move more steadily than before with his items returned to him. Feeling fully prepared he turned to look for his fellow traveler.

Trem was bowed over a spit roasting the rabbits and cutting up slices of salted venison for the journey. "Watch these, I won't be a moment."

Jovan complied, kneeling to turn the spit slowly and mentally calculating the number of days they had meat supplies for. Trem entered his home and walked to the bedroom. Removing a long, squat chest from under the bed he eased it open with an ominous creak. He flinched as if struck when he saw the torn and faded blue tunic, but he recovered quickly and made himself rummage through the items beneath it. First he reached in to pull out a sword, barely squeezed into the trunk diagonally from behind the folds of cloth. A battered and scuffed scabbard of a longsword rested in his palms for a while as he took the time to study every inch and absorb every unnerving, disquieting thought it brought to him. Calm at last, he set the blade aside and continued his search. He pulled out a thin but finely made leather shirt, which he put on immediately over his green tunic. He then removed a light, long armed suit of chain mail and draped it over his body. The added weight felt abnormal, but he knew it would take him only a short while to adjust. After another brief inspection of the other odds and ends, he slammed the chest shut and went back to his entry room to grab some spare traveling clothes and a worn knapsack.

Trem swept out of the house closing the door softly behind him. He was clad in the thin and lightweight chain mail over the brown leather bodkin. He wore his usual lightly tanned high boots of deerskin and had strapped on a wide belt for his water flask and sword. On his back was strapped the small pack of provisions with his unstrung bow, both mostly obscured by a long and heavy hooded forest cloak. The cloak stretched down to his ankles and as he approached Jovan it blew back slightly to reveal the longsword riding easily at his hip. Jovan stared at him wide-eyed, and Trem anticipated the question on his mind. "As I said, I've found many items of all kinds in my time here."

Adjusting his belt and cloak, Trem paused outside and turned. He studied his home, the haven from the world he was preparing to return to. He thought about how easy it would be to change his mind, to go back, and as he studied the downtrodden abode he wondered if he was making the right choice. He glanced over his shoulder at Jovanaleth, waiting patiently with his touseled dark hair, and steeled himself. Looking back once more to give a last farewell to his home he turned and said simply, "Let's go."

Jovan did not argue. He followed the shrouded figure out of his small clearing into the forest. Neither man would ever see the cabin again.

They traveled quickly for the first few hours of early morning. The first several miles of the journey was spent in silence moving through the thicket of Silverleaf's trees. Trem did not speak out of choice, and Jovanaleth because he was struggling to keep an eye on his guide, whose shifting cloak was difficult to follow in the shady green of the forest. Trem's pace was deliberate but quick, finding small animal trails that made the going easier. Around midday they emerged from the woods onto Old Southron Road.

Trem stopped here and turned to address his companion, "This is about four hours march from what used to be called the Plains Way, which was, I believe, the southern road leading to Gi'lakil. We are further south than you were when your party was attacked, and if we continue to follow this road south we will reach the Plains Way by early evening. I suggest we continue an hour north toward Gi'lakil from there and then camp so as to avoid being caught at a crossroads."

Jovan agreed, the plan was good and would hopefully avoid any confrontation with other travelers. They continued without another word, Trem passing back nuts, berries, and some roast meat to serve as their marching lunch. The road wound lazily south and was wide and easy to travel. Jovanaleth lost track of time and soon they arrived at the old crossroad that once served as the main way connecting the continents of Southron and Legocia. In the years before the assault on Aves, this road had been the main artery of trade between the two lands. These days the Plains Way remained little more than a thin trace of a trail just wide enough for one man on foot.

Trem did not pause but followed the faded tracks marking the road rolling north to Gi'lakil. Jovan hurried to follow, focused on the last hour of their hike, beginning to feel the wear in his somewhat untested legs. Normally he would not have been tired, but his time in bed had drained some of his old strength. It would return in time though, and until then it was bearable. He focused on putting one foot in front of the other with a stoic's deliberate stride, unwilling to slow their progress or appear weak in front of his partner. His muscles burned and his side ached, but Jovan was also invigorated by finally being back on the hunt for his father.

Trem stopped an hour later, as promised, and announced he would find a suitable campsite several feet into the woods and off of the road. Once a feasible location had been chosen, Jovan followed and sat down thankfully between the large roots of an old tree as Trem took out the two thin bedrolls he had thoughtfully packed. Jovan thanked him for his as Trem passed it over. After spreading their bedding out Trem dug into the pack and pulled out some hard but still edible bread and more dried meat.

"Sorry, there is not much else that will last very long out here," he remarked.

Jovanaleth accepted his share gratefully and leaned against the oak to eat. He watched his traveling partner as he did. Trem ate slowly, as though considering each bite before taking it. He stared at the ground or off into the trees at things only he appeared able to detect, or perhaps he was just deep in thought. Jovan finally decided to ask the question he had been pondering since he awoken in the cabin, "What made you become a hermit Trem?"

The half-elf paused mid-bite, considering the question. "When the war ended I decided I'd had enough violence in my life. I walked into Silverleaf Forest one day and simply never walked out."

"But you chose to fight, volunteered you said, what made you change your mind so suddenly? After all, the knights won the war." The tone of Jovan's inquiry was a touch demanding.

"Our side won," Trem admitted, putting his food down. "We were able to repel the enemy and they scattered across the land. That does not mend severed limbs or take away the guilt of having ended another's life. I was done with all of it, so I simply removed myself from the rest of the world."

Jovan seemed to accept the answer in part. "Why help me now then?"

Trem picked up a piece of meat and chewed slowly. "Your father was a good man, and I feel I owe him and his family some measure of loyalty."

"It is appreciated."

"Tell me," Trem said wiping his hands on his breeches. "Why did your father leave Bladehome? Do we have any idea where he might be?"

Jovanaleth leaned forward, his eyes searching the ground before him. "Some years ago another invasion began. Even if you had been outside of Silverleaf, it's likely you would not have heard of it. A large army did the unthinkable, crossing the Frozen Reach and sweeping down through the Napalian Empire, sacking her towns as they went. The High Thane of Napal City and the houses loyal to him put up a valiant defense, but the most trusted man in their ranks betrayed them all. The city gates were opened for the invaders when they reached the capitol and the massacre was reportedly horrible. Now the lands north of the God's Bones Mountains are ruled by the invaders, their leader apparently goes by the name of Wolfbane."

"Wolfbane? That's an odd name."

"Yes, apparently it is a title he gave himself. He's from the west, as is most of his army. A massively strong man, the rumors say, wielding a great axe in battle. His army and followers call themselves Nerothians and say they serve the will of the God of Death, to conquer and claim all the lands and unite all mortals under one banner. It is said that Wolfbane believes he is doing a great service for the people of our world, but the methods of those loyal to him are wretched, and those are just the actions we have been able to confirm."

"What does this have to do with your father?"

Jovan sighed and rubbed his head. "You have to understand, and maybe you remember from when you knew him, my father is not someone who delegates responsibility. Even less so when it involves great personal danger. When he began to hear rumors of torture, dark magic, and a great fortress in the east that had pinned the nation of Angladais within their valley homeland he became gravely concerned. Wolfbane has also made it no secret he will not stop at ruling Napal, he means to take over all the lands of Legocia, including ours. Worse, while Thane Greymane Squall committed the worst single act of treachery by betraying his High Thane at the capitol and let the enemy in, other houses worked long behind the scenes to help the invaders emerge victorious. There are elements in Napal that want Wolfbane in command, who are willing to throw their support behind him and Neroth in the hopes it will bring them power and wealth. All of this suggested our homeland, so young and hopeful, was in danger."

"So your father went to see this threat for himself. Was he kidnapped?"

Jovan shook his head. "No, he did not go as an ambassador or member of our order, he was going as a spy."

"But as the ruler of Bladehome and a prominent figure in the War of the Lion he could not home to be unrecognized, even in the north." Trem's expression was puzzled and a bit incredulous at the foolishness of Jonathan Blade. "He had to know they would seize him once he was through the Windpass."

Jovan smiled slyly. "My father has many gifts from his pirating days, disguise and deception among them. He also had the help of my mother, who has some skill in the arcane. He was protected, and we never received word of his capture or death. If the Nerothians and this Wolfbane had found him they would have made it known. As it stands, his last communication was a letter sent by carrier pigeon from Ozmandias, over six months ago."

Trem understood at last. "A long time, and even in the north and disguised he should have been able to send a note of some sort."

"Yes," Jovanaleth said quietly, "that is why we need to go to Gi'lakil first. I need to know if he made it north at all or if he was met upon the road and taken. Or worse."

Trem did not respond, unsure of what to say. He would have liked to reassure his new friend, but it was not in his nature to do so. Instead he returned the uneaten rations to his pack and said stiffly, "We have a long day ahead of us tomorrow. You should get some rest."

Without another word he rolled over and covered himself in the thick cloth of his cloak against the chill of the early fall evening. Jovan sighed and removed his own belt and boots. Rolling over onto his mat he could not help feeling frustrated. He had begun to like Trem, at least in most respects, but his apparent discomfort with discussing the realities of the world in plain terms grated at times. Perhaps it was a byproduct of his time away from others and his decision to follow that path at such a young age. As Jovan lay down he wondered how long Trem would truly stay by his side. It seemed that their chance encounter had drive his fellow half-elf from his state of self-imposed sequestering in the forest, but Jovanaleth drifted off to sleep unsure if he could even expect to find Trem with him in the morning.

The rat scurried rapidly across the room, careful to stay under the shadows of the looming furniture about it. It had learned from the mistakes of its previous brethren that only in the darkness were they safe, and rarely at that. Pausing to sniff the air it detected the rank odor of something near death, already partially rotted. This was surely to be its meal for the night and whatever it was lay just a bit further down the tunnel.

Dashing quickly along the blackened wall the rat followed the corridor until it reached the barred room at the end of the hall. Here it could smell the food, but it also detected something else, something dark and cold. Looking carefully into the light the rat saw a figure cloaked in a black shroud of cloth. The manlike form was tall and thin, with a sense of power, chill, and, most of all, death emanating from it. This was the source other than the food, the one blocking it. Patience would give the rat its chance, once this hulking form left it would be free to feast.

The dark one spoke from the glow of the torch in his hand. His voice had a bizarre and twisted echo like that of a wind from some deep crevice. Whenever he spoke a slight crackling came underneath his words, like snapping parchment in the air.

"Why do you continue to evade me? Your friend has forsaken you, protecting him is pointless, give me his location and I will kill you quickly before the rats eat you alive."

From deep within the chamber came a second futile voice of another man, sounding alone and forlorn. His speech was slurred as though he spoke around an obstruction or perhaps his lips were somehow stuck together, "Never you fiend, I'll never give you what you want."

The dark figure sighed and shook his head. "Still you insist on being foolish, even after he betrayed you and your whole miserable city. Stop shielding him and tell me what you know."

"Greymane was tricked. Lied to."

"Your blind stupidity and pointless resistance bores me. I can find him through many other methods. Very well, the rats may have you."

With that the shadowy mass swept out of the room, slamming the steel door behind him. As he walked down the hall he flicked his wrist in the cell lock's direction and it clicked into place. Swiftly, he moved along and was soon around the corner out of sight. The rat stirred itself and hurried forward, leaping between the cracks of the cell bars. The meal squirmed as the brood closed in on it. The rat could feel more of its kin writhing alongside it. Hopefully there would be enough for everyone.

Chapter 3

Jovanaleth awoke as the sun began its early climb into the sky. He stretched and looked out towards the road through the morning haze. He found it hard to tell if his lack of visual clarity was from lingering mist or his own foggy mind. Jovan reasoned that it was only a little past dawn but he had slept easily and comfortably on the forest floor. Trem was nowhere in sight but any doubts from the night before were assuaged by the bedroll that was neatly folded and attached to his pack, leaning against a tree. A small fire was boiling some water and a slim leather pouch was lying close to it along with a wooden cup. Jovan carefully removed the copper pan and poured some water into his cup, adding a touch of the leather pouch's contents. He smelled what he presumed was one of Trem's teas, a strange mixture; it was certainly some sort of draught he had never experienced.

Taking the cup with him he walked to the fringe of the woods and saw Trem at the edge of the road sipping from his own simple wooden receptacle. He nodded as Jovanaleth approached. Walking to stand beside him, Jovan looked north with Trem.

"It doesn't look like anyone passed us in the night."

Trem did not answer, but continued to watch the road before them. Trying to engage his companion, Jovan asked, "What's in this tea anyways? It smells odd."

Trem actually smiled a little. "Why don't you try it?"

Jovan obliged taking a small sip. It was sweet and smooth, almost like honey. Then suddenly it turned shockingly, deeply spiced and bitter and he gasped aloud. Unable to contain himself, he spat it onto the road. "Phwaw! Uhh! What is this?"

Trem was laughing openly now, patting his gagging companion on the back he said, "The elves call it Sugarburn Tea, made from the plant of the same name. It takes time to develop a taste for it."

Still laughing softly to himself Trem walked back to the campsite shaking his head in mirth. Despite the terrible taste in his mouth, by the time Jovan had emptied his cup onto the road he was chuckling himself. The two gathered their things and resumed the march north in congenial silence. The weather was cool but not unpleasant and before an hour was passed they had begun an amicable conversation about their destination.

Jovanaleth had been to the town a few times before and described it to his companion, who only vaguely remembered it. Near the end of the Age of Emergence, men and elves had dragged great collections of lumber from the Silverleaf Forest to the center of the Dust Plains, atop a large rise in the stony earth. There they had founded the wooden walled town of Gi'lakil, which had been a hub of travel, rumor, and information since its very inception. The thick, high wooden walls were ruled over by even more massive round wooden towers formed from the largest logs that had been brought to the site, allowing a clear view for some distance around the township proper. The interior of the wall held several temples, taverns, shops, houses, and the famous Inn of the Four Winds at the center, where the two main roads crossing the Dust Plains met. This intersection represented the importance of Gi'lakil, a settlement that had been founded by so many together that none were actually certain who had ruled it when it was formed or where the name had come from.

When the road to Southron became harder and more danger-ous to travel due to increased numbers of gnolls, followed by the glut of new bandits marauding the roads from the fallout of the War of the Lion, Gi'lakil became the stopping place for those on their way across the continent. Its high walls offered safety to those within and the militia was always well stocked with volunteers and occasional visi-tors willing to lend a hand in the town's defense. The population had numbered just shy of seven thousand within the walls, and around a thousand outside, but recent events had driven many to Gi'lakil in search of refuge. The number of would-be residents had ballooned to over eleven thousand, many sleeping on the streets inside the palisade or, if trapped outside, against the wooden barrier itself, as though proximity would afford them greater protection. Where the city had once been a cultural crossroads it had become a beacon of hope for those with very little left. The burden on the residents was understandably difficult to bear.

Gi'lakil had begun as a small town, blossomed into almost a true urban center, like nearby Ozmandias, and throughout it all had adjusted to the necessary expansions. The inn had grown into a three-story building with two floors for sleeping quarters and a large common room for traveling performers and mealtimes. The trades to be found in the city expanded from the fundamentals of smiths, carpenters, and masons to more exotic occupations like alchemists, jewelers, and even a mage with her own shop of arcane parephenalia. The town had prospered and everyone gained more revenue from the increase in visitors. Thus, it was a place that had weathered danger before, particularly the gnoll campaigns rebuffed by the orcs and Angladaics many years ago. However, the city had always remained a beacon of independence and self-sufficiency. Never had the people been asked to take on the role of saviors and supporters of the larger region and the strain of accommodating the sudden influx of refu-gees was real.

The gates were solid and well maintained. The volunteer mili-tia of the town, usually composed only of those who lived within the walls, took turns at the entrances. Of late they patrolled in groups of four as a precaution. The threat of assault from the Broken was real and growing more serious by the day. Jovanaleth had explained to Trem the growing sense of impunity among raiders. Broken clans had stepped up assaults on the eastern towns and there were words of terrible pillagings and razings of entire villages, all without response from any of the region's powers. Gi'lakil had determined to remain exempt from all conflict for now. The town was never meant to be the fulcrum of a nation and wished to remain uninvolved in the violence of the Dust Plains. Any refugees from the eastern towns were openly welcomed and housed, if they could afford it, but that was the extent of Gi'lakil's involvement. As long as they did not blatantly defy the Broken's incursions, they hoped to at least delay the necessity of dealing with them. That delay, Jovan had advised, would kill the town in the end. No matter how high they built the walls or how many guards patrolled them the Broken still possessed a weapon unlike anything Gi'lakil had seen: their gnoll allies.

A gnoll was something like a cross between a wolf and an unnaturally long-limbed man. With large, heavy arms and thick chests they often were forced to lean on one hand rather than stand, and usually did so except in battle. Their rear legs were thinner, like those of a wolf, but in time some strengthened them to the point where a fully-grown gnoll could walk and fight on their hind legs for hours at a time. Standing on two legs, a gnoll would easily reach seven or eight feet in height, dwarfing almost any opponent. Erect or in a crouch, they wielded massive halberds, broadswords, and battleaxes with one hand, weapons a strong man might find difficult to lift with two. Further enhancing their battle prowess, their skin was as tough as hardened leather and difficult to pierce with anything save a close range crossbow bolt or a very strong sword arm. Trem had killed his share of gnolls, though he made no mention of this to Jovanaleth, but he had always taken care to fight them in small groups. Jovanaleth had implied that hundreds of gnolls might be serving with the Broken now, and Trem shuddered at the thought.

Gnolls had long been a problem on the Dust Plains. Their numbers ebbed and flowed with time, but they had required the combined efforts of several groups to be culled in the past. Gnoll society is nomadic and establishment of pack dominance integral to the whole race's survival. Gnolls follow the most powerful among their number and assault targets ripe in potential supplies. In packs, gnolls communicate like wolves or dogs with barks, howls, and snarls, but many are intelligent enough to learn the common tongue and speak it haltingly with other mortal races. Rarely is this skill applied however, as gnolls are a veritable force of death and destruction, communication not being high on their list of valued skills. Rumors said that the gnolls followed the Broken because they ate the flesh of slain enemies and where the Broken raided there was always plenty of food. The value of a contingent of gnolls in any army could not be underestimated, their raw power and speed made them as punishing as charging cavalry and their strength and size gave them the ability to tear down even well designed defensive structures. It was difficult to tell exactly how true the word of the gnoll involvement with the Broken was, as Jovan implied there was such fear of them that most wanted to bury their heads in the earth and pretend the devastation in the east was not really happening.

Such was the case in Gi'lakil, and the city did not have the capacity to withstand a gnoll assault if it came. Perhaps they would have been able to secure aid from an outside force, like Ozmandi-as or the Eagle Knights, but they appeared unwilling or unable to acknowledge their own precarious position. Gi'lakil had chosen to ignore what was happening around it, too drunk with its own recent prosperity to see the trap being plainly laid out to snare it. As they walked, Trem shook his head at the foolishness of it all, Jovanaleth clearly in agreement and lamenting the shortsighted leaders of the hub city.

Reaching the edge of Silverleaf at last they paused, looking at the vast expanse of land that stretched out before them. Rolling hills of bare grass and thin shrubs spread for miles all around and Trem could plainly see dirt and dust swirling for a great way off in the distance, the few trees across the land sticking out of the rocky earth like giant splinters. Jovanaleth stood at his side, their conversation forgotten as they took in the scene. After a moment, Trem adjusted his pack and weapons. "We may as well keep moving. The town won't get any closer with us just staring at the road."

"Right," Jovanaleth replied as he moved to follow. "I hope we can find news of my father. It was so long ago that he should have passed through Gi'lakil, if he ever did. I wonder if anyone will even remember him if they did meet."

"If memory serves," Trem said thoughtfully, "the Inn of the Four Winds is a place for storytellers and travelers and your father was a well-known man even if disguised. Someone will remember a guest asking questions about the invaders and the situation in the north. That is one region where few travelers come from, as the Napalians have always kept to themselves. No one would be actively asking about those invaders unless he was looking for trouble, and an inn-keeper always marks the guests that could cause trouble."

"You don't think the innkeeper would throw my father out?"

"If he did," Trem answered, "then we will be sure to repay him in kind."

Jovan did not respond, noting the dangerous light in Trem's eye. As they moved down the road he glanced at Trem's side, beneath the cloak. He saw the shimmer of the old sword hilt beneath it and not for the first time wondered where he had aquired such a unique looking and finely made weapon. Shaking the thought from his head, Jovanaleth concentrated on putting one foot in front of the other as Trem's piercing eyes scanned the horizon in search of any danger that might be looming about them. His wound throbbed and he felt fatigued, but the energy of acting at last spurred him on towards their destination.

In his dungeon laboratory, Daerveron strode about hurriedly, searching through his vast array of materials and spell components divided seemingly without intent among a great number of tables and shelves. He wanted to complete his tests to perfect his latest incantation before being summoned again. That meant he had to hurry much more than he normally would have, and hurry might mean error, which infuriated him. Daerveron hated to be rushed. Time should not be a factor by which he was governed anymore. Death was no longer a looming fear for the wizard. After all, he had experienced dying once already, and did not intend to go through the process again.

Many years ago, in a time he had only broken recollection of, he had been a sorceror of no small fame and talent. In fact some might have called him the greatest mage of his time, perhaps even of all times, but with that greatness had come knowledge. It was the knowledge that he would never have all that magic could grant him, because eventually he would die. There was simply not enough time to unravel all the secrets of his art, so he sought a way to avoid that annoying little thing called mortality.

Daerveron found his loophole in the power of Neroth, the God of Death. At that time, contact with avatars and other varying degrees of immortal manifestations on Teth-tenir were not as rare as they had since become. Neroth, with his unmatched understanding of mortality, knew how Daerveron could obtain the power to undo his own demise. Such an incredible feat came with a price of course, incurred both in the moment of agreement to Neroth's terms and for all time afterwards. First, Daerveron had to pledge himself to serve Neroth's larger goals, lest the god turn his full attention and ire on him and recall his soul to the realm of the dead where it belonged. This unveiled the second portion of the bargain Daerveron had to make. He was not being allowed to continue living indefinitely, but granted a return to his corpse once he had expired. In the end, he had to welcome death to overcome it.

Even this did not come easily. Despite the immense complexity of the rite, Daerveron was not rendered invincible and could still be killed, which he discovered when he rose up out of his coffin and was attacked by the horrified priests laying him to rest. Determined to be free and pursue mastery of the arcane once again, he defeated them with his magic, but not before one managed to pick up an old sword from one of the tombs in the crypt and slice his right arm off at the elbow. Daerveron never noticed until he tried to use his arm after fleeing the crypt, for he felt no pain and saw no blood. He had escaped from his tomb and returned to the mortal world, but Daerveron was furious. His magic required the dexterity of both his limbs, and now he was without one. Once again Neroth aided him, this time with no catch involved, for he was also useless to the God of Death without his arm.

In place of his mortal limb, Daerveron found a strange appendage formed from the souls of the dead. The hand and arm were black, barely holding the form of their former living tissue and looked more like smoke than anything flesh. But it could manipulate magical components, wield utensils, and draw runes as adeptly as the human hand it had once been. Daerveron designed a gauntlet made of black-steel, a rare metal forged in volcanic fire with obsidian and magic, to cover his arm up to the elbow. The foul hand's touch ripped apart the spirit of those who felt it even for a moment, and despite the terror this could inspire it was often an inconvenience. Daerveron believed that his fearsome appendage utterly erased his victims from existence, though he had not taken the time to study its effects formally.

For centuries Daerveron had been permitted to do as he wished in the art of magic. Hiding far to the north in an old abandoned house just outside the town of Tianis, he perfected old spells and invented new. His ultimate goal was to master the six schools of arcane magic completely, an accomplishment no wizard of any race or nation had ever managed, not even the infamous God-Sorceror. Soon he realized that in order to do this he would need to gather magical tomes and scrolls at a rate far faster than he alone was capable of. Worse still, his isolation in the barren Frozen Reach made it difficult to obtain supplies for his experiments, further slowing his progress. In frustration, he toiled alone and in secret. Though he did not long for company, Neroth's demands that he keep his existence hidden forced Daerveron to use complex and often delayed means of acquiring components for his work. His time near Tianis highlighted the rift between Neroth and his servant, for Daerveron cared not at all for the God of Death's vision for the mortal world, but was insatiable in his quest for magical supremacy. Their allegiance was one of convenience. Neroth had given Daerveron time and means to complete his work, and Daerveron offered the God of Death a powerful presence on Teth-tenir to oversee his goal of dominion there.

Unfortunately, it now seemed Daerveron's dream was never to be realized, for his benfactor still held him to his end of the bargain and the wizard's duties to Neroth increased almost daily. It was only four years ago that he was told to leave his work and go to assist another in service to Neroth, a barbarian from the west commanding a great army. Daerveron had met Wolfbane and his allies in the staging area the westerner had established in the shadow of Mount Iceblade, near the Gulf of Thunder. Daerveron was mildly impressed with the intelligence of this man, but found his lack of subtlety in the application of physical might and total disregard of magical knowledge to be insufferable. Of course, this was why he was supposed to help him. With Daerveron's assistance Wolfbane had won the war with the Napalian Empire and gained a foothold for Neroth on the continent of Legocia, the land that most interested him. Why Neroth cared so much about this place Daerveron did not know, and he prided himself on knowing everything. It was no secret he was highest in the God of Death's ranks, and by his own doing he was also the most feared. Daerveron reveled in the cowering forms of the lesser members of Neroth's following, as it provided a way for him to keep them from disturbing his greater work.

But for all his power, death, while it had not claimed Daerveron, did infuse him with a few less desirable traits. Worn and dry-rotten as a corpse, his body was held together only by the magic that had resurrected him. Over time he had lost much of his physical shape, reduced to a graying flaky skin around hardened, shrunken muscle and old, creaking bone. His magical reanimation imbued him with unnatural strength and allowed for many other benefits, like shedding the necessity of sleep, but being conscious of his appearance, Daerveron avoided allowing his face or body to be seen by wearing a cloak, robe, and silken wrap about his decaying jaw when in the presence of others. That was more for their benefit than his. Fear was a powerful tool, but it could be a hindrance on some occasions, and his role required that once in a while he had to converse with the rabble that scurried about the fringes of his domain.

So now he carried out his immortal lord's personal agenda from his labyrinth in the dungeons of the newly christened Castle Bane, formerly Napal City Castle. Here he continued, at an even more exasperatingly slow rate, his experiments that had begun in the isolated hovel to the north. He was also tasked with finding two men Neroth was deeply concerned about. These two apparently posed an actual threat to the God of Death's many plans, though Daerveron did not understand the precise danger to his schemes. All he knew was in them lay the potential to prevent Neroth from achieving his goal of utter conquest of the mortal realm of Teth-tenir. Daerveron had been informed there was reason to believe other deities were trying to assist the two mortals he sought, so it fell to the mighty, undying wizard to locate them and be sure they were dealt with.

Daerveron had made some progress in ascertaining the whereabouts of one of the two mortals, but none of his methods had located the second. The first was currently in Gi'lakil, and where the other was could be anyone's guess. The mage was pleased with his progress, knowing his patron had not expected such results so fast. He was troubled that of the second individual he had not learned anything, but considered it a mere matter of time. Instead, Daerveron focused on what he had accomplished, for by his calculation the first of his targets would be dead in Gi'lakil before the night was through.

Finally, what Daerveron had dreaded most occurred. A bell rang softly down the corridor in his chambers. He was being summoned to a meeting with the fortress council, led by Wolfbane. Respect for Wolfbane he had, but his subordinates were fools, in Daerveron's opinion. They lacked the occasional cunning and guile that their leader possessed, with the exception of one. He looked, to untrained eyes, to be a young man of some elven lineage, but his quick wit and oddly colored, sharp eyes held an older kind of wisdom and had enabled him to learn more than he was supposed to. Daerveron sighed with a hiss like steam out of a loose valve. He had to convince Wolfbane that the lost elf known as Edgewulf el Vac was too dangerous to keep around.

At that moment, that same Edge el Vac was unaware of Daerveron's dire plans for him. The young commander had ridden hard from the edges of the Great Northern Waste to reach Napal City that evening and was now trotting his fine warhorse through the gloomy streets of the metropolis. Napal City was a dark, industrial maze with four great hills and narrow, steep streets of irregular pavement or cobblestone. The buildings of Napal City loom over those thin alleys like dark judges, observing unblinkingly even the most furtive of passersby as they wind their way through among the high walls of windows and stone about them. The main roads are slightly less imposing, and efforts were made in the past to build parks of a kind to offer more open views of the sky, but even these attempts cannot quell the constant noise of loud voices, baying animals, and banging items that never fully ceases even in the dark of night. It has never been a city welcoming, even to its own people, but it has been home to many.

Yet when Edge came to Napal City he came not as a traveler, but as part of her conquest. Under the tyranny of Wolfbane, Napal City had been culled in a day. The end of the Empire was mercifully quick, but the suffering of her former citizens had lasted for months now, with no sign of relief forthcoming. Edge tried to keep his brilliant, entirely green, eyes in front of him, avoiding the lost and dead looks of the populace as he passed their battered and worn homes. He had not wanted this. Following his master, his hero Wolfbane, from the west he had expected to find a mission of noble intent. Instead he had become part of a great shroud over the corpse of this once proud nation.

Down the main road he steered his mount. Before him he could see the gates to Napal City Castle, now cruelly renamed Castle Bane. Spikes stood all about the entrance like sadistic fangs, each holding the head of an enemy of the Nerothian army or those who had dared to join the Napalian resistance once their nation fell. Edge had brought some of these men to their fate here and each time he rode past the weight of his involvement in the tragedy of the Napalian Empire's ignominious end was suffocating. Nearing the heavy doors to the castle, he heard the great chains commanding them pull back as they opened and he slowed his gait as he passed them by, coming to a stop within. Handing the reins to one of the soldiers that came to assist him he inquired after Wolfbane's whereabouts.

"Upstairs, Lord Edgewulf," one of the men informed him, "he has called a meeting in the war room."

Without a word, Edge marched to the central castle and the guards unquestioningly let him in. The main hall of Castle Bane was now used only for ceremonies of surrender. Before the invaders arrived it had contained wall paintings and grand tapestries depicting the building of the Napalian nation out of a region mostly consisting of dead frozen tundra, led by thanes of the oldest families in the north, many of whom had been scourged from their homeland. Wolfbane had torn down the tapestries and covered the walls in the weapons of his defeated foes. The former fortress of Napal now held the broken shields of its own housekarls. In place of the fine woven rugs, Wolfbane had furs and skins of exotic animals leading up to a monstrous throne built of iron with thin streaks of silver woven in like crashing lighting behind the heavy seat. Decked out in its barbaric finery, it was the most intimidating place to be in the fortress, until one went to the war room.

Edge lingered momentarily in the main hall, his eyes scanning over the shattered shields and tattered banners. He did not sense Daerveron, standing plainly in the entryway from the stairs of his dungeon chambers that led to the upper floors, watching him silently. Edge closed his eyes and thought of the past, the time when he believed they were coming to save the people of Legocia and all of Teth-tenir. The optimism of that time seemed defeated completely by these symbols of conquest and destruction. Sighing, he walked past the throne and to the servants' stairwell at the back, beginning the arduous climb to the war room.

Up a long flight of over a six hundred stairs was the strategic heart of Castle Bane. Located in the highest point of the castle it was accessible only through a well-concealed entrance near the servants' corridors that looked, even upon careful examination, like a blank wall. Having watched Edge el Vac scan the hall, Daerveron gave him time to begin his ascent before following. He strode determinedly across the throne room and to the same secret stairwell Edge had passed into before him. Through the narrow entryway Daerveron swept, having made his way quickly but unhurriedly. He was always emphatic that he should never appear rushed by anyone, for he answered to no mortal and especially none in this fortress.

Daerveron made his way up the sinuous spiral staircase with ease. The eeriness of its climb did not escape him. No decorations adorned the walls and it gave the illusion that one had been climbing into space for days. In reality, it was only about ten minutes before the mage reached the heights of the tower. He knew beyond the room he was about to enter lay Wolfbane's private chambers containing a forge, map room, and makeshift bed, although the general slept little. Upon entering the main chamber, bedecked with furniture and other concessions to the public nature of its purpose, he was pleased to see he was the last of the six commanders to arrive. Sweeping an icy stare around the room, he appeared to flow over to his black iron seat, and settle onto its small cushion. Comfort had never been as big a concern as intimidation to the ancient wizard.

Daeveron sat opposite the general himself. No man except for Edge, who had traveled with him prior to the general's arrival in Legocia, knew Wolfbane's true origins, though the rumors were many. Wolfbane was in his late forties or perhaps older, a human with an incredible muscular build who wielded a massive twin-bladed battle-axe in combat. His aggressive combat style and willingness to wade into the fray on his own front lines told Daerveron that somewhere in his past he had been accustomed to fighting his battles himself. The mage found it hard to believe any man could overcome Wolfbane in single combat, but of course his magic would render the commander helpless if it were deemed necessary.

Two cross-straps adorned with strange bits of spiked metal over a massive bare chest held Wolfbane's smaller throwing axes. He was renowned for his deadly aim with them, and had killed more then a few men from great distances before they even got close enough to see him. He had on heavy leather pants with metal studs and thick-soled war boots made for long marches. Wolfbane was quite plainly not a native Napalian or even Legocian. He had shaggy black hair, streaked with grey at his temples, together with a full beard and hanging mustache covering his tanned and weathered face. His eyes were narrower than those of Legocia and along with his darker complexion marked him as a Theiman man, from the desert known as the Pirate Sands in the west. Unusually for those people, Wolfbane's eyes were an icy gray in color and stood out starkly from his tanned and earthen tones of hair and skin. Regardless of his origins, those who sat around him feared him almost as much as they did Daerveron, though not in the same way.

The two sat across from one another to display the assumed equality between them in the current state of conquest. A simple nod was exchanged and Daerveron looked around at the other four men, and one woman, stationed about the table. All of them had played a part in the downfall of the Napalian Empire, some directly and others less so. Among them the wizard found little worth noting. They were small pieces in a much larger game, one they could not even hope to understand. As such, he found these meetings tedious and frustrating.

To Wolfbane's right sat Frothgar Konunn, publically holder of the title High Thane of Napal. Frothgar had risen to power through his small army of archers, the criminal empire of Napal City's dark underworld, and a secret cabal of assassins. He was a wiry little man hidden in his shifting black cloak. Beneath the frail looking features was a body hardened and toughened by many knives in the back and minor doses of poison to make him resistant to the deadly efforts of his myriad enemies. House Konunn was one of the founding houses of Napal City, but Frothgar himself was better known in Napal prior to joining Wolfbane's ranks for his network of spies and cutthroats, as well as many illegal operations he ran within the city. Together, he and Daerveron had worked the secret political war behind the physical violence of Wolfbane's conquest.

As the newly named High Thane, his power should have increased immensely, but everyone knew the title was meaningless despite Frothgar's attempts to assert authority. His strength still came from his old trades in prostitution, gambling, and various mind-altering herbs and chemicals sold on the street. Frothgar had close to a hundred followers skilled in the craft of intimidation and assassination, along with nearly a thousand archers who had once manned the walls of Napal City for the former High Thane. By Frothgar's own orders, several of his spies and murderers answered only to Daerveron, an attempt to curry favor with the powerful mage. The man knew how to cast his lot with whoever was likely to come out on top, and his desire to obtain wealth and power had made betraying his own country an easy decision. For his part, Daerveron considered Frothgar an irrelevant rodent.

The man on the High Thane's right was even lower in Daerveron's eyes. A mage from the city of Ozmandias, trained in the wizards' fortress, but originally from Napal, he had come to the side of Wolfbane on orders given to him by his god, Neroth. His power was puny compared to Daerveron's own, but Saltilian was strong for his time. The younger mage was always nervous, eyes shifting back and forth and running his fingers up and down his staff's runes. He stammered often too, a defect many suspected had been beaten into him during his time under the care under parents who had never wanted another child, let alone one so disinterested in the martial tradition of the Napalian Empire. He was unnecessary to the cause, as far as Daerveron was concerned.

Valissa Ulfrunn was the only female at the table. A very attractive woman, she had pale blonde hair and weather tanned skin over a lithe, but muscular, body. Though many foolish enough to doubt a woman's battle prowess would not have thought it, she was the best sword fighter in all the northern lands. She had fought against Wolfbane and the Nerothian army during his invasion, her skill convincing him to offer her a place in his ranks rather than having her killed. Her family had fallen during the first phase of the invasion, when the town of Tianis and seat of House Ulfrunn was taken by the Nerothians with no aid coming from the other Napalian thanes.

On the surface, Valissa would have been considered a simple study. Frequently she dressed in clothing that could be politely described as scandalous, using her beauty and cleverness to manipulate men into doing what she wanted. In truth, she despised most men completely because the male-centric culture of Napal had restricted her rise to a position of command and respect within the military, despite her obvious qualifications. The only man she was said to tolerate, and perhaps even hold affection for, was Wolfbane. His personal interest in her as a warrior, not a pet or subservient lover had been all it took to convince her she belonged with the Nerothian forces, even if her faith in the God of Death was nonexistent.

Daerveron watched as Valissa turned and whispered something to the youngest council member sitting to her left, bringing the mage's gaze quickly around to him. His unearthly eyes narrowed and he focused harder on this individual than he had any other. Edge replied with something that made the woman nod and met Daerveron's gaze unfalteringly. Edgewulf el Vac appeared, and was treated, as the youngest seated in the room but he had a sense of honor and respect for fairness that had no place in Daerveron's schemes or those of his master Neroth. Edge had startlingly white hair over a smooth and, Daerveron supposed, handsome face. Built thin but strong, he was extremely agile and very good with a halberd. The most astonishing thing about him was his eyes, which were entirely green and glowed slightly. Daerveron doubted very much that even Edge knew this marked him as a native of Haddon Mirk and a lost elf.

Daerveron knew much of the Haddon Mirk people. They were isolationists, utterly disinterested in the world outside of their islands. And yet, many years ago several prominent families had sent missionaries to other locales around Teth-tenir to bring the knowledge of the lost elves to them. One such family had been el Vac, and it was likely one of these pilgrims to whom Edge could trace his lineage. Daerveron admired the traditionalism and unbending law of the lost elves, and found the few who still existed outside Haddon Mirk to be poor imitations of that greater culture. Several had tried to bring change to the world, and as near as Daerveron could tell they had all failed.

Daerveron continued his study of the outsider. For all his youthful appearance, Edge was almost as old as Wolfbane, his race being one of the first mortals, and many living two hundred years or more. Edge wore silvery chain mail over his dark blue tunic adorned with a strange design to his cloak clasps, a pair of skeletal hands that held a connective chain between them. Where these had come from, Daerveron had always wanted to know, but he let his examination halt for now. Instead he turned his attention to a quiet conversation between Wolfbane and the last member of the council, Caermon Erefoss.

The conquest of the Napalian Empire had required the enlistment of elements within it that would make overthrowing the government and nation easier and less bloody. Caermon Erefoss had, in some ways, been a valuable asset in that process, but he was also a man deeply wedded to his house's history and longing for revenge on those he believed had wronged his family. The Erefoss people had a long-standing feud with the Napalian Empire and particularly the Squalls, who had held the role of advisors to the High Thane before Wolfbane's successful invasion. The brutal execution and imprisonment of the Squall family, after their patriarch and thane, Greymane Squall, opened the gates of Napal City to the invaders in exchange for a quiet, shameless exile he never received, had been strongly advocated by Caermon. Wolfbane had justified the death of the Squalls and Greymane in particular as a necessary action, eliminating a potential threat to his absolute dominion over the north. Moreover, Greymane had not negotiated for the lives of his people or sanctity of his nation, but for the preservation of his own reputation. This was because Frothgar had caught him in a web of lies of omission. Before the invasion had even commenced, the thane of House Konunn had acquired promises from Greymane to overlook his illegal operations in Napal City, which by all rights Greymane should have shut down upon discovering. When the invaders reached the city, Frothgar had then blackmailed Greymane into opening the gates, promising his family's honor would not be destroyed in the process. It was one of the greatest lies Frothgar had ever told.

Greymane could not have known Caermon Erefoss was among the invaders, or he might have realized Frothgar's deceit and stood fast in defending the city. Daerveron believed the former thane of House Squall to have been a fool for trusting Frothgar at all, for he was clearly little more than a gifted liar and criminal. Regardless, Greymane had bent under the threat of exposure and been broken. His family died in the main hall of Napal City Castle or amid the dungeons, and though he had managed to escape before his own execution, he was undoubtedly a shell of a man. It was Caermon Erefoss who had relished the obliteration of House Squall the most, for his family had been driven from the town of Glaciar and across the Great Northern Waste in the founding days of the north by the Squalls and had sought revenge for generations since.

Wolfbane had stood by Caermon's zealous insistence at killing or imprisoning most of the Squall family. As for Greymane, Wolfbane claimed he could not keep a traitor who would offer up his whole nation in exchange for his name and legacy. Daerveron had seen the flaw in that logic, after all Frothgar Konunn had remained an integral part of their council and had committed many acts of betrayal against his own people, but the lives of the Squalls meant nothing to him and he saw no benefit to intervening on their behalf, except for one. Daerveron had detected an unusual spark of magical energy in one of Greymane's daughters and had her spared, as she might prove useful to him later. It was a small benefit to a bloody business that had become most trying to the dread wizard due, to the unfortunate escape of Greymane Squall. His flight had caused an unnecessary interruption in Daerveron's studies, as Neroth seemed determined he be recaptured or, better yet, killed. For his part, once Daerveron found Greymane he intended to make the former thane pay dearly for inconveniencing him.

Daerveron returned his attention to the moment at hand. The meeting was beginning. Wolfbane stood and removed the round sigil from his belt and placed it on the table. It depicted a black wolf's head with white eyes and fangs on a red field, the symbol of the Blood Wolf Mercenaries, Wolfbane's first conquest in his road to this new Nerothian kingdom he was forging. In a deep, rumbling voice he pronounced, "As a servant to the God of Death, Neroth, I hereby call this meeting to order. May the Shepherd of Souls spare us until our work is done."

Slowly, the others followed suit with their own symbols of office, and the meeting came to order.

Chapter 4

Trem and Jovan reached Gi'lakil shortly before nightfall after four full days of travel across the plains. The brisk pace set by Trem had continued unabated, despite his recognition that Jovanaleth was struggling to keep up. In Trem's mind time was of the essence, and his companion did not complain or ask him to slow his progress, so Trem did not. Nor would Trem check on him; he merely kept them both fed and made sure they were able to camp in sheltered and relatively safe areas during their journey. Trem allowed no fires during the long march, and he was rewarded by the two having no encounters with anyone, traveler or bandit, on the worn and fading road.

There was a distinct mood to the town as soon as they reached the outskirts. The sprawl of desperate people outside the walls was visible from afar, and when they were still some distance off Jovan remarked that it looked like there were ants crawling about the base of the city walls. Trem made no response, instead keeping his mind focused singularly on their purpose for coming here. As they came close enough to distinguish the individual people all around the palisade he glued his eyes to the gates, trying to avoid any acknowledgement of the desperate situation all about him.

Jovanaleth was quite the opposite. He took in the ragged crowds of hopeless and exhausted faces, scanning the entirety of their number as they approached and made their way to the main gate. It was clear many of the refugees were without food, or at least had very small amounts of it, but they made no attempt to beg or plead coins or supplies from the two travelers. Their walk up the road was unimpeded. In fact, many stepped aside to allow them through. To Jovan it was clear this was a great mass of defeated people, not those who had fight left in them and were going to seek aide from passersby. He also noted, among the worn frames of makeshift tents and camps, bloody rags and grievous wounds. War had come to the Dust Plains, and these people were merely its harbinger.

Trem and Jovan reached the gate, looming high and sturdy before them. Four guards stood outside the entrance they came upon, thoroughly eyeing them both but not asking any questions. Above them, Trem could see several archers keeping a sharp eye on the newcomers. Those outside gripped their pikes and watched them tensely, clearly aware of their responsibility but uncomfortable with it at the same time. Trem slowed his approach and they halted a safe distance from the guards. They pushed one of their number forward, and he attempted to assume an air of authority. "What business do you have in Gi'lakil?"

"We are seeking the whereabouts of a man we believe passed through here." Trem answered.

"Do you have coin? We can take no more within our walls who cannot pay."

"Some," Trem pulled a small pouch from his belt and held it up so the guards could see. "Enough for a room for a night or two."

This seemed to satisfy the guards and they motioned for the gates to be opened. Jovan had expected questions about their weaponry, for the two were heavily armed for simple travelers, but in truth the presence of more fighting men and women in the city was looked at as favorable by most. Violence in the streets was clearly not the concern, what lurked beyond the walls was the real source of their fear. The great doors of the palisade swung open and the two walked in, the town of Gi'lakil stretching out before them.

The guards watched until the pair turned a corner off of the main road, trying to find a street not packed tight with the bodies of refugees and their meager shelters. The town itself was a cluster of thatched roofs supported by solid wooden or mud-brick houses. These uniform structures dominated the majority of the town, but a slightly larger building with a smoke hole in the hut top and the rhythmic clanging of hammers clearly stood out as the blacksmith, some distance to the east if Trem had to make a guess. The eeriness of the sounds in the streets was unnerving. Children from the town were not darting around playing at being heroes or engaged in games of tag. In fact the few that were out were under the careful eyes of concerned mothers who would not let them stray too far, due to the other occupants of the roads.

Being about dusk, the streets were still relatively full, full with the most run down people Trem had ever seen. Most of them were humans and halflings, smaller and stockier humanoids who were fond of farming and the countryside. But all of these people, regardless of race, appeared to be those who had retreated from destroyed villages to the east to find someplace safer than where they came from. A few true elves dotted the street sides too, but they were heavily outnumbered by the others sitting forlornly beside them; those elves that were there looked to be dead already, with sunken eyes and distressed faces, their halfling and human counterparts not much better off.

Trem expected at least some of them to beg for coins or other help, but like their fellow refugees beyond the walls they just sat as though defeated. Perhaps, he admitted, they really were. The crowd continued to stare beyond he and Jovan as they passed by, travelers clearly no longer brought much notice, even unique ones. Their beaten appearance kept Trem focused on the hundreds of refugees, despite all his efforts to ignore the dire situation. Trem could not make his eyes turn away, but Jovan tugged at his sleeve pulling him out of his thoughts.

"There's the inn, I bet that is the best place to find rumor of a traveler."

Trem nodded murmuring, "There are lots of travelers. Only it seems many have nowhere to go."

Jovan looked at Trem sadly, clearly the scene on the street disturbed Jovanaleth as well, but he knew there was nothing to be done. Trem watched a woman come out of the inn and hand loaves of bread to the people on the street. There wasn't enough for even a quarter of the people there and a few scattered fights broke out. He spotted two children, little over seven years, flailing and striking at each other to steal just a scrap more of food. Leaving Jovan's side he walked to them and took the piece of bread they were fighting over, holding it away above their heads while they watched angrily knowing they could do nothing.

Trem smiled as disarmingly as he could manage. "This is not worth fighting over. If I split it between you then you will both have something to eat. You can take this too." He pulled some dried meat from his pack and gave one piece to each. The boys stared wide eyed at meat they probably had not tasted for months and then, as though they feared he might rethink his generosity, they ran swiftly away from him. Trem watched them for a while and then shook his head to clear his thoughts. He felt rather foolish for his charity in that moment.

Trying to shake off his conflicting emotions, he walked over to Jovanaleth. His companion patted him on the shoulder remarking, "For a loner you seem to get along with people well."

"It was a foolish decision; we will need those supplies as well."

Jovan was somewhat taken aback by Trem's hard tone. "Starving children can have my share any day. I would not call your actions foolish."

Trem did not reply, still a bit out of sorts, and followed him to the inn door. The building was large and rambling with three above ground levels. The base of it was clearly the common room. Trem could hear a minstrel singing the grand ballad of Bullwyf Margrave and the War of the Lion. He paused before entering the main room, and Jovan looked back questioningly. Trem swallowed and said, "Go get us a table and a room. I need to take a walk." Jovan seemed to hesitate and Trem tried to reassure him. "Don't worry, I will not be long."

Jovan decided even should he want to, he could not convince Trem to come in now. Besides, he thought, there was very little trouble Trem could get into that he could not get out of in this place. The hermit, despite his youth and inexperience, had a deadly walk, one that appeared trained into him and something he would never shake off. Jovan nodded and said, "Alright, but don't be long, some of these people are more desperate than they look. And do not get lost."

Trem solemnly turned and started off down the main road at a brisk pace, away from the larger crowds of refugees. Jovanaleth hesitated, wondering if he ought to follow and chose against it. Trem wanted to be alone and Jovan decided he should respect that. Thinking that this was probably the best thing he could do, Jovanaleth entered the inn and was immediately swallowed up in the noise and rush of dim light.

Trem felt guilty for abandoning Jovan at the inn, but the story he had heard coming through the door, one he knew better than any bard, had driven much of the old fear back into him. Moving quickly away from the refugees he pushed between the homes of Gi'lakil's citizens looking for someplace to rest and collect his thoughts. Almost without thinking he walked through an open doorway to a small granite building and pressed against the wall within, letting out a great sigh.

Feeling somewhat better, Trem looked around and a sense of trepidation came over him. He was in a temple to one of Teth-tenir's many gods, though Trem could not say which from the few plain trappings about him. His wariness for the immortals was overcome by a sudden twinge of curiosity as he spotted the small pedestal at the center of the tiny building. Walking towards it, he realized it held an hourglass with a slowly filling base at its center. Leaning in for closer look, Trem was caught off guard when the sound echoed in his mind. *I would appreciate it if you did not touch that, Trem Waterhound.*

Straightening in surprise, Trem looked about him and then, seeing nothing, turned to the hourglass again. Realization dawned on him as he knelt closer once more. "Kurven. I should have recognized your symbol."

Perhaps, though I will not hold your forgetfulness against you. There was a pause before the voice continued. *So you chose to leave.*

"Yes. I am not certain I am happy with my decision." Trem glanced about him as though suddenly reconsidering the encounter. "I ought to get back to Jovanaleth."

Trem made as though to leave, but the voice echoed sternly in his mind. *You must hear what I have to say Trem.*

"Why?" Trem crossed his arms in defiance, "Nothing a god has ever deigned to tell me in waking or in dreams has ever led to anything good; even you, God of Time."

Kurven spoke steadily, *I pressed you to leave your exile and I wish to repay you for your decision, though you may not see my gesture as a kindness. Tell me, why did you give up trying to find your mother?*

"My mother?" Trem whispered, "What does it matter... I... I do not know how to answer that question. She left me when I was an infant. I suppose I simply decided I no longer cared."

A lie, Kurven said matter-of-factly. *I can understand leaving Aves, abandoning the knights and their inexplicable disgust for your elven heritage, but I presumed you would take up your old quest.* There was a pause, and Trem sensed Kurven was coming to the point of his rambling. *Besides, your mother had no choice in leaving you. To fulfill my duty I had to make her give you away.*

"Your duty?" Trem's wrath began to overtake him. "What possible benefit could there have been to making a mother surrender her child to strangers?"

You did not know your mother, Trem turned as he sensed movement in the room. The hourglass rose slowly from the pedestal and began to rotate. *She was an angry young woman, Trem. Moreover, you were not something she had planned on. Her people had been destroyed by the rash influences of immortals upon mortals and the surge of power beyond even the reckoning of we gods. She wanted revenge, and asked me to grant her, my servant, the power to exact it. But she was not strong enough.*

The hourglass completed its revolution, the sand now beginning to fill the empty half as it slowly lowered back down. *Your mother was not strong enough, but I could sense that you were. I agreed to give you a piece of myself, that you might cease to age and the great powers of elf and man would resonate at their strongest within you for as long as you remained alive. This was to give you power and the time to understand and wield it with wisdom. That is why I made her surrender you to the Waterhounds. Her wrath, her lust for vengeance, it would have infested you and turned you into an instrument of her will. I wanted you to be your own person, to reach your own conclusions about the world and your place in it. This is what I wished to give you, in exchange for your trust in my advice.*

"I acted despite your advice, not because of it, and I want no part of the world," Trem said defiantly, "in my past I only wanted to meet the woman who gave me up and ask her why. I suppose you have given me that answer."

She is very different now than what she once was. I think perhaps you may meet her someday and get the reconciliation you seek.

Trem slashed the air with a dismissive hand. "There is no need anymore. I am not here for myself, Jovanaleth and his mission are my only purpose."

Tell me Trem, Kurven's voice became calmer and soothing, *what makes you wish to help Jovanaleth? Is it because you lost a mother and he seeks his father? Do you not believe the similarity of Jovan's circumstances to your own speaks to you in some way?*

"I do," Trem replied. "And perhaps that does drive me to assist him. But there is also still that sense of anger. Anger at my mother, at you, at all the gods for cursing me with this pseudo-immortality and thrusting me into a conflict I do not fathom nor care to understand. I have wondered so many times why it was done to me? Why I could not be left alone to rise or fall like every other soul on Teth-te-nir?"

Kurven did not respond at first, but Trem waited. *These are fair questions, Trem. The answers are not simple. You were chosen because you were capable of absorbing my essence. There are few in all of history who could do so. And as to why you cannot 'rise or fall' as you put it, you still can. I admit that I tried to drive you from your home; though I also believe it is what you truly wished to do regardless of my influence in the matter. What happens to you beyond that is in your power, do not doubt that.*

Trem sighed. "Yet you told me that my leaving meant a chance to prevent some cataclysm that awaits Teth-tenir. You pretend at clarity, but you talk in riddles."

No riddles, Kurven continued calmly. *I, more than even other gods, have dwelt ever in realms apart from the visible world. There are powers beyond our own, too utterly beyond thought—I dare not tell you more of. I say this not to speak without clarity, but because such couched language shields you from the danger of knowing what should not be known.*

"That is a convenient excuse to speak so cryptically," Trem said, but added begrudgingly, "though I believe you are trying to protect me in your own way."

I am, and as unbelievable as it may seem, so too is Neroth. Yes, we gods manipulate and vie for command over our creations for selfish reasons, but all our worlds are under threat.

"So what do I do?"

What you believe is right. Nothing more or less can be asked of you.

Trem sensed the god was fading, leaving him behind in the temple. "But what if I do not confront the troubles of the world? What if I decide to return home?"

That, Kurven whispered faintly as his voice slowly faded from the chamber, *is always a path that shall remain open to you.*

A great pressure left the room and Trem felt as though he had been released from a trance. Stepping outside he saw that at least an hour had passed, though it had felt like no more than a few minutes. Making his way back to the Inn of the Four Winds he stopped, standing at the center of the town where the two roads intersected. Looking south he imagined he could see Silverleaf Forest, his home. Turning his head west he saw the inn where Jovanaleth was waiting. He hesitated a moment there, remembering what Kurven had said about choices. Then, with a stern determination and defiance, he stepped with fierce intent to the west, and opened the door of the inn.

Edgewulf el Vac faced a choice of his own at that same moment. He tried hard to keep the tears from welling in his eyes as he crossed the main hall, emotions roiling within him. Edge could not afford to let on that he was sickened by Wolfbane's behavior or the plans that had been unearthed in the meeting. He could show no weakness until he got Wolfbane alone, then he would loose all his pain and frustration on the man he had trusted for so long. But at the moment he had to lose Valissa Ulfrunn. She had followed him after sensing his distress since the meeting; though Edge was certain she thought it for reasons other than the truth. At last, she reached out a hand to halt him as he turned a corner towards his rooms.

"Speak to me young one. What troubles you so?"

Edge turned slowly, taking in Valissa's attractive features, hardly concealed in a low cut leather chestpiece complete with a dangerously short armored kilt and high hunting boots. Her seductive voice had drawn the answers she wanted out of many a man, Edge knew, usually right before she turned them over to the guards and they spent their years wasting away in a dungeon, or worse. The tears he had feared might appear moments ago went dry in an instant. He could hardly bear to speak to this insult of a woman.

"It is nothing, Swordmistress, I am merely tired."

She studied him with a hard eye. Valissa took a special interest in the protection of Edge, mainly because he belonged to Wolfbane, and in her eyes was one of his favorites. Edge knew this was fortunate, for refusing to answer Valissa truthfully would have earned anyone else a blade between his or her ribs.

"You must not be so distressed. Wolfbane merely holds you back from the excursion to the Dust Plains so he can preserve your skills for more important duties. You are too valuable, and attractive, to lose conquering some meager rural settlements. And if some foolish farmer is lucky enough to hit you with a stray arrow Wolfbane would never forgive me." She smoothed his cloak on his shoulders pressing a bit closer than was necessary. "If you are indeed tired then go rest, though I wonder if there might be something that could reinvigorate you?"

Forcing himself not to shove the despicable woman off of him, Edge managed a sickly grin. "Thank you, another time though. I truly do not need to be any more exhausted than I already am."

Valissa curled her catlike smile and stepped back. "Very well, young warrior, get some rest then." And without another word she brushed past him, heading for the training grounds.

Edge managed to contain himself until he was within his chambers, where he tossed his chain mail tunic onto a nearby chair. He then he made a sharp motion of dismissal at Lolenas, his elven

servant supplied to him by Daerveron after the cruel beast had removed the man's tongue. The elf closed the door softly behind him as
he left, perhaps sensing his master's mood. Removing his cloak and
his cloth tunic, Edge tossed them aside and strode to the washbasin,
splashing some warm water onto his face. Looking up he saw his
unusual green eyes staring back under a head of striking white hair.
Dark rings were around those eyes. He had not slept well again. He
could not even remember the last time he had.

Taking a towel he dried his face and walked into the main room
where he slumped onto his bed. Squeezing his eyes shut he tried
desperately to think. Wolfbane was mad in his conviction and likely
had been for a long time, but Edge had clung to the hope that every
once in a while he saw the old light of sanity in the man's eyes. It had
blinded Edge to the fact that even he himself was now in the service
of a violent dictator. The same man who had saved Edge and the
island town of Ilanis from a grim specter of death and mayhem now
brought those plagues on an entire nation. Edge had been raised in
the temple of Neroth, he and his brother left there by their mother
who could not, or would not, raise them alone. Wolfbane had taken
them in when he came to Ilanis and solved the mysterious murders
plaguing the town. Together, the three had sworn to serve Neroth in
his quest to seize control of the mortal world, a mission Edge once
considered noble and for the protection of the people of Teth-tenir.
Now, after such violence and bloodshed propogated in the name of
safety he knew protection was not the goal, but subjugation. Wolfbane was leading a campaign of coerced loyalty maintained by the
blades of the conquerors.

Edge remembered how he worshipped the great warrior. He
remembered watching him practice with the immense axe that Edge
could not have dreamed of even budging. He remembered seeing
Wolfbane make that axe seem light as a feather when he fought and
killed the slyth, the murderous beast that had been taking the forms
of its victims and casting a shadow of fear over Ilanis. The slyth had
been the servant of Balthazain, God of Betrayal, and had killed close
to thirty people in his name. Before Wolfbane, none had been able to
uncover the cause of the deaths. He had arrived at Ilanis and swiftly
become a hero, had been a defender to the small island's people and
a living legend. Edge closed his eyes and sighed. He had not seen his
home in several years. He wondered what they would think of Wolfbane, and him, now.

Wolfbane had taught Edge and his brother, trained them, and
enlightened them in many ways. Not merely a master of the axe,
Wolfbane was skilled enough with the halberd that he was able to
create a man better at it then himself, or so he had told Edge. Edge
was not so sure he had surpassed Wolfbane yet, which was one reason why no weapon would be on his person when he confronted him.
He realized at last that this was the one remaining option to him, to
confront and possibly, through some miracle, turn the former hero

from his path to damnation. It seemed impossible, but Edge felt an irresistable compulsion to make the attempt.

Wolfbane had practically preached honor in defending the weak and less fortunate, now he was ardently opposed to such action. The weak had to be quelled and controlled, made to serve their superiors. If anything Wolfbane's insurmountable strength had increased since he began his march of conquest. Wolfbane told Edge it was his destiny and right; he little realized or perhaps he simply did not believe that Neroth was using his skills as a leader to further his own plans. Wolfbane always doubted the potency of the gods. Edge, having grown up in the temple of one, was wise in their ways; he knew that the ancient feud still raged on among the immortals. Alinormir and Neroth, the most powerful of the gods, had long ago been driven apart by their vision of the world of mortals. It was for their pettiness that Wolfbane now fought, whether he understood that truth or not.

The situation could not be so far gone that it could not be reversed. Edge stood up, suddenly awake and energized. There had to be a way to make Wolfbane see that there was no grand reward nor any sudden acceptance and immortality awaiting him for his loyal service to the God of Death. Surely some glimmer of his old self lingered inside the man that now ruled with an iron fist. "I'll find it," Edge whispered to himself. "I have to find it."

Leaving behind his chain mail and weapons, Edge threw on his cloak with the skeletal clasps and walked quickly out into the corridor. He carefully checked to make sure no one was behind him, then walked down the hall to the servant's quarters where he sought out Lolenas. Edge was unable to find him and began considering where he might have gone, but another worker caught his eye. He was a large man wearing the red and blue livery of Frothgar, working diligently on repairs to a suit of armor. Edge walked over to him, the man kept his eyes on the leather he was patching as he spoke, "The silent one has not returned yet, young master. He scurried off in the opposite direction when he left your quarters."

Edge hissed a sharp intake of breath. "Were you spying on me servant?" he asked, his tone frosty.

The man shook his large head. "No sir, not built for that type of dishonest work, just saw him as I was bringing this back from the training rooms."

Edge realized the man was quite tall and stocky, the type that would normally be a soldier in one of Wolfbane's elite groups, as the general favored large powerful men like himself. Edge wondered why this man was reduced to a role as a mere servant? The worker must have understood the reason for the silence because he lifted his right arm up for Edge to see. "Hard to fight when you only got one hand to hold a blade in. I do the best I can." Edge scolded himself for not having noticed the man was using his teeth to pull the thick stitching through the leather, his powers of observation apparently greatly diminished in his worry and scheming. Still, Edge had larger problems, such as how he was supposed to get the supplies he wanted to spirit Wolfbane from the fortress. Lolenas was trustworthy enough, but where was he? Knuckling his brows Edge tried to decide what his next move should be.

"If it is something you need I can get it as easily as your quiet servant my lord." The one-armed man grunted. "I have nothing else to be doing today." He looked up at last into Edge's eyes and displayed a worn face with a short but rough graying beard. Edge would have placed him at perhaps forty years. "Just tell me what and where." He provided a quick grin for encouragement.

Edge looked at him and finally said, "Alright. I need supplies for three for one month in packs, plus a set of hunting knives and short swords. Leave them by the north barracks and have it there within four hours, alright?"

The servant nodded and returned to his work. "Have it for you on time my lord. Don't worry yourself over it."

Edge nodded once, than a second time more emphatically and started out of the room. "Thank you, servant." He added as he was departing.

"Not a problem my lord Edgewulf, not a problem," The man whispered to himself, and chuckling he returned to his work.

Trem braced himself, his hand on the knob, before opening the door of the inn. He had been in many public houses in his time and was used to the noise and chaos of too many people in too little space. However, that had been some time ago and he was not sure he was ready to dive back into the fray, especially given the encounter he had just had in the temple. "Stop worrying," he said to no one in particular, "no point holding back now, you're stuck in this and you know it." With that and a deep breath he opened the door and stepped inside.

The slight hint of pipe smoke hit him first, but with it came the distinct smell of old stale mead and roasting meat. Standing next to the entrance he closed the door and took his time observing the establishment. Directly across from him was the bar with about twenty stools that wrapped from the left wall to take a sharp, ninety-degree bend into a rather snug corner at the far end of the main room. On the left wall, where the bar began, were two raised corner stages so that the inn could sport several entertainers in the common room at once. On the stage side of the room, from left to right, were tables and benches against the wall opposite the bar and kitchens beyond. This stretch of seating led to the far end of the room, which had a blazing fireplace that made the whole space warm but not overly so. The bar bent away from the fireplace, reaching about ten feet to the back of the inn and there were two small wooden booths, currently unoccupied, that looked made for more privacy. By now it was evening, cool trending towards cold and making the places near the fire more appealing, and as a whole the year was getting into the mid-fall months. Trem realized he did not even know what month it was, and decided he should ask Jovan when the young man was in a less suspicious or concerned mood. The inn's common room was packed; save the two slightly separated booths, and every chair and stool seemed filled and there were people standing besides. Many of the patrons appeared to be regulars, sitting in groups and conversing lightly but rather nervously. Others were more easily recognized as outsiders given their dress and attitude, most seemed rather quiet and absorbed in whatever they happened to be drinking or eating.

Both stages were occupied, though only one performer was currently amidst his routine. A bard tuned his instrument and waited his turn, while opposite him a young human boy, probably hardly out of his teens, if that, was performing a few illusions and sleights of hand for the benefit of those present. He was dressed in a shoddy and weather worn robe that, but for the fraying of the cloth, looked almost like one of an authentic wizard. His short black hair was tightly cut round his head, though it was barely visible beneath his large and drooping hood. What was more astounding was the illusionist's partner, a large and brightly flame-colored cat. Standing on its hind legs, the cat was doing its own performance by balancing on its front paws, then on one, and then on only its head. On all four of its paws it wore several leather straps with bells attached that jingled with every graceful movement.

Having performed its section of the show, the cat returned to its master's side, standing at what Trem guessed was just shy of seven feet, dwarfing the young man. Currently, the latter was making coins randomly appear from nearby people only to vanish and suddenly reappear in his hand. Those watching laughed, though the losers of what they thought to be their coins began to get a bit testy. The bard, perhaps in an attempt to assist the other performer in winning over the crowd, began playing some background music on his strange six-stringed instrument. As the mood seemed to be getting tenser, the minstrel sidled over and whispered in the boy's ear. Quickly he jumped forward and snatched the last coin out of the air from a grinning, beady-eyed man, and pocketed it. The rather fearsome looking patron growled something, but waited to see what the boy was up too. Trem crossed his arms and leaned against the wall beside the main door to watch.

The young man raised his arms that were almost lost amid his worn, mousy gray sleeves, and called out in a clear voice, "Sorry folks, last trick of the night! But don't worry, my friend here surely has some tales he looks forward to sharing with you!" Some people called for more than one last trick, but others simply applauded politely as the bard smiled reassuringly.

95

"Alright then, this one requires some very powerful magic now, so keep your distance and do not disturb me!" The young man then closed his eyes and spread his hands beginning to chant in a strange singsong voice, imitating quite well by Trem's memory actual spell chants. Trem's elven blood would have given him a tingling sensation were there true magic in the air, and it remained unaffected by the grandiose verbage coming from the young entertainer. The robed performer's voice rose steadily till finally he shouted a last word; "Kataz!" and then he froze where he was, arms outstretched.

Slowly he brought his arms together, cupping his hands and covering what they held. The audience was leaning forward, straining to see what he was about to reveal. Then he whipped his top hand back and showed nothing more than a common acorn.

The people watching exploded. Some laughed thinking it a joke, others yelled their complaints but the young man was not done yet. He held up his free hand for silence and moments later it was restored. Winking, he said loudly enough for everyone to hear, "Of course that's not the whole trick."

A few people laughed, but most remained silent, waiting for the big surprise that was coming. Holding the acorn in the palm of his hand, the boy extended it out as far as he could and whispered a word under his breath, hardly moving his lips at all so that Trem was certain only he had noticed. Suddenly he felt a tingling in his hands and it rapidly shot up his arms and soon he could feel a dull hum throughout his whole body. The acorn suddenly split open and a griffin, half lion and half eagle and steadily growing, crawled out of it. When it reached the size of a small dog it leapt from the boy's hand and flew around the inn's common room several times, causing people to duck their heads and cry in surprise. The griffin flew by once more and then alighted on a table where it suddenly shriveled up into an acorn again.

There was a period of dead silence while a man at the table picked up the acorn, turned it cautiously in his hands, and then replaced it where the creature had landed. Trem feared the boy might have overplayed his hand, for surely those there would realize it was no simple parlor trick he had performed, and some might react out of fear with violence. But then the room erupted in applause and as the young man strode to the table, grinning at the shocked acorn examiner while he received many hearty claps on the back from several patrons. One of the most incensed clappers near the bar Trem recognized as Jovanaleth.

Taking his hand off the hilt of his sword, unaware he had reached for it at all until that moment, Trem watched as the boy retrieved his acorn and slipped it into his robes. He had performed a very real and very powerful illusion, a spell he should not be even capable of reading at his young age without having his eyes burned out of their sockets. Yet he had cast it, well enough to fool even Trem but for his elven heritage. His respect and wariness of the boy grew.

Trem was not the only one who was intrigued by the display and not all the audience were so amused. The man who had lost the last trick coin stood up, blocking the boy's path to the corner at the far end of the bar.

Leering down at him through bleary eyes, perhaps a bit clouded by the establishment's ale, the man stood as straight as his tipsy legs allowed. The rest of the common room, aside from the man's cronies, was now focused on the minstrel reciting a love story to the occasional twangs of his instrument. The boy looked right back at his intimidator, betraying no emotion. In his mind Trem urged the illusionist not to do anything rash. The man growled at the boy, "Yer gonna be givin' me that coin son, else there'll be trouble. I know yer kind and their tricks, killed plenny in my time."

The boy simply stared back, unmoving, but his cat had paused in the stowing of their equipment into a large leather pack. It was staring frozen at its master and his confronter. The man grabbed the boy by his front robes, lifting him off his feet and bellowed, "Are ya deaf boy? I said gimme my money!"

In a flash the cat was between the two, holding a longsword to the man's throat and a dagger to the temple of his closest friend, who had started to draw his club. Trem noted the long, finger-like paws of the cat creature and how they seemed to envelope the entirety of the handle and hilt of its sword and dagger. But the others were more interested in the standoff. The youth stared at the man, whose chin was nearly perpendicular to the ceiling with terrified eyes angled down at the boy still clutched in his fist.

"Put me down and I will tell Neep to let you go." The young wizard said with exquisite calm.

The man instantly dropped the boy and ran out of the inn, followed by his companions. The sword and dagger immediately disappeared into sheaths at the cat's back and leg respectively. The cat retrieved the pack it had been stowing their gear in and, with its eyes following only its master, walked to one of the corner booths and sat down, its tail poking through the back of the bench and swishing just off the dirty floor. Trem watched the inn return to its normal noisy self, the silence that had been complete once the man grabbed the magician shattered, and the minstrel took up his tale with a light joke that erased the tension.

The bartender for the evening, a rather large and wide woman, came and spoke to the two unusual performers, smiling genuinely and bringing them some stew from the kitchen. The boy thanked her and the two started a quiet meal.

Deciding he had observed all he needed to, Trem turned to find Jovan crossing the room. He had a rather grim look on his face as he commented, "Glad that cat took care of the drunk. He looked dangerous."

Trem smiled and the two walked toward the corner of the bar where they sat on neighboring stools. "The stew should be safe,"

Trem commented. "The cook is fat, it means she must eat well." Jovan laughed out loud and called the woman over. Before she arrived, Trem added almost as an afterthought, "You were wrong about the drunk, he was harmless."

Jovan looked at him curiously and Trem returned the look, now quite serious. "It's the boy who's the real danger. He's a mage."

Chapter 5

Edgewulf el Vac walked out of the servant's quarters and paused, considering what to do next. It would be easiest to abscond with Wolfbane as close as possible to the time when Edge's supplies would be in place. Thankfully, this gave him a few spare moments to make other preparations. Walking back to his rooms he retrieved his armor and tunic, tossing his hooded black cloak on in place of the silken one he had been wearing, carefully swapping out the clasps as he did. Taking his large halberd from its corner in the wall he examined its blade and spearhead. The weapon was a foot taller than Edge, well over six and a half feet from haft to fearsome, spiked tip. The spearhead was diamond shaped and had a large axe head just below it. The concave axe blade was curved in two places, making a central flaring point and two more sharp tips at the top and base. This gave it a rather large, serrated look, as though it should have been part of an immense knife. The haft was of black ironwood from the Forester woodlands in Silverleaf. Edge had made the weapon himself upon arrival at Napal City, a means of distraction from the somber spectacle of the fallen city. It was now his most prized possession. Using it like an oversized walking stick he walked out of his room with the hood pulled down over his face.

Once back in the hall he checked both left and right, then went down the passage opposite the servant's rooms, he had visited earlier, heading past other high-ranking officer's rooms, including those of Valissa and Frothgar. At the end of the hall he turned left from the commanders' private smithy room, where his halberd had been forged. A large double door stood before him and he opened it, entering the courtyard of Castle Bane.

The yard was vast and there was no shortage of activity within it. The entire space was surrounded by a ten foot wall with tightly placed ramparts topped with spikes that curved from their tops down the wall's outer edge to prevent scaling. Solid gray granite a foot thick made these impressive bastions of defense. Frothgar's personal guard trained as expert archers were atop the walls, spaced about every three feet and armed with daggers and crossbows. The only way in, barring coming over the walls, was the massive main gate made of two eight-foot-high ironwood doors backed by two equally impressive blacksteel portcullises. Flanking the entrance were two four-story stone towers with murder holes facing inward so as to protect the entrance. Within each of the towers were the mechanisms for one of the portcullis gates. Thus, in order to control the entrance into the fortress, one had to hold both of the towers.

Even in such an event, there was an interior fortress with four towers, the largest rising some twenty stories high, fifteen more than the other three attached to the inner castle. The highest tower, used by Wolfbane for council meetings and his personal chambers; had been constructed by Kundren Dolg, also know as the Mad Thane. Most subsequent rulers of Napal City had considered it an eyesore, but Wolfbane had thought otherwise and claimed it as a way to assert his authority and power. After all, demanding his council climb the great number of steps to its peak for any meeting assured they remembered who was in command.

The rest of the castle was taken up mostly by the large entry hall, though there was also a gigantic kitchen occupying a decent portion of the ground floor and a vast expanse of dungeons beneath it. The other floors above the main hall contained several substantial libraries and a few small storage areas or cluttered bedrooms. The dungeons were Daerveron's almost exclusively, the kitchen supplied the entire compliment of fortress defenders with their rations, and the libraries were strictly for the use of the two mages who had the entire authority over the fortress; excepting Wolfbane's tower. At its very top, which Edge had left just over an hour ago, was where Wolfbane kept his private items and spent the majority of his time, often not coming down even to sleep in his more practically positioned bedroom located on the third.

On the interior of all the outside walls excepting the location of the gate, were barracks, north, east, and west. The western end also held the officers' living quarters, and was where Edge was currently standing. In front of the castle, Valissa was drilling her fighters in several sword forms. Despite his total dislike for the unscrupulous woman, Edge respected her skills with a blade. Often those who rose quickly in her ranks of trainees would be forced to fight her. Those that could last more than five minutes were entered into the elite troop commanded by Valissa herself. Most did not make it more than thirty seconds without being disarmed or seriously wounded, and Valissa offered no apologies for her brutal methods.

To the north of the castle stood a few Nerothian soldiers practicing with ranged weapons against tattered, vaguely humanoid targets. Few remained out in the darkening light, but those that did were opposite Edge's path, firing arrows or hucking axes and conversing casually with one another. Edge strode out and into a narrow gap between two of the barrack bunkrooms. Following the darkened pathway, he moved north until he was facing the wall. Keeping it to his left, he turned right and walked until he stood outside a small cottage shielded from the rest of the fortress by the surrounding barracks. He knocked quietly, checking over his shoulder to see if anyone was with him in the alley. The door opened a crack revealing shimmering firelight from within. A tentative, but almost musical voice called, "Yes, who is it?"

Edge smiled in spite of himself and replied, "It's Edge, Raymir. Can I come in?"

The door swung open. "Of course you can!"

Edge set his halberd outside and stepped into a comfortable one-room cottage with a blazing fire, a small cot, and two chairs with an uneven and unmatched table. Edge picked up one of the chairs and set it in front of the fire, warming his hands as his companion brought over her own seat to join him.

For some time they merely sat there letting the heat of the fire wash over them. Edge looked over at Raymir while she was staring into the flames, enjoying the features of her face. Raymir had unusually bright red hair that hung several inches past her shoulders. Her small nose was set under two bright green eyes that he sometimes swore were just like his own. She had high cheekbones and an intoxicating smile completed by small dimples. In short, she was the most beautiful person in the world, by Edge's account. He came to see her at least three times a week whenever his responsibilities left him free. Raymir worked in the castle libraries, documenting and sorting the various books for the two mages. More often than not she was released earlier than other servants and treated well, for it was known where she served the army. Some suspected her to be an illusion, for surely no mage needed a woman to assist him, but Edge knew she was very real.

Looking at her, he suddenly noticed a small lump on her forehead, partially hidden by her red hair. He reached out to brush it back making her meet his gaze. He paused a second before asking, "How did you get this?"

Raymir blushed. "It was Saltilian. He found me looking at a book I should not have. Its alright, I'm fine, I told him I was just looking at the pictures and he believed me." Raymir grimaced. "He still leers at me when he thinks I don't see him. After he saw the bruise he apologized and tried to heal it for me, but I would not let him. I do not want his magic touching my skin." She shuddered slightly and Edge cupped her head in his hands, moving the bruise into the light.

"I can put a poultice on it right now, it would not take long." She protested, though not much, as he applied a small weaving of leaves along with a few drops of a concoction he had stowed in his gear brought from the castle. He did not tell her Saltilian probably made the medicine, knowing he would never get her to accept his help in that case. She held it to her forehead while smiling at him, and he grinned back before taking a deep breath and reaching for her hand. Holding it in his, he moved her fingers front of his face, while keeping his eyes down.

Concerned, Raymir tried to bring his eyes upward. "What is it Edge? Something is wrong."

He looked up, now smiling, and ran his hand through her hair. "No, love, everything is fine. I have just made up my mind, that's all. We are leaving, if you still have that escape tunnel you told me about." She nodded, trying to contain her excitement. "Have you tested it?" he asked.

"No, I would not go through with truly leaving until you decided to come with me." She grimaced slightly. "My father showed it to me once when we still served our people in the castle. At least he did one noble thing in life, even if it was unintentional."

Edge sighed; Raymir's father, Greymane Squall, had betrayed his people in the hope that his family would be spared. In the end only he and Raymir survived Wolfbane and Caermon's violent retribution for his traitorous bargain. Raymir was forced to watch her siblings killed and her mother waste away in the dungeons of the fortress while her father made a seemingly impossible escape. Raymir blamed her father for everything; Edge blamed Wolfbane's blind corruption.

"Well, if you are sure we can go tonight than we will go tonight. I have a pack with some food and anything else you need, warm clothes, that sort of thing. We have to travel lightly, though, or we will not get far. My things will be here in a few hours, a servant is bringing them and he will leave them outside. Once he leaves, bring them in here. I will come by a little later with Wolfbane."

"Wolfbane?" she asked him, not sounding angry or shocked but more skeptical, "Are you sure he will come? I know he was your friend, and like a father to you, but Edge you have to realize he is different from the man you knew...." Her voice trailed off. She was clearly very worried and looking at him imploringly.

Edge stood and put his cloak back on, turning to her, his face grim. "I have to try, at least, Raymir, and even if he won't come I doubt he would hunt me down. Our friendship still runs that deep. It has too."

She stood and walked to him, hugging him suddenly and fiercely. He held her for a few glorious moments and then she stepped back with tears in her eyes. "Just be sure you come safely, please. I promise to be ready."

"I will, love, I swear. Remember, just a few hours, waste no time." And having spoken his piece, Edge kissed her hand lightly and turned, sweeping quietly out the door and into what was now becoming a rainy evening.

Raymir stood at her lone window and watched him walk down the alley and turn left, away from the wall. She crossed her arms and looked at the floor taking a deep breath. Raymir had lived so many hard days since the fall of her nation that she had lost count, or chosen not to attempt keeping track. Her pursuit of magic and knowledge within the library had sustained her and given her purpose, but then Edge had come along and once again she felt she had something to lose. She looked out the window into the soft rain now falling more and more steadily outside and whispered, "Just let him come back. Please let him come back."

Perhaps if he had any idea how worried Raymir was Edge never would have left her home. As it was, he was more interested in rescuing Wolfbane from his misguided reign and bringing him freely out of the darkness to a new life, one that would be more like the old days of heroism and virtue. His step was lighter both from these thoughts and knowing that no matter what happened with Wolfbane he would still leave with the woman he loved and perhaps find someplace, anyplace, to ride out the storm of war. In truth, Edge felt he had already seen enough of battle and was ready for a quiet life in relative seclusion.

Through the rain now pelting down on his head the stealthy warrior walked, eyes down to conceal himself and to keep out the wetness. Even in his heavy cloak he felt the cold seeping into him slowly, making him shiver. He chanced a glance upward and saw the towers of the castle in his wet eyes. Nearly there, he sped up a bit, holding his halberd halfway up the pole and off the ground, trotting for the archway of the castle gates. Two guards were huddled in the entrance, but they ignored him. Anyone who came to the castle was permitted entry without question until they reached the third floor, where Saltilian and Daerveron had set a few wards to detect intruders within their domain. Edge knew from Raymir that there was a servant's stair leading to the northwest tower's giant spiral staircase, which was not warded. Dodging left halfway through the main entrance hall, lit by several immense flaming braziers, Edge entered the kitchen. Already the cooks were preparing the next day's meals and no one paid him much heed except to step aside when he came forward. No servant dared challenge an armed man in Wolfbane's fortress.

At the far end of the kitchen was a door that appeared to lead to a storage room. Edge used his halberd to pry it open and check for occupants. It was pitch black within, so he borrowed a thin torch from the kitchen and slipped back behind the door. Once inside he turned to see a small stair leading up to the second floor, complete with another door. He went up and past it, following the next flight beyond the first landing until he reached the third floor that had no door to the library; hence the lack of magical wards. He took the last staircase, which ended in an apparent blank wall. Feeling the wall to his right he pulled the loose brick out and watched the false wall slide aside opening up the foyer to Wolfbane's tower stairs. After checking left and right for any other presence he started the long trek up the spiraling stairs. The entire walk of over six hundred stairs carried one to a dizzying height only after a tiring climb. So flushed with hope and exuberance was Edge that it took him a far shorter time to reach the top than any of his previous ascents. He paused, catching his breath and straightened his cloak so as not to look disheveled before the commander. Edge did not want to appear a runaway or Wolfbane might not even take the time to listen. With a final nod to reassure himself, he opened the door by pressing another false stone in the wall.

The large meeting room spread out before him, adorned with its massive table and many shield and weapon displays from fallen enemies. Strangely it was sparsely lit and only a wavering torchlight shone down the far hall where Wolfbane's makeshift bedchamber was. Edge was surprised that the warrior was sleeping already, he had anticipated finding him in his study poring over his maps, but the hall end lights were out. Moving quietly toward the back so as not to startle Wolfbane, he reached the doorway and called out, not loudly but too aggressively. If he skulked around, Wolfbane might mistake him for an assassin and he would be dead in seconds. "My lord? Wolfbane? Please, I need to speak to you urgently."

There was no response, so cautiously Edge stepped into the room. Wolfbane had ordered a large mat and several plush pillows moved into one of his smaller rooms along with several hanging curtains to give the sleeping area more of a bedroom look. A large assortment of sweet smelling candles lit the room faintly, explaining the shimmering light Edge had seen earlier. Wolfbane was slumped on his stomach breathing extremely slowly and heavily, apparently in a very deep sleep. Edge leaned in close and tried to nudge him awake, but there was no response. He had known Wolfbane was a light sleeper; surely he would have awakened before Edge could have even touched him.

"Ah, the young fool is here after all. How perfectly predictable."

Edge whirled around, holding his halberd in front of him. Daerveron materialized out of the gloom from the hall, his loose hanging and dislocated jaw showing under the thin silk wrap over his face. Edge would have sworn he was smiling, though he was not sure if that was possible. Daerveron walked to within reach of Edge's weapon, clearly unperturbed by its presence. The mage shook his finger sardonically at him. "It is not wise to be wandering after dark. One might almost think you were up to something." He laughed, and it sounded like a pit of snakes, "Did you honestly believe no one would find out? I have eyes and ears everywhere. Your elven servant happens to be one of my favorites. They are so much more useful once you remove the tongue."

"What have you done to Wolfbane?" Edge growled.

Daerveron shook his head dismissively as he answered, "No need to be concerned about him. I merely gave him a sleeping draught. I convinced him that rest would give him the ability to think clearly. Fortunately, he is too bull-headed to ever become truly clear minded, even when well-rested." That shimmer of cloth betrayed another almost-smile and Daerveron sighed. "Ah well, he is no longer your concern. You will not be taking him anywhere. I need him still, for now. As to you, troublesome whelp, your escape ends here tonight. And shortly thereafter she will be joining you." He laughed loudly at the anger contorting Edge's face.

"You leave her out of this! She has done nothing!"

"True," remarked Daerveron thoughtfully, "but you will suffer so much more knowing you are the reason she died. Goodbye, fool!"

Before Edge could react Daerveron called out and shoved his hands toward him. Edge flew backward, striking the wall a few feet behind him and dropping his halberd. He clenched his teeth in pain and tried to clear his head. His weapon was useless against the undead fiend's magic, but he had to save Raymir.

Daerveron advanced, already chanting the spell that would snuff out his victim's life. Edge looked around wildly and spotted his halberd lying next to his foot. Without thinking he brought the toe of his boot under its axe blade and kicked up, hard. Throwing his weight forward, he slammed his shoulder into Daerveron's, breaking the surprised wizard's concentration. Catching his weapon as he struck the withered spellcaster, Edge swung it hard and low taking out his enemy's legs with the haft. Rushing forward past the sprawling form, he sped toward the stairs.

Daerveron roared his unearthly fury after the retreating man and regained his footing. Rising swiftly he hurried after his quarry and saw him duck behind the door to the stairs. *"Elgata,"* the mage commanded and the door swung open so forcefully it shattered on the stone wall where it struck. Stalking to the doorway, Daerveron raised his hands and started chanting, his voice now surprisingly clear and terrifyingly free of its usual dry crackle, *"Asgatinth lo manoths, en vathce del calloth!"*

Edge was running and leaping rapidly down the stairs, careening off the wall when necessary, and was almost to the bottom when he heard the mage finish his chant. Instinctively he dove, rolling down the last twenty or so stairs and slamming into the floor splayed out, knocking the wind from his lungs. A searing orb of heat hurtled around the corner he had just tumbled down and smashed into the secret entrance he had come from, blasting the stone to bits and cutting at his hands and face. Regaining his feet, Edge rushed down the stairs to the bottom floor, shoving his way through the kitchen and out of the keep doors.

The guards on watch stared at him as he burst forth but did not attempt to stop him. Edge paused, trying to reorient himself now that he was outside. All he could think of was that he had to reach Raymir immediately. Suddenly a figure appeared in one of the third floor windows in the keep. Daerveron spat at the guards in rage, "Get him you fools! Kill him!"

Unquestioningly the guards hefted their spears and positioned their shields to protect their bodies. Quickly they circled Edge, cutting off escape on both sides of the keep. Their reach would prevent him from simply running past, and returning to the keep would mean certain death. Edge turned to face the guard to his right. The man readied himself and started pressing in with his longer reaching weapon, Edge backed up slowly, being sure not to check over his shoulder at his other opponent. Keeping his eyes on the other man's face he saw him glance behind Edge's shoulder meaningfully and reacted instantly. Spinning, he ducked low under the thrust that would have taken him through the back and stepped forward swinging the heavy balancing spike of his halberd behind him. He caught the thrusting guard squarely between his shoulders and broke his spine with a sickening crunch. The guard grunted and gasped, stumbling into his partner who was slowed as the dying man's weight pressed into his shield. Without glancing back, Edge had already started running and was now heading north along the eastern wall of the castle.

Speeding through the archery range, now thankfully abandoned by any lingering soldiers, Edge hurried down the narrow alley toward Raymir's cottage. Suddenly a figure rose up in front of him, just outside her door, and without thinking Edge drove his blunt pole end into the shadow's gut and grabbed its shirt collar, pressing the intruder up against the wall of the cottage. "Where is she? Damn it! Tell me where she is!"

"Edge! Edge stop! I'm right here, I'm fine!"

Raymir stood poised in her doorway, holding a lantern, which she shone on his face. "Oh Edge, you're hurt! Quickly, get inside!"

But Edge used the light to examine the trespasser, immediately dropping him upon seeing his face. It was the one armed servant from before. Bending over to catch his breath he held up a large and full pack. "Beg your pardon my lord, I was not trying to skulk, you just said to bring these quietly so I did." Edge stepped back and helped the man straighten.

"I am sorry, but we have to leave right now, Raymir. You too," he gestured towards the servant, "we are all of us in grave danger. Daerveron was waiting for me, Raymir; he drugged Wolfbane so I could not even talk to him. He knew about my whole plan and about you, I thought... I was afraid...."

Suddenly she was hugging him tightly and sobbing into his shoulder. Edge embraced her just as tightly and squeezed his eyes shut. His fear, his pain at having thought she was dead had passed. The servant coughed, hefting the pack he had brought. Edge and Raymir separated, Raymir blushing and pretending to be fixing her hair, though she was still crying a little. Edge looked at the older man. He met his gaze with surprising ferocity and said, "If you know a quick way out of here, my lord, I suggest we take it immediately. The guards will be here soon."

Raymir composed herself and straightened. "He is right," she said looking at Edge, "we have to get away first, come on, once we are in the tunnel and I seal it off, they can not get to us. No one knows where it comes out."

The three hurried into the cottage and stood before the fireplace. Raymir whispered a few words and the blaze winked out immediately, leaving them with only the lantern. The servant grunted and Edge looked at Raymir wide eyed. She grinned mischievously. "You did not think I spent all that time in the library without learning something?"

Edge shook his head in awe as Raymir lifted an iron hinge from under the ashes and threw it back. She winced as she did so. "I'm afraid I burnt my hand, forgot magic fire is still fire." Without another word she dropped into the tunnel, followed by Edge and then the one-armed man. Urging them forward she returned to the entrance, taking what looked like a string between her fingers. She whispered some words and suddenly it began burning. Edge saw that at the other end was a small barrel, filled to overflowing with a strange black powder. Raymir hurried up to them, grabbing the two men and shoving them forward. "What are you waiting for? Run!"

The three sped down the tunnel ducking to keep from scraping their heads on the low roof. Moments later there was a resounding explosion behind them and the shockwave knocked them all flat. Rising quickly from the dust Raymir pulled the other two up with surprising strength. "It's just a few more yards, hurry!"

Running forward quickly, the three suddenly shot out of the hole into a large open cavern with a small spring running out of its walls and flowing down a gentle slope. The moonlight lit the cavern from a small opening in its roof. Edge and the others hit the stone hard as the tunnel caved in behind them. Looking at Raymir, Edge grinned; they were safe from pursuit at last. She smiled back, and suddenly leapt up, her face a mask of fear and shock, Edge started to rise when a firm hand grabbed him around the neck, the other holding a dagger blade to his throat. "Do not move now, miss. I will not hurt him if you stay still, but he's not someone I can let run wild. He was in league with Wolfbane and I cannot just let him run free."

Edge's chin was pointed to the sky, but his green eyes burned in hatred at the face over his shoulder. The worn and bearded visage leaned forward to grin knowingly at Edge from behind two good hands. How had he gotten his arm back Edge wondered? The grin quickly turned sad, as the hand with the dagger came up. "Sorry lad, I liked you, I really did. But you are just too dangerous to trust."

The dagger came down, Raymir screamed, and everything went black.

Chapter 6

Jovan stared at Trem for a moment as if considering whether or not he was serious. "A mage? You mean a real one?" Trem nodded as Jovanaleth leaned back to get another look at the young performer. "No, he can't be. He is far too young to have completed his training, he'd still be in Ozmandias at that age."

The matronly cook dropped two bowls of stew before them along with a pair of mugs. Trem tossed her some coins and reached for his ale. Taking a long sip he turned to face his friend with a small smile. "It's been some time since I had a real drink. Now to your point, I agree, but the fact remains he is still a wizard." Jovan started to protest but Trem silenced him with a wave of his hand. "Oh, he had a couple of common street acts like you said, but that last one, nobody performs a trick like that with only sleight of hand. That was a mage's illusion, through and through. I can sense these things."

Jovan gave his stew a gingerly slurp before responding, "Sense? What do you mean?"

Trem looked at him with a puzzled expression. "You should understand," his eyes drifted to Jovan's ears, which had visible but not excessive points. "Your blood and mine, it is of the same ancestry."

Jovan reached up to touch his ear points and smiled slightly. "You mean half-elven? But you have more elf in you than I do, Trem, and I am some years beyond my nai'valen. What few elven gifts I once had have faded in the past years."

Trem took a bite from a large chunk of meat in the stew and said around his mouthful, "Yet you do not remember the tingling of your blood around a wizard as they invoked the arcane word?"

"Ah," Jovan nodded, "I do recall hearing of that with some half-elves, but it was very rare and took a great deal of magic for most to experience. You are saying your elven blood can feel the presence of magic?"

"Often times, yes. It is not true for all elves. I hear those of Silverleaf are far less likely to feel it's presence. But I can, and when that boy unveiled his last trick I felt the sensation strongly. He is a real mage, Jovanaleth, most assuredly."

"But then how is he out here? He can't be more than twenty years at best and Ozmandias keeps most of their charges a decade longer than that, sometimes more."

Trem took another slow sip of ale. "Sometimes those who practice arcane magic do not stay in Ozmandias, dangerous as the alternatives can be."

Jovan looked at him a moment longer and was about to question him further when the man sitting to Trem's left leaned in and whispered, "Your friend is correct boy, that was no mean flight of fancy. He pulled the wool over everyone's eyes with his other tricks first but that last feat, well, take it from one who knows; that was real magic."

Jovan and Trem both turned to study the speaker, who smiled at their sudden attentiveness. He had long black hair graying through his temples and most of his forehead, along with a very gray beard surrounding his face in short curls of bushy hair. His smile was slight and gave away nothing, but his eyes were hard as rock and grey to match. He wore muddied and battered plate armor and a heavy white cloak, which must once have been very expensive, but was so travel-worn and dirty that only a beggar would be interested in now. Trem mostly noticed the battered and curved scimitar at his side. It had a ruby-jeweled handle and looked to be worth more than the whole inn put together. When the man noticed him looking, he swiftly swirled his cloak to cover it. His smile broadened unconvincingly. "You have the look of well-traveled men, though perhaps not so worn as myself." He laughed, a gruff but nevertheless amiable sound. "Where have you come from?"

Jovan returned his smile, though more freely. "We came from the south, through Silverleaf Forest."

The man's eyes widened and he took another look at them, this one more considering than before. "Well now, you certainly must have some ability with those weapons to make it out of those woods. Folks around here tell me they are haunted." He took a swig from his own mug and looked at them as though he expected a heroic tale of how they valiantly fought their way clear after days of travel without rest. Trem disappointed him quickly.

"You are truly not a local. The woods are about as haunted as this inn, from what we saw. I used to live there and I never saw a single spirit."

The man sighed and took another gulp from his cup. "Too bad, I was hoping for a rousing adventurer's tale. You two had the look, despite being a bit young. Me, I hail from the north, been in too many scrapes to remember every one, might as well try remembering every stone I see on the road."

Jovan was intrigued. "You are from the north? I fear I must ask you a question of dire importance. Did you ever meet a man from the city of Bladehome? He would be about your age, maybe older, might have carried a worn sword like my own...."

The man was already shaking his head before Jovan finished. "Sorry lad, have not heard of him. Is that where you are off too, heading north on a mission to find this man? I suggest you think again.

110

The north is safe for no one nowadays. There are things up there worse than Broken or gnolls. It took me many weeks just to get clear and even now I am far from safe." He paused as though he suddenly thought he had said too much and grunted into his mug, taking another swallow. "Then again it is your skins not mine, so do what you will. I just hope this comrade of yours is worth looking for."

Jovan eyed him hard. "He is my father. I have not seen him in months and intend to bring him home, alive."

The man changed his tune rapidly. "Ah, sorry boy, I didn't know. Look, if it is that important to you then I think I can help you, but I would need your help first. I have a package I need to retrieve. It's only a few weeks south through the woods, but I would be in need of guides and I cannot find anyone willing to travel that far. If you bring me through and we get what I seek then I will take you north, and if your father is there, friend, than we will find him. I know the north better than any man. What do you say?"

Before Jovan could respond Trem jumped in saying, "You will have to pardon us sir, but I think we ought to discuss this privately before we give you our decision. I hope that won't inconvenience you too much?"

The man smiled that non-smile again and stuck out his hand. "Fair enough. I have to get a room anyway, so you just talk it over until I get back." Trem grasped his extended hand and the man gave him a rather rough handshake. "Call me Ghost. Just Ghost if you have to ask after me, I'll tell the innkeeper to show you my room if you need me in a hurry."

Trem returned the shake just as fiercely never letting his gaze slip from the man's eyes. "Very well, Ghost, my name is Trem and this is Jovanaleth."

"Well met then, whether we work together or not. Speak with you both later." And with that and a rather promising wink, Ghost hopped from the stool and was gone in the crowd.

Jovan looked at Trem accusingly. "Why did you act so coldly to him? I questioned the innkeeper before you got here and she knew nothing. That man may be the only one who can help us!"

"He may also be just the person to slit our throats if we are not careful." Trem responded angrily, "You can not trust every man you meet in an inn. We have to be certain of his intentions."

"I apologize, you are right." Jovan said, recognizing the wisdom of Trem's words. "He may not be safe for traveling with, but I think he told the truth about being from the north and knowing it well."

Trem nodded his agreement and took another bite of stew. "Yes, I would say he is a northerner and that is why he could be dangerous. The north is a treacherous place even to those who live there. I would also like to know exactly what package we are supposed to help him get. From his tone of voice it did not sound like something he wanted other people to know about."

"But he could be part of the Napalian resistance. There are still a few trying to fight the invaders up north, and if he is I say we help him. My home could be next on their list and with no word from Angladais since the invasion, who knows what may have happened to them? Without their paladins and armies the rest of Legocia is in grave peril. No other country is large or powerful enough to stand against this invasion if the rumors are true."

"If all the nations united that might be enough to drive out the invaders."

Jovan laughed mirthlessly. "They will never unite! The Eagle Knights turned down my father, once one of their own. There are too many differences going back far too many years, and not a single common bond to hold us together. Once the invaders are knocking on their doors, they may realize their foolishness, but it will be too late."

Trem sat pondering the situation. Like Jovanaleth he could not believe the invaders would be satisfied with just the wintry north-lands. Once they got beyond the Dragonscale Mountains, they would be in the rich farmlands of Dragon's Watch, and the Broken tribes would become the least of the free people's worries. Trem wondered briefly again if he had made the wrong choice, but he pushed such dark thoughts aside.

"Eat your food," Trem said, "or else it will get cold. Give me time to come up with a plan. Maybe we will be leaving with this man Ghost after all. Just let me handle the negotiations."

Jovan took a bite and smiled contentedly. "Alright Trem, I can follow your lead."

"Good," Trem stirred his spoon thoughtfully. "I do not doubt your good sense, Jovanaleth. I have just seen enough of the world to know that most people have a darker side than they present."

"I understand, though you seem a bit more on edge than you were earlier." The man from Bladehome searched his companion's face for some sign of confirmation for his suspicions.

Trem met Jovan's eyes and shook his head in confusion. "I cannot explain it, but since we met Ghost I have had a chill running down my spine," Trem gazed over his shoulder out the window into the night. "Something is coming, Jovanaleth. Be sure your sword is loose in the sheath."

With the night having rapidly come on, as it did nearing the end of the fall, the guards at the gates of Gi'lakil had to deal with the rapid loss of their line of sight over the plains. Typically, the open flat spaces allowed them a chance to spot any incoming travelers to the small town, or to see a Broken attack party on its way in time to seal up the walls and raise the alarm. When night fell, the guards became more alert, for Broken night raids were not unheard of, and with the reports coming from the east the guardsmen were all on shorter nerves than usual. The two men stationed at the northern gate had a more relaxed attitude this night. All sightings of Broken troops came from the east after all, and there was rarely a traveler coming from the north. Very few Napalians had escaped farther than the Windpass or the southern foothills of the God's Bones Mountains.

Bode and Wellin were two of the youngest guards, recently appointed because they were young and fit, if a little rambunctious at times. Being friends and new to the job, they had been assigned the northern gate in the hopes that it would offer them little enough time to get in trouble. But, as the saying goes, mischief loves idle hands, and these two were no exception. Without much chance of a visitor and having received the night shift, they had opted to smuggle some of the Inn of the Four Wind's famous Autumn Ale out the back earlier that afternoon. With their own beat-up tin cups in hand, they had tapped the small barrel minutes after the sun disappeared, and now an hour later they were deep into it, and it into them. Talk had ranged from the prettiest girls just up for marriage to the possibility of fighting Broken, something both looked forward to with the foolish eagerness of youth. After all, the Broken may once have been well-trained soldiers in the Army of the Lion, but they had deteriorated in the thirty-odd years since the legendary siege to a ragtag horde that won battles by the sheer weight of their numbers. At least that was the common opinion.

It is therefore not surprising that they never noticed the five riders that seemed to materialize out of the gloom just a bare three yards in front of them. Even if they had not been deep into the inn-keeper's best brew it is unlikely they would have noted these particular five horsemen. More annoyed than alarmed by their sudden appearance, Bode and Wellin rose unsteadily to their feet in surprise, but determined to follow their orders. Being intoxicated as much with their own heroic chatter as with the ale, they made a brave show of it. If they had been more themselves they might have noticed the exceedingly emaciated appearance of the five steeds, and perhaps the cold emanating from the dark foreboding cloaks and hoods of their riders. They did not, however, and with encouraging cries from Bode, Wellin rashly threatened them with his spear, ordering them to camp a mile outside the walls and wait until morning to enter like everyone else. When the lead rider made no reply and his colleagues showed no intent of turning around and doing as ordered, a rather unsure Wellin daringly pressed forward to pursue their departure further.

Neither saw the black blade sliding out of its scabbard until it was too late, although Bode immediately turned to rally the guards once he saw Wellin's head neatly sliced from his body with nary a sound. Unfortunately he never got the chance to cry out. One of the back riders shot him in the shoulder with a heavy black shaft, and its poison turned his cry into a foaming sputtering gasp. The leader sheathed his sword and his companion replaced his bow. Riding up to the gate, the first rider waved his hand before it and the heavy slide bolt splintered and snapped. The doors swung wide with a small creak that the tower archers did not respond to until the mysterious riders had trotted silently into the town. No one was left on the main road to see them. No begging was taking place once night fell as the refuges had retired to the smaller street alleys, huddled masses near the towers, and a few fortunate ones to homes of kindly folk. Nobody saw the five black figures ride slowly through town, turn to the west, and head for the inn.

Trem and Jovan were enjoying their meal, each one lost in his own thoughts when the inn door was hurled open. Most of the people in the building looked up, though a small hum of conversation and raucous laughter continued, but not for long. Gradually the entire inn turned and stared at the figure in the doorway. Despite himself, Trem stared too, for he had never seen a larger orc in his life. Jovan's hand was gripping his broadsword hilt in a white-knuckled fashion, and he was not the only patron who looked ready to fight, though more were prepared to run out the back door.

The orc was wearing a large wolf-skin kilt that hung past his knees and a heavy half-moon axe was glinting from over his left shoulder where it rode easily strapped to his back. Two cross belts were strung tightly over his unclothed chest, both containing a vast assortment of throwing knives and axes. This all would have been extraordinary for any adventurer even if he were not also clearly a pure bred orc. Dark green skin and sharp, almost elven ears marked him out clearly. The ears were the only characteristic orcs shared with elves, for the rest of their appearance was fearsome and bestial. This particular specimen's lower protruding fang teeth had been sawed down and blunted over a cleancut and massive chin. He wore his hair down to his waist, braided in several lengths and tied with orange cuts of cloth. Despite his fierce appearance Trem noted that he was well groomed and civilized looking, unnatural for the tribal, minimalist living conditions preferred by most orcs. Most remarkable, he had a large tattoo over his heart of a bird of prey taking flight, a symbol Trem did not associate with any orcish clan.

The large beast turned to address another figure standing behind him, hidden by the tall and broad creature, "Aye, Logan, this do be lookin' like a suitable establishment." And with that he stepped aside, nodding respectfully to the inn's guests, and allowed the obstructed figure to enter.

The man behind him was also unmistakable, but not in the same way as his strange partner. He wore shining plate mail, expertly designed to allow plenty of free movement along with unparalleled protection. Trem had seen the same make only once before, but he knew it instantly. The beautifully worked carvings of his armor shone bronze even in the moderately well lit inn. The same bird, which Trem now recognized as a hawk, was clearly represented in the center of the chest plate. Trem realized then it was an Angladaic Highlord's family marking. Trem guessed the suit of mail was an inherited one, based on the impressive intricacy of the armor's design. Jovan leaned over and whispered into his ear, "The orc has the same symbol on that man's breastplate tattooed on his chest."

Trem glanced briefly back at the orc and nodded. "I noticed. Certainly an unusual pair."

Trem knew the marking meant that, for whatever reason, the orc was also a member of the same Angladaic house. He would not be a knight, only humans were permitted to pursue a paladin rank in the Angladaic regime and knighthood was the first of many exclusive steps. The man had dark brown hair cut short and precisely, with a rough unshaven face excepting a tuft of hair on his chin. He looked worn and haggard from travel, but he was also youthful, perhaps in his late twenties. His clear blue eyes were depthless, though, and spoke of years more experience, and Trem would have bet confidently on his ability to use the fine sword at his side. The very presence of these two outside of their famed kingdom was unusual, and despite his preference for keeping out of such matters, Trem was curious as to why they were so far from home.

The knight bowed to the overweight matron as she approached and announced just loudly enough for all to hear: "I am Logan Angladais, of the Hawking House of Angladais, son of Arvadis Angladais, current blessed ruler of that kingdom and Paladinis's hand on the mortal plane. My companion is Grimtooth Angladais, also of Hawking House and my bloodbrother. We seek a meal and a night's rest here if you are able to house us. We can pay you good coin." All but the last was spoken with an air of a tiresome chore, although Logan's voice did sound with pride when he announced Grimtooth his bloodbrother, as though daring anyone to challenge the claim. No one did.

Such an announcement was startling not just because of the unusual tradition, bloodbrothers being an orcish creation, but because of the mere existence of Grimtooth. The orcs had been a race in great decline for several decades, perhaps longer. It was difficult to determine the inner workings of their society, as they lived in secluded holds in the mountains around the Dust Plains. As far as Trem knew, only the Icemoon Clan was still active, but even they were rarely seen outside their hold. His knowledge of their race was limited, but he doubted very much that this orc had grown up in the traditional surroundings of his kind.

The fact that Logan was Grimtooth's bloodbrother was arguably the most astounding portion of his pronouncement. Orcs used religious rites of blood to bond with those of their clan and form tighter, more familial relationships within it. Many tests and trials had to be passed, oaths had to be taken, and pain endured. It was said the exhausting ceremony lasted for as many as five days during which little sleep and no nourishment were permitted to the two striving to become brethren. The idea that these two had gone through such a trial was what most fascinated Trem. He understood such mergings of bloodlines to be rare, and he had never heard of such a union between an orc and someone not of their clans.

What Trem knew of the Angladaic people was more than he did of orcs, but still limited, for even during his wandering years he had never ventured there. The kingdom was in a region called Cloud Peak Basin, sheltered on its western and southern ends by the most dense and dangerous section of Silverleaf Forest, a nest of thick branches and tangled vines that was impassable in most places. This provided a barrier impenetrable to all but the most intrepid adventurers, and no army would ever pass through it swiftly or safely enough to threaten the kingdom. On its eastern end were expansive cliffs that towered hundreds of feet over the rushing roaring waters of the Longwater, the fabled sea that had no end. The only passable entrance to Angladais was between the Pillars of Light, two massive stone spires of harsh brown rock. Easily thirty miles in diameter, they rose at an almost perpendicular angle from the earth, their tips invisible in the sheltering clouds. The western peak began at the edge of Silverleaf Forest and its twin along the high cliffs brushing against the Longwater. The space between them was wide enough only for three horseman to ride abreast, and not comfortably. The long narrow pass could easily be defended against any invaders. The geography of the kingdom would have made it a legend on its own.

But the society itself was the real magnificence of the Angladaics. The greatest city in all Legocia, Alderlast, built like a great eight-spoked wheel with glistening stone walls and towering pearl white buildings held the greatest concentration of the kingdom's people. There were other, lesser cities and many citizens who farmed the rich lands of the Basin. Rumors claimed that in Angladais no one was permitted to go hungry, crime was swiftly and brutally punished, and the rulers were wise and caring. But the inner workings of the Highlord Houses were far less noble. Violent competition and merciless attempts to overthrow and eliminate rival houses were day-to-day occurrences. Kept quietly hidden from the public eye, these secret battles of politics were waged constantly among the many minor nobility and the greater Highlord Houses. The reason stability still existed in the land at all was that the ruling house of Angladais fell to the Highlord who had the support of the people. The Hawking House had maintained hold on the throne for over four hundred years, despite repeated attempts from other Highlords to seize it.

The Highlords were all supposed descendants of the first men ever to settle in Legocia, only they and their children could rise to the position of king. Among their number was the family responsible for commanding the legendary paladins, named for the God of Honor, Paladinis. Paladins had to pass not only strenuous tests of physical prowess, but also incredibly trying tests of purity and faith. Only around five hundred paladins were ever active at one time and all served for life. Perhaps ten or twenty would make the rank every year, during bloom periods. Logan was likely a knight in his father's house, possibly a captain or other higher rank, but he was no paladin. Trem had heard paladins carried an aura about them of incredible power and spoke with an almost otherworldy voice, blessed as they had been by Paladinis in his temple when they were deemed worthy. This man Logan looked the part, but nothing in how he spoke or presented himself marked him as a sanctified warrior.

Only one Highlord oversaw the paladins, there were others whose duties extended to seven additional key components of Angladaic society. Each Highlord kept their own private guard, all at least theoretically fighting for a common cause. Especially in times of war and conflict the people of Angladad were known to be extremely loyal and focused. No questions were raised by any soldier in the army about rank and house, especially the lowerclass men who were relatively free of concern in those areas. In the past, the Angladaics had fought beside orcs to cleanse the Dust Plains and protect the people there. Perhaps Logan and Grimtooth signaled a reinstatement of that ancient alliance.

What confused Trem, given what he knew of the Angladaic armies and their abilities, was why they had not responded to the invasion of the Napalian Empire. Though the Angladaics usually chose to assist those they deemed defenseless, a great invasion of the lands just outside their own should have garnered a response of some kind. It seemed every corner of Legocia knew what had befallen the north, and surely the Angladaics were aware as well. The half-elf determined to learn what he could of the fabled nation's role in the conflict, especially given the opportunity that had just presented itself in the inn's newest guests.

Trem watched the two foreigners walk to a back table just in front of the young wizard and his cat. The large feline was wary at first, but a reassuring murmur from its master quickly calmed it. The knight took his seat, settling back heavily, as though exhausted. The orc dropped his belts and weapons on the bench and casually walked up to the bar, leaning in between Jovan and Trem. Jovan appeared to be waiting for the large creature to attack but he merely nodded to both of them and hailed the bartender who had returned to her duties, "Two ales an' some food marm, if ye please." The rather nervous woman nodded quickly in agreement and hustled off to fill the order. Trem watched the orc return to his bench and glanced at Jovan. Winking, he stood and walked to the odd pair's table.

The two had been exchanging a few brief words when the half-elf came over. Logan studied him quickly and immediately decided he should be on his guard. The scuffed scabbard at the man's side and his worn bow sugested a well-seasoned fighter, not to mention his guarded appearance and careful stride. Here is one, the knight thought, who gives nothing away unless he has to. Grimtooth turned to examine him as well and Logan watched him make the same short assessment and quickly tense in case there was trouble. Behind him followed another youth, perhaps five or six years younger than Logan. He too looked well trained, but far less relaxed. The first half-elf stopped between the two and bowed respectfully low to each in turn. Logan returned the welcome with a slight nod. "May we join you, sir knight?" asked the half-elf neutrally.

"Of course, and you may call me Logan. This is Grimtooth, my bloodbrother." Logan waited for any sign of disbelief or doubt at his relationship to the orc, but the newcomer betrayed nothing more than a smile of thanks for the invitation. The speaker sat next to him while his companion warily eyed the limited bench space next to Grimtooth.

The orc grunted, "C'mon, lad, I dinnae bite boys."

Logan stifled a laugh as the youth went red with shame and anger, but he took his seat and settled in, trying hard to look unconcerned. The man beside Logan spoke again, "My name is Trem Waterhound, and this is Jovanaleth of the Blade. We are roaming in search of a friend who may have gone north. You both appear to be well traveled and hail from Angladais, I was wondering if perhaps you had seen an older man from Bladehome in your kingdom?"

Logan shook his head. "We could not tell you. We have been away from our home for nearly four years, fighting bandit uprisings in the God's Bones and Dragonscale Mountains. We attempted to return through the thickest woods of Silverleaf a week ago, but found the Broken forces to be too great a presence in the region. We never even got to the edge of the woods." The bartender bustled up with food and drinks for Logan and Grimtooth, asking the others if they would need any more but Trem waved her off. Logan took a swallow of ale and stirred his thin soup, adding as an afterthought, "Indeed all passage east appears blocked, and to the north as well. We may have difficulty returning home at all."

Trem pressed him a bit more. "What of the situation in Angladais? Why have they not responded to the invasion?"

Again Logan shook his head. "Something is preventing my people from reacting. I know that if they could have mobilized they would have by now. Grimtooth and I are the only ones outside the kingdom at the moment. That we know of anyhow." The orc nodded his stalwart agreement.

"I know what is keeping your people back."

The entire table turned to see the young boy who had been performing earlier leaning over the back of his own bench to speak with them. His protective cat was sitting in its chair still, but looked ready to act at a moments notice. She had shed the bells and other costume attire for an armored kilt of segmented leather with metal studs along with a single strap to hold her sword and assortment of daggers.

Grimtooth cleared his throat, "An' 'ow would ye know that boy?"

The youth frowned and answered, "The name is Diaga, and Neep and I can travel where we want, unseen, if it is necessary." He refocused his attention on Logan. "A fortress has been constructed in the very rock of the Pillars of Light that frame the entrance to your kingdom. And with the Broken holding the eastern side of the wood, no messengers can get through. The fortress is rumored to have appeared in a day. It's a sheer black wall with no gate that can be seen by the naked eye, or so the men passing by there told me."

Logan looked troubled and skeptical. "How could they raise such a fortress in only a day? Its impossible, it would take months."

Diaga lowered his voice slightly, "There are some forms of magic, great ones, which might make such a thing possible."

This statement was met by complete silence by the others seated around the tables. What Diaga suggested was dire news indeed. Most mages were contained within the wizard fortress of Ozmandias, or otherwise careful to remain inconspicuous. The Arcane Wars long ago had devastated the reputations of those practitioners of the gods' language. Too active a wizard might draw the attention of groups who hunted their kind, and outside Ozmandias there was no protection from their brutal interpretation of justice. Yet if Diaga was right, a mage of some immense power was trying to seal the Angladaics within their own kingdom.

Logan and Grimtooth exchanged a look. "If this is true we shall have to force our way north. There might be a way to break in if it is done by just the two of us. Your news is most dire, Diaga, but most valuable as well. Thank you for it."

The young mage inclined his head. "I only wish it could have been for the better. I suggest you find more aid before trying to go north though. It is crawling with these Nerothian invaders and the Broken. They do not seem to be fighting each other."

Trem sighed and leaned back. "Nothing is simple anymore. The world grows more dangerous every moment."

Nothing could have summarized what occurred next more accurately. The door of the inn was suddenly thrown open and five black forms strode in, taking a staggered formation in the center of the room, blocking the exit. The leader, standing at the head of his troop, appeared to survey the room. Trem could not be sure what he, or it, was looking at. The face was completely hooded in black cloth, and only a drawn and pale chin was partially visible jutting from within. Shadows upon shadows seemed to mark his face, if there were one. Trem was not even sure it was a man or woman, but he recognized trouble immediately.

The patrons cowered at the sight of this dark figure, sinking back into chairs, frozen in fear. Not a sound was heard. Even the minstrel had gone silent. The leader finally spoke, a hiss of steam escaping from a crack in the rock, "We seek the traitor. Tell us where he is and you will live. Refuse, and you will die."

No one answered. Nobody appeared to know who the dark shape was looking for. Trem, fearing the worst, was about to move behind the bar when he caught sight of a figure coming slowly down the inn stairs. Trem's gaze also took in the jerking, stuttered turn of the hooded heads of the intruders as they turned to face him. They moved in a way that was unnatural and disrupted somehow, as though their bodies could not fully follow the laws of motion that gives a soothing fluidity to living creatures.

Ghost strode to within five feet of the cloaked forms and there he stopped. Hands on his hips, cape thrown back to reveal his sword he faced them grimly and without fear. The leader took a step forward, hand moving to his sword. "Time to die, traitor!"

Ghost let the figure draw its weapon, watching the other four mirror the motion and then with blinding speed he drew his own blade and struck. The black figure parried the blow with a swift twist of its shrouded arm and swung quickly into a counterattack that Ghost barely managed to avoid. The wrenching, broken movements of the figures in black became more pronounced as they drew weapons and closed in on the embattled northerner. Jovanaleth was on his feet and had drawn his own sword before Trem could stop him. Jovan looked at Trem with a fierce intensity. "We have to help him!"

Without waiting for an answer he leapt forward swinging at the nearest figure. The creature parried his blow, shifted a foot to his left, and struck back, but Jovan was agile, dodging aside from the swinging blade of dark steel. Trem was already next to him, fighting another of the black-cloaked apparitions, hoping his body still retained its once masterful skill with a sword.

Logan and Grimtooth were suddenly there as well, sword and axe working on the other two figures, but no matter what speed the rescuers fought with the cloaked forms countered just as quickly. Trem could see Ghost starting to tire as he tried to keep up with the lead shade's rapid attacks. He was now completely on the defensive. Suddenly a streak of bright orange appeared between Ghost and his assailant. Neep, Diaga's cat, had jumped into the fray to help Ghost, who was rejuvenated by the sudden appearance of aid. As the two redoubled their efforts on Ghost's foe the black creature left an opening. Ghost struck, slicing the thing's arm from its body and a piercing cry roared across the sounds of clashing metal. The limb, corpse-white, clawlike, and scarred with swirling patterns fell to the floor and dissolved, just as Ghost's blade began to melt in his hand. He threw it away and stumbled back as the thing came at him, but Neep was in its way again, barely holding it off. Trem nearly lost his own arm as he watched the thing's missing limb slowly extend, remade, out of the torn cloak, a black shadowy substance he could not name reforming into the deathly pale appendage.

Trem understood immediately that their weaponry would be of little use against the abominations in the inn. Before he could warn the others, he heard Diaga's voice rising in a chant off to his left and, in the same moment, saw that Jovanaleth was losing his battle with his opponent, stumbling to one knee. Before Trem could intervene a streak of blue flame lanced into the black form looming over Jovanaleth and the beast screamed, louder and more terribly than its leader had. In seconds it and its cloak were reduced to a pile of ashes and the three forms battling Trem, Logan, and Grimtooth turned in an attempt to confront this new danger.

Trem was the only one between Diaga and the black monsters coming for him and in an instant he knew what he had to do. Before he could change his mind, he held his ancient sword before him in both hands and closed his eyes, focusing on the blade and whispered, *"El dath du hakin."*

The sword flared suddenly as previously hidden runes now shone like molten fire across the steel. A thin sheet of red flame encompassed the blade and Trem swung it threateningly in front of him, watching as the black-clad figures retreated a short distance. The leader stopped its brutal assault on Neep, who nearly fell backward from exhaustion as it turned from the feline warrior to fix its black gaze on the sword burning in Trem's hand. "El Vac!" it cried as though it were a curse, and with a howl of rage fled through the inn door, followed by its dark company.

Logan and Grimtooth pursued the figures outside, but the other fighters came forward to stare at Trem's glowing sword in amazement. Jovanaleth in particular seemed stunned by what had happened. Neep had recovered and was now protectively leaning on Diaga, who reassured his companion with soft words and a gentle stroking of the cat's ears. Trem swiftly released his focus on the sword's enchantment when he saw the others staring, and the fire and runes vanished. Ghost came forward, now weaponless, breathing hard. "You've got more than a few tricks up your sleeve. I do not doubt it." He leaned on the counter. The inn had emptied as soon as the fighting began, and the dark figures had made no attempt to stop the fleeing patrons. Ghost kicked at the ashes of the one shade that Diaga had killed, speaking softly to himself, "I never thought they would find me here, at least not so soon. Wolfbane's arm has grown long."

Trem sheathed his sword and faced the older man. "You had better tell us what is going on and quickly. I want to know what the devil those things were, and now."

Ghost met his gaze with a quick, oily grin. "Afraid we haven't got the time, half-elf. They will be back before too long and I will not be waiting to greet them. We have to leave and now. You had best come with me. They will be hunting you too, for interfering with their mission."

Jovan looked at Trem, his unvoiced question coming through clearly in the brief glance, then he turned to Ghost and said, "We can not do that. I must find my father. We need to go north."

Ghost whirled on him, suddenly angry. "You don't get it do you, boy? Those things are from the north! They were made there and they will be hunting from there! If you go north and you might as well count yourself dead right now!"

Trem grabbed the man by the collar and spun him so they were face to face. "And what is it you propose we do then? Follow you, surely, but to where?"

Ghost glared at him, but made no attempt to remove his hand. "We go south, like I said. The item I seek will aid us against these creatures, but we must leave now and first go east. We cannot risk the main road. There is another way, older, south by the town of Delmore."

Diaga's head came up sharply. "What road is it that you intend to take? There are dark paths beyond Delmore, deep in the Silverleaf woods."

Ghost shook his head and crossed his arms defiantly. "That there may be, but there are darker places elsewhere. Believe me, I have seen them. This is an ancient road, one that can take us south without fear of being attacked."

Diaga stared at Ghost piercingly and said sternly, "All ways I know of in that region should be left alone."

"You are not coming anyway." Trem said decisively. "Those things will be following Ghost and I. Jovanaleth too, I suppose. There is no need to get involved."

"I just reduced one of those things to ash," Diaga's voice was deathly calm. "It would be fair to say I am involved. And I am sick of parlor tricks and drunks. It's time to put what I have learned to some use. I will be helpful, you can be sure."

Ghost smiled and clapped a none too pleased Diaga on the shoulder. "Undoubtedly! After all, you're the one who knew how to kill those things. It is settled. You are coming if that is what you want. Innkeeper! I will be needing six horses...."

"Four," Trem interrupted, "the Angladaics surely have their own."

"Three then," added Diaga, "Neep does not need a mount."

Ghost waited a moment to see if there were further interruptions, and then grated, "...and I can pay you extra if I can have the beasts now."

The large woman's frightened face rose from behind the bar, but upon seeing the monsters were gone she toddled over swiftly and nodded nervously in agreement with Ghost's request. "My husband owns the inn and handles such transactions," she continued swiftly when Ghost's brow furrowed in irritation, "but I'm certain I can do this for you. But it will take some time to saddle the beasts."

"Forget that, we will do it ourselves. Just bring us some food for a few days and that will be all." He tossed a bag that jingled with coins at the woman. The frightened matron snatched it and hurried off to prepare the supplies.

At that point Logan and Grimtooth returned, breathing hard. They stopped when they reached the others. "We could nae catch 'em, they rode off wit' some black steeds. Looked ta be rightly ill ones, too."

Logan sighed and slumped into a chair, "We didn't have time to mount up and ride after them. I doubt we could have caught them anyway, they flew out of the west gate like they had wings." He paused a moment before adding, "They killed two guards at the north gate, just boys. It seems they broke the slide bar from the outside. How they managed that I have not the slightest idea."

Trem faced the two. "We are leaving with Ghost to head east and from there we need to ride south. He has a package he intends to retrieve."

Logan looked at them all questioningly. "You intend to go to Southron? Well, we may as well come too, I have questions that need answering and they all seem to involve at least one of you. Regardless, we cannot go home. South is as good a direction to wander in as any."

Jovan broke in quickly, "It will only be for a short while, then we head north to find my father; perhaps we can help your people as well."

"Very well." Logan heaved himself up from his chair. "We will go south and then we will see what we can do to the north. Alright with you, Grimtooth?"

The orc merely nodded his consent to the decision. Ghost cleared his throat and declared, "Well this is more help then I dared hope for, but if you are all willing to follow than we best get going, we can not afford to lose any time."

The travelers packed quickly, bringing only their bare essentials for the journey and the new provisions provided by the innkeeper's wife, who despite her considerable gain in coin seemed happy to see them off. They rode out of the east gate a few hours before dawn, Ghost in the lead on his own large black horse. Trem and Jovan followed on smaller, light stepping brown geldings from the inn with Diaga and Neep after them, the cat padding softly and swiftly on foot. She was remarkable, moving with an eerie grace, and as they went eastward she would wander awaw from the road and reappear beside Diaga as if from nowhere. The mage seemed unfazed, but Grimtooth was fascinated by how stealthy and, simultaneously, fiercely loyal to Diaga the feline was. Though Neep would not ride, Diaga said the cat could keep pace with them at any speed the horses chose and all evidence supported his claims. As a rearguard, Grimtooth and Logan rode atop the warhorses they had come to Gi'lakil on. Grimtooth's steed, Thunder, was probably the largest horse Trem had ever seen.

As Trem looked back over the strange company he could not help wondering if things would have been this way if he and Jovan had stayed out of the fight. It had not been their conflict anyway, and now these fearsome hunters were after them because of it. Somehow, he suspected this would have happened anyway, whether he had helped Ghost or simply stood by. His focus turned to the man they had all rescued. He suspected Ghost had as many secrets as himself, and if that were true he should not be trusted. Something was very wrong about him. Trem felt it as he would a cold breeze. Nothing but trouble would come of this march south.

His focus shifted to Jovanaleth, riding beside him. Trem stopped thinking about betrayals and hardship and instead thought about the young man he had sworn to help. Whatever happened, no matter what, he would find Jovan's father and rescue him if it had to be done.

Trem had given his word.

Chapter 7

The dagger descended onto the back of Edge's head faster than Raymir could react. Hilt first, it struck the base of his skull, knocking him out instantly. Before his body had sprawled onto the cold stone of the cavern floor Raymir was already moving, rushing the man crouched over the one person she had left in the world. Weaponless, she dove at him, trying desperately to pin him while screaming unintelligible threats in his face.

The man was thoroughly stunned. He had seen the girl perform a few minor magic spells, but the strange elf had seemed to far surpass her in potential danger. As she tried to get her hands around his neck he quickly tossed his dagger aside, not wanting to stab her accidentally. Grabbing her firmly by the shoulders he flipped her over easily and by straddling her back and pressing her arms down he was able to hold her in place. He had already sustained a few bruises to his face and was in no mood to suffer more.

"Come on, miss, just relax for a minute. I'm not going to hurt you or your young man. I need to ask him some questions without the risk of him attacking me if they are ones he doesn't like. I need to make sure he is really on my side."

Raymir stopped struggling and stared fiercely at her captor over her shoulder. "What side would that be?"

Feeling her relax just a bit he smiled and said, "The resistance, I am a servant of the city of Hethegar. If I let you sit up, can I tell you my story without worrying about another assault?"

Raymir paused a moment to consider the offer, then nodded. She reasoned that if he had not simply executed Edge right away, he must not be one of Frothgar's assassins or loyal to Wolfbane's cause, otherwise what would have been the point? No, if he wanted them dead he would have killed them both already. Listening to him could not hurt, and if his story proved false she was prepared to go back on her word using a few more tricks from her time in the Napal City Castle's library.

Accepting Raymir's promise the servant eased himself off of her back and stepped away, hands held palms outward and maintaining a reassuring smile. It was a smile that calmed Raymir as she sat up to meet his eyes. The man cleared his throat, "First of all my name is Romund, Romund of Hethegar, and I was sent by the remnants of House Hethegar still loyal to the memory of the late Thane Fernal to infiltrate the Nerothian army and learn what I could of their greater plans. The thane's wife gave me this," he held up a thin chain of silver, to which was attached a small amulet of narrow bronze wires that surrounded a glowing crystal. "This is a Mirage, a special elven amulet that lets a person alter his or her appearance for as long as they choose, though the change is limited. I couldn't have become another person entirely, as convenient as that would have been. Once a Mirage is activated it can only be removed by the wearer and once removed it can never be reactivated."

Raymir nodded in understanding. "Your arm, you made it appear as though you had lost it."

Romund nodded, grinning. "It was a rather obvious solution once I came to it. No one hires a one-armed man to become a soldier. When I reached the border of the Whitewood, near Napal City, I activated the enchantment and sought out the bulk of the Nerothian army. I made up a story of having served as an armourer and soldier before I lost my arm hunting. The Nerothians are not stupid, they know several of their soldiers are former Napalians who simply want a solid job with good coin, honest work or not.

"So I convinced them after a time that my mending skills were worth placement in the fortress, patching up armor for leaders and the elite soldiers. People never think much of servants, they say a lot of things they should not in front of them. There I learned of the attack that was being plotted in the northwest tower last night. Not the specifics mind, but enough to know something big is beginning to happen to the south, the raids over the next few days on border towns are merely a distraction. I had to get out of the fortress and reach my people, or those elsewhere if necessary, and warn them before it was too late.

"But getting out was far more difficult than getting in. Any soldier or servant that fled the fortress was rounded up quickly and executed; I needed a failsafe way to get out, one where they would not follow me. Then I saw your young friend there, knew him from before, knew he was high ranking and could tell from his face he was looking for an escape. I offered to help as discreetly as I could, figuring he must know a safe exit and betting I could beg to be taken along. Never figured he would get himself into a fight though. What was he doing, trying to kill the general?"

"They were friends once; Wolfbane trained Edge in his youth. He made him into a fine fighter." Raymir shook her head sadly. "Edge had to watch him go from an honorable man to an evil tyrant. He thought he could convince him to flee with us, but something went wrong, I don't know what. Maybe Wolfbane tried to make him stay or maybe the guards found him out before he could even explain. Whatever happened he must have fought his way clear somehow."

Romund watched the gaze of the young girl drift from him to the unconscious man on the cavern floor. There was such love and devotion in that look, for a moment Romund sharply regretted knocking him out. I had to be sure though, he thought; one can't be too careful, especially with strangers. To Raymir he said, "I am sorry I hit him, but I had to be sure he was against Wolfbane. It was risky leaving him in a position to kill me when I had just gotten free."

Raymir managed a slight smile, "I understand. You did not have to hurt Edge though. I'm a Napalian myself, and I trust him. He and I were intending to go north and hide until the war ended. Well, that was Edge's plan. I'm not so sure that's enough for me. The Nerothians have taken my home and my family. I've been looking for a way to strike back since the fall of the city. I worked in the library of the castle, helping the wizards, and something I found in Saltilian's notes struck me as quite odd."

Romund became curious. "How did you access his notes?"

"My role in their library was tending to their books and other needs. Saltilian was scatterbrained; he left a lot of handwritten papers strewn about. I found one, written in shorthand and hard to decipher, but there was something about 'breeding,' 'arcane vessel,' and 'Daerveron's connections.' It had a lot of ramblings on a place called Twisted Spire and there was a history book on a woman from the ancient times called Istrain Cutwave, who supposedly learned how to prevent her own death. It was very strange, but from what I understood, it seems Daerveron was communicating with someone from this Twisted Spire about some undertaking to aid the invaders. Saltilian seemed very interested in the Frozen Reach and someplace west of the Gulf of Thunder and Mount Iceblade. He kept asking me how one would most easily cross the wastelands north of Sheerwater Cove. It sounded like he intended to find this Twisted Spire and learn for himself what Daerveron was up to."

Romund rubbed his chin thoughtfully. "That shall certainly have to take some consideration, but I think we should first wake up your young man and see what he suggests. If you wish to go on your way I will not stop you, but I need to know what happened to him this night and anything else you can tell me about the Nerothian plans."

Raymir, now considerably confident in this man's honesty, nodded agreeably. "I will wake him for you, probably safer."

Romund's smile shone. "Probably, miss."

Raymir moved swiftly to Edge's side, removing his pack and weapons she leaned them against the wall of the cavern before taking his head gently in her arms. The dagger had left a nasty lump on the back of his skull, but the fair white hair showed no sign of blood. Romund had indeed been careful to do only as much damage as necessary. Stroking his hair softly Raymir murmured one of the few healing spells she had found in Saltilian's books. The mage had been far more interested in the schools of Ruination and Degerneration than those that might have helped people. Still, Raymir was confident she could do something about this fairly minor injury.

A soft glow emanated from her hands as Raymir pressed them on Edge's temples. In front of Romund's eyes he watched the man begin breathing more rapidly and finally gasp as he regained consciousness, the lump now gone. Romund was impressed. He had known few mages in his time, but enough to recognize the girl was certainly a novice, though a decidedly skilled one. He suspected she could become very powerful in time.

As Edge sat up sharply up his green eyes went from a dull to a sudden sparking rage. He spun, not realizing Raymir was still holding him, and locked onto Romund. The man had a sharp jolt of fear, and actually thought of diving for one of the short swords on the cave floor before Raymir restrained Edge.

"Relax, he is on our side Edge. I promise."

The glaring look lessened only slightly at first, but as Romund and Raymir jointly explained Romund's story, Edge became calmer in stages, though he still kept his eyes on Romund. Finally, he stood gingerly and looked hard at the man before him. Edge took in the aged but rugged features, the strong arms and shoulders, the glint of experience and confidence in his eyes with just a hint of mischief. Edge extended his hand and Romund took it, smiling reassuringly. "We are of one mind, young sir. I apologize for doubting your character. Perhaps you would explain how you came to us so battered and rushed?"

Edge seemed to snap out of his reflection as the events that had preceded the cave came back to him. Sitting down once more he gestured for the other two to join him, Raymir staying close, her hand in his. In a quiet and troubled voice, he described his journey into the castle, becoming more and more furious as he related the battle with Daerveron and the guards, at last ending the tale with his flight to the house and the caverns. When he was done he sat back and squeezed his eyes shut and said quietly, "I never even got the chance to turn him, not even an opportunity to say goodbye. I know he is different now, but once he was like the father I never had."

Romund grasped the boy's arm in reassurance. "You did all you could. Wolfbane would never have left, not even for you. He is in the full sway of Neroth and his vision of our world. We can do no more for him. If he breaks free it will be from his own determination, not ours. There are other things we must take care of now."

Edge looked hard at the man he was rapidly gaining respect for. "What is it you propose we do?"

Romund stood and sighed, turning his back to them and running his hand through his hair. He seemed slightly unsure of what to say next, but finally he turned and after glancing at the floor of the cavern for a moment nodded and said, "You are both young and have been through much already. Raymir seems to know the lay of the land around here well enough. Your chances of fleeing the region safely are probably quite good. I would love to join you, or even return to Hethegar, but Raymir's other news, that of the Twisted Spire, I cannot ignore. If somewhere in that tower there is a cohort of Daerveron's helping formulate something that will sway the tide of battle even more in Wolfbane's favor, I must go and at the least find out what undertaking it is, and prevent it's completion if I can." He shook his head, looking desperate but determined all at once. "I do not know if I can even find this place, but if it lies north of the Frozen Reach I may find someone in the mountains who can aid me."

Edge looked at Romund thoughtfully. Little did the older man realize what he was proposing was madness. When Wolfbane and Edge had originally landed on Legocia two years ago they had been in the Frozen Reach region, a vast stretch of wind, ice, and snow northwest of the Dragonscale Mountains. The journey with over ten thousand men and wagons had been one of constant danger, from rabid wolves and their larger, fiercer cousins known as wargs, to the biting cold air and freezing nights. They had only managed to bypass the mountains alive because Daerveron had found them amid the swirling snow and brought them by fleet through the edge of the Gulf of Thunder to the town of Crestwind, using his immense arcane power to hold off gales and crashing waves. The act of keeping the army alive had exhausted him, but without his magic Edge was certain they would have perished entirely.

What Romund wanted to do was noble, and Edge was intrigued as to what Daerveron was up to as well, but he could not fathom the task he was setting before himself. Edge had Raymir to think about, she had made it this far on her quick wits and skill with minor magic, but a journey north, even for a native Napalian, would be far too dangerous. Edge could not believe he was thinking of making the venture himself. But simultaneously he could not just let this older man who had, intentions aside, helped get them safely out of Castle Bane, go into untold danger without someone to watch his back. At least Edge knew something of the land they would be traveling through. He could take Raymir back to Glaciar first, her grandfather still held some authority there. Algathor Squall could shelter her until they came back, if they did. Most importantly, Edgewulf el Vac felt a great need to atone for his part in the fall of the Napalian Empire. At the very least this quest would give Edge a chance to do something in repayment for his missteps with the Nerothians.

Edge looked at Raymir. She stared back, saw the truth in his eyes and sadly nodded. She knew they had to help this man. They needed to do something about the current state of affairs in the land. Wolfbane's total conquest could not continue unchecked. Even if Edge failed to shake the foundations of his army he might still hinder the plans of Daerveron. Raymir hugged him tightly and pressed her face into his shoulder. Sitting there on the ground with her held tight, he thought of how lucky he was to have the most beautiful woman in the world to himself. He also thought how terrible things could become for them both if Wolfbane continued to sweep, unabated, across the world. Stroking her hair, he looked at Romund, who still stood hands on his hips, now facing the interior stream on the cavern slope. Now that he truly studied the man, Edge saw the years weighing his shoulders down, the grayness of his hair was more apparent, the stoop was clearer and he wondered how he had not noticed it before. This man must have his help.

Edge gently took Raymir's hands from him, and with great care placed her slowly on the floor, as she had fallen asleep. He paused, looking at her red curls and soft, innocent face. Raymir should not have to live the rest of her life in fear. Edge rummaged through their supplies and pulled forth a bedroll that had fallen out of his pack, placing it over Raymir to keep her warm. Assured that she was all right for the moment, he turned and walked somewhat stiffly to Romund's side. Romund was still studying the stream in front of him, his eyes raptly following the flowing water. Edge knelt and cupped his hands, drinking some of the icy liquid before standing and addressing Romund in a calm but self-assured tone, "You cannot find the place you seek on your own, Romund. It is simply not possible for someone who is unfamiliar with the Frozen Reach and its dangers. You are going to need my assistance to get anywhere, and even then I don't know if we will survive long. It may be late fall, but in Napal, winter is eternal."

Romund looked at him, surprise clear on his haggard face. "You cannot do this, Raymir needs you. You both have long lives in front of you. I will not let you throw them away for a crazy old man's desperate gambit."

Edge shook his head. "This is no trivial thing you seek to do. This is a blow to the enemy; to the fiends I have been so blind as to assist in their conquest of this land. I cannot sit idle while that happens. If I take you north, I give myself a chance at redemption."

Romund inclined his chin in the direction of the blissful sleeper. "And what about her? What has she said about this matter? I will take you willingly, Edge, you are obviously a warrior and trained in the art of combat. But she, she is just a young woman with a few mystical tricks. She does not have the instinct to last in the wild for as long as we may be there. You cannot get her involved."

"I know. She will not be. Raymir still has kin in Glaciar. Her grandfather is a respected man there, although he has fallen on hard times. He can keep her safe within his estate." Edge glanced over at the man he had chosen to ally himself with. "Besides," he said smiling slightly, "you already admitted you are an old man. A young counterpart might keep you alive a little longer."

Romund smiled and clapped the youth on his back. "Another pair of eyes never hurts. I would be glad to have you along."

The two walked back to the cavern wall where Raymir still slept. Edge pulled out two bedrolls from the packs Raymir and Romund had brought, tossing one to his companion he said, "As good as you are with a dagger, you might find a sword more useful. Take one of them."

Romund complied, pulling free one of the battered blades and its scabbard, and along with the bedroll offered to him, he retired to one end of the cavern. Edge left the other sword next to Raymir. It was small enough she might be able to wield it if it should come to that. He intended to keep her free from danger if possible, but he was not naive. Edge took his bedroll and settled against the wall next to Raymir, keeping his halberd resting on his right shoulder where he could reach it easily. Edge no longer suspected foul play from Romund, who was already snoring loudly at his end of the cavern, but he was also a very careful man. Wrapping his bedroll around his shoulders against the evening cold, Edge closed his eyes. He was tired, but his years of campaigning had taught him to keep his other senses active while asleep. If anything changed in the cavern that he could hear, smell, or feel Edge would be alert instantly. Wolfbane had trained him well.

In the soft calm of the cavern, Edgewulf el Vac finally accepted the loss of his friend and guardian, Wolfbane. From now on, Edge would have to make his own way in the world and at least he would not have to start his journey alone.

There was very little weeping over the loss of Edge at Castle Bane. Daerveron spent the remainder of the night in meditation to restore what magical energy he had expended during his battle with the escaped lost elf. The fearsome wizard was not in a pleasant mood, not that he ever was, but his general attitude had become even darker. The fact that Edge had escaped with a manservant and, more importantly, the young woman who had worked in the library with he and Saltilian, bothered Daerveron deeply. Raymir had never gotten close to his personal files or records as he had kept them in the dungeons where he conducted his most serious work, but Saltilian was well known as a meddler and could be counted on to leave potentially valuable information lying around. While Daerveron was certain that whatever Saltilian had left available to the girl was of no consequence, the idea of her escaping with knowledge of anything contained in the library enraged him.

So Daerveron rested in a deep trance for several hours, coming out of his static state just before dawn. With the sun still down in the west he decided to make a connection with his god Neroth, informing him of recent events that may have passed unnoticed. Daerveron's runners had arrived during his meditation and the silent messenger Lolenas had left him a simple note from his Night Cloak captain. It had not been pleasing, but neither was it terribly bad news. The one he sought had evaded his minion's clutches in Gi'lakil, but was now traveling in rather large company, and one that would be easy to track. While he had not succeeded in capturing his quarry, he knew that he would not evade him much longer. Patience Daerveron had, he only hoped Neroth would share his view.

Walking down the dismal hallway to his summoning chamber, Daerveron mused over what else Neroth would need information on. The God of Death would likely order the pursuit of Edgewulf el Vac for practical purposes, though with Edge no longer arguing against Daerveron's council, the overthrow of Wolfbane's mind should become even more complete. As for the other tasks he had left to his disciple, Daerveron had all but accomplished two of them. It was the mysterious second individual, not the one the Night Cloaks were now stalking on the road from Gi'lakil, which continued to utterly evade him. The whereabouts of his target had been narrowed down to Silverleaf Forest or perhaps the region of Dragon's Watch, but little else was known. If Daerveron's target had chosen to remain secluded and in exile from others then the necessary depth of investigation could not really commence without the removal of the Eagle Knights, the Foresters, and Order of the Blade; all of which would take time. But Wolfbane was clever and his Broken allies were moving swiftly toward their goal of becoming a fully functional and disciplined army. The mass assault on western Legocia should begin soon.

Daerveron ran his hand along the ancient stone walls of the dungeon hall. Unlike the rest of the castle, the dungeon was very, very old. When first he had found this place, long before leading Wolfbane's army south, it had been a mere staircase under the castle disappearing into the earth and expanding into a massive underground labyrinth so huge as to seem limitless. It was here that he had discovered prison quarters and rooms for his use as a private library, alchemical lab, and study. The deepest level of the dungeon was completely abandoned, and only the ancient casting chamber there was Daerveron's to hold total sway over. Neroth had forbidden the revived wizard from wandering anywhere else, and Daerveron had not truly relished the thought of going beyond the confines of his workspace. It would be too easy, even for him, to become lost in such a massive nest of tunnels.

Daerveron took the stairs down to the deepest level and strode to the old metal door of the summoning chamber. With a mere wave of his hand coupled with a few precise movements of his fingers, he undid the five locks and several wards on the door. As it swung easily open, he stepped forward into the chamber. It was large and circular, perhaps twenty yards in diameter. At its center stood a circle of red paint dotted about with many blue runes. Before it stood a smaller white circle with a few green runes in its circumference. Daerveron approached the smaller circle and entered it. Casting some powdered bone into the larger circle he chanted softly, forming the connection between the world of the gods and that of the mortals. This would allow Neroth to enter Teth-tenir, though he would be confined to the circle that had been created for him.

The Sword

The great task that had been laid before Daerveron when he entered Neroth's service had been to rediscover the secrets of forming these summoning circles, a feat long ago abandoned by wizards of the ancient days. In the past, the gods had been able to come to Teth-tenir still immortal, flush with the power of their worshippers and their own immense strength. Yet some time ago, after the Arcane Wars and during an event Daerveron had heard referred to as the Immorbellum, the ability to reach Teth-tenir had been lost to the gods. He did not understand how it was possible, nor was he so foolish as to ask Neroth to explain. When he had first begun working for the God of Death, Daerveron had learned to make smaller, weaker circles for Neroth to project a part of himself into. Now he could bring his full strength to the one in Napal City, but the secret to allowing Neroth to break free of the confining ring and return to the mortal world still evaded Daerveron. On one hand, he hated not knowing how to accomplish a feat of invocation magic, but on the other the study necessary to gradually break down the barriers between their worlds was tedious and uninteresting to him.

Daerveron neared the end of the ritual, the wall sconces erupting in a shimmering blue flame and receding slightly, to burn steadily in the background and illuminate the chamber. As the chant ceased a large black cloud billowed up from the floor and spread slowly, filling the room. As the smoky substance faded a figure became visible. He was gaunt, yet muscled, wrapped in flowing black robes. A sword hilt of fearsome, jagged steel with a fine leather scabbard could be glimpsed under the folds of the waving silken cloth. This was the God of Death, and to mere mortals his image sprayed fear like blood from a wound. But this apparition did not affect Daerveron as it might others, for he was not frozen at the mere sight of his master. Upon being given his existence, such as it was, back, Daerveron no longer felt true fear, though at this moment he felt a heightened sense of awareness. While he was relatively confident he knew of no opponent who could defeat him, Neroth was something else entirely. Daerveron knew beyond a shadow of a doubt that if he desired, even in his ethereal form, Neroth could rip the life he had given Daerveron from him in the blink of an eye.

Neroth's eyes were his greatest power. From the drapes of his hood two gleaming black orbs shone, and now Daerveron felt a spike of unease but it passed, eventually. "What news of the mortal world?"

Daerveron's mind swayed with strange detachment, as the power of the god undulated against the barrier of the circle. His strength had increased greatly since their last meeting, only a few weeks prior. Neroth appeared more solidly before him now, a sure sign his ability to bring more of himself into the mortal realm was increasing. Daerveron touched the cloth over his ruined face and spoke, "There is much that has changed my lord. The youth, Edgewulf el Vac, has fled the castle with his mistress and a one-armed servant. I failed in my attempt to slay him, but he did not have a chance to turn Wolf-bane's mind against our efforts, I saw to it."

"Wolfbane's loyalty is not a concern," Neroth shifted slightly, "and your failure is not great in this matter. Better you had killed Edgewulf, but he has little hope of causing our mission any harm, trapped in the north as he is. What of the Twisted Spire? Was Valroth successful in the first phase of his experiments?"

Daerveron nodded confidently. "Our associate has done well, he claims that the fusing has been completed and now the training will begin. He fears the powers of his creation may extend farther than we could hope to contain without your support here, but he will teach what he can."

"This is good. If we succeed in this venture then it will be due to your strength of will and cunning, Daerveron, Valroth is not easily swayed to do anyone's bidding."

Daerveron scowled defiantly. "He is not as hard to break as one might think."

"This you have proven true enough."

Daerveron cleared his throat, eager to make his report and re-turn to matters more of interest to him. "As to the issue of the targets you asked me to locate and deal with; the Night Cloaks trapped one to the south, but found he had aid in the form of several formidable allies. They fled Gi'lakil last night. I have sent more of their kind to join them and further the attempts to end his life before he brings you further trouble. I received word the Night Cloaks intend to push him and his new associates east, where the shades or the Broken can dispatch them all against the eastern foothills and edge of Silverleaf as they continue to pillage farther south."

"Drive them east and have the Night Cloaks make contact with the Broken army. Use the raids south to trap them against the woods of Silverleaf, but tell your spectral hunter and his followers not to expose themselves to the enemy unless they must. I do not wish to reveal the full extent of our might so soon. What of the other I seek? Have you learned nothing?"

Daerveron shifted uncomfortably. "I fear I still have no word. No scouts have been able to thoroughly explore the Dragon's Watch region due to the patrols of Eagle Knights and Forester elves. Perhaps once the Broken take the region...."

"This is not acceptable. I have no time to wait for Wolfbane's puppets to complete this task, which is why it fell to you. Drive those from Gi'lakil east and trap them, but do not neglect our second tar-get. I can sense him again, though he strives to hide himself from me. He represents a far greater foe, and potential ally, than the first. Find this other, or I will place my trust in someone more capable of doing my bidding."

And thus Neroth evaporated suddenly, sucking the light out of the room in his departure, leaving Daerveron alone and squeezing his dead hands tightly. His fear of the God of Death was impossible, yet something gripped him in that moment. Daerveron had to find the other mortal or Neroth would surely cease to reward his efforts. The God of Death had made it clear that the invasion was secondary to the discovery and elimination of these two threats he seemed so wary of.

Frustrated and on edge, Daerveron departed quickly, slamming the door shut and snapping the locks into place with a sweep of his departing hand. He bounded up the stairs in a rage, violent in his indignation at his own weakness. In his study he found Lolenas, the mute elf, waiting for him. Glaring at him he barked, "What is it?"

The elf signed hurriedly that Wolfbane requested his presence at the war room immediately. Daerveron went into a blind rage. "He requests me? I shall make him grovel on bended knee before this war is through, then he will come crawling at my decree!" As he howled his last statement he shot his gauntleted hand out and grasped Lolenas' unprotected neck, bringing the elf's face closer to his he hissed, "All of them will, every, last, one."

Daerveron accented each word by squeezing the elf's neck tighter, until his throat simply collapsed and his lifeless body hung limp in the mage's hand. Daerveron let Lolenas fall to the stones of the dungeon floor and sat in his chair, staring at the volumes on his desk. A hundred lifetimes to acquire all the knowledge in the world, and he had but cracked the surface of its secrets. Slamming his fist down Daerveron split the sturdy table in two and whirled out of his seat, snatching his dark purple cloak from the hook on the wall, along with his most regal silk scarf. Wrapping this around his decomposed face and hurling the cloak over his shoulder he stormed up the stairs and collected himself at the trap door to the fortress. Stepping up and tossing the hidden door open, he seemed to appear in the central hall of Castle Bane, just as a terrified servant was passing by. Without looking Daerveron reached out his gloved, still partially whole, hand and caught his tunic. "There is a mess downstairs I want you to take care of right now." He waved his free hand to dismiss the illusion hiding the entry to the stairs below. "Go."

The servant took off, glad to be free of the fearsome mage, and Daerveron marched to the war room.

Once again, Daerveron found himself the last arrival at the meeting this day, noting with some satisfaction the empty seat that had once been Edge's. This time Wolfbane did not wait for him to sit down, he rose as soon as the mage entered and growled, "Where is Edge, dead one? I hear he fought with you while I slept!"

Valissa could not be held back either. "One of my guards is dead and a servant missing! What happened, mage?"

Caermon looked on with mild interest, while Frothgar and Saltilian remained meekly silent, though Saltilian leaned forward as though interested in how Daerveron would respond. Daerveron though how pleasant it would be to tear the man's bones from his legs and pin him to a wall with them. Crossing his arms, he faced Wolfbane. "We did indeed battle, in this very chamber, my lord, where I chose to guard you so you might rest peacefully and safely. Edgewulf el Vac came here with the intent of murdering you as you slept. It seems he foolishly sympathized with the Napalians who opposed you. I believe he escaped with my young librarian and the missing servant."

That response brought Wolfbane slumping back into his chair and silenced the others in the room. Saltilian sat back in his chair as well and rubbed his chin, now looking far less pleased with himself than before. Satisfied, Daerveron sat in his own seat and waited for Wolfbane's reaction. There would naturally be some grief at learning his beloved ward had deserted him, and more so after hearing he had tried to kill him first. What a hindrance emotions could be, thought Daerveron, conveniently forgetting his own bout of unease only a few minutes before.

Wolfbane shook his head and looked up, clearly shocked at the news. It was far easier to believe that Edge had been driven out by the foul mage across from him, an ally whom he utterly mistrusted. Such a revelation as mutiny was hard to swallow, but he made a decision then and there, one that Daerveron would not like, and also had no choice but to support. Straightening he glared directly across the table at the wizard as he made his announcement, "We will have to hunt him down to learn the truth. If indeed his intent was what you say it was, we shall treat him like any other traitor. If not, well, then the circumstances change dramatically don't you agree?"

Daerveron stiffened, but kept his composure. "Indeed."

Wolfbane smiled dangerously. "Then it is settled. I would search for the lad myself, but I am needed to command our mission of conquest from the fortress. Frothgar, you have your responsibilities to the south; I imagine you intend to leave today?"

Frothgar sat up, surprised to be included in the meeting. "I move when you say my liege."

"I say. You go now, bring several of your men with you, perhaps a score or two. Gather the Broken army together in the northeast and steer them south through the farmlands, then west towards the home of the Eagle Knights. We will cut off the three western kingdoms by taking their central and most easily defended point: the Fortress of Aves. That should prevent you from meeting any truly formidable defensive effort. How long do you expect the campaign to last?"

Frothgar sat even straighter, realizing he was suddenly being treated as important. "Difficult to say, my lord, but if I were to estimate then I would guess at perhaps two or three weeks to unite the Broken from across their scattered clans and another four or five to move them all west. Then naturally a few days afterward to array our plans and coordinate the attack." Frothgar realized his estimation might not please Wolfbane and tried to correct course. "I might be able to spur them on faster my lord, perhaps with more men."

"No," Wolfbane shook his head, "a month or two is not long, Frothgar, and the Eagle Knights have made no move to bring their forces to bear now. I doubt they will suddenly be driven to do so in the weeks to come. The fools are still too suspicious of the Order of the Blade and Foresters to desert their one stronghold on the coast, even if the east is virtually under siege."

Frothgar seemed to relax. "Then forty-odd men should suffice, if I may have my own choosing."

Wolfbane nodded his ascent. "You may. Leave immediately and get eastward as quickly as you can. Find our contact among the Broken and get him behind you, the others should join quickly after that."

Frothgar stood and placed fist to heart. "For the God of Death I shall do this. Safe be your crown, Lord Wolfbane."

Wolfbane dismissed him and the ceremonial phrases with a wave of a huge hand. Frothgar departed swiftly, intent on accomplishing his mission as soon as he could. Wolfbane now rounded on Daerveron, pointing one massive finger at him he addressed the mage, "You will go to Marlpaz and ensure that all her defenses are in order," Daerveron eyes narrowed and he was ready to protest but Wolfbane rolled over him, "and you shall stay there until you are certain that the Angladaics pose no threat, if it takes a day or a year. Do not test me, sorceror, at this stage the great Neroth still prizes my skills in war over yours in wizardry."

Daerveron forced himself to yield, though the urge to hurl a bolt of fire at the man across from him was strong. Wolfbane was his commanding superior, or was intended to believe so. The God of Death would look foully on any action taken against him and Daerveron doubted he could have defeated him and the other three on his own, even if they were caught off guard. He was more inclined to strike from the shadows, and he could wait to kill Wolfbane. In the meantime, the trip to Marlpaz would not be a disastrous move for him. It would be easy to reach his Angladaic contact there and see how plans for the nation were progressing. Yes, a trip there would give Wolfbane time to forget his suspicions and let Daerveron plan a bit. This was acceptable.

Wolfbane was now silent, seemingly deep in thought. Finally he rumbled to life, his chin resting on his hands. "Valissa, you must go with Frothgar. Keep me informed on the troops and be sure to watch relations with the Broken; we need them. Crush any resistance you find, though there should be little. I would bet against any trouble at all, but then I am no gambler. Also, bring as many of your own soldiers as you need and make certain that fool doesn't mar negotiations with the Broken. I'd prefer to use them against the armies in Dragon's Watch over my own men."

Valissa looked displeased but merely nodded her consent. Wolfbane eyed Caermon Erefoss briefly, rubbing his beard in thought. "I could send you to find Edge, or to the south to assist Valissa and Frothgar, but neither seems necessary. No, you may remain here for now, Caermon, and assure things run smoothly as we assimilate the last remnants of the Napalian Empire into our new kingdom."

Caermon dipped his head in acquiescence. Wolfbane now rounded on the final member of the council. "Saltilian, you are the only one who does not serve a much greater need to me here or elsewhere. I charge you with finding Edgewulf el Vac and the servants he escaped with. I care not for them, but he must be brought back alive so I can deduce precisely what happened. Understand if he comes back injured beyond what I deem necessary, you shall receive the same, even if Daerveron has to administer the beating himself. Do you follow me well enough?"

Saltilian seemed unsure of himself and the sudden responsibility being foisted upon him. Usually he was left alone during the meetings. It was out of order to even hear him speak more than once or twice. At the mention of Daerveron, he paled considerably, but rapidly seemed to regain his backbone. "Aye, Lord Wolfbane, I can f-find him for you and h-have no fear, I will return him unhurt, I s-s-swear it."

Wolfbane gave him a considering stare and then dropped the matter. "See that you do. You are all dismissed. Go about your tasks immediately. I will not tolerate sluggishness in these matters. They are of the utmost importance."

There was no formal intonation during the departure, everyone merely stood and left. Valissa Ulfrunn delayed briefly trying to gain Wolfbane's ear, but when he ignored her she flew down the stairs past the others in a huff. Daerveron had no doubt some loudmouth soldier was in for a painful meeting when she crossed him. In the meantime, the wizard thought he might enjoy laying into a passing servant himself, for his fury was immense. Wolfbane had more than undermined his authority, and he had opened the door for Saltilian to poke around in his other affairs without Daerveron to keep a watchful eye on him. The dread wizard fumed, but held it in. Whatever Saltilian uncovered, Daerveron was certain that he would die before Wolfbane learned any of it. He was determined the man would not make it back to Castle Bane still breathing.

Saltilian was unaware of any threat to his person. The timid mage was too giddy with joy and shock to pay attention to the smoldering fire in Daerveron's dead eyes. He could not believe that he now had the ideal opportunity to inspect the project Daerveron's notes had hinted at. It had taken Saltilian nearly three months, stealing one page at a time when he was assured it could be returned before Daerveron noticed it was missing. Those few moments with the sheets and their cold, spidery handwriting had been enough to learn much.

Saltilian was not foolish enough to think that he could directly cross Daerveron. He knew the other mage was far too powerful for him. What he wanted to do was eliminate him and obtain his tomes on ancient magic, something Daerveron was supposed to have a great deal of knowledge about. To do that Saltilian needed Wolfbane on his side, but that would only happen with proof that Daerveron was plotting behind his back. Saltilian had finally acquired the first clue toward that proof, and now had the good fortune to be granted the means to examine it.

Back in his room on the library floor, a smiling Saltilian leafed through his reams of notes looking for the one blank sheet that was more precious than any. Saltilian's room was a small one, cluttered to the point of ridiculousness with scrolls, books, and scraps of paper. Only half his bed remained cleared; he had trained himself to lie perfectly still so as not to disturb the stacks of tomes at his feet. Saltilian lusted for knowledge as other men lusted after beautiful women, though in the case of Raymir Squall he had made an exception. Truthfully, while he was thrilled to be given the chance to investigate the dark machinations of Daerveron, the opportunity to lay claim to Raymir was almost as enticing. He had watched her since the first day she came to the castle. He admired the curvature of her body and the delicate sheen of her skin, longing to know it better. Now he would, and he could finally put the frustrations of the past behind him.

Saltilian's time at the library fortress in Ozmandias had led him to believe that no one had more arcane wisdom than Daerveron, not even the reigning High Wizard, Q'thal. Saltilian's training as a mage had been harsh and unforgiving, but he had rapidly outdistanced all his other fellow students, except for one young boy who had been there for a time before Saltilian left. This rival had been the most powerful mage in many ages and instantly became Q'thal's new favorite, but the child had not believed, as the High Wizard did, that the arcane practicioners of their time should be preparing for some sort of cataclysmic war. Eventually, Saltilian's rival, whose name he could now not quite recall, had left the school of his own accord, allowing Saltilian to curry favor with Q'thal once again, though he never gained access to the most precious books he sought in the fortress. But soon they would be his, once Wolfbane's army took the city of magic along with the rest of the continent.

Very little was important when placed next to Saltilian's aspirations of power and wealth. Long had he lusted after the great fame and the admiration of others, ever since he had been a lone child on the streets of Napal City. His younger days had been harsh, sold by his own northern family to another Napalian household as a slave and servant, far from his home in Lowinter, unwanted by his parents who could not, or would not, accept another mouth to feed. He had escaped his baleful purchasers and was forced to fend for himself in the city. Without friend or family he had sought aid from those in Napal City that were charged with helping the less fortunate, and in repayment of his trust had been violently abused in the streets and engaged in many unscrupulous practices before learning he had a gift for the arcane. That aptitude resulted in him being driven out of the north and finding his way to Ozmandias, where his ability was fostered and grew. His increasing sense of power was all directed towards one goal: revenge on those who had wronged him. When Raymir Squall had come to the castle he had added her to his list of planned conquests, and now he only needed to track her and Daerveron's correspondent down to get what he sought.

Rummaging through his papers he finally found what he was looking for. Saltilian smiled into the sheet of blank parchment in his hand. He had learned a few useful tricks for stealing information in his time at Ozmandias, and this was still his favorite because it was difficult to detect and impossible to unveil unless one knew the command word. Saltilian uttered his with relish, "Alk'avar."

The paper glowed softly and words began to appear like glowing embers on the sheet. Gradually they hardened and solidified until Saltilian's triumphant clue stood glaring at him from the paper. Saltilian had copied precisely Daerveron's spidery hand to the blank sheet and then sealed the knowledge from view by the naked eye. He had pored over this parchment many times before, but now that he could make use of its words he studied them with a fiercer focus than ever. Sweeping several large stacks of books carelessly from his lone chair, he sat and began to devour the contents of the document in front of him.

It said very little outright. Daerveron had written almost entirely in his own unusual shorthand and clearly with great haste, which seemed odd for someone who had had centuries of time to gather knowledge and wisdom. Saltilian focused in on the one passage so vital to his intents and began picking it apart: *The creation of a vessel that could absorb such an essence appears, on first study, an impossibility. My duties here give me no opportunities for such an undertaking, but he claims there lies, farther in the north and therefore within the grasp of the Twisted Spire, one of the few entities that could be used in such an attempt. From there the matter of creation can become one more of alteration, the transforming of tissue as well as soul into another being entirely....*

The passage went on some more about the possible deterrents and obstacles to the vaguely described experiment, but did not contain enough to prove Daerveron was conspiring to create something that he would use to take command of Neroth's mortal army. Saltilian needed to find this thing for himself, hold it in his own hands, so that he might understand and even use it against Daerveron. The remainder of the passage suggested immense, even unlimited, arcane power, enough to make Saltilian salivate merely in reading it. Saltilian suspected that once he understood the nature of the spell or item being worked on he would be able to wield it without much difficulty, such was his confidence in his powers. There was no thing ever created by gods or men that he doubted could be his. Saltilian settled back in his chair and sighed in contentment. All he had to do was find Edge, perhaps he might even coerce him to aid in the search for this Twisted Spire, and once he had what he wanted he could return him to Wolfbane. If he was unwilling to return well, Saltilian would just cripple him and then he would have Raymir to himself. The hunt would last a very brief period either way, of that Saltilian was certain, and then he could fabricate the difficulties of finding Edgewulf el Vac and explain how he "stumbled" onto Daerveron's plan and just let it fall into his hands. It was a brilliant idea if he had ever had one.

Saltilian fingered the runes on his staff nervously as he thought. He adorned his thirty-two-year-old frame with as many trappings and signs of his power as possible, perhaps beyond what was necessary. Always he felt a need to show others his strength, to make clear his station in life. Saltilian was only comfortable when he felt people saw his status clearly, understood his authority to command them. Even as a young man he had wanted to gain the prestige he thought he deserved. In adulthood he had climbed out of the pit of his youth through diligence and study, yet his success did not make women find his spindly frame, thin face, and sunken eyes any less unattractive. Saltilian never bothered to try to explain that his physical appearance came from studying magic texts in the wee hours of the night and that he ate only when he was about to keel over from lack of sustenance. Saltilian had long known he would never be the fighter revered in the Napalian histories, but he had enjoyed watching many who aspired to that archetype die, withering slowly under the effects of some of his most disturbing incantations. Yet the mage did share one trait with the Napalians, a tenacity for glory had taken hold of him from his youth. Saltilian was determined to outdo all others in success and fame, and now he felt close to that goal.

Straightening, the wizard grabbed a small set of saddlebags from his wall hooks and quickly filled them with whatever scrolls he thought might be useful, folding the slip of stolen paper into one of his many hidden pockets. Gripping his staff tightly he strode out into the library and down the spiraling stairs to the entry hall. The guards saluted him as he passed through the main entrance, though not as smartly as they might have had he been one of the other commanders. One day I will make them grovel at my feet, he thought. The idea made him smile slightly, which was not a pleasant sight. Once outside, he headed for the parade grounds where he could see Valissa working her soldiers into the ground in shifts. She shrieked out commands if they did not move swiftly enough to suit her, which they never did. Saltilian walked up behind her and waited. Valissa never took her eyes from the soldiers as she addressed him, "What do you want, wizard? I am busy here."

"I r-require some of your s-s-soldiers, and h-horses."

She turned to glare at him, then glanced at his staff and the silver runes of his dark purple robe and thought the better of what she had wanted to say. "I will send you twelve of the best as soon as they are done here, with horses. Is that acceptable?" she ground out the last word as though it pained her.

"As long as they are n-not overworked," Saltilian snorted.

Valissa's glare sharpened but she turned away. "One hour, mage."

Saltilian inclined his head at her back. "As y-you say, woman." He grinned as her stance stiffened, confident in his own safety under Wolfbane's orders. Saltilian would let her keep him waiting, but he refused to be lowered too far without taking her down with him. Still smiling sickly to himself, he headed toward the stables to retrieve his own horse. It will be a long journey, girl, he thought, but when I return I will teach you who truly rules here. The staff flared with a bright light as arcane energy coursed through in his body. "Oh you will learn that lesson well," he sneered.

Saltilian snapped at the stableman as he entered, "S-saddle my horse, boy, and make c-certain he is fit for r-riding when you do."

He enjoyed the way the man scampered under his eyes. In his mind glorious visions of servants fearfully doing his every bidding danced before him. One day they all will serve me, he thought, and a chilling laugh escaped his lips.

Chapter 8

The seven fugitives from Gi'lakil rode until dawn then collapsed to rest in a small grove by the roadside. They arose again after only a few hours to race onward to the east. "We cannot give those foul things time to find us," remarked Ghost briefly, "the faster we move the better."

The town of Gi'lakil had faded in the distance shortly after the party had crested the first rise. The Dust Plains are, truthfully, more hills and mounds than actual plains. The region is large, covered in low brush, rounded and jagged rocks of various sizes, and ample amounts of dirt and grime that give the territory its name. In the dry season, especially the fall and late summer, the dirt and sand rises with the winds and obscures the vision of most travelers for some distance. As the party left Gi'lakil they kicked up a great cloud of dust behind them, but saw few others on the road eastward. Logan posited they had all fled west already, though Diaga suggested perhaps there was no one left to flee at all.

As Trem scanned the horizon at each opportunity, he could have sworn that he saw, mingled among the dust clouds, more uniform swirls of smoke coming from the northeast. Trem made no mention of these to his companions, but he believed as Diaga did that they suggested a much darker reason for the absence of other people on the road. Their own travels were already unpleasant enough. Over the course of the journey, lasting a harrowing three days, Ghost's thin mask of charm and concern faded, and perhaps it had never truly been there at all. Within a few hours of leaving he was barking orders at the others and demanding greater pace and berating those, like Diaga and Jovan, who were simply not in any condition to keep up.

It would have made sense for Logan, given his pedigree and knightly bearing, to stand up to Ghost at that time, but he did not. Logan instead kept a quiet eye on the two weary riders along with Grimtooth, pointedly ignoring Ghost's verbal abuse without openly challenging his authority. Indeed, it was Trem who became the oddly calming and reasoned voice among the party. He seemed utterly unimpressed by Ghost's efforts to order them about like his personal army, and offered words of encouragement to Diaga and Jovanaleth when they began to tire. This caused the others, even Logan and Grimtooth who were veteran campaigners, to warm up to the seemingly younger Trem quite swiftly. This fact got deep beneath Ghost's skin, though he tried not to let it show too often how infuriating he found the undermining of his authority.

Diaga also became quite fond of Trem in a short time, and it seemed his trust of the half-elf meant Neep accepted him as well. When Diaga was struggling to guide his horse on the second day, dazed and half-asleep after barely two hours of rest, Trem took the reins and led him onward. Neep reacted sharply, appearing between Trem's mount and that of her beloved master, but she kept her weapons sheathed and simply padded along between them, sparing perhaps a few extra cautionary glances for Trem while she did. Logan and Grimtooth took it upon themselves to follow Trem's lead, and watched over Jovan so as to give Trem more time to help the young wizard. The unity of purpose among those six meant that Ghost was soon set apart from the group, and Grimtooth in particular became especially disdainful of the northerner's vicious and confrontational leadership style. Ghost could sense he was losing the respect and support of those who had only a short time ago saved his life, but he also seemed unwilling or unable to change his approach, and the divide between them grew larger.

They continued at a breakneck pace for three days with only occasionaly stops to rest and water their mounts. Eventually the travel began to wear on everyone, even Ghost and the other more experienced campaigners. Diaga and Jovanaleth were virtually falling out of their saddles in exhaustion, but Ghost would not slow the company. Finally, as night fell on the third day, Trem approached him. "We have to rest for a while. The others will not make it much farther and we need to double-check the supplies. That innkeeper was too frightened to really count how much she gave us."

Ghost eyed the half-elf. "I don't like your tone, boy, but you may be right. Those tenderfoots will not make another hundred yards without some rest. As to the supplies, we will need to stop at the next town with a blacksmith anyway. I need a new sword."

He turned sharply and called a halt. Grimtooth practically carried Jovan from his saddle to a bedroll and laid him down. Neep helped Diaga to his own place then curled up beside him, orange tail flicking back and forth protectively. The others tied the horses and Logan went to look for wood while Trem and Grimtooth went through their supplies.

Grimtooth scowled at the meager rations. "'Ardly enough ta feed a wee gel, much less seven grown men." He paused and added with a grin. "Well, six grown men an' one fat cat."

Trem smiled ruefully. "One loaf of hard bread and ten strips of dried meat is not my idea of a feast either. We will just have to make the best of it."

Grimtooth gestured to Trem's bow. "Could ye maybe catch us some nice bunnies wit' ye spear thrower?"

Trem shook his head. "Too dark for hunting tonight."

"Dinnae ye 'ave the elven night sight?"

"Not as strong as a full blood elf."

Grimtooth shrugged. "'Cuse me lad, Ah know little of ye kind. No insult meant ya undahstand."

"No harm done," Trem answered, then feeling a bit braver he said, "Do you mind if I ask you a question Grimtooth?"

The orc flopped himself down and tossed his cross straps to the earth. "Nay, Trem, Ah dinnae mind."

"Where did you get your accent from?"

Grimtooth looked at him a moment, then burst out in a bellowing laugh. Ghost looked sharply in their direction, but Trem waved his concern away and the Napalian scowled and stormed off away from the fire. The orc regained his composure and grinned toothily at Trem. "It be noticeable? Ach! Ah thought Ah'd been getting' a wee bit bettah. It's just tha way orcs talk ya know, not so many strange T's in our tongue."

"What do you mean strange T's?"

"Well," Grimtooth rubbed his chin as he tried to explain it. "In orcish we dinnae end words wit' T's 'ardly ever, so Ah forget," he emphasized the sound on the end of the word with a look of concentration, "sometimes. But shorta words is easiah to say clearah, like 'but,' 'cat,' and tha' sorta thing. The damned Ah's though, I cannae say 'um 'less they be neah a 'ard sound, like in 'ard!" He grinned, "And I cannae evah say ta H's that be startin' words."

"So it makes the common tongue a bit harder to pronounce then?"

"Aye."

They sat in silence awhile as Grimtooth sliced the bread and Trem carefully divided the rations. Jovanaleth came shambling over and sat with them, unbuckling his sword and leaning back on the hard ground with a groan. Grimtooth nodded at him and Jovanaleth took the opportunity to converse, "Grimtooth, did I hear you call your horse Thunder?"

The orc grunted, "Aye lad, Logan said when 'e trots trew ta streets of ahh 'ome it be soundin' like rollin' thundahclaps."

Trem smiled slightly. "One might expect that from the world's largest horse."

"Aye, it do be takin' a big animal ta 'old me."

Jovan put his hands behind his head and looked up at the stars. "It is something to be out here, under the night sky. I find I don't miss home at all."

"Ach," Grimtooth shook his head. "Ah would be givin' anythin' ta be back 'ome this moment."

"Why are you so far from home?" Jovan asked, "Are you and Logan on some rite of passage?"

"Well lad, it might be somethin' ya could call a rite." The orc shifted nervously as he struggled, but was able to get the word out clearly. "'Twas more like we 'ad to leave."

Trem noted his tone. "Why would you have to leave?"

"Ah cannae tell ye, Trem, not anythin' personal, but suffice ta say we 'ave to atone fer sins committed."

Ghost, apparently somewhat recovered from his irritation with the orc, came over briefly from his watch to take his share of the food without a word. Grimtooth watched him walk away. "That un is no leader. We be 'eaded for a long an' 'ard journey with 'im at our front."

Trem said nothing but instead took up his rations and began chewing methodically. Finally he leaned back against a small stone and said, "Tell me, Grimtooth, how did you come to be Logan's blood-brother?"

The orc sighed and also reclined, having wolfed his food down quickly and without complaint. "That'd be a long tale for ye, Trem, an' I no like ta talk much."

"Maybe it is better I tell it then."

All three glanced up as Logan appeared with the firewood and dropped it down between them. "If you would be so kind as to start the fire then I think I could be convinced to tell a little tale."

The two went at the wood with flint and tinder. Soon a comfortable flame was going and Logan had a small, carved pipe lit. He too settled back and sighed. "Now that is much better. It is no prince's lounge but it works just as well."

"You are a prince too?" Trem glanced at Jovanaleth. "I am traveling in awfully royal company."

"No, not really." Logan stroked his chin as he explained, "My father is Arvadis Angladais Hawking, current King of Angladais, and so that makes me something of a prince I suppose. But I have no real ties to the Highlords or any governing body. Mind you, that is just fine with me." He took a long draw on his pipe. "No, my oldest brother, Vorasho, is the prince and heir, as long as the family is permitted to hold the throne."

"What do you mean permitted?"

Logan spoke around a puff of smoke, "In Angladais there are laws to intercede if an heir is believed to be unworthy. We are of the Hawking House and thus, like all other Highlords, have a claim to ties to the first founders of Angladais. In order to hold the throne one must be met with the approval of the other Highlords and of the people. My father has had little trouble winning the people," he grimaced, "it is some of the Highlords that chafe at his reign."

"Why is that?"

"My father does not live in the palace, nor does he hold sway for long periods in the throne room unless absolutely necessary. He lives in a cottage, a nicer cottage than most but a cottage all the same, among the commoners on the Zenith Road, one of our raised central avenues. The Highlords of the city each have their own district to govern, and most have manors all just barely lesser in grandeur than the Royal Palace itself. They find my father too earthy for them, although the people of our kingdom love him for it."

"And you?"

Logan looked at Trem with a slight grin. "Have I ever regretted my father's decision? Do I pine for wealth and the recognition of other austere gentlemen? No, Trem, I love my people. What the Highlords often forget is that the common peoples' ancestors built the kingdom, both cottages and palaces. They are still its foundation. My brother Vorasho is more inclined toward keeping good relations with the other nobility, but even he has a much softer heart for the common folk than most. I think it is our love of the everyday man and woman that led my father and his sons to travel so much. That is how father found Grimtooth after all.

"It was some years ago, a dozen now I think, when the gnolls were becoming a growing threat in the Dust Plains. Father wanted to send aid to the people of the region, just as the Angladaics had done in times before, but many of the Highlords were unwilling or uninterested in aiding those outside our kingdom. Only Runiden Calavar, Highlord in command of the paladins, agreed to help. The two came through the Windpass to the Dust Plains and learned the Golden Sun Clan was under massive assault. They were our oldest allies. Cran Broadaxe gave his life defending Gi'lakil many years ago, alongside our people. My father could not leave them to be slaughtered."

Grimtooth's countenance darkened as he spoke up quietly, "Ah remembah seein' 'im come inta mah 'ome. Mah parents was dead, all of um was dead, and Ah was all that was left. Ahvadis, 'e took me ta Angladais wit' 'im, made me 'is son. Ah would be dead now if 'e 'adn't found me."

Logan nodded gravely as he replied, "My father had only recently been named king, and he took a lot of jeering from the nobility for welcoming an orc to our kingdom. No one cared that this same clan had fought beside our ancestors many years ago. They all saw a monster and threat to our traditions." He shook his head. "Ridiculous, all of it."

Trem looked at Logan and Grimtooth quizzically before asking, "So you were both raised by the Hawking House? How did you become bloodbrothers?"

Logan smiled. "Grim was eighteen when my father brought him to live with us, he was still a true orc through and through. As for myself, I had no real friends as a youth, except my brother. When Vorasho got older he started taking his duty to Angladais very seriously. We did not spend much time together then. But Grim came along, and soon we became a common sight around Alderlast. We mingled with the locals, spent time policing the streets with them, solving disputes and reveling in small celebrations. It was an easy decision for me to complete the orcish ritual, and my father was very proud when we decided to join our bloodlines. The blood joining is not just a formality. The process uses rites that bind the two brothers' lives, if one of us dies, so to will the other. Technically, ours remains unconsecrated. We need a powerful orc shaman to complete the process. We thought we would find one when we came southward, " he paused, "of course it has been more than two years now since we left."

Trem pressed the opening. "Is there a reason you have not been able to return?"

"In truth, we have not made any great effort to go home." Logan shrugged slightly at the thought, though his eyes showed a hint of sadness. "This journey is supposed to be my final test of worthiness, so that I may receive the mantle of Paladinis and obtain the grand title of paladin, yet it is not honestly a responsibility I seek. I enjoy being a simple knight, a friend to the people." His face darkened and his tone grew grim as he added, "Though if our young illusionist is to be believed then there is foul magic afoot in the north. Angladaics distrust the magical arts. We rely primarily on the power of faith in our god to grant us holy might. If what Diaga says is true this fortress is an affront to our very beliefs." Logan seemed to drift off for a moment before adding softly, "Yet another roadblock to our eventual return."

No one spoke for some time, and then Grimtooth silently rose and went to his bed followed shortly by Logan. Jovan and Trem sat at the fire for a long time, silent. Trem poked at the flames with a stick and said with a sly hint of a grin, "You know, there's evidence enough Logan is truly Angladaic royalty, but you have not shown me anything to prove you're really a prince."

Jovanaleth smiled at the mischievous glint in Trem's eyes. He reached behind him into his knapsack and drew forth a heavy round metal pin, tossing it to his companion, "That is the sigil of the Order of the Blade. You'll find others know the symbol well."

Trem turned it over and gave a sharp intake of breath, for he recognized the scene depicted on the pin. A blade, wreathed in flame, was being dipped into a pool of water. He thought back to the Inn of the Four Winds, his foolish actions there. His face now serious, Jovanaleth leaned forward and asked the question that had kept him from seeking much needed rest that night, "Where did you get that sword, Trem?"

Trem had not been prepared for this moment, and he shifted uncomfortably before answering, "I told you that I served in the War of the Lion, along with your father. You know where the sword came from."

"I know of one sword that could be covered in fire. The sword that belonged to the traitorous Vactan el Vac." Jovan's tone grew soft. "It became my father's symbol for the Order of the Blade, the extinguishing of the fire on Vactan's sword, a last testament to the bloody end of that war. Vactan killed the Commander of the Eagle Knights, Bull the Warrior, with that same weapon."

"Yes," Trem said, his eyes still on the pin in his hand, "so the story goes."

"That story also says that Vactan himself died by the hand of an unknown soldier from Aves. A man whose name was never revealed and who left when the final battle was over." Jovanaleth leaned in closer to Trem. "But it can't have been you, Trem, you would have been just a boy."

Trem rose, turning away from his companion, surprised at how upsetting the distrust in Jovanaleth's words was to him. "I found the body of that man, away from the battle. I took his sword and fled to Silverleaf Forest; he needed it no longer."

Jovan considered this silently then said, "How did you know the arcane words to summon the fire?"

Trem's eyes came round sharply. "Everyone in the fortress had seen Vactan set his blade alight. He used to intimidate those he trained by calling the flames when he was sparring with them. We all knew the words, it was just a matter of having the sword." Trem tossed his stick in the fire and said, "I am done with this matter. We both need rest. Good night, Jovanaleth."

Trem tossed the pin to Jovan, who had to snatch it quickly from the air before it was lost in the darkness. Jovanaleth watched him walk past the fire, not waiting for a response, and settle down by his belongings. Jovan wanted to follow him, to press him further with questions, but he did not. For now, Jovanaleth determined he would have to wait until Trem was willing to tell him more. He was certain there was something wrong with his story, just as he had been certain the weapon he used back in Gi'lakil was the same one depicted on his family's sigil. Exhaustion clouded further thought and he stretched his bedroll out by the fire. Lying back on the ground, the young man from Bladehome closed his eyes and was soon asleep.

For Trem the dream was a familiar one. He sat at the edge of the stream, watching the otters play in the shallows. Occasionally he would throw some fish from his abundant catch towards them, gradually coaxing them to his hand where they would rest their furry heads. Trem loved the otters as much as his parents. His father said they were just dogs trapped in the water, water-hounds. That was his name, Trem Waterhound, son of Emond and Gilda Waterhound. He was a simple herder's son, a decent hunter, a nobody.

The dream was all the more pleasant because Trem could see it so clearly. His old home was a ramshackle log cabin his father had built and his mother maintained while he and Trem were off selling cheese, meat, and other goods in various markets in nearby countless nearby villages. He glanced over his shoulder at the homely place in the distance; what a mess it was. How he loved these days. Trem was twelve again, just a boy beginning to learn a man's responsibilities. His home was his world, his loving parents the universe, his gods the river and its many secrets. He could have stayed at the riverside for his whole life. Deep inside, after having gone to so many other places, it was his secret wish that he had stayed. There was nothing in the world he found that made this seem poor or unfulfilling. As always, the brief joy of the dream began to fade and Trem's attachment to the dreamscape it.

Only as he was fading from the familiar sight did he suddenly notice he was not listing off into dreamless sleep. Trem felt himself pulled, though moved was a better word, but he could not explain how. Suddenly, he stood in a great hall with an oddly made table spanning its length. He was not twelve anymore, he was himself now, dressed in his worn clothes from the trunk in Silverleaf and older in years than he appeared. Trem could not explain how he came here to this odd room, empty but for its single table, the hall devoid of seats. He lingered, his hand touching the edge of the table and tried to recall something he had read once.

Mere walls and windows must soon drive to madness a man who reads and dreams too much. Do you know this place?

Trem's head came up at the echo of a voice in his mind. Across from him was a blue shimmering form with sharper blue wide slits where he believed eyes should have been. Kurven hovered beside the table, and the world about them wavered slightly as Trem steadied himself. He now knew where he was. "The Archway Temple, the meeting place of the gods."

Yes, though at the same time it is not. This is still a part of the dreaming world. It would be impossible to bring you to the real temple in the Godly Realms, unless you were dead.

"'A man who reads and dreams too much,'" Trem quoted the god. "Were you thinking of me?"

Perhaps, but the warning is the same for everyone.

"And how did you bring me here?"

In the dreamscape such things are possible for those who know how.

"I'm not sure I like you being able to do that," Trem crossed his arms, "or your cryptic way of introducing yourself."

I apologize, I merely thought to give reference to your past self and the daydreams you once had as a child. You have that dream often I know, it seems a comfort to you.

"Everything is about dreams isn't it?" Trem leaned on the table as he spoke, "I only wanted to spend my time asleep in a place of comfort. I did not seek the counsel of you or any other."

Not directly, but I gave you a piece of myself once. I can occasionally use that to exert some control over you, in the realm of dreams especially.

"Pleasant." Trem said sarcastically. "Is there something else you want to threaten or cajole me into? My personal history has already raised doubts within the man I came to help."

Kurven did not respond immediately and Trem looked up from the table where he had been studying his reflection. *I asked if you recognized this place, and you do. I believed you would, given your penchant for reading and study as a boy. I wanted to show it to you and to offer you some counsel.*

"Kurven," Trem's voice was exasperated, "you have now three times come to me, twice in dreams and once in your temple. It is hard for me to believe that you are not trying to manipulate me, just as other gods once did before I fled to Silverleaf Forest. If I'm being honest, you're only making going back look more appealing each time you come to me."

We gods have sworn oaths many times, in this very chamber, to stay out of the lives of mortals, but many of my kin violate these agreements with impunity. I have never done so, until now, but you must believe me when I say I only desire to help you.

"But why? You were right in saying I read much, of gods and mortals, when I was young. I remember you. You are not like the others, so dependent on the many people of Teth-tenir for your existence and strength. Some of the texts I read even implied you might not share kinship with your own kind, let alone us mere mortals."

It was hard to tell, given his formless shape, but Kurven seemed to flinch at Trem's words. The God of Time spoke softly in Trem's mind, *I gave you a piece of myself. In many ways, I have more of a connection to you than to any being in this or any other world. I have watched you and, yes, interfered in your life. Perhaps I have been too intrusive, but I have done so out of a desire to help. It is because of me you have no mother....*

"Don't," Trem cut him off sharply. "You are not my mother or my father. I believe you when you say you want to help, so speak your piece, God of Time, and then let me rest."

I wished only to say that you should tell Jovanaleth the truth.

Trem's laugh was short, a barked chuckle without mirth. "Now, when you say things like that it makes it harder for me to believe you wish to help. Rather, I think you are actually trying to get me killed, immortal."

Eventually, your lies will catch up with you.

"They may. But what do I gain by telling them I do not age? Are you hoping they will see me as some sort of savior? A hero? I am none of those things. I only wish to help Jovan."

But the ideal still intrigues you. The possibility saving a young man so like yourself, in some small way to help the people you have tried to hide away from. All these things harken back to the young, idealistic version of yourself you buried years ago. Perhaps a reawakening of that ideology is a good thing, but you should remain wary. Trem remained unmoved and said nothing in response, though the God of Time waited a long while. *Very well. There is one thing that I can show you now that is over dire importance: beware allowing yourself to drift from the dreamscape.*

"Beware?" Trem was, despite himself, intrigued. "What do you mean?"

Your mortal world, Teth-tenir, is bound by laws of physics that the gods put in place to give it some degree of order and logic. When the first mortals were made they were driven mad or taken over entirely by the total freedom of power and unbounded existence we have in the Godly Realms. In truth, even most immortals are not capable of handling this limitless, formless world restrained only by imagination and strength of will. Many of my kind form realms like your own, with physical objects and barriers that exist only to create the illusion of boundary, but the illusion also helps preserve sanity.

The dreamscape is a strange blending of the two worlds. In truth, we gods did not make it and have no idea how it came into being. Dreaming was not something we envisioned mortals doing, nor did we expect you could learn to manipulate the more pliable realm of dreams. As little as most mortals understand about the dreamscape, we know only slightly more. But, as you have found, the creation of places from memory and sensation are entirely within your power, as is projecting yourself outward to find other dreamers and converse with them.

"And the dead," Trem added. "I have heard that the dead can enter the dreaming world rather easily. Some say they occasionally get lost there and cannot return to the Godly Realms."

This is true. The dead travel, intentionally or sometimes unintentionally, into the world of dreams. Some do not understand that they have traveled there and remain, unable to get out. But you have focused on a small part of the danger of the dream world that affects only the deceased of your kind. Can you not see the dangerous implications for mortals? Even dreamwalkers, who have honed their craft over many nights, run the same risk.

"I'm not sure what you mean. Being trapped in the dreamscape like the dead? Remaining unable to awaken?"

Perhaps, but the greater peril lies in projection of one's power. It creates a beacon that can be spotted and, as I have demonstrated, manipulated.

"But you said that was because you had a piece of yourself within me."

It made finding you easier, but bringing you here I could have done on my own once I located you in the dreaming world. As could many gods and, Trem felt his head begin to throb, the beat of his heart to thump against his ribs and the pulsation to ring in his ears, *their power can harm you. Do you feel the pressure of your own blood against your physical form? I can, with enough focus, break your mortal body in many horrible ways.*

The terrible, overwhelming sense of his blood fighting against its confines subsided and Trem fell to one knee as he felt the loss of control recede. "You could have killed me."

Yes, but I did not.

"You are saying others of your kind might? Tell me the truth, Kurven, is there another immortal hunting me? I deserve to know."

But the God of Time was drifting away from him. *You should learn to harness your strength and vision of the dreamscape, Trem Waterhound, before you have to meet another of my kind in less amicable circumstances.*

Trem tried to clutch the side of the table, to rise, but it was shimmering, wobbling, and fading out of view. He fell backwards and the floor did not catch him. Spinning, he fell, fell forever through visions and sounds that were not comprehensible. He could not say how long he swam in the cacophony of noise and light, but it was slow in ending and his mind never quite rested.

Trem awoke suddenly, shooting up from his prone position on the ground with a loud gasp. The sun was well into its daily climb and he realized he had slept far beyond dawn. He looked toward the remnants of the night's fire to see Jovanaleth stirring the ashes with his belt knife. Upon seeing Trem was awake Jovan rushed towards him. "Trem, are you alright? We could not rouse you, Diaga said to just leave you alone until you woke up," he grinned sheepishly, almost apologetically. "I guess I feared you might not wake up."

Trem grunted and rose to his feet, quickly gathering his belongings. "Thank you for watching over me. I had a restless sleep."

He turned away and went to saddle his horse. Jovan caught himself staring and muttered, "Let him go, no sense pestering him now."

The company moved on shortly after Trem's awakening. No one mentioned the comatose state he had been in for most of the morning. In fact, no one said much of anything for a long while. As afternoon came on, Jovanaleth joined Ghost riding up front, the grizzled older man relating some of his greatest adventures for the spellbound youth. Logan, Grimtooth, Neep, and Diaga rode a few yards behind them both, the pace light enough now for conversation. Trem was still farther back acting as rearguard. Logan glanced back and turned to the young mage. "You are certain he is alright, Diaga?"

The refreshed wizard followed his look then grinned. "Trem? Yes, he's fine, he was in some sort of trance this morning, but I have seen that type of thing before."

Logan was taken aback. "When?"

Diaga's smile faded a little. "Well, truth be told, I used to go into such catatonic states a lot, usually when I was studying too many magical texts at once. Sometimes your body just has to shut down to process all the arcane energy. It is a great strain, it becomes difficult to remain awake and active."

"You think Trem was studying magic?"

"No, but something significant has happened. He is certainly not the same man he was when we stopped last night."

Logan nodded and Grimtooth grunted, "'e's not the one that concerns me Ah tell ye. It be that 'un up there," he gestured towards Ghost. "Ah dun think it's a great idea lettin' 'im be the leader of this little trip."

Diaga eyed the orc with a skeptical look. "You really think Ghost is in charge?" Logan and Grimtooth both turned their attention to the youth. "If anyone is truly leading this expedition, it is Trem," Diaga concluded.

"How would you figure that?" asked Logan.

"He is obviously the only one who can tell Ghost what to do, he has been watching out for Jovanaleth and I since we left Gi'lakil. He called for a stop last night and after what he did in the inn with his sword... I know a magical weapon is not enough on it's own to make a man or woman a leader, but there is something about him that even Ghost has to respect. Think of it this way, wouldn't you be more apt to listen if Trem suggested a course of action than if Ghost did?"

Logan looked thoughtful. "I suppose I would."

"Aye," agreed Grimtooth. They looked sharply at each other, then at Diaga, then back at each other and burst into laughter. When they had recovered, Logan asked a now broadly smiling Diaga, "How did a young wizard grow so wise so quickly?"

"That," remarked Diaga, "is not a terribly pleasant story for such a beautiful day, but I can tell you if you want to know."

The other two nodded their ascent and Diaga cleared his throat to oblige. "Well, it's best to get the details out of the way. Firstly, I am an orphan, but unlike some I have a family name from my parents: Cursair. My parents had a small home outside the Whitewood in Napal. One night, something or someone killed them. I do not know what, and no culprit was ever found. All I have been able to learn was that the murder itself was especially brutal and violent. So, with no relatives to take me in, I was raised by one of Napal City's most auspicious orphan houses." He winced as if physically remembering a whip. "They were most unkind.

"My parents left me one gift, aside from their name, before they died. They had been educated people, and I later learned both were renowned poets in the north before they retired to solitude near the forest. I knew how to read reasonably well, even at a young age. In the orphanage, I was always smaller and weaker than the other boys and fighting for food was common, but there were also books there and I didn't have to fight anyone for those. The owner of the place would not let any of the children die outright, so his workers begrudgingly made sure I was fed just enough. I filled the gaps in my meals with reading. Among those books were several no one, not even the masters of the orphanage, could make sense of.

"I was not yet ten years old, but I began to understand some of the meaning in those pages. I discovered I had an affinity with powers I did not understand. I could call upon words in a language I had never heard. I began to set my tormentors' clothes aflame when I felt in danger. I had devoured every book in the orphanage and began asking for more, of every type and language. My masters, perhaps unnerved by my method of dealing with the more brutish boys, became less abusive and more fearful. Eventually I was packed off with a shipment of goods to Ozmandias. They left me at the front gate of the fortress with a note tied round my neck: 'Mage, do not return.'

"Ozmandias was a good experience for me. There were other children my age with the ability to fathom aspects of the arcane. Moreover, my studious behavior was encouraged by wise, older wizards and for a time I was happy. But then a different man, one named Q'thal, replaced the High Wizard of the fortress. He had a very dark view of the world and often spoke of a great conflict coming, wherein those of us who studied the arcane would need to arm ourselves against great enemies. Many times I heard him speak of the Arcane Wars and he even dared to utter the name that has become a curse in our time, that of the God-Sorceror.

"Q'thal saw how gifted I was. He attempted to convince me to turn my skills to the schools of Ruination and Degeneration, believing that I could grow strong enough to devastate entire armies by myself. I had no love for that magic, though I admit it has always come easier to me than the other schools. I wish that I was more adept in Regeneration or even Disruption or Conjuring, but it simply was not the case. I do not think Q'thal meant me any ill, but he grew frustrated with my resistance to my gift. We had something of a falling out a few years ago, and I left Ozmandias. I have never been back, nor corresponded with Q'thal since."

Diaga paused and glanced towards Neep who was trotting alongside him. "I had to escape, I simply did not believe I could remain any longer. I did not know what I wanted to do with my life, but I knew eventually I would give in to Q'thal's insistence I focus my energy on destructive forces. To my shame I stole several volumes from the library and departed under cover of night. In retrospect, perhaps I should have used a jump spell."

"A jump spell?" asked Logan.

"A random teleportation spell, sending the caster far away from his location to one he cannot determine. It would have been a foolish gamble, Q'thal would immediately know I had cast it, though luckily it's one of the few spells that cannot be traced. I opted not to, fearing where it would land me, perhaps in the ocean or among the high peaks of the mountains. Ultimately I chose to walk back to Napal. I attempted to make a living in the city for a time, but I had no skills outside of the arcane. In the Napalian Empire such gifts were frightening, hence why I had been sent to Ozmandias in the first place. At the time I had no idea what to do, so I left and started walking north. I had no money and no concept of where to go, but I knew the city was not the answer.

"In my travels a fearsome storm rose up, as often happens in the Great Northern Waste, and I lost my way. I stumbled, snowblind and near unconsciousness, into a small cave. I was fortunate to find shelter, and more fortunate that it was occupied." He looked at his feline companion, running effortlessly beside his trotting horse. "That is where I found Neep, or more aptly put, she found me."

Grimtooth was astounded. "Ye tellin' me that flamin' orange cat a' yers is a gel?"

Diaga smiled. "Yes that is exactly what I am telling you. Neep kept me warm through the storm that night. She was like me, an orphan. Her parents had died in that cave, far from the warm lands in the south firecats are native to. I think perhaps they had been driven out of their home and just kept wandering. They were caught in the sudden descent of winter and were too weak to survive. I would have met the same fate that night if not for Neep.

"When I woke up I was shocked to find a cat about my size covering me from the cold, and even more surprised to see it was a firecat. As I said, firecats are a rare breed, normally residing along the base of the Skytable Plateaus amid the heat of the Endless Sands in Southron. They are prized and hunted for their brilliant coats, though they are also considered one of the most intelligent bestial creatures in the world. That morning she went out of the cave at great speed once I awoke, and I suspected I would never see her again. A few hours later she came back with several rodents in her jaws, and lucky for me too, as I had barely managed to find enough wood for a meager fire and a few roots I thought might be edible.

"Neep was smaller then, though to be fair I was but fourteen years myself, and clearly neither of us was ready to be on our own. For a few days we made due in the cave, with her hunting down game nearby and I building fires for warmth and scrounging for herbs and anything else we could eat. Before long we were inseperable, and she allowed me to seal her parents' bodies in the cave. We had to move on, but we never would have been able to alone."

"Did she always walk upright?" asked Logan.

"Firecats are stronger in their hind legs than other felines, even the lions of Westia. Neep watched me, and then one day she was simply walking beside me, studying my movements. It gave me quite a start the first time she did it!" Diaga laughed at the memory. "They are amazing creatures. Some day, I'll have her show you her front paws. They have long fingers that curl into more traditional cat paws when they are on all fours, and in place of a dewclaw they have a long thumb. That's what gave her the ability to hold weapons and take part in our performances, and as I explained she is a fast learner. We made a decent living in the north for a while, performing in small inns and earning enough for a meal and a bed for one or two nights. It was a happy time."

Logan looked at the young mage, enthralled by his story. "But you came still further south, why?"

Diaga sighed. "I missed people. It seems odd for a beaten orphan to long for the presence of others, but I did. I thought Neep might abandon me eventually as she grew older, but she has remained. She has always stunned me with her ability to adapt to our world. She was entranced by armor and weapons from the time I met her, hence her armored leather kilt and bracers, she's added more over time as she studies people and their ways. She has always been good with daggers, but even I was amazed how comfortable she is with a sword. At first I thought it would just be good as visual intimidation, but she has real skill with a blade." Diaga looked down at Neep with genuine affection and care. "From the day we met, I have tried to teach her things. Walking upright, juggling, even to talk."

Logan's eyes went wide. "She talks?"

Diaga laughed. "Well not really. She cannot seem to grasp the concept quite yet. She has the vocal capacity to speak as well as you or I, but she only knows her name. Right, Neep?"

The firecat, who had been watching the groups' flanks the entire time for any sign of danger, turned her head and sharply in the wizard's direction and called, "Neep!"

Logan laughed loudly and Diaga smiled happily. Grimtooth was so dumbfounded by the sudden pronouncement that he nearly fell from his saddle. Instead he took to muttering to himself, "'Alf way 'round the world wit' that no brained brotha o' mine an' we got a blinkin' cat that talks. Gods save me, Ah nae asked fer this."

When he had recovered, Logan wiped his eyes and asked Diaga, "So why Gi'lakil? I fear we may have dragged you to even greater misfortune in your young life."

Diaga shook his head. "There is no joy in life without sorrow. We came to Gi'lakil to avoid the fighting in the north, now it appears that war will leak south. I am just trying to make sure I am with the right people when it does."

Grimtooth leaned over and clapped the youth on his back, nearly knocking him from his saddle. "Not ta worry laddie, we always be on the right side. Win or lose."

Logan nodded sagely and voiced his agreement, "Win or lose."

"Hey!"

The three looked forward to see Jovan riding toward them and Ghost sitting calmly on his mount at the next rise in the road. The young ranger sped up to them and halted, his horse rearing up slightly as he did. Jovan looked excited. "There's a village up ahead. Ghost says we need to stop there and find a blacksmith to make him another sword."

"We should also ask after directions to this road south." The group turned to see Trem had caught up with them from the rear. "After all," he remarked, "I certainly do not know where it is."

Diaga smiled and moved his horse aside. "Lead the way, Trem."

Chapter 9

The village the companions rode into was a tiny, nameless one. Yet, it appeared the people here had prospered either from travelers moving east and west or by their own trade. There was no sign of fear in them, despite the rumors of bloody fighting to the east. A few guards, likely mercenaries, were positioned at the entrance to the town on both ends of the road to drive refugees clear of the village. But once they saw the party was well-armed and moving east they stepped aside without question and let them pass.

Five fine stone buildings with real slate-tiled roofs around a community well made up the main square of the village, though there were a few low wooden homes beyond the central hub that Trem could see. Children played in the streets and townspeople carried on conversations while washing the laundry or fetching water from the well. As the group made their way into the square they were met with stares and whispers. Neep and Grimtooth drew the most discussion, but there were ample fingers pointed at the others. Ghost, having overtaken the others once they reached the outskirts of the village, rode through the town like a conquering general, looking neither left nor right but moving unstoppably onward and the people gave him a wide berth. By contrast Grimtooth and Logan waved and smiled at the children, who shied away in doubt and fear, while Trem and Jovan merely looked about them in curiosity. Diaga was farther back at the end of the line whispering to Neep in a soothing voice. The firecat seemed to grow less and less tense about entering the village as he spoke, but it was clear she was not fond of populated areas.

Trem wished he could relax, but he remained on alert, scanning the gaps between the buildings and attempting to ascertain the purpose of each structure and what lay beyond them. Too many times he had ridden into places such as this to find an ambush or some other danger looming. Jovanaleth however, was all smiles. "It's like being in Dragon's Watch again, a tiny section of Bladehome in the middle of nowhere."

Trem eyed him as he answered, "Does it truly resemble your city?"

Jovan nodded. "Bladehome was built entirely from stone buildings and there's no thatch anywhere. Much harder to burn in an attack."

"Ah, of course."

"The wizards of Ozmandias helped us raise it. One of them even remained once their work was complete to advise my father and mother, and to tutor me."

"Tutored by a wizard!" Trem was mildly astonished. "Did you learn any of Diaga's magic tricks?"

Jovan laughed. "No, I was taught history, mathematics, poetry, all the key subjects for a young lord. Dilekatha was a good teacher. He made everything seem interesting and important."

Trem considered his young companion. "Do you miss your home?"

Jovanaleth paused thoughtfully before replying, "I suppose I miss Bladehome, but with my father gone... in the end it is naught but cold wood and stone without friends and family to warm it."

"What about your mother?" Trem asked.

"She is very like my father," Jovan said, "and wouldn't stand by while the invaders built up their forces to come further south. She was readying to go to Aves and attempt to orchestrate some kind of treaty with the Eagle Knights when I left. In some ways, her mission is more impossible than our own."

Trem did not reply, sitting lost in thought as their group rode on through the center square of the town to the lone inn just beyond. Unlike the sprawling structure in Gi'lakil this was a small and squat place, very simple but well kept. The innkeeper, a kindly looking older woman, met them before the door. "I fear we may not have enough rooms for all of you, my lords."

Trem was the first to dismount, smiling and taking her hands in his. "Rooms are not necessary good woman, but we would like to stable our mounts for the day. We can pay you of course."

She smiled pleasantly at him. "Of course, my lord, of course."

Introductions were made and the kindly woman was careful to instruct the travelers on conduct while in the town. "You do not look the type to start trouble, but you do carry weapons. Be careful to keep them to yourselves now."

Grimtooth made a surprisingly elegant leg for his size and addressed her graciously, "Mah good lady, there be nothin' ta concern yer beautiful self with, Ah shall keep these 'ooligans in line."

The innkeeper nodded sagely and said, "Thank you, master Grimtooth. See to it that you do." With that she disappeared inside, leaving the travelers alone on the street. First Logan, swiftly followed by the others, burst into laughter at Grimtooth's gentlemanly display. Jovan wiped tears from his eyes and Diaga laughed so hard he sat on the ground holding his ribs, causing a confused Neep to drop next to him protectively.

Only Ghost was unmoved by the display. "I will head to the blacksmith if you fools can keep your wits about you for a few hours without me."

Logan, still laughing, waved him off and the Napalian strode away, angrily shifting his armor as he did. Diaga, now somewhat recovered, declared he would go perform some parlor tricks for the town's children until it was time to leave. Jovanaleth eagerly asked to join him and the two, along with Neep, headed for the town square talking excitedly. Logan watched them go and asked Trem, "Do you suppose they will be alright without us?"

Trem sighed and shrugged his shoulders to indicate he thought the answer mattered little. "If Diaga keeps his tricks simple they should be fine. We cannot treat them like children. They are old enough to look after one another."

Logan eyed Trem sideways. "An odd thing to say for someone who is about the same age."

Trem was unsure how to respond but Grimtooth saved him when he nodded agreeably and said, "Well then if that be ta verdict Ah say we 'ead inside an' grab some drink. It be too 'ot in the sun fer this orc."

"Grimtooth," Trem redirected the conversation quickly, "can I ask why you have that tattoo? I realize it is the symbol of Hawking House, like on Logan's armor, but why have it set into your skin?"

It was Logan who responded, "My father is responsible for that. Grim wanted to hold on to some of his orcish heritage, such as having the Hawking House tattooed on his chest like a clan sign. Many of the people in Angladais were aghast at such a 'barbaric' display, but it demonstrates how wedded Grimtooth is to both his traditions and the family he now calls his own."

The orc nodded sagely. "Sometimes it be ya roots that do 'old ya in ta ground ta most."

Trem and Logan exchanged smiles of approval and they went into the inn's common room. The place was compact but well lit and as nicely kept as it had appeared from the exterior. The furniture was all lovely carven wood, and though there was little of it it was spaced comfortably about the cozy room. The weather had been pleasant of late, so there was no fire, but there was a halfling man with a small instrument perched on a stool on a makeshift stage. He was in the midst of a cheery song and plucking away as they approached the bar languidly, taking in the scene.

> *"Come hither my lads, with your tankards of ale,*
> *And drink to the present before it shall fail;*
> *Pile each on your platter a mountain of beef,*
> *For 'tis eating and drinking that bring us relief."*

Apart from the performer, who was dressed audaciously in brightly colored cloth of white, blue, red, and gold, there was only one other patron. He was not far from the stage, a figure of human height but of race indeterminable due to his heavy black cloak and robes. He leaned against the wall, no food or drink at hand, and watched the three travelers enter the inn. The halfling also eyed the newcomers, and gave a wink and nod to them when they caught his eye, but continued his song:

> *"So fill up your glass,*
> *For life will soon pass;*
> *When you're dead ye'll ne'er drink to your king or your*
> *lass!"*

Grimtooth and Logan were admiring the wall tapestries and paintings while Trem went to the bar to order three tankards of house ale from the grizzled barkeep, who he assumed was the inn-keeper's husband. He could not help but continue to listen to the strange song, which had begun with and maintained a cheery tune, yet seemed to be veering darker in subject matter. As he was wait-ing for the man to fill the glasses he turned and leaned on the bar, watching the strumming halfling a bit longer.

> *"But fill up your goblets and pass 'em around—*
> *Better under the table than under the ground!*
> *So revel and chaff*
> *As ye thirstily quaff:*
> *Under six feet of dirt 'tis less easy to laugh!"*

Grimtooth and Logan seemed quite impressed with the perfor-mance, chuckling at the black humor and nodding in approval. Trem brought their mugs of ale over and the three took a seat near the entrance of the building, softly clinking cheers before they took their first sip. The ale was well made and Logan closed his eyes contented-ly. For his part, Grimtooth downed half the mug in one pull, breathed satisfactorily, and grinned impishly at Trem. The half-elf smiled back and was about to speak when he felt a tug at his traveling cloak and turned to see the halfling from the stage smiling toothily at him. "Hullo!"

Trem was confused and a little wary, but he answered, "Hello, can I help you?"

The halfling was of middle years for his race, perhaps fifty to sixty, and cheery enough. He had short curly black hair and a ready smile that betrayed his openness. If that alone hadn't told Trem he was a mite flamboyant, his bright blue tunic, complete with the red and golden puffy arms and elaborate trim, all atop sheer white breeches, certainly did. He was dressed well enough to be a noble, but outlandishly enough for a traveling jester, or Trem supposed, a child's idea of a minstrel.

The smaller man extended his hand. "The name's Gend, Sylras-tor Gend, renowned hero, performer, lover, and thief."

Trem smiled in spite of himself and returned the handshake warmly. "Trem Waterhound, a simple traveler. What brings you to me, Master Gend?"

The halfling waved the title away. "Just Gend, old boy, Gend will do." He gathered himself as if to ask something significant and gestured to the dark clothed figure in the corner. "My friend Rath and I, we wondered if you and your mates might join us for a round or two? It's terribly lonely here and the townsfolk are dreadfully boring. Most don't even come to hear me play, and I dare say I'm rather good."

Trem eyed the cloaked shadow still leaning against the wall in the back. "No offense, Gend, but your friend does not sit well with me."

Gend looked back at Rath as if seeing him for the first time. "Really? Must be all that black he wears. Not to worry, he's a simple adventurer like me, not as well known I assure you, but a member of my trade nonetheless." He looked at Trem beseechingly and said, "Please, Trem, we only want to swap stories."

Trem sighed. "Well Gend I suppose if that is all, but we have few stories to share."

Gend clapped his hands. "That's fine, fine! I like telling stories almost as much as hearing them!"

Trem followed the unusual character back to his table, waving over Grimtooth and Logan, who were back at the bar to refill Grimtooth's drained tankard. The two exchanged glances and shrugged, bringing over their drinks and nodding politely at the two strangers. The half-elf sat first, eyeing the smiling Gend and his shady companion, who nodded slightly. Trem could see that he had brown eyes but that was all he could discern. The rest of his body was hidden completely by black cloth wrapped round his head, face, and even his hands. He appeared tall, elven tall even, yet strong, as he filled out his ample robes just casually leaning. Logan and Grimtooth sat, introducing themselves and getting enthusiastic shakes from Gend and the same slight inclination of Rath's head.

"Well now, isn't this nice!" Gend rubbed his hands together excitedly. "Finally some real people to talk to, not these dreary townsfolk. I am from Delmore country originally, it's a few days ride east of here and I must say I have not been this bored since I left home."

Logan sipped his ale before asking, "You left home out of boredom?"

Gend nodded emphatically. "Oh yes, I had many skills that were not looked kindly upon there. Lockpicking, horse thieving, anything involving risks and stealth, I am your halfling! Perhaps you have heard of me?"

Trem shook his head. "I am afraid I have not been away from home in some time."

"We are from Angladais," Logan added soothingly, "we may have missed some of your more famous escapades."

Gend was slightly downtrodden. "Still I would have thought the tales would have spread that far by now. Ah well! What about you, any grand adventures to share?"

Trem answered him swiftly, "Actually, we met but a few days ago. We intend to head to Southron with a few other companions."

"Southron. That is a distance quite far to travel."

It was the first time Trem or the others had heard Rath speak. His voice was rough and almost guttural, reminding Trem of a wolf or bear growling. The strange man continued in an accent none of the travelers recognized. "You intend not to travel the woodland road? You seek, perhaps, another way?"

Trem immediately felt wary, but he remembered what he had told the others. They needed someone who could show them a way south and this Rath sounded like he knew of one. Trem gathered himself before replying, "One of our company claims to know a road south exists, beyond the town of Delmore, but any path to Southron is what we seek. Could you explain one to us? It sounds as though you've been there before."

Rath suddenly grew very tense. "This way, it is not safe. You would do better to go back as you came."

Logan placed his hand on Rath's arm, pulling his attention back to the Angladaic. "We cannot go back. Now do you know a way or not?"

"You will not touch me again, knight." Rath's eyes burned into the armored man and he pulled his arm free and moved suddenly away from the wall and began making his exodus toward the stairs of the inn. "Gend I must gather my things. We should leave soon."

Gend waved him away. "Oh get going you! You're ruining my fun! Go on, go on!"

Rath swept across the common room and up the stairs. Trem's eyes followed him, but then Gend was gesturing to the others to lean in, as though he had a secret. Trem turned his focus back to the halfling. "Listen, Rath does know a way to Southron, and it is dangerous, but I know it too! I have been through it a few times! I could get you there and quickly out again better than anyone alive!"

Trem and Logan exchanged a brief glance. The half-elf took the lead. "Gend, this is a very appealing proposition of yours. We need to consult our friends first. Will you and Rath wait a while for us?"

"Of course, of course." The halfling was all smiles, but suddenly his face grew very dark. "But hurry, Trem! I do not know how long I can convince him to wait. We should leave swiftly, especially if your mission is dire." He pointed a diminutive finger at the half-elf. "You must not dawdle. Go!"

Trem and the others were outside quickly and exchanged mixed opinions on the odd pair they had found within the inn. "Ah dinnae like 'em, Trem, either one."

Trem was surprised. "Either? Gend is a harmless talespinner, and if he knows the way."

"I agree with Grimtooth, Trem," interrupted Logan, "Rath may seem more dangerous, but I doubt Gend is as famous as he says. He could get us lost on this road of his, or worse."

Grimtooth nodded. "It would be better ta wait fer more reliable fellows. Or ta simply follow Ghost's road, whateva it is."

"There is no need to convince me, I am not the leader of this little expedition!" Trem's explosive outburst caught the others off guard. "You two may do as you please, I am going to find Ghost."

Logan tried to quell Trem's sudden temper. "Alright Trem, if that is what you want." The half-elf made no move to respond, walking swiftly away from the bloodbrothers. Logan sighed, "Maybe we are wrong about Gend. We do need a guide."

Grimtooth shouldered his axe. "Aye, and mebbe Diaga was wrong about Trem."

The orc strode off toward the town center, leaving his companion alone with his thoughts. Realizing he might be by himself for a while, Logan shook his head and started after the orc talking softly to himself, "What does it matter anyway? Every step we take south leads us farther from home. I wonder if we will ever get to go back."

Trem stormed off in the direction of the blacksmith shop, his thoughts in turmoil. Logan and Grimtooth's behavior had infuriated him because it put a weight on him he did not desire. Trem's sole duty was to Jovanaleth, even if Kurven had made inroads to show him the greater weight of his actions. Trem had no desire to be in a position where his decisions affected the fates of others, given how hard it was just guiding himself. He picked his head up and realized the distance to the blacksmith was quite short and so he slowed his pace. There was no proper building; just a large brick and mortar forge with a heavy canvas awning. Trem did his best to gather himself before getting any closer.

As he reached the blacksmith shop he paused, glancing under its heavy canvas awning to watch Ghost and the smith. Ghost was leaning back on a stool against one of the shop's heavy support beams while the smith was toiling away, apparently guided by several sketches that Ghost had given him. The Napalian spotted Trem looking in and motioned him over.

Trem sat next to Ghost without comment. For a while the two remained there, unmoving in the eerie glow of the smithy's dancing flames, and then Ghost turned to Trem. "It should not be more than five or six days hard ride southeast before we get to Delmore. Before I came to Gi'lakil, I had heard there is a road south from there, past the forest and leading to the desert beyond. The trick will be finding it."

Trem nodded and said, "I heard the same from someone else." He related Gend's tale and offer, emphasizing that he thought it might be their only option.

Ghost shrugged and furrowed his brow in thought. "Rather dangerous to go trusting strangers on a perilous road."

"I trust Gend."

"And the other?"

Trem paused. "No, I do not like the feel of him."

Ghost accepted this without comment and they sat in silence a while longer, listening to the rhythmic clanging of the smith's hammer. Finally Ghost spoke again, "Unfortunately, I have no choice. We must get to Southron at all costs, and if this Gend knows the road well enough to have traveled it before, he's a better guide than I."

"Why are we in such a hurry, Ghost?" Trem turned to face him. "Evading the creatures from the Inn of the Four Winds? Fair enough, but we've seen no sign of them and you continuously pull us southward. For what?"

"I told you, I must retrieve something in Southron."

"What is it?"

Ghost suddenly became angry. "Why should it matter half-elf? You are stuck with me now!"

"I will not be partnered with a man who has evil intents."

Ghost laughed. "Oh I see, Trem Waterhound has had nothing but honest causes all his life. You are as pompous and foolish as that damned Angladaic."

Trem spat on the ground angrily, rounding on Ghost. "My causes are not of your concern! I promised you nothing. I only swore to help Jovan find his father. Anything else we take by choice alone!"

Ghost stood then, leaning close to Trem. "And if the boy wants to join me when he learns what we are after? What will you do then? You want to know what I seek, fine! Bring the others here, ready to ride, and I will tell you what you want to know."

Trem spun on his heel and walked out of the smith's shop. Ghost's voice followed him out of the heavy curtain as he brushed it aside: "Just remember Trem, you chose to help him. What if he decides he doesn't want your help any longer?"

Diaga and Jovanaleth found time to chat as they made their way to the town square. Jovan was curious to a fault, and the display of power Diaga had shown in the Inn of the Four Winds had caught his attention. He had heard the story of Diaga attending a sort of mage's school at Ozmandias, though he was not entirely clear on why the younger man had to go to a school to learn magic. As they walked, he put the question to the young spellweaver, "I thought that magic was something you were born with, not a discipline that you studied?"

"To a degree magic is bred into a person," Diaga explained. "Though no one knows how certain people develop an affinity for it. Still, a mage, someone like me, has a capability to use magic, but will never truly learn to without instruction. We mages must study the language of the gods and learn to speak and even write it properly, so we may lend power to the words we invoke. There is a price to be paid however."

Jovan looked at him quizzically and Diaga continued, "When a mage casts a spell he must give something of himself to provide it with arcane energy. Simply knowing the proper words, gestures, or scripts is not enough. The more powerful the spell the more that one must sacrifice. The more one studies and uses magic, the more arcane strength they can give to their spells. It exhausts the caster once they use too much and we must enter a deep resting state, much like the one Trem was in this morning, to regain what we have given of ourselves. This is not the only method of using magic. There are other forms, priests for example."

"Priests?" Jovan looked puzzled. "Do they not also study the language of the gods?"

"In a way you are right, but a priest serves a particular god, and does not study their language so much as their ideology. When a priest uses the magic of their deity, they must pray for the gift of that god's power. The stronger their conviction the greater their ability with magic and the more powerful they become. They study the teachings of the god they serve. The more they study and believe in their faith the greater their mastery of their boons. Take Logan, if he serves Paladinis well he will become a paladin and receive many boons from him, the stronger his belief in him the more potent his magical strength will become. Regardless of how one summons magic, they must spend time in meditation and study of a kind to harness it."

Jovan felt he understood. "So there is no inherent ability to wield magic. It takes a dedication of some sort."

"For the most part yes," Diaga glanced at him, "though there are some who are believed to possess magic in their blood."

"Trem explained that to me, like how some elves can sense arcane power."

Diaga shook his head. "No, I mean those who can truly wield magic as if it were a part of them, though only one race is believed to possess such power. The legends call them the Revenants."

Jovan looked at the mage in amused disbelief. "But they are just that, legends."

Diaga shrugged and replied, "Some believe they exist, but are rare and in hiding. Revenants are said to be born with magic a part of them, as surely as our arms and legs are a part of us. A Revenant wields magic like a physical extension, though his or her power is not unlimited. The stories claim that a Revenant specializes in a type of magic and enhances their skill in it through constant use. A Revenant may learn to call upon lightning and focus his exertion in that ability, but his strength with conjuring fire or ice will never match it."

"So it is like training with a weapon, the more you use a sword the better you become, but you will never be as effective with a bow."

"And like physical training it takes effort. A Revenant must use magic frequently to become stronger in it, just as you must practice forms with your sword to stay skilled."

"I think I understand," Jovan said thoughtfully, "but they are still a fairy tale. No one has ever even seen a Revenant."

"None of you had ever seen a firecat before, and yet Neep exists."

Jovan digested that comment with a smile and patted Diaga's shoulder. "Well then I shall suspend my doubt for now, and call you wise if we ever meet a Revenant."

Diaga grinned. "A deal, Jovanaleth. Now, let us see if we can rouse the attention of these townsfolk."

Diaga had learned parlor tricks from many of the wizards and students during his time at Ozmandias. Even before he was enrolled there, he had developed a deftness of hand that enabled him to perform basic feats with his thin fingers. None of these skills involved magical talent, but rather dexterity and sleight of hand. The ability to control something like a coin so fluidly as to make it seem alive as it danced through fingers improved an aspiring wizard's skills of concentration and weaving runes or sigils. The complex hand motions required to effectively use magic took years of practice, but the naturally developed motions of a common street illusionist could give an aspiring sorceror an advantage.

Unlike his counterparts at Ozmandias, Diaga had taken all of these tricks quite seriously, and they had fed him and Neep when they would certainly have gone hungry without them. Still, Diaga's real passion was performing for children, whom he deeply loved. His own broken childhood made him almost desperate to brighten the youthful moments of others. While the other members of the party were gathering information or resupplying, Diaga was thoroughly enjoying himself.

Once the children of the village had realized the mage was not going to turn them into toads, they began to watch him more carefully, with curious rather than fearful eyes. Diaga had walked from the inn to the town center, dancing a coin through the fingers of both hands. Jovan had walked alongside him, as agape as the children who watched from the shelter of their doorways. Neep prowled along behind, looking directly ahead and drawing as much attention as the mage through her sheer uniqueness.

When Diaga completed the five-minute walk from the inn to the town's central well he had a gaggle of intrigued townspeople, old and young, behind him. Once he entered the square, he turned to face the crowd, which stopped short, still apparently unsure of the mage. Diaga smiled slightly and tossed one of the coins into the air. The crowd followed the shimmering gold with their eyes, losing it in the afternoon sun. They waited but the coin never came down. All eyes turned to Diaga as he sighed heavily. Suddenly he glared at a young boy in the crowd and cried, "You there! You little thief! Give me back my coin!"

The stunned boy looked around hoping the man in the grey robes was speaking to someone else, but as Diaga approached the crowd backed away from him, leaving the child alone to face the mage. "Well?" Diaga said, "Where are you hiding it?"

The boy shook his head emphatically. "I don't have it mister."

"Do not lie to me! I saw you grab it out of the air!" Diaga was right in front of the boy looking very grim, when suddenly he gave a knowing smile. "Oho! I see it now, good try, but I believe this is mine!"

Diaga's hand shot forward and pinched the boy's ear. The child cried out and clutched the side of his head to be sure the appendage was still there. Then the crowd, which had gone deathly quiet, burst out in uproarious laughter. Diaga held the coin aloft. "Fancy that, a boy hiding gold in his ear!"

With a smile he handed the coin to the stunned boy, who still held the left side of his head, and turned back to the well followed by thunderous applause. From then on, the show took off with further sleight-of-hand tricks, juggling routines done by Neep, and the occasional illusion tossed in to spice things up. Jovanaleth applauded as hard as anyone else and laughed louder than most as Diaga and Neep continued their good-natured pranks on the villagers.

Then Diaga turned to Jovan, stretching his arms wide and calling out in a booming voice, "And now, to perform feats of incredible mastery with his magnificent sword, Jovanaleth, Prince of the Blade!"

The applause was deafening, but a shocked Jovan did not respond until Diaga jerked his head several times to get his attention. With a nervous smile, Jovan walked up to the wizard, whispering in his ear, "Diaga, I do not know any sword tricks like your coins."

Diaga did not even glance at the warrior, but kept smiling at the crowd. Then Jovan heard him mutter from the corner of his mouth, "Just do some forms with your sword, typical practice maneuvers, they should be impressed by that."

Jovan swallowed and nodded, forcing a smile for the benefit of the crowd as Diaga announced his name again. "And Jovanaleth, do not make a fool of yourself," the mage ribbed him, "Grimtooth and Logan will never let you forget it."

As Diaga slipped aside, Jovan glanced at the crowd to see Logan and Grimtooth standing at the back. The orc, who had a small child from the town perched on his shoulders, waved one huge hand at the prince. Logan only winked broadly.

Jovan steeled himself and drew his sword. Holding it before him in both hands he felt the perfect balance of his family blade and suddenly a fire erupted within him. The crowd had gone silent as he closed his eyes, and when they opened Jovan began to move.

He started simply, shifting from one basic slash or thrust to the next. Then he began to whirl faster and the forms grew more and more complex. Jovanaleth had never mastered all the exquisite movements his father tried to teach him when he was in Bladehome, but he had seen them and he remembered. He spun like a roiling storm, yet his exertion was limited and he felt no fatigue, he only felt alive.

As Jovanaleth spun from a thrust and into a swift vertical cut, he felt his blade strike something hard. There stood Trem, his own blade drawn, holding Jovan's sword on the crosspiece. Trem smiled at him and whispered, "You practice well, so let us see how you fight."

The crowd roared at the sight of a challenger and the two stepped back and saluted. Grimtooth cried from the back of the audience, "Set 'im on 'is arse, Jovanaleth!" The audience exploded in laughter that quickly tailed off as the fighters dropped into crouches. There was an audible gasp as the two rushed each other and their blades locked. The battle began.

Jovan had only seen Trem fight in the inn at Gi'lakil and he had been impressed then, but this was far more daunting than he had expected. Trem seemingly flowed from one strike to the next and for the first several moments all Jovan could do was parry or dip out of the way and retreat. Trem was effortless in his movements. He simply struck, shifted and struck again. Jovan found himself dodging, trying to make Trem miss utterly so that he could counter, but the former hermit was always a step ahead.

Jovanaleth finally chose not to deflect an oncoming slash, but instead ducked quickly as Trem swung lazily at head level. The warrior seemed surprised when his blade passed unimpeded over his foe, connecting only with the air. He was even more surprised when Jovan swept his feet from underneath him. The half-elf recovered as he fell; rolling away and springing swiftly back to his feet. The crowd was applauding Jovanaleth's sudden return to the fight. Trem reset himself and smiled, but Jovan was into the battle now and he lashed out quickly.

Trem found he was now the one on the defensive, warding off Jovan's blows with his sword. His attempts to get back in control of the fight were lax. Jovan was battling like a man possessed. Launching himself forward, the prince finally put himself off balance, and Trem swung downward to disarm him, but Jovan had roped him in. He spun as Trem slashed aggressively, and his blade hurled Trem's away. The prince stood, his chest heaving, and the stunned crowd was silent for some time before bursting into whoops and cheers of delight.

Jovan stood, surrounded by villagers who were patting him on the back and exclaiming at his skill, unsure of precisely what had just happened. Then Trem was there in front of him, sheathing his sword at his side and placing a hand on the boy's shoulder. "That," he shook his head, "was most impressive."

"I'm not sure what happened." Jovan shuddered and blinked as though coming out of a trance.

Trem gripped him by the shoulder. "Your instinct took over. Your father would be proud."

Jovan looked at the blade in his hands as if seeing it for the first time. "It was like he was here with me."

"I noticed."

The two stood silently for a moment while the crowd dispersed. Jovan slowly sheathed the heavy broadsword and finally began to look around. Logan and Grimtooth were there with him, holding the reins to his horse and their own. Diaga was coming toward them leading his own steed, with Neep loping at his side.

"We are leaving?" Jovan asked.

Trem paused, then nodded slowly. "We have to pick up some friends on our way out."

Jovan seemed to gather himself. "Alright, well, let's move on then."

They turned and headed back to the inn. Grimtooth and Logan praised Jovanaleth up and down for his skill in combat, but the young man was only half aware of their presence. Trem and Diaga had their heads together in front of them, talking quietly, and all Jovan could see in his mind was the effortless movement of Trem's blade and his own, seemingly inborn, response. His mind remained clouded a moment longer, then he pulled himself back to the present and fumbled through a few gracious responses to the Angladaic and the orc as the edge of the village loomed before them.

Ghost had by now met with the infamous Gend and was not, as Trem had been, amused. He found the halfling annoying and thought he talked to an extent that was unnecessary. Given his distaste for the flamboyant taleteller, Ghost had attempted to communicate with his strange companion instead, but Rath refused to open his mouth despite all of the Napalian's efforts. This had, in turn, led to Ghost being in a foul mood, so he sat in silence on his powerful warhorse waiting for the rest of the companions to arrive. All the while Gend sat on his diminutive pony below the saddle of the Napalian, chattering away about great adventures involving places and people that Ghost had never heard of and doubted really existed.

In the drone of Gend's incessant rambling, Ghost drifted to other thoughts. The Napalian was old, too old for all of this travel and adventure. He was supposed to be home, his children on his knee, his military salary rolling in steadily and keeping them safe and fed.

Tears threatened to cloud his vision for a moment as Ghost sought his conviction. There was no more family, no more hope for his military career. There was only revenge, and that would keep him going longer than rest or peace ever could. Gend was still talking about his ridiculous escapades, but Ghost blocked him out. He could now see the others coming in from the town square. Ghost prepared himself. He was not given to long speeches. This explanation Trem demanded was not required. The half-elf never said he would leave the party if he did not get one, yet Ghost was going to explain, and he could not truly say why, but he felt a great need to expound, at least in part, on his mission.

The others rode up slowly, stopping before the three who had been waiting. Ghost nodded to each in turn, waiting first for Trem to retrieve his horse from the inn's post before speaking. He cleared his throat, "I have been asked to inform all of you of the mission we are going to undertake. If what I say is not acceptable to anyone, you may leave once we are safely out of Legocia and I will not hold it against you." Ghost's eyes said differently, but he had spoken what in his mind was expected of him. This speech was going badly already. "I told you that we had to reach Southron, to retrieve an item. The nature of that which I seek I had originally planned to keep secret, but I have been persuaded to do otherwise and perhaps when you understand what I am after, why I am being hunted, it will make you realize you see why you should help me."

Ghost paused and the others waited for him to continue. "I am, rather I was, a Napalian soldier, an officer. When the invaders took our country they killed my family, my wife and my children. I had two sons and two daughters, as precious to me as their mother, and they were all of them taken from me. The Nerothians stole my entire life." Ghost took a deep breath, his moment of vulnerability passing quickly and replaced by the unending anger. "I want them to pay. I want to kill the bastards, and this thing that lies to the south could be what allows me to do it."

Trem crossed his arms and said quietly, "Ghost, we need to know what it is you seek."

Ghost looked at him, and the fervor in his eyes was frightening. "There is a city in Southron, amid the Endless Sands. Once, when the roads through Silverleaf were still active, some used to trade with the people there. The city's name is Yulinar, home to a race of black-skinned men we Napalians call the Sun People. They prize knowledge and understanding of the world over all else, worshipping each god equally and dedicating a great number of their people to the cataloguing of history and legend. In my father's house there was a book, supposedly written by one of these men, which spoke of weapons forged by the gods themselves. I am going to this Yulinar to find out where those weapons are."

The others withdrew to smaller debates as they considered Ghost's mission. Trem eyed them all in turn. Grimtooth and Logan were in deep conversation with one another, Jovanaleth appeared to be lost amid his own thoughts, and Diaga was merely watching Ghost with a fierce interest he had not shown before. Gend was looking thoughtfully at Rath, who had not shifted his gaze from the Napalian as he spoke. For himself, Trem was not sure how he felt about Ghost's quest; it stank of too much zealous rage. It was also undoubtedly dangerous, and Trem was pledged another duty, a responsibility that struck him as right and honorable. And yet, like Ghost, the potency of these weapons called to him and that nearly forgotten time when he was enamored with heroes of legend. What if this was a real chance to seize the dreams of his childhood? Despite himself, Trem found he was far more intrigued than he had expected to be.

The half-elf realized Diaga was speaking, "As intriguing as this tale is you have no way to know if the city exists, where it is, if the weapons are real, or even if they are whether these Sun People know where to find them. It sounds like too much of a gamble to me."

Logan cut in ahead of Ghost's reply. "But if it does exist, Diaga, we could save Angladais, my father, and my people. You said yourself that fortress was made by powerful magic, and these invaders claim to be acting in service to the god Neroth." Grimtooth nodded in sage agreement.

Ghost spoke quietly, reverently, "It could save us all, Angladaic."

They were silent, even Gend, who had opened his mouth several times to chime in, but missed his chance. Trem roiled in the silence, his logic battling emotion. Something told him that this was wrong, very wrong, that he and Jovanaleth should leave. But that was not what he did. Instead he sat up straight in his saddle and looked Ghost in the eye. "Weapon or not, this seems a mission bred from honorable intentions. I will go."

Ghost nodded, visibly thankful. Jovanaleth followed on Trem's heels saying, "I will go too."

"Aye," said Grimtooth, "Ah 'ave lil' else ta pass mah time doin'"

Logan agreed. "If it can save my people, I will follow."

Diaga looked briefly at Neep, and then sighed in resignation. "We will go," he said quietly.

"Well then," Ghost turned to Gend, "you had better know the way, halfling."

Gend brightened considerably. "Oh yes certainly! Well I must say this should be a very rousing expedition indeed, yes!"

Ghost grunted, "Then get going, move!"

Gend spun quickly and spurred his small pony southeast, followed immediately by the silent Rath, the dimunitive halfling still chattering away enough for both of them, "Well, I say, we are on our way to this adventure rather fast. I do hope this pace slows before long!"

The others were soon behind Ghost and their guides, Diaga turning to wave at the few lingering townspeople one last time before launching his steed after the others. Jovan and Trem were the last two to depart, Jovan swallowing and smiling nervously. "Well, I never expected any of this when I left home."

Trem shifted in his saddle. "Things never go quite the way you expect, do they?"

Jovanaleth looked at him. "You learn that through your own adventures?"

Trem shook his head ruefully as he replied, "No, I learned that from fighting you."

Jovan laughed and then whooped in surprise as Trem slapped his horse, launching it forward and nearly unbalancing him. Jovan glared back as his mount pressed onward to catch the others, only to see Trem laughing so hard he was fighting to stay in his own saddle. As the half-elf regained control and rode after the others he neglected to notice the gathering storm clouds, far to the east.

Chapter 10

The Great Northern Waste is a treacherous land, full of unseen ice chasms, thin frozen lakes where the frosted coating is no thicker than a sword blade, and ravenous predators that will kill anything to stay alive. The Napalians, a nation of hardy humans renowned for their toughness and courage, call the Waste home, along with the dreaded forest of Whitewood, and the even more desolate lands of the Frozen Reach. Most people would look at the lands north of the God's Bones Mountains and leave them be, or remain entirely on the thin strip abutting the northern foothills of those mountains called the Springtide Steppe, where the weather is at least seasonal. Not the Napalians. From the very beginning they have been explorers and settlers, carving out homes in the worst of the cold climes. The houses of Napal formed slowly over time, with violent battles for supremacy marking most of the nation's early history. In fact, the Unification of Napal did not take place until the Age of Faith, as most of the thanes were unwilling to swear loyalty to a singular ruler.

Apart from Napal City, a great bastion of civilization in an uncivilized territory, there are several scattered towns of significant size, formed from the efforts of people across the inhospitable landscape. Napal City lies at the edge of the Springtide Steppe, with Lowinter to the east, just north of the Pillars of Light. In contrast, the towns of the Frozen Reach, which rarely see temperatures warm enough to completely thaw the lakes and streams of their land, are small and compact. Crestwind, Tianis, and Winter's Folly form a stretch of fishing towns and mines for the precious dark ice, valued by smiths and mages across Teth-tenir, all of which allows the residents to narrowly eke out a living each year. The region west of the Dragonscale Mountains is almost bereft of wildlife or arable land, and only Sheerwater Cove along the western coast houses a concentrated number of people. The lands around Whitewood, just north of Napal City, hold the two most populous towns in the nation outside of the capital. Hethegar, to the east, is a hunting and logging town of considerable size, but it is Glaciar, a walled town nearly as old as Napal City, that has played the largest part in the nation's history.

Glaciar has been besieged and severely damaged several times. Upon its founding, an internal feud over mining rights had led to the formation of House Erefoss, whose members were sealed beneath the Dragonscales and managed to find passages west that eventually brought them above ground on the other side of the mountains.

During the Unification of Napal, Glaciar was the target of Vladar Konunn, the self-proclaimed High Thane of Napal City, and the people of Glaciar had to call on the orcs of the Sundered Blades Clan to overthrow the mad ruler. When the Arcane Wars led to the invasion of the Napalian Empire, the forces of the God-Sorceror had besieged Glaciar, a fight they only overcame with the aid of the entire Napalian nation and several foreign entities. In each case, House Squall had been the ever-present force in Glaciar. It was they who had sealed the mines and trapped their foes of House Erefoss within, it was Uthgar Squall who had rallied the people of the north against Vladar Konunn, and it was Alfhilda Squall, at only sixteen, who had led her people against the armies of the God-Sorceror.

The first towns of Napal taken by Wolfbane and the Nerothians had been those in the Frozen Reach. Caught unaware and unprepared, they had fallen without much of a fight. Most of the thanes who ruled those towns were permitted to keep their titles and continue their duties, but their brethren from Hethegar and Glaciar had responded by trying to fight back and free their countrymen. Algathor Squall had been the renowned and beloved thane of his house for some time before the invasion began, but had passed on his duties to his son, Greymane, with the ascension of Reghar Holt as the new High Thane of Napal. Under the leadership of Greymane Squall, commander of the Napalian armies, a disastrous counterattack had been attempted in the north that resulted in the death of Thane Fernal Hethegar. Greymane then fled Glaciar and his home with his family: his wife, two daughters, and two sons. Algathor chose to stay behind and hold onto the family's longhouse out of pride and no small amount of stubbornness. The rest of the Squalls reached Napal City and its high stone walls ahead of the oncoming Nerothian army, where Greymane set to advising the young Reghar on the defense of his city and castle.

What Algathor could not have known when he abdicated command of his house to his son was that Greymane, while a gifted military leader, had entered into agreements of questionable foresight with Frothgar Konunn. The thane of House Konunn was involved in all manner of illegal activities within the city of Napal: prostitution, gambling, and the trafficking of slaves. Greymane agreed to look the other way as Reghar Holt's military advisor in exchange for Frothgar helping to build his reputation with the people of Napal City via his network of rumor-spreading spies and thieves. Frothgar quickly turned his knowledge of Greymane's lax enforcement of laws to his advantage, first by blackmailing him into delaying his venture north to aid the towns of the Frozen Reach, under threat of exposing his turning a blind eye to the corruption within Napal City. When Greymane finally did bring his army northward Frothgar had bought Wolfbane time to lay an ambush that decimated the Napalian forces. The spymaster then continued to use his influence over Greymane to work his greatest deceit of all.

Daerveron had, by that time, infiltrated the city and made himself at home in the dungeons of the castle, undetected by those living there. It was he who, under Frothgar's guidance, went to Greymane and offered him a deal. If he would betray his people and open the gates of the city, he and his family would be spared and permitted to leave, while the illusion that Greymane had stood by the High Thane and resisted to the last would persist. The traitorous Napalian, knowing the depleted forces of his army could not withstand a siege from the greater force of Wolfbane, agreed. One night, he surreptitiously opened the eastern gate of the city and watched, ashamed, from the battlements of the castle as the enemy took his home street by street.

When the invaders strode triumphantly into the hall of Napal City Castle, Greymane was there beside the young Reghar Holt advising him to surrender for the sake of his people and himself. But Reghar, though young and inexperienced, was also proud and valiant. He would not kneel to Wolfbane or his army, preferring death instead. Admittedly impressed by the younger man's bravery, Wolfbane had him thrown in prison beneath his own castle. What has become of Reghar since his imprisonment is unknown.

But for Greymane the outcome was far worse. When he took Reghar's place as the authority surrendering the city and empire to the Nerothians, Wolfbane revealed that Frothgar had been working for him all along. He called Greymane the worst kind of traitor, one who turned his back on his duty for personal pride and survival rather than belief in some greater good. Wolfbane ordered Greymane and his entire family arrested, but the thane's sons, Squalls through and through, fought back and were killed. His eldest daughter tried to flee and was captured and reportedly raped by several of Frothgar's men before dying in the dungeons with her mother and sister. Greymane was imprisoned near them, and he heard his own family curse his name as his wife, her heart broken, died shortly after his daughter. When he managed to orchestrate his escape from his cell, Greymane went looking for his lone surviving daughter, but the chamber where she had been held was empty. The former thane of House Squall fled the castle and city, and no one knows what became of him.

What Greymane had not known was that his daughter, Raymir, had survived. Daerveron had taken a personal interest in managing the prisoners in the dungeons of the castle, and he had sensed her emerging potency in the arcane. Hoping to turn her into a loyal and useful servant, he was rebuffed by her staunch adherence to the Napalian nation and her, now greatly reduced, family. Greymane had fled, leaving his name to his only remaining daughter, and Raymir had proudly done her best to uphold her ancestry. Even as it became apparent to Daerveron that she would never serve him, the frustration her continued survival brought to Caermon Erefoss pleased him to no end. Raymir was allowed to remain in the library of Napal City

Castle, where the dark wizard watched Saltilian's futile attempts to woo her fail miserably.

For over a year, Raymir had to stand by as her people were exploited and enslaved, sometimes killed for the slightest violation of the new, draconian laws of Wolfbane's regime. Valissa Ulfrunn, once a servant of the Napalian Empire herself, sided with the harsh treatment of the people, openly decrying the weak rulers who had let her family of Ulfrunn and the town of Tianis fall without resistance to the invaders. Raymir became angrier and angrier, though she directed her fury not at the invaders, but at her father whom she deemed responsible for these atrocities. Raymir suspected that her father had managed to escape the city and flee to an easier life elsewhere, spared the shame of his sins and the righteous anger of the people he had abandoned. As far as she was concerned, he was dead and gone.

Meeting Edge while working in the library was the first time in that hard year she caught a glimmer of hope. He had been standing in the main room, which was well kept and dust free unlike the stacks around it. He held an ancient, leather-bound volume in one hand and leafed through the pages with the other. Once he found what he wanted he smiled contentedly and settled into one of the room's overstuffed armchairs to read. Raymir watched him with only cursory interest, but made it a point to check what volume he had selected from the shelf, since she expected he would simply abandon the book when he was done for her to find and replace. The location of the chosen tome surprised her, and she observed him further.

Given his appearance, Raymir thought the text would be military strategies or accounts of great campaigns. She was surprised to see it was instead *A History of Teth-tenir: Legends and Myths*. It happened to be one of her own favorites. She was drawn toward Edge before realizing she had exposed herself, and when he gestured her over she was too frightened not to obey. But rather than question why she was staring at Wolfbane's favored commander, he instead asked, "Have you read this?"

Taken aback Raymir hurriedly replied, "Yes, my lord."

Setting the book down, Edge turned to her and his powerful green eyes stunned Raymir from the first moment they met her own; entirely green eyes. "I am no lord, my lady, just call me Edge."

His smile was genuine. "Raymir." She extended her hand.

"Delighted," he answered taking it gently, "now, I would like to know: what do you think of this book?"

There followed that afternoon, and well into the evening, a long discussion of the massive volume of fact and potential fiction on the history of their world. It was apparent, perhaps from those first few moments, that love had blossomed between them. From then on, Raymir became happier and more optimistic once again. Edge would visit her late at night, sometimes happy, often depressed. He told her all about life with Wolfbane before he had accepted this dread task of conquest and domination. How he and his slighter twin brother Aydwulf had followed the great warrior, learning his trade, mastering their own weapons. Aydwulf had been left behind in Ilanis as the invasion was planned, and where Edge had seen changes for ill in their master, his brother had seen ambition well placed. Aydwulf's task had been to rally the people in Westia to Neroth's cause, and since leaving him Edge had received no word of his twin. Raymir comforted and consoled him, and together they had hatched a plan for escape. The addition of Romund had been an unexpected turn of fortune.

Following the harrowing flight from Napal City, the three fugitives had left the caverns and headed north towards the traditional Squall seat of Glaciar in search of provisions and a map to find the possible location of the Twisted Spire. Glaciar would be few days north and west of Napal City, through the thinnest stretch of the Whitewood and the least imposing section of the Great Northern Waste. But even given the mildness of the region, the going was surprisingly easy for the northland. Still in the southerly region of the Waste, the party was not subjected to as much danger as they would be further north. Edge was glad that Raymir would not be around for that leg of the journey.

Despite his age, Romund was a rugged traveler carrying an equal amount of the supplies and pushing the pace rather than holding it back. Several times they had to hide at the roadside to avoid armed patrols of Nerothians, fearing one of them might recognize Edge even as he tried to hide his face and garb. Raymir became more and more upset upon seeing soldiers she had known under her father's command in Nerothian livery. Edge tried to comfort her but to no avail, her fury remained white hot in her eyes.

Even with the occasional patrols, the small group arrived at Glaciar without event or injury. The town with its low stone wall still showed the ravages of its initial capture a year before, though the burnt stone and broken buildings could have come from any number of previous staunch stands of resistance to would-be conquerors. The Nerothians had repaired none of the damage they had incurred and the townspeople were too few and stretched too thin to spend time cleaning up their broken lives.

Getting inside proved slightly more difficult than expected, as they could not enter the main gate where the guards accosted and searched every incoming traveler, taking his or her select goods and money as an "army tax." Aside from that, there was the issue of whether they were being pursued by their foes. Edge had an easily recognized face and they had heard from passing patrols enough to know that he was to be captured on sight, and killed if absolutely necessary. Romund finally solved the problem when he found a jagged hole, low in one of the walls and wide enough for them to crawl through. Edge went first, shoving his halberd in front of him. Raymir and Romund followed quickly and they took stock of their surroundings within the town.

There were signs of destruction everywhere in the alley they had entered. What had once been a shop of some sort was broken on three sides, only the wall that had once held its business sign still stood. Other buildings across the street had holes in roofs or walls and all were deserted. Romund was mesmerized. "Where are all the people?"

Edge hefted his weapon. "They are dead or in hiding. Wolfbane ordered any resistance was to be met with no quarter."

Romund shook his head in sadness, saying softly, "Such hatred, where does man harbor these vicious intents?"

Raymir walked forward determinedly. "Deep inside, but apparently not deep enough."

The main road the alley led into was little better. A few structures still stood and were apparently serviceable, but the people were haggard and weary. To Romund they seemed little more than listless bodies, just moving corpses mechanically going through old routines. The soldiery took what they wanted from the few food stalls along the roadside, paying for nothing, and the vendors had seemingly learned not to complain. Edge led the small group along the broken buildings and into another alley before the guards could notice them.

"We can't hide in the crowd, seeing as there is none," he remarked. "Raymir where does your grandfather live?"

The young woman thought a moment then pointed. "It's not far from here."

"Can you get us there quietly?"

She nodded again and the three took off swiftly through back alleys heading toward the rear of the town. Glaciar was built against the mountainside of a small peak of the same name, nestled in the lowest mountains of the Dragonscales that loomed large like a heavy backdrop on the settlement. Against this nearest rocky rise sat the Squall estate, a small rundown manor in the style of the longhouses of old, in which Raymir had grown up. Now only her grandfather remained with his servants, Renatus and Anhager.

When the trio reached the gate Raymir feared it was locked and that her grandfather had gone or worse, died. But when she touched the frosted iron bars she found they swung open easily. Slowly she entered the courtyard of the manor's garden. The bushes, evergreens really, had withered and died despite their resistance to the cold. The entire snow-covered entry had the feel of a graveyard rather than a home. The three crunched tensely up to the big oaken doors. Taking a deep breath Raymir grasped the heavy door knock, hanging from the house symbol of a jagged mountain, and thumped it three times slowly.

They stood waiting, Raymir remarking, "Renatus should have been here before I finished, he was always quick to answer the door."

Romund did his best to console her. "Perhaps he and your grandfather are at their afternoon tea, child."

They waited a few minutes longer, and just as Raymir was about to knock at the door again, it opened a crack, then flew wide as an elderly man, clad in light leather armor with a short sword at his side pulled it inward with a gasp, "Raymir! My gods I thought you were dead!"

The young woman lunged forward, embracing him fiercely. "Grandfather!"

Edge eyed the manor entrance. Several guards seemed to be investigating the exchange at Squall's front door. "Thane Squall, would you mind if we came inside?"

The old man eyed the soldiers at his gate and nodded grimly saying, "Come in, please, to the study with you. Raymir, show your friends the way while I bar this door."

The weary travelers followed Raymir into the small study while Algathor Squall, last of the male Squall line, watched the Nerothian soldiers turn and march back to the town gate before barring the door to his home.

Saltilian did not wait for the guards to report what he already knew through rumor, that the traitor and his accomplices had indeed entered the Squall manor. This would please the guards' captain, who had been looking for an excuse to evict Algathor Squall since he took command of the town's defenses. Saltilian could care less about the old man: he wanted his granddaughter back and her green-eyed lover captured or dead. The third man spotted traveling with them he knew nothing of, but seeing as he had aided in their escape, he too could die when Saltilian caught them. The wizard had been driven to great anger at learning they had managed to reach Glaciar unnoticed, and had rushed swiftly from just outside Napal City to reach the town before the three moved on.

How they had evaded his patrols he did not know. Once it became apparent they had escaped through a collapsed tunnel in Raymir's cottage within Castle Bane, Saltilian had felt certain that they would be heading back to Glaciar, her ancestral home. The only road from Napal City had been thick with the mage's patrols, told to stop any and all travelers looking for a red-haired woman and former lieutenant Edgewulf el Vac. The plan had failed, yet he did not like admitting he had been outsmarted.

Still, they had not been clever enough to see the wisdom in avoiding the Squall home. He had known where they were heading, and it had been simple enough to allow them to "sneak" into Glaciar. Once there, they would be cornered, with no passage out except by the front door, where he would be waiting with the soldiers of the Nerothian army. If necessary, he would force his way inside, take

181

Raymir, and burn the manor to the ground. A simple plan, but he consoled himself with the wisdom that the best plans often are the least complicated. He sat in the dining room set aside for him at the inn closest to the Squall estate. He had ordered the entire building cleared so he could set up shop where he liked, though in truth he had issued the command more to demonstrate his authority than out of need. The occupying force's captain came in after a sharp knock and Saltilian's stammering permission to enter.

"My lord," the captain saluted, "they are indeed the ones you seek."

"Excellent c-c-captain," Saltilian told him, "t-take your s-s-soldiers into the c-c-courtyard and wait for m-my signal."

The captain saluted again. "Yes, sir!"

Saltilian smiled as the guard left to muster his troops, enjoying the way in which he swiftly followed his orders. The haggard mage took his moment of solitude to reach into the large satchel he always carried and pulled forth a strange volume. It was small, not thick or built to the normal proportions of a magical text or history book. It looked, from a distance, more like a personal journal or carefully crafted notebook. Upon closer inspection, it was quite obviously something very different. It had a leathery coating dyed a deep purple, with a deeply-pressed silver symbol on the cover in the shape of a swirling vortex. Saltilian could have easily slipped it into his robe or boots had he wanted to conceal it, but, as he was alone, he held it before him and grinned with a satisfaction and pleasure that would have been unnerving to any observer.

Gently, reverently, he set the book on the table in front of him. He caressed the surface, too smooth and delicate to have been the skin of any beast, and felt the undulations of the swirling symbol as his fingers skimmed it. This had been his great accomplishment, the uncovering of a book that Daerveron had overlooked in the mass of texts in Castle Bane's libraries. Saltilian suspected its small size had made him pass it swiftly and without notice, but he himself had felt compelled to pick it up and open it. The text within was written in a strikingly choppy hand and was difficult to read, both due to the strange lettering and the fact that it was an odd mix of the common language, the arcane script of the gods, and other writing he did not recognize.

Oh, but the delicious wonders it contained! The book was a fit of ramblings and incoherencies, but where he had been able to understand anything, the shock of that clarity had been like a bonfire suddenly alighting in the deepest darkness. Saltilian had been trained, like all wizards of Teth-tenir, to believe that there were six distinct fields of magical study: Ruination, Disruption, Natural, Conjuring, Regeneration, and Degeneration. But this wonderous item implied another kind of eldritch magic, one far older and greater than that of the established schools of study that now seemed trivial in their organization and narrow in the scope of their power. This text was something else. Something greater, and the longer Saltilian had possessed it the more compelled he felt to read it, to caress it, to simply assure its presence was ever near. With this book he had felt the need for sleep and sustenance recede, for its might was such that it alone could give him life and he knew that soon he would pull from it the secrets it contained and use them to seize the future he felt was meant for him.

To the south in Napal City, Daerveron, returned from his deliberately brief excursion to the east, was doing some plotting of his own. The undead wizard had made his trip to Marlpaz, as promised to Wolfbane, and come back in secret. He knew he could have argued against his exile and won, but it was easier to simply avoid the debate altogether. Besides, his visit had the good fortune of aligning with a foolhardy attempt to sack the fortress by the Angladaics, and much of Daerveron's frustration had been taken out in the destruction of a great many in their assaulting force. The mage also understood that Wolfbane was an important component in the larger scheme of Daerveron's master Neroth, and until Edgewulf el Vac was dead or returned to the fortress, where Daerveron could silence or frame him as a traitor in front of the commander, the invoker needed to demonstrate loyalty to him. Otherwise their relationship would become too contentious and cause unnecessary delays, which would be unacceptable. Daerveron had to return to Napal City and his dungeons anyway, for he needed to report on his progress to Neroth. In the dread chamber beneath his laboratory, he met once again with the lord of death.

"The Night Cloaks have not caught up with them yet?"

Daerveron crossed his arms. "My lord, a small number of them are keeping a reasonable distance from the target, but will prevent them from turning back west. As you ordered, I am driving them eastward and into the path of the Broken army."

"Good." Neroth paused a moment before continuing. "There is a road south from the town of Delmore that leads to a great underground passage. Should the Broken fail to destroy this group, have the Night Cloaks kill them on the road to the caves or force them within. I have contingencies in place there, if you should fail me."

Daerveron bristled at the insinuation of his incompetence, but held his tongue. Then he asked, "May I know, God of Death, what other entity is aiding you in this matter? Perhaps I could more effectively coordinate this endeavor with greater understanding of all the plans in place."

"You know all that you need to. Slay them before they reach the passage and it will not matter who else was acting on my orders."

Though frustrated, Daerveron chose to let the issue go. "Your Night Cloak commander is ready to depart once more and reinforce the others to the south."

"Then make it so Daerveron. I will reward you well when you are successful, but this venture must not fail or I shall be greatly displeased."

The image of Neroth vanished with his ominous words hanging in the air. Daerveron shrugged off his thoughts of precisely what would happen if he did fail, confident that this would not be the case. Striding assuredly from the summoning room he mounted the stairs to his laboratory and marched down an unlit tunnel that stretched far beyond the reaches of the city. A long walk of nearly two hours down the cold and dripping halls eventually gave way to biting cold and bright moonlight as Daerveron came out of the tunnel just south of the city walls, pushing open an immense sewer grate as he stepped onto the cold earth of an aging graveyard.

In the pale moonlight a multitude of black-mounted shapes sat astride dark horses. The largest of the group moved his mount slowly toward Daerveron. "What is your command, master?"

Daerveron eyed the hissing figure. These riders, perhaps a kind of undead like himself, were the most terrifying and unnatural forces he had leave to command. The Night Cloaks, they called themselves, and they served Daerveron at the order of the God of Death himself. Even Wolfbane did not know about them. These strange beings remained wrapped in long black cloth most of the time, but Daerveron had seen underneath the folds. They were pale white and sometimes appeared to glow in the light of the moon. He knew the rumors, few and lacking much detail, of their origins and some evidence supported those tales, but where they had come from mattered not to him. The Night Cloaks had served Neroth in secret with a fierce loyalty that was unwavering and were far more powerful than nearly any mortal being on Teth-tenir. Their first venture south had gone poorly, which was a great surprise, for they claimed to have encountered a wizard that had killed one of their kind, and a weapon that was a danger even to them. It was something Daerveron had not expected, and been curious to know more about. It had not been fear or sadness in the eyes of the leader when he told Daerveron about the death of one of their number, but cold anger and a hint of an insatiable need to seek vengeance. It is said the dead know no fear, but they are unused to any challenge, and their response to one is most unpleasant.

"Take all of your company, ride south. Do not stop. Find the God of Death's enemies and keep them heading towards Delmore. The army will smash them there if they linger, but if they continue onward ensure they go south. Kill them, especially the one you sought in Gi'lakil if you can, but should you fail keep them moving southward. Once they enter the tunnels others are in place to do what our lord commands."

"As you say."

With an unearthly cry, the mounted horrors turned and raced from the graveyard, following the black steed of their leader. Daerveron watched them go, his robe flowing in the sharp, cutting wind of the night. When Valroth had sufficiently prepared his work in the Frozen Reach, there would be no stopping the Nerothians. They had too many forces of strange origin and mighty ability serving them. Once the enemies of Neroth were dead, Daerveron could return to looking out only for himself and his interests. The thought was comforting and had he been capable of it, Daerveron would have smiled then. Instead, now consoled, the dark mage reentered his passage and returned to the laboratory.

The tiny village of Florin had burned like a dead twig. No sooner had the Broken army reached the wall-less hamlet then it was little more than smoke on the wind. The few who had survived fled south to warn those who were next in the path of the relentless army. The commanders from Castle Bane sat on a hill above the burning houses and farms, listening to the screams of the dead and dying. Valissa, mounted on her warhorse, watched the orgy of slaughter with a practiced look of indifference. Frothgar, who stood next to her holding the reins of his own mount, was more disgusted than uncaring. "They are like animals! You can't fight a war with such rabble! They hardly know which end of a spear to stab with!"

Valissa smiled. "Frothgar, the Napalian's poor and simple High Thane," the last words were spoken with obvious derision, "what did you expect? These people have fought for years as a disorganized mass of rage. Most have no military training and those who once did have long forgotten it! They only know how to kill the defenseless and the outnumbered!"

Frothgar grimaced. "Then why are we not here with our own soldiers? We could take the whole of Legocia without involving this useless lot."

Valissa turned to the assassin leader with a look of annoyance. "Because our own soldiers number little over ten thousand, and even the massed army in Napal is not much better trained than this one. Also, we are scattered, soldiers in Marlpaz, all across that damned unending winter of our homeland. We do not have the time to join our forces and make a concentrated move south. This rabble, as you call it, is our best hope."

Frothgar grunted, "The armies of the Order of the Blade and the Fortress of Aves are the best trained on the continent, barring Angladais. Numbers or no numbers, this lot do not have the skill to match them."

Valissa was getting tired of Frothgar's attitude. "We have over fifteen-thousand Broken, which is not including close to four hundred gnolls. They account for more than enough Eagle Knights to crush them alone. We are going to burn, rape, and maim every person from the east inward until that castle is all that stands in our way. This is not an army, it is a force of vengeful nature. The divided and self-absorbed semi-nations of Dragon's Watch will crumble in days."

The assassin was about to respond when the Broken chieftain, Goranath Megrim, appeared, cleaning off his bloodied dagger and sheathing his hefty curved cutlass. The Broken leader was a vicious looking man, scars crisscrossed his face and he wore a black head rag with a patch covering his missing left eye. The patch prevented one from seeing the undoubtedly horrific wound beneath it, but did not do enough to conceal the puckered white scar running from above his forehead to well below his left jaw. He wore red breeches that might once have been bright and proud but were now stained with blood and grime to a dark, forboding color. Over them he had black leather boots, clearly made for long marches, coupled with a worn red tunic similar to the breeches and torn leather armor of the same dark black tone. Goranath was a vicious, ruthless, and impassive commander of men. Once, he had been an officer among the Army of the Lion, and unlike those who had first tried to return to Westia by boat he had chosen to stay in Legocia and carve out a bloody empire for himself and his wandering tribe of cutthroats in the Dust Plains. Without his allegiance, the invaders would have been hard pressed to gain the Broken's help. Caermon Erefoss had brokered the deal with Goranath, being a man of rather sadistic hobbies himself, but Frothgar was not as impressed as his fellow thane. Still, he had to admit Goranath and many of his men were a fearsome sight in their bloody, ragged dress and hodgepodge of fearsome and sometimes improvised weaponry.

Goranath halted a few paces from the two and spoke in his gruff baritone, "We burned the village to the ground. All the people are dead. We are ready to move south."

Frothgar sighed, "None escaped this time?"

Goranath eyed him darkly. "My men want plunder more than blood. I cannot always kill those smart enough to flee quickly."

Frothgar took a lecturing tone, "You should plan your attack better then, barbarian. If you knew anything of military strategy we might not...."

Goranath interrupted him, "My men are winning these wars, not you. Keep your tongue between your teeth or I'll cut it out."

The Broken commander turned smartly and marched back to his raging horde of killers, leaving the Napalian spymaster sputtering with rage and some degree of fear. Regaining himself, Frothgar turned on a sniggering Valissa. "Well, he'll certainly have alerted Delmore with this charade. Laugh if you want Valissa, but Delmore is a town not a village. It may not have gates and guardhouses, but it has a wall of solid wooden logs to bar intruders. With enough preparation, they could hold that small town for a time, especially if they know we're coming. We could lose many men that we need later, in real battles."

Valissa's mood sobered up somewhat, but she remained confident. "So some of the Broken die, what of it? We have more men than leaves in an autumn wind. They aren't our own, if they fall so be it. There will still be enough left to take the Fortress of Aves and everything in between."

Frothgar was still unconvinced. "It's foolish. You do not waste soldiers if you do not have too."

Valissa was fed up with him at last. "Go play with your knives, Frothgar, and let me worry about the soldiering. You kill individuals, and I kill armies, so you will defer to me, understood?"

Without answering, Frothgar turned and rode back to his waiting men and gathered them to return to the camp. He had preferred the Valissa at Castle Bane that went round dressed provocatively and used her body and sweet tongue to manipulate others, not this new woman who had come dressed in practical plate and leather armor and with a general's keen mind. He felt her undermining his authority at every turn, and he had not manipulated matters to become the High Thane of Napal only to lose his position to some woman. His men gathered around him, dressed in the dark blue and red of House Konunn and bearing forth his banner, a three bladed dagger. Each blade represented one component of the Konunn's triumvirate of power: knowledge, coercion, and force. Frothgar contemplated which of his ancestral methods would be best for dealing with the upstart from House Ulfrunn.

Valissa watched Frothgar leave with little interest, but thought briefly of how far she ought to push him before starting to worry about her own safety. She knew the materialistic and soft Frothgar would spend some time taking down his tent and packing his collection of clothes, exotic foods, and other luxuries before heading south behind the main body of the army. Valissa had respected Frothgar, to a degree, before leaving for the lands south of the God's Bones Mountains, but now she utterly detested him. The man worried too much and his posturing infuriated her, but his archers would be essential to defeating the Eagle Knights at Aves. For now, she would need to be somewhat more respectful, at least until this miserable campaign was over with.

Chapter 11

Raymir seated Edge and Romund before she went to find her grandfather. She caught him entering the study with four beautifully carven thin grey stone cups and a small, matching stone teapot. "I am afraid," he said, "that I have run short of spirits for my guests."

He placed the tray on the old table at the center of the study and settled in behind his beaten war desk. Raymir poured the thick, aromatic tea made from the moss and lichen of her homeland for all, and they sat in silence for some time. Finally, she turned to her grandfather and asked, "What happened to Renatus and Anhager?"

The old man smiled slightly. "When the invaders came, those who survived were looking for a way to escape and head south where it was still safe. I was too old to lead such an excursion, and I was praying you or one of my grandchildren might be alive somehow. I heard the rumors from Napal City, but I would not, could not, believe them. Renatus and Anhager went south in my stead. As loyal housekarls, they were more than reluctant to leave me, but my house arrest had turned them into little more than personal servants. They have been trained as warriors just like every person in the north. They deserved the chance to fight back, even if it was not by my side."

"Where did you send them?" Raymir asked.

Algathor paused in thought. "There are few safe places left in the world that will take in refugees from our home. They talked of making for the Whitewood, where Fernal Hethegar's surviving family have rallied much of the resistance, but I told them to seek out the Order of the Blade or the Eagle Knights. I even suggested they go to the Foresters if they could find them. This war is not over, and those lands will be next. The God of Death has always believed that mortals must be brought firmly under control, for our own good he claims. I have no way of knowing if either of my most loyal men made it.

"Your father though, Raymir, he was here."

Raymir shot a hard look at her grandfather, her voice rising in fury, "You let him back in this house? After he killed mother? And Grethann? And Kaylina? She was only fifteen and they raped and butchered her because of him!"

Algathor stood slowly, palms extended slightly towards her, trying to calm his granddaughter. "Please, Raymir, please. Let me explain."

Raymir still looked incensed, but she stopped her rant and held back her tears long enough to hear out her grandfather. Taking a long draw from his tea, the eldest Squall began, "It was not your father's hand that took your family from you. Yes, his betrayal of our homeland caused their deaths, but it was never his intention. I firmly believe that."

Algathor leaned on the back of his chair and looked at the floor. "Greymane came here in complete shame. At first I would not let him in, and Renatus wanted to fight him in the courtyard himself, but I forestalled more violence within the family. I let him in when he told me he just wanted some books, he said he had found a way to make things right, that he could still save his people."

Algathor shook his head. "I told him he was beyond redemption, but that if he would swear never to come back, I would let him have his run of this study. He was here only one night, he took nothing with him as far as I could tell, but I found several open volumes on the history of Teth-tenir and the Immorbellum in particular. He insisted when he was here that something greater than any mortal was among the invaders, that Neroth would return to our plane someday soon. It is of course impossible, and I think perhaps he went mad with grief."

Raymir shrugged dismissively. "It was no more than he deserved."

"I agree child, but something told me not to desert him, just as I will not desert you."

Raymir smiled. "I know you won't."

Algathor nodded in satisfaction, his tale told. "Now, with that unhappy business done tell me how you came to be here, and with whom you travel."

Edge stood quickly and stiffly, saying, "Sir, my name is Edgewulf el Vac. I was formerly of the Nerothian ranks, but I deserted when I bore witness to the atrocities my former friend and master Wolfbane committed."

Algathor said nothing for a time, but studied the young man before him. Finally he spoke, "You were with him when he sacked my home, yet now you fight against him. I have never agreed with turncoats." He turned to his granddaughter. "You trust this man?"

Raymir looked very seriously at her grandfather. "I love him."

The old man did not appear surprised. "Then that is enough for me, you are safe in my house, young Edgewulf. Our family once had the help of a man from Haddon Mirk who bore your same name: Xantes el Vac. He died valiantly defending this very town." He cocked his head slightly as if trying to remember something. "Indeed the name sounds quite familiar, even recent, to me. But no matter, who is this?"

Romund stood and bowed low. "My name is Romund. I serve the resistance in Hethegar, though I spent much of my time disguised as a worker in the Napal City Castle. I too, can vouch for the lad."

Algathor nodded solemnly. "My thanks, Romund, consider my worry assuaged. Though I fear you have come to me for help at a time when there is little left for me to give."

Raymir stared at her grandfather. "Do not say such things...."

"I cannot deny that which is inevitable!" Algathor cut in. "The guards watch my house night and day. It is a matter of time before they find some reason to bring me out, and I will not go quietly."

The old man sipped his tea and silence fell again, a somber and forlorn quiet. Raymir suddenly noticed her grandfather was shaking, though with fury or sadness she could not say. "Why it is me who should live only long enough to watch my people wither and die I do not know," his eyes stared at Raymir, sunken and fading. "That my family should fail so spectacularly. My own son should be the cause of my country's destruction. I wish I knew what I have done to bring this blackness on my house."

Raymir rose and took his hand. "You did nothing my lord, and your leadership has been a beacon for our people."

Edge interjected as well, "I will not allow Wolfbane's greed to destroy your homeland, sir."

The Napalian's eyes fell hard on the foreign warrior. "As bravely did I once speak when I was young. You will find in time, my young friend, that brave words come as easily from fools as from heroes."

Romund, still seated and stirring his tea calmly, spoke softly, yet commandingly, "And sometimes the aged forget what power the young still hold." His eyes burned with an unearthly passion at Algathor. "Sometimes, youthful determination out does experience."

Raymir gripped her grandfather's wrist, expecting a scathing retaliation, but none came. Instead the old man seemed to straighten and his shoulders set themselves daringly. "The people of Hethegar have always been quite wise in ways of war. It seems perhaps I have forgotten some things myself." His gaze took in all of his guests as he spoke wit conviction, his voice rising in passion, "Let the black hordes come, they will still find one Napalian here willing to die for his people."

As he spoke, there came a sudden knocking crash at the door. A shout rose from the courtyard, "Open up in the name of Wolfbane and the Nerothian Legion!"

Edge hefted his halberd. "It seems they heard you my lord."

Algathor swept quickly from the study. "And glad I am! Raymir, fetch me my spear, it is time I showed these bastards from the west whose land this truly is!"

Raymir rushed from the room to her family's armory while her grandfather made for the door to greet the intruders. Edge looked at Romund standing beside him. "We cannot fight them all, there are far too many."

Romund drew his short sword and followed the aged Napalian. "Don't have much of a choice, do we lad?"

Far to the east, some say beyond the land where the sun first rises, sit the great peaks called the Pillars of Light. Huge monoliths of sheer stone, they rise far into the clouds, surpassing the most imposing mountains of the God's Bones by great heights. Riding between the Pillars brings travelers to the sheltered Cloud Peak Basin, home of the most noble nation in Legocia, the Kingdom of Angladais. Famed for their prowess in battle, their great sacrifice to people in need, and their never-ending war with any force of evil and suffering, these brave servants of good live for the God of Honor, Paladinis.

Cloud Peak Basin is a rich farmland full of heavy, crop-bearing soil. The many farms spread across the nation are prosperous and peaceful, as are the few small towns that rest against the mountains or along the sheer eastern cliffs. But all of these wonders pale in comparison to the magnificent city of Alderlast, in the southern third of the nation cupped on three sides by the thick and imposing Silverleaf Forest. The city is divided into eight equal districts, each falling under the jurisdiction of a powerful Highlord, one of the oldest families in the nation who claim to be able to trace their roots back to the first founders of Angladais. The eight roads lead to the center of the city, where the towering structure of white marble and beautiful polished crystal, the Angladaic Palace, sits. The roads themselves are raised three stories in height and act as dividers of the districts, suitable for the defense of Alderlast as well as her logistical organization.

The palace is a hulking representation of the peoples' devotion to justice and honor, for no one lives there permanently but the God Paladinis and the current King of Angladais. The structure rests on a great raised platform, higher even than the eight roads that form the spokes of the wheel from the outer walls of the city to the palace grounds. This elevated seat holds the palace, whose massive main doors face the Zenith Road, and which has consecutively larger octagonal platforms descending from the entrance down to the level of the roads. For the people in the districts, the palace rises so high into the sky above that, at the brightest points of the day, it appears a shining beacon of hope and purity reaching up to the realms of the gods themselves. It is here, in this great tribute to the might and devotion of Angladais, that their criminals are punished, heroic excursions are planned, and great wisdom is imparted to all.

In the council chamber of the Highlords sat the current King of Angladais, Lord Arvadis Angladais of the Hawking House, alone for a rare moment. He was an imposing figure in his burnished bronze tinted armor bright as the sun, exquisitely carved and sculpted in flowing patterns of silver amid the bright russet of his plate. Some claimed that Arvadis resembled Paladinis himself, but for his white moustache and hair. He rested one careworn gauntlet on the armrest of his heavy, padded wooden chair, its back stitched in the Hawking House colors of bronze and white with a great hawk taking flight. He was pensively drumming his fingers with one hand while in the other was clutched a grimy, bloodstained report. It was one he had read over and over, as though it would change what it said in the repetition of the reading.

The council chamber was simple, holding a large round table at which Arvadis sat. The other seven chairs of the powerful Highlords of Angladais loomed empty before its glossy finish. Those same eight Highlords, said to be able to trace their lines back the founders of the nation, were absent by Arvadis's own orders. Each of their families was responsible for a different aspect of the Angladaic society: Hladic the priests, Bwemor the army, Calavar the paladins, Vendile the commerce and trade, Irindein records and histories, Xarinth agriculture, Galden construction and maintenance, and finally Hawking, who kept watch over the law of the nation known as the Angladaic Code. Despite Arvadis's insistence on time to think in solitude, the seats would soon be filled. Once word of the massacre in the north got out all the Highlords would have to be consulted, whether he liked it or not.

The heavy, iron-trimmed doors opened and a single wiry figure heaved them aside with great effort. Arvadis grimaced in distaste. He did not trust the man coming, head bowed subserviently, towards him. Where Arvadis was a noble, scarred, and fit elder man this one was of age indeterminable, unkempt, and conniving. Arvadis wished dearly he could send him from the kingdom, but he had uncovered no crime committed, nor any grounds to bar him from the city or the palace.

The newcomer knew this and more about the king's thoughts on himself. He was a messenger and merchant of information. He had won his living off knowing as much as he could and selling it to the highest bidder. It had been so for years. Despite his appearance, which was such that he fell into that strange place where age was impossible to ascertain, Arvadis suspected he had been at this particular craft for a long time.

The man's name was Freyan, a former Broken seer, or fortune-teller, turned spy and possibly worse. He had latched himself onto one of the Angladaic Highlords, the power-mad Karsyrus Vendile of the Vendile House. How he had come to Angladais, none seemed to know. He acted as Vendile's advisor, though he really helped play the role of usurper, aiding Karsyrus' plans to remove the current king and take his place. Such a victory would place Freyan firmly at the top of the Angladaic society and make his authority, through Vendile, very great indeed. Arvadis watched his slow approach, pale and sinister in his colorless robes. He knew what Freyan wanted, perhaps not in the particular moment, but in every waking hour of his existence: to rule.

But for now this old man barred his way.

It was not as simple as murdering the current king with poison while he slept or staging a hunting accident. Freyan had contemplated such actions and proposed them in passing, but Karsyrus had been clear about the ways one might become king in Angladais. Murders or accidents were treated as one and the same and they were certain to be heavily investigated, running risks despite Freyan's calm assertion that he could evade all detection. Their game had therefore become to discredit and demean Arvadis. Freyan had sold Vendile on slowly developing a vision of the king as weak and inept. The plan had, by happy coincidence, coincided with the emergence of a dark fortress between the Pillars of Light, trapping the fabled Angladaics within their own lands. It had begun the spiral downward for Arvadis, as every attempt to negotiate or expel these invaders had failed, and after each failing Freyan had been there to highlight the king's shortcomings in the matter. Freyan was well practiced in these tactics, but had found Arvadis and his family difficult to hook on his lures, for despite his success so far, Arvadis remained stubbornly entrenched on the throne.

Bowing as he reached the old man, Freyan began his inquiries. "His majesty feels well today, I hope?"

Arvadis glanced coldly at him. "Indeed."

There was no illusion between either, both knew the other to be their hated foe, and returned that hate tenfold. Freyan adjusted his long grayish robes, hoping he looked as stately as he intended. His black hair was parted down the middle and flowed to his shoulders, held in place by a thin gold coronet bearing House Vendile's insignia, a black bat gripping a coin, on its crown. The man wore his entire appearance with a great ease, but seemed put off by the circlet around his head, as though its weight made him uncomfortable. Still feigning deference, Freyan smiled slightly. He did not regret the challenge of this man, for he had met and defeated many in his time. He considered himself a shrewd master of manipulation, and the king a worthy adversary. Soon Freyan would make the decisive move in this little chess game, and the king would fall.

First he had to maneuver his victim, make him vulnerable so that he would blunder most opportunely. Circumstances had conspired in ways that suited his plans. Sidling up to the king, Freyan twirled a gold leaf goblet taken from the table beside Arvadis' seat. He said as offhandedly as he could, "Word has reached Lord Vendile of news from the north. Perhaps there was some good fortune in the pass?"

Arvadis eyed the detestable man sideways and responded as curtly as politeness allowed. "Had the news been good I would have sent word to the people long ago."

"Then things have not progressed well?"

Arvadis glared at the advisor. "Call the council if you will, Freyan, and you shall hear all you want to know."

Freyan bowed, only slightly. "As his majesty wills."

The snake-like man departed slowly from the council chamber, but Arvadis was not to be left alone long. Moments after the great doors closed another figured entered, opening them far more easily than Freyan had. He was a big man, strong and young. Clearly an Angladaic lord, he dressed unusually in light mail that covered his chest and groin, leaving arms and legs exposed. Forsaking the favored heavy plated armor of his ilk, he dressed in mail of elven craftsmanship, light and designed for mobility. His long brown hair hung well past his shoulders and he carried a simple steel helm beneath one arm. Bowing low before the king, he spoke fervently. "May the Goddess of Life bless you this day my King."

Forgoing all formalities Arvadis stood and rushed forward to hold the young lord close. "Vorasho! Ah, my eldest! I did fear for you when you did not bring me the report personally."

Vorasho grasped his father in return. Ever stern and serious was the young lord, but beneath his calm exterior emotions raged. Love for his father, and fear for him as well. "I saw Freyan coming out, has he been harassing you again?"

Arvadis waved the inquiry away as he poured them both a small amount of wine. "A fly among wasps that one. He need not concern you."

Vorasho sipped the wine his father handed him and eyed the king seriously. "A fly on the wall can learn more than a wasp in his nest."

Arvadis smiled and placed a hand on his son's shoulder. "You are indeed a wise one. It must have come from your mother." Arvadis settled back into his chair, gesturing for his son to join him. "Tell me what transpired in the gap."

Vorasho pulled up his own seat from the wall, forgoing the chairs of the Highlords as protocol demanded. "We went north with the full compliment of two hundred paladins, per your request, and found the great fortress between the rocks. It is a massive place, a tribute to the evil of its making. Somehow the builder fused it into the Pillars. There is no way in but through the black walls of the fortress." Vorasho paused, his face growing dark as he spoke, "There were men on guard, maybe a hundred or more at best. With that few we thought perhaps a force of sixty or more paladins could break through, with the rest to support them when the breach in the gate was made through Paladinis's blessed wrath. We never even got to the wall. A black clad mage strode atop the ramparts as our force rode closer. He dropped fire and lightning on us like rain. We lost eighty men, the sixty I sent forward and a score more trying to save them. There were few wounded, perhaps ten or less. Those struck often did not survive long.

"I wanted to march in with the infantry, lead some of our force to where we could reach them with archers. Captain Gildanes refused to allow me and he instead led them himself. I fear he did not live through the attempt."

Arvadis was silent, pondering. "We lost how many?"

"Two hundred and seventy one men, sir."

Arvadis' heart sank. "Their families?"

"Know nothing."

"As well they might not." He removed his gauntlets and ran one gnarled hand through his fading hair. "We must let the people know what we face."

"Father," Vorasho stood very close and leaned in, "Freyan and Vendile mean to use this against you, to put the fortress forward as a sign of your weakness. They will try to take our kingdom from you."

Arvadis looked at him in defiant fury. "The people, my people, they trust us still! They will not allow that snake to take command."

Vorasho nodded in agreement. "Yes father, but the Highlords are greedy and will take money over happiness. Vendile could find much support if we do not solve this problem soon."

Arvadis stood, pacing the floor in perplexity. "If only your brother were here. We might rally the people behind us, we three, and scare the others into submission."

Vorasho adjusted his mail. "We can still try it, you and I."

Arvadis paused in consideration, and then shook his head slowly. "I no longer possess enough allies to sway the council, only enough to keep it at bay. Tell me, of the other seven Highlords, who sides with us?"

"Vendile and Hawking are polar opposites of course, leaving only six to choose their side. Houses Galden and Xarinth remain neutral and sidelined with fear, fear of retribution in picking the wrong horse in a dangerous race. Irindein is firmly with us, as is Calavar. Runiden will not forsake our family with or without support from others. Yet Vendile has persuaded Hladic and Bwemor that wealth and dominion will come to them with him on the throne."

Arvadis grunted as both Hladic and Bwemor's names were mentioned. "Xarinth and Galden are led by children. We cannot blame their advisors and guards for telling them to stay on the sidelines. Vendile may even have threatened them and their families. The division is a difficult one. Hladic commands the priests, and Bwemor the army. We could not be more ill supplied for a fight." He eyed his son sadly. "I am afraid we have been handed a war we cannot win."

Vorasho paused and sipped his wine once more. He looked about the high-ceilinged council chamber, at the room that stood for truth and justice and all the things he believed in so strongly. He longed to tell his father how much he loved him, how he would do anything for him, but he was not the emotional family member. Vorasho was the brain and the rational, logical one, while his brother Logan was the heart and the fire. They had grown up together, Vorasho training his younger brother, but only when his father could be pulled away from him. The two had been inseparable, as inseparable as Logan and Grimtooth now were. Like his father, Vorasho approved of his brother's companion, despite some of the Highlords' collective distaste for him, but he also knew things about Logan his father did not. A secret so dark that it would spell exile or worse were it known to the wrong people in Angladais. Even with all his jealousy at Logan's ability to express his emotions and his anger at his brother for stealing the attention of their father, Vorasho would never divulge his brother's sins. Though in truth he could not say why, perhaps because of the lingering fear of his own darkest desires.

Arvadis noted his son's black countenance and forced a smile he did not feel for his benefit. "I am sorry, my son, I have pressed the gloom of an old man upon you. Do not despair, Vorasho, Paladinis is with us!"

Vorasho swallowed the last of his wine, intoning the appropriate, trained response, "As he has always been."

The Highlord Karsyrus Vendile lounged in the overstuffed cushion of his bedroom chair. He was a sturdy, well groomed and handsome man; very tall and imposing when standing and not as aged as Arvadis. Karsyrus was also a man with far fewer ethical scruples. Vendile's house was famous for their covert strikes amid the Highlords, undermining others' efforts for personal gain and status. Murder and suicide could become one and the same in the hands of House Vendile; for suicide was simply a murder that no one could quite prove a party responsible for. There was great advantage in the commoners not knowing anything of Highlord house intrigue; had they seen the dark underworld of Angladais, they might grow daring enough to rise up and strike the Highlords they had for centuries followed unquestioningly.

House Vendile certainly conducted its business with far less honor than the nobler houses like Hawking and Irindein. Karsyrus was proud of telling his followers he was the most ruthless lord in a long line of infamously ruthless Vendile leaders. As he sat in his lavish bedchamber, in a home only slightly smaller than the royal palace itself, he stroked his chestnut brown trimmed goatee and allowed himself a small smile. When he was king he would take over the palace, add several additions for his personal use, and reopen the torture chambers below the dungeons that his ancestor of over four hundred years, Malvor Vendile, had built. Malvor had been the last Vendile to hold the position of king, a position that he had been forcibly removed from.

And naturally, a Hawking had stolen it from him. Now, ever since that disastrous fall, the kingship had belonged to that despicable house, with their patronizingly weak ways among the common folk and their idiotic penchant for peaceful negotiations and cooperation with weaker nations that the Angladaics should rule! Vendile liked this new invading commander. Wolfbane he was rumored to be called, and true to his name he ruled with steel and flame, the way it should be. Angladais had always been a nation that restrained herself, despite the military superiority of her forces and the power of their faith. What use was there in being the most honorable of nations if you could not use the weapons your loyalty to Paladinis had earned you? When Karsyrus Vendile was king he would ally himself with this newly risen warlord, then find a clever way to take his place.

Vendile's pleasant thoughts were interrupted when a contrite young serving man entered his room, averting his eyes from the insanity burning in his master's. "The advisor Freyan is here, my lord."

Vendile waved his hand indifferently. "Send him in then."

Freyan strode in without being told by the servant, who was happy to leave. He poured himself a glass of brandy and swirled it slowly, waiting for Vendile to speak. The Highlord had little patience. "Well? Report you sniveling cur! Tell me what has happened at the pass!"

Freyan sipped his brandy and waited a few more moments before settling into a smaller chair than Vendile's. Fiddling with his robes until satisfied with their placement, he spoke to the fuming Highlord, "Captain Gildanes is dead. Over eighty paladins reportedly fell before even reaching the alleged fortress. It was thought that Vorasho Hawking died as well, but it seems he was held back from the charge by Gildanes and has returned just today."

Vendile sighed in disappointment but could not help looking pleased. "So it was an utter failure then. The great Arvadis has blundered. I presume he shall call a council meeting?"

"I did mention it to him, sire."

Vendile smiled that sly grin of his again. "Excellent work, Freyan, truly marvelous. Now we can begin to corner him, pull the other Highlords to our side. Once they are firmly behind us we can arrange a little mishap for our friend Arvadis."

Freyan raised one manicured hand. "Might I suggest, my lord, that Arvadis be left alive?"

Vendile rapidly became a raging beast. "What! Leave him alive, around to challenge me? I don't want him breathing! I want the crown! I want it all! I want to kill him myself!"

Freyan put up both hands to mollify his master. "But sire, if he lives and is dishonored, say by evidence you yourself uncover."

Vendile stopped flailing about and turned to his advisor. Slowly a terrible smile covered his face and he began to laugh. He couldn't stop, he howled. When he finally recovered he brought his face close to Freyan's, forcing the seated man to stare unperturbed into his maddened eyes. "Yes! Yes, that is it! We'll dishonor him but imprison him! He'll watch his House fall, and all the things he stands for crumble! Then when he is safely in the dungeons, his execution can be carried out quietly, no one will even know it occurred!" The insane Highlord stood triumphantly and rubbed his hands together, his right hand drifting to his breast to stroke the odd metal pendant hanging from a thin chain. It was a finely made piece, with three heavy, dark stones set in the steel at equal intervals around the plain round setting.

Freyan noted his master's obsessive rubbing of the bauble and smiled to himself. "I see you still admire the gift I brought you from the Dust Plains?"

Vendile looked up sharply, then down at the pendant and said, "Yes, it seems I do not feel whole without it near me."

"I am glad it pleases you, my lord. I wish only to serve."

"Of course," Vendile regained his composure and sat back in his chair. "You will be well rewarded for your loyalty, Freyan, well rewarded indeed!"

The former seer sipped his drink. "My lord is most kind."

Far to the south, along the road from Delmore in the east to the Fortress of Aves in the west, the traveling adventurers had paused perhaps a day or more outside of the township of Delmore. It was late and they huddled around the campfire as the first truly cold fall evening fell on southern Legocia. Diaga had long since retired, claiming the trials of the earlier days had stolen his second wind. The young mage had been very withdrawn since they left the village, paying only absent-minded attention even to Neep. His condition concerned Jovanaleth, who had taken a strong liking to the wizard, but the others seemed more preoccupied with the quest that lay before them. No one else gave his sudden change in condition and demeanor a second thought.

Their trek would take them through the town of Delmore and then south to the forested nest of Silverleaf, forming the border of the continents Legocia and Southron. Sylrastor Gend had explained the condition of the road they must travel, a long tunnel going for at least three day's journey under the Sunteeth Mountains that hugged the eastern coast and extended a fair distance east along the southern border of Silverleaf Forest. It would be dark, as there was little to no natural light, and Gend would need to take his time finding the way to ensure they did not get lost. The thought seemed to make all concerned rather uncomfortable, excepting Rath and Trem. Ghost sat sharpening his new scimitar, far plainer and with a less expertly made curvature than his older one, given the smith had no experience with forging weapons of its kind. He asked whether the shades would follow them beneath the earth, gauging what their chances of evasion might be. On this matter Gend admitted he wasn't sure. He said that dwarves were rumored to live under those mountains, founding a settlement there many years ago and trading with Delmore while also providing safe passage to Southron and the greater dwarven kingdom of Hulduvarn. Still, none in the Dust Plains had seen the dwarves or traded with them for a great many years.

To Trem, sitting silently and observing the discussion, it all sounded a bit too simple. When he had traveled across Legocia in his earlier days he had encountered difficulty at nearly every turn. He had faced segregation and mistrust from those who found his mixed heritage an affront to both races, and he had wandered in lands where violence and right by might were common. Despite the time that had elapsed, Trem still felt exhilarated from his spar with Jovanaleth and also sensed a strange pull to uncover this item Ghost was so fervently chasing. The former hermit struggled to stay grounded in the reality of the moment. Kurven's ominous warnings about the dangers of the dream world lingered in the back of his mind, though all he wished to do was seek out some tiny part of his own redemption. How his part in this journey was going to affect the larger matters at hand remained beyond him, but he had noted a disturbing interest from Jovanaleth in the ideas of Ghost, Logan, and Grimtooth about enacting some greater service for the world. In truth, Trem wanted the scope of their partnership to remain simple. The locating and potential rescue of one man or one object was enough of a challenge for him. Trem had no intention of actually being present when the greater forces of the world began to come to blows.

Tired, Trem rose quietly and went to find his bedroll. The others kept talking, oblivious to the half-elf's departure. Trem had not noticed that Rath was apart from the others, just as he had been. The black clad figure suddenly appeared beside him, his piercing eyes boring into him. Rath spoke in an urgent whisper, "You and your friends cannot pass through the mountains, Trem Waterhound! It is an evil road."

Trem replied evenly, "We do not ask you to travel with us, Rath. Gend knows the way, you do not have to go if you do not wish to." He tried to brush the man aside but he grabbed Trem's collar and held him fast.

"There are those among you who cannot be trusted!"

Trem glared at him. "I've noticed." And he shook himself free and went to find a place to sleep.

Rath hissed in frustration, "You are going there to die, fool!"

Trem did not pause or answer, but faded into the darkness and went to his rest.

Chapter 12

Exhaustion from travel and his inner conflict sunk Trem into a dreamless sleep. He floated, suspended in space and time. He exulted in the peace, hovering far from the dangers of mortal life, safe and carefree. It was impossible to say how long he dwelt in this place of recovery and calm, but slowly a voice began to pierce the darkness. Trem gradually came to a state of semiconsciousness, as it grew stronger about him.

"Trem Waterhound," the tone and inflection was unfamiliar but not threatening, "hear me, lend me your ear."

"Kurven?" Trem asked the darkness, still unsure of who was out there or how they had found him when he had remained apart from the dreamscape.

"You are in grave danger, Trem." The voice grew stronger. It was a male voice of a mature owner, but Trem could not see where the words came from. It was not but black and quiet all around. "I knew you sought me before but were unable to find me in this world, but I did hear your call. There is a threat in Delmore that will divide your newfound company. You must make the proper choice when the time comes."

"Grandfather Forest?" Trem questioned, but knew the answer instinctively. "Is this about Rath's warning to me earlier?"

"Perhaps. Any of your companions might be a danger to you. You must remain cautious, Trem, and stand by yourself above all else."

The dreaming world had begun to find stability and substance as Trem drifted back to the voice. He was unable to solidify his vision of Gerand Oakheart, he suspected because he had only known him as a soul encased in a natural vessel, and Gerand likely projected his own vision of himself as he had been in life. Still, the vague and jittering form he was able to bring before him was clearly humanoid in shape. "Your advice has changed since we last spoke. Was it not you who told me to leave Silverleaf and help Jovanaleth or else risk 'not living'?"

"I have had time to reconsider my position in some ways. I would not wish anything ill to befall you."

"And there is some looming threat you foresee? More than the strange beings that haunt our steps or the violent rumors from the north?"

There was some hesitance in the reply, "I have learned only of something which will come soon and the danger it poses to you."

"You know," Trem said, doubt creeping thickly into his response, "I would have trusted another who has been kind enough to aid me with predictions of my future, but he refused to give me too much information. Kurven has begun to seem more reliable of late, though he can be irritatingly unclear at times. But in truth it seems he wants me to make my own decisions."

"Immortals look out for their own, half-elf." The tone was harsh, almost threatening, "I remember my mortality. I wish to prolong yours."

"I see." Trem tried once again to focus on the figure floating unclear and insubstantial before him. "Give me your advice then, Grandfather Forest, I shall do my best to abide by it."

The frustration seemed to fade from his visitor and the response came through more sympathetic and fatherly, "In Delmore the choice will come: to remain and cling to a failing fight for survival, or to move onward towards the possibility of hope. You must do the second, no good will come of the first."

Trem found he could not see the form of his host clearly, but it seemed to him some fraction of his face came through a bit clearer in sudden, jerking moments of clarity. "So we cannot pause in Delmore. I think this was already our intention, Gerand, you need not fear."

"But you must!" The voice and what little of the figure Trem could see began to fade and he squinted and tried desperately to make out what was before him. For a brief second, the face seemed to snap into clear form and he saw graying brown hair and striking blue eyes, sharp and oddly frightening. "Do not tarry there, Trem, move on for your own sake and that of those with you."

There was a sharp cracking sensation, and the voice and figure were gone. Trem felt very unsure of the entire interaction, perplexed by the warning and the sharp, insistent tone of Gerand Oakheart's lingering essence. Something struck him as amiss, but his tired mind pulled him back to quiet sleep and recuperation. As he drifted down into the depths of his rest, the memory of the encounter became jumbled and faded. Soon, he was back in void, floating quietly through the night.

As Trem slept on the other travelers made small talk and soon went to their own rest. Shortly after Trem had walked off, Gend had begged to rest as well and been relieved from his brief watch. The halfling found Rath already asleep in his many black strands of cloth, free of a bedroll or other comforts. In Gend's place, Ghost opted to take first watch, with Logan to be wakened, then Jovanaleth. The others filtered into the inky night to sleep, and Ghost set himself against a small boulder near the roadside.

The Napalian had felt a strange comfort come over him the past few days. With his purpose more or less exposed to the others he had grown more at peace, both with himself and with the experience of traveling with these people. Originally he had sworn to involve no one else in his mission, but that had proven impossible even before the incident in Gi'lakil. He would never have made it out of that inn alone, but he doubted the journey southward would be any easier. They were a motley band to be certain, but there were real skills among them and the older man knew his chances of success were far higher as long as they remained with him.

Ghost could also inherently sense that Trem, despite his youth, was a kindred spirit. The half-elf might not realize it yet, but Ghost could sense the internal motivation to be someone or something of significance emanating off of him. Somewhat troubling, the others seemed drawn to the half-elf. He was intelligent, certainly, but something else, something unexplainable, lent him a kind of authority that unnerved the Napalian. There was an aura to him that simply drew others in. Ever a man obsessed with authority and control, Ghost would have expected such a rivalry to infuriate him, but he found Trem's presence to be an odd comfort. Since his departure from his homeland, he had struggled to find purchase in this weak world of the south, where his blunt, assertive behavior was seen as threatening and even insulting to those who would be his followers.

A sudden snap to his left made Ghost whirl around, sword drawn, but he saw it was only the young mage. Coughing loudly to cover his brief moment of distraction, he sheathed his blade. "Dangerous to be sneaking up on a fellow like that. Why aren't you sleeping, boy?"

Diaga leaned on his staff and eyed him. "For once, I cannot. As to my safety, surely you would not harm a fellow Napalian?" He paused. "Then again I believe you already have."

Ghost was immediately on guard, "I do not know what you're talking about boy but…."

"No, of course not," the young man cut him off. "You would have blotted out that terrible memory, Thane Squall."

"You know not of what you speak!"

Diaga took a step forward and remarkably Ghost recoiled at his approach. "Oh, I know exactly of what I speak. Your real name is Thane, rather former Thane, Greymane Squall. You opened the gates to Napal City; you sacrificed your own people. You even let your own family die!"

"That was not the way it was to be! They were supposed to spare us. My family was to leave with me!"

Diaga scowled and thrust a lecturing finger at Ghost as he said; "You sold out your home, for what, a promotion? Gold?"

Ghost pointed his own finger back at Diaga defensively. "Froth-gar had blackmailed me, painted me into a corner by paying me to turn a blind eye to his illegal trades! My reputation would have been ruined!" His voice grew fiery with conviction. "I was the one who would elevate our house. Become the pinnacle of Squall family great-ness, and I was handed a war I could not win amid traitors I could not expose."

Diaga shook his head. "You could have died a hero to the peo-ple. If you truly wanted to protect your reputation you would not have opened the gates, you would have fought to the last."

"You talk bravely for a whelp who has never seen combat."

Diaga ignored the insult. "How did you escape the dungeons?"

Ghost shuddered at the memory. "I broke free. One of the guards got too close to the bars, so I snapped his neck. I went looking for my wife and children, but they were already dead. The Nerothians have to pay. Wolfbane has to pay. That is why I must go south."

Diaga watched the man seeth emotionlessly. "Vengeance will not ease your guilt."

Ghost tried to regain his composure asking, "How did you know?"

"I have suspected since Gi'lakil. When you mentioned there was an item you sought to strike back at the invaders, the fervor and hate in your voice when you talked of revenge, then I knew. I grew up admiring you and your house when I was an orphan. I even spent my afternoons trying to catch a glimpse of you in the streets until I found my magic and was shipped off to Ozmandias."

Ghost sat heavily, his head in his hands. "The Squall line is dead. All I can hope for is the eradication of the men responsible. Frothgar. Caermon Erefoss. Daerveron. Wolfbane."

With each name Ghost's fists clenched tighter and his pronun-ciation became more guttural. Diaga knelt beside him whispering in his ear, "You can make this right. Find what you seek, fight the invaders, but do it justly. Do it to free the Napalian people. Do this for something more than revenge."

Ghost looked up at this young man. Until now he had consid-ered him little more than a burden on their travels. He was no longer so sure of his worthlessness, but his imploring words did not change Ghost's conviction. He was young and weak, and there was no turn-ing back. "I am incapable of anything but revenge, boy. It is a fact of my life I have embraced. You'd be wise to join me in my quest for it."

"You should not expect all of us to follow you into oblivion. Our paths are the same now, but if you pursue this selfish road they will diverge." Diaga paused before adding, "You may keep your identity to yourself, Greymane. After all you are no longer the man you once were."

With that Diaga melted into the night, leaving Greymane Squall, traitor to his people, to finally die. Since he had fled like a mad beast from Napal City, Ghost had been at war with himself, or rather with the man he had once been. Now, with Diaga's harsh reminder of his past, he no longer felt the need to hold onto what shreds of his former self remained. When the morning light came, Ghost had still not awakened the others for their watch. He had buried his past. In that one night all traces of Greymane Squall were burned from Teth-tenir. Only the ashes of an old man's memory remained, and the true life of the vengeful spirit named Ghost had finally begun.

Two other Squalls were in grave danger of dying in a more concrete sense that morning. While Algathor had managed to rebuke the first attempt of the Nerothians to enter his home, it would surely not be the last, and two men who had beat upon his door were far easier to intimidate than a squadron would be. He and his guests now remained on alert, for it was obvious that the presence of Romund, Edge, and Raymir was well known. For his part, Saltilian was furious. His plan had been to gather a large force and storm the house without prelude, but the overeager guards had ruined that trying to curry favor with the wizard. Saltilian had them beaten, and dispatched far to the north where the winter chill would teach them a lesson, if they survived it at all.

Saltilian opted not to change his strategy, however. A frontal assault would certainly overwhelm an old man and three tired fugitives with nowhere to go. He gathered the entire garrison of Glaciar outside the home and delivered his instructions to the guard captain: "Y-you will k-k-kill all of them, s-save the g-girl. I want t-the traitor's h-head for W-W-Wolfbane to see."

The captain saluted and went to relay Saltilian's orders. The wizard hung back just outside the gate so he could watch his plan unfold in safety.

Having driven the guards from his front door with a series of threats and meaningful gestures of his spear, Algathor Squall had set himself in the small study next to the main entrance and was watching through the curtain for a renewed attempt to gain entrance to his home. Romund had been set to rummaging through the cellar for supplies, as the head of the Squall home was determined his guests should move on and swiftly, hopefully to avoid bloodshed they all seemed assured was coming but determined not to mention, as though leaving it unspoken would somehow prevent it from oc-curring. Raymir walked into the room and sat near her grandfather without speaking, her clothes changed into more practical garb for traveling. She wore a heavy olive-green dress with leather boots, belt, and bracers. The dress had slits up the sides almost to her hips and she wore tan deerskin pants beneath. She eyed her grandfather, dressed for battle in what would have seemed a comical fashion given his advanced age, but for the glint of danger in his old eyes.

Without looking at her, the older man said, "I am glad I kept some of your things here, my dear. Otherwise, you'd have had little to choose from."

Raymir brushed her knees self-consciously. "I could have made due, grandfather."

"Yes," he said, "I'm sure you could have. You're a Squall through and through. A fierce lover and deadly foe all at once, and able to switch between both at a moment's notice."

"Grandfather!" Raymir laughed and blushed slightly. "What could possibly give you a reason to think that?"

His eyes turned towards her and Algathor smiled sadly. "I know what you have been through and what you must go through still. You are a hard woman, Raymir, not a girl any longer. I am proud, and also very sorry that it came to this."

His words struck her deeply and Raymir did not answer for a time. They sat there in quiet, watching the windows together, before she said, "Edge would leave me here. He means to help Romund, I can sense it, but he thinks I have to be sheltered from the world."

Algathor scoffed. "He's a fool, and in love. You can't blame him for wanting to protect you. In time, he'll learn that we Squalls pro-vide our own protection." Algathor turned to her then and said, in a gentler voice, "But do let him shield you from harm, my dear. I wish to see you survive these dark days. I know you cannot stay here, you must not stay here, but please don't throw your life away either. You are all I have left."

Raymir felt tears welling in her eyes and saw the same on the face of her beloved grandfather. She went to him and the two embraced for a moment, then she turned away and he back to the window. She wiped her eyes and said, "I should see if Romund needs help in the cellar."

Algathor did not respond but waved her away. She left the room and he sat there a while longer as morning passed into afternoon. Some hours later, the Nerothian guards began to gather outside. Within the house, Algathor, now joined by Edge, sat at the front win-dows while Raymir and Romund slept briefly on cots in a back room. The old man was now fully armored, heavy steel plate covering his far thinner leather cuirass; and wearing a helm of layered crags of metal extending from over the forehead to the rounded peak. He heft-ed his spear and eyed the young stranger. "My granddaughter seems to have been greatly taken with you."

Edge was cautious in his reply. "I am also with her, my lord."

Algathor grunted, "Oh do stop calling me that, you fool, the name is Algathor. Alright?"

"Yes, sir, I mean, Algathor."

"Good, that wasn't so bad was it?"

"No, sir."

Algathor chuckled slightly as Edge tried to recover. "You are young aren't you? I don't remember what the other was like too clearly, but he was about your age maybe."

"I'm sorry Algathor, I don't understand what you mean."

"Your name, lad," Algathor leaned on the shaft of the spear and studied Edge closely, "el Vac. A name that, in these lands at least, still carries great respect. I told you our family once fought with a lost elf from Ozmandias named Xantes el Vac. Well once, when I was far younger, another of your kind by the name of Vactan el Vac came asking after Xantes's story. He had the same odd cloak clasps you've got on now."

Edge touched his shoulder where the hands held his cloak chain and said, "I've heard Vactan's name spoken of more as a curse."

"Yes," Algathor replied, "he supposedly killed Bullwyf Margrave, the Commander of the Eagle Knights in the Fortress of Aves before being run through himself."

"Why do you say supposedly?"

"Because even in my memory full of cobwebs and half-images, I recall the make of the man. He was not a traitor, though perhaps my inability to detect such qualities in those close to me makes my opinion of no importance in this regard."

The mood darkened significantly and they sat in silence a while longer, until Edge finally spoke quietly, "What will we do if they come in force?"

The old campaigner looked at him. "You fear for your life boy?"

Edge shook his head resolutely. "Only hers."

"A good answer." Algathor smiled, then his face grew grave. "When they come, because they will soon enough, we will do nothing. I will hold them off while you escape."

Edge was puzzled. "Escape, Algathor? There's only one way out of the city."

Algathor shook his head. "Glaciar was a mining town first and foremost. We dug those tunnels deep, and one of them is how the damned Erefoss bastards escaped, only to come back again and again to pester us like an infestation. But it has been the duty of the Squall family to watch over the old mines and the way through the mountains to bar their return, or in this case the pursuit of your enemies. There is a narrow path behind the manor that opens up against the side of the nearest mountain. Raymir knows of it from her childhood, though she never knew its purpose. You will see it just beyond my backdoor. Try to block the exit of this place when you leave, to slow them down. I have left a little surprise for any who do follow you into the pass." He paused a moment before adding, "You will have to carry Raymir, she will not want to leave me."

Edge's eyes widened in understanding as he said, "You can not really mean to stay, Algathor, we could all escape."

The old man rounded on him. "I am not young enough to survive the Frozen Reach, but I can fight, boy, and like a true Squall I will give myself to buy time for those I love." He grabbed the young man by the front of his tunic and Edge was surprised at the strength of his grip. "You will take my granddaughter from here, Edgewulf el Vac, and you will love her all your life and give her everything she desires. You will build her a home far from the madness of this world and grow old with her. That is an order!"

He released Edge and the lost elf was surprised to see tears fill the old man's eyes, which seemed to him suddenly far, far away. "You will protect the last of my kin with all your might, and be kind to my great-grandchildren, tell them of their dear ancestor Algathor. Tell them," he paused wistfully, "tell them I died a warrior of my people."

There came a roar outside the manor gate as the guards charged the house. Algathor and Edge stared sharply at the rushing mob. Then Edge was hurled down the hall by a powerful shove of the old man's arms, stumbling toward where Romund and Raymir lay resting. "Save my grandchild, warrior! I will hold them as long as I can!"

Edge paused a moment, watching the older man ready himself, then he spun and charged down the hall as the last great warrior of the Squall line burst from his home to meet the enemy. Edge sobbed as he heard the clash of metal and the roar tearing from Algathor's ancient chest, "Come to me, you lucky devils! Let me carve the way to the Dead Realms for us all!"

Raymir and Romund were awake already, he standing in the doorway, ready to join Algathor's mad assault. Romund clutched his sword and caught Edge's look as the lost elf ran towards them. Raymir suddenly launched herself from the room hearing her grandfather's cries. "Grandfather! I am coming!"

But Edge held her fast, keeping her from tearing down the hall to her grandfather. She beat at him wildly as Romund stared in shock. "Edge! What are you doing? We have to help him!"

Edge shook his head, his eyes running freely. "There is a way out." Romund looked unsure still. "Damn it Romund! I promised him!"

That seemed to settle it for the man from Hethegar. He grabbed Raymir by the waist, tearing her from Edge, and started down the hall. "I've got her, see if you can help Algathor! Where is it?"

Edge was already moving towards the front door. "There's a back entrance, end of the hall!"

Romund redoubled his efforts as a screaming Raymir kicked and contorted, trying to break free. He hauled her down to the end of the hallway. "Raymir! Raymir, listen to me! Your grandfather is giving his life for you! Now we have got to go now! Help me open the door, quickly!"

Raymir pushed him away as she gathered herself and at first he thought she might attack him, but instead she stood staring at a large bookcase at the end of the corridor. Suddenly she snatched something from the shelf then grabbed the sides and hurled the obstruction aside with strength born of inexpressible grief. Wrenching the now-revealed door open, she stumbled forward a few steps and fell sobbing into the gently falling snow, unable to move. Romund made sure she was staying put and had nowhere to go, then drew his sword and ran back down the hall to rescue Edge.

The old warrior of House Squall had pushed far from his front door and into the courtyard. Algathor was bleeding from dozens of cuts all over his body, yet he was surrounded by dead and dying guards, and those unscathed refused to get any closer to the whirlwind of death his spear and sword still created. The guard captain made a desperate lunge at him with his own blade, and fell with his face split down the middle from an expertly swung spear as Algathor danced his way to his doom.

Saltilian could see the warrior was tiring, though he could not believe such an aged man could have killed almost a score of young guards. He screamed over the roars of the ancient Napalian, "Stand c-clear you f-fools! He'll b-b-bleed out s-soon enough!"

The guards complied, happy to step back from the raging maelstrom of steel before them. Algathor called out to the mage, his lips flecked with blood. "Come on, you coward! Fight me yourself!" Saltilian did not move. Algathor grinned like a mad thing. "Then I shall come to you!"

He began to rush forward and the ranks parted as the guards continued to distance themselves from this man who would not die. Saltilian shrieked for them to close with him, to stop his charge, but none listened. Mere feet from the mage, Algathor stumbled, as did a terrified Saltilian, falling onto his back and cowering like a child. The old man raised his spear, a blank stare coming over his face. He tried to focus, but it seemed there were several mages prostrate before him, all little more than vague shapes in the slowly falling snow. Algathor could not see, he shook his head to clear his vision, but he heard the voice of his son's murdered family calling to him. He fell to his knees, a smile coming over his cragged face. "Children? My grandchildren, at last, I have found you."

Algathor fell into the blood-reddened snow, his soul fleeing his body to join his descendants, and so passed the last legendary Thane of the Squall family warriors.

Edge arrived at the doorway in time to see the great man fall. He groaned in despair, too late to drag Algathor back from his doom, as the figure slumped in the snow. Almost immediately, the guards were upon him. They had seen the inexplicably unstoppable Algathor fall and felt a renewed surge of bloodlust and anger at the deaths of their fellow men. Edge whirled his halberd, killing the first two to approach the door, but the press of bodies forced him to back into the entryway. He felled another intruder before taking a sword in his thigh and he stumbled back still farther, trying to narrow the avenue for his enemies to attack from.

Suddenly Romund was at his side, thrusting his blade and driving back the enemy with the ferocity of his own attack. He grabbed Edge and yelled, "Hold onto me, hold on!"

They each swung one last time, then whirled and lurched down the hall to the rear exit. Romund heaved Edge with all his might through the gap then spun and threw himself at the door in time to close it. The guards pressed against the other side, sliding Romund back a few steps. Then suddenly Raymir was beside him, forcing the door to shut. She slammed the slidebar bolt into place and they turned together, grabbing either side of Edge's shoulders and racing for the narrow pass in the distance.

They tore across the deepening snow. Edge hobbled along, leaning heavily on Romund as they did. Raymir was in front, forcing her way forward determinedly. They reached the narrow opening in the mountains and Raymir spun, her heavy outdoor cloak swirling behind her. The backdoor bulged and cracked as the guards battered against it. Edge lurched his way to her side and Raymir grabbed his free arm and together she and Romund pulled him into the opening of the narrow pass. As they rounded the corner, Edge could see thick ropes extending out either side of the trail under the snow and running up the mountainside rising above them to the north and south.

Romund heard the explosion of timber and the shouts of the guards. Raymir slowed and shoved him to the right crying, "Grab the rope and pull, be ready to run!"

Romund did not stop to argue, grasping the coarse, heavy cord and pulling sharply. He was surprised when the rope came loose easily, though he heard a low, thunderous sound from above him, rapidly building. Romund looked skyward and saw, perhaps halfway up the mountainside, a gathering cloud of rolling snow coming down on either side of their position in the pass. Raymir screamed over the gathering roar, "Romund! Help me!"

That broke the trance. Romund grasped Edge's arm and together the three raced as fast as they could drag themselves away from the avalanche. Edge could not hear anything except the incredible noise of the careening whiteness behind them. It felt as though it was rushing to swallow them up like some ravenous beast. A great gust of wind hit them in the back and the three fugitives flew forward, landing safely in the soft, newly fallen snow. Romund turned on his side to look back at the pass, now completely erased by the destruction of the deluge. Raymir rose slowly, exhausted, and threw herself sobbing into Edge's arms as the weight of what had just transpired finally hit her.

Romund slumped against the pillow of snow opposite the two and closed his eyes. Eventually, Raymir cried herself to sleep and the two sat alone in the eerie silence, the sun falling rapidly behind the mountains. Romund opened his eyes and stared at Edge. "There are only a few moments in my life that have been as dark as this one."

"Were you lost in the frozen north those times as well?" Edge asked gloomily.

Romund sat up a bit. "Lost?"

"Algathor never explained where this pass goes. Even if we end up near a campsite we could miss it from a bare ten yards if the weather is the way it was when I first came here. Not to mention it seems winter has come on earlier than I expected."

Romund seemed to understand. "It's nearer to winter than it should be, an ill omen if I've ever seen one. It's possible the weather will be worse than when you arrived by the time we get through the mountains. But we'll be alright, no matter the situation."

"You seem upbeat for a man with limited supplies in a frozen wasteland without any sense of direction."

Romund grinned. "I think your brave young lady may have the answer to our prayers." He pointed to the sheet of parchment on which Raymir had loosened her fierce grip in her sleep. "That looks from here to be a map. It seems old Algathor did not send us out blind after all."

Edge smiled fondly. "I should have known. He would never let his granddaughter leave without guidance."

Romund heaved himself up from the snow and walked over. "Let me see that leg."

Edge moved his limb slightly, felt a lancing pain, and gasped. He tried to put on a brave face saying, "I don't think it's too deep."

"All the same," Romund pulled forth some clean cloth and undid a leather strap from his waist, "better to get some pressure on it now and we can see about healing it more thoroughly later." Romund tightened the belt around Edge's leg, ignoring his wincing as he did so. The blood soaked into the cloth, but did not seem to be worsening. Satisfied he had done all he could, Romund returned to his side of the path, undid his bedroll and laid it down.

Edge looked at the man he was now indebted to for so much. "You saved my life back there, Romund. I will repay you."

Romund's head came up from his blanket. "Repay me? I believe I owe you for a welt on your head and my safe passage from Napal City. No, my brave young friend, you owe me nothing. It was the least I could do."

Edge smiled, which quickly turned to a yawn. Pulling Raymir protectively closer, he adjusted to a more comfortable position, and soon joined her in slumber. The moon, now rising quite high in the starry sky, shone brightly over them as they fell into an exhausted sleep, the gentle snow still falling silently all about their weary bodies.

Saltilian's sleep came much harder. He was both furious and relieved. Furious at losing his prize, and relieved that his failure had not cost him his life. He had stayed clear while the remaining guards buried the Napalian, afraid the sight of him might once again cause him to vomit as he had when he foolishly scrambled away from the specter of the dying man. Saltilian had locked himself within his private quarters of the inn he had claimed, until the guards came to tell him Algathor was truly dead. Even then, Saltilian stayed in his quarters, trying to stop the shaking, nauseous sickness that came over him. Eventually, he settled on studying his spellbooks, reciting incantations he should have known by heart, only to find he had forgotten them. Even that was not enough, so he finally removed the oddly-sized and bound text from his robes and sat with it. For several hours, it remained unopened as he simply stroked the surface of it, calming his frayed nerves.

His fear slowly turned to curiosity, and a strange, unexplainable need to open the book. Saltilian, who had been laying on his bed twitching and convulsing until he began fondling the odd tome, rose and set it on the small end table. He flipped to several pages mechanically, but at last one caught his attention and he held it open before him. The words, still incomprehensible, swam before his eyes for several seconds and he felt transported to another place. He could not say how long he sat there, frozen, but he snapped suddenly out of his entrancement and knew immediately what he must do. Still, it took him several moments to even begin to consider closing the book, and when he did he found his mind still swirled with images and ideas of which he could only fathom the barest portion.

When Saltilian had finally cleared his head enough to call in a guard, he had a plan. He listened indifferently as the guard informed him that twenty-two men had died taking the manor, eleven more when the pass the fugitives fled through was blocked by a sudden avalanche. The guard started to inform him of the recent appointments and promotions following the disastrous affair, but Saltilian cut him off. "I understand t-t-that you managed t-to w-wound the f-former officer, Edgewulf?"

The guard nodded. Saltilian stood from his bed, where he had been sitting aloof throughout the report. He walked to the small armoire that was the only furniture in his sparse quarters, aside from his bed and end table, and poured himself a glass of wine. He turned slowly to face the guard, taking in the drink's alluring aroma. "Y-you will f-f-find s-some of his b-blood, it n-n-need not be f-fresh. B-bring it t-to me."

The guard stood as if waiting for more, then hurried out of the room when he realized there was to be no further direction. Saltilian turned back to his book to wait, staring at it as though it spoke to him from its quiet seat on the table edge. He set his wine down on the cabinet once again and looked up at the wardrobe, whose doors had several fine, mirrored glass panes at the top. Saltilian examined his face, with its pale, almost dead skin. His sunken eyes and hooked nose, his dead, limp, black hair, slick with grease. He snarled, revealing crooked yellow teeth and hurled his wine glass at the armoire, shattering it and the mirrored glass of the doors.

Saltilian stared at the shattered pieces on the floor and breathed, short ragged breaths. Memories from Ozmandias flooded back to him, the cruel lesson Q'thal had tried to teach him before he departed. Each wizard, upon graduating to independent study and arcane practice, was given a gift from his teachers. When he learned his was to come from the High Wizard himself, Saltilian had been elated and arrogant to be chosen for such an honor. But the gift from Q'thal had been nothing more than an elegant golden hand mirror. It was to remind him that the power he sought could do nothing about the condition of his appearance, which had always driven his hate. The mirror was supposed to teach him to accept, to forgive the disgust others felt for him and turn to them with kindness. Q'thal swore that then his image would change, and he would see his true self, his inner self.

Saltilian had long ago realized that his inner self was the image he already saw. That same foul visage that had always drawn stones and insults from others as a child was his true self. His soul was as twisted as his face, and he found now that he could comfortably embrace that. He had smashed that mirror on the stones of his quarters in Ozmandias, leaving its broken shards to be found and removed by the servants. In the end, he had dismissed both the gift and the lesson.

A shuffling of feet behind Saltilian interrupted his reminiscing. He turned to see the guard he had sent out standing there, a bloody sword in hand. Wordlessly he took the weapon from the guard and, using his long fingernails, scraped the semi-dry blood into a fresh wine cup. Muttering in an ancient language, one reminiscent of the arcane words of the gods yet somehow older and more twisted, he wove a complicated spell that set the wine glowing a faint blue. His audience, the young guard, was curious enough to come closer, eyeing the concoction.

Saltilian looked at him, his voice suddenly clear and distant as he asked, "You want to know what this will do, this little potion of mine?" The guard nodded silently. Saltilian bent and picked up a large shard of reflective glass from the floor. "It will show me where our friends are, once it is complete."

The guard looked puzzled. "You need glass to finish the job?"

Saltilian smiled slightly. "No," He rammed the shard into the guard's throat, holding the wine glass beneath it to catch his spurting blood, "I n-need f-f-fresh life to f-find them."

Saltilian grimaced as he heard his stutter return. Ignoring the spasms of the still bleeding guard, he gulped down the now brilliantly violet potion and focused his mind on the form of Edge el Vac. The dark magic took him, knocking his physical body senseless as he slipped into a storm of sights and sounds, flying from his body and the room on black wings of determination. As his spirit floated away a crooked smiled lay transfixed on his face and in the fevered dreams that followed the uncovering of el Vac's location, Saltilian sat on a bloody throne time and again, lording over the destruction done in his name by beings so grotesque and inhuman as to be beyond descripton.

Edge woke to the throbbing pain in his leg. He managed to peel back a corner of the bandage, and could see the blood was mostly dried. While he certainly wasn't going to die from loss of blood, he thought the pain might do him in. Through the haze that was his vision, he saw that Romund had left his makeshift bed, having his pack neatly prepared for travel. From the soft pressing weight on his shoulder Edge knew that Raymir still slept on, seemingly unperturbed by the dark tidings that had befallen her of late. Edge sighed and closed his eyes. The pain didn't fade, but he could focus on images in his mind rather than those in the pass, which only reminded him of their seemingly insurmountable situation.

He heard boots on the soft snow and looked to see Romund returning, clad in his leather armor with metal studs and covered in a thin layer of snow. He clutched his short sword in one hand and a strange plant in the other. Kneeling by Edge, he extended the plant to him. "Chew on the stem, it should ease the pain."

Edge complied, and soon found the pulsation of pain punctuated by the occasional sharp twinge had dulled down to a mere ache, with occasional spikes of real discomfort. He watched Romund shake off the snow he had inadvertently collected and pile a small stack of twigs in the center of their path. Using flint and tinder from his pouch, he set the pile alight and rested his back against the hard base of the mountain.

Edge shifted slightly, careful not to wake Raymir. "Did you find anything? Clearly the end of the trail is not far from here."

Romund nodded. "It took me an hour or so at an easy pace to find it. On your leg it may take us two."

"Where does the pass open up?"

Romund grunted, "Amidst the mountains. I would say it's some sort of valley in the center of the Dragonscales. How we get beyond them will depend on Raymir's map."

"No towns nearby then?"

Romund shook his head. "None. The Sundered Blades Hold is supposed to be near Glaciar, but like any orc tribe they are unlikely to seek us out and we won't spot them unless we have a clear sense of where to go."

Edge rubbed his fingers over the wood handle of his halberd. "They won't attack us either, I suppose that's something. We will have to get out of the mountains quickly. Our supplies will last us but a few days and we have to begin at least partially replenishing them."

"We will have plenty of wood to burn, at least; that way we won't freeze."

They sat in silence for a time, each dwelling on their dire predicament. Edge nearly drifted off again when Romund spoke hesitantly. "I heard you talking to Algathor before, about your ancestry. Exactly where are you from, Edge?"

The young warrior eyed the older man with a wry smile. "It took you some time to ask that question. Most just stare at the stark white hair or my green eyes. I've heard many call my appearance unnerving."

Romund shrugged as he said, "Didn't want to be rude about it."

"No fear of that. You likely know of the lost elves, found mostly in Haddon Mirk?"

"Yes, one of the first mortal peoples. Isolationists, if I recall."

"Indeed, they are said to scuttle ships that sail too close to their islands. But once there was a great flurry of desire to connect with the other mortal races of Teth-tenir, and the lost elves sent out missionaries to chosen locations. It was a great sacrifice, for those who went were never allowed to return. The el Vac family sent many of their large house, and it is to one of their lines I owe my descendance."

"An old family," Romund agreed, "and one recently in disgrace, so the tales say. Did you ever think of changing your name?"

"No, it is my name. I will not run from it."

Edge's tone was defiant and Romund chose to let the matter drop, instead saying, "I read about the emergence of the elves once, as a child. Many mortal races, including elves, are supposed to draw their ancestry from the first mortals, the Revenants. It is said the Revenants were the first race the gods created, that they retain some of the immortals' innate magical powers and that even after the Great Exodus some still can be found in Southron."

Edge waved his hand. "I know nothing of them but what you have said. Of my own people, I have ever only known one other, my twin brother Aydwulf. Wolfbane found both of us on a small island in the Syrrion Sea, in a town called Ilanis. The island had a temple to Neroth, whose priests raised us when no one else would take us in. We never knew how we came to live there; it was kept a secret from us. Maybe the people of Ilanis never knew themselves."

"Where is your brother now?"

Edge turned to look down the windswept trail. "I do not know. He was with me on the island. We trained under Wolfbane there. When I left with the army he was still there, but I do not think he would have stayed. He was always more a fan of cunning and guile and Wolfbane talked often of Aydwulf's role in Neroth's grander scheme, but I do not know what part he was meant to play.

"Aydwulf and I were ostracized for our differences. Even though the townspeople took us in, they feared us as well. You have noticed my eyes, of course. Why they glow green I do not know, none of the lost elves do. Supposedly it is the defining trait of our race, but it frightens people. As much as I have trained myself to kill, to wage war indiscriminately, I wanted to be recognized as a man of other qualities. I am not a heartless killer, and neither is my brother, but he seemed to embrace the distrust and actively work to foster qualities that make others fear him."

Romund swallowed visibly and paused a moment before forging into a topic he knew would be dangerous to discuss. "I can tell you why they fear you."

Edge looked up sharply asking, "Beyond my appearance you mean?"

"It goes back to the War of the Lion. You said you knew about the el Vac name, but perhaps not about why it is so reviled. Vactan el Vac, the man who destroyed his family's name, did so in a fashion so repulsive it is infuriating to even hear the tale."

"Algathor mentioned him killing the Commander of the Eagle Knights, though he seemed skeptical it was actually his doing."

"He should not have been!" Romund's tone was harsh and emphatic. "There is much mystery around Bullwyf Margrave's death, certainly, but it is the motive of his killer that eludes history, not the man's identity."

"You seem to be certain of this."

Romund eyed him and proceeded more cautiously in his response, "I had not heard the name el Vac in many years. I do not think that a name or even relationship to someone who has done evil means that they will also be flawed in the same way. I believe in my heart that Vactan el Vac killed Bull the Warrior, but I also believe you are not the same man as he was regardless of your connection to him."

Edge sat in silence while this took hold on him. He had never met or known any of his ancestors, nor where they came from. Never had he known another lost elf other than his brother Aydwulf, and in his childhood only Wolfbane had possessed any knowledge of their people. Now it seemed as though his history was as black as the service he currently fled. Perhaps he was cursed. He felt compelled to inquire further, "Algathor said el Vac was killed shortly after his betrayal."

Romund continued the story. "Vactan el Vac was one of the most empowered officers among the Eagle Knights, some believed him second only to Bull himself. He was a fierce fighter and harsh leader. Many feared him and rightly so, legend has it he was the greatest swordsman of his time. Yet, the story goes a young recruit, only just raised to the order, slew him in single combat upon learning he had murdered Bull the Warrior."

"Who was the recruit?"

"No one knows. He too disappeared after the battle. Vactan's legendary sword, said to be enchanted with the power of flame, was never recovered. Stranger still, when the soldiers of Aves returned to retrieve their fallen brothers they found the body of Vactan el Vac missing."

Edge's brow furrowed. "Can they be certain he did not somehow survive?"

Romund shrugged and answered, "Some claim he cheated death and lived, but those who saw him fall insisted death took him before he struck the earth."

Edge's face had been ever darkening with black thoughts and misgivings, which Romund had taken note of and now felt it his duty to rectify. He coughed to get his attention. "I mention this not to hurt you, Edge, but only because this happened within my lifetime, and it is possible you were related to this man. Regardless, it speaks not to your character. Honesty, courage, love, these things are not passed through blood. You have proven yourself a man of quality many times over. Whether or not you have a relation to Vactan el Vac does not matter. You are Edgewulf el Vac, a noble man and a very good friend."

Edge felt himself relax then. Romund had somehow, with simple words, dissolved all his fear. Whatever past he had, whether it included some connection to this Vactan el Vac or not, it would not determine his future. He knew the path he would take. He, Romund, and Raymir would deal a blow to Wolfbane's mad plan and then fade into the background of this greater conflict. He would keep his promise to Algathor and protect his granddaughter, no matter the cost. They would be happy somewhere, anywhere, else.

Edge was about to express his gratitude when Romund appeared next to him, a comforting hand on his shoulder. "This is too much to digest immediately, I think. You should rest some more, we've slept a bare number of hours these past few days. Sleep, and know that Romund of Hethegar will watch over you."

Edge patted his hand thankfully. "I will undoubtedly sleep easier than I ever have, Romund, thank you."

Romund nodded and moved down the pass to take his post on the gradual incline of the mountain slope. The last thing Edge saw before drifting off to sleep was the older man crouched by his meager fire, a monolith of strength and determination. Edge dreamt himself into that same position, Raymir behind him, as he held off the darkness for her. She slept undisturbed in his shadow, and the evils of the world ran from the warrior with no past, for he had much future before him.

Chapter 13

Arvadis had retired to his small home along one of the main avenues of Alderlast. The Zenith Road, the further it got from the Royal Palace, was more market and gossip center than a royal street, at least on the southern side where the district belonged to the Hawking House. Arvadis preferred this part of town further from the palace, the royal center being a place where he felt closeted away from the people. The king had taken his oath as ruler very seriously. Part of the oath stated that the king of Angladais "will protect, justly and honorably, the people above all else, including himself." So it was that Arvadis was prepared for the possibility of his demise for the good of the people. He knew that in his compromised position he was a perfect target for Highlord Vendile, who had lusted after the throne his entire life. Arvadis only hoped that if Vendile assassinated him, his son Vorasho would be wise enough to uncover the scheme, and finally put the self-serving Highlord into exile where he belonged. If he played the games some of the other Highlords did, Arvadis would have killed Vendile long ago, but he would not stoop to that level. He would not allow a murderer on the throne, even if it was himself.

Arvadis's had no counter to Vendile's next move, whatever it would be, for there was very little he could do. He had announced the deaths of the paladins and other soldiers to the people and declared a day of mourning in their names. At this moment, the king would have to wait and see how his foe would try to capitalize on this disaster. Worse, Arvadis could think of nothing that would extricate Angladais from the current predicament. He had no idea how to battle a wizard in an impenetrable fortress built into the very stone of the Pillars of Light, and Arvadis feared that the only hope for his people lay beyond his borders, perhaps if another Legocian nation came to their rescue. He laughed softly at the idea. Angladais was the defender of the lesser nations of Legocia. They came to the rescue of others; it would be unthinkable to any realm that they could defeat a foe the Angladaics could not. No one would be able to save Angladais if she could not protect herself. Arvadis and his kingdom were well and truly alone.

The aged king rose from his wicker chair and walked slowly along the upper level of his modest home. Battle-worn shields decorated the walls all along the hall and in most of the rooms. They were shields that went back to the very founding of his great nation. They represented the great men and women of his family, going back many centuries. The Hawking house had always defended the people with their very lives, fighting for those who could not fight for themselves, and upholding the greater code of the nation. They had broken their spears on the shields of all Legocia's great enemies, and now one damnable mage was stopping him. A sorceror, a wielder of magic despised by all Angadaics, barred the way to the outside world. The cruel truth that a master of an art forbidden to his own people now held them trapped within their homeland did not escape Arvadis. What frightened him more was what the invaders were doing to the world beyond the Cloud Peak Basin with Angladais trapped in their own lands. The invaders did not set their roots between the Pillars to crush Angladais, but to enclose them. They would destroy Legocia first, and then come for the noble nation when it was all that remained. Arvadis wondered how long it would be before the smoke of burning villages would cross the thin border of Silverleaf to the south and east.

Arvadis ran his aged hands over the shields. His family's honor was held in those bits of wood and steel. He glanced out the window of his bedroom, with its blank space on the wall for his own shield. Arvadis watched the people moving silently back and forth along the dark streets clad in black robes. He wondered if they would hang his shield for him as they had his father's. He feared those who came after him might burn it to ashes instead.

A commotion from the other side of the house brought him around from his musing. Walking to Logan's old room he stared out the window and was shocked to see Highlord guardsmen coming down the street, attempting to push his two personal wardens out of the way. Graham and Derek were refusing to budge and blood would be spilled if he did not interfere soon. Arvadis rushed downstairs.

The two Hawking men held their posts firmly. Graham had been in Arvadis's service for over twenty years and he was as tough as stone. His gruff and curt voice carried loudly from the street to Arvadis's ears within the manor. "You cannot see the king without a grievance or council decree," the elder guard said, "and I see neither in your possession."

The lead guard, of Vendile's house, gritted his teeth in frustration. "Listen, you old sod, we had a decree and your young friend here tore it to shreds!"

Graham was unperturbed by the flustered visitor. "Well that sounds quite unlike Derek. You must have been very rude."

The Vendile men looked ready to draw swords. Arvadis remained in the shadows a bit longer, studying the contingent. They contained only guards from Vendile, Hladic, and Bwemor with a smattering of unsure and nervous looking members of Xarinth and Galden. Those two had the customary three representatives for providing escort to nobles called before the council for violations of the Code, but the others had more than twice the traditional number. Representatives of Houses Calavar and Irindein were nowhere in sight. Things were not looking well for the king, but he had bloodshed to avoid. "Friends," he announced, entering the faint lamplight at last, "enough good men have died tonight without adding to that number now."

All present were surprised by the king's sudden appearance. Graham tried to warn him back into the house, but Arvadis's look silenced him. If one of them were going to fall, it would be he alone. Arvadis turned cordially to the guards saying, "State your business with the king, sirs."

The lead man, Vendile's guard, turned a frustrated gaze on the king and seemed to hesitate. Fear of Vendile overtook him and he found his tongue. "The Highlord Council has issued a decree, you are to come to the meeting hall at the palace immediately."

Arvadis remained silent a moment and Graham jumped in. "You cannot take him anywhere without a formally written decree."

"We had one until this cur ripped it apart! You want me to pick the pieces off the cobblestones?"

"No, I'd rather you dig through some horse dung for them."

Arvadis interjected before the furious Vendile guard could draw his blade. "I see no reason not to travel with you to the palace. Otherwise, I will never learn the nature of this decree. Let me dress more appropriately, and I shall be with you momentarily."

The escort looked as shocked as Arvadis's own guards, but he consented. Arvadis went inside to change into his more formal garb. He put on his traditional Hawking House colors of gold and white, covering the fine garments with a shawl of silver and gold design, the colors of the Angladaic kings. He reappeared in his doorway shortly. Graham and Derek had not moved, but both gripped their spear hafts tightly. Graham put a restraining arm on his king's shoulder whispering, "This is wrong, sire. You cannot be taken in such a disgraceful manner. Make them bring the traditional number and order as the Code decrees. They dishonor you!"

Arvadis ignored the man's fears and instead pulled him close. Graham was stunned both by his firm grip and fiery eyes. "I will not run from this, Graham. Now listen to me, this may be my last order as your king. You will stay here with Derek until my son Vorasho returns. You will tell him what has transpired and give him this letter from me. He must follow it precisely as it is written, and you will do as he says. Understood?"

Graham took the thin parchment, sealed with the Hawking stamp, and slid it under his mail tunic. "It shall be as you say, my king."

Arvadis smiled. "Thank you. Be steadfast in your faith, Paladinis shall deliver us."

Graham could not muster the words to respond. As Arvadis walked toward the escort Derek suddenly spoke up, "My lord!"

Arvadis turned to the young and soft-spoken guard. "Yes, Derek?"

The young man snapped a formal salute. "My life for you, sir!"

Arvadis smiled sadly as he returned the gesture. "And mine for you."

He turned and was swept into the guards and ushered along towards the palace. As he walked, people noticed the flash of white among the black garb of the forlorn populace, and whispers traveled swiftly. King Arvadis marches to the palace, they said. He walks in the clothes he wore on his coronation, he wears white, but seems to carry his own shroud. Suddenly, the mourning black took on new meaning for the people of Angladais. Many feared they had now lost a king as well as many of his bravest men. One particular pair of eyes had witnessed the exchange before the king's home. Graham and Derek kept their silent vigil over the empty house, and the people were too afraid of their response to ask where the king went this night. The same watcher observed quietly from the shadows, and waited for the people to disperse before approaching the guards.

"Halt! Who goes there?" Graham's voice had a strained edge to it. He examined the cloaked figure before him. Its form was too slim to be an armored warrior, but this night was hiding many surprises. "State your name and business, shadow, or I will see if you bleed a mortal's blood."

A silken voice responded with boldness, "I bleed the pure blood of the Angladaic faithful. I must speak with the prince."

Graham shook his weary head. "He is not here, and only he will be allowed into the home of the Hawking House."

"My master bade me give you this." The figure, now clearly recognizeable as a woman, held forth a round object for the guards to see.

Graham's eyes climbed up his brow. "Of course, m'lady. I will admit you at once."

The two guards ushered the strange woman inside and returned to their posts. Derek asked no questions of his older companion. They had both seen the object the woman carried and known immediately she must be brought inside. As the night thickened around him, the young Derek felt the tension within subside slightly. Perhaps some hope did exist.

The palace halls were dark. Arvadis strode sternly through them with his unwanted company of Highlord guards. They seemed fearful of him, for they knew they were violating the Code in this act, but would not speak of it. Perhaps the silence eased the guilt on their souls. Arvadis turned to one of the men who wore the sigil of Xarinth over his mourning black asking, "Why do you lack the men of Calavar, Hawking, and Irindein?"

The young guard swallowed hard. "They would not come, my lord."

"And why?"

The guard looked ready to run under the king's scrutiny. He stammered, "Lord Vendile ordered your arrest and that of Highlords Irindein and Calavar. Their men either ordered by their masters to stand aside or were killed, but none would participate in the escort."

Arvadis acted as though this surprised him. "Indeed? I would think such men would be honored to act on behalf of their kingdom, if they felt the summons to the palace was just."

The guard could not fathom how to respond to the thinly veiled insinuation. Arvadis pressed it no further. Vorasho had pointed out the separations among the houses and clearly Vendile had not won them all over, but Vendile would also not call the council to sit without the Highlords present, as such a transgression would ensure civil war. He had the army and priests by way of Gelladan Bwemor and Brusius Hladic. Most likely Runiden Calavar and Fremont Irindein were being forced to sit in under guard, even if they had agreed to come in an effort to avoid bloodshed as Arvadis had. He almost smiled to think of how Runiden would react when he arrived. The gruff leader of the paladins would be furious at his own late night eviction, but even moreso at his friend's. Yet, if Vendile had called the council he must be confident of success in whatever lay waiting for Arvadis in the palace. The thought soured the brief moment of the king's amusement as they reached their destination.

The council doors loomed before him and Arvadis steeled himself. For the first time in his life he recited the oath of the Napalian Army he had heard long ago, "No retreat except by coffin, no ground given without my blood to water it."

The young guard looked at him in near horror, and Arvadis's smile was determined but equally unnerving. "You think I will step down so easily?"

The doors opened, and the king entered his council room.

Vendile's good mood was ruined by the appearance of a silver and gold clad Arvadis. The old fool would not simply move aside. Arvadis had to know that Vendile was assured of victory if he had sent a guard escort not fitting the requirements of the Code. That miserable document would be the first thing Vendile would destroy when he took the crown. Now the Highlord had to bend his will towards that goal, Arvadis could not be allowed a chance at resistance. Freyan's plan seemed solid, but it all hinged on the fear inspired by Vendile's presence and his promises of glory and wealth for all the Highlords. This had not convinced Calavar and Irindein, but they would be imprisoned along with Arvadis for defying the new ruler if it became necessary. But the old king was slow in leaving.

Arvadis swept into the high-ceilinged room and stopped as the guards from his escort filed around the outer ring. Arvadis took in the details of the council chamber he knew so well. The banners of every house hung from the eight pillars of the circular hall, swaying slightly from the movements of the guards spreading about the room. It was smaller than the grand hall, where public audiences were held, and the council chamber was a more intimate setting meant to house only the eight Highlords who ruled over the nation and their own district of Alderlast. The table was round and it took up most of the room. Eight panels extended the colors of each house to the center of the table, where a winged helm of silver on a bronze field, the symbol of Paladinis, showed the kingdom's devotion to their god. The entire room glowed with the gentle light of the moon that leaked through the small glass dome at its height. Arvadis could feel his soul rise with the majesty of the hall he stood in, and it fell when he saw Vendile lean on his end of the table, symbolically opposite to Arvadis's own.

The Highlord eyed his opponent triumphantly, but before he could speak a word he was beaten to the punch by the irate cries of the fiery Highlord Calavar, "This is blasphemy of the highest order, Karsyrus! I will see your head on a pike before the end of this meeting!"

Vendile glared at the old campaigner. With the fashionable mustache and well-groomed hair of the paladins, Runiden Calavar looked imposing even in his nightshirt. The two guards flanking Calavar had his shoulders in a firm grip, barely keeping the infuriated old man in his seat. For all his fifty years, the Highlord Calavar seemed to have grown harder; he was nearly beating off the strength of two much younger men. Vendile walked over to the furious Calavar, reveling in his superior appearance and authority in the purple and black silk tunic with silver trimming. Vendile felt superior to the regal and blustery warrior for the first time in his life. The image of power was power itself, and Vendile proved it by viciously backhanding the Highlord with his mailed fist. "You will keep silent old man, or meet the fate you presume to hand to me."

Calavar had reeled at the blow and his nose and lip were a ruined, bloody mess. His head fell forward in defeat and Vendile sneered and turned on his heel, nearly running into the current king. Vendile was temporarily taken aback. He hadn't heard Arvadis come around the table, even moving so swiftly and aggressively. He shouted to his guards, "Seat him! He is not to touch me!"

Arvadis was dragged back to his place at the table, his brilliant blue eyes boring into his hated foe. Vendile recovered from his moment of fear and surveyed the other Highlords. Fremont Irindein was guarded doubly in a fashion similar to that of Calavar. A younger lord than his close friends Arvadis and Runiden, Fremont was a calm and calculating man, but he too wore only his bedclothes. By contrast, Hladic and Bwemor were dressed as finely as Vendile, but not so extravagantly that they might have outshone him. The allies of Karsyrus Vendile commanded both religion and the machine of war in the kingdom of Angladais and thus were his trump cards in this dangerous bid for the throne. Observing, and perhaps only partially comprehending, the vicious feud playing out before them, were the leaders of Xarinth and Galden, whose Highlords looked frightened and stunned. Arvadis wondered if they realized that it would be they who would sway the outcome of this meeting. Touching the pendant hanging from the chain given to him by Freyan, Vendile began his carefully planned speech, "Almost three months ago, we learned that our kingdom was imprisoned by a great threat that appeared suddenly using methods beyond our understanding. A foe was allowed to dig in their claws on the very doorstep of our kingdom. Why? We were trapped because, my fellow Highlords, our esteemed king was lax in the defense of our nation. He allowed the enemy to camp at our door! He allowed him to murder our people and those who would come to us for trade and wisdom! He allowed our very existence as a country to be put into jeopardy! And worst of all he has done nothing to effectively correct this predicament. Nothing!"

Vendile had been walking slowly around the table as he spoke, and when he finished he emphatically brought both fists down before Highlord Galden, who flinched so badly he nearly fell over in his seat. Vendile paused, but only briefly. "Highlord Bwemor has assured me that if he had been allowed to expand our reign beyond the Pillars of Light, this incursion would never have happened! It is the foolish policy of the Hawking kings that we stay confined within our meager borders. We are the most powerful nation on the continent of Legocia, we should be an empire and not a mere kingdom in a valley!"

"And I suppose you would be the one to do this for us, Vendile?"

Highlord Irindein's inquiry was voiced softly but firmly. Vendile turned blazing eyes upon him but did not respond. Instead he began pacing again, gesturing emphatically as he made each of his points. "We are too long held captive to fight out of this corner. We must negotiate with the invaders."

Calavar raised his bowed head in desperate protest. "You are a madman! We cannot parley with murderers! It would be a blasphemy to the ideals of our most holy god!"

Vendile sneered at the paladin leader, "And what would you say our god would have us do? Attack again? Your men have had their chance and failed, it is time for a new route to be taken. I propose we parley with these invaders, seek to find common ground and understand them. Then, when the time is right, we will strike at them when they least suspect it and take back what is ours."

"These people have slaughtered innumerable innocents in the name of the God of Death. They have burned, pillaged, raped, and murdered. Neroth's intentions are clear, he means to bring the world to heel by force. These people are not our allies, nor can they even be bartered with. They are our sworn enemies and enemies of Paladinis!"

"Ah Irindein you fool." Vendile wagged his finger at the Highlord. "Have we not maintained that same form of control over our own people under the guise of justice and law? How is that so different from Neroth's own goals? And if we took command of all that we could, with our mighty armies and strength of belief, would the other peoples of Teth-tenir not be happier ruled over by Paladinis rather than the God of Death? The rightful place of Angladais is as the mightiest nation in all Legocia. That destiny should be our guiding light, not the fear that Paladinis will strike us down for daring too much."

Irindein was livid. "How dare you blaspheme the Lord of Honor in this holy place? Hladic, how can you allow this foul beast to speak so?"

The leader of the priests smiled benevolently as he replied, "My upstart young Irindein, you seem to think that our good Highlord Vendile is shunning our god. To the contrary, he is embracing him by seeking to both embrace and spread his doctrine. Yes, some of that message may be delivered through the dark art of combat, but in those moments come many opportunities for our people to prove their valor before Paladinis himself. Highlord Vendile even plans to usurp the authority of this Nerothian force at the opportune moment, freeing many in the northern lands from the yoke of oppression. My priests and I have conferred and believe Paladinis himself would wholeheartedly approve of this path."

Arvadis blocked out the rest of the argument and observed the sitting Highlords. Irindein was young, perhaps twenty-seven years, but no more. His stately posture was quivering under the outright foulness present in the room as it bombarded his faith in his country and sense of duty to what it was meant to stand for. Arvadis would have liked to soothe the loyal Highlord, but this was not the time or place. Galden and Xarinth were younger still than even Irindein, Xarinth barely over fifteen years. They were being forced into this somehow, but Arvadis could not unravel the methods that Vendile was using to coerce them. The elder men were equally divided between his camp and Vendile's. The two lackeys of this coup looked extremely confident, and even Bwemor's chin stroking could not conceal his grin of satisfaction. Whatever plan they had concocted, it was working out as they expected.

Arvadis decided it was time to stop that. "My dear lords," he said interrupting Hladic and Irindein while rising almost effortlessly despite the eyes of the watchful guards. He noted that they feared to touch him, suggesting he still held some authority here. "I will be the first to admit I have failed us. I have not led an adequately prepared kingdom against our foe. However, the only open aid I have received has come from House Calavar's paladins and Irindein's own personal guard." Arvadis wheeled on Hladic suddenly demanding, "Where were your priests when my men were bleeding out after the first assault on that dread fortress? And where was the army I called for, Bwemor? I have yet to see a single soldier that did not come in defiance of your own orders to remain clear of the Pillars of Light."

The two Highlords started to stammer out answers but they could not speak. Vendile made as though to interject, but a look from Arvadis cut him down from his pedestal and he closed his mouth quickly. "We cannot, and will not, ally with these barbarians; not even in deceit. We must unite, which will not happen in circumstances such as these. We face a greater foe than we have ever known and only our combined efforts can thwart him."

It was a kingly appeal given with calm and authority. Vendile could see the effect it had on even his minions. The youthful Highlords Galden and Xarinth were nodding slightly, while Hladic and Bwemor looked terrified and ready to abandon the scheme. Vendile sensed the moment and plunged forward, leaning onto the table and striking it with his fist, trying to quell the fear swiftly. "Enough! You have had your chance, Hawking, you have failed. It is time for a new leader, a strong leader. You are unfit to govern this kingdom, and I ask that a council vote make this not a mere statement of opinion, but a declaration of truth. I call for the forceful abdication of King Arvadis Angladais of the Hawking House!"

The reaction was not quite what Vendile had expected. The sitting Highlords paused at the dramatic delivery, and even his own fellow conspirators seemed slightly unsure. Arvadis spoke calmly, "It will take a majority in the council to oust me from the throne, and I do not believe that you can force so many hands against my person."

Vendile sneered as he retorted, "I am aware of the requirements for dethroning a monarch, Highlord Hawking, as you recall the only royal family ever removed from the position was my own. As you no doubt also remember, it was a Hawking who led the call for his loss of title. The irony of the moment is palpable, to say the least."

Arvadis shook his head. "Your ancestor was dethroned for multiple violations of the Angladaic Code; what do you presume to hold as grounds for my removal?"

"For failure to govern our nation as a responsible monarch should, for contributing to the deaths of our most noble soldiers, but most of all for incompetence through inaction and stubbornness. You have refused to recognize the need for our nation to expand. Too long have we stayed confined to our lands watching over the squabbles of weaker kingdoms. Our nation should command this continent. With our power we could end the vast and disparate petty feuds throughout Legocia!"

"And perhaps we might become unimaginably wealthy in the process, yourself in particular?"

Vendile had been relishing his speech; certain his argument had been clear and without error, but Arvadis' insight drove all semblance of control from the Highlord. Marching over to the proud current monarch, he struck Arvadis viciously across the face, knocking him back into his chair. Calavar was on his feet in an instant, despite the blades at his throat and sides, "How dare you! You fiend, you aren't worthy to lick the mud from his boots! By my honor, you'll not touch him again!"

Calavar's flushed cheeks subsided as the current king waved him silent with his left hand. Wiping the blood from his own face with the other, he stood again. His fierce glare forced Vendile back. In that moment, the malicious Highlord forgot he was surrounded by guards, and all he could see were Arvadis's measuring eyes before him finding his very existence wanting. He could feel his death in their stare and he forgot himself. He recoiled and began to shelter behind his seat, but a resolve took hold, beaten into him from a young age by his cruel father, and Vendile managed to assume his commanding position once again. He thrust the two nearest guards forward. "Enough! Your reign is over, Hawking. I once again move that the council vote to dethrone Arvadis Angladais."

The guards hesitated, but to their relief Arvadis sat without being forced. Calavar seemed ready to fight still, but he saw the defeated slouch of his king and friend and suddenly it seemed his own years caught up with him as well. The fire in Calavar's eyes went out and he too slumped into his chair. Vendile glared at Highlord Bwemor until the seemingly distracted man realized his part in the plot had come. With as much conviction as he could muster he said, "I second the proposed action."

Vendile nodded curtly. "Who else is in favor?"

Slowly, Hladic placed his signet ring upon his section of the table to signal his agreement. Bwemor and Vendile hurried to formally cast their votes, placing their official rings near the center circle to signify assent. Angrily Calavar removed his and slammed it to the table edge, announcing his defiance. Irindein did the same with somewhat more deliberate calm. Arvadis also placed his ring along the table edge and three sat opposing three. All eyes fell to the remaining houses, Xarinth and Galden.

The young Highlords looked petrified to have such responsibility fall on their shoulders. Galden tried to assume a proud and what he must have felt was mature posture, but he could not shake off the youth of his seventeen years. Xarinth stared at Arvadis as though pleading with him to help, to understand. Suddenly the king recognized the unspoken threat hanging over both, knowing now that they were already under Vendile's heel. With a consoling smile he nodded his head, forgiving them. Xarinth barely choked back his tears, but he removed his ring and threw it at the table's center. Galden swallowed hard and did the same. Calavar sat stunned, Irindein shook his head sadly, and Arvadis merely sighed in resignation. Vendile was standing tall with a malicious and victorious grin upon his face.

It had seemed impossible, but it was happening. Freyan's plan had worked after all. Karsyrus could barely contain his glee.

Vendile strode around the table and stood proudly before the fallen king. "Arvadis Hawking you are hereby found guilty of crimes against the Kingdom of Angladais. You will be imprisoned until an appropriate sentence has been passed."

Calavar was enraged. "Execution perhaps? Then take me too you cur!"

"So be it." Vendile wheeled on the Highlord. "Irindein and Calavar you shall also face the same sentence as your fallen king."

"And what gives you the right to make such sweeping motions in this council, Vendile," said Irindein softly, "the Angladaic Code decrees that only the King can propose imprisonment. Even then the council...."

"There is no more council!" Vendile erupted smashing his hand onto the table emphatically.

Every Highlord froze in their place. Vendile was a tower of rage, his face blood red and his eyes burning. His mailed fist came down on the table once again, this time shattering the portion bearing the Hawking symbol as he howled, "I am the council, the throne, and the law! Now take these men away!"

The guards pulled the Highlords from the room, though it was not an easy task. Calavar fought tooth and nail. Irindein walked, and though it was unforced he did so with a firm expression that made clear he chose to make the journey, but would not accept the sentence handed down. Arvadis was dragged forcefully out, staring daggers at Vendile the whole way. The victorious Highlord watched him go with a twisted grin, fingers laced before him and pressed to his face in victory, and the cool metal of his strange pendant, clutched in one hand, felt wondrous against his flushed face. Then he turned to the remaining members of the council. "Hladic, I wish to go through the private crowning by tomorrow afternoon so I may assume official governmental command. The public ceremony may be delayed so we can provide the appropriate degree of stateliness. Bwemor, you will provide the army and a list of crimes the imprisoned Highlords are charged with for my announcement. Galden and Xarinth, you will not be present for my crowning. You shall to return to your estates and stay there under my protection."

The next king of Angladais sat slowly in his chair, arms folded in front of him. "Now go. And Bwemor?"

The Highlord stopped halfway out the door and bowed slowly asking, "Yes, my king?"

"Bring me the head of Vorasho Hawking. I want that cursed line ended. My reign must be consolidated."

"Of course, my king, it will be done."

Bwemor turned to leave, but Vendile called after him, "Oh, and Highlord Bwemor," Vendile smiled in deepest satisfaction, "next time, bow lower."

Bwemor nodded, then reconsidered and bowed deeply to his new ruler. Walking from the council room, he had his first doubts about the new bearer of Angladais's crown. He had known Vendile was somewhat mad, but he could not be sure the extent to which he would go to destroy his enemies, both real and imagined. Doubt crept into Bwemor's mind in that moment, but then he was leaving the chamber and among his men again.

Stepping into the main hall of the palace, Bwemor was joined by his personal guards. His captain, newly appointed for exemplary service, was a powerful looking man named Renon Ordlan. His name was unusual for a commoner. In Angladais, the noblest families had auspicious and high-sounding names, like Gelladan Bwemor himself and the other Highlords. To have taken a name like Renon, and possess a family name such as Ordlan, this guard must have some connection to a minor noble house, perhaps one that had fallen on hard times or been disgraced and forced Renon to take up military service to make his way in the world. Regardless of where he had come from, Renon Ordlan had proven a reliable soldier. Young and strong, he took up the position next to his lord. Bwemor eyed the bodyguard, taking in his unshaven features and the silvery sheen of armor decked out in red plume and cape, his clasp bearing the Highlord's symbol of a charging boar. Bwemor stopped and waved the other guards away. "Renon, you were named my personal guards' captain this week?"

"Yes, Highlord."

"And I have heard you advanced so rapidly due to your willingness to carry out any task, as ordered, without question. Is this true?"

The younger man stopped his deliberate stride and met the Highlord's eyes firmly saying, "I will do anything you command of me, Highlord Bwemor. It is my duty."

"Good. Then I think it is time you proved your loyalty to my house."

Bwemor pulled Renon into a small alcove and laid down plans for murder.

Beneath the Angladaic Palace the old dungeons had rotted away from years of disuse. The predecessors to Arvadis Hawking had banned their employment as a method of correction some time before his reign, choosing to focus on rehabilitation through faith and service rather than imprisonment, which many in the kingdom believed to be unnecessary and barbaric. In the case of serious crimes, Arvadis had resorted to exile and conscription for more minor ones or repeat offenders. The result had been a severe drop in violence and crime within the kingdom, and an increase in available soldiers for defense and public works. Not merely sealing the dungeons had done that, further emphasis on aiding and providing care to the poor and sick had reduced criminal activity, and the nation had the wealth to support such efforts. Now Arvadis was a victim of a practice he had tried to destroy completely during his reign. Chained to a wall in one of the damp, ill-lit cells, he sat with his arms held against the cold stone. Arvadis could see rats milling about in the distance of the unlit hall. He, Irindein, and Calavar had separate holds, each dimly visible with one slow burning but weak torch. How long they would burn for the imprisoned was difficult to say, but the captive royal knew that once they went out their true fight for survival would begin.

Calavar's groans from his cell caught the Arvadis's attention. He was concerned for the Highlord. Calavar had resisted and been severely beaten by the guards. Arvadis could not say how extensive his injuries were, but he feared for his life. Irindein was beyond Calavar in the farthest chamber. Arvadis called out hoarsely, "Fremont? Fremont, are you alright?"

Arvadis heard shuffling and a long sigh. "Well, my friend, I am alive. That is always something."

Despite himself Arvadis smiled. "This is true, Fremont, we are alive. Can you see Runiden?"

"I'm afraid not, my back is to him, can you?"

"No, I have a wall between us. Have you any idea how long our torches will last?"

"Well, Arvadis, I am no expert on conflagration, but I would venture to say the torches will burn until they go out."

"Of course, how foolish of me," Arvadis paused and in the silence he could hear the rats shuffling just at the edge of his vision, "but let me ask you this, how long will we last?"

Arvadis could hear his friend's dry laughter as he answered, "Well, Arvadis, that would be until someone rescues us now, wouldn't it?"

"You really think someone will?"

Fremont Irindein nodded knowingly to himself in the waning light. "It has been my experience that people sometimes forget kings and queens, but sons very rarely forget their fathers."

In the darkness of the guttering flames Arvadis allowed himself a small smile and the faintest glimmer of hope.

Chapter 14

The journey to Delmore was silently plagued by the inner turmoil of each of the travelers. Ghost had not spoken since Diaga confronted him during his watch, and the pall that had fallen over the former thane kept the others quiet. Now with his past laid bare, Ghost had found a new sense of himself and his purpose. He was not going to let anything stand in his way, and if anything had changed it was only that he was more committed to his plan than he had been before. Revenge was the only thought recycled over and over in his mind. Ghost eyed the riders about him distrustfully. How far could he expect them to go? Ghost was committed to his quest, and willing to do anything to achieve it, but he was not sure the others could be relied upon. The Angladaic and his pet orc had that entitled sense of self-righteousness found only in those ignorant of the great inequalities of the world. The others were young and impressionable, and Ghost knew enough about himself to understand he was more a taskmaster than a honey-tongued orator. To bring the others along with him, he had to put forth proof that life was hard and brutal, and moreover that to survive meant striking back with decisive malice. It was an attitude many of those he now journeyed with were likely to reject.

Trem in particular, despite what was in Ghost's eyes the weakness of his half-elven heritage, seemed important to hold onto. His companion, the younger and distinctly more human half-elf, was too green, and the orc and Logan were too righteous. Ghost needed people who were not afraid to bend the rules of morality when necessary. Vengeance was not a virtue, as Diaga had said, but Ghost had no use for virtues anymore. He was a killer at heart and it was time to use that skill in the name of someone other than himself. Ghost's life had been about his career, his reputation, and his name. He had been a warrior, a brilliant commander when tested, but his pride had made him want to be the most famous Squall in history and now he never would be. His ambition had been his downfall, but he knew it was also the core of what he was. The other thanes of the Napalian Empire had whispered that his drive would either lead to his meteoric rise or disastrous fall, yet his father had passed the responsibility and opportunity of leading the Squall family to him despite the risks. Everyone had believed he could be the greatest thane of his time, but they had cautioned him not to attempt to find swifter inroads to his success.

Ghost knew now they had been right. His attempt to orchestrate a more rapid ascension to legendary status had been what undercut him in the end. He was no longer a Napalian; he was a man haunted by his failure and driven to bring punishment upon those who had assisted in his fall. At the last, with his back against the wall, he would have fought for the highest bidder, even the Nerothians as Valissa Ulfrunn had done, but they had dismissed him for his betrayal. Perhaps their reasoning had been sound, but the horrors brought upon his family would have to be answered for. Ghost could still see their faces when he closed his eyes, could hear their screams at night. He himself had never been innocent, but his wife and children had been clean of sin. As a man deeply stained with his own immoral actions, he was at least capable of doing whatever was necessary to avenge them.

The dark clouds in the north had moved steadily towards the party, and by now blotted out most of the sunshine. The weather was as gray as Ghost's shaggy beard and it's mood half as foul as his own. He rode in front of the others, wrapped in his dark cloak and darker thoughts, hoping to spot Delmore before nightfall. Jovanaleth rode with Logan and Grimtooth, talking softly and laughing lightly at tales from the Angladaic homeland. Behind them rode Diaga and Rath, an odd pair, but deeply locked in an engrossing conversation, even if it was one-sided. Neep trailed solemnly behind, eyes always moving over the hills and thin woods. Gend was alone for once. The halfling had seemed nervous and edgy since he woke, and this was the longest he had been silent since the others had met him. His usefulness had been minimal thus far, getting to Delmore was as simple as following the eastern road from Gi'lakil, but once there the halfling's knowledge would be tested.

Trem was riding rearguard, but quite a deep rearguard. His thoughts were scattered. The arrival in Delmore would bring a decision he was not eager to make. If the band of travelers, loosely bound as they were, chose to take different paths what would he do? That was his burning dilemma. Trem had a deep and indescribable need to see this thing Ghost was chasing after, a yearning that felt branded to his bones. At the same time Jovanaleth was an innocent child in Trem's eyes, with a simple and noble desire that spoke to his own past. Trem believed he was unaware of the vicious nature of the world and that brought out a protective side of the former hermit. Both Kurven and the spirit of Gerand Oakheart had each, in their own way, implored him to confront his own personal demons. Trem feared that the moment when they reached Delmore would mean more than a choice of staying or moving on, but the choice between Jovan and Ghost.

Trem was snapped out of his miserable contemplation by the arrival of Diaga, shadowed as always by Neep. The young mage smiled, and Trem responded in kind, though a bit halfheartedly.

"We must talk, Trem," said the young mage, "I fear we face great danger in Delmore."

Trem matched the wizard's pace, hiding his alarm at Diaga's words. "Of course we can talk, but what makes you fear for us in Delmore?"

"It is only for particular members of our company that I fear. In the case of others I am wary of their intentions."

Trem eyed Diaga sideways. "Like whom?"

Diaga shifted uncomfortably in his saddle. "The man who professes to lead us, for one."

"Ghost," Trem stated flatly.

"Indeed, he troubles me. His intent is revenge and a bloody revenge at that. Such a vendetta is dangerous to the other members of our party and possibly those outside of it. I do not think Ghost will look out for anyone who is not necessary to the completion of his goals."

"I agree, Diaga," Trem said, "but he also possesses a lead that might allow us to locate a powerful artifact capable of accomplishing great things. We cannot allow what dark Ghost holds in his heart to condemn what good his knowledge might do for us. You yourself came from the north; don't you want to see your home liberated if it can be done?"

Diaga nodded slowly. "Of course, but there is the question of how such a thing is accomplished. We also have to consider the more immediate danger we might be facing. You have perhaps heard of the pillaging of the eastern villages?"

"Naturally, there were refugees in Gi'lakil after all."

"Then you also know that is not a cloud darkened only with the promise of rain," Trem looked sharply at the young man, "it also carries the heavy smoke of death."

Trem nearly stopped his mount and Diaga rounded before him. "We are riding into a war, Trem. Delmore cannot be far from the front of this destructive army cutting through the Dust Plains."

"That may be true, but we do not have to fight. Our task lies south, away from the town. We simply keep moving and stay alert."

Diaga looked at Trem in genuine confusion. "Would you not try to help those who might need it most? I know Ghost will be single minded in his actions, but you," Diaga shook his head and pointed down the road, "I guess we will find out soon enough. You see those broken carts on the hill ahead? Those are the remnants of the farmer's carts from Delmore. Once we reach that rise, we are less than a mile from the town limits."

"What are you driving at, Diaga?"

"Nothing, except that perhaps you ought to prepare yourself for what we find once we get there." Diaga turned down the road and trotted after the others. Trem, unnerved by the exchange and his own personal fears, delayed a moment before following. His eyes strayed from the road before him to the north where the heavy weight of the dark sky was becoming more oppressive by the minute and he now thought he could smell the burnt wood and other matter on the air. He leaned over the neck of his horse, and forced himself to keep his eyes on the path ahead.

Edge emerged, limping; from the pass at the base of the largest mountain he had ever seen. Looking around, he could see nothing but wind and snow. He turned back and swept his cloak about him, half walking and half lurching his way to the relative safety of the trail between the mountains. Edge shook off the heavy snow and removed his hood. "Well, we are definitely north, I just don't know how far. And I think we may have reached the end of the pass. It's all snow as far as the eye can see."

It had been almost ten days of forced marching. Their relatively light packs and the lack of new snowfall had made it easier than it might have otherwise been, but the constant movement had also slowed Edge's recovery from his leg wound. Raymir unrolled the leather parchment she had procured from her family home. "Grandfather's map says were about fifteen days south of Mount Iceblade, going slowly, and from there we go northeast and...."

"And from there we hope we find this mysterious tower," finished Romund. "The map doesn't by chance have a location for it?"

Raymir shook her head. "The only thing I can tell from this map is that our family did not know what was in the northeast. That would make it the only place where this tower could possibly be."

Edge chuckled softly saying, "I did not think that you could go further north than Mount Iceblade, it seems so massive it must be the edge of the world."

Romund laughed with him. "I can understand that, how big is this rock?"

"It is well above the clouds." Edge shook his head in wonder.

Raymir grabbed Edge's sleeve. "Wait!"

"What is it?"

Raymir eyed Edge nervously as she laid out her thoughts. "Well we don't know for sure where this tower is we only know that it is far to the north, most likely northeast."

Edge nodded.

"And we know it's a large structure away from the mountains."

Edge nodded again.

Raymir shifted her feet as she got to the point. "What if we climb Mount Iceblade and try to look from there?"

Edge and Romund's eyes widened, then they looked at each other and back at Raymir. Edge rubbed his chin thoughtfully asking no one in particular, "Could we actually climb Iceblade? How sheer is the rock face?"

"I do not know, but if we climb even partway we might be able to see the tower." Romund shrugged in a half-concession to the plan.

Edge remained doubtful. "But how far could we see, truly?"

"Our eyes might not see much beyond a hundred miles, but I have something that will help." The man from Hethegar smiled slyly, and he produced from his pack a strange item wrapped in a thick, soft cloth. Removing it carefully, Romund held it out for the other two to see. It was a long tube, perhaps six inches, with a narrow end that gradually widened to a large lens at the opposite side. He pulled on the wide end, and the device extended outward, now over a foot in length. "The seafarers of Hethegar use these to spot land and other ships from a distance. It would give us a significantly longer view than our own eyes. From Iceblade it would see quite far indeed, and really it is the only reasonable course of action. We can see the mountain as we approach it and we cannot see the tower, even if we knew its location exactly. We'll easily find our way to the mountain, ensuring we don't get lost and give ourselves a chance to get our bearings."

Edge looked from Romund to Raymir then back to Romund. Finally he looked at Raymir again for a long time. "Can you make it?"

Raymir punched him lightly. "You dumb ox, of course I can make it! It's you we should be worried about."

Edge grabbed her hand. "I'm serious, Raymir. I have been here before, it's dangerous enough with a storm brewing let alone gusting."

Raymir glared at him in steadfast defiance. "I have lived my whole life in the shadow of the Great Northern Waste. I know you planned to leave me behind in Glaciar," Raymir silenced Edge's protestations with a sharp look, "and you're a fool to think I'd have allowed that. Besides, now there is nowhere for me to go. I am a daughter of Napal and I would be willing to bet I know the dangers of this region better than either one of you."

"She's right my friend," Romund said confidently. "We need her more than she needs us out here."

Edge sighed then held up a hand in acceptance. "Alright," he wrapped his arms around the shoulders of his companions. "Let's go to the mountain, all of us."

The three pulled their furs and thinner apparel about themselves as tightly as they could and stepped from the mouth of the mountain trail and into the blizzard. Raymir squinted as the wind blew her hair back. Edge threw a hand in front of his face and they walked northward together, Raymir's arm in his. Romund pulled his hood lower and moved to follow. Before long the hidden opening in the rock was covered in snow and the footprints of the three adventurers were fading under new forming drifts. Raymir squinted at

Edge calling over the wind, "They call this place the Bowl of Storms. The wind is constant and snow ever present."

Romund grunted as he forged ahead. "Lucky for us."

A few hours later, a shadow came across the pile of snow that hid the opening to the pass between the western Waste and Glaciar. Stepping through a strange rift was a heavily clothed Saltilian, clinging to his staff, its runes glowing brightly with magic. He gripped his portal stone tightly in his left hand, leaning on the dimming staff with his right. Releasing his grip on the gem snapped the portal shut and Saltilian lowered himself to the ground, sitting solemnly in the snow. He tucked the gem into his robes and relaxed his body. They had been here, but where did they go now? There were no towns in this region. They had nowhere to turn. They would die from the cold or hunger before they got to shelter. Perhaps he ought to abandon his pursuit.

No, he cast the possibility out of his mind. Saltilian could not take the chance. He wanted Raymir back. She was his, and he also felt a growing urgency to kill the upstart lost elf. Saltilian would rip his eyes out with his bare hands, making him suffer in front of her. Saltilian would show Raymir where real strength lay. The wizard had kept a lot of artifacts, ones that Daerveron had no use for or did not understand, but Saltilian had the advantage of being from this land and time, thus some of the newer items made more sense to him. The portal stone had been tossed aside by Daerveron as an unnecessary trinket. Saltilian's other artifact was a medallion he wore around his neck. This particular item was not a scrap thrown him by Daerveron; Saltilian had found it depicted in an illustration in the strange book he now kept pressed close against his body. Amid the storage rooms off of the Napal City Castle library, he had stumbled upon it and been drawn to remove it for himself.

The medallion was quite old, but shone with an unearthly sheen as though the metal was freshly polished. He pulled the wolf's head from beneath his robes where it had rested heavily against his chest since he left the inn and stared at it. The beast had red eyes in a snarling face full of fangs. Saltilian met the gaze of the red orbs and his head swirled. He forced himself to focus and the medallion sucked him in. He sought the wolves running on the cold grounds of the land about him, but they turned him away refusing to serve him. Saltilian raged and they fled his anger as he delved deeper, far beneath the snow and ice. Suddenly he reared up out of his sitting position as something larger and far older than any wolf extended contact back towards him. Saltilian was held in place, riveted by the power. A dark language of rumbling menace snarled in his head, *Human.*

Saltilian fought for control. *Help... me.*

Kurok helps no mortal, only himself.

Salitilian steadied his mind and he lashed back at the creature. *You will help me!*

238

Saltilian felt the thing lurch in pain and unspeakable anger. Then it subsided, Saltilian was not in control, but he was no longer being assaulted. He tried to communicate again. *I have prey for you, here in the Waste.*

The resistance weakened further but did not disappear. *Where?*

Saltilian smiled, knowing he had succeeded in baiting his quarry. *Come to me.*

The creature barked savagely in Saltilian's mind, *I will come.*

The connection was broken. Saltilian fell back in the snow, still smiling. His already worn mind was fraying even further, but of course he did not notice. The mage was not even aware as his hand strayed to the book, brushing softly over the binding. He would find Raymir and make the other two scream for mercy. She would be unable to resist the might of the newfound forces he called to his side. Saltilian, with great effort, sat up and waited for Kurok to arrive.

Vorasho Hawking walked from the hospital tent and to the washbasin outside. He paused as he was about to dip his hands in when he realized the water was already a deep red. The field surgeon walked out of the tent and replaced the bowl with a fresh one, pouring the contents of the old bowl onto the grass and handing it to a servant. Vorasho began washing his hands and whispered, "Thank you, Nemil."

The surgeon eyed his lord askance. "Do not thank me, Vorasho, I should thank you. Every pair of hands helps. Without the priests, we have to tend to every wounded man here and too many are dying that could have lived." Nemil glanced at Vorasho and inquired nervously, "Where are the faithful healers of Paladinis?"

Vorasho wiped his hands on his tunic and sighed. "My father has ordered their appearance at the front. Hladic has stalled."

Nemil grabbed Vorasho's wrist. "He cannot be allowed too! Damn it, Vorasho, I am proud of my trade but I am used to minor wounds or working when the priests have worn out their powers. I am not capable of caring for this many men. I can't watch this many people die under my care."

Vorasho turned to his companion and placed a hand on his shoulder. "Nemil, I cannot change what is beyond my control. You are doing everything that you can, and all I can ask is that you have to keep helping my men, at least until I find a better solution."

Nemil pushed his hand away and turned back to the tent. "Of course I will keep helping them, I'm a blasted doctor." Nemil turned back to Vorasho and pressed his finger against his chest speaking sternly, "But do not think I will forget this. That Highlord should hang for letting our people die when they could have lived."

Nemil turned and shrugged his skinny, shirtless shoulders as he went back to the tent. Vorasho sighed and bent to retrieve his tunic from the foot of the basin's pillar. They were camped several miles from the Pillars of Light, less than a day's ride from the twin towns of Beroh and Dunagen, and a few days march further from Alderlast. Vorasho had returned to help Nemil and his companions stitching up the warriors who survived the attack on the vile fortress. Nemil was a good man who had served the kingdom well. Too squeamish to be on a battlefield, he overcame his fear of blood when he knew his actions could help people. The result was his own inventive form of military medicine. Many had called him a blasphemer or faithless citizen of Angladais. Nemil had chosen the practical path of science and experimentation to supplement the powers of zeal and loyalty. It had been meant to augment and support the priesthood and their magical methods of healing the injured, but had upset many. The Angladaics are a people whose national identity is so closely tied to their god that any alternative to his immortal gifts is, to his most passionate followers, seen as an affront to their culture, but several Highlords had vouched for Nemil and others like him. Now their support of his art had saved many lives, though his anger at the absence of the faith-empowered healers was justified.

Vorasho pulled his shirt over his head and paused, sensing others moving about him. Men had entered the dark clearing between the camp tents. Vorasho instinctively reached for his staff and remembered he had left it in his own temporary quarters along with his armor. There were five of them, armored in heavy mail and wearing red cloaks. Vorasho watched one of them approach with his sword drawn, recognizing the charging boar symbol of Bwemor on his armor and tensed for a fight. "What is the meaning of this?"

The lead soldier kept coming forward slowly then stopped just out of arm's reach, saying evenly, "I was ordered by Highlord Bwemor, who took orders from Highlord Vendile, to kill you."

Vorasho stumbled a bit but recovered himself. He took a step forward and lifted his chin to his would be assailant. "You are here to kill me? My father will not sit idle if he learns I have been murdered."

"Your father is no longer in a position to help you or anyone else."

Vorasho swallowed but refused to back down. "Were you sent to kill him too?"

"No, he is imprisoned."

"Who would dare?"

The soldier chuckled, "Who but Highlord Vendile, the same man that demanded your death."

Vorasho's shoulders slumped and he half-turned away, his mind working swiftly on how best to catch the five off their guard. But he was distracted by the news that his father was now in prison. Vorasho had predicted this, but of course his law-abiding father would never have struck first. Now his son, his only hope, was trapped far from the capitol. Vorasho considered calling for Nemil, but that would only result in another innocent life being taken. He eyed his adversary. "If you intend to kill me then at least show me your face, unless you are afraid to have me know you."

The soldier removed his helm, showing short black hair and hard unshaven features. He was a rough looking man, a soldier by profession with a grim eye. To Vorasho's surprise he then knelt holding his sword up to the prince. "My lord, I was sent here to kill you by a man who was too cowardly to do it himself. I will not commit murder any more than I will be party to an unlawful usurpation of the throne. I came here to find you and bring you to Alderlast. Allies await us at the home of your father."

Vorasho stared awestruck at the kneeling soldier, then gestured quickly for him to stand. "Allies?"

The man rose and sheathed his sword. "As much as I would like to, my lord, I cannot free your father alone, and neither can you. Your father's men can tell you better what they plan to do and who has come to our aid."

Vorasho stepped close to the guard, doing his best to hide his growing respect for the man. "Who are you that would defy a Highlord and newly named king for a marked man?"

"They call me Renon Ordlan, sir, and the way my men and I see it, the only marked man is my master." Renon paused in consideration before adding, "And that snake Vendile."

Vorasho grasped Renon's forearm firmly and pulled him in. "This will not be forgotten, Renon."

The guard returned the grip. "I ask for nothing but the right to serve a king I believe in."

"Then let us go get that king, together."

Renon nodded and motioned to one of his guards, "I had your armor and weapons brought from your tent and we have fetched you a fresh horse."

Renon pulled his own mount close and heaved himself into the saddle. "If we leave now we could reach Alderlast before dawn, riding hard."

Vorasho nodded and pulled on his armor. "We will have to be careful. Vendile will have guards on watch."

Renon shook his head. "He is keeping the succession a secret until his public crowning tomorrow afternoon. The guard won't change until then, but we expect the city will be locked down afterward so that he cannot be opposed by any outside protest. You have to get into Alderlast tonight."

"Then my father's house is also unguarded?" Vorasho asked as he pulled himself into the saddle.

"Nothing can appear out of the ordinary until Vendile wears the crown." Renon assured him.

Vorasho wheeled his horse and snapped the reins. "Then let us ensure him a short and unhappy rule."

Vorasho tore out of the camp followed by the five killers turned saviors. As he galloped into the darkness he grew angrier and angrier. That Vendile would actually order the imprisonment of his father appalled Vorasho. As a child he had fallen in love with the ideals of Angladaic society only to learn as he grew up that those ideals were just that to most people. His father had dared to fight for his beliefs and it had put his people and himself in a dire predicament. Vorasho was determined to rectify the mistakes of his father, and punish the foolishness of his enemies.

Chapter 15

The companions stopped on the hill of broken wagons to survey the scene below. The town of Delmore was sizeable, though not as large as Gi'lakil, and formed from tightly grouped houses that doubled as walls. It had no gates, just three gaps in the buildings, and where there was any barrier between the structures meant to slow incomers it seemed halfhearted and poorly made. Trem speculated that these were more likely to contain wandering children and domesticated livestock than actually serve as a defense against assault. The buildings were wood and hard mud bricks, not as fine or well-built as Gi'lakil. This was a rural town, a hub for farmers and herders and a community for those who traded with them as well. Those who didn't live in the town limits likely were not far from them, for safety's sake. It was a typical and simple defensive country philosophy, and it stood no chance of resisting a full-blown military assault.

The town of Delmore looked to be in a state of utter panic. Carts were lined up facing the eastern road, as though the populace intended to depart west as one long, desperate caravan. It was a mass emigration and it was badly organized. A few men were running around in tattered armor and carrying old bulky weapons trying to get things moving in one direction, seemingly being overseen by a striking woman in brilliant white robes. There was an air of fear all over the town. People were running through the streets without purpose or any apparent reason for their actions, they simply were hurrying to get something done without any plan for how to do it efficiently.

The travelers watched all the chaos in silence from the hilltop beneath a massive dead tree. Ghost took a pull from his water canteen and stared impassively at the terrified town. Wiping his mouth with the back of his glove, he eyed the party behind him. They bore mixed expressions; concern, grimness, but Trem had the oddest of all. It was an expression Ghost never expected to see from him. It was fear.

Jovan edged closer to the scene. "They look like they are running from something."

Grimtooth grunted, "Aye lad, an' when it looks like runnin' then it prolly means runnin'."

"Indeed," agreed Logan. "The real question is what are they running from?"

The remark brought no response from the group, as the answer had been provided in Gi'lakil and through numerous rumors on the road. Ghost tucked his canteen away and gritted his teeth. "Not our problem. Whatever is driving them out they are choosing to leave and we are choosing to enter. We let them be and move on. Gend, where do we go from here?"

The halfling started in surprise and licked his lips. "Uh, well, once we're inside the town we turn southward and ride towards Silverleaf." Gend pointed to the gap in the fence right of their vantage point. "We go through there and follow the road to its end. That will bring us to the where the hills rise up among the trees close enough to hear the Farwater striking the cliffs. From there, well, that is when the road goes underground."

More than one head turned upon hearing the last word. Diaga, who had not been privy to this stage of the journey until now, was alarmed. "Underground, surely you cannot mean the Passage of Cronakarl, the one that goes beyond Sunhall?"

"Yes that is the name!" Gend smiled. "I had quite forgotten."

Diaga shook his head and said gravely, "None have traveled that road in hundreds of years. The dwarves left the halls long ago, or so the legends say. There has been no contact with those beneath the ground in many lifetimes. We cannot be sure there is anything left, and what may remain could be that which we do not want to encounter."

"I went through once and it wasn't so bad." Gend shrugged dismissively. "And Rath tells me he has gone that way as well."

Logan turned to the black clad figure, his body almost totally obscured by the folds of dark cloth. "You have made the journey?"

Rath tilted his head towards the Angladaic slightly. "I have walked the road before, knight, yes."

"And it is safe?"

Rath watched Logan a bit longer then turned his gaze back on Delmore. Gend quickly interjected, "Don't mind old rain cloud. It's safe, alright? Wide enough to take a whole army through, too! Well, in a few parts at least. Not that I have you know."

Ghost glared at Gend, sternly remarking, "We do not want an army with us, halfling."

Gend waved his glower away with a laugh. "Oh, do not worry. I'll seal the door behind us. If you really want me to, that is."

Trem spoke softly, "How do you know about all this, the path, the door, everything?"

"My family used to live nearby." Gend smiled that disarming smile again. "An old dwarf was our neighbor, told me all kinds of great adventure stories. That's how I started my own travels. One of the stories about that old cavern just happened to be true."

Trem nodded slowly, accepting the explanation. Jovanaleth shifted in his saddle uncomfortably. "Well, I suppose we ought to get into town, then. Perhaps buy some supplies before we head for this passage?"

Ghost shook his head emphatically. "If they are leaving for good any supplies they have will be sold at high price, and besides, how long is this journey?"

"About a week, perhaps a week and a half if the going is slow," Gend remarked.

"Then we will not need any supplies, we can get them on the other side."

With that, Ghost began riding slowly towards the town followed by Logan and Grimtooth. Rath and Gend quickly fell in but the others hesitated.

"This will end badly," muttered Diaga. Neep eyed him quizzically and he glanced at her, before smiling slightly, "But only good men make quiet journeys. Great men make dangerous ones, right Neep?"

Neep meowed softly and started toward the town, her master in tow. Jovan heard none of Diaga's musings and neither did Trem. The boy sat stiff in his saddle watching the panicked people run to and fro in the distance. He jerked when Trem placed a hand on his shoulder. "Are you alright?"

Jovan shook his head grimly. "I have a terrible feeling about this place, Trem. Something dark is in the air."

Trem eyed him carefully then spoke slowly, "I am not sure I get the same sense, Jovan. Perhaps those people are in some danger, but it is not our concern. We move in and move on. They will be alright." He smiled then rode forward to join the others. Jovan watched him go perplexed. He sounded so much like Ghost, emotionless, even uncaring. Where was the man who had been so moved by the refugees in Gi'lakil?

"Who are you?" Jovanaleth asked after the departing figure, too softly for him to hear, but the only way for the young man to learn was to follow.

Renon Ordlan was as good as his word. The riders reached the gates of Alderlast still under cover of darkness, just shy of dawn, and the guards on duty waved them through without hesitation. Once within the city, they took dark alleyways and back streets to reach the home of Arvadis Hawking. Their arrival came just before sunlight began to creep over the horizon. Vorasho climbed down from his horse, tired but determined. He glanced at Renon, who stood calmly beside him, his guards arrayed stealthily around the house perimeter to watch for inquiring eyes. The soldier bowed low. "I must take my leave and report your demise to Highlord Bwemor. I do not know if I will be able to aid you further, but there is a house north of here, close to the marketplace. There will be a small Hawking banner hanging in the window. You can leave a message there, if need be. I will send word of any developments in the palace if I am able."

"You have done me much service already, Renon, I thank you."

Without another word, Renon leaped back upon his horse and started towards the palace. Vorasho hoped his lie would be enough to deter the soldiers of Vendile from scouring the city, but the false king had always been notoriously paranoid. Vorasho turned to his father's house and quietly rapped the door. There was no response. Glancing around and pulling the hood he had worn since he entered the city closer about his head, Vorasho knocked again a little louder. The door cracked open and the grizzled head of Graham poked out. "No visitors tonight, his majesty is taken ill."

Vorasho removed his hood saying, "I hear he is more taken than ill. To the palace I was told."

Graham's eyebrows rose and he shoved the door open. "Get in here quickly, my prince, quickly!"

Vorasho swept in and the door slammed shut behind him. Graham dropped the heavy door bar into place, jolting the young Derek from his brief slumber where he sat propped up by the wall in one corner of the room. Vorasho noted only one other in the entryway, a dark hooded figure that sat proudly at his father's table. Vorasho moved to sit at his usual place, the chair to the right of his father's own. He eyed the figure beside him in an attempt to discern which of his family's loyal guards it might be, but he soon realized it was no guard. "Lena?"

The figure stood and removed her hood. Lena Engrove was a thin, fair-skinned woman with raven black hair and deep brown eyes, an intoxicating combination of pride and mystery lurking in them that had ensnared many men. One of those men Vorasho knew particularly well. He stood and stepped cautiously toward her. "Why are you here, Lena?"

"Your father left you a note, Vorasho," the young woman said quietly gesturing to the small paper on the table, "he believed he would be imprisoned in the dungeons by Vendile. He wanted you to know you might be in danger."

Vorasho shook his head and sighed, "His warning reached me a bit late."

Lena cocked her head slightly and looked questioningly at Vorasho. The two had never been friends, but consequence often made them unwilling allies. Lena kept her palms on the heavy wooden table and Vorasho could not help but notice the Hawking family ring she still wore on her left hand. "Do you wear it all the time?"

Vorasho had not meant to ask the question so chidingly and Lena's sharp look told him she was offended. He went ahead in a lecturing tone anyway, "It is dangerous. I explained this to you. Why are you here?"

Lena crossed her arms in her velvet travel cloak and eyed Vorasho for a minute then said softly, "I saw them take your father."

"To the palace?"

Lena nodded. Vorasho spoke quietly, "So why are you here, you know it's dangerous to you and...."

"I know. I can help you."

Vorasho looked at Lena skeptically. "Help me? What exactly can you do to help me?"

"As your father feared, they took him to the dungeons. They would have to. Where else can they keep him out of sight? I can bring you there unseen."

Vorasho paused and considered with growing understanding. "By way of the servants' quarters. That might be an idea."

"You have to let me help," Lena reached out and grasped Vorasho's hand, "Please, Vorasho, Logan would have wanted me too."

Vorasho pulled her close and whispered urgently, "You will keep that quiet! I must protect my brother, now more than ever."

Lena averted her eyes and Vorasho lessened his grip. "I'm sorry, Lena, I am not myself."

"It's alright," she whispered.

Vorasho decided to let the conversation go. He turned to Graham and Derek, who were also standing, still fully armed and armored as though awaiting orders. Graham shifted and cleared his throat. "M'lord, your father was taken some time ago. If we are going to get him back...."

"We cannot do it now," interrupted Vorasho, "we need to rest, all of us. If we try to rescue my father as day is breaking, exhausted and frantic as we are, we will be more likely to misstep and end up sharing a cell next to him."

"We also cannot linger too long," said Derek. "Highlord Vendile will execute the king before as soon as he is able, and then come looking for you."

Vorasho chuckled, "He already thinks I am dead." He explained Renon's rescue and return to the palace.

Graham stroked his moustache; "Well that gives us a few allies inside Vendile's nest. We will need them, m'lord."

Vorasho murmured his agreement and raised his hand to stall further talk. "Rest while there is still light. We act tonight under cover of darkness. Lena, you can stay in my brother's room. You two may use mine and my father's."

Derek tried to reason with the prince. "You have ridden all night, my lord, and I just rested. You take your room and let Graham have a break. I will wake one of you at midday. We can't be without a watch."

Vorasho nodded reluctantly. "When you wake me, I shall have a plan."

Despite his protests, Graham went upstairs with Vorasho, and was soon fast asleep in Arvadis's bedchamber. Vorasho had removed his tunic and was shirtless in his own room, standing in a daze of sleeplessness and worry. He examined the heavy bedposts on his old bed and ran his thumb across the initials he and Logan had carved in them so long ago. It was before Grimtooth had come along and he had begun to lose his kinship with his only brother. The two had been great friends as children and Vorasho had looked out for his younger brother in fear he might be hurt or led astray. It was his conviction, his utter faith in the Angldaic Code, which had broken them apart.

Logan was rebellious, adventurous, and he defied the conventions of his highborn status, preferring to mill among the common people. As his father had admired the people, so did Vorasho, but Logan identified with them, even loved them as his own family. Arvadis protected the people as his subjects, where Logan defended them as though their trials were his own. Vorasho understood why he and Grimtooth had become so close. His father admired Logan for his connection to the common folk, and Vorasho could not help but resent him for it. With his passion, Logan had won the love of his father and become the favorite son of the citizenry of Angladais. By remaining steadfast in his sense of duty and place in the world, Vorasho had become ostracized from those he was sworn to defend.

"Why do you hate it so, your brother's defiance of nobility?"

Vorasho turned to see Lena in his doorway, clad in a simple woolen dress of pale blue. He dropped his hand from the bedpost and turned to her. "You should be resting, Lena."

But Lena did not leave. She stepped in and went to the same bedpost, running her thumb over the initials as Vorasho had. She spoke without looking at him, "He loves you as much as Grimtooth, you know. He told me, one of the nights we were at my home. He told me...."

"I do not need you to tell me of my brother's love."

Lena shook her head in frustration and turned to Vorasho. "Yet you do, because you do not believe it yourself. He loves you, Vorasho, because you have always protected him."

Vorasho slammed his fist against the wall and shouted, "All I protect him from is you!" He regained his composure and continued more calmly, "The only thing I have done for my brother is to shield his reputation. I have not consoled him, nor have I bled for him. I am so little his brother that he seeks that bond from another. My father would not be imprisoned if Logan were here. He would have smelled the trouble and been there to fight Vendile himself!"

Lena placed a hand on Vorasho's arm but he jerked it away. She looked at him pleadingly. "You have acted according to the law, Vorasho! Your father knew what was coming and the people are not blind to Vendile or his cohorts! You did exactly what he wanted; you refused to play the backstabber. There is nothing more you can be expected to do."

Vorasho leaned on the wall and stared at the floor. "Therein lays my fault. As I have always done, I acted according to the Code. Logan defied it and became a hero to the people who have kept my father on the throne. Angladais respects me, yes, but they love my brother."

Lena stood close to Vorasho and pulled his chin upward so he looked straight into her eyes. "I, of all people, know how far your brother has gone in breaking the Code. But it does not make him any less ashamed of it. Your Code took him away from me, and I cannot forgive it for that. His other offenses were only minor compared to what we did."

Vorasho simply stared at her. Lena sighed and whispered, "Say something, at least. Something that will make me believe you finally forgave your brother."

"I forgave him before it even happened."

"And me?"

Vorasho placed his hand on her shoulder. "I never faulted either of you, only myself for not preventing it."

Lena looked at him in confusion. "For not preventing love?"

"Do you think that is what you had?"

"Yes."

Vorasho stood silent for a moment and considered her words. "I think perhaps I blame myself for sending him away."

Lena nodded, "You were not his brother then. You acted as his superior."

"I did what the Code demanded. I gave him a quest to remove his sin."

"He does not blame you for it."

"I treated him like a whoring nobleman."

"Yet you told no one that it was such a quest. They think he is taking the Rite."

Vorasho glanced back at the bedpost. "Maybe he is. My brother may come back a paladin. He may live by the Code as ardently as I when he returns. But a part of me prays he does not."

Lena smiled slightly. "Why is that?"

Vorasho returned his gaze to her saying, "Because the Logan that left here was one destined to do great things, but should he change and become as rigid as every noble warrior of our highest rank. Well, then he shall do only good and just things as dictated by our laws."

Lena placed her hand on his face consolingly. "And what of you, young prince? What sort of things will you do?"

"I will do what is right. I will save my father and my country."

Lena smiled then and dropped her hand. "Naturally."

She turned to leave, and as she stepped through the doorway Vorasho said, "Lena? I know you used your ring to gain entry. What did you tell Derek and Graham?"

She stopped and eyed the prince over her shoulder. "That I was a loyal servant of the house for many years and that I could be of service to you. I said nothing else."

Vorasho nodded. Lena walked down the hall and closed Logan's door. He was alone again. Vorasho closed his own door softly and examined his room once more. As a child he had sat in this same bedroom planning the rescue of princesses in distress. Tonight he would plan something strangely similar. It seemed odd to him that he might be the hero reminiscent of his long ago imaginings. He had always pictured Logan to be the one completing such feats of legend. Vorasho lay down on his bed and wondered where his brother was then. What would he have said about their father's predicament?

Vorasho laughed softly. He knew what his brother would have done. He would have looked at Grimtooth, then at Vorasho, then drawn his sword. "Well," he'd remark, "I hope there are enough of the villains waiting to satisfy all of us."

Vorasho could not hold the image in his mind as he drifted off. When sleep overtook him, his smile was gone and in his mind he was watching Logan ride away from Angladais. Away from the woman he had been told he could not love. The woman he had lain with before she was his wife. And it was not the paladins or the priests sending him into exile, it was his own brother.

The Code had demanded it.

While the area that contained the many small isolated communities of the nation of Napal was called the Great Northern Waste, the name might have fit better for the region known as the Frozen Reach. The two locales were similar in environment, but the Reach was colder by a significant amount through most of the year and had almost no permanent inhabitants outside of several huddled towns. Even animals avoided the Frozen Reach if they could, preferring to linger near Whitewood or the mountains. The western side of the Dragonscales now being traversed by both the Napal City refugees and their mad pursuer was known as the Bowl of Storms. The Bowl was so called for the curvature of its mountains, which trapped the arctic gusts coming across the north of the Sirrion Sea. This made the region incredibly dangerous to travelers since the visibility even on a relatively calm day was typically less than one hundred feet.

The weather during the stormier days was far more severe. Then visibility shrunk down to inches, if that. Unfortunately for the three fugtivies, they had chosen one of the worst times to make their short journey. It was late fall, winds were high but not wintry enough to freeze those caught in the open. And yet, the billowing and blowing made the soft snow into a white curtain that surrounded the three lonely wanderers. For Saltilian things would have been much the same, but his madness had awoken a sort of latent sixth sense. He needed no footprints to follow, nor did he need the keen nose of the daemon wolf, Kurok. Saltilian was certain of his path and so he hardly glanced up from his feet shuffling steadily forward through the increasingly higher drifts of snow.

The meeting with Kurok had gone well. The beast had sensed the summoner's madness and it immediately felt confident that it could manage the situation if things became counter to its liking. A hunt had perked the monster's interest. It had not tasted fresh blood in many years, but this summoning guaranteed at least one kill. The demands of the pitiful mortal who had summoned it had been needlessly detailed: "Do not touch the girl, wound the tall elf with the green eyes but only enough that he cannot flee. Kill the other if you like."

Kurok did not care why the mage had summoned him or what sort of vendetta he had against the three. The daemonic beast would certainly kill the third for sport, and probably the others if it felt ravenous enough, the wizard's instructions be damned. Then it thought it might go south and terrorize a few villages. It had been too long since Kurok had fed on the weak peoples of Teth-tenir, and in his awakening he now remembered the rush of adrenaline he felt when he killed each victim. It was time, and he was ready.

Edge slogged through the knee-deep snow in the lead, despite his injury. His youth and strength had overcome his wounded leg. It was stiff, but the snow made him move stiffly anyway, so he hardly noticed. Romund was bringing up the rear as best he could, theoretically trying to keep Raymir on pace. They had moved like this for five days, Edge breaking the packed snow in front and the others following in his wake. Romund had taken the lead a few times to relieve him, but for the most part the grim lost elf held the point. Edge kept a methodic plod, stabbing forward with the heavy shaft of his halberd and then driving his legs one at a time behind to meet it. His hood would not stay on and his tender pointed ears were chilled beyond feeling. Raymir kept her eyes down and did her best to stay on the worn sections of Edge's path. Romund's head remained up and he would replace her hood each time it fell while making sure she stayed steadily on the path. Sometimes Edge glanced back to make sure Raymir wasn't dragging too much. If he believed she was he would slacken his pace or call a brief rest.

At night, they had been forced to stop and carve out a small hole under the snow to keep warm. Edge's long halberd served as a marker for where they had to dig themselves clear in the morning.

Speed was key. Once on the mountain there would be less exposure to a potential storm, which thankfully had not yet arisen. Edge was counting on a slowed pace to give them time to recover before they had to venture onto open ground again. The winds would be worse on the mountain, but cover would be more readily available amid the rocks; at least that was the hope.

Romund was more concerned about making it to the mountain at all. He had kept close watch on Raymir and knew that the travel was wearing on her as much as it did on him, but for all the lost elf's determination Edge was faring the worst. He had an injured leg that he was largely ignoring, but Romund had seen his gait slow. He knew about the occasional slackening of pace for Raymir, but she was fine. Edge's own pace had been dying down since yesterday and it made Romund fear that he was pushing his injury too hard and fast.

Romund saw a stumble through the blowing snow and stopped his own movement, "Edge! Maybe we should… " Romund froze. He could not explain it, but he felt something behind him. "Down!" he shouted over the shrieking wind.

Romund dove forward, taking Raymir towards the earth with him while also moving off the path Edge had made. Raymir yelled something he could not hear, but both felt a rush of air pass where they had been standing. He heard Edge grunt and saw him fall as something struck him and moved on at an impossible speed.

Edge heard Romund shout but only turned in time to see some kind of strange form leap out of the swirling white. It smashed into Edge's side sending him spinning off the path into the snow. Edge was stunned, but Romund reacted quickly. He hauled himself up and drew his sword, peering into the driving white flakes. Raymir was up as well and rushing to Edge's side. Romund called out to them both, "Can you see it?"

Edge heaved himself up to hands and knees just as Raymir arrived next to him. "I am okay, really."

Romund kept turning from side to side, trying to spot whatever had attacked them. Something darted past his left shoulder and he spun swiftly, but saw nothing. Edge had grabbed his halberd and was starting to heave himself back up when he caught sight of something hurtling towards Raymir and him. Acting quickly, he shoved Raymir away and tried to hop aside to avoid whatever was coming. Edge was dealt a glancing blow but remained upright, if teetering a bit.

Romund saw the attack and without thinking swung his sword low in a sweeping arc. The thing ripped past him, but Romund felt his blade bite into flesh and heard an unearthly howl as the beast blew by and rolled, crashing into the snow just within his field of vision. Romund looked over his shoulder and saw Edge trying to stumble towards him. He turned back in time to see the beast get up. It was massive, almost five feet wide at its shoulders and at least six feet in height. It moved on all fours but wasn't close enough for

Romund to make out any other distinguishing features. Even in the obscuring flood of driving white, he felt a tingle of fear and hysteria creep up his spine. This thing was not of this world.

The creature had righted itself and began moving in a low, crouched stalk towards the three battered figures. Romund took a step back, and then froze as the creature became more clearly visible, "Alinormir, protect me," he whispered.

Raymir had regained her feet and looked up gasping in horror, "What is that?"

Edge was moving far more quickly now, the pain secondary to his desperation to protect the other two. With his halberd gripped in both hands and cocked back for a heavy swing he called out, "Raymir, get behind me," but the girl was frozen. "Get behind me!" yelled Edge again.

Raymir moved, but then stopped as the monster before them became more clearly visible through a lull in the winds. The creature was hideous. It had grey and black fur that looked singed and stood out in sharp, jagged tufts across its body. The wild hairs covered only some of its form. The rest was devoid of skin or hair and was a pulsing red like a beating heart. It had fearsome claws as long as Romund's sword blade and a monstrous maw of teeth, which its snarling, dark lips curled back to reveal far too many of. What captivated Romund most were the thing's eyes. They were white with red veins, but no pupils, just vein-streaked orbs of madness. It crept a little closer in a slinking crouch, blood dripping from its foreleg where Romund had wounded it. *Do not resist fools. Just let this be and you will not suffer.*

Edge hissed at Romund, "Is it talking?"

Romund grunted in disbelief, "In our minds."

He does not want the girl harmed.

Romund was confused. "He?"

Raymir clapped her hands to her mouth in horror. "Saltilian!"

"How did he find us?" Romund said.

"I don't know," murmured Edge. Then he spoke to the creature, "Leave here beast. I have no quarrel with you."

A strange vibration went through Edge's mind and he realized the thing was laughing. It reminded him of a wolf but also a bear, like some nightmare combination mixed with other horrors he could not fathom. Raymir's thought entered Edge's own: what was this thing?

I am a daemon, young elf, and I am only the beginning.

With that, the monster reared up and let loose a bloodcurdling howl that caused its foes to recoil. Romund recovered and stood his ground, twirling his sword in anticipation. Edge shuffled his position to the left of his companion, giving himself full range to swing. The creature landed on all fours with a snarl and lunged at Romund with one of its titanic claws. Romund leaned back as the talons streaked past his face, narrowly avoiding his flesh. The creature then leapt at Edge before completing its first swing, catching the young man off guard. He threw his haft up to deflect the blow and was knocked stumbling backward as the monster landed its weight against his weapon. Raymir began chanting almost without thinking and extended her hand towards the creature. Flames leapt out from her fingertips, uncontrolled, knocking her back as well, but the flare scorched the creature and drove it away from Edge.

Kurok was caught unawares. It had expected the men to be dangerous, but this female was a surprise. She should not have been a threat, for Kurok would have sensed the magical spark in her had it been greater. That explained why she could not control the spell she unleashed to defend the elf, but it had still done Kurok harm. Burned and in pain, the beast roared in anger and flexed its powerful muscles. Shaking off the attack, it tried to regroup against the fallen lost elf and take him out of the fight, but the annoyingly durable human had come and placed himself between Kurok and its target.

Romund spread his legs so as to set a base and waited for the thing to attack. He could not see if Raymir was moving, but she had been knocked high and far by the blast she let fly at the beast. Fortunately, it at least seemed hurt by her explosive burst of magical energy. He had doubted, upon first seeing it in all its horror and despite his lucky slash to its leg, that they could even harm the abomination. Its fur was singed to go along with several hanging flaps of blackened flesh; surely it would have slowed somewhat. Romund could feel the burning anger of the monster as it eyed him and gathered to strike. He tried to preempt the assault, swinging for its shoulder. The blow landed, but the thing did not seem to notice as it backhanded Romund and sent him flying almost twenty feet into the snow. Romund landed hard and tried to regroup immediately, but his legs nearly buckled as he rose. The blow had shaken him and the creature was already closing the gap.

Romund just managed to stand and tried to bring up his guard, but the beast snarled and batted his blade away. It went spinning into the snow and Romund tried to make a grab for it but the beast struck him with its shoulder. Romund went down and the thing moved over him, its fangs a mere foot from his face, jowls dripping with saliva. It reared back and Romund knew he could do nothing to stop the killing blow, when suddenly Edge's halberd struck the thing in its side.

Kurok spun away in howling spasms of fury and pain. It had been intent on its victim and had not seen the other male recover and make a desperate swing to save his friend. The monster had felt its ribs broken under the force of the blow. Once again it had underestimated its enemy; the lost elf was incredibly strong and shockingly resilient. Edge wrenched backward and pulled the halberd blade free of the creature's hide, steadying himself as the thing writhed and turned to face him. Edge used his weapon like a spear, thrusting the point at his foe to back it away from Romund's prostrate form.

Kurok was at a loss. The girl appeared to be unconscious after releasing her spell and it had battered the two warriors enough to know they were hurting, but the lost elf had wounded it severely. Kurok was considering whether or not to flee before it became more seriously injured. Then it saw the human crawling towards his sword. Feinting to Edge's right, Kurok turned the quick clawing jab into a lunge to its left. The lurching motion exposed Kurok's wounded side, but it was intent on taking out at least one adversary. Romund saw the beast turn for him but stayed focused on his sword. Once he had the hilt he immediately swung upward in a curving arc.

Unprepared for such a sudden motion, Kurok caught the blade directly in its face. The strike sliced across its muzzle and through its left eye. Kurok spun away in rage and pain. Flailing about madly, it tried to regain a sense of its location, but its good eye refused to co-operate. The pain blinded Kurok completely and it never saw Edge's overhead chop that split its skull, putting an end to the fight forever.

Unnaturally dark blood exploded from the ruined head of the monster. Flecks landed on Edge's cloak and face as the lost elf stood over his kill, breathing hard. Romund looked up from his place in the snow at the young man as he tried to recover his wits. Heaving himself up, he surveyed the chaos of their battlefield. Blood soaked most of the ground around them and the beast's body was massive even as it lay prostrate in the soft snow. Romund stood and tested his legs for stability. He felt pain all over, but that did not surprise him. He had not been slashed, thank the gods, if he had he was certain he would already be dead. Edge released the haft of his weapon and fell hard into the snow.

Romund caught him in time to keep him in a sitting position as the youth leaned against him. "I owe you, again."

"We are even, Romund."

Romund glanced at the body. "That's not my blade in that thing's head."

"A lucky swing."

Despite himself, Romund laughed loudly and helped Edge to stand. "Can you walk?"

Edge gritted his teeth, but nodded as he gained some balance. Romund moved quickly to Raymir's side as she began to gingerly rise and checked her hands for injuries. She held them out, and despite her the torrent of fire she had invoked they were unharmed. Against her protests, the man from Hethegar hefted her arm over his shoulder just as Edge gave a sharp intake of breath. "Romund, look."

Romund turned slowly and saw Edge holding his bloody weapon watching the body of the creature turn slowly to ash and collapse into a pile of dust. The blood on Edge's blade dried and fell away as well, like water being soaked up in a desert. Romund held his own bared blade up for inspection and noted the same strange effect.

Edge hobbled over to him, but kept his eyes on Raymir. "Are you alright?"

"Fine," Raymir said unconvincingly, "just a bit dazed by the blast. Sometimes that happens when you use a spell you are unfamiliar with."

"Where did you learn to do that?"

"I don't remember."

Edge nodded wearily in acceptance. "I had no idea you were capable of something that powerful."

Romund patted Raymir's hand hanging over his chest. "I doubt she knew it herself. You saved us, young Squall."

"She would," said Edge proudly, then surveyed their position and grew serious, "We need to move."

Raymir was close to fainting, and Romund convinced her to let him sling her across his back and be carried for a time. He adjusted her body across his shoulders saying, "Let's get as far as possible before we need rest. Saltilian is clearly tracking us somehow."

The two turned and began slogging their way ever north to Mount Iceblade. As they plodded off, Edge suddenly thought of something the monster had mentioned; about being only the beginning. He looked briefly over his shoulder back at the hole in the spinning snow the body had left and terrible images came to his mind. What if there really were more of those things somewhere? Edge pulled his cloak tighter about him, for the wind suddenly seemed much colder.

Saltilian felt the death of Kurok minutely through his medallion but it held no real sway over his thoughts or plans. He did not slow nor increase his pace, for in the spinning of his twisted thoughts he understood where his quarry was going. Mount Iceblade was nearby, and if they had chosen to go north there could be only one place they sought. Saltilian had kept careful record of Daerveron's contacts. Anything he mentioned even in passing was filed away and later written down for permanent documentation. There was only one reason they could be moving north instead of fleeing south to relative safety. They had uncovered the same mystery that the mad wizard had.

Raymir had worked in the library at Castle Bane where Saltilian had browsed the many texts for hours on end. He had the run of the place, for the most part, as Daerveron insisted that the majority of Napal's tomes were of no interest to him. His arrogance had allowed Saltilian to openly research this mysterious structure called Twisted Spire, a name uncovered in one of his furtive explorations of Daerveron's personal notes. All Saltilian's labors had allowed one rare slip to reveal so much, but it seemed he had not been the only one spying on his fellow mage.

He knew by now that Raymir had likely found his own carelessly scattered notes in the library. Only she would have been able to see them; the servants never lingered long on the levels set aside for the wizards' use. Saltilian had underestimated her potential. He had not known she was capable of magic, but through his connection to the daemon he understood that she had wielded a significant enough incantation to wound the creature. Saltilian's lust had only increased and his plans now changed. He wanted Raymir to see his arcane might was nigh infinite in comparison to her own. More importantly, he wanted her to understand only he could unlock her potential. The others in her life were worthless.

Twisted Spire was important to the war effort, but even Saltilian did not know why. He had already concluded that Wolfbane knew nothing of it either, making it of even greater importance. His quarry was looking for it as well, and perhaps they thought Mount Iceblade would give an ideal vantage point to try and spot it. Saltilian would let them get up the mountain and allow them to waste more energy. Kurok must have injured the men, at the very least. He would let time weaken them further. Once they reached the height they sought, Saltilian would strike. He would use his magic to come upon them unseen before they knew what had happened. Saltilian was certain he would not tire like they must, for he was driven by the strength of his forbidden knowledge, tucked safely within his windwhipped robes.

Chapter 16

The faces of the people mulling about Delmore barely registered the incoming riders before they erupted in shrieks of terror. The citizens turned as one and fled, even as Logan attempted to calm them with shouts of, "Peace! Peace! We are but travelers passing through!"

None listened. The people of the town fled indoors, dropping all their possessions in the street as they ran. Logan continued to try to quell the panic, but Ghost roughly pushed by him, guiding his massive warhorse into the crammed streets. "Leave them, knight, we move south. They will know our intent when we are on our way."

Logan shot a fierce glare at the grizzled soldier. "I will be on my way when I know what has frightened these people so."

"There's a damned army of murderers bearing down on them, Angladaic. I'd say the cause of their fear is easy enough to determine."

"Then we ought to be staying to help, not passing them by in their hour of need."

The two squared off, still arguing as the others squeezed through the western entrance, brushing against the rough old wagons littering the road. Diaga shielded his eyes from the dust kicked up by the terrified townspeople and tried to take stock of the situation. Grimtooth was edging near his increasingly upset bloodbrother as he and Ghost continued exchanging choice words. Neep looked around bewilderedly, as did Gend, who stood beside her. Only Rath seemed unshaken by the tattered appearance of what Diaga would later call a storm of human debris.

Jovan and Trem were bringing up the rear slowly. Trem led, but Jovan was trying to sneak past him to see the condition of the dwellings beyond the wall. Trem opened his mouth advising, "Stay behind me. We do not...."

The town is dead. People still move about the buildings, but they are just shadows among the grave-like homes they have erected. Trem could not see them. They were all hiding. The road into town was cobblestone, very nicely made and unusual for a frontier town.

These people had worked hard, and all they had raised was a carcass.

There was still one person out there, at least, a hardened but unimposing man whittling beneath a great tree at the town's center. Trem needed supplies and he would have to ask the only person who seemed willing to talk. He approached the figure as openly as he could so as not to startle him.

"Trem, Trem are you okay?"

"What?" Trem snapped out of his trance, Jovanaleth was at his side shaking him slightly, he looked very concerned.

"I said, are you okay?"

Trem shook his head and blinked a few times, "Yes. Yes, I am all right. It was just a hazy memory."

Jovan stared hard at his friend in obvious concern, and then released his shoulder without pursuing the bizarre instance further. Trem had frozen stock-still and seemed to be staring off in the distance, to the east, at something beyond even the horizon for several seconds, oblivious to the escalating turmoil around him. Logan and Ghost's argument had reached a boil inside the town walls and the people were beginning to edge out of their homes, curiosity getting the better of their fear. At the front of those brave enough to venture back into the street came a slightly hunched older figure with the white clad woman they had seen from afar at his elbow.

"We are not here to aid farmers, knight! We have a job to complete."

Logan spun his horse and brought himself alongside the larger beast Ghost rode. "You have your quest and I have my vows. I defend the defenseless, help those in danger, and I will know what is wrong in this town!"

Ghost's warhorse snapped at Logan's own steed and the calmer mount cantered back a few steps. Ghost sneered cruelly as he replied, "Even your horse knows better than you do. It seems Carock has as much distaste for you as I, knight. There will be no more of this, I am in charge here."

The elderly man wearing beaten leather armor and carrying a worn bow stepped forward, his younger, white-robed female companion remaining a bit behind him, and addressed Logan in a weathered voice, "Are you truly a paladin of the Angladaic kingdom?"

Ghost turned on the daring townsman growling through clenched teeth, "Stay out of this, aged one, it is not of your concern."

Diaga intervened then, having circumvented the argument on his smaller horse while Neep, Grimtooth, Gend, and Rath watched from a small distance. The young mage was enraged at last, something none of the other companions had seen. "So you have not changed, Greymane Squall! You remain a coward and a bully bent on his own personal gain!"

Ghost whirled on the mage, and simultaneously drew his scimitar, holding it a short distance from the quietly mounted young man. "That name is dead!"

Logan's eyes had gone wide. "Greymane? Thane Greymane? The one who betrayed his own people to the Nerothian invaders? Who let his own family be murdered to protect his skin?"

Ghost rounded on his new accuser, shouting, "They were to live! Our safe passage was to be exchanged for control of the city!"

Neep was already closing on the cornered Napalian with her sword drawn. Ghost saw her moving and roared, "Keep the cat away, mage, or I will skin her alive!"

Diaga spoke calmly, "She is wary of your blade being so close to my chest."

"It will be in your guts before she comes any closer."

"I think not."

It was not Trem or Jovan who intervened then, nor any of the other travelers who had made the journey from Gi'lakil together, though they were all present. It was the old man who had spoken to Logan. His bow was drawn and pointed straight at Ghost's head. For all his years the arrow never wavered from its target and there was no tremor in his arm. His eyes glued to the stern face watching him along the notched shaft, Ghost slowly lowered his blade.

The situation was far from diffused, however. The old man had relative control with the riled warrior staring down his arrow, but he could not hold his weapon taut forever. Ghost attempted a disarming smile, but it was little more than a baring of teeth. The aged archer never took his eyes off of him as he addressed Logan, "I wish to ask again, are you indeed an Angladaic paladin, young man?"

Logan paused a moment before replying. "Not yet. My quest is to prove myself worthy of becoming one."

"And how would you do such a thing?"

Logan caught the look of the old man's eyes and saw the masked desperation in them. "By helping those who need it."

The stern elder relaxed his bow slightly and looked the young knight squarely in the eyes. "I can think of a few people who might take you up on such an offer."

"No!"

Heads spun as Trem let out a cry that sounded like a man having his very soul torn from his body. The old man also turned and he froze, his bow clattering to the ground when he saw who had uttered such a terrible sound. He stared hard as Trem looked upon him in unspeakable confusion and horror. "How can this be?"

Trem clutched at his saddle as he tried to maintain his balance, "Not again, not...."

The man beneath the tree was kind but firm. Trem could have no supplies; the people had barely enough to fend for themselves, let alone to share with a weary traveler. Trem sensed something was terribly wrong. Foolishly, he inquired as to what it was. The lone representative of the village was slow to tell him, but he relented before the intense eyes and strangely powerful demeanor of this young half-elf.

The village was besieged. Only a week ago, a party of men had gone out to the fields to recover the harvest for that month. Only one had returned, dying. He spoke of terrible monsters that looked like wolves but walked upright and carried massive axes and spears. The young survivor told the townspeople these creatures had burned the fields and devoured his companions even as they lived. He said these abominations were coming for the town. The oldest among the people recognized the things of which he spoke as gnolls, an ancient plague on the peaceful people of the Dust Plains.

Trem had digested this calmly and without remark. The stern older man informed him that they expected the creatures sometime that night, as they had been seen coming closer and closer each evening prior. Their shapes were massive and hulking things in the dark. There were many of them, far too many to stand against, and yet there was nowhere to run.

Against his better judgment, Trem sat and listened. Even more against his own good sense, he inquired as to the plans for the town's defense, the numbers of able bodied warriors, even as to who would lead them. They were questions that this seasoned man could not answer readily. He had tried to organize resistance, as he alone had once been a soldier, but he had made only small headway with those determined to resist. The people needed more than his voice to find their courage.

Trem could feel the decision coming. He knew it was the wrong one, he knew he should just keep moving or find a way to get the people of this village safely on the road to a larger, better defended settlement. He knew he should wish the man well and encourage the people to attempt a desperate, if impossible, flight under cover of darkness, perhaps going so far as to harass their enemies from a safe distance to buy them time. Naturally, he did none of these things. Instead, he remained and began to conspire with the spokesman for the doomed hamlet.

Trem snapped out of the trance again. His head was spinning and his horror was now beyond containment. Trem was shaking visibly in his saddle and Jovan's steadying hands were the only things holding him atop his horse. The old man was moving closer to the stunned half-elf as though he himself could not believe his eyes. But rather than horror his face seemed lit up with a new sheen of hope. "It is you! You aided me and my friends, helped us once! You must do so again, Trem Waterhound! Please!"

The shock on the faces of those around him was the final straw. Trem threw his hands to his temples and cried out in a haggard, pained voice that none of his companions had heard before, "No! This is not happening! I will not...."

The thrashing hermit could not be contained even by the strength of his friend's firm hands. Trem hurled himself from his horse and smashed to the ground in a limp mound. Logan jumped down from his saddle and rushed to his prostrate form, soon followed by Diaga and Grimtooth. Ghost could only sit shocked in his saddle at this sudden turn of events. All he knew for certain was that things were rapidly spiraling out of his control.

Jovanaleth was on his knees beside his friend trying to revive him. Logan appeared quickly at his side and helped turn the prone half-elf over. Trem's eyes were still open and his mouth was moving. Jovanaleth leaned in, attempting to hear what it was his friend was repeatedly whispering. His eyes widened in horror as the words became clear. He turned to Logan with a mixture of fear and disbelief on his face. The knight grasped the younger man's shoulder asking, "What is it Jovan? What is he saying?"

Jovan could not stop the descent of several tears as he listened to Trem's rambling, "Logan, gods save us, Logan."

"Jovan, what is it?"

The young man turned back to his friend's shaking form, but he could not bring himself to repeat what he heard. Jovanaleth motioned Logan closer and the knight leaned in so he could hear the faint and strained voice of the half-elf. The Angladaic's face fell as he made out what Trem was muttering and all he could say was, "Trem, my gods Trem, what have you seen?"

The man's name was Joseph, and despite himself Trem felt a great deal of kinship towards him. He reminded the half-elf of his foster father, and maybe that was why he stayed in the town, even though every fiber of his being urged him to simply move on or drive the residents to flee. Trem had learned quickly that whenever he stopped somewhere for too long, he would wear out his welcome among the people. His elven heritage made him unpopular among most of the residents of the Dust Plains. In Meana, the halflings had welcomed him, and in Gi'lakil he was just another half-elf passing through, but the farmers and settled people of the towns and villages often saw him as a threat. He had come to this new village out of curiosity, as it had sprung up north of Meana seemingly overnight, based on rumors of iron deposits found in the nearby mountains.

He had meant to pass through, perhaps to push westward in search of aid, but Joseph had convinced him to stay. His stalwart calm and reserve, his seeming fearlessness of the terrible threat facing his village: Trem found it was infectious. He listened as Joseph explained what odds they were up against. An entire pack of gnolls, he suspected perhaps twenty based on the account of the victim of their first assault, was intent on making the town their personal playground of slaughter. There were only a hundred or so people in this fledgling hamlet and many of the younger men had already met their fates at the hands of the gnolls while wandering outside the light of their new-built homes. Joseph brought Trem to the inn where most of the citizenry had barricaded themselves. There he introduced Trem to the people as the Warden of the Plains, and Trem promised he would come up with a plan to defend the town.

Trem had spent several years thanklessly patrolling the Dust Plains, defending the people from bandits and small groups of gnolls that threatened them. His swift legs and strong bow had helped save many farms and merchants, but few were as pleased with their salvation when they met him up close. The Forester Elves of Silverleaf had long ago taught the people of the Dust Plains to fear their kind. Battles between the elves and the knights of Aves had left scars on the people here, and the resurgent Eagle Knights had spread their message of the purity of human blood, leading to stronger animosity towards half-elves and other races. Trem had continued his quiet guardianship of the lands and their residents, but a growing anger at being mistrusted was simmering in him. Initially, that was why he had planned not to stay. It was a daunting task to face down even a few gnolls, and he believed that even successfully driving off a whole pack would do little to change the minds of the people here.

But the older man had been convincing. Joseph himself was a former soldier. He had fought in the battles against the Merkath goblins years before and was calm in the face of such danger. Despite being human, Joseph did not care about Trem's mixed blood. He had heard tales of the Warden saving people on the Plains, recognized Trem's huntsman attire, long heavy cloak, and leather armor. All Joseph wanted was someone who was willing to help them. Though he had tried to change his ways in the face of the disgust and dismissal of many he had aided, Trem still harbored dreams of being seen as a hero. Joseph saw and fed into that desire in order to convince him to stay.

The two toured the town as Joseph pointed out the many alleys and opeings between the homes that the gnolls would use to infiltrate it. Gnolls had broad shoulders that might prevent them from using the narrowest of openings effectively, likely funneling them to the main street of the town. Trem concluded the best method of defense would be to gather around the great tree in the center of the village and await the attack. There were two main avenues to the northeast of the settlement, leading to the main road that would be easy paths for the gnolls to follow. Trem proposed setting up rickety barriers in each street, and when the creatures appeared the defenders could rush to the appropriate spot to head them off. Ultimately, it might be enough to slow them or convince them the attack was not worth the cost it could potentially incur.

Joseph was hopeful they could buy time. Word had been sent southward and also to the north, where it had reached Trem in Meana, so it soon would pass to Gi'lakil and perhaps the Eagle Knights would send a patrol to aid them. Trem agreed with the possibility, both men pointedly ignoring the rumors that Aves was dealing with threats from across the Sirrion Sea that would pull their forces back to the fortress. In situations as dire as the one Joseph described, Trem knew that hope was an important factor for success.

Trem knew gnolls, had fought them on a few occasions, and he thought he understood them. Gnolls attacked without considering strategy, they overwhelmed through power and the sheer ferocity of their assault. Monstrous creatures, they were strong and swift enough to overpower trained soldiers in great enough numbers. Joseph knew there were not enough townspeople experienced in combat to defend both roads, and feared that assuming the gnolls would attack from only one angle would leave them open to flanking. Trem insisted that if they did not defend one alley, they would be forced to hole up in the inn, which would only lead to disaster. Joseph conceded and they set to building ramshackle barriers from furniture and scrap metal, using the benches from the inn to provide archers with a clean shot over the makeshift wall at their attackers.

Trem discovered Joseph was not as old as he appeared. Years of campaigning in his younger days had given him a weathered and worn appearance, though he was barely fifty. Despite years of fighting and injuries, Joseph still moved with a grace and power that Trem recognized as a great asset to their efforts. The older man's very presence seemed to lend courage to his fellows, and his vocal support of Trem was enough for the villagers to trust him. As they worked together, the two became almost symbiotic, the one knowing precisely what the other needed from him. Joseph and Trem were invigorating in their enthusiasm for the defense and as they orchestrated the communal efforts the people of the town slowly began to believe they might stand some chance.

Joseph's primary concern was the safety of the women and children. He wanted to shield them from danger within the inn, but some of the women refused to stay out of the fighting. Those who would not stand down were armed as best they could be, the rest holed up in the barricaded structure with the children and elders. In case any of the gnolls slipped by the defenders, the innkeeper provided a heavy bell to be rung if the sheltered group was in danger. By nightfall the preparations, such as they were, had been completed and the tiny detachment of combatants huddled about the great oak awaiting the monsters. As the darkness deepened, the tension rose and much shifting and clattering was heard among the citizenry.

Trem stood stock still, listening and straining to see into the inky blackness with his stronger, elven vision. Joseph was leaning on his bow next to him, his eyes focused more on the defenders than the potential assailants. As the hours passed, the older man relaxed slightly, turning to his companion he said, "Perhaps they will not come this night."

A spine-chilling howl came ripping out of the dark. Trem raised his bow and notched an arrow, but did not draw it. Joseph and the others followed suit as Trem gave instructions in a clear, calm voice, "When they come, aim for the neck or the legs. Their chests are thick and bony, so a killing shot has to strike the neck. If you cannot strike the neck aim low, their legs are long and weak. Hitting one will slow them considerably and buy us time."

A young man next to Trem was shaking so badly that his arrow was rattling against the wood of the bow. Trem paused his speech and grabbed the shaft of the arrow. "If you are nervous, pick up a spear. An errant shot will help no one."

As the youth complied, Trem took a step forward and continued speaking in an even voice, "We will use bows until I say otherwise. We must avoid close combat as long as we can. When it comes, we fight in shifts, half with bows in back while the spears fend off the attack." Pausing, Trem turned his head over his shoulder. "One last thing: they are large and fearsome creatures. You will be afraid when they appear. Remember those you are fighting for."

More howls came through the alleyways, but there was no way to tell which direction they were coming from. Joseph was on edge, fearing they would not see the gnolls until they were on top of them, and their carefully prepared strategy would prove useless. He was about to say something to Trem when the half-elf swung his bow upward and loosed a shaft into the leftmost street, though there was nothing in that direction that the others could see. Even so, there was a cry of pain and rage. Trem's response was instantaneous. He rushed to the left barrier shouting in earnest, "Fire away! Hold them off!"

The townspeople were next to him in a heartbeat, firing arrows as quickly as they could. Many seemed to be flying wildly, but the barrage did not stop. There were more yelps of shock and rage and now the defenders could hear the monsters running, their clawed paws scraping viciously on the cobblestones. Then a massive wolf-like creature burst into the torchlight, bleeding from several arrows that had found their mark. The effect on the men and women was terrible.

They froze in place and some cried out in horror, even Joseph paused in shock, but Trem did not wait. The half-elf shot an arrow into the creature's throat and it gurgled and sputtered as it collapsed to the ground. He readied another shaft. "Do not stop firing! Fight!"

The defenders renewed their counterattack with vigor. More arrows flew faster and with greater accuracy into the now visible, oncoming fiends. At first they all fell before reaching the barrier, but then a large contingent came rushing forward in a pack that the archers had difficulty thinning. Trem drew his long hunting knife and jumped over the barrier. "Keep shooting and stay on the wall!"

The half-elf met the three gnolls that reached the barrier calmly, blade held downward with his thumb on the pommel, positioned readily at his side. They came hurtling towards him recklessly and Trem neatly swept between them, slicing effortlessly across the abdomens of the first two. They clutched at their bellies in pain and stumbled into the barrier as Trem whirled and thrust his blade into the back of the last monster's neck, causing it to rear upward in pain. Over the barrier, several spear tips thrust down to finish off the other gnolls. Trem hopped backward, away from the one he had just stabbed, when Joseph shouted a warning from the wall. Trem turned just in time to see another pack charging forward. Without a clear way to get back over the wall he motioned the others away from the barrier as he prepared to meet the new threat. "Fighting retreat! Spears up!"

Trem managed to avoid the first two gnolls and wound the third along it's arm before the haft of a weapon struck him solidly in the chest, sending him flying through the air, clear of the makeshift fence, to land hard on the stones of the town center. Joseph was at his side in an instant, but Trem waved him away as he heaved himself to his feet. The villagers were fairing badly and more gnolls were coming into the light of the torches. Trem pushed Joseph forward. "Help them, quickly!"

"There are more than I ever expected," the older man sighed, "more than we can handle."

Trem rushed to assist the spearmen. "Then we will keep them away from the inn as long as we can!"

As the pack descended on the barrier, the townspeople, men and women, held forth their improvised weaponry and thrust it fearfully but aggressively at their enemies. The gnolls seemed to be all about them, but they could not penetrate the line of sharp weapons bristling before them. A few more arrows struck the congested mass of monsters, and though a few grasped spear shafts and pulled their wielders off-balance or to a grisly fate as they came too close to the beasts, the assault was slowed and then halted altogether. Trem saw the despair of Joseph was misplaced and roared incoherently as he struck back with the people of the village, trying to break their assailants' spirit with a powerful counterattack.

Trem watched as the lead gnoll, taking a spear in the chest howled, and spun away from the fight. Waving its massive axe in the direction of the darkness beyond the town, it began to retreat. The dozen or so creatures among the town fell back as well, rushing back down the left road from which they had come. The villagers relaxed, but Trem jumped in front of them to wave them onward. "Drive them out! Chase them clear of the light! We must make sure they know never to come back!"

The wounded hung back as the able-bodied men and women followed the half-elf down the dark street, firing arrows and yelling wildly. Trem was in the lead, his face beaming as the survivors about him cheered in celebration. A few clapped him on the shoulders in thanks, and despite himself he smiled at their gratitude. Joseph was by his side, laughing as the gnolls disappeared into the night. When their howls had quieted he turned and clapped the half-elf on the back heartily. Trem smiled fully then and the two stood, arm in arm, tired but proud. The would-be warriors were sobering up as they recognized those among them who were missing, wounded or killed in the attack. Trem and Joseph made ready to lead them back to the town center.

Then the bell in the inn rang out in earnest. Trem's heart sank to the floor as the blood fled Joseph's face. The gnolls had deceived them. It had all been a diversion. Trem realized his gambit had gone terribly wrong. The half-elf raced down the street, the people of the town following him in a desperate sprint to reach the inn. Trem rounded the corner first and his greatest fear was realized. There were over twenty gnolls crashing against the doors and windows of the building. Inside, Trem could hear the screams and cries of the terrified people.

As he rushed forward to attack the creatures a shout went up behind him and more screams, terrible cries of suffering and horror. Trem spun and saw more gnolls, hidden in the street they had used to circumvent the defenders, tearing through the ranks of survivors like they were threshing wheat. Trem was caught in the center of the maelstrom, the beasts abandoning the attack on the inn to complete the destruction of the town's untrained militia. Trem held his ground, rage driving him as much as the guilt at his failure. He took several gnolls down before a spear drove into his shoulder and he was tossed off the point like a rock from a sling. Trem crashed to the ground and could not rise. He waited there, blood seeping down his side, for one of the monsters to finish him off.

But someone else found him first. Joseph had realized they had been duped once he saw the inn surrounded. Knowing he could do nothing but die with honor, he had tried to fend off the beasts that had attacked the rear of the defenders. Then Joseph had seen Trem tossed through the air like a ragdoll and determined then and there he would save at least one life that night. The gnolls had killed most of the fighting men and women and their bloodlust now drew them to the inn. Joseph slipped behind the foul beasts into the shadows and hurried to the beaten form on the ground. Trem was hurt and could not rise. The older man grabbed his cloak and dragged him behind a nearby house, hauling him into the darkness where they could hide. The half-elf struggled, assailing Joseph with demanding cries, "No, leave me! Leave me!"

But Joseph would not listen. He pulled Trem into a small garden and laid him among the tall stalks of corn and wheat where they would not be seen. As best he could, Joseph staunched the bleeding with a cloth and forced liquid from his waterskin down Trem's throat. The half-elf fluttered in and out of consciousness, but when he was awake all he could hear were the screams of the dying people in the inn as the gnolls tore them apart. Each time he awoke he tried to rise, but Joseph held him down, refusing to let him throw his life away. Even though the true brutality of the slaughter was likely over in a matter of hours, it would be days and weeks on end that Trem would awake to the shrieks of children in unspeakable fear and pain, just before their unearthly cries were cruelly and abruptly silenced. Long after he wordlessly left Joseph, Trem had been haunted by visions of the deaths he had not seen, but heard so profoundly that their voices seemed to follow him everywhere he went since that cursed night.

Trem's eyes suddenly regained focus as the words stopped spilling from his mouth. He could see Jovan's blurred face before him, etched in fear and concern. Logan was just over his shoulder, a more knowing glint in his eyes. Trem realized he had been raving as he relived one of the most terrible nights of his life. That was the only way to describe it. He had not revisited it or recalled it. He had been there again. Suddenly he could not contain himself. With unnatural strength, Trem surged from the ground, throwing Jovanaleth onto his back and causing Logan to stumble away from him. His soul burned with the pain of the vision as he searched for the man who knew too well what he had seen. Joseph's ancient eyes met his and the onlookers could feel the crackle of electric recognition between them.

Trem took a few steps nearer the old man, still not believing what he saw. Joseph was even more alarmed, for Trem was the same as he had been when Joseph met him almost twenty-five years ago. Now a man of over seventy years he was accustomed to, even comfortable with, the effect that age had on everyone, but this half-elf seemed untouched. No, that was not entirely true. His eyes appeared older than any Joseph had ever seen.

Trem stopped a few feet from the old man he had once tried to help and found he could not speak. Unimaginable horrors were still flitting through his mind. They had lain in the basement of one of the homes for weeks, Joseph sneaking upstairs to find food and gradually nursing Trem back to health. Trem had left as soon as he could stand, wandering aimlessly until he stumbled into the Aves and service to the Eagle Knights. Each day he prayed something, anything would erase that night from his mind or snuff out his life altogether, and now it was here, in the flesh, before him; a living testament to his failure.

The two men faced each other silently but Joseph noted the strange quivering in Trem's body as he sought control over his memories and emotions. The old man approached and laid a hand on Trem's arm. Trem jerked away sharply and his eyes burned into Joseph's. "Please," the old man whispered, "please, help me again."

Trem met the worn man's gaze and the conversation with Gerand Oakheart began to ring in his mind. There was a choice to be made here and the choosing had terrible implications. Despite his fear, Trem felt that old desire to play at being a hero rising from somewhere deep within, long suppressed inside him. He began to feel a twinge of resolve, an intent to strive for action that was just and good, but then an image flashed harshly in the back of his mind. It was the body of a child, its sex indeterminable, with an arm chewed off at the elbow. Trem lurched backward and with great effort forced himself to retain his standing position. It was not possible, he had tried to walk this mythical path of heroism before and knew it to be an illusion, a fable. He met Joseph's eyes again as his own suddenly grew hard and unyielding. "No."

The old man felt his as though he had aged another fifty years at the firm pronouncement from the one person he thought he could trust amid these travelers. His eyes sank and Trem broke free of his stare long enough to wrench himself away. He turned his back on Joseph, on the town, and started walking south.

Ghost, still mounted, spurred his horse forward and ripped the reins of Trem's own mount from Logan, who had been holding onto the riderless steeds. "Stay if you want, Angladaic, but it seems your friend knows better than you when the course of action is clear."

Ghost wheeled away and brought Trem his horse. Logan looked on solemnly with his bloodbrother beside him. "He cannot really mean to leave these people."

Grimtooth placed a huge hand on his brother's mailed one. "Ach! Ah am afraid we 'er wrong brotha. 'E is nae the man we thought 'e was."

Diaga was calmly watching the procession as Gend passed him by. "Well, er, I suppose I ought to be going too, leading them on and such. Good luck, young mage, I hope you do not suffer too painful a death!"

Diaga did not even glance at the halfling's extended hand, nor did he notice Rath pass by and tug the little guide along with him. His eyes remained fixed on Trem's retreating back as inwardly his mind raced. Trem and Joseph knew each other from before. Long before. How was that possible? Neep sidled up to him in an attempt to comfort the puzzled youth, but Diaga was trapped within his own mind, cycling over the possible explanations.

Only one person was not frozen to the spot by the sudden turn of events. Jovanaleth of the Blade, prince of his people, seemed to have suddenly found himself. He rode forward and past the departing travelers, stopping before the southern entrance to Delmore. Ghost smiled reassuringly, if not kindly, at him. "I see you too have come to some sense?"

Jovan's glare would have knocked the old campaigner from his saddle had it been able. "Do not speak to me, traitor. I would just as soon pretend we never met."

Trem stopped beside Ghost but failed to meet the burning eyes of his young companion. Jovanaleth pulled his horse closer and tried to move his face in line with Trem's. The half-elf finally managed to return the look, but Jovan's stern grimace caught him off guard. "Come with us, Jovan. This is not our problem."

Jovan's eyes widened in fury, as he said, "Not our problem? There are innocent lives at stake here! Are you the same man who fed those refugees in Gi'lakil? Or who nursed me back to health? What of your promise to aid me until we found my father? What happened to the man I started this journey with? What happened to my friend?"

Trem's blank eyes looked back at Jovan unblinkingly. "We were never friends, Jovanaleth. I only made a promise out of the guilt I feel everyday for the people I have failed to help. You were just a way to ease my conscience. And now, now I realize that, after all I have seen, there is no conscience left to me. I cannot be responsible for these people, or for you." Trem turned away and gently nudged his mount forward. "Goodbye Jovan of the Blade, I trust we will not meet again in this world."

The deserters moved on past a stunned Jovanaleth and out of Delmore. As they passed, Jovan found his vision increasingly blurred by the tears seeping out from his eyes. He could only barely see the last figure that passed him, draped in black cloth. A soft whisper escaped the fabric, "Fear not, young warrior, his life will not last much longer than your own."

And then they were gone.

Chapter 17

The grand city at the heart of the Angladaic kingdom lay still. Alderlast had experienced its most chaotic day in recent memory. Early that afternoon, all trade, bartering, labour, and even routine movement seemed to have been stopped. The word had spread rapidly through writs posted on every street corner, storefront, and at every lamppost. Arvadis Angladais was deposed and Karsyrus Vendile now held the throne. There was no explanation for this shocking turn of events, only strict new regulations on the people and the implication of taxes to come. The citizens were given no recourse or outlet for what grievances they might have had, so they went back to their homes and tried to pretend nothing had changed. But no one could help noticing the increased presence of guards, almost exclusively from houses Vendile, Hladic, and Bwemor. No one saw any paladins, nor were there any house guards from Hawking or his allies.

These were disturbing signs to say the least, and no amount of armed enforcers could quell the rumors in the streets. People watched the Hawking's home carefully looking for any hint of the former king, but saw nothing. The word spread quickly that Vendile had finally succeeded in his scheme to rid the people of their beloved king. It was a dark day in the city of Alderlast. Despite the new ruler's urges to get back to their daily work as though nothing were amiss, the people had made their own choice. All houses were closed and everyone wore black, mourning the former king they feared was now dead.

Vendile himself sat pensively on his throne in the hastily refurbished palace. His quarters had not yet been cleared out and redecorated, but soon he would have a grand expanse of rooms at his fingertips. To think that Arvadis had used those expansive chambers for storage! Bwemor had brought to Vendile the grand news that Vorasho was killed only a short while ago, and the new king had insisted upon meeting his enemy's executioner face to face so that he might reward him personally. Despite the lack of the prince's head, Karsyrus had been assured the deed was done, so well in fact there was nothing left of the head in question from the encounter. Unfortunately, rumors of the peoples' sadness and self-imposed mourning had alsoo reached the tyrant and his previously elated mood had darkened considerably despite the general success of his coup. Leaning on his elbow, draped in the violet cloth of his house and twirling the heavy crown of Angladais with his free hand, Vendile listened to the ring on his index finger creating a strange and undulating sound as it ground against the interior of the circlet. Vendile rubbed his bent nose, his hand stealing to the pendant resting heavily against his chest, and waited for Freyan to report.

The now well-dressed advisor eased open the heavy mahogany and steel doors and shuffled his way across the carpet to his master. Taking great care to bow low before speaking, Freyan eyed his unhappy king. "The servant of Bwemor, whose presence you requested, is here my lord."

"Make him wait," grunted Vendile as he stared idly at his crown. "What news from the city?"

"The people still mourn the death of Arvadis, my lord."

Vendile gritted his teeth but his rage did not boil over, he was too pleased with his victory to become angry. "Why must they do this? Can they not simply move on and accept me?"

Freyan spread his hands, and his tone was placating. "It was sudden, my lord, and a period of shock and distress is not a surprise. Within the month, they will have forgotten Arvadis ever existed, especially once we have made peace with these invaders. Also," he added slyly, "the grand public ceremonial crowning by Highlord Hladic has been scheduled to occur in the next few days. I am certain the paladin order will be forced to attend if the priests are present. That will solve the matter of quiet resistance from Calavar's house."

"You have done well, Freyan, very well indeed. Hladic and Bwemor are more than satisfied with their share of the kingdom's spoils, and before long we will have an entire continent to claim! I can assure you that your reward will be most substantial."

"I am here only to serve, my king."

Vendile's smiled then, his previous glower replaced with a manic happiness. "As always, Freyan, you put me in a good mood! Send in the loyal servant of Bwemor, that I may make him my own. I believe there is one more task he might perform for me."

Freyan nodded in acquiescence and departed quietly from the presence of his king. The advisor smiled slightly to himself as he neared the entrance of the hall. Things had proceeded splendidly in the last few days and, if he read Vendile correctly, the fool believed it had all been his own doing. This was proving an easier task than he had expected. Reaching the door, he cracked it open and beckoned the young man into the throne room.

Renon Ordlan held back his shock at seeing the Vendile colors flying throughout the massive, high-ceilinged hall. When Arvadis had been king, the room had been used for private councils and open audiences with the people, with all the Highlord banners displayed in small stature compared with that of the Angladaic nation itself. The young soldier was accustomed to seeing a large, long table as the room's only real furniture or decoration. Now a velvet carpet of purple stood out against the shining white marble of the floor and the many grand vases and newly hung chandeliers of fine crystal. For all its opulence, it was the gently rippling banners of Vendile that made Renon's skin crawl. Walking slowly down the long path through the pristine flooring he kept a tight grip on his sword hilt. His armor was plain but well kept and shone in the flickering torchlight that pushed back the gathering night in the massive hall windows. Renon knelt and bowed his head before the throne, noting the vile man before him sat unarmed and unguarded.

Vendile stood and stepped down from his throne, taking the man by the shoulder and pulling him up. Renon could see the new king was much taller even than himself, and Renon considered himself a large man. The dark eyes and black hair stood out in the rough and somewhat contorted face of the smiling king. Renon found himself on the defensive, though he could not say why. He wisely released his sword hilt.

Vendile put his arm about the young man's shoulders and walked him a short way from the throne. "Ah yes, the loyal servant returns! I hear you have done your king a great service, young soldier, and you must know it will be rewarded."

Renon swallowed. "I followed my orders like any good servant would, your majesty."

Vendile's grin widened. "Your majesty! Why, I like the sound of that! Tell me, my fine warrior, what is your name?"

"Renon, sire."

"Renon, a bold name for a mere warrior, though I must say I approve. Now, Renon, rest assured that a grand prize for your service is forthcoming, but first I must ask you to prove your loyalty once again, for I feel only you can be trusted with the task I am about to hand down."

Renon tensed but forced himself to respond calmly, "Whatever you desire, my lord."

Vendile pulled the young man still closer and his mad eyes danced. "Now that, my good Renon, is precisely what I wanted to hear."

Vorasho awoke to find that it was already nightfall and, cursing his own frailty, he hurriedly arose and dressed. Strapping on his light cuirass and grabbing his heavy steel staff, he readied himself. As he stood in his room holding his weapon, he paused to examine it. Runiden Calavar had gifted it to him when he reached the paladin rank. It was a beautiful piece, an eight-foot thin steel staff with a scaled grip design on the shaft. At each end, claws held wide orbs, heavy and dangerous. Only a truly devout warrior could find the strength to lift such a weapon. Vorasho could wield it with ease, and he hefted it now, thinking of the moment he had received it and the pride that had washed over him.

Vorasho cut his revelation off forcefully, and walked quickly downstairs to find the other three already awaiting him. Eyeing them, he strode to the table and laid down a map of Alderlast he had brought from his room. "Were you planning to let me sleep the night away?"

Graham cleared his throat. "Begging your pardon, m'lord, but it has only just darkened outside and we thought rest would do you good."

"And if I rest all day, Graham, when do you expect me to plan?"

The older man opened his mouth to reply but could come up with nothing. Vorasho waved him into silence. "Fear not, my friend, I had hatched a rough idea of our course before I slept. You both know that Lena here was once a servant in the palace?"

The two guards shook their heads. "Well, suffice to say she was, and her work there will allow us to rescue my father swiftly and with little interference. There are passages within the palace only accessible by those who know them, and most who do know such secret ways are the servants. Previous kings wanted their retainers able to easily cater to their every whim but to do so out of sight. These passages can take us anywhere in the palace and also keep us somewhat hidden. From what I was told, they can even bring us to the dungeons."

Lena nodded. "I have had reason to use those very passages before. Getting you inside will not prove difficult."

Derek cleared his throat and inquired, "Perhaps, my lady, but what of the others we will bring with us?"

"There will be no others," Vorasho said softly, "we cannot run the risk of word reaching Vendile, nor can we take the chance that with so many in our midst we might be discovered. The fewer in number we are there are the better our chances for success."

"So only the four of us then." Graham's tone was somewhat hesitant. "What about your friends within the palace?"

"We do not have time to await Renon's help, and also have no way of knowing where he is or even if he can aid us." Vorasho said decisively, adding, "We must look to ourselves and not count on his aid."

The others exchanged looks of acceptance and determination, and then they turned to study the map with Vorasho. Lena placed a thin finger on it near the northwest end of the city. "The servants used to live exclusively in this part of Alderlast, so the entrances all originate here. Since the palace is at the center of the city, it will take us at least an hour to even reach the passages that lead to the palace proper. Finding the correct passage and the cell where Arvadis is being held may take longer. We should leave now and move swiftly before it gets too late, or we will not be fleeing under cover of nightfall."

"We will get inside, find my father, and flee the city to rally our allies near the Pillars of Light." Vorasho met the eyes of his fellow conspirators one at a time, willing his own determination into them with a look. "Then we can start taking back what we have lost. The people will flock to their true king and Vendile's reign will be short indeed."

A sudden knock at the door jerked the four from their examination of the map. Derek moved swiftly to stand by the entrance as Graham went to answer the door and Vorasho pushed Lena protectively behind him. Graham eased the door open and as the figure outside started to step in, Derek grabbed the tunic of the intruder and flung him to the floor. It was a young boy, perhaps thirteen, and he was carrying a letter in his left hand. He stared wide-eyed at Derek as the soldier held his blade near the boy's throat, "It's only a child, my lord. Looks like he is delivering a message."

Vorasho strode over and knelt by the frightened boy, asking, "Who sent you?"

"M-my brother Renon," stuttered the young man. "He said it was urgent. He said you needed to come quickly."

"Let him up." Derek heaved the child onto his feet and Vorasho took the hastily scrawled and crumpled letter from him. Opening it he scanned it swiftly and his eyes widened. He grabbed the boy's collar and pulled him in close. "Your brother, when did he send you?"

Lena tried to calm Vorasho. "He's frightened, let him go!"

"Tell me!" yelled Vorasho. "When did he send you?"

The boy was shaking. "A-an hour a-ago. I h-had to come from across the city!"

Vorasho dropped the youth unceremoniously onto the floor where he stayed seated. Grabbing his heavy dark cloak from the back of his chair Vorasho flung it on saying, "We have to go now. Lena, I need you to get us inside as quickly as possible."

The young woman crossed her arms and refused to budge. "Slow down, Vorasho! What is going on? What did the letter say?"

Derek and Graham were already dressed and waiting. Vorasho chucked Lena's dark cloak to her. "Vendile sent Renon to kill my father. He wants the same man who killed the prince to execute the king. Renon said he would not be with friends this time, he is going into the dungeons with Vendile's own guards."

Lena hurriedly threw on her cloak and checked her belt knife. "Then we have no time to waste. Follow me!"

She led the way out of the house, followed by Graham and Derek. Vorasho brought up the rear, and as he closed the door, he turned toward the boy. "Stay here and do not leave. If we are not back by morning, flee the city and go north. Find the army encampment and ask for Nemil. Show him this," he tossed the boy his house ring. "He will know what it means."

Vorasho shut the door and followed his companions through the inky blackness of Alderlast's back streets. The boy watched from the window until the figures disappeared, then he curled up in the corner to wait, nervously shaking the ring in his cupped hands.

Edge and Romund were taking turns carrying the exhausted Raymir up the sides of the massive mountain. They had been fortunate that there were ample footpaths to make the ascent considerably easier than they expected. Raymir had not gained consciousness since falling into a deep slumber after they escaped the daemon wolf's attack, but Romund had assured Edge that she was merely resting. Still, the younger man was concerned. Even if Raymir were merely exhausted from the immense expenditure of herself that went into her magic in the battle with the daemonic Kurok they needed her awake, if only so that she could make the climb on her own.

Romund, strong as he was, could not maintain the hard rate at which they were ascending with Raymir on his shoulders. Edge had done the majority of the carrying, but even he was weary from the long hours and lack of sleep. Romund finally stumbled as they were beginning yet another steep, hairpin pathway winding back from where they had slowly plodded for several hours. Despite his protests, Edge insisted they stop and rest. The two set Raymir down gently under an overhanging cliff that sheltered them from the now-nonstop snowfall. Romund leaned back, exhausted, with his eyes closed. Edge reached into his dwindling pack of supplies and pulled out the remains of his kindling. Clearing out the snow as best he could, he set down the sparse dry wood and pulled out his flint and fought with the stone until he got the meager fire burning.

Romund kept his eyes closed but he groaned and muttered, "Is that the last of our wood you are burning?"

"I am afraid so."

"Well, I hope it lasts. Personally I am a little tired of this white, cold wasteland."

Edge didn't answer. He focused on coaxing the small fire to greater heights. Romund stayed silent a moment longer then asked, "How far do you suppose we are from the summit?"

Edge thought a moment. "Perhaps two days, maybe three?"

Romund opened his eyes in concern and glanced at the warrior. "Do you think we'll find any wood there?"

Edge shrugged. "It is exposed, which might mean it is too cold, but it could also mean that the sunlight actually reaches the top. There may be soil there as well."

Romund shifted, trying to make himself more comfortable. "And how do we cut down any fledgling growth we might find?"

Edge looked at him. "My halberd has an axehead that should manage."

Romund chuckled. "As long as you are the one who ends up swinging it."

"How is our food supply looking?"

Romund reached into his pack and felt around. "Well, on a rough estimate I would say we have about two weeks worth left, maybe three if we really stretch it."

"We do that and we won't have the energy to climb back down the mountain or even get across the plains."

The hard man from Hethegar shrugged. "Then I guess we better hope this tower of yours isn't too far from here."

"We are in a bit of a tight spot, wouldn't you say?"

Romund laughed lightly. "Please, my friend, this is a holiday compared to the dark times I have seen." Romund patted him on the arm. "Now you get some rest and I will take the first watch, though what I could possibly see in this swirling blanket of white is beyond me."

Edge was too tired to argue and before long he was fast asleep with his head on Raymir's shoulder. Romund watched them for a while with a small smile. Somehow, this far from home, in a frozen wasteland, he felt the warmest he had in years. Adjusting his armor and flexing his legs, he pulled his feet underneath him and leaned against the strong rock of the mountain. "Just hold me together a little longer, and I promise I will get them out of this."

Romund stared into the shifting cloud of snow uncertain as to whose aid he was calling for, but strangely confident that his prayers would be answered.

Jovanaleth was still sitting astride his horse, lost in his bewilderment, at the southern entrance. He did not even realize he was crying until Logan appeared standing beside him. "Come on, lad, and let's get inside for a bit."

Jovan complied without really knowing he was. Logan eased him out of the saddle and Grimtooth led his horse behind them. The orc followed them as Logan escorted Jovan towards a small thatch-roofed home in the center of town. Diaga and Neep were sitting outside on two barrels, talking quietly to some of the more inquisitive townspeople. The hubbub of fear that had permeated Delmore was gone with the sudden split of the travelers. The townspeople were waiting now. Waiting to see what would happen next, almost as though their own predicament no longer mattered.

Diaga watched Jovanaleth approach silently, but he kept his mouth moving and his hands working simple tricks for the adults and children in front of him. Logan stopped in front of the door and grasped Jovan by the shoulders. "Listen to me, Jovanaleth," the young man met his eyes briefly and Logan took that to mean he had his attention, "listen to me. This is Joseph's home, the old man who knows Trem. You need to speak to him. Trem was your friend and he is gone now, but I do not think we have seen the last of him. I told Joseph that Trem was helping you. He wants to tell you something and he wants to tell only you."

Jovan's eyes came up and this time held Logan's own. "Why?"

Logan shook his head. "I am not sure, but if we want to help these people, we need his cooperation and to get that you need to talk to him first."

"I understand that, Logan, but why does he want to talk to me? I'm not in charge."

"That, my son, is irrelevant." Jovanaleth turned to see Joseph standing in the doorway to his home. "I am not looking to talk to the one in charge or I would have spoken to the Angladaic already. I want to talk to someone who knows him."

Jovan faced the old man. "You mean Trem?"

Joseph shrugged. "His name is also irrelevant."

Jovanaleth crossed his arms. "Then tell me, sir, what exactly is relevant?"

Joseph smiled. "Why don't you come inside, and I will tell you."

Jovan paused, and then he walked inside, closing the door behind him. Joseph walked over to his table and pulled out a chair. "Sit, please. Are you hungry?"

Jovanaleth moved to the chair but did not seat himself. "It sounds like a rather large army is about to descend on your town. Shouldn't we move this along?"

"When you are as old as I am, time no longer seems to matter."

"Well, I am afraid I am not old enough to think like that," Jovan said as he sat slowly.

Joseph turned from his cupboard smiling. "Your name is Jovanaleth, I heard the wizard say you were a prince. I am Joseph, I was once a soldier."

Jovan took a chunk of the cheese that Joseph offered him and eyed the worn figure holding the tray. "How did you meet Trem?"

Joseph sighed and sat down opposite the younger man. "He tried to save my village once over twenty years ago."

"That's not possible, Trem can't be more than twenty-five himself. What was he, a child savior?" Jovan's tone was incredulous and bordering on exasperation.

"I heard you were friends before he saw me and chose to flee." Joseph's voice no longer attempted to feign hospitality, recognizing Jovanaleth was not interested in it as it was. "I know why he left. Trem failed when trying to help me long ago, and he fears he will fail again. Regardless of what you might think you know about him, I believe none of us truly know anything. I believe he is someone, something, we cannot even begin to comprehend."

"And what makes you think that, Joseph?"

The wizened man suddenly reached across the table and grabbed Jovan's hand. "Because, boy, I have seen over seventy years in my time on Teth-tenir, and no one, no one, has ever had eyes like his."

"You are judging him based upon his eyes?"

Joseph cocked his head slightly in thought. "You have seen them. Tell me they did not send a shiver down your spine. Tell me they didn't look right into your soul."

Jovan stared back at him beginning to wonder if the old man was a bit short on his senses. "I don't know that his eyes ever looked through me. But there is something about him, I will admit to that."

"Let me tell you something only time will reveal," Joseph released his hold, "Your friend, he is unique in a way beyond individuality. He is, well, I am not sure what he is."

Jovan stood and shoved his chair back into its place. "Must you constantly refer to him as my friend? He was just someone who helped me once."

Joseph was quiet for a moment then he asked, "And what is he now?"

"Nobody." Jovanaleth looked at him as though expecting further dispute, but when none came he said, "I am not concerned about him anymore. My only concern is doing what he would not. I am here to help you and this town."

Jovan turned to go, but Joseph stopped him at the doorway saying, "Do not be so quick to judge him, young man. When Trem tried to help me so long ago his efforts could not prevent the terrible deaths of my friends. It does not surprise me that he is afraid to help me again." Joseph stood and walked to the door, leaning in close and whispering, "Are you so sure you want to make the same mistake?"

Jovan turned to meet Joseph's gaze. "I would pay any price to help people in need, any price at all."

Joseph's hard face lightened into a genuine smile. "Then it sounds like we are both headed toward the same end. Let's go talk to your Angladaic friend."

Jovanaleth and Joseph emerged from the older man's home to find the entire town had arrayed themselves before the house while they were inside. Logan had taken up a position on a broken down cart near Joseph's door and was addressing the populace, "People of Delmore! Listen to me! Within a few hours there will be a large army of Broken attacking your town. It is a fight that you cannot win."

A voice called out from the crowd, "Tell us something we don't know, Angladaic! Why waste our time listening to you when we could be fleeing west?"

Logan addressed the unseen voice from his position, "Because if you flee west you will also die. There is no safety in Gi'lakil, even if you could reach it in time, and you cannot."

"So what are we supposed to do?"

Logan glanced down at Diaga who was leaning against the cart. The young mage looked back, shrugged, and nodded. The knight took a deep breath and spoke, "You cannot flee west. You must go south. There is a road through the woods leading into old caverns there. We will take you."

There was a massive clamor of noise at the mention of going south. Women shrieked and men were yelling. One voice came through the noise; "To go south as you say would take us into the haunted caves of the dwarves. You ask us to choose one death over another!"

Logan tried to quell the increasing swells of rage but he no longer had a hold over the townspeople. Diaga left the wagon and came over to Jovan and Joseph. "You have to do something," he said to the elder, "otherwise these people are just going to argue until you are all dead."

Joseph looked at him then glanced at Jovan. The young man asked Diaga, "Is there any chance we make it safely south?"

"It will be difficult." The young mage sighed. "I believe the caves are dangerous, but Gend is not the only one who knows them. I read about them once, I think I remember enough to get us inside. After that we are in the hands of the gods."

Joseph paused as though considering, then he rubbed his careworn palms together and patted the young mage on the back. "A chance is better than nothing at all. We'll need Khaliandra to get them calmed down though."

Diaga cocked his head in confusion, asking, "Who is Khaliandra?"

"That would be me." The woman they had seen briefly upon entering the town stepped forward, ignoring the tumult behind her. Jovan and Diaga felt themselves bow instinctively. She was clad in a sheer white robe, with a round, caring face and dark hair. Jovan would have guessed she was older than Diaga, but not by much. Her attire was simple, but she wore a steel pendant with the open and accepting hands that were the symbol of Endoth, God of Healing, etched on it. She smiled at their bows and said, "Please, if you could get everyone's attention?"

Jovanaleth helped the old man up onto the cart. Joseph nodded to Logan who stepped aside. Gradually the crowd quieted as they saw one of their own poised to speak, Khaliandra standing beside the barrel, but shining like a beacon in her white robes. Joseph put up his hands and they turned to him. "My friends listen to me. These people are honest travelers who are offering to help us for no reason other than they are good folk like us. Now this young man," he gestured to Diaga, "says that he can find a way into the caves and after that they will do their best to guide us out. I say we go with them, because if we do not we are certainly going to die."

The crowd was silent as they took this in. Joseph gave them no chance to respond. "Please, my friends, you have trusted me in this time of danger. Do not stop now."

Khaliandra's voice rose powerfully from beside him, "People of Delmore, trust in these men. They could have fled when the others did, but they have stayed only to help us."

The crowd rumbled and then a voice called out, "I'll go with you!"

"Aye, me too!"

"And us as well!"

"I'd rather die with friends in a cave than with monsters in my own streets!"

And just like that, it was decided. Joseph nodded solemnly amid the cheers and cries of his people. Grimtooth took his place and began issuing orders for the carts to be repositioned and barriers to be erected. The people went at their tasks with renewed hope and fervor. Logan aided Joseph once again as he clambered down from his makeshift podium. The old man thanked him as the other companions joined them. Jovanaleth looked at Logan. "You are the most experienced. How do we make this happen?"

"It will not be easy." Logan looked around the town and seemed to be making a great number of critical calculations as he did. "If there are fewer than two hundred people to get out of Delmore, we can have them moving well before the army arrives. Otherwise were going to have to make a stand long enough for the people to get safely away."

Diaga leaned on his staff while Neep crouched beside him, sharpening her sword on Jovan's whetstone. "What are our chances if there are more than two hundred?"

Logan shrugged. "Not good. We have to cover two entrances with only ourselves and every able-bodied fighter left in Delmore. I don't imagine that leaves us many defenders, most of those outside the main town left before things got so dire."

Joseph interjected, "And you will need someone to lead the wagons and get the refugees organized."

Jovan had fetched a recurve bow from Joseph's home at the older man's offering and tested the bowstring as he pondered their predicament. "How many men do we have?"

Joseph thought a moment before saying, "Perhaps a hundred, maybe a score more."

Logan rubbed his chin thoughtfully. "That leaves us about fifty apiece for each entrance, were going to need some barriers."

"How long do you think we can hold once they attack?" asked Diaga.

Logan shook his head. "Perhaps an hour if they do not come in full force."

"And if they do?"

"Less than half an hour, at best."

They stood there digesting this information. Jovanaleth watched the people milling about the streets, urgently moving things and trying to get the flight going as swiftly as possible. "I will take the north entrance. Logan, you and Grimtooth take the western one. Diaga, you and Neep stay with the wagons, see if you can get them moving any faster...."

Logan interrupted, "The north end is going to be the hardest hit, Jovan. They are marching right into it. Why don't you let Grimtooth and I take that post?"

"I can handle it." Jovan stood a bit straighter and his expression broked no argument. "If you are at the west entrance, you can help Diaga with the townspeople.'

Grimtooth crossed his massive arms. "Ah'm nae lettin' ye guard the north alone, lad."

"I can aid him and you as well," Khaliandra said softly. "Endoth will come to our defense."

"And he won't be alone," Joseph removed his bow from his shoulders, "I will go with him."

Jovan looked at Logan expectantly. The Angladaic had led small companies before, but the gravity of their situation far exceeded the minor campaigns he was used too. He knew if he sent Jovanaleth to the north end of town, flight would be almost impossible once the attack began. He also knew that the young man would not accept no for an answer. Feeling trapped in a situation not of his own making, he sighed and said, "Alright. Jovan you and Joseph take fifty men and go north. Grimtooth and I will take the rest to build the barriers and then send a few more your way. No reason to split our force halfway when most of the action will be headed towards you. Diaga and Khaliandra, see if you can get these people moving. Grimtooth and I will clear the west end houses as we move to the entrance. Use the broken wagons and anything else you can find for the defenses."

Diaga looked at Joseph. "How many people are we evacuating?"

The old man returned his gaze solemnly. "Over five hundred, mostly women, children, and the elderly."

The silence that followed was like a black cloud over the defenders. Logan chuckled ruefully. "Well," he said, "no one ever became a hero without beating the odds."

"I don't want to be a hero," said Jovan, "I just want these people to have a chance."

Grimtooth smiled sadly. "Aye lad, an' a bloody good chance we be givin' 'em!"

The trip through Alderlast was swift with Lena in the lead. Vorasho hurried to keep up as Graham wordlessly took the rear-guard. Derek expected he would need to do his best to keep the older man from falling too far behind, but found Graham actually pushed him onward. Lena moved so silently that Vorasho had to stay close enough to keep her in sight. As they moved she whispered questions, "Why are we striking so soon? I understand the urgency but you said this Renon was a friend. We should have planned this before we did anything instead of rushing in. We don't know...."

Vorasho cut her off, "Renon's letter said that he was called in to an audience with Vendile. The new king ordered him to complete his mission. He is on his way to kill my father right now."

Lena stopped briefly. "But he saved you! Why would he kill your father?"

Vorasho pressed her forward. "He wouldn't, but if Vendile's guards are there he will have to, or he'll die fighting. I cannot let that happen, so you better find the right passage to the dungeons quickly, or we are all going to die tonight, one way or another."

Lena saw something in Vorasho's eyes that terrified her, but it spurred her forward. They had reached the northeastern corner of Alderlast, the district belonging to Highlord Bwemor. It was thick with his guards and the rescuers flitted between shadows, running from doorway to doorway and the small alleys in between. Alderlast's more densely populated streets were a nest of handmade cobble-stones and fine wooden buildings, the elevated window and walk-way balconies and railings popular in the city providing some cover for them as they moved deeper into the district. Lena brought them quickly to a dead end street far beyond the other houses. This area was more rundown than the others they had passed and there were several buildings fallen into disrepair. Vorasho was somewhat taken aback by the worn and beaten look of this portion of the city, for he had believed Alderlast to contain no such disheveled corners. There was a rickety old wine cellar door at the street's end, the house it belonged to long abandoned. Lena heaved the door open and waited for the others to clamber in.

Once inside, they waited a moment while she struck flint and tinder to light a wall torch. The cellar was old and covered in cobwebs, several worn barrels and crates, many broken, taking up the majority of the space. Lena ripped the torch clean from its stone mooring. "The whole place is weak like that," she warned, "do not brush up against the walls too hard and don't touch the supports or we will not get out of here. The tunnel is quite narrow so move cautiously or we will bring the whole thing down."

Vorasho knew Lena was directing the words at him. Graham, despite his aggressive pace on their way through the city, was wheezing from the effort of running down the streets of Alderlast, and slowing their progress would leave him fit to fight when they reached Arvadis's cell. Derek kept a wary eye on him as they slowly shuffled down the hall. The slowed rate of movement also gave Vorasho time to think and clear his head. He stayed as close to Lena as he dared so they could talk. "I am sorry I was so short with you."

She glanced backward at him. "Don't be, it's Logan's father too."

Vorasho took that in and kept moving. He watched Lena's sleek, raven-haired form move silently before him. Derek and Graham were quiet behind Vorasho. Lena whispered back to him, "Will Graham be alright? He doesn't seem to be holding up well."

Vorasho chuckled softly, "He is an old man but not a weak one. He just can't run as quickly as I was demanding of him. Once we get into any sort of combat he will be just fine." Vorasho eyed her as they kept up the steady pace down the now twisting tunnel. Inside, he felt something was very wrong about this place. Vorasho reached out and grabbed Lena's arm, nearly knocking her into the old dilapidated wall.

"What are you doing?" Lena was angry until she saw Vorasho's face, the concern unmistakable in his eyes. "What is it, Vorasho?"

The grim, dethroned prince looked her straight on and spoke softly, "Promise me something Lena."

Angry now, she hissed back, "What? Not to be seen by your father? You want me to leave before I can be seen at all?"

Vorasho held her gaze. "Yes, but not because of that. Promise me you will get clear once we find my father. That you will leave here and go home once we are inside. Promise me!"

Lena met his burning eyes. "Why, Vorasho? Why do you suddenly care?"

Vorasho swallowed, but he offered her no explanation. "Just make me the promise. You have done all you can do anyway."

Lena dropped her eyes from Vorasho's. "Very well, I promise."

Vorasho nodded as though to convince himself. "Lead the way."

Graham and Derek stayed stoically silent as they watched the exchange. Once the would-be rescuers began to move again Graham nudged his less experienced friend. "You listen to me, youngster. You and I have been together a long time, and protected the interests of our king for as long a time. No matter what happens once we get inside, you keep an eye on that woman, keep her safe understand? I am too old to do it."

Derek had never heard Graham speak so seriously or for so long. "Yes sir, I will."

Graham nodded as though it were settled. "That's a good lad. Now let's keep up."

The two trailed hard after Vorasho and Lena, the younger man grabbing his own wall torch. Derek kept pace behind Graham, urging him on as hard as he dared. The older guard had told him to watch the girl and he would, but he determined to also keep his other eye on Graham. From the way she moved, Lena was used to taking care of herself; Graham was about ten years removed from that point in his own life. Derek owed everything he had learned to the master of Hawking's guards, and he would do whatever it took to keep him alive.

Vorasho saw Lena stop a short distance in front of him. She ran her hands over a slightly discolored section of the wall. No, Vorasho realized, it was not discolored. This wall was newer. She searched an area that became smaller and smaller as she ran her hands over the stone. Finally she settled on one brick with a fine crack down its center. Pressing it gently she then applied pressure to the wall itself, but it refused to budge. Vorasho threw his shoulder into the heavy stone and felt it give. Derek cried out from behind them, "The walls are coming down! Hurry!"

Lena swept inside with Vorasho close behind. Graham and Derek were right on their heels. Lena rushed to seal it and Vorasho hurried to help. The door closed and he heard something click as it snapped into place. The rumblings of the old tunnel caving in could be heard but not felt. Lena looked at him as they waited for the noise to subside. When it did, she slowly moved her torch around to reveal the room they had entered. "Closing the door should have prevented us from being discovered. The tunnel was loud when it went down but the walls muffled it."

"Where are we, my lady?" asked Derek.

Vorasho ran his hands along the rusted iron bars in front of them, saying, "I would say we are precisely where we want to be, Derek. We are in the dungeon."

Graham coughed loudly as the centuries old dust shot up his nose. "Clearly, m'lord, but the question is, where in the dungeon?"

"Where indeed," wondered Vorasho aloud, then he heard noises. "Those sound like boot steps."

Lena was already moving. "They are coming from above us, come on!"

"Lena, wait!" but before Vorasho could catch her she was already running down the dark hall toward the stairs. Derek and Graham unsheathed their swords and moved to follow. Cursing, Vorasho hurried to keep up, before it was too late.

Chapter 18

Goranath led his sea of warriors over the hills of eastern Legocia. The leader of the Broken had become legendary for his cruelty and cunning. Thanks to the efforts of Wolfbane, he had obtained a following of over five thousand men who would otherwise have remained divided by clan conflict. The Broken were once soldiers in a powerful army that nearly conquered Dragon's Watch. Now the remnants of that army had no recollection of their former duty and only fading memories of their home. Those who had not managed to assimilate into the nations of Legocia had turned to banditry. The Broken only lived to rob, cheat, kill, rape, and conquer. Disorganized, they had no chance against any of the cohesive and properly trained forces on the continent, but consolidated their numbers were staggering and enough to overwhelm some of the best-trained opponents they might face. Shatrix, the chieftain that had led the assault on Bladehome some years ago, had only controlled a quarter of the total horde of Broken. Goranath had secretly orchestrated Shatrix's fall, but had also learned from his predecessor's mistakes at the head of his Broken army.

No Broken chieftain would willingly follow a fellow Broken leader. It took a larger fighting force and the authority of one's reputation to bring others to heel. But the Broken were even less interested in fighting for an ousider. They knew their own kind were backstabbers and traitors, but they also believed in rule by the sword and there was a kind of cruel unwritten law among all within their brutal culture. They had an inherent distrust of others, and normally would not ever have welcomed the Nerothians into their midst. The solution came to Goranath one night in the form of Caermon Erefoss, who represented the interests of the invading army in the north. He promised Goranath that if he led the Broken, they would be under one of their own and allowed to conduct their war as they saw fit, provided they allowed Wolfbane to select their targets. In addition, he offered more disciplined and specialized soldiers to bolster Goranath's own, and a promise of the majority of the spoils to the Broken from their campaign.

Goranath had commanded a sizeable number of his own men before being handed a much larger compliment of Broken soldiers driven to him by the opportunity to conduct larger and more lucrative raids. His own men had numbered over one thousand and were supported by a substantial contingent of gnolls. Goranath had convinced the other clan leaders that he could avoid the influence of the invaders and preserve the Broken's unique way of life. In the end it was all rather irrelevant, because the result of this massive army's raids would be more important than why it was held together. Spoils went to the victors, and no member of this horde doubted that this great force would always be triumphant over all who stood in their way. For Goranath, the challenge lay in maintaining the iron grip he had on all of his followers. There was always a lesser chieftain looking for any sign of weakness to exploit and take command of the largest Broken army in history for themselves.

The more significant difficulty presented to Goranath was that he didn't want to see his army dissolve once their march of destruction was over. His private ambition was to maintain his control and quietly expand it, becoming as deadly a force in Legocia as the invaders themselves. And so, while his subordinates thought he was busy arguing with Frothgar and Valissa, he was in fact consenting to most of their demands and plotting the demise of his enemies within the Broken ranks. This next target, the town of Delmore, would offer such an opportunity. Goranath had discussed with Valissa the importance of testing the loyalty of the gnolls in a combat situation. She agreed that the time was ripe. The gnolls had to be battle-ready before the more significant clashes began with disciplined opponents.

In truth, Goranath knew there was no questioning the effectiveness or loyalty of the gnolls. He had them in his pocket already, though he had kept that a secret. The gnoll's pack leader, a massive creature almost nine feet in height and with darkly bronzed skin, was unfailingly his. Gren was intelligent as gnolls could get. He could speak the common tongue quite well, and had a firm grasp of Orcish, even though it was no longer especially useful. Gren was not what Goranath would call educated, but he was calculating and driven. Gren liked Goranath because he treated the gnolls as a society, not simply as disposable weapons. Where the other leaders had always made the mistake of thinking the gnolls were stupid creatures, Goranath had patiently studied them and discovered they were as intelligent as any Broken and could be taught to maneuver like the best of the professional soldiers in Angladais. The result was his massive gnoll division that had been the primary bargaining tool in his bid to unite the clans. Anyone who was unwilling to bow to his authority was given a demonstration of the gnolls' terrible aptitude for murder and death. Resistance had been minimal and brief.

It was this maneuvering, a task which had taken Goranath many long and patient years, that led to him now standing at the top of a large rise with the smoke of burning towns left in his wake behind him, twirling his cutlass in one hand while Gren waited impassively at his side. The two could see the distant outline of Delmore and the long line of Broken companies marching toward it. Gren fingered the haft of his battleaxe resting easily on his shoulder. The gnoll studied the marching humans without interest, keeping a close eye on his own company of raggedly armored war beasts to make sure they stayed in formation. "They become lazy. Not hold order."

Goranath tossed his blade into the air absentmindedly before catching and sheathing it. "They only just began learning, Gren. You cannot expect perfection already."

"They will be perfect." Gren glared at the human commander. "If they no perfect they die."

Goranath sighed. "As you say, I just do not think it is that desperate a rush. You will have a chance to test them on the puny defenses that Delmore will offer."

Gren remained silent. He eyed the human beside him. Goranath was relatively short but fearsome with his coal black hair and missing right eye. His black silk eye patch stood out among his tattered and beaten armor and his torn cape. Many of the other Broken dressed in finer clothes to denote their importance, but none fought as well as Goranath. While the others wore the bright crimson of the Broken out of tradition, only Goranath understood what that tradition meant. He remembered the days of the Army of the Lion, the dream of conquering Dragon's Watch and going down in history as a part of one of the most successful wars ever. All of Goranath's cloth attire, excepting his black cloak, was red, and in some places you could see where darker crimson had bled into the red dye. Gren knew when he first met him that Goranath was a real warrior, and that was why he trusted him as far as he did.

The gnoll was a deep bronze color from the tip of his tail to the end of his snout. His browner fur tufts even had a slight metallic sheen. Not even Gren knew where his strange coloration came from, but he was not concerned with such things. He was not the leader of the gnolls because his appearance was unique. He was their leader because he could have mutilated any of his kin with his bare hands with little exertion. Gren was massive, intelligent, and unbelievably cruel. Once, he had cut the arms from a rival gnoll in combat and then sent him to lead a charge against a well-defended village. Armless, the creature had tried to refuse, but Gren beat him until the monster followed his orders and died a grisly death, unable to defend itself. Despite his brutality, Gren could also be calm and patient, unlike many of his kind. This had served him well in battle when things became chaotic, because the gnoll lord never lost his cool.

Despite all his physical advantages, Gren still found himself serving a human half his size. Many of the more foolish gnolls mocked Gren behind his back for following such a puny, and in their eyes inferior, man. Gren had let Goranath know about this so the human could kill the dissenters in combat himself. Gren was wise enough to see that Goranath held the cards of negotiation and that his own followers were too few to act independently to accomplish all the things they could do with the Broken. Goranath could converse and make alliances with the invaders, which Gren could not. The Nerothians, who believed gnolls to be too unpredictable, did not trust his kind. Thus, Gren needed Goranath to communicate with the invaders, and Goranath needed Gren's gnolls to assert his power over the Broken. Together they were now thriving and apart they were disposable. For now, Gren was comfortable with this symbiosis. The gnolls got a nice cut of the spoils, and he could raid places beyond his usual reach with relative impunity.

Goranath shared his understanding of their relationship. They needed one another. More importantly, there was no benefit to separating anytime soon. They were accomplishing great things acting as one. The only question that had begun to cross Goranath's mind was why did they need the others?

Gren seemed to sense his partner's thoughts. "You want them made dead?"

Goranath glanced at the hulking Gren. "The other chieftains? Yes, of course, but not just them."

Gren turned slightly and twirled his battle-axe excitedly. "Who? Who else dead?"

Goranath patted the monstrous gnoll's arm. "Why not kill our fellow commanders as well? They have nowhere near our numbers. When the time is right, you and I will rule all this land together."

Gren's face split in a terrifying grin. "Together, much blood for us."

Goranath chuckled as he answered, "Oh yes, as much blood as we can spill, starting today. I want your gnolls to have a slight lapse in discipline during the assault on Delmore. Perhaps they will have some trouble distinguishing friend from foe?"

Gren's massive smile widened still further. "Ah, we make mistake, maybe."

"Yes, maybe you will."

Atop another small rise, Valissa and Frothgar sat on their horses, once again surveying the passing forces below them. Valissa's eyes scanned the countryside with the practiced discernment of a general, taking in all the minor shifts in movement before her. Frothgar's stare remained fixed upon the figure of Goranath, roughly a hundred yards away. The assassin had no love for the brutal leader of the Broken. His methods were too direct and he had no tact, and a blending of violent necessity with artful misdirection was Frothgar's ideal of how to wage war. Goranath was a barbarian, and Frothgar liked to think of himself as a sophisticated man, placing Goranath and his heathens beneath him.

Valissa was of another mindset. She had no illusions about Goranath. He was a power-hungry warlord with a surprising amount of veiled intelligence. His soldiers were the key to Wolfbane's scheme and she had to keep them happy. Thus far that had been easy; they pillaged and burned everything and thus kept the bloodthirsty army satisfied. When the killing was over there would be a new problem, sating the insatiable. Goranath was king of his people, the first they had ever had, and he would not give that title up for nothing. Valissa was determined to make sure he also remained an ally, if not to the Nerothians then at least to her. She had every intent of getting out of this hornet's nest alive.

Inwardly, Valissa was unhappy with her assignment. The Broken disturbed her, though she would never admit it to Frothgar. Their propensity for violence and bloodshed had nothing to do with strategy or reason, they enjoyed killing for killing's sake. Valissa Ulfrunn had been raised in Tianis, learned to fight before she was twelve years old, and had killed a thief on the run by age fifteen. Death and harshness were not new to her, but in the north there was a purpose behind those ugly acts and there existed laws, written or unwritten, which were understood by all. This was less a campaign of establishing order and more one of sowing fear. Wolfbane had explained the intent of such a plan, and Valissa had seen his reasoning at the time, but the longer she spent overseeing it, the more she had grown to detest her role in the Dust Plains.

Moreover, Valissa had been a consistent companion of Wolfbane since she joined his forces at the fall of Napal City, and this had pulled her away. In more ways then one, they had shared everything when she first joined the Nerothians, but recent times had seen him become more distant. Valissa was disturbed by the sudden insubordination of Edge, for he had seemed to worship the man who had brought him to Legocia. It made her wonder how drastically Wolfbane had changed and what she had gotten herself into. She had accepted the offer to fight beside him because Reghar Holt and Greymane Squall had let her home be swallowed up and her family, loyal to the Napalian Empire, be killed trying to hold Tianis for the High Thane. Unlike them, Wolfbane had been a man of action, and with her rational approach to war and violence Valissa did not harbor a grudge against him for the deaths of her family. She understood the cold calculus of war. Napalians had always lived brief and often trying lives. What Valissa had been infuriated by was the fear, the lack of pride, in her former nation's leaders. Wolfbane had reinstilled that sense of belonging and comradery.

Wolfbane's mood had darkened greatly since Edge fled. Valissa had attempted to talk to him about what had transpired in Castle Bane, but he had closed himself off to everyone. Part of her wondered if he had sent her away on purpose, to keep her from pressing the issue further. Wolfbane seemed unable to grasp the fact that Valissa was his one true friend amid the dangerous collection of barely-loyal advisers that made up his council. Being sent away had not only wounded her feelings of kinship towards the man, they had made her begin to doubt her place in this new order.

Admittedly, Valissa was in charge of Wolfbane's greatest undertaking, the conquest of the southern lands. That meant she certainly had his confidence, but that he would send her with this lout Frothgar was inconceivable to her. Had he sent Saltilian or Daerveron she would have been merely uncomfortable, especially around the reanimated mage. She distrusted magic, but recognized its purpose and its effectiveness. Frothgar was worse than them both. He was a coward, a shadowy puppet master employing night stalkers and thugs, who preferred his machinations remain unseen and hated direct conflict either verbal or physical. In short, he was the wrong man to send on a mission of conquest. The only bright side was that he provided them with a number of skilled archers who should at least be mildly useful in future battles. Otherwise he whined and whimpered so much Valissa was longing to stick a blade in his belly and be done with it.

The little toad was eyeing his nemesis across the hills. It was difficult for Valissa to grasp at first why Frothgar detested Goranath so much until she understood that the assassin saw what she did. Goranath was in charge of the entire endeavor, more so than Frothgar, who was an outsider and whose repertoire of skills was useless in these environs. His method of addressing this sense of inadequacy was simple, but no less infuriating. Frothgar did everything he could to oppose any idea that Goranath put forth. It was pointless and often made a simple task of conquest into a harrowing and tedious affair as the two exchanged thinly veiled insults and quibbled over unimportant details. There might be larger factors driving Valissa to doubt her place among the Nerothians, but there were none that she found nearly as irritating as those two.

The Broken leader understood the bitterness between he and Frothgar all too well. He glanced over his shoulder and saw the nominal High Thane staring his way. Goranath offered a mock salute that did not bother to hide his contempt. Frothgar grimaced and nudged Valissa, who eyed him askance. "You see? He thinks we are his lackeys! Must we always remind him who we serve?"

Valissa snorted her response, "Stow it, Frothgar. You are just mad he has proved so effective. You have been waiting for him to slip up since he brought his army here."

Frothgar grunted and conceded the point, but it wasn't long before he was complaining again, "Still, you have to admit his gnolls haven't been especially useful so far. We do not even know if they will be able to function in a real battle yet."

Valissa shrugged. "Look at them, they can handle a halberd that I could barely lift with one hand. They may be brutes Frothgar, but there is something to be said for sheer strength and intimidation, whether you like it or not."

Frothgar stayed quiet. He knew Valissa was right, but he still did not enjoy the fact that his own services were being overlooked. He watched the marching column of gnolls as they moved deliberately towards the front of the army. "Is this the time that we will finally get to see his beloved pets in action?"

Valissa nodded. "Goranath thinks that Delmore will prove a perfect testing ground for the gnolls. They know we are coming and the inhabitants who remained behind this long cannot run now, so they will have to make something of a stand. The gnolls will be our battering ram into the town. Once they break through we can begin taking the place apart at our leisure. Besides, I want to see the effect those creatures have on a defense's morale."

Frothgar chuckled, "I can tell you what that will be. The defenders are going to run as hard as they can in the opposite direction of those monstrosities. We had just better hope our own troops do not do the same."

Valissa eyed the smaller man from her higher position in her saddle. "Well, Frothgar, I doubt Goranath's men will flee. After all, they were trained to fight in battles, not just shoot at them from a distance."

Valissa rode off, leaving the biting remark to burrow under Frothgar's skin. The thane of Konunn was annoyed but not angry. His profession did not permit such an emotion. Valissa and the other leaders did not find Frothgar particularly useful, but because of him they hadn't had their sleep interrupted by a dagger in the night. Of course if Frothgar chose to deliver the knife himself, they would never even know their dreams were interrupted when the blade drove home.

Goranath eyed the approaching woman with a half-turned head. She was attractive, for certain, but he had had many women as a clan leader and found none of the things they offered came near the rush of taking another person's life. Fortunately, he could see that Valissa understood this as well. While Frothgar saw only a woman playing at soldier, Goranath saw a warrior who just happened to have the body of a woman. She rode up to them speedily and he kept his attention focused on the marching horde before him. Gren nodded as she approached and then broke into a lope that quickly carried him towards his gnolls as they moved unerringly for the head of the army.

Valissa positioned herself to Goranath's left and observed the moving soldiery with him for a while. The two did not speak, but simply watched the rising sun of the morning glint off the spears and swords of their massive legion. Valissa finally posed the question Goranath knew she had come to ask, "The plan of attack will be a swift and direct overrun?"

Goranath turned slightly and eyed her with a crooked smile. "The gnolls will break through whatever meager defenses these people offer and several of my clansmen will be hard on their heels. I want to see how quickly it can be accomplished."

"As do I. In fact, I want to see if you can conquer the town within an hour."

Goranath turned to fully face Valissa, who was still watching the slow moving army. "I too would like to see if that could be done. I take it your master wants you to speed up our little venture?"

Valissa glanced at the Broken lord and nodded. "We must reach the end of our march before winter comes, or else we will leave this land with the chance to unite against us."

"A valid point, my dear Napalian. Today we shall test the use of my gnolls against the defenses of the town of Delmore, and soon we will know how quickly we can make this land into a beautiful burnt cinder."

Valissa turned her horse to ride back to her post, now joined by her small personal guard. "Then gather the clan leaders for your assault. I want your men to be the first into the breach."

Goranath bowed low to cover his wide grin. "I will choose only the best for you, my lady."

He watched her ride quickly away toward her small group of mounted swordsmen. Goranath stayed on his hill, still smiling in satisfaction. By the end of the night, his opposition amid the Broken would be dead and gone and he alone would hold sway over them all. It was a shame to think that someday he might have to do the same to the lovely Valissa, after all they thought along similar lines when it came to military strategy. Still he could console himself with the fact that a warlord can always attract the most alluring of women through his plunder and lands alone, and Goranath stood to inherit a lot of both very soon.

The army moved relentlessly towards the town of Delmore, and as it marched the dark clouds gathered overhead. Before noon a slight rain had begun to fall, moistening the road by which the horde traveled and buying the defenders some time. Goranath allowed Gren to take the lead and he marched quickly up and down the line inspecting his ragtag soldiers and trying to whip them into a killing frenzy. As he did, he would periodically pull aside old rivals with an uncharacteristic arm about the shoulders and sell them a tale of his remorse for their past disagreements and lament how foolishly he had acted. They were wary of him; Goranath was not known for singing the praises of friends, let alone foes.

But Goranath wooed them all. He spoke of his jealousy as the reason he had made them his enemy. He told them how wonderfully and loyally they had performed thus far in his service. He encouraged them to continue to be examples to the other men following him because he needed their support. When they finally began to believe, he delivered the selling point: in light of their service he was giving them a great gift. They would be the first through the breach along with five of their closest allies. The looting of the town would be theirs, the best trinkets for their taking alone.

Every man Goranath pulled aside fell into his scheme perfectly. They would lead the charge with their most loyal followers and once they got through the wall into Delmore, Gren and his gnolls would set them upon. Goranath might even enlist the assistance of Frothgar to rain arrows upon his rivals on the pretext that they were cowards fleeing a battle and should be treated as traitors. It might even confuse the worm and make him think Goranath actually held him and his meager offerings in mild esteem.

The Broken chieftain was happily strolling along with his personal band of killers, a small smile on his scarred and battered face. Within his mind, a thousand beautiful burning fires raged as he scorched this pitiful land. Lost in his thoughts, Goranath almost missed hearing the trumpet sound at the head of the army, announcing the proper sighting of the town of Delmore. The Broken leader immediately picked up his pace to a swift lope, his strong legs carrying his body rapidly forward. As he passed by, he called orders to his men to form up wide ranks and disperse about the hill from which the town had been sighted. Those he had chosen were to congregate near the center of the target so that their assault would be head on. The word raced through the ranks and the soldiery began the slow process of maneuvering into position.

Goranath was steadily making his way towards the mound from which the scouts had seen the town. He kept his head down until he heard the noise of approaching hooves. Looking up, he saw Frothgar on his slight brown steed riding hard towards him. The assassin reared up and turned to keep a light pace with the warlord. "You must hurry, Valissa would like to attack the town as soon as possible. Let me carry you to the front."

Goranath laughed loudly, "No, thank you, Lord Frothgar, my legs have always been good enough for me. Tell the Lady Valissa I will be there in due time, the town is going nowhere."

Frothgar grunted in frustration, but he merely spurred his horse forward and galloped to the meeting point. It took Goranath some time to finally reach the spot, but he was neither winded nor concerned. Valissa and Frothgar were already there, along with Gren and several of each's lesser commanders. Frothgar looked unhappy about the presence of the gnoll chieftain, but he tried to give off an air of uncaring. Valissa approached Goranath, saying tersely, "You should have come sooner. I want this attack to begin now."

Goranath was nonplussed. "Even if I came the moment the horn was sounded, it would not have made the attack start any sooner. We have to wait for the army to get into position, we cannot simply charge in blindly."

Valissa realized the sense of his comment, but she still seemed agitated. "You should speak to the scout. There are some visitors in the town we were not expecting."

The man in question, an older soldier, came forward. He bowed slowly to Goranath then began his report simply and directly; "There were many people in the town, perhaps four or five hundred. They had seen the fires of our march and I expected to find them running and disorganized. However, when I arrived I noticed that they were instead moving about purposefully and they had constructed rough barriers at their north and western entrances. Any and all points where even one of our men could have infiltrated the town were walled up and being carefully watched. I managed to visit some of these unseen, but the only way in will be to break down the barriers themselves."

Goranath shrugged and glared at Valissa in annoyance. "This is nothing new. We encountered plenty of villages with walls before and we broke them all. Why is this place suddenly a bigger challenge?"

Valissa returned the glare. "Let him finish."

The older man cleared his throat and continued, "The organization surprised me, as I said before. I soon discovered that several outsiders were aiding the people of Delmore. There were five of them who were clearly foreign. One was a young man from the land of the most-hated Order of the Blade, he bore their insignia pinned on his breast. Another was massive and seemed to be green as the earth around him, bristling with weapons, it seems impossible, but he looked like an orc warrior. There was also a giant cat with bright orange fur and it seemed to be the servant of a young man directing the townspeople in a worn robe. There was, most importantly, a knight who clearly hailed from a powerful kingdom, perhaps Angladais or Aves by the make of his armor. I think he was a companion of the strange green one, but they were all working together."

Frothgar started and stepped forward. "An Angladaic? They aren't supposed to be here! They are trapped behind the fortress amid the Pillars of Light!"

Valissa silenced him with a look, but Goranath took Frothgar's side. "He is right. You told me the Angladaics would not be present here. My men cannot win against a force from that land."

Valissa threw up her hands and cried, "It is one knight you fools! Our bigger concern is if the one in the robe is a wizard of some kind. Even young and alone he could be quite dangerous."

"This mage is not the one. We seek only the one."

Goranath felt, for the first time in his life, a true stinging pang of fear. Somewhere from behind Valissa a figure emerged, hooded in long black folds of cloth, its body impossible to define under the wavering material. The shadowy thing seemed to undulate before him, and it emanated a blackness that was too dark even for the overcast day. He could see no threatening stance or weapon in its possession, but he gripped his cutlass handle tightly nevertheless. Valissa turned to the thing and unthinkingly took a step back as it glided into the circle of commanders. Goranath glanced at Frothgar who was now edging toward Gren, seeming to prefer the gnoll to whatever devilry this creature was. Valissa leaned in and spoke quietly, "This is why I wanted you to hurry, Goranath. We have a new ally now, sent from Neroth himself."

The Broken leader swallowed. "You mean this thing is on our side?" He couldn't decide if he should be relieved or even more unnerved. "What sort of friends do you keep Valissa?"

The Swordmistress emitted a dry laugh. "I would not call this thing's master a friend. No, certainly not. This creature is called a Night Cloak, one of the dead mage Daerveron's servants. He and his retinue are apparently seeking someone in Delmore."

Goranath was appalled. "There are more of these things?"

"About fifteen."

The Broken leader shook his head in disbelief. "I have no quarrel with them. They are welcome to take the town themselves if that's what they want."

The apparition turned towards Goranath, though as it did he wished it had not. "No, we seek two within. Two men: the traitor and another. They must die. You will do this."

"Me?" Goranath was incredulous despite his nerves. "I thought this was your mission."

"We cannot attack in this brightness. We must wait for night. You will go now, in the sun. Kill the outsiders or drive them out, we will do the rest."

"What sun? The clouds have blotted it out, it looks more likely to storm."

"And yet it is in the sky and we must wait. You will go."

There was no debate, the horror simply turned and seemed to glide, in fits and starts, away. Goranath felt his body return to warmth; he had not even noticed how cold he had been. There was a deathly silence over the gathering. Frothgar turned to the Broken commander saying, "Well, Goranath, I am glad it is you who is leading this attack. I would not want to disappoint whatever that thing is."

The Broken leader did not respond. He was still in mild shock. Gren strode over and tapped his shoulder, bringing him around. Even the hideous gnoll was a welcome sight after the harrowing encounter with the specter. Goranath seemed to snap out of his trance and he turned to Gren. "Get your pack in position and spread the word along the lines. We attack as soon as possible. Drive for the ones the scout described. Kill the outsiders. We will pillage once they are dead. Do not mention the mage, our people are too superstitious."

The monstrous gnoll nodded slowly as he tried to digest this sudden change in information. Goranath waved him off and the creature bounded swiftly to his awaiting brethren. Goranath turned to Valissa and Frothgar. "I will send my best men to the north entrance and loop a smaller force around to the western side to feign a two-pronged approach. I do not want them meeting me with a united front, even the gnoll pack will stuggle to overcome that. Frothgar, use your archers to keep them busy on the north end. Gren will lead the breach at that side once we soften them up enough from a safe distance. Let's get this over with and those things can be far away from us by nightfall."

It was almost noon.

Chapter 19

Delmore was a hive of activity. Things were moving so swiftly they might have seemed chaotic, but this was an organized turmoil. Diaga Cursair was hustling people into wagons along with all the possessions they needed. He positioned himself with a few of the elder men of the town at the end of the wagon train and dispensed orders to the men, women, and children as they passed by. Diaga had been giving direction for over three hours and he was tired but remained determined. His experience as an orphan had led Diaga to feel that if people experienced even a minor kindness they would then learn to do the same for others. Besides, these people had no one to guide them. By remaining with them and directing their efforts to escape the coming assault, Diaga felt he was passing on a lesson of courage and charity in the face of doom.

The work also served to keep his mind off the fracturing of their little band of travelers. The departure of Trem confused him deeply, and he found that in the rare idle moments he had he inevitably puzzled at the causes of Trem's peculiar actions. Diaga had not learned precisely what transpired between Jovanaleth and this man Joseph, but the more he pondered the old man's reaction to Trem the more things had begun to make sense. Diaga understood from the beginning that Trem was unique. The mage's experiences with the arcane had lent him a sixth sense for all kinds of oddities. From the beginning he had suspected there was more to Trem than there appeared to be, but not until encountering Joseph had Diaga started to wonder how unusual the half-elf actually was. It was impossible for Trem to have known Joseph almost thirty years ago. Even taking into account his elven blood, which would have prolonged his youth and lifespan, Trem could not be a day over thirty now based on his appearance. Yet, somehow, he had helped the Joseph in a predicament similar to their current one. This had brought all sorts of strange ideas to Diaga's mind, but also raised arguably more significant questions: how old was Trem really, and why did he appear untouched by the passage of time since his nai'valen?

But even an explanation for that oddity would not entirely clarify Trem's sudden departure. It was an action taken out of fear and doubt, or perhaps even a selfish sense of preservation. Trem had sworn to help Jovanaleth, that much Diaga understood, and yet when he learned Jovan wanted to risk himself for people in need, Trem had abandoned his friend for the more logical, if heartless, path south. There was a large piece of this story missing and Diaga was determined to uncover it, if he was given time. For now, all he could do was worry about living through this ordeal and getting as many others out of Delmore with him as he could.

That Jovanaleth was conflicted over Trem's departure was obvious. Logan seemed convinced that the young prince had a death wish and he appeared to have accepted this with a soldier's dutiful understanding. Diaga was not willing to allow such misguided nobility to go unquestioned. Whatever foolish belief led Logan to think Jovan's sacrifice was in some way right was one he disagreed with completely. Jovan should not be allowed to pursue his suicidal defense of the north wall simply to make a point about the value of his ideals in the face of death. The wizard thought that it would make more sense to give Jovan enough time to realize that Trem's betrayal had less to do with their relationship than it did outside circumstances, and to understand that dying would in no way undo the hurt he felt at watching his friend turn his back on them all. Diaga had advocated removing Jovanaleth from the dangerous northern barrier in favor of a more experienced warrior, but Logan had insisted that if Jovanaleth wanted to be there he could not, and should not, be stopped. Grimtooth had merely shrugged his shoulders. Only Diaga seemed to believe Jovan was risking his life in a futile attempt to prove something to an absent Trem.

Diaga had his own responsibilities to worry about, though. Thoughts of the others only briefly passed through his mind as he had little time to think beyond handing out orders to the people of Delmore. As they moved swiftly past him, he or a militia member would stop a man or woman and direct them to return some unnecessary item or to hurry along with the rest of their family. They discouraged multiple trips back to the home because Diaga feared it would make the families determined to stay and cling desperately to the familiar. He well understood their desire to hole up where they were comfortable, but he also knew they would die if they did not leave.

Neep was of no small assistance. Being an animal herself, she had a great affinity with the horses and oxen being used to pull the carts and wagons. Her confidence that Diaga would not leave his post allowed her to wander down the line and help calm the beasts so that the process of loading them became easier. Many of the people seemed wary of a large orange cat with a menacing sword, but they seemed to have accepted her as a friend for the moment. Diaga watched her during a lull as she held and stroked one of the horses' heads and was surprised at the emotion it solicited in him. He had known Neep for a large portion of his life and had always simply expected her to be there when he turned around. He was so accustomed to it that he realized he could not envision life without her. In fact, the thought scared him.

Diaga's revelrie was interrupted by the necessities of his duty. He halted a farmer carrying a large sack of wheat grain on his back. "Sir, I am sorry but you can't bring that. We have enough supplies to last a few weeks, but we simply can not wear down the animals with too much weight."

The man did not acknowledge Diaga, but in compliance he turned to move back to his home. Diaga stopped a mother with several bundles containing clothes and told her to leave them. "We will get you some new ones once were out of danger." He attempted a friendly smile and got no response, but she dropped the sacks. Diaga sighed. He wished Logan with his charismatic demeanor and proud presence was doing this job instead of him. He simply did not know how to connect with people he'd never met.

A small tug at his robes brought Diaga's attention to his left. A young boy, hardly five summers, was sucking his thumb and looking imploringly at him with a small sackcloth bear tucked under one arm. Diaga crouched down low with a genuine smile to reach eye level with his young visitor. "Hello there. What's your name?"

The boy did not respond but simply sucked his thumb and stared at Diaga. The mage tried another ploy. "Is that your bear?" The boy nodded. "Does he have a name?"

That brought the thumb out of his mouth. "Coal."

"Coal. So he's a black bear then?"

The boy nodded again. "He's a nice bear though."

Diaga smiled. "I am sure he is. Is there something I can do for you and Coal?"

The boy looked quite seriously at him. "Will you really save us from the bad ones?'

Diaga's smile disappeared and he put a gentle hand on the boy's shoulder. "I won't let anything happen to you, or Coal."

The boy seemed to feel that decided things. "Okay, thanks mister."

"Diaga," the young man said. "You can call me Diaga."

"Thanks, mister Diaga."

Diaga looked around. "Where are your parents? You should get into a cart."

The boy stuck his thumb back in his mouth and spoke around it; "I don't have parents anymore."

Diaga was struck dumb. It took him a moment to realize he was just staring at this young child before he pulled himself together. "Well then, how about I take you to one of the carts? I will find you another nice boy to sit with."

The child nodded and put his hands up. Diaga hoisted him into his own arms and was stunned to realize how small the boy actually was. He turned and began walking down the line of carts. As they walked the boy tapped his shoulder. "Yes?"

"Mister Diaga, my name's Samuel. Samuel Jovian."

"Nice to meet you, Samuel."

"You too, mister Diaga."

Diaga kept walking and when he found the cart he wanted, he realized that Samuel was asleep with his head on his shoulder. He was bewildered, unsure what to do. Fortunately, the priestess of Endoth, Khaliandra, was there with another child, slightly younger than Diaga's little friend, and smiled at him. "I can take him."

The living warmth in his arms had mesmerized Diaga and his reaction was delayed. "What's that? Oh! Oh yes, thank you, miss."

She smiled again as he gently passed Samuel to her. "No, my lord, thank you."

Diaga blushed muttering almost to himself, "I am no lord priestess, just someone trying to help."

"Well, that makes you better than a lord already. Bless you, sir, and your friends."

Diaga did not know what to say, so he simply nodded and made a gesture that might have been a wave and walked back to his post. The guards were still stopping the odd member of the town, but for the most part it seemed things had finally been prepared. Diaga nodded to one of the guards just as Jovan came running up with his bow out and strung. "We spotted them! They are just a half mile off up on a hill. They're spreading out, no idea when they will attack."

Diaga glanced at the sun. "What time is it?" he asked the nearest guard.

"Almost noon, my lord," he replied.

Diaga looked at Jovan. "Soon then," the ranger said. "I should get back to Joseph."

He began to hurry off but Diaga called after him, "Jovanaleth!" he stopped, and Diaga found he wasn't sure what he should say, so he said the first thing that came to mind. "Be careful, alright friend?"

Jovan looked at him confused, then seemed to understand and nodded. He was gone a moment later. Neep came up next to Diaga and leaned slightly on him. Diaga absently stroked her fur and dismissed the militia assisting him with a wave of his hand. He looked at his companion and smiled, though it felt rather forced. "Well Neep, I always said I wanted to have adventures. Come on, I need to study my spells in solitude before things get too dangerous."

The two wandered to the eastern side of town to find a suitable home for Diaga to meditate in.

At the western gate, Logan and Grimtooth were still directing the construction of their barrier. The huge orc was wearing only his wolf skin kilt and hefted massive planks and tables from nearby homes with frightening ease, carrying them with a steady pace to set across the entrance. The townspeople hurriedly used smaller planks to bind the larger pieces together under Logan's careful direction. They had accepted Grimtooth's presence slowly, but his good humor and incredible strength of will won them over. Their fear subsided for the most part and some even offered him a hand with the heaviest pieces.

Logan had shed his armor and was directing the placement of the defenses shirtless in the gathering shadows of the dark clouds. If it rained it would work in the favor of the defenders by making the ground muddy and slick, but it would also hide their opponents and dampen the bowstrings of the archers. Logan had a team of men busily digging up the soil outside the barricade as far out as they could to create a mud pit in the event the rain started before the attack. For the first time in all his years as a soldier, the knight found himself in charge and was not particularly fond of it. He was a warrior, but not a leader. Logan had always inspired through his actions not his direction. His moment of bravado on the cart had been a mere expression of his beliefs, not an attempt to assume command.

In the back of his mind, Logan also wished Trem were there with him. Even Ghost, or Greymane Squall as he supposed he should be called, would have been a welcome presence. He knew that Ghost had, under his former name and title, commanded armies before, and there seemed every hint that Trem had combat experience as well. Logan had taken up this mantle because he felt he ought to, but he was uncomfortable and awash in self-doubt. He knew that at the very least, the two knew how to handle themselves in a fight, and right now he could use all the fighters available. Moreover, he had grown to like the half-elf and if he was being honest, even the strange events when they had reached Delmore had not changed that.

Trem's flight from the town had not permanently tarnished his image in Logan's mind because he could at least see the logic in his decision. Logan had trouble accepting Trem's choice to leave Jovan behind more than anything else. To take the more practical road, particularly when one was not bound by duty to remain, was sound reasoning, but to toss aside a friend whom one had sworn to aid at the first sign of danger was unthinkable. He recalled his conversation with Diaga, who had expressed great concern for Jovanaleth. Jovan was with them, and he was in danger, and he most certainly seemed to have a strong desire to risk his life and limb to prove that this venture was worth undertaking. Logan had seen this sort of thing before among young Angladaics, a desire to fight in the most dangerous places to prove their devotion to the cause. He suspected Jovan was trying to prove to Trem just how worthwhile this fight was and it was a motivation Logan recognized and felt had value.

Diaga had shaken his head at that reasoning. He had asked how anything could be proven to a man who was not even there and what possible purpose taking such brash risks could serve. Logan replied that it did not matter if Trem were there because the doubt had been sown in Jovan and so it was in him that the faith must be found to keep on going. Diaga merely insisted Jovanaleth wouldn't be going anywhere if he died. Standing there amidst the chaos of the preparations, Logan had blocked out this thought. In leading this desperate rescue, he had decided that he must become more like his brother. Vorasho was calculating and harshly logical. There was no point in risking many lives to save one. Logan must accept that Jovanaleth was choosing to endanger himself of his own accord and that, as the leader of this effort, it was his duty to use what time the young man would buy him to save as many innocent lives as possible.

Grimtooth was well aware of what his bloodbrother was doing and he disapproved. While the orc did not dislike Vorasho, he much preferred Logan. This act of detachment was not like his bloodbrother. War was a naturally emotional state and even though those who removed themselves seemed to succeed more often than not, this time it struck him as wrong. There would be young men dying here this day well before their time. Their passing should be avenged and, if possible, guarded against. This was an act of love in the orc's eyes. It was love of these people and regret for their predicament that made Grimtooth stay, and he would fight to the death for nothing more than that blind faith in standing up for those who lacked the strength to defend themselves. It seemed a betrayal for his brother to detach himself from the internal struggle of Jovanaleth, a struggle that was causing the young man to place himself at the forefront of the maelstrom descending upon them all.

Hefting yet another table from the nearby inn, Grimtooth kindly turned down the help of a young boy who attempted to take hold with him. It was surprising to the orc that the youthful gravitated towards him more easily than the elders. Grimtooth speculated that perhaps it was because they had not experienced enough of the harshness of this world to distrust people based upon appearance. The elders of the town had come round to him slowly, but the distance remained. These young people though, somehow they saw through it all. Logan had once told him, back when they were in Alderlast, that this was the innocence of youth. Grimtooth wished the world had a bit more of their accepting attitude.

The orc marched down the line of the makeshift wall with the massive table on his broad shoulders. At the end, a crew of men waited with small planks and nails to bind it with the rest. They had nearly finished the barrier. One more table would likely cover the whole gap. Grimtooth dropped the heavy wooden mass into position and held it there for the men to seal into place; then he made his way back to Logan.

The knight was conferring with one of the townspeople. The man was nodding again and again until finally Logan sent him on his way. Grimtooth approached and his bloodbrother handed him a wineskin filled with clear water. The orc downed it in one gulp while Logan talked.

"I told them to add some planks from the lumberyard to the barrier in a vertical fashion so the wall is a bit higher. I am afraid I will need you to carry some of the long benches from the inn behind the wall. That way our archers can shoot over it from a covered position."

Grimtooth wiped his mouth. "Aye, sounds like a fine plan. Mayaps we should tell young Jovanaleth ta do the same?"

Logan nodded. "I already sent a messenger to him."

Grimtooth eyed his brother. "Ya know tha' lad be in grave danger."

Logan stared straight ahead. "I know."

"An' ya also know we should be lookin' out fer 'im."

"I do."

Grimtooth sighed, "Well then 'ow do ye propose we do tha', Logan?"

The knight looked up at his towering companion. "He is with Joseph, and I trust that man. For now we will have to rely on him. Fetch me those benches, Grimtooth, and send some other men to bring a few to Jovan as well."

Grimtooth stared at his brother a bit longer then nodded. "Aye."

Logan watched him go. In his mind he began to form the orchestration of the defense. They would need to coordinate it perfectly in order to make everything work, but if they did it would save many lives. He surveyed the construction of his barrier quietly until he noticed the messenger he had sent was standing next to him at attention. Logan turned and made a gesture of apology, but before he could speak the man blurted out, "They have been spotted, Sir Logan! Lord Jovanaleth saw them from his position! They are spreading about the surrounding hills!"

Logan digested this calmly. "It will take them some time to position themselves. Send word to Jovanaleth that I want him to meet me in the center of town. Have someone else to find the wizard, Diaga. We must converse before they attack. Hurry now!"

The messenger rushed off to convey his information. Logan called out to the workers to hurry along, and arm themselves once the job was done. He left Grimtooth in charge and told him to meet him at the junction of the west and north roads as soon as he could. Logan retired to a nearby home to arm himself. He pulled on his beautifully engraved steel armor and carefully tested and retested each leather strap. Logan considered putting on his heavy riding helm, but thought the better of it. He would need his peripheral vision once the fighting began and he would sacrifice the added protection to preserve it. Logan took out his heavy sword and twirled it a few times, feeling the elegant balance. He held it before him and traced the fine carvings on the blade with his eyes, marked the dual blood channels, then sheathed it and stepped outside.

Grimtooth was waiting, battleaxe in hand and wearing his leather chest straps. Logan eyed his bristling collection of throwing axes and knives before nodding. The two started a slow walk toward the center of town. After only a few strides they heard a roar of thunder overhead and the sky opened up into a steady rain. Grimtooth glanced beside him and Logan half-smiled. "Well" he remarked, "at least we can be sure it's raining on them too."

Grimtooth chuckled. "Aye, tha' be fer sure."

Jovan watched the army on the hills with growing apprehension. He had lived through his people's wars with the Broken when they had attempted to siege Bladehome, but this was something far different. Then he had been in a walled central castle within a city, only rushing out to fight when the bulk of the enemy had broken on that heavy stone bulwark. Now he was no longer distanced from the initial fury of assault by a fearsome wall. Instead, he was the first line of defense behind a rickety barrier of wood. Jovan had not dared to tell the others that he had only been in live combat a scant number of times, and how his last real fight had ended poorly, just before he met Trem. That had been a mere skirmish compared to this. In the inn at Gi'lakil, he had barely done anything. Trem had saved them and now Trem had abandoned him.

At that thought, Jovan's anger rose boiling to the surface. To have been forsaken by a man he trusted at the drop of a hat. The conversation with Joseph had done him some good, but he still could not comprehend Trem's departure or his apparent alignment with Ghost and his deplorable sentiments. The two had seemed complete opposites in terms of doctrine, and their unification had been stunning. Jovanaleth supposed he had trusted Trem too quickly; he had no basis to expect heroics from him. As Trem had alluded to, they had just been words.

Yet the thought that he had saved his life would not dissipate either. Jovan knew he would be dead if it were not for Trem's healing in Silverleaf Forest. He also thought they might all have died in that inn without his strange sword coming to their aid, regardless of how he had acquired it. But that same weapon supported the theory of Trem's dubious past. Jovan did not believe Trem's account, so where would he have acquired the sword of Vactan el Vac, the most hated man in western Legocia? It was possible that the creature leading the attack on the inn was mistaken when it had named the previous owner of the blade, but Jovan thought it unlikely given his own familiarity with the weapon's history.

So this man he had had the foolishness to call a friend was quite possibly something else altogether. After all, Trem was following a man both Diaga and Logan had identified as the traitor of Napal City. How could someone follow Ghost and not fear a knife in the back or involvement in a scheme of dubious motivations? Jovan shook his head violently. These thoughts, they were clouding his mind. He needed to be focused on the task at hand. He could see the horde of Broken soldiers massing on the surrounding hills. Jovanaleth knew all too well what they would do once they were inside. His duty was to hold them off as long as possible, Trem be damned.

Joseph leaned on his bow beside him. Despite many of his reservations about a man who seemed to think Trem was of vast importance, Jovanaleth liked Joseph. This was a man much like his own father, a warrior by trade, a constant combatant and a wise one. Jovan thought he would have fit in quite well in his own home. Joseph surveyed the construction of their barrier with a practiced eye, stressing the reinforcement of certain areas and the necessity of height. Jovan simply nodded at his suggestions, there was no use pretending he knew more about warfare than this veteran.

Unlike the wall at the west entrance, this one had been constructed with breadth in mind. The thickness was essential to maintaining its strength and would also serve to slow the invading army. Joseph had insisted on bales of dry hay being placed inside the wooden furniture making up the majority of the wall. In this way he hoped they might be able to set the barrier alight quickly when it looked as though the enemy was ready to break through. Jovan eyed the sky and wondered how well this plan would work if the rain came. Almost in answer to his thoughts he heard a boom of thunder and it started to drizzle at a soft but steady pace.

Jovan eyed Joseph askance and the old man simply shrugged, reading his thoughts. "Well, it might still burn if the hay stays dry."

Jovan didn't respond. He watched the crews hurriedly adding some height to the outer edge of the barrier. Joseph tapped his shoulder and he turned to see several men approaching with three benches. Jovan eyed them quizzically and the lead man spoke, "Sir Logan suggested you use these for your archers to shoot over the wall."

Jovan nodded and the man continued, "He also asked that you meet him at the junction of the west and north roads. He said the others were waiting."

Jovan nodded again almost as if not hearing. Joseph patted his arm. "Go, young man. I can manage here for a while."

Realizing he had no excuse to delay, Jovanaleth shouldered his bow and started for the center of town. Joseph watched him go with a small sigh. He was an old man. These young people came and went in his lifetime and he was powerless to stop it. Eventually he had ceased trying, he had put down his sword and hidden in a small village far from war, or so he thought. Perhaps only he understood how Trem really felt after what had happened twenty-odd years ago. He knew why, because he had done the same thing. He had tried to hide here, but his past caught up with him yet again.

The thought came to him again that Joseph was an old man, and to many he was a very old man. He had lived more than long enough already. In his earliest life he had made a living on his sword. He had killed so that he could go on living. Never had Joseph bothered to ask if it had done anyone any good, he was only fighting to serve himself. Later he had tried to make up for his misguided youth by taking up causes he thought were noble, only to learn of the gray lines between nobility and villainy. Here in Delmore, at this final stage in his life, he was wondering if he had ever done a decent thing for another human being, a single self-sacrificing act in his whole existence. It was so difficult for him to think of his last selfless decision that he had made a choice when he saw Trem and the others earlier this day. Joseph decided he would correct the selfishness of seventy odd years. Whatever happened, he would make sure that this young man Jovan lived to see the next dawn.

Jovan was of course oblivious to Joseph's thoughts and he would not have believed them had he known. He was within his own mind now. His walk was heavy, knowing this would be the final meeting with his companions before the battle began, that this might be the final time he would ever see them in this world. It was a sobering thought for an already-drained young prince. Jovan was realizing now, for the first time in his life, exactly how lonely things could be. He had made friends here, but he had other friends at home he had known his whole life. They were not here to help him and he might die never seeing them again. He might never learn what had happened to his father.

As he plodded slowly through the now muddying streets of Delmore, Jovanaleth was overcome by the harsh reality of life as a would-be hero. If you wanted to help people, the price you paid was your own sense of independence. It was indeed a great irony that Jovanaleth of the Blade had been notorious for trying to avoid any semblance of his duties to his office as a prince. In fact, Jovan had departed Bladehome to avoid the responsibility pushed upon him by the absence of his father. When younger, he had tried to prevent his behavior from reflecting poorly on his family, but now as an adult, he found he also did not want to take on the mantle of a leader of a great nation. He had feared the damage that a mistake could make, the lives ruined with the simple stroke of a pen. Yet at least in that prison one had a sense of home. That was not the life of an adventurer. On the road, you lost the right to die among friends and family, you could be killed anywhere at anytime, and the facts of your passing might never make it home.

But this dark thought was countered by what was, to Jovan, the moral purity of his actions. Jovan knew he was risking his own life to save others who did not deserve to die in a terrible invasion. There were young children in those wagons who would have a chance at life now because he was willing to give up his own. This was calming and allowed him to detach his fear and emotions from the events around him. Logan would have a plan that would help the people of this town and Jovan would have an integral part in making certain it worked. That kind of responsibility, newly foisted, he found he liked.

Jovanaleth had kept his eyes upon the muddy road of Delmore as he pondered his life up to the present. Now and then he lifted them and scanned the area around him. People were no longer hustling through the streets to retrieve their belongings. Delmore had reverted back to the town they had discovered when they first arrived. It was a corpse, a memory of a town. Jovan shouldered his bow and picked up his pace to reach Logan and the others more quickly. They were circled around a pile of stones and sticks in the middle of the junction. Logan, Grimtooth, Diaga, and Neep were all present.

Jovan slowed and strolled into the circle with only a nod of acknowledgment. Logan got down to business immediately. "This," he pointed at one pile of sticks near the edge of the rocks, "is the north entrance. And this is the west. The attack must come at one, or both, of these points."

Jovanaleth surveyed the hodgepodge of items and realized they were a rough representation of Delmore itself. Logan continued, "The primary assault will likely fall on the north entrance where Jovan and Joseph are situated. The distance from where we stand right now and that point is roughly twice the distance from the western entrance to here. What we expect is a focused attack at the north and a smaller, likely even a diversion, attack to the west. We will therefore use these distances and the expected intensity of the assaults to our advantage.

"The attackers will break through eventually. In fact, they will break through too quickly for us to give the people enough time to escape. Once within the town they will have to be harried, ground given slowly and the narrowness of their attack channel exploited. This means we must organize our men into units, preferably three different groups at each barrier. Each group will fight in a rotation allowing the other groups to rest. They will defend in a stacked fashion, one group in front with a second supporting and the third out of the action in the rear. Of course we cannot expect this pattern to hold, but the longer it does the more time we buy. The fighting retreat should be based upon need. We will not back down if we do not have to. Jovan, your unit will likely reach the center of town before mine. If you do, you must wait for us to join you."

Jovan understood. "If I retreat too quickly you will be surrounded."

"Correct. The plan is to unite our forces where we are standing now, then fall into the final stretch of road and gradually filter out men to join the people fleeing the town. We will have to try to buy them, at the very least, two hours. They are already leaving the town as we speak and are on the road, but they will not be able to travel far or at great speed."

Jovan looked at the knight. "What do we do once we get beyond the town?"

Logan glanced at Diaga. "That depends on whether our resident mage can open the entrance to the caverns Gend is leading the others to."

Diaga shrugged. "I can unless Gend seals them permanently with some sort of spell or mystical item. If he wards the doors or even brings down the cavern entrance in a cave-in, it will be beyond my ability to open. If not, I will need some time to decipher the stone locks. I have been reviewing my spells and I took some time to study dwarven locks as well. They do not appear complicated."

"But if the cavern is sealed?" Jovanaleth asked.

"We are going nowhere."

There was a brief silence as the warriors considered the implications of that fact. Jovan finally chuckled mirthlessly. "Well, it is still better than waiting for them to come. Any plan beats no plan."

Diaga smiled slightly. "I do believe I have a few surprises for our foes as well. I have enough energy to heal the wounded for some time, but I might expend some in a more offensive manner if I find it necessary."

"I can help as well." They turned to see Khaliandra, having left her cart, walking to join them. "I am not a fighter but I am a servant of the God of Healing. I will be among you and will attempt to help those in need."

Logan nodded curtly. "Just be sure you both stay clear of the fighting. I do not want you getting injured trying to save someone else."

Diaga locked eyes with the knight. "Neep can protect me, Angladaic. I would be more concerned about myself if I were you."

Grimtooth grunted, "Aye, that be where I come in, savin' Logan's arse."

There was a genuine moment of mirth among the assembled defenders at Grimtooth's quip. Then they heard a horn blast from the north. It was echoed by more and more horns until the deafening sound mimicked the thunder overhead. As if in response, the rain came down all the harder. The company gave one another a last glance then made for their posts. Logan reached out and caught Jovan's arm. "Keep them outside the wall and in the mud pits as long as possible. That should slow them well enough. If you see any gnolls, send word."

Jovan nodded and swallowed hard, as he had forgotten about the gnolls. Logan was already turning to Diaga and Khaliandra to inquire about the progress of the people of Delmore. Khaliandra assured him she had seen them safely out the south entrance with a capable guard in the lead. Logan nodded and he and Grimtooth made a hasty dash for their entrance. Diaga saw Jovan watching them and waved. Jovan returned the gesture and then he was off and running to his own post. Diaga watched him a moment longer, as though he meant to go after him, then along with Khaliandra he followed Logan's path to the west gate.

Chapter 20

The troubles of Delmore were far behind Ghost and his converts as they made their way south under the dark sky of the gathering storm. They had ridden for most of the morning and had only slightly slackened the pace with the pouring rain. The former Napalian was confident he had put enough distance between his new followers and their softhearted former companions. A part of him still understood the sacrifice that the Angladaic had chosen to make and even agreed with it, but most of that remnant of conscience still within him had died much earlier. That sense of duty to the weak and defenseless was from an older version of himself he had long since shed. Ghost had personally seen the way in which selfless men were recognized. Their heroics were praised, but they received nothing but words. Deep within, he knew his singleminded attitude was a betrayal of the legacy of service that had marked the history of the Squall house, where honor was not measured in titles and gold, but in responsibility to the people.

Ghost could hear his father's words echoing in his head. The stern voice telling him his ambition was misplaced, that the gods would reward him what was his due and no more. Until the day he died he should conduct himself as a man of the people, with their lives his primary duty. Greymane Squall, the man Ghost had once been, had given up that sacred obligation in pursuit of one more selfish. His bargain with Frothgar Konunn had been meant to secure his place at the High Thane Reghar Holt's side for years to come and put him in position to grow his family's fame. Instead, his attention had been drawn so far from his duty to his own personal achievement that it had blinded him and cost him everything.

Throughout all of the tragedy he had brought upon his house, Ghost had remained arrogant and confident, qualities that are essential to any great military commander. What made this a poisonous mixture was the fact that he did not possess the patience or patriotism that makes such men satisfied with the more fundamental duties of a soldier. Ghost had not loved the military, though he was gifted and talented in its necessities. He had adored power and the admiration of others. His betrayal had been shortsighted, only an attempt to further his sphere of influence and the legend of his family. What it had done instead was destroy any thought of fame and glory. Ghost had lost his family, whom he had never truly cared deeply for when he had them, but whom he discovered had meant the world to him once they were gone. This rending of his soul had shattered what had once been an unbreakable ego, and Ghost had not shed the poison of his ambition, he had merely added to it the venom of hatred and blind revenge.

Those young men back in Delmore, who had so valiantly stood to defend the innocent, were in his mind inexperienced fools. Ghost had lived long enough to learn how fruitless such ventures were. Battles for what was right over what was practical left behind only the bodies of the brave and forgotten. The only way to accomplish anything was to let those issues which were not of immediate concern pass you by. Permit the deaths of people who could not swing the tide if it bought you time to turn around and strike back. His strategy was single minded and its goals were to spill blood, not prevent it from being shed.

Ghost was pleased to see that Trem understood the uselessness of standing against impossible odds, the futility of martyrdom. Their former companions back in Delmore might make one grand stand, a valiant defense in the face of impossible odds, but their names would fade. The victors would be the ones who would carry on the legend of their deeds. The fallen became only footnotes in the great story of history. If there was anything Ghost had maintained in his transition from his past life it was the fear of being forgotten. He hoped he could pass the importance of making one's mark on to the half-elf.

Trem had once been one of these fools, these would-be martyrs. Men who thought their sacrifice was worth more than living on and finding fame through careful selection of causes and battles. Ghost was learning this lesson now. People like Ghost and Trem had a gift for war. They could offer the world much more than a corpse killed by good intentions. If Trem proved to be the fighter he had been in the inn, he would be a deadly ally. The two of them could accomplish great things and the Napalian would be able to have his revenge in full. In Ghost's mind, the two were parts of the same creature and that beast could channel its anger into a bloody rampage across all of Teth-tenir.

The brooding of Ghost's thoughts was balanced out by the silent agony of Trem's. He knew now what Gerand Oakheart had tried to warn him of, this terrible choice. He had expected to feel relief having done what the spirit had suggested, but instead he felt only guilt and shame. How coldly he had dismissed the young Jovanaleth, a man who reminded him of all the good parts of himself. Jovan was a true innocent if ever there was one. Trem was consoling himself with the repeated mantra that his one sword could not make that much of a difference in the slaughter to come. He knew how these brave stands for the defenseless played out. Everyone ended up dead except him. Their suffering was terrible, but it would end. On the highest planes of his own madness he felt certain he would not die, the torment's end would not come. The pain of living through another violent massacre was too much. Jovan would not follow Trem, and he could not remain long enough to convince him of the misplaced bravery of their desperate last stand in Delmore.

The realization that he cared about not just Jovan and the others, but Delmore and the people there tried to penetrate the stalwart defenses of Trem's mind. It was repelled by the continuous notion of his fated hand in the deck of life. He had been foolish to follow Jovan in the first place. That Trem would think he could help a young man with such pure intents as his was laughable. Looking around at his remaining company, he knew he belonged in this rogue's gallery of betrayers and assassins. Gazing at the black form of Rath he began thinking perhaps they were not so different. In his mind, Rath was most certainly a coldhearted killer, though Trem admittedly had yet to see him take a life. Gend was a liar through and through, though otherwise harmless. Trem had lived enough of his own lies to see the halfling's were only to protect his ego. He could not see him harming anyone but himself with his deceit, yet he could not be certain.

Ghost saw Trem's eyes studying the riders before him, and their empty look shook him, despite his resolve to treat this odd half-breed as nothing more than a mighty tool towards his own ends. Inside, he could still feel that nagging understanding that Trem was superior to him in a way he had not been able to decipher. Ghost suspected that Trem's strength would only be brought out if he wanted it to be, otherwise it would remain sheltered behind his denial of whatever he was beneath the surface. Thankfully, buried was where he seemed to want to keep his authority. Ghost peered ahead through the driving rain trying to see the rising, rocky hills he knew they must be nearing. It was less than twelve miles from the town through the fringes of Silverleaf Forest to the caverns, according to Gend. Ghost wanted to be there and gone, the rain and his soaked clothes were starting to irritate him.

"We will need torches."

Ghost nearly fell from his saddle in surprise, but Trem did not notice. He cast a dark glance at the half-elf who had ridden up silently behind him, but Trem was staring ahead into the storm. Ghost took a moment to recall what he had said, "Ah yes, torches. We will need those in the cavern of course. I am sure we can find some wood to bring inside with us where it can dry. Once there we will be able to seal the entrance behind us and our pace can slow a bit."

Trem shot him a surprised glance. "Why seal the cavern? You know the army will be busy with Delmore, there is no reason to think they will come here."

Ghost grunted, "If those fools we were traveling with actually manage to get out of the town alive, I do not want them coming on our heels."

"But if they are fleeing the army, they will have nowhere else to go but the caves. They will be trapped."

Ghost snorted, "And whose fault is that, Trem? They were witless enough to stay in Delmore. They do not deserve to make it out."

Trem snarled suddenly, deep in his throat like a wild beast. "You cannot just leave people to die!"

Ghost reined in his horse and rounded on Trem, a sneer on his haggard face, "Can't I, Trem? I already have and so did you! You left them to die when you joined me on this journey south, and it was the right decision. You are no hero, half-elf, people will not write passionate stories about your kind or mine. No, we will be spoken of like dark specters haunting the night, and I for one will accept being remembered fearfully over being forgotten. I chose to leave them to their fate and I will not falter once we reach our destination."

"I...." but Trem was speechless. What Ghost was doing was akin to murder, cutting off the only possible escape for people he had only days ago asked to help him. But he was right; Trem had done the same thing. He had sentenced them to death as surely as if he had swung his blade. His mind reeled; he had refused to stay because he had trusted the words of a being he thought had his best interests at heart. But in doing so he would leave the others dead and he alone alive in this guilt-riddled state. His decision for self-preservation had been as murderous as Ghost's made in order to bring about a deserved but brutal revenge on his enemies. Trem gritted his teeth in anger, for it seemed his choice had been more hateful even than the Napalian's. Trem looked at Ghost anew and his face widened in horror.

Ghost saw the change and suddenly realized what the half-elf was thinking. "It is too late, fool! Do not throw your life away!"

Trem's countenance firmed, his eyes grew harder than steel and Ghost found himself suddenly frightened of this youth before him. His words blasted the veteran campaigner like shards of ice. "I already did when I left with you. My life is forfeit as well as my soul, just like yours. Well, I will not let them die alone. I will die with them."

Trem reared his horse up, terrifying the larger animal that Ghost rode and hurling him into the mud. The half-elf spun his mount around and tore down the road back to Delmore as Ghost pulled himself up in a fury. "I won't wait for you half-breed! I will leave you out there just like the others! You are a blind fool, Trem, and now a dead one as well!"

Rath and Gend were staring at him from atop their mounts, and Ghost's rage boiled over. He struck the pony that Gend was riding and roared, "Take me to the caverns, halfling! Unless you would like to die as well?"

Gend sputtered, "Of course, Ghost. Yes, it's not far. That is if you're certain about Trem?" The halfling turned, trying to soothe his mount and began slogging south toward the caverns in deep thought.

Ghost tried to wipe the mud from his armor but found it too thick and clinging. He ignored the halfling's question angrily and looked up to see Rath holding his horse's reins. The dark figure dropped them rather than handing them over and the Napalian reddened still further, but before he could erupt Rath whispered, "Letting Trem Waterhound go is a grave mistake."

Ghost was silent as he grasped his reins and heaved his sodden body onto Carock. Once he was situated, he eyed his now depleted band and sighed in frustration. "Well what else am I supposed to do? Tell me! What else can I do?"

Gend averted his eyes but muttered, "We could go back too."

Ghost almost exploded in anger but somehow restrained himself. He glanced at his remaining followers again and knew they were right, but his pride would not allow him to turn back. "We go to the caves." Gend looked up in shock but Ghost did not let him interrupt. "Now! We have wasted enough time already."

He turned and started south again. Rath and Gend exchanged a look and the assassin shrugged indifferently, turning to follow. Gend watched him a moment and then looked down the road where Trem had gone, his eyes approaching something near panic. He looked both ways a few times before realizing he did not have the courage to return to Delmore or to disobey Ghost. Fearfully, he spurred his animal after the Napalian and away from the coming battle.

Jovan rejoined Joseph at the barricade to see that the Broken had shifted positions and were now slowly approaching their post. They were still almost a mile away, but already he could see the army splitting into attack groups and could estimate the numbers being redirected to the flanking position along the west side of Delmore. The majority was coming at his barrier, almost one thousand men to his one hundred. He could see a unit of gnolls not far behind the main group. Things were not looking good.

Jovanaleth eyed Joseph beside him and asked, "You are certain they can only come in through the main gates? There is only a livestock fence surrounding the backs of the buildings."

Joseph said reassuringly, "There are hardly any gaps between them, such a maneuver would be a waste of time and besides," he grinned ruefully, "they know they have us outnumbered."

Jovan found this information made him feel only more nervous about the coming battle. He adjusted his metal-studded armor and checked his bowstring yet again. It was still taut and dry, exactly as it should be. He took a deep breath and tried to calm his nerves. Joseph patted him gently on the shoulder. "We will be alright young man. Just stick with the plan."

"Of course, we stick with the plan."

The young ranger watched the column moving towards Logan's position speed up and pass the others. There were about five hundred men in that group. That left reserves within the opposing army of a size more than twice what was being hurled at them. Despite himself, Jovanaleth was impressed with the careful and methodical maneuvering of the Broken. They were functioning much more like a trained army than a mass of rabble, which was contrary to his own experience when he had faced them in the past. In the end though, it was their numbers they would rely on. And yet, this coordination would make them far more dangerous. Jovan's eyes continued to follow the flanking soldiers who moved in a straight line towards him, then suddenly banked a sharp turn to the west for the gate. It had been an attempt at a feint at his position to draw men away from the west entrance. Apparently the Broken didn't know the defenders had already split their forces, a rather small consolation.

Jovan watched the larger section as it also increased its pace. He removed his bow from the watertight leather sheath holding it and selected an arrow. The men around him followed suit. Joseph began talking calmly about what they were to do; "They will come at us in a mass without order or plan. Aim for the center of the attackers, that way if your shot is off it may sail short or wide and still strike a target. Do not abandon the wall to reload, duck down, string a new arrow, then stand and fire. They will have their own archers, so be quick about it."

The men silently digested this information as Jovan stepped up onto the bench and gauged his position. His chest was revealed to the opposition, not a wise thing to do, but he had a much better line on the oncoming army. The others clambered onto the bench beside him and Jovan spoke, "Wait until I fire, we want them close enough that we do not waste arrows."

Again there was no response. Jovanaleth watched the enemy coming toward him. They had increased their gait again and were now moving at a steady jog. Their faces were becoming less blurred now. They were about a quarter of a mile away. Jovan saw the lead man raise his sword and take up a bestial cry of rage. The others around him followed suit and now the entire column was charging at a breakneck pace, lungs bursting with their roar. Jovan raised his bow as they closed and drew back his shaft noting the rest of the defenders mimicked him. He spoke loudly, "Hold! Wait for them to close!"

The men beside him were shaking slightly, their arrows clattering against the curved wood of the bows. Jovanaleth glanced to either side and saw the fear, knew it was his own and swallowed. He looked back at the attackers and saw they were about to be in range. He drew his bow back farther. "Now!"

Jovan's shot flew straight and true followed by forty or so other shafts that were of varying accuracy. He watched them thud into the mass of incoming bodies and heard the cries of agony. Almost instinctively he yelled, "Down!" and the defenders atop the bench ducked to restring fresh arrows. One man was too slow and an enemy shaft caught him in the throat, sending him gurgling into the others below the barrier who had no bows and were waiting with spears and any other implements they could use as melee weapons. Jovan found himself transfixed by the dead man's body, where his eyes seemed to stare accusingly at the young man.

Joseph's hand landed on his shoulder and heaved Jovanaleth to his feet. His eyes alive with a fierce light, Joseph hissed, "Shoot, boy, now!"

Jovan snapped out of his trance and turned to loose another arrow, strike another foe, and then duck down again. This time none of the defenders was hit with an enemy shaft. Jovan looked at Joseph and nodded, the old man grinned madly and turned to fire again. Jovan rose quickly and did the same, noting that the enemy was now close to the mud pit. He heaved himself up again and fired blindly, but was rewarded with a cry from beyond the wall. The routine began to seep in, and Jovan found himself acting mechanically and thinking almost serenely about how Logan was faring.

Logan had a slight advantage in facing a much smaller force, but he had noted that his opposition was behaving rather oddly. He had heard the battle cry of the men assaulting Jovan and had assumed he would be dealing with the same bloodlust filled charge but instead this column had slowed and spread out into a great line. Logan stood atop the bench with Grimtooth, eyeing the enemy and speculating at this new development.

"I dinnae like it, Logan," Grimtooth spat and fingered the edge of one of his throwing axes. "They be actin' too strange fer Broken."

"I agree," said Logan, "but we have no choice but to wait and see what they do."

Grimtooth studied the group before them a moment longer, then reached out and grabbed his brother's gauntleted hand. "Logan! Look, ta the nawth!"

Logan followed the orc's pointing arm and saw it, a massive ballista being towed swiftly by a troop of well-muscled gnolls. The machine was like a titanic crossbow on wheels of wood rolling creakily but steadily into position. The string was thick and taut, looking more than capable of launching the heavy bolt that was thicker than three spears. It had a huge metal point fixed and ready, waiting to be hurled like some terrible steel comet at their meager barrier. Logan grunted and said matter-of-factly, "We have to put that thing out of commission before they can use it or they're going to be through the barrier and among us in short order."

Grimtooth tucked away his smaller axe and leaped off the wall to grab his weighty battleaxe from the house against which he had leaned it. Shouldering the huge weapon, he called to his bloodbrother, "Gimme some covah on mah way back!"

Logan waved to signal he had heard, but he was already shouting to his men to move away from the wall in case the weapon was fired before Grimtooth could reach it. They seemed confused; watching the massive orc disappear down the street in the direction their families had gone. Logan struck a fearsome stance and cried, "Forget him! We have a battle to fight! Archers to the sides of the wall and out of sight! Wait for my signal! Everyone else get under cover!"

At this command, the men quickly moved to obey. Logan took up a position kneeling on the wall to watch. He rubbed the pommel of his sword; anxiously waiting for the sign that Grimtooth had made contact with the enemy host and trying not to betray his fear for his brother.

Grimtooth trotted down the street to the stables, which had been conveniently located along the west side of town, therefore allowing him a straight shot to the enemy. He strode in and let his gigantic warhorse, Thunder out of his pen, allowing the steed to nuzzle his huge shoulders a moment before saddling her quickly and steering the beast to the entrance of the stable and whispering, "Dinnae move, ye great dunce. Ah'll nay 'ave ye 'urt breakin' loose of 'ere. Stay right still now."

Turning he took his huge axe in both hands and gazed at the back wall of the stable, judging the location of it to the field that it faced away from. Settling on a location he hefted the weapon, took a deep breath, and let out a roar, "Angladais!"

Grimtooth swung his axe and hurled his body forward behind it, exploding through the wooden wall of the stable and stumbling out into the open field around Delmore. He could see the enemy and the approaching ballista now almost in position some hundred feet or so behind the line of Broken soldiers. Grimtooth made sure they had not seen him, focused as they were on their assault, then whistled sharply and his mount trotted to him obediantly. He slung himself into Thunder's saddle, grabbing the reins in one hand and thrusting his axe into the leather strap across his back. He spurred the great horse onward, out and around the enemy force using the rolling hills for cover. With his free hand he selected an axe from his seemingly endless collection about his midsection and tested its weight. Smiling to himself he urged his horse to greater speed, circling the Broken contingent as swiftly as he could.

Goranath had heard the main force let loose its battle cry and was unable to restrain a small smile from crossing his face. His foolish rivals would never see the force of gnolls, over fifty of them, until it was too late. True, perhaps killing several hundred of his own men was not a strategically sound move, but he could not allow them to live and grow in confidence to eventually challenge his own command. Hopefully his own soldiers who he had sent with the main force would remember to peel off from the attack so as to avoid the wrath of the gnolls coming in behind them. It would be a shame to lose more than the three hundred men he wanted dead because their greed spurred them to the front of the attacking line.

For his own part, Goranath was ready to put an end to this battle swiftly by blasting a hole into the town with his favorite war machine, the ballista. It was a massive and murderous contraption. The ballista took all six gnolls with Goranath directing them to drag its wheeled girth, leaving massive troughs of upturned dirt in its wake. The bolts it could hurl were three times as thick and powerful as a spear or javelin. The siege weapon was made to do only one thing: smash through opposition and any defenses they might employ. It had not failed Goranath yet.

Coming behind the few defenders this town had been so foolish to leave was going be great fun. Goranath always preferred the look on the faces of men caught with a knife in the back. It had irked him at first to see that the people of Delmore had split their forces to prevent his plan from being perfectly executed, but his good mood had returned when they abandoned the wall as his siege engine appeared. Goranath stood at the center of his line of men, watching the ballista move into position with the effort of the six gnolls towing it. A bigger smile split his scarred face. This was going to be a bloody fun day.

Suddenly a cry came from the right side of his line and he turned to see a lone rider charging toward his cherished weapon. The mount and its occupant were massive, the rider certainly not human. Goranath was mesmerized, unsure precisely what this lunatic intended to do against six armed gnolls. He watched the figure raise one hand then snap it forward in a blindingly rapid motion. To his horror an axe hurtled into the lead gnoll just turning to face this threat and spilt its skull into chunks. Goranath was stunned only for a moment, and then he was screaming to his men, "Stop him! Go! Kill the rider! Kill him now!"

Grimtooth had already released his second missile and crushed the chest of another gnoll as the distance between them and his racing horse diminished swiftly. The others had grabbed maces and swords and were crouched, waiting for him. Grimtooth did not hesitate, he charged directly among them. Standing in his stirrups, he released the reins and pulled out his huge axe, holding it above his head. He clicked his tongue as they neared the first gnoll, a black skinned monster holding a titanic mace ready to swing.

Thunder twisted to the left as he launched himself from the saddle and directly at the gnoll. Gnolls are large creatures with long arms and a terrible reach that is beyond that of any human, but orcs are massively built and terribly fierce. Grimtooth swung sideways in a large arc and the gnoll's snarling head went ten feet to his right. Landing, he turned to face the next creature with its heavy broadsword closing the gap between them. Grimtooth waited, and then swiftly sidestepped the beast as it lunged towards him. In an almost casual manner he thrust his right hand up and grabbed the monster's throat in his powerful grip, crushing the windpipe, and in the same motion he turned and hurled the body at the other two who were charging at his exposed left side. The corpse took one creature full on, knocking it flat, but the other managed to stumble aside, right into a vicious uppercut from Grimtooth's half-moon battleaxe. In two strides he was beside the final creature and delivering the killing blow with the butt end of his axe haft.

Breathing heavily, the mighty warrior looked behind him to see that the Broken force was coming back towards their war machine. Among them he say a red-clad man laying about with his sword in a rage, trying to drive the raiders onward still faster. Turning his back and knowing he did not have much time, Grimtooth grasped the base of the ballista, dropping his axe to the ground. With a roar of exertion he heaved upward, his muscles bulging, and tossed the ballista back over front, crashing it into the oncoming attackers.

Goranath was quick enough to dodge the splintering wood of his prized ballista, but it buried a score of his men under its great girth. Drawing his cutlass, the Brokan leader, in his rage, hurtled toward the titan that had dared to insult him with his attack, determined to kill him himself. As he closed the distance he realized it was an orc he was dealing with, and even Goranath was surprised to encounter such a fearsome enemy here. It was even more of a shock to find the creature was fighting for the defenders of Delmore. Almost within range, thinking he would have a chance to express his rage against this foe, Goranath instead found he had just enough time to throw himself aside as the orc's warhorse blew past him and his hated foe pulled himself into the saddle and began riding hard for the western gate.

Goranath recovered swiftly, shouting, "Follow him! They will have to open the gate so he can return!"

The Broken fighters were in a state of shock but it quickly turned to anger as they spun to pursue the demon that had shattered their assault. Grimtooth rode hard at the gate, knowing he could not hope to jump it on his mount, nor could he ride to the hole he had created and allow the Broken to follow him. Unsure of what else to do, he simply spurred Thunder forward as though divine intervention would solve the problem for him. In a way it did. Knowing as well as his rider that he could not clear the barrier, Thunder skidded sharply to a halt and sent Grimtooth flying over the wall directly into his waiting brother.

Logan tried to avoid the living missile hurtling down upon him, but his bloodbrother was far too large to sidestep. The two crashed to the ground below the wall, Grimtooth atop his armored friend. The orc was breathless, but he managed a grin, "Well, Logan, 'ow was that?"

Heaving his bloodbrother off of him, the knight grunted, "Top marks for the deed, but you and Thunder need to work on your escapes."

Helping Grimtooth to his feet, Logan called to the archers, "Get on the wall! They will not be far off!"

In answer to his words a hail of arrows came over the barrier, striking several of the defenders just mounting it. Logan felt two shafts clatter off of his heavy mail and Grimtooth grunted in pain as one found its way into his shoulder. Snapping the thin wood he tossed it aside in annoyance. "Ye'd think they might at leas' wait 'til Ah was settled in."

The two rushed back to the wall, which Grimtooth's horse had abandoned for the comforts of his stable. Goranath was too enraged to watch the path of the animal back to the hole in the defenses or he might have been in the town by then. Instead, he was standing behind his men, beating the stragglers onward and urging them to the barrier. They stepped into the massive pit of mud, sinking to their knees in the rain, and found themselves easy targets for the defenders. Goranath yelled to his own archers, "Keep those bastards' heads down! The rest of you, use the others' bodies for purchase! Get over that damned wall!"

Grimtooth was standing in plain view, taking careful aim as he launched light throwing axes into the enemy ranks. Logan stood below him calling up questions about the enemy as he fought. "How many?"

"'Bout five-'undred, mebbe!"

"Is the mud holding them?"

"They be usin' the bodies to get onta the wall."

Logan grimaced in frustration. He hadn't anticipated that. Looking into the street, he saw Neep and Diaga approaching the barrier. Neep stood near the young mage, who knelt by the wounded men and took their heads in his hands, whispering strange words. A pale blue glow enveloped their heads and his hands and their wounds seemed to improve, with the bleeding slowing and their pain subsiding. Diaga paused at every fallen man, even those clearly dead; to make sure there was nothing he could do to help. Logan called him over and the robed boy kept his head low to avoid errant arrows as he reached the wall.

"Yes, Logan?"

"I need you to go to Jovan's position and see what you can do. I do not have anyone to spare as a messenger so you will have to play the part. He likely has more wounded as well." He eyed the wizard up and down. "How are you holding up?"

Diaga shrugged and said, "I have not exerted myself greatly yet, but the battle has just begun."

"You told me earlier you might have a spell to help us in the actual fighting. Do you stand by that?"

"Of course."

"Then save your strength, mage, we are going to need it." He glanced up at the wall as Grimtooth bent down, snapping a second arrow from his shoulder. "Hurry, Diaga!"

The young man turned and started running towards the north gate.

Chapter 21

From his position at the northern barrier, Jovanaleth stood mesmerized by the scene before him. The majority of the attacking Broken had split off to the sides and a smaller contingent had rushed into the mud pit and was being systematically slaughtered by the defenders. There seemed to be no reason for this except some kind of personal grudge between the Broken soldiers, as those who had not charged into the trap were jeering and mocking their wounded and dying allies. Jovan and his men were still firing arrows at those in the quagmire, but there almost seemed no point. Those attackers trapped before the barrier were unable to reach the wall. Joseph ducked down beside him to take a breather and the two discussed the situation.

"Odd," said Joseph, "they seem intent on just letting us kill these men. It's as though we are being served up free victims. Could they be out of favor with their commanders?"

Jovan paused thoughtfully. "I think I saw some clan armbands amid the men below. That usually denotes a chieftain or his personal guard."

"A political execution then?"

"So it would seem."

The two sat silently a moment longer as Jovanaleth counted the arrows he still had left. Suddenly a cry of horror came from both beyond and along the wall. Jovan leapt to his feet to see a mass of armored gnolls approaching the town of Delmore at breakneck speed. The men who had peeled off from the attack gave them a still wider path and the monsters collided with the mass of wounded and immobilized Broken and began massacring the soldiers in the mud pit with incredible ferocity. Jovan was stunned and it took him a moment to realize that the next place these beasts would assail was his position. He yelled to the defenders, "Forget the Broken! Shoot the gnolls! Shoot the...."

An arrow drove Jovan off the wall and hurtled him to the ground where he lay still. The defenders about him glanced his way, and his still form left them convinced he had died. Before there was a chance to take this in, a huge gnoll wearing a hodgepodge of steel plate armor clambered onto the wall and swept five men from the bench with a single swinging blow of its long spear. Jovanaleth blinked and shook his head to clear it. He looked up to see a concerned Diaga kneeling over him and the gnoll overtaking his defensive barrier. Diaga placed a hand on Jovan's chest where the arrow had buried almost a quarter of its length into his flesh. "Let me help you."

But Jovan was not listening. He shoved Diaga away and stood, grasping the arrow. With a howl of pain, he broke the shaft at the point of entry. He was filled with a blind rage, watching the gnoll take the wall, his wall. Jovanaleth pulled his broadsword from its sheath and ran to the fence where the monster was now keening to the thundering sky. Reaching the bench, Jovan jumped up on it and thrust his blade up under the worn chest plate of the beast, burying it beneath its ribs. The gnoll gurgled and looked at him in stunned silence then toppled from the wall, dead. Jovan stepped up in its place, and, ducking an arrow that sailed over his head, he jumped down into the mud and began laying about with his sword.

The shock amid the gnolls was palpable. They were not used to a human, especially a fairly lithe one, attacking them with such visceral rage. Jovan felled three more foes out of the sheer force of his blows, shattering rib cages and skulls with his heavy weapon. Joseph was above him launching arrows into the other monsters, and, shockingly, the two were driving back the gnolls with their assault. Others joined the old man on the wall. Some fell to enemy arrows, but most held their positions and soon the now dark red mud was clear several feet from the defensive line, giving the people of Delmore a brief moment of respite.

Diaga appeared above Jovanaleth and extended a hand. "Come on! Get out of there!"

Jovan was in something of a trance and could not understand why Diaga wanted him to leave. He turned back to the enemy now several feet away and saw a gnoll over eight feet tall with deeply bronzed skin towering over his fearsome brethren. The creature snarled at him and began to move forward. Jovan's good sense overtook his daring and he scrambled up the wall with the help of Diaga and several others. Once on the bench behind the ramshackle defense, he ducked down with the mage and Joseph. Diaga reached for his wound again. "Let me see that, Jovan."

The young man pushed his hand away. "Later! I need you to warn Logan that we will have to start our retreat soon. How long have the refugees been gone?"

Diaga closed his eyes in thought as he replied, "Perhaps an hour, maybe less."

"That gnoll is going to break this wall within minutes." Jovan turned to Joseph. "Get the men without bows back, we have to keep the archers here as long as possible to slow them. Go, Diaga, and tell Logan to hold them as long as he can. We will manage here."

The mage looked as though he were about to speak, then he shook his head in frustration and turned away. Jovan spun back to the wall and reached for his bow. Joseph handed it to him from the ground beneath the bench and Jovanaleth started firing arrows back into the enemy forces, but it was a futile effort to hold them back. He spent more time ducked behind the wall to avoid the increasing number of Broken arrows than he did shooting his own. Jovan felt the barrier shudder and looked over it to see the gnolls had reached the rickety wooden structure and were battering it with their heavy weapons. The larger gnoll stayed back a few paces, then let out a guttural cry and threw itself at the brittle defense. Jovan tried to shove Joseph clear, and then he himself was sailing through the air and landed in the slop of the street in a stunned heap.

Dazed, Jovan picked himself up and cast a look around to see where his bow had gone. Then he saw the wall, or what was left of it. There were five gnolls already in the town and the archers who had not been blown entirely clear by the monsters were quickly falling victim to their vicious assault. Jovan stumbled to his feet and found Joseph, along with the reserve men, holding spears beside him. Pointing his sword at the enemy, Jovan roared, "Charge!"

The tiny detachment launched themselves at the gnolls and began flailing their weapons about in desperation. Jovanaleth felled one creature and ducked as another nearly took his head from his shoulders with a hammer the size of his torso. Joseph stabbed under the monster's guard with his short sword and the beast yelped in pain and retreated. The spears were thrust forward as the men of Delmore attempted to hold the gap a while longer. Jovan stepped back a moment, trying to see through the debris where the enemy host was and then suddenly three gnolls jumped from the top of the remains of the barrier and attacked the defender's flanks. Jovan spun on two of them, parrying a large worn axe and narrowly dodging a long spear that tore his leather armor. He kicked the weak legs of the first monster, causing it to stumble and delivered a second kick to its wolf-like snout that knocked it over. The creature with the spear stabbed down and its blade found Jovan's thigh.

Jovan screamed in pain and chopped downward, breaking the spear haft. Grabbing his leg in one hand he tried to slow the bleeding but he had no time to assess the extent of the wound. The beast he had kicked grabbed his uninjured leg and threw him onto his back. Jovanaleth swung blindly downward, cutting the creature's arm from its body. Flailing, the monster collided with its companion, which had been about to finish Jovan off. Jovan took the opportunity to swing his blade with a backhanded motion and slash the creature's face, cutting out its right eye. The defenders came to his rescue then, having killed the other beast by sheer weight of numbers they managed to finish off the two Jovanaleth had been sparring with. Joseph appeared at his side with someone else's bloody shirt, which he tore in half and pressed forcefully down upon Jovan's wound. Jovan gritted his teeth and gripped his sword handle fiercely as he sat on the bloody, rain soaked earth. Joseph quickly tied the second half of the shirt around his thigh and pulled it tight. They exchanged only a look, knowing they had little time to rally what was left of their men before the gnolls would be among them again.

Jovanaleth heaved himself up and ignored the screaming pain in his thigh. The spearhead was still in him, which should slow the bleeding, but his entire leg was covered in his blood. He looked at his remaining men and realized less than half still remained standing. They were hurriedly backing up as more gnolls came cautiously through the gap in the wall, measuring the tenacity of the remaining defense, Jovan cried out, "To me, men! To me! Retreat down the road, the gate is lost!"

The defenders of Delmore, what few of them were left, responded swiftly. Some had retrieved fallen bows and were firing missiles at the enemy as they backed away, hoping to keep the attackers at bay for even a moment. Jovan moved down the road as fast as his hobbling gait would allow, searching for a place to hunker down and try to make a stand. Joseph was beside him, watching lest he should fall in the slick mud. The others kept pace about them and Jovan finally decided to make for an overturned wagon that had been crippled and abandoned during the first panic within the town. Turning, he could see the advancing Broken, led by almost a score of gnolls with the enormous bronzed creature at their head. Ignoring the constant pain he urged himself onward, striving to get to any place he might be able to defend even for a moment longer.

Diaga had rushed back to Logan in anger. It was not anger borne at Jovanaleth for his stubbornness or even Logan for allowing him to make such a suicidal stand. It was at himself that Diaga directed his frustration. He should have intervened and gotten Jovan away from the gate. Instead, here he was playing messenger boy for the real warriors. Diaga had managed to heal a few injured men at Jovan's position, but there were too many beyond his skill to aid. Khaliandra had taken most of the severely wounded and been able to assist them, but even she would tire before long, and he was little help when it came to the most grievous wounds. For a brief moment he regretted not having spent more of his time focusing on the Regeneration school of the arcane, but he did not allow that to infest his mind with doubt. He must believe in his ability and keep his focus on the spells he had prepared for the battle or he would be truly useless. He kept reminding himself that Logan had said it might be necessary to unleash his power in this fight.

Neep jumped suddenly, a moment before Diaga heard the rending crash of the northern barrier breaking. The two exchanged a glance, and Neep started back towards the gate, but Diaga restrained her. She looked at him, knowing he wanted to go back, but he shook his head. The two continued on to the western position to find the Angladaic. Rounding the corner to the short length of street off the main road, they saw bodies strewn below the defensive wall. Diaga hurried forward, healing those he could while trying to assess the situation. Logan was atop the wall, struggling to fire a bow in his full suit of steel armor. He eventually gave up and grabbed a long spear and began stabbing over the wall at enemies that must have been just below him. Grimtooth was taking massive swings downward upon the heads of the Broken, and from the crimson staining, his axe looked as though he was connecting more often than not. Still they had lost many men and the hail of enemy arrows had not ceased since Diaga left.

Logan glanced back and saw the young mage. Urging his men onward, he jumped off the wall and rushed to his side. Diaga looked up at the bloodstained face of the warrior questioningly. Logan paused to lean on his spear and said, "Could you destroy that wall with your magic?"

Diaga paused to consider the inquiry. "I could, but why?"

Logan wiped his forehead saying, "I have a plan. How big would the explosion be?"

"How big do you need it?"

Logan looked at the youth to be sure he was serious. "It has to be big, but I want the remains to burn a while. Buy us some time."

"That I can do, when?"

"I will signal you." Logan turned to go back to the wall.

"Wait," Diaga caught his arm, "Jovan is in a tight spot. The gnolls broke through the wall. I heard it just now. He said he would retreat and to hold on as long as you could, but I think they are in grave danger."

Logan considered this. "Then you had better be ready soon. Wait for the signal."

Logan hurried back to the wall and began calling out orders to his men. Diaga passed his staff, without looking to Neep, who took the simple metal-bound shaft of soft pine gently from him. Neep carefully strapped it to her belt, sheathed her sword in her back sling, and stood waiting. Logan was ushering the men off the wall, surrendering it and ordering them to hurry back to the position where the young mage stood. Grimtooth remained on the structure for one last swing, and then Broken warriors began to appear at its top and he abandoned his post to aid Logan. Most of their men had reached Diaga at this point, and the young mage needed no signal to understand it was time to act.

Diaga rolled up his sleeves and pulled a thin yew branch from out of the folds of his robes. Whispering softly to himself, he began to carefully draw a circle in the mud before him with expert flicks of his wrist. As he did so the mud began to steam and give off heat as though a fire burned beneath it. Diaga finished the finer points of detail within the circle and straightened, tossing away the now burnt stick he had drawn with. He relaxed a moment and closed his eyes, lowering his hands, palms up above the circle.

Diaga began a slow hum that seemed to further heat the muddy water. Sparks began to fly from it and a small flame appeared. The people around him were staring now in open awe, some had been healed by him and respected his arcane ability, but their looks were changing to something closer to fear. Diaga was not aware of anything about him. His eyes had rolled back into his skull as he focused on summoning the spell. Above him, a great black cloud was swirling in a funnel of darkness, lanced here and there with crackling shafts of narrow lightning. The people about him began to move away, some dropping their weapons and recoiling from the scene as they sought a safe place to hide. The streaks of lightning grew thicker and a massive thunderclap exploded overhead. As Diaga's humming grew louder, he snapped his hands palm downward and began chanting, *"Ith atar mer iferno, at mitah iferno, kan himil iferno, lan gratiast iferno!"*

At the last word, the increasingly large flame began to suck itself into Diaga's hands and envelope them. The young man's eyes rolled back downward and he watched the process with elation, pulling more and more of the magical fire from the earth to him, drawing on his inner strength and the depths of his attunement to the arcane. He determined at last that he had pulled enough and the pool of fire suddenly went out, like a candle being snuffed. The flames still held firm in his hands, a raging inferno of heat and destruction. Diaga's downcast eyes now snapped up, seeing Logan standing before him, something like terror creeping into his face. Diaga spoke, and his voice seemed that of a man much older, "Move."

Logan complied, and as soon as he was out of Diaga's line of sight the wizard could see the wall before him, now teeming with jubilant Broken men, their impending triumph raging through their bodies as they began to enter the town. Diaga saw the leader, a man wearing an eye-patch and carrying a scimitar and long knife. He focused on his image and smiled. Goranath, from his position on the wall, sensed something amiss and looked upward. As soon as he saw Diaga and his eyes burning into him he turned, knowing what was coming, and started to launch himself off the barrier.

Diaga thrust his hands forward and the hellish fire erupted before him, racing faster than the eye could follow towards the wall. As it did the crackles of lightning began to snap downward and lash at the Broken within the town, striking them like fiery whips of vengeance. The fire exploded outward and smothered the people around it, who were entirely engulfed in flame one second, then simply obliterated the next. The fire raged and flicked about, lashing at scattered Broken like a living thing as the lightning danced among their ranks alongside it. The screams were horrific, the ferocity of the fire seemed incalculable to Logan, who was now looking at Diaga in stark shock.

The young mage watched his work, then suddenly his eyes rolled back and he sank down in a faint.

Neep caught him expertly and carried him like a child away from the barrier. The men of Delmore gave the firecat a wide berth and eyed her burden askance. Logan waved Grimtooth over and they began to follow the mage and his guardian. The rest of their soldiers filed along behind them at some distance. They reached a small over-hang that might have once been the entrance of a shop, where Neep rested Diaga against the building and somewhat sheltered him from the rain. Logan sent Grimtooth and the remaining defenders to check on the situation at the north end of town. The Angladaic knelt beside Diaga, glancing at Neep who had now removed a cloth and dampened it with some clean water from a pouch at her side. She gently dabbed it on Diaga's forehead and the young man seemed to stir at last.

Glancing up, Diaga first saw Neep, and then Logan next to her. He smiled at Neep and at Logan but the feeble joy died when he saw the look of the knight. He shifted slightly under his gaze and murmured, "So now you know."

Logan said nothing, for he could not find the words to express how he felt about this young man now. Before the demonstration of such forcefulness of will he had considered him a nice youth with some affinity for magic. Now he was being made to assess him differently, as a mage, a truly gifted wizard. In Angladais, those who dabbled in the arcane were persecuted and exiled, or worse. Only the holy priests and paladins were allowed to study magic, and that came from their faith in Paladinis himself. Magic of a destructive nature, like that of wizards, was highly distrusted as a weapon of evil, but Logan had traveled with this boy for sometime, even liked him. This new development left him confused, a bit frightened, but more than anything sad. Diaga had never struck him as a vessel for destructive forces, yet it was clear that his greatest power lay in causing immense harm to the world around him. To Logan it seemed a lonely, sad life.

Diaga processed the eyes of the Angladaic in his mind and spoke softly, "It has always been this way for me, for mages everywhere. You want us to be there in a battle, but once you see what we can do the fear takes over. We are like a sword you cannot control, a blade that thinks and is infinitely more destructive.

"But consider this, my dear Logan: I chose this life of revulsion. These people here, they will never look at me the same for what I have done today and neither will you." Logan attempted to speak but Diaga cut him off, "Do not try to shield your conscience with an apology, Logan, I know how you feel about me and I accept it. I was alone as an orphan and I grew accustomed to it. You might say I have been training for this life from the day my parents were taken from me. My masters at Ozmandias warned me this was my path, just as it had been theirs. I tried to run from it with my parlor tricks and Neep's acrobatics, but this is who I am."

Logan watched the young man before him as he shuddered from the cold of the rain soaking his worn robes. When he had lived in Alderlast, Logan had tried to make himself a man of the common folk, to understand their struggles and dreams. Now, as he made his journey through Teth-tenir, he was beginning to see what it really meant to be a part of the wider world. Diaga was parentless and without property or family, there was no home to return to. Logan could always go back to the house on Zenith Road and disappear into the luxuries of his esteemed name and lineage. Diaga had nowhere to go. He was trapped by the ostracization of his chosen life and his only companion was a silent, feline bodyguard. For the first time, Logan could picture the two of them traveling the roads from Napal to Gi'lakil alone, Diaga carrying on a one-sided conversation with his only friend. A man more powerful than most mortals in the world, and because of his magic he was apart from them all. As the understanding came through more and more clearly, Logan felt his heart sink.

He put his hand on Diaga's shoulder and the mage, who had turned his head away, looked up at him. In that moment he saw Logan for who he was as well, saw the age lines in a man who could be no older than his late twenties, saw the graying hair and battle scars. Most importantly, Diaga saw in his calm, brown eyes the care that dwelt there for him. Greater still, he saw it was genuine. Neither spoke a word. They merely studied one another for perhaps the first time. Then Diaga reached a hand out for Logan's shoulder saying, "Help me up, knight, we have work to do yet."

Logan lifted Diaga with some effort and Neep passed the young man his metal wrapped staff. Diaga leaned heavily upon it as he tried to recover his strength and balance. He glanced up and caught sight of Grimtooth barreling towards them. Logan spun as well and saw the sadness in his friend's eyes. "What? What is it?"

Grimtooth halted, his chest heaving. "It be Jovanaleth. 'Is men an' 'im, they be surrounded."

Logan pulled his sword free and started forward. "Then we must go to him."

Diaga placed a restraining hand on his shoulder. "I think friend Grimtooth is saying more than he lets on."

Logan looked at both of them and the orc sighed heavily. "'E's trapped Logan, the gnolls be keepin' us outta the street. They want 'im dead before they go anywhere else."

Diaga looked hard at Logan. "It will buy us time to escape, his stand."

Logan shook his head in fierce refusal. "I cannot just leave him there. He is my responsibility! I have to go back for him. I will not let him die alone."

"He will not, Logan."

The four turned in astonishment. Before them, sitting astride his grey horse in a mud-spattered cloak and chainmail armor, was

Trem. His eyes were on the road in front of him, his sword was drawn and the hand that held it white knuckled. Diaga gaped in surprise, Grimtooth shook his head as if he was staring at a ghost, Neep eyed him distrustfully, and Logan's only reaction was to scratch his head. The half-elf finally glanced down at Grimtooth and his eyes were burning hot. "Where?"

Grimtooth pointed down the road and Trem started forward. "There be too many of the bastards Trem! We got tah get clear o' 'ere!"

Trem called over his shoulder, "Get the people out! I will deal with this rabble."

Grimtooth looked at the others in shock. "Ya cannae mean tah send 'im alone? We cannae let 'im go!"

A thin, mirthless smile crept onto Diaga's face. "We do not have a choice."

Logan threw up his hands. "Enough! We have to save what can be saved. Get these people moving, Grimtooth! Diaga, you retrieve our horses, quickly now!"

Logan watched them go and started down the road out of Delmore. As he did he paused and glanced back. "Good luck, half-elf," he whispered, and then he was trotting for the stables.

Jovan had not anticipated that his enemy would be as clever as they were. His men had regrouped in the center of the road, about halfway from the intersection that led to the western barrier, a distance of about two hundred feet from their original position. They had pulled in any debris they could find to form as much of an obstacle around the wounded man from Bladehome in the road's center. Jovanaleth knew the road was too wide to be held by the just over thirty men he had left, so he had decided to hunker down until enough time elapsed to make a full retreat feasible. He had not expected the gnolls and Broken to simply bypass them, cutting off escape for the small group by skirting the barrier and surrounding them completely. They did not advance into the town, but simply formed a line blocking the road south. Joseph wiped rain from his brow only to have it replaced by the downpour above them. He grunted and nudged Jovan saying, "Looks like we will not be going anywhere today lad."

Jovan snorted, "Neither will they."

Joseph smiled. "You're starting to sound like someone else I know."

Jovan shot him a look of confusion, but Joseph was moving about the small circle of defenders, offering encouragement. The men needed little, they knew they weren't making it clear of this fight but their deepest pride had been awoken. Jovanaleth could only hope they would buy enough time for those riding south to escape. He intended to make this a glorious last stand. Placing his back against the wagon that was the centerpiece of his defense, he pulled out his bow and counted the remaining arrows. Twelve, a nice even dozen, and in his moment of desperation Jovan found himself laughing. Horns sounded behind the waiting lines of gnolls and Broken. They had paused in entering the town and they now stood about the small circle of Delmore's men in anticipation. Jovan waited, certain something was about to happen. From the ranks of enemy warriors the massive bronzed gnoll strode out. He was enormous, easily dwarfing his own kind and rippling with taut muscle and sinew. Jovan swallowed his fear as the monstrosity walked about before him, sneering at the tiny contingent of defenders. The beast had a huge battle-axe, one that dwarfed the weapon Grimtooth carried. The creature stopped its pacing and shot a glare at Jovan, then pointed the weapon at him. "You! Boy! You are leader of these, yes?"

Jovan replied, "I am."

The gnoll leader smiled evilly. "Choice for you, then. Surrender, die quickly. Fight, die slowly. What you say?"

Jovan stared at the gnoll and his mind reeled briefly, could he allow the men to suffer if they were somehow captured alive? He looked about him at their faces, grim and bloodstained. They wanted to fight. A smile crept over his face and Jovanaleth whipped his bow upward, drew his hand to his shoulder, and loosed an arrow into the creature's chest. The monster stumbled backward and nearly fell, its face twisted in pain and shock. Looking down, Gren snarled at the shaft, then roared in rage. Ripping the arrow from his chest, Gren left a gaping wound he seemed not to notice and cried, "Kill! Kill them all!"

The Broken and gnolls rushed to the attack, but the men of Delmore were ready. Inspired by Jovan's defiance, they leapt to the defenses, shoving spears into the faces of their opposition. The attackers were repulsed and danced about the circle of biting spears, seeking a way in. Jovan and Joseph rained arrows upon those outside, carefully selecting targets for their limited number of shafts. Jovan was nearing the bottom of his quiver when three gnolls hurled themselves onto the spears of the defenders, taking mortal wounds but laying about them so viciously they killed or drove back several men from Delmore and opened up a huge gap in the defensive line. Dropping his bow, Jovan hefted his sword in two hands and balanced on his good leg, waiting for the enemy to reach him.

Joseph drew his own small sword and hefted a spear in the other hand. He put his back to Jovan's and yelled, "I'll cover your rear, lad!"

Jovan didn't have time to respond. Three Broken were closing on him quickly, with weapons raised. Jovan had learned a lot about fighting the Broken from his father. Lifting his blade high, he began a swing at their chests but at the last second cut hard and low, hewing the legs out from underneath all three. The swing nearly toppled him and his leg was shrieking in pain, but he gritted his teeth and ignored it, refusing to drop to the ground. The next to attack him was a gnoll with a rusty spear. Jovan parried the blow but the gnoll came in close, snapping at his throat. Enraged, Jovanaleth howled and drove the steel hilt of his sword into the thing's face, smashing its snout. The monster cried out and tried to back up, but Jovan reached out and grabbed its shoulder, keeping it close. He bashed his hilt into the thing's face again and again until it was nothing more than a bloody mess.

Joseph could not equal the young man's ferocity. He fought with tact and patience, measuring his opponents as they came to him. As efficiently as he could he dispatched the attackers in his range with smooth fluid motions, trying to keep the enemy clear of his younger ally. He disemboweled the first two Broken with his spear and stabbed his short sword into another's chest before swinging his blade out and down upon the man's head to finish him off. Gnolls seemed to ignore him, but the fight he and Jovan put up was drawing in the other defenders, and soon a small circle of ten or so men had formed. They kept their weapons in constant motion, swinging them in spinning arcs to ward off attackers. The man next to Joseph took a spear in the gut and collapsed, as good as dead before he reached the ground, but still swinging defiantly as he bled and writhed in pain. Two other defenders met with gnoll halberds and went down. Joseph finally received a wound, a sword slash hit his spear arm and in pain he dropped it, though the attacker lost his head to the old man's sword. Joseph slipped then and went down among the feet of those still standing around him.

The loss of four men left the circle too open, and Jovanaleth was soon battling enemies on three sides. He fought like a demon, killing anything that got too close. He impaled one gnoll and in his fury swung his sword so hard and fast the beast was sent flying into the line of his allies. Then the massive gnoll Gren was before him, battleaxe hurtling about, killing his own men in his haste to reach Jovan. The young ranger deflected the first blow and swung for the evil creature's legs, hoping to topple it, but the monster was too quick for him and deflected his blow with ease. The two were locked in a bitter struggle, neither able to strike the other cleanly, but refusing to back down. Gren tried a punch to the young man's face with his free hand, but the warrior ducked and delivered an uppercuting fist of his own that shook the gnoll to his core. Spitting out one of his fangs, Gren roared and redoubled his efforts with his large axe.

The swings from the gnoll became increasingly powerful and soon Jovan was straining to hold his own against them, lurching out of the way or desperately throwing his blade up at the last moment to avoid a crippling blow. He futiley tried to counter, but his sword moved as though it was under water. Finally, one of Gren's blows caused him to stumble, putting his weight on his injured leg, and he fell hard in the mud. Gren stood over him, howling triumphantly and pulled a dagger from his belt to dispatch this annoying man like a pig for slaughter. As he brought his long dagger down to impale Jovan, Joseph made one last desperate effort and dove in the way. Gren's blade bit into the old man's chest instead, and Joseph gasped in pain and shock. The gnoll grunted in frustration, tossing the older man aside he raised his axe this time, intent on finishing his work.

A feathered shaft seemed to erupt from his shoulder. The force behind the arrow was so strong the point came out the back of Gren's muscled frame. He howled in rage and surprise and fell back a step only to be struck again, this time in the gut, with another brutally powerful arrow. Blindly, Gren lashed out and his axe caught something; an animal, he thought, and the beast whinnied and fell, its neck broken. Trem careened off of his mount and delivered a two-footed kick to the gnoll leader's chest, sending him sailing into his own army.

The half-elf landed lightly and stood slowly, protectively, before Joseph and Jovan's prone forms. The young man was weak now from his fall and the loss of blood, but he saw the lengthy hair and its long matted curls above him. He noted the sword gleaming in the rain as it rested lightly at the figure's right side, etched with strange runes. Jovan gaped and uttered in disbelief. "Trem?"

The half-elf glanced back over his shoulder and Jovan read the sadness in his eyes, but there was no time for an apology. Gren was out of the fight but his followers were about to renew their attack and only one defender still stood before them, this strange newcomer. Trem swept his blade up and held it before his eyes, kissing the steel gently in a mocking salute. "Well," he asked quietly, "who would like to die first?"

The unlucky victim was a Broken soldier who lunged suddenly, hoping to catch Trem by surprise. In mid swing, Trem whispered so softly that Jovan would not have recognized the words had they not been spoken once before, *"El dath du hakin."* The sword in Trem's hands flared to life and the red flame ripped through the man before him, leaving his body in two smoldering halves. The attackers paused a moment, then in a rush they hurled themselves at the solitary warrior.

Trem began to dance, for that was the only way to describe it. He moved so fluidly from one attack to the next that Jovan could not understand how he kept track of his own motions and yet not a blade touched him nor did any foe enter the small circle he held around Jovan. The half-elf was wonderfully horrifying. He moved in such a hypnotizing way that Jovanaleth almost missed the incredible pain he was inflicting, severing limbs and heads with every flick of his wrist. Trem turned foes' weapons upon one another, driving Broken blades into their ally's own bellies. His own weapon was just part of his arsenal, he kicked and careened off his opponents like chain lightning, striking everything in his path. With a widening sweep of his blade he spun, and in doing so drove the circle of foes back even farther. He yelled to Jovanaleth, "Hurry, Jovan! Grab Joseph and get clear of here! I will keep them distracted!"

Jovan heaved himself to his feet and lifted the groaning Joseph, calling to his rescuer, "I can't just leave you!"

"You aren't; I left you. Now go!"

Jovan looked at Trem, unable to move as the circle began to tighten around him. Trem's eyes found him outside of the maelstrom and he screamed, "Flee!"

The Broken were no longer concerned with the young man or his wounded older companion, this new devil needed to die and die quickly. Jovan forced his way out of the throng by laying about with his sword until he had a clear path. He stumbled out of the heap of bodies and bumped into something massive and armored. It snorted. Jovanaleth looked up to see Ghost astride his titanic warhorse. The man was grim, but looking determined. "Trem, is he in there?"

Jovan could only nod. Ghost handed him the reins to another horse he had brought with him. "You get going, young man. I cannot leave him in there."

Jovanaleth was too confused to respond, and as soon as he had the reins in his hand, Ghost was careening into the battle, throwing the bodies of his foes about him like the wake of a ship. Jovan hoisted Joseph onto the horse first then managed somehow to pull himself up as well. Leaning heavily upon the horses' neck, he turned it slowly and began trotting out of Delmore. Joseph groaned behind him and Jovan gritted his teeth against the jarring pain. "Hold on, friend, hold on."

Trem was battling to extend his life by seconds at a time, and he knew it. He had never intended to survive. From the moment he turned his horse around, he had known he was riding to his doom. Forsaking the words of Gerand Oakheart and embracing the realization he would die had been surprisingly comforting. All he wanted to do was hold their attention a while longer. If Jovan made it clear of Delmore then Trem could consider his sacrifice worthy. A sword blade narrowly missed scalping him as he quickly dispatched the wielder, but too many slashes and cuts had reached him, and though he had avoided any serious injuries, he was bleeding from many small wounds. Trem fought on, waiting for the blow that would finally end the siege and his life.

Suddenly, there was a commotion behind him and the attackers seemed to flee from his blade. Trem spun round to see what had caused the sudden retreat and to his astonishment there was Ghost upon his mighty warhorse, Carock, slashing and thrusting with his scimitar. The older man glared at him saying, "Get on the horse, fool, I cannot do this forever!"

Trem grabbed the saddle and wrenched himself upward and onto the great horse. Ghost took a few last-second swings, then turned the animal and was off, riding hard for the south. They were soon clear of the army and the Broken didn't seem eager to pursue them. The older man sheathed his sword and Trem finally released his hold on the spell that kept his own blade burning, shoving it into the sheath at his side. As they passed the last house on the edge of town Ghost slowed his pace and Trem relaxed a bit. The two rode in silence for a moment, then Trem asked tentatively, "Jovan?"

Ghost grunted, "I gave the young oaf the horse you were supposed to have. He had that damned old man with him too, though he looked to be on his way out. They have probably met up with the Angladaic and the mage by now."

Trem sighed in relief, confident that Jovan was free of Delmore and danger, at least for the moment. He watched the graying length of Ghost's hair bob up and down before him and then said softly, "You saved my life, all our lives."

Ghost glared over his shoulder. "I do not want to hear any of it. I did not do it out of compassion, you understand? I need you, all of you. I cannot reach Yulinar alone and gods know what other trials may lie waiting in Southron. Besides, if you come along maybe the rest will too, and the more weapons at my disposal the better. None of this was about you; it was about me. My revenge, that is all that matters now. I will do anything to repay the debt I owe those back in Napal City."

Trem sat in silence after this pronouncement and knew it to be true. What Ghost had done he had done for himself, for he could not accomplish his goal of driving out or killing the invaders without help, and so far the only help he had was from those he had met in Gi'lakil. As the rain continued to come down, Trem thought about the aftermath of the fighting in Delmore. It seemed that, against all odds, the others had survived. He doubted they would all be happy to see him. Trem wondered what sort of reception they were riding towards.

Ghost spoke once again, drawing his horse to a halt, "And look at all you have accomplished, half-breed. Look at your handy work."

The two gazed upon the fires of a now burning Delmore in silence. Ghost continued to talk somberly, "All those lives lost back there, all the blood paid for the escape of a few people who will never be able to raise a sword against their punishers. Was it worth it, Trem? Was staying there and having so many die in vain worth the efforts of your friends? Think of the young man you were so desperate to save, is he better off after seeing what he has seen and accomplishing nothing at the cost of his own innocence?"

Trem considered this. "I think that, of all of us, I understand you best. You want to fight on ground of your own choosing, against foes deserving of your rage. Maybe the people of Delmore will never be able to avenge the crimes committed today, but they will live, and that matters. It would have been a waste to let Jovan and the others who made it out die back there."

Ghost shrugged. "I suppose for once, half-elf, you might be right."

The two turned back to the road, but Trem kept his eyes on the burning village. In his brief ride through the town he had seen the vastness of the army waiting above Delmore and knew they had seen but an inkling of the power of the invaders today. The horrors that awaited them would be far worse than the glimpse given in the blood and muck of Delmore. Yet, as he watched the fires burn under the driving rain, Trem had a calming thought. Eventually, those fires would stop and the rain would wash away the dirt and grime of battle. Delmore would be empty, but some of her inhabitants were still alive and well. A new town might rise from the ashes of the old, stronger than the one before it. Perhaps some of those they had helped escape would one day return to bring about this new era.

Trem had not lied to Ghost. He did understand him and his single-mindedness towards the world, he even agreed with it in many ways. In some lives, maybe revenge was all that could keep a person going, but for most it seemed that the hope of something better was all the motivation they needed. Trem still did not think lingering in Delmore had been the right choice. It had been an unnecessary risk that would now bring with its success new challenges the weakly-bound companions would have to overcome. But he understood why they had wanted to try. Faith sometimes overrides sensibility and logic. Guilt, a close cousin to faith, had driven him back to Jovan in the end. Now he would need to consider the outcome of his decision and the consequences that would come with it.

Chapter 22

The dungeons underneath the Angladaic palace were rotten with disuse. Vorasho was paying little attention to their decay as he raced to keep up with Lena. She held a torch aloft in one hand as she ran, her long cloak trailing like a moving shadow behind her. Vorasho tried to keep his eyes on her and her trailing black hair as it sailed out behind her, but he couldn't keep up while carrying his heavy steel staff. He could also hear Graham and Derek running behind him, the older man wheezing as he struggled to stay near them. Vorasho ignored the guards and picked up his own pace, as they had a torch and he didn't. For Vorasho, Lena was the only guide.

Vorasho's hand brushed back the remnants of cobwebs along the walls that Lena had broken. His father had left these bowels under the palace to be forgotten. It pained Vorasho to think that Arvadis was now suffering in the very place he and his ancestors had tried to bury. Vorasho watched Lena's light pause, then turn and disappear around a corner. In almost complete darkness he hurried forward. "Paladinis take that woman if I get lost! She is not even supposed to be here!"

Vorasho turned where he thought Lena had gone and stepped into a dark hole. He felt around and realized it was a steep spiral staircase. Taking the steps as rapidly as he dared, he reached the top. It was still completely black. Guessing, he turned left and started ed tentatively walking in the direction that he had come from on the floor below. The floor felt the same as it had in the level beneath him, and there was nothing to indicate what direction to move in. Still, he chose to push onward. He thought he could hear voices now, coming from the direction he was traveling in. Vorasho paused, trying to pierce the gloom with his eyes. "Lena!" he hissed.

A hand closed over his mouth. Vorasho instinctively reached back and grabbed the attacker's arm ready to toss him to the floor when Lena whispered, "Stop! It's me!"

Vorasho released her, but she remained close to him, talking softly, "They are ahead of us, the guards. I heard one of them mention Renon's name. They must have reached their cells a moment ago. I cannot hear their boots anymore."

"We must not wait, Lena, we have to help Renon before he gets himself and my father killed."

"There were six of them Vorasho. We need Graham and Derek."

Vorasho shoved her off of him. "There isn't time."

341

Vorasho moved swiftly but silently forward. He could hear voices down the hallway. He crept low and silent, trying to get as close as possible without giving himself away. Vorasho could see torchlight now and hear voices clearly. There was a conversation going on, apparently between his father and Renon. He could hear Highlord Irindein's voice as well, speaking calmly and rationally. Something brushed against his shoulder as he crouched at a cell entrance watching the dim torchlight. Lena knelt beside him. "Go back," he whispered.

Lena didn't move so he huddled there, listening. He heard his father's voice, "Are you really so bent on completing a false king's foul deed? One he cannot do himself, in his cowardice?"

A voice Vorasho did not know, presumably a guard's, spoke, "We serve a king. What are you, old man? Nothing but a lowly prisoner, and it is time for your sentence. Sir Renon, I believe the honor is yours."

Vorasho looked back, he could see dim light. Graham and Derek were close. "Lena, go and bring them here quickly."

Dark eyes regarded him coolly. "What will you do?"

Vorasho hefted his staff. "Renon needs my help."

Lena was given no chance to argue, Vorasho was already moving. He was quiet, keeping his staff high but angled to try and avoid its metal causing glare from the torch. Vorasho neared the cells holding the Highlords and knelt again, barely twenty feet away from his quarry. Renon stood there, proud and stiff in his newly acquired purple cloak and shining armor. He wore Vendile's insignia, but even Vorasho could read the disdain in his eyes. There were six guards with him, all Vendile's and likely his best and most loyal men. Vorasho watched and waited.

Renon opened the gate and stepped inside. He was certain of his fate now; he would die here with his king. He pulled forth the sword he had carried for Arvadis for so long, held it high, and saluted the bound monarch.

Arvadis's grey eyes regarded him sadly. "Death by an unknown hand, is it?"

"Perhaps," said Renon, "but not my hand."

The knight spun and struck. The first guard was not expecting treachery and took his blade full in the face, splitting it in twain. The others reacted swiftly, drawing their swords and rushing to meet the rebellious man. Renon closed on the entrance quickly, parrying the first weapon, but taking a second off his armored chest, knocking him backward. He surged back towards the cell door, trying to block the entrance with his body.

Vorasho struck then. He materialized out from the shadows with his staff in two hands. The first blow smashed a guard's skull and the second buffeted another a short distance down the hall. The Vendile loyalists were now yelling, "Traitors! Invaders in the palace!" But there seemed to be no one to hear them.

342

Vorasho spun his staff swiftly in a circle about his body to keep the enemy at bay. His face was emotionless as he whirled it, creating a wide radius around him. The still living guards split their force, two to battle each would-be rescuer as Vorasho spun the weapon effortlessly in arcs, finally stopping with it across his hip and pointing at his opponents. "If you recognize the true king of Angladais, you will leave now and let us be on our way."

The guards paused as though considering this and then Vorasho heard shouting down the tunnel. Graham's voice came down the hall, "More coming! Hurry, m'lord!"

Vorasho glanced at Renon, "Well, I guess it is just us then."

The guards lunged at both their foes at once, trying to take the prince unaware. Renon leapt between the two assailing him to protect Arvadis, taking a blade in his side that snuck in under the armor. He only grunted despite the pain, and smashed his mailed fist into the man's face, crushing his nose. Vorasho nimbly dodged a blow and swept his staff low, toppling one of his attackers. In the same motion he brought the heavy iron weapon down on the man's head, killing him instantly. The second guard struck, but again Vorasho was too quick, deflecting both wild blows and kicking him against the bars of his father's cell. The dazed guard swung blindly and missed as Vorasho ducked, striking the wall instead. The prince finished him with an upward swing of the staff.

Renon had downed both of his remaining opponents as well, but he was holding his blade barely above the stone as he struggled to stop the bleeding from his side. Vorasho looked at his father who nodded to the knight. Renon glanced at the prince and motioned dismissively with his sword. "I am fine, my lord, attend to the king."

Lena and the others came running down the tunnel. "At least a dozen guards are milling about the entrance to the dungeons, Vorasho," she gasped, "and more are sure to be coming behind them."

"My men will be attacking the hall above us now," said Renon, "they were to buy you time to reach your father."

Lena looked at the knight and then Vorasho. The prince paused, then Irindein spoke calmly and evely, "Free us first, Vorasho, and I will attend to Calavar. It does no good to formulate a plan while some of us are all in chains."

Vorasho grabbed the keys from the body of one of the guards and tossed them to Lena, who unlocked Irindein's cell and bonds. The Highlord thanked her and took the keys to Calavar's cell. Graham pulled some cloth from his belt pouch and tried to assist Renon with Derek looking on, wide-eyed. The king forced himself upright in his shackles and met Lena's eyes, which were watching him from a safe distance. The two stared at each other, barely noticing Irindein's return with the keys to free the king. Lena took them and silently slid near him, releasing the bonds. Arvadis kept his eyes on her. "Thank you, young lady."

Lena cast him a look askance, answering, "Of course my lord."

"Have I seen you before?" asked Arvadis, "You seem familiar somehow."

Lena smiled shyly. "My name is Lena Engrove and I know you my king, but I doubt you know me."

As the manacles came loose Arvadis said, "I know your name now, and I will not soon forget it."

Arvadis rubbed his wrists and brushed his now filthy robes as well as he could before he moved stiffly to Calavar's cell. Graham, Renon, and Derek stood blocking the hall, looking for trouble from back in the direction of the palace proper. They could no longer hear any footsteps approaching, and Vorasho was urging them to be quiet in case those within had not been alerted to the prisoners' escape. Calavar was unconscious and badly beaten. Irindein glanced at the king and his son then nodded solemnly, exiting the cell. Arvadis clasped hands with Vorasho at last. "You should not have come, as I tried to warn you," their eyes met, "but I thank you, and I love you, son."

Vorasho swallowed emotionally before uttering, "It is what Logan would have done. I would have left you here. It would have been the intelligent thing to do."

Arvadis smiled. "I made an entire reign out of doing the unintelligent thing, you know."

"I know."

"I am proud to have raised such a man, Vorasho, as proud of you as I am your brother. I realized, sitting here waiting to die that I never told you that."

Vorasho shrugged. "Your obligations...."

Arvadis seized him. "My obligations were to my family, my family and the people. I failed some of both."

Vorasho shook his head. "I have never admired a man more than you."

"Admiration is not love, son. I have never wanted to be admired. I only wanted to be loved."

Vorasho met his eyes. "I do love you, father, but I am a son not of yours but of our teachings. I do what I do because I was trained to do it. This is the first time I have ever done anything remotely against my training."

Arvadis chuckled softly. "I must say, you picked a good time to start."

Despite himself, Vorasho smiled, though he tried to hide it, then he grew serious. "How are we going to get Runiden out of here? Can we even move him?"

Arvadis sighed. "Could we get him to wherever it is you came from?"

"The tunnel collapsed behind us, we cannot go that way."

Arvadis considered this a moment. "Than that would mean our only way out is down that hallway and through the palace itslef, where many more guards await us."

Irindein strode softly into the room. "We have other problems, my king. It would appear your gallant servant Renon is badly hurt as well. How we are to get both he and Calavar from here I do not know."

"Renon said he had allies among the guards," Vorasho said thoughtfully, "if only we knew how to contact them."

Irindein shrugged. "We have not long, the other guards surely heard the commotion and are now concerned with the long silence. We must make a decision and quickly."

Arvadis put up his hand to quiet the others. "There is a way out of here other than going up. We must descend even further."

Irindein cocked his head to one side. "What might that accomplish, my friend?"

"We came from below you, father, there cannot be much beyond those depths."

Arvadis grunted, "I am afraid there is a great deal beyond those lower levels and the going will not be easy, but if we make it clear we should be past the city walls."

Lena came into the room then. "There are lights starting to come down the hall, my lords, we must move quickly if we are to beat them to the stairwell."

Arvadis shook his head. "There is another way down at the end of this hall, and it should buy us some time. Vorasho, take Calavar and have Graham and Derek assist Renon. Lena and I will lead the way and you, friend Irindein, can cover our rear."

The solemn Highlord bent down and picked up a sword from one of the fallen guards. "I will do my best."

Arvadis retrieved one as well while Vorasho hefted Calavar onto his back. The old Highlord groaned but did not waken, and his girth was great, wearing down the young prince. Derek and Renon came shambling forward, the brave knight leaning on the younger guard. Graham and Irindein took up positions at the rear and with Arvadis leading the way they began moving deeper into the dark of the dungeons. Only Lena still held a torch, so the party had to stay packed in tightly to avoid losing sight of one another. They moved as fast as they could and then faster still when they heard the shouts of the guards as they found their companions' bodies.

Arvadis hurried forward and came to a great stone wall with a massive gargoyle protruding from it. The cells about them were pitch black, but Lena edged near the king thinking she heard something moving in them. Arvadis patted her on the shoulder and whispered, "Do not stray from the center of the hall, there are things down here far worse than the guards."

Irindein said casually, to no one in paritcular, "Always important when selecting an escape route."

Arvadis reached up and thrust his hand into the mouth of the gargoyle. He pushed his arm upward until his elbow nearly disappeared then he tugged down hard and whipped his hand clear of the mouth. The statue groaned almost as though it were crying out then fell forward slowly, resting on the protruding claws of the beast and revealing a black portal beyond that seemed to open downward into the earth. Arvadis helped Vorasho through first, then Renon and Derek. Irindein insisted on waiting until all were inside before clambering after them himself.

Once beyond the hallway, Graham and Arvadis pulled at the great iron handle on the back of the statue and it rose slowly to its former position. Having completed their escape for the moment the party turned, and from Lena's torchlight observed their new surroundings. It was a great cavern they stood above, with a wide pool below and huge stalactites hanging almost to the floor. The place itself gave off an eerie glow, so much so that Lena's torch seemed unnecessary. Amid the rocks and moisture dripping from the ceiling sat great cairns and heavy stone coffins of incredibly ancient design. The party was positioned high above the pool of dark water and the tombs surrounding it, a long and winding staircase descending almost immediately from the secret door they had just stepped through. Even from the great height, they could see another stair leading upward on the far side of the underground chamber, similar to the one just before them, one they would have to reach by passing through the still water that occupied the center of the huge cave.

Arvadis walked forward to the edge of the steps and surveyed the scene before him quietly. Graham and Vorasho exchanged uneasy glances before Renon spoke, "What manner of place is this?"

It was Irindein who answered him in a voice that belied his nervousness, something rare for the even-tempered and well-read Highlord. "It is the Cavern of Ancients, a tomb lost in memory to all. Well, apparently all but some."

Vorasho looked at his father asking, "How did you learn of this place?"

The king spoke calmly as he stared down at the great yawning depths, "There are some texts available only to the rulers of Angladais and one such book is the Tome of Cerestus, the first king of our people. He chronicled all the ancient and dark secrets of the founding of our nation before we became who we are now, and among them he included this place, the Cavern of Ancients."

Irindein continued, "In the lore of Angladais, this cavern was thought to be no more than a myth. It is said the weapons these dead are buried with contain almost unlimited power and the treasures residing in their caskets would be enough to buy our kingdom three times over."

Arvadis added, "Cerestus also said that this place was a source of unnaturally strong evil. The shuffling we heard in the cells above is but a taste of the darkness amid these tombs."

Irindein cleared his throat. "Then might I ask again, old friend, why we are attempting this particular road?"

"Indeed," said Graham hoarsely. "I would rather face an enemy I understand than some dark magic I do not."

Arvadis turned to them. "We are here because Cerestus noted that passing through the Cavern would not be difficult if one came there out of need and touched nothing of the dead. They will not strike us as long as we leave them be. But be warned my friends, the creatures may be bound by the laws of their imprisonment here, but it does not mean they will not try to entice us with their words and magic. Touch nothing! The exit is only just across that pool of water and we shall take the shortest route straight through it and be on our way."

The weary party glanced about at one another for a time considering the king's words. Then Lena gathered herself and stepped down upon the high stair leading to the cavern floor. The others paused as if waiting to see what would happen, but as she continued to walk unhindered they too found their courage and began the trek downward. Vorasho followed her, still carrying Calavar on his shoulders. He peered intently before him, as though he might be able to spot the danger below before it revealed itself. Down they went, and the descent was farther than they had anticipated. Soon they had traveled so deep Irindein speculated they might be as much as a mile below the palace. It was an unnerving revelation and an uncomfortable experience, the silence of the cavern broken only by faint echoes of dripping water.

Lena watched the dust flee from her soft boots as she came down the carved stone stairs. The air was alive around her and she could hear it whispering to her. As she descended it became louder and more insistent in her head and the rate of her tread slowed. Arvadis caught her from behind with a gentle hand on her shoulder. "Do not heed the voices, child. Move swiftly and surely through the water. Go now, while we are still under our own power."

Lena felt the reassurance in his grip and continued onward. The stairway curved and she felt the living air cool drastically with each step. Suddenly, without realizing how, she was at the bottom of the stairs and only some few feet from the water's edge. She glanced at it, noting the dark cold the water seemed to house in its reflection, and then Arvadis was beside her again. "Hold my hand, and we shall go together." To the others he called, "Lock hands, do not break the clasp of your partner!"

The king took her hand gently and stepped into the water. It was a completely silent entry by all, no splashing or even rippling disturbed the unnatural peace of the cave, as though the water was not even liquid at all, but something more sinister. It was cold, so cold it frosted the armor on Renon's hanging chest-plate and he paused to warn Derek and Graham of the phenomenon. The cold was clinging and Graham muttered that it seemed to creep above the water and into his chest, but Irindein harshly silenced him from the rear.

They were only a few feet away from the shore with almost a quarter of a mile to cover across the strange pond when the voices began to resonate clearly about them all. They came out of the tombs on tendrils of promise, whispering of great deeds and greater treasure. At first the very nature of their origin made ignoring them easy. Then the constant speech, icy as the water they were passing through, began to seep into the bones of the fugitives. Arvadis kept his path straight, loudly whispering words of encouragement, "Heed them not! Keep with me! We are almost to the middle of the pool."

Do not listen to this false king, he knows not of us. He cannot even recall who we were in days gone by.

Yes, do come take our gifts, take them for a meager price.

They are powerful. You in your bright armor could be even greater than those you sacrifice to serve. You could be true heroes if you will but take our offer.

The words were like webbing and the weakened Renon could barely resist them while the cold seemed to slow him even more. He shook his head to try and clear it, but it felt as though something stuck to his forehead and he released the hand of Vorasho before him, separating the prince, who was holding onto Lena and by extension Arvadis, from the rest of the line. As soon as Renon broke the chain something interceded between them and his hand froze in its raised position.

The loyal subject! Does your wound trouble you? We could heal that in a moment, but a trifle for our power.

The thing before him was mostly transparent, a strangely clothed figure with an indistinguishable face and undulating body. Renon tried to see deeper into the visage and found his thoughts were turned inside out. He could not remember where he was or even who he was. He began to panic, releasing the hand of Graham behind him who was yelling, trying to get him to go around the apparition before them. Irindein reacted swiftly and lunged forward grabbing the bewitched man and hurtling him through the figure towards Arvadis. "Time to be gone, my lord! Enough walking, make haste!"

Arvadis turned briefly to see what had happened but Lena and Vorasho shoved him forcefully towards the far shore. Derek shouted a warning and suddenly there were strange figures all about them, whispering in a maddening frenzy, and the party could do nothing more than forge ahead. Derek had his sword out and was back-pedaling, desperately looking for a foe to strike at, but there was none. Vorasho, who had braced Calavar across his shoulders well enough to free his hands to hold onto Renon and Lena, now let go of her hand so he could speed his motion forward without dropping the Highlord. This created another rift for the specters to divide them and soon there were divisions throughout the party. However, each of them in their small pocket clung together and blindly moved forward, the strong voice of Arvadis pulling them towards the far shore.

They pressed onward. Derek swiped at a few of the figures and it brought only maniacal laughter rebounding off the cavern walls. He turned and ran hard for the rest of the group, sheathing the obviously useless steel blade. Derek nearly knocked them all over when he reached them, Irindein having passed him when they began to flee in earnest. The Highlord stayed him, and they turned their eyes forward. The strange creatures surrounded them and were indeed flitting among them, but the group had packed itself together tightly enough to be able to see one another. Arvadis was at their head still, facing off with a large specter, this one with a much clearer appearance.

It was thin and tall, elflike perhaps, but possessing far too much height and not enough girth. The thing had no visible eyes or nose but a mouthful of terrible fangs and long, thin ears. It hovered before Arvadis, hands in its long thin robes with that deathly grin upon its horrid face, and the king, for all his daring, plainly had no intention of challenging whatever this thing was. The beast floated there, its strange minions behind it and suddenly the rampaging voices and pleas ceased and all was silent in the cavern. The desperate rescuers and those they had come to help stood in the dark water watching the thing size them up before it threw back its fanged head and laughed so sinisterly that they all visibly shuddered.

What do you mortals think you are doing in my cavern? Refusing my hospitality? Surely your noble selves would not turn down the gifts of my people? It is an insult punishable by death in my realm, and this is my realm, Arvadis Hawking.

The king steadied himself. "I apologize, I was only attempting to pass through on my way from my city."

Another terrible laugh came from the monstrosity. *You do not pass through the realm of those in limbo, foolish king. You either pay tribute to the Forgotten or you join the waiting, and we have not had company in a long while. I am tempted to invite you to entertain us for several more eons. We could keep you in perpetual suffering for some time, I think, before your minds crumbled under the relentless pressure.*

"We are not staying. I am crossing through your realm because it lies within mine. You will move, demon, or I will simply pass you by."

A rage overtook the creature and its face was terrible to behold as the mouth opened and many more teeth appeared, a number beyond reckoning. It howled and brought the sharp daggers near the face of the king in a shriek of hatred, but Arvadis would not be moved. The creature regarded him with its eyeless gaze then laughed again. *There is no departure without my permission, mortal. You will have to pay a price of some kind to me. I assure I can make it reasonable.*

The king shook his head. "We can simply step around you, specter, and be on our way."

Can you? The cold of the water intensified, and the gasps of several of the others behind Arvadis told him the frost was painfully sharp. *I rule this place, and one of you is already succumbing to my will and wishes to join my thralls. He is already wounded and weak, give him to me and I will grant the rest of you passage.*

Arvadis held up his hand to silence the protests of those behind him and answered, "His life is not mine to give. Suggest a toll to procure our passing, and I will consider it."

More laughter echoed from the strange specter. *How very noble! Then my price is simple. You, being mortal, will eventually die and your soul pass to the Dead Realms or whatever god you deserve to join, however there are ways around such an end. You might join another group of souls, perhaps even one such as my conclave? Or perhaps, another would take your place?*

Arvadis stood silently a moment then spoke, "This seems a high price just for letting me pass through your homeland."

Then perhaps you would like to turn back and take that road? Assuming you and your companions can muster the will to walk that far.

The fiend knew this was no option for the king, it had put him in a position where the only offer he could accept was the one it presented. Arvadis was furious at having placed his companions in such a predicament. He should have studied Cerestus's writings more carefully; as it was, he had remembered this place from casually glancing over the book once in an idle moment. He pondered the situation before him. Selling his soul to this monstrosity would be quite difficult to undo once he agreed to it, but they would never survive the journey back across the water, never mind the dungeon halls where undoubtedly Vendile was searching for them with the full complement of his guard. Arvadis met the beast's eyes gravely. "I accept your offer."

A massive grin split the thing's face. *Wonderful! Then I shall see you, or a worthy descendant, sometime in the near or far future, for we Forgotten can wait a long time for what we desire. I hope the bargain was worth the price to you, Arvadis Hawking.*

"I suppose I will know soon enough."

Then farewell for now, mortal king, until you come here to meet the fate your ancestors have avoided for centuries. I dare say only one of us will look forward to it.

The specter melted away into the walls, the cackling of its minions echoing off of the stone. Vorasho grabbed his father's shoulder and spun him in a rage. "What have you done?"

Arvadis regarded him calmly. "I did as was necessary for those under my protection."

Vorasho was exasperated. "You gave your life away!"

Arvadis nodded. "And I saved the lives of my friends. It was a sacrifice worth making."

Lena intervened then, saying quietly, "It was a king's decision, Vorasho. Someday you may have to make the same kind of choice, and the price may be as high."

The prince found he could not dispute the obvious wisdom of this statement, so he simply shut his mouth and adjusted Calavar's body on his shoulders. Grimly, he strode forward out of the dark pool and began climbing the staircase to the light glowing dimly far above them all. Lena gave Arvadis a look of understanding and even sympathy before she moved to follow Vorasho up the stairs. The others passed by slowly, Derek clearly relieved to be free of the strange water. Graham appeared saddened, but could not seem to find the words to express his emotions, so he simply paused as though prepared to speak, then walked onward with Renon leaning heavily on him. Irindein was the only one who did stop, though he made sure they were both clear of the strange water first. The prudent Highlord regarded his friend calmly. "What you have done was not wise, but I also know there were few other choices."

"We could not have gone back."

"We could have, it would just have been difficult and some of us would have died."

"An unacceptable solution."

Irindein frowned at him. "To you perhaps, but the selling of one's soul is not something to be done in haste, and you did so. You did not even consult the others or me about your decision. Who is to say we could not have forged past those creatures?"

Arvadis returned the look. "You know we could not have."

Irindein gritted his teeth. "That does not mean I would not have rather tried."

The Highlord swept past him and up the stairs. The usurped king was alone at the foot of the steps in the now rapidly darkening Cavern of Ancients. Arvadis glanced about him at the coffins and tombs resting in the shallow water and something caught his eye. An ancient blade lay in its sheath above the liquid, seemingly floating over the pool as though the water was afraid to touch it. Arvadis leaned near and the sword floated towards him. Despite all of his own warnings, he reached out for it and the hilt slipped into his palm. The king raised the blade before him. He turned it in his hand, caressing the sheath with his palm. It was gilded in fine silver and depicted a great bolt of lightning crashing down between the Pillars of Light. It was an Angladaic blade, to be certain. The king took the sword in hand and began to climb the staircase.

Before he even reached the third stair, the toothed specter appeared before him. The beast was grinning again, its triumph apparently imminent. *It seems that you did not want to wait out your years, Arvadis. You wish to join my brethren and I sooner yes?*

"I think not."

Indeed? You have taken from my people's trove and that means you are subject to our law. Your life is forfeit.

Arvadis grew angry and he stepped closer to the foul being, thrusting his face into its own. "This blade is of my people, not yours. If you are going to demand so high a price of me, than I think I will take this in exchange. If you want to claim your prize, then come and get it yourself."

The monster was baffled by this sudden show of defiance. It reared back, the smile disappearing into a look of indignation. It seemed to recover quickly, but was still unsure of itself. *Very well, king, take your blade and know that soon I will have something of more value for myself.*

There was a brief moment of evil laughter, somehow less convincing than before, and the creature was gone. Arvadis looked down at the sword, wondering what had possessed him to seize it in the first place, then began the ascent. It took him some time, and when he finally reached the entrance at the top of the stairs the others were waiting anxiously for him. They could see the first hints of bright sunlight of a new dawn and the gentle late fall breeze, bringing smells of life and from the wakening day. Arvadis paused at the exit to take in the feeling of freedom, for he felt he had been imprisoned for years, though in truth it had been mere hours.

Upon seeing him at the tunnel entrance, Vorasho rushed forward. "Father! Are you alright?"

Arvadis waved him away. "I am fine my son, just fine."

Irindein was still brooding over his king's decision in the cavern but it did not stop him from seeing his strange prize. "What is that, Arvadis, a parting gift?"

"Let us just say I negotiated the terms of my contract."

That was all that was spoken on the matter and the party looked around, clearly unsure of what to do next. Calavar was still unconscious, resting on the earth where Vorasho had gently set him. The others were battered and weary but relieved to have escaped the dark underground. Arvadis handed the hard-won sword to Irindein and then turned to eye his company of loyal followers. "Well, where have we emerged?"

Lena answered him, "The woodlands, just outside the city walls."

Arvadis nodded in satisfaction. "Good, now we need to find a safe place to camp out of sight of Vendile's patrols."

Lena pointed to the road just beyond the trees. "I recognized this area when we emerged. There is a road just beyond these woods, and my home lies not far down it."

"Excellent, then let us retire there for the moment, until I have had time to come up with a plan to get back my kingdom. Now, if someone would see to covering up the opening to the caves, just in case."

Arvadis went silent. The company turned to see that the rock that the cave had seemingly emerged from was now solid, with no sign of seams or cracks denoting a door. Graham shuddered and moved away but Derek tapped it with his mailed hand a few times to be certain they had not made a mistake. "It is solid, completely."

"But how," Renon said softly, "we just came from there."

Arvadis waved away the questions. "Let us not trouble ourselves over it, we have much work to do. Off we go."

The finality of the last statement settled things and soon the exhausted party was up and moving again, down the road and away from Alderlast. Vorasho paused to take one last glance back at the strange stone and could have sworn he saw a foul figure hovering near it, smiling at him. The prince adjusted his armor harder than was necessary and moved stiffly after the others. He tried to put the events of the night behind him. They had, as his father rightly said, much work to do.

Chapter 23

In the young days of Teth-tenir, the Great Northern Waste was a more fruitful place, and consequently had a less foreboding name. In the early years of the planet's long life it had been a more temperate region with many deep valleys of often-fallow fields. In those days there had been more inhabitants who would settle there, spending time upon the surface and within the mountains, farming and mining for their living. Beneath the earth they had delved and worked great tombs for their lords as well as wondrous homes for living in the mountainsides. It was said by northerners that from these first people the dwarves had come, but the elves of Silverleaf argue that they were those early northern people and the dwarves merely copied their old and vulgar habits of altering the nature of mountainous stone. The dwarves themselves refute both accounts and have their own story of their origins.

The land was thus once and was not so any more. Where Edge and Romund laid Raymir down, there had once been a plateau of gardens belonging to the first people in the north and now they found only mounds of snow. What was once the Great Northern Waste now went by the name of the Frozen Reach, and the border between the two was unclear, but by design neither name was especially inviting. The mountains extended out and above their position so that Edge thought he could see only rock around him on all sides, and thought there might be nothing but cliffs left in all the land. Romund, who had never been this far north, not even passing by as Edge had, was similarly mesmerized. The two men sat, weary and cold, watching the great expanse about them and marveling at the sheer emptiness of the land.

They had climbed for an entire day while sharing the burden of Raymir's sleeping form. She had roused briefly while they rested at the lower level of Mount Iceblade, but had then fallen back into a deep slumber. She seemed to be breathing easily now, which was more than could be said for her companions. Romund remained standing, looking about as he sucked in the chilled air in deep gulps. Edge had collapsed in a heap beside Raymir. He had carried her most of the way in the past few hours, allowing Romund to break the deep snow before them as they went. She stirred slightly and her eyes fluttered open but closed again and her body relaxed. Edge patted her hair back gently and watched as Romund looked about. "What are you expecting to find?"

"I expect to find nothing," the older man grinned ruefully, "but I am hoping to find some wood before it gets too dark."

Edge picked his head up slightly. "Try over there, I see something sticking out of the snow. It might be a tree."

Romund shrugged. "I hope it's a nice country cottage, but I suppose a tree would suffice."

Edge laughed as Romund moved stiffly away from him. Raymir stirred again and this time her head came up slowly. "Edge?"

He turned his brilliant green eyes on her and smiled. "I am here, love. How are you feeling?"

Raymir rubbed her eyes. "Quite tired still. Where are we?"

"We are climbing Mount Iceblade, a little over halfway up the rock."

"How long have I been asleep?"

Edge pulled her close. "Don't worry about that. You saved Romund and me with your magic, but I think you may have overexerted yourself."

"Yes," Raymir felt consciousness come back to her. "I only remember fear for you both and crying aloud words I read in one of Saltilian's books, and suddenly I was knocked flat."

"Romund said the spell was beyond your power to cast. What you did you did out of desire to protect us." His face grew solemn. "I was just afraid you might not recover from it."

Raymir smiled weakly. "It is the cost of magic. You have to give a piece of yourself for a time, though it will come back. I will just need to rest for a while longer."

Edge nodded though his eyes still shone with concern. "You may rest as much as you can. I carried you from the battle and up Iceblade this far. I can manage a bit farther."

Raymir rubbed his cheek gently. "I think it is time another one of us rested. Sleep love, I am here to watch you."

Edge seemed about to resist, but his body cried out for respite so he accepted the offer. As he settled down in the snow Raymir helped him burrow in for warmth and threw a worn travel blanket atop his armored body. Edge looked at her, his eyes struggling to remain open. "Romund went to find wood, he should be back soon...."

Edge drifted off in complete and total exhaustion. Raymir watched him a while then kept a wary eye about her for Romund or any other guest. Before long a shape emerged before her in the thick, slowly falling snow. Romund was carrying a collection of miraculously dry dead branches in his arms. Raymir laughed at the sight of him, for his hair had gone from a silvery grey to a great cap of pure cotton white and he had acquired a moustache in his travels. Romund was caught a little off guard by the sound, but he soon realized his comical appearance and dropped the kindling to brush the snow aside. He shrugged and laughed as well, happy to see Raymir was awake and apparently healthy as ever. The two quieted and went to work making the wood into a small, comforting fire. Romund spoke softly with her as they did, recounting the journey up the mountain and the final fight with Kurok after Raymir had collapsed.

When the fire was ready, Raymir finally noticed a gnawing hunger in her belly, which Romund was quick to insist on quelling. He gave her a double share of food, including most of his own, and after eating she found the weariness in her was gone and she was ready to move, but clearly Edge was going nowhere for a time. Romund lounged in the snow, watching it fall from the sky above him with a small smile. Raymir studied him and saw the care lines in his face and the battered look of his clothes, yet something in him made him seem to shine before her like a wondrous lord of some ancient kingdom. She had suspected since he first revealed himself that Romund was more than he let on. Now, watching him recline on the mountainside, she was certain of it. He held himself with an air of power and command that he had projected calmly throughout their journey. He reminded her suddenly of Algathor.

"Romund," she asked softly, "tell me about your home. I've never been to Hethegar."

The old man eyed her with a small smile and sighed. "My home, my home. This is not an easy thing you ask me to explain but I can try." He seemed to fumble for the right words, speaking in generalities and half-measures. "It's mostly logging and hunting, you know. We have our big wooden homes, warm fires, and long days. Work is life in Hethegar, like most of the north. Labour keeps you fed, keeps you safe." As he moved from vague descriptions of the town to things more personal, she sensed him perking up slightly. "I have a wife, and a son as well. He's around your age, I think, though I've not seen either of them for some time. She's older than me, but the most beautiful woman you've ever seen, and wise. Certainly her patience and logic keep me in check. My son is more like me, rash and daring."

Raymir shifted in the snow and spoke again, "I would dearly love to see your home, Romund."

Romund's eyes met hers and at the same time seemed far away. "Perhaps, my dear, we will all go there one day when this deed is done. You will be my guests, and I can repay you for your kindness and faith on this quest of ours."

Raymir studied him a moment before asking quietly, "Why did you help us, Romund?"

"My responsibility is to my home and its protection," he responded. "People loyal to what was once Napal charged me to gather information on Wolfbane and bring it back so we might concoct a plan to bring him down."

"Then why delay reporting to the resistance by aiding us?"

"Your search for this tower seems of the utmost importance, and to be perfectly frank, I like you both. Sometimes you can cause more good by doing a small thing than in setting out to accomplish a great one. It is these lesser deeds that in the end can affect larger events. This is my goal, a great accomplishment through minor doings."

Raymir smiled. "What you do for us is not minor."

"Well, every man breaks his creed once in a while."

Raymir laughed softly and they settled into comfortable silence. Romund burrowed down into his blankets and snow, warm for the moment, and fell asleep. Raymir lay awake a while longer, watching the two men about her as they rested. To her, it seemed they were but variations on the same core being. Edge slept on clutching his halberd and Romund's hand stole to his hilt every minute or so, as if assuring himself it was still there. These dangerous men, wrapped in the tension of ever-present threats to themselves, had proven loyal to her and one another. Even though they still dozed they radiated a constant awareness, and they seemed oddly suited to this harsh and alien environment. It was not the first time Raymir questioned her purpose among them, but her mind would not allow her to doubt herself for long. Her value was in her faith and spirit, not her physical strength. Her wits would be of help, as much as their courage and ferocity. After the battle with the daemon wolf, she was still more assured of this fact.

Raymir had grown a great deal since the tragic deaths of her family. When she had been faced with her own demise in those moments, she had felt a steel resolve within her she never knew she possessed. In the dungeons of the fortress, defended for centuries by her ancestors, watching her mother wither away to nothingness, she had felt that resolve tempered and hardened further in the suffering she bore and witnessed. Her skulking about the library and secret study of magic had been the first real steps on her new path to becoming a true Squall. Her family had always been steadfast and defiant, though until the Nerothians had come there had been little to set their mind toward combating. Now, the lone survivor of the family had tapped into a secret strength and her tentative dabbling in the arcane would need to become true study. Raymir could feel, even in her exhaustion, the wellspring of energy she had called upon against the daemon pulsating within her. She might be in the company of dangerous men, but she could now see that with enough time and diligence she might be their guardian instead of they hers.

In this resolution Raymir determined to watch over them now as they slept, but the peacefulness of their surroundings and her own weariness conspired against her. Despite her good intentions, Raymir drifted off to sleep again, passing into sweet rest as the snow floated down around her. There was nothing to disturb any of their dreams on this part of the mountain. Surely no living beast could climb so high. Yet not far below, unknown to the travelers, a deadly malice was slowly ascending. Saltilian had rested briefly, and now pulled his thin body up the rock face with bleeding, clawed hands. Each motion brought more blood oozing from beneath his remaining nails, but he continued to climb, his madness deepening with each lurching motion. As he groped along the face of the rock, he muttered to himself words with no meaning, talking in his own tongue to the creature inside him. Tattered robes billowed out behind him like a funeral cloak, yet he pushed onward.

Raymir and her companions were unaware of the danger, still some distance beneath them. The snow fell steadily like a new linen sheet upon their bodies, obscuring them from view. A cold white fog of flakes fell softly, melting in its own time about the circle of their small fire. Despite the cold, the wind, and the ever-increasing snow, the flame burned on, its glow keeping them safe from the deepening darkness about them. Below, the night crept upwards behind maddened eyes and still the adventurers dreamt and caught not the stench of hatred steaming from the stone about them.

The great Karsyrus Vendile, soon to be King of Angladais, sat brooding upon his throne in a terrible rage. He was erect in his new, massive iron-spiked seat intended to intimidate and overawe those who came to audience with him, staring straight ahead as thoughts raced through his mind. That devil Arvadis, whom he had intended to murder shortly after his imprisonment, had evaded him, all due to a treacherous knight. Foolish soldiers and their concepts of honor! It was what made this kingdom weak! Vendile relaxed his death grip upon the arms of his throne and gazed around, the view of his purple wall hangings and decorations of vicious armaments soothing him slightly. He rubbed the stones of his metal pendant and waited for the act to bring about some further measure of calm, yet it seemed to have no effect on his agitated mind. Still, this was his palace and his kingdom and he must remember that. Already, Freyan was seeing to the recovery of Arvadis Hawking and his despicable son. They would be captured before the night was over. Vendile was still unsure how they had evaded his guards in the dungeons, but fortunately for them all the appointed executioners of Arvadis had been killed in his escape. Otherwise Vendile would have prolonged their demises over several days.

The guards loyal to Vendile were at the temples receiving care from the priests for the many wounds they had suffered at the hands of the traitorous men aiding the despicable Renon. One of the rebels had been captured alive, and Vendile was awaiting his arrival so he might learn where Arvadis had fled, and thus corner and slaughter him at last. In the meantime, he had sent out his army to place every citizen under house arrest until the crownless king was captured. Surely he was hiding amid the unwashed masses he so dearly loved. Vendile would put a stop to that soon enough with a more aggressive campaign of suppression and martial law if it became necessary. He was not against sacrificing a few thousand innocents to flush out his hated foe.

The doors to the throne room were heaved open and the High-lords responsible for the coup came through. Vendile was keeping Xarinth and Galden under tight house arrest with his own guards for their "protection." He did not expect them to try anything, but their descendants had reputations for bravery and independent action, something he was not going to allow to develop in the latest heirs to their titles. It was Bwemor and Hladic that slunk through the doors of his hall, both looking proud and yet rather nervous. They noted their king's mood and were wary of it, fearing heavy retribution was to fall upon them for the events of that day, of which they knew only the basest information. Both paused some distance from the dais and bowed low, keeping their eyes upon Karsyrus Vendile and also looking about them for possible assassins, or worse, hidden behind the wall hangings.

Brusius Hladic made a show of brushing off his red and gold robes over his corpulent body before greeting his king, "My lord, how fare you this evening?"

Vendile snorted and did not respond. Bwemor, the military man that he was, assumed that his king wanted a report on the situation at hand and so he launched into one. "My king, we have located the survivor and are in the process of bringing him to your dread presence, but we had to send him to the priests first in order to refresh his condition."

Again Vendile made no response so Bwemor forged ahead, "We have sealed all the homes in Alderlast per your request and are beginning a search of every store, warehouse, and residence immediately. I assure your majesty we will leave no corner of the city untouched. Any who resist or harbor any rebel will be imprisoned at once."

"No," Vendile's voice was soft yet commanding. "Kill them if they show any sign of opposing me. Do not leave behind any voices of dissent. Once enough die, they will no longer attempt to resist my rule."

"Very good, my lord, an excellent plan."

Hladic spoke up, nervously rubbing his smooth shaved head and fondling the knots of office about his waist, "My lord, I have dispatched priests to the front near the Pillars to assure that the army withdraws, since some of their members have appeared unwilling to cooperate with your commands."

Bwemor glared at the priest, his already ruddy complexion deepening to crimson. "There will be no problems with the army, what happened was a minor moment of dissent amid my men!"

"Minor!" Hladic scoffed. "The man released Arvadis Hawking! That is anything but minor!"

"And what have your precious priests done about it? They sit in their white temples of marble and read the day away! Tell me, will you find the location of the traitor in one of your precious books, Brusius?"

"Enough!" Vendile stood up before his throne and tossed back his cloak, staring hard at the men before him. "You have caused plenty of trouble and done no good between the two of you. Why I ever allowed you to enter into this conspiracy with me I have not the faintest idea! Do not forget I gave you what authority you have now! Were it not for me, Gelladan Bwemor, you would still be commanding grunt infantry in a forward post! And you, Hladic, would be with your priests leading the morning, noontide, and evening Calls to Paladinis, not wallowing in your private harem! You owe all this to me and yet a former bandit seer has done more good than the two of you combined!

"I will no longer tolerate your incompetence. Spread your followers to every corner of my kingdom. Go to every village, every outpost, every squalid shack, and find that bastard Arvadis Hawking! Do not return to me until you have his and every traitor's head on a spear before my palace gates! If he wants to oppose me I will make him pay in blood, the streets will run red with it, and then we shall see if the Highlord Hawking is truly as noble as he claims to be."

Bwemor and Hladic bowed low and scurried away to their respective posts without another word. Vendile collapsed into his throne and grasped his pendant before running his now trembling hand through his black hair. The metal chain caught the edge of the heavy crown and knocked it from his head. It tumbled to the floor where one of the inset rubies cracked and fell from within the circlet. Vendile sat silently, alone in his throne room, staring down upon the broken crown at his feet. This was how Freyan discovered him when he swept past the guards into the room some time later. The former bandit paused, examining the grim sight, then rushed forward to his king and whispered in his ear, "My lord, I have brought the surviving traitor here for you to question personally. We believe he and those who fought with him were in league with the knight Renon who betrayed Highlord Bwemor and yourself."

Vendile did not respond, but continued to look down on the symbol of his power. Then he rose, swept down the dais and hefted the item. "Naught but a chunk of precious metals, it means nothing to me." He hurled it from him at the door to the throne room where it shattered into a hundred pieces. Then he spun on Freyan with a mad light in his eyes. "Bring the foul betrayer to me that I might show him what king rules here!"

Freyan bowed low, concealing his look of distaste when Vendile had hurled the crown and walked swiftly to the door. He cracked it open and three guards ushered in a bleeding and beaten man, still wearing his heraldry, through the entrance. Vendile bitterly noted that he possessed the red and black colors of Bwemor, though the black boar on his breast plate was battered and misshapen with the beating it had taken. This man should have been loyal to him and his Highlord! What fools he had to work with. The guards brought the traitor before the throne and Vendile stood atop the stairs, gazing down on him.

Freyan moved slowly beside him and commanded, "Bow to your king, fiend."

The disheveled man looked up. His youth surprised Vendile. He could not have been over eighteen years of age. He spat blood upon the robes of the advisor. "I see a fiend here, but it is not me."

The guards drove him to his knees and Vendile approached, studying him carefully. He picked through his blood-matted hair with one bare hand, then swung it backward forming a fist and smashed the man across the face, knocking loose several teeth, "Fool! You are not enough to oppose me! Your little feat has accomplished nothing! Tell me who else among the army conspired with you!"

The guards released the man, who nearly collapsed, yet he willed himself to remain upright, blood forming a pool at his feet as it fell in a thick stream from his mouth. He opened his jaw, releasing two of his teeth onto the carpet as he did, and looked up at the fearsome king with a crimson smile. "I have done my duty. That is all I desire to say."

Vendile roared ferociously and struck the man again, bowling him over onto his back. Freyan intervened quickly. "My lord, do not kill him! He may be our only opportunity to learn where Arvadis has fled!"

Vendile managed to contain his anger, barely. He rubbed his knuckles in his free hand and spoke, "Tell me where the rebel has gone and I will assure you that you die quickly."

The guard groaned on the heavy carpet and hefted himself onto his hands and knees. He wiped his mouth, found that it did no good as the blood simply kept flowing from his face, and chuckled again. "I know not where my true king has gone, pretender, however I can show you where to begin searching."

The guard lunged forward, reaching for one of his captor's blades, but his wounds were too many and he was weary. The loyal henchmen sidestepped him and delivered a vicious mailed boot to his face. The rebel's head snapped backwards too abruptly and he rolled over, eyes staring unseeingly at the ceiling. Vendile watched the body convulse briefly then snarled and kicked it himself. He whirled on Freyan and paused, thinking better of striking his only competent advisor. "Find me Arvadis Hawking! And get this miserable cur's body out of my palace! Hang him outside the gates as a warning, and when I awaken on the morrow he had better be joined by at least a dozen more like him! Go!"

Vendile stormed out of the throne room through the back door to his private chambers. Freyan regarded the guards and body briefly, then motioned them to move it away. Stepping lightly around the bloody pools in the rug he moved onto the marble floor and made his way almost disinterestedly from the throne room. Outside he grabbed a passing commander of Vendile's personal soldiery. "Take your men out into the city. If you find anyone on the streets at this time ask no questions, seize them and bring them back here for execution. Every one you find, do you understand?"

The guard nodded and moved off to do the advisor's bidding. Freyan stood before the iron doors of the new king's hall to make certain that the soldiers went about their business quickly. Then, with a sigh that betrayed his irritation, he turned back to the throne room and tramped past the massive chair to the palace's library doors at the end of the great hall. Tossing his cloak back, the advisor swept inside and quietly slid the lock into place.

Arvadis was far from the city by that time. The strange cavern beneath the palace had taken them nearly a mile outside the wall, not far from a nameless outlying hamlet. This was near Lena's home, and yet the tunnel had been quite far from even that, north of Alderlast's wall in the fringe of the Silverleaf woods. This section of the woodland, to the north of the main stretch of forest, was considered especially treacherous. Those who ventured too deep into its woods often never returned and many shepherds and hunters in the area referred to it in fearful whispers as though the trees themselves could hear them. Despite its reputation, this region of Silverleaf had made for a great natural defense, as it wrapped around the western and southern lands of Angladais like a dark blanket.

The progress of the escaped captives had been slow. Derek had taken Runiden Calavar on his shoulders now, and while he was youthful he was not as strong as the prince. Vorasho was exhausted from his flight to Alderlast and subsequent mad dash to save his father. The eldest son of Arvadis was no longer capable of bearing the Highlord Calavar. Irindein was helping Renon continue to move forward as best he could, but the young knight had lost so much blood he could barely keep himself going. Lena refused to let them stop, however, insisting they come to her home before nightfall, lest the guards had made it into the outlying towns. Arvadis seemed unconcerned. "It is unlikely they will expect me outside of Alderlast."

"Nevertheless," Irindein advised, "we need to be cautious."

So they traveled all through the morning, reaching the edge of the small settlement a few hours before noontide and circling about it so as to avoid alerting the townspeople. Lena's home was on the northeastern edge, slightly removed from the village proper. They crept up to the backdoor and were ushered quickly through. They stepped into the cool basement, containing farming implements and broken wagon parts long out of use. Lena urged them to stay there and hurried upstairs to retrieve blankets and other necessities.

She returned moments later and soon they had laid Calavar and Renon upon two thick bedrolls and were treating their wounds with the herbs Lena had been able to gather from her stores. Runiden appeared to be better than they had expected, having suffered a few broken ribs and nasty bruises, but there were no severe punctures to his skin and none of his injuries showed signs of infection. Renon was worse; his wound was deep and swollen, and he was hot from an internal fever that was likely stemming from the thrust he had taken under his armor. Vorasho and Irindein tackled his illness with everything Lena had, mixing every herb Irindein could find amid their supply that had some healing property. While they worked and forced the foul tasting concoctions down his throat, Arvadis stitched up Renon's side as best he could with needle and thread. The knight floated in and out of consciousness the entire time, but finally he seemed to relax and his unnatural warmth subsided slightly.

At this point the weary rested. Derek and Graham had insisted on posting themselves at the entrances to the basement, but upon Lena's urging everyone bedded down for the night without a watch. Then she departed, going upstairs to busy herself baking bread to sell to the people of her hometown so her absence would not be noticed and thus spark curiosity. Indeed, there were many questions from the townspeople for her, but most revolved around what she had heard from Alderlast, since she had told them truthfully the day before that she must travel there on an errand. She related nothing more than general rumors of usurpation and rebellion. The village, being loyal to the Hawking House, grumbled and returned unhappily to its familiar pattern of life. Soon Lena was able to close up her bakery and seek some brief rest for herself.

She awoke late in the evening, hearing movement downstairs, and stole quietly from her small bedroom, carrying a dagger tucked behind her back. Fearing the worst, she glanced around the corner of the stairs and saw the flicker of flames in the stone fireplace at the back of her shop, which also served as her personal dining room. A figure sat rocking gently in her family's oldest chair, staring into the flames. Lena edged forward and realized suddenly that it had not one but two occupants, the second much smaller than the other. She drew a sharp breath and rushed forth in fear, but even then knew it was too late.

Arvadis sat in the rocking chair with a young boy of perhaps four years on his lap. He was relating a great tale to the child, the legend of Keldan Calavar, gesticulating as he spoke of the Gnoll Campaigns, about the Angladaic allegiance with the ocs of the Dust Plains, and the terrible monsters that came down upon the people of Gi'lakil like an all encompassing storm. The young boy was entranced, watching the old man, whom he knew by sight as his king, envisioning the heroic feats of Keldan, his personal hero. Lena stood at the edge of the firelight, her hands covering her mouth as her son listened intently to the tale he knew so well, probably the most famous telling he would ever have the privilege to enjoy.

Arvadis paused in the story as he spotted Lena and smiled. The boy followed his gaze and his face lit up. "Mother!" he rushed forward and hugged her legs but Lena did not move. The boy looked up at her. "Mother? Is everything all right?"

Lena stroked his hair gently. "It is late, Logan. Go to bed and perhaps our king would be kind enough to finish his tale in the morning."

"But...." the boy paused and glanced at Arvadis.

Arvadis Hawking looked at him sternly. "Mothers come before kings, my boy. Even Keldan Calavar knew that."

The youth jumped in immediate compliance and sprinted upstairs, determined to fall asleep before he hit his straw mattress. Arvadis rose and guided Lena to the chair he had occupied and sat the bewildered woman down, pulling up a stool for himself from behind the bakery counter. He leaned in and, taking her hands in his, met her eyes. "After all that you have done for me why should you fear that I know you bore a child out of wedlock?"

Lena averted her eyes and whispered, "It is not as simple as that."

"Then pray tell me, fair lady, how complex is it? Nothing you could tell me would diminish my love for you and the thanks I deeply give for all you have done for me."

Lena looked up. "Did nothing about the child seem unusual?"

"He is a boy who loves his adventure tales!" Arvadis laughed heartily. "I have yet to meet one who does not!" Lena remained silent and Arvadis grew serious. "Truth be told, I do not know why my meeting this boy has suddenly made you fearful of me. You have saved my life. There is nothing that you can admit to me that would incur my wrath."

Lena looked up once more, now with tears in her eyes. "The boy is closer to you than you know. It was not by chance that his name was chosen!"

Arvadis caught her look and paused. Suddenly his eyes widened and his hands dropped from hers. He glanced back at the stairs the boy had fled up, then at Lena again. Bewildered he spoke in a whisper, "That child is of my blood?"

"Your grandson," Lena almost choked as the words came out, "I named him after his father."

Arvadis was speechless for a time before asking, "Does Logan know?"

The distraught woman could only shake her head. Arvadis looked back at the stairs and spoke as the obvious became clear to him, "He has the same features of my son, the autumn brown hair and the square, firm chin. Logan would listen to the same tales for hours from Graham and I, but always beg for more. I must have told him the tale of Keldan Calavar a thousand times over, and now," he paused, "I have begun to tell it to his son."

Lena stood swiftly and paced the room in desperation. "Please!" she cried, "Do not think badly on Logan because of me! I love him! I have always loved him!"

"How has this been kept from me for so long?"

Lena ceased her hurried stride and faced the king. "We met years ago, when we were young. He came riding through here with Vorasho. They were traveling to the cliffs in the east above the Far-water and stopped for supplies. My mother was still alive then and she ran this shop. That night, when they took a room at the inn, we met in the center of town beneath the statue of Paladinis. We did not arrange it, we never even spoke of it, it simply happened."

"You were connected without even speaking the words," Arvadis said softly. "I can remember a similar thing occurring with myself and Logan's mother."

"We met off and on again ever since. Either I visited Alderlast when I could get work as a servant or when I stayed here we would find each other. Logan would claim he was traveling out to go hunting and instead come here. He came in the same way that you and the others did today. Always careful, always unseen, he did not want you or anyone else to know, lest it harm your reputation."

Arvadis digested this before inquiring, "And my grandson?"

Lena blushed a deep red. "He knows his father is a knight, but not who he is. The others from the village think he is a boy I adopted from Alderlast. I have helped feed that rumor by allowing Logan to tell them he is the son of a knight who died in battle. He is a smart boy though. He asks to meet his father often now."

"You have kept this great secret from everyone, for so long?"

Lena averted her eyes. "Not from everyone. To deceive you was not difficult. You love Logan unquestioningly and have never doubted his virtue but his brother... Vorasho is cautious. He watched Logan for a time and learned of our meetings, of the affair. He demanded we put a stop to it, that we end our relationship before you were aware and Vendile used it to undermine your authority. I had to hide from him the fact that I was pregnant, just as I hid it from Logan. When Vorasho learned that we were lovers, he went mad with fear. He thought that such news, if made public, would ruin your reputation. He also demanded that Logan take the Rite to redeem himself of his sins."

Arvadis' eyes widened. "His Rite! That is why my son went to try and become a paladin. I had always doubted his commitment. Logan was satisfied with knighthood. To be a paladin would take him too far away from his people, and they have always come first for him." Arvadis rose and walked forward towards the distraught Lena. "What you have done is not wrong, child, indeed it gives me more happiness than any news I have heard in many days. To think that I have a grandson!"

"Yet he is illegitimate!" Tears welled in Lena's eyes. "And your son is gone, my would-be husband is not even allowed to be a father, to know he is a father! All that I have done these past few days has been what Logan would have wanted me to do, not what I would have done. My only act of defiance came in my son's name, a point of pride for myself alone. I care not for you and your royalty nor your elder son and his traditions and codes. I love Logan and him alone! He would not allow his relationship with me to drag his beloved father down. Even if it meant leaving the woman he cared for."

Arvadis pulled Lena's hands from her face and brought her close. "What you have told me both lightens and weighs upon my heart. I have wanted nothing more in these last years of my reign than to see my people and my family happy, yet to learn that my rule has jeopardized the love of two wonderful people and hidden a child of my own flesh from my son and I is more distressing than I can express. I also realize the resentment you must bear for Vorasho, and for me, but please let that pass. Let us not be hateful of one another any longer and instead find peace between us, for you are my daughter, Lena, and shall be treated as such."

At those words the young woman collapsed into convulsing sobs, held in Arvadis's arms. The king was somewhat bewildered to be holding a crying woman, but at that moment it was the least alarming event in his life by quite a fair amount. He held her there, shaking, and it felt right. So much wear came off his shoulders, to do as simple a thing as comfort another person in need. These were the opportunities a king missed out on simply because he was a king. Arvadis found it made him think of his own wife, now long dead, but the pain of the memory was fresh in the feeling.

Both heard the cellar door open and footsteps upon the heavy wood boards. Vorasho stood before them, his face a knot of confusion. Lena released Arvadis. "I told him, Vorasho. I told him everything."

Vorasho looked at her in wonder and then stared at his father and instantly became defensive. "I kept his secrets to protect our kingdom. It seems now they matter least given our current situation."

Arvadis sighed and went to him. "I have trained you too well, my son, in the customs of our people. There are some things in this world that go above the law and the Code. Our family, your brother, is most certainly one."

"His behavior violated the honor of our house. I did not send him away merely to protect you father. I sent him to atone for his sins before Paladinis."

"Our love was a sin?"

Vorasho returned her look coolly. "Love out of wedlock, in the eyes of our priests, is a most grievous offence."

Arvadis placed a hand on his son's shoulder. "What you did, you did because you felt it was the right thing to do. Let there be nothing more said of it, we are allies here." Then he turned to Lena. "But that is my grandson upstairs, and hitherto he shall be treated as such. Let him know who his family, your family, is."

"Father, what you do, however I might feel it is kind and just, will tarnish you and your reign...." Then Vorasho's eyes widened in understanding. "A grandson? Logan and Lena had a child?"

"Your brother does not know about young Logan," Lena said softly. "It happened after he left, several years ago."

Arvadis stared hard at his son. "Right now, my boy, I have no kingdom to rule over and no image to tarnish with Logan's scandal. If it concerns you so much what the Hawking name takes upon itself, perhaps it is you who should journey abroad seeking redemption for the family."

"I only advise what is most logical!" Vorasho's anger flared. "To take on Lena and Logan's child is to invite disaster and will provide ripe fodder for rumor and doubt when you reclaim the throne!"

Arvadis waved his hands calmingly. "We will see to those doubts when the time comes. I am already known for my generosity in family matters. I accepted an orc into our house, did I not? I think a grandson out of marriage will be received better than that."

Vorasho crossed his arms. "And what of Logan? He cannot attain the power and blessing of Paladinis with such a sin on his conscience."

Lena stepped forward. "Your brother knows better than you the price he has paid. He cares not for the oaths of a paladin. He only went away on the Rite to appease and prove himself to you. This quest of his is not one he has taken lightly. He wishes to win back your heart Vorasho!"

Vorasho stared at the floor ashamed. "My brother has always had my heart," he looked up at Lena, "as have those he loves."

She took him gently and embraced him. "I know."

They separated and Arvadis drew himself up, glancing at both of them. "Well, it has certainly been an eventful evening. I will never claim my latter years waned in excitement. Still, the great task before us lingers, and we must rest so that tomorrow we can plan. I am not letting Vendile sit atop the throne any longer than I have to. I cannot begin to think of the horrors he will inflict upon my people."

At those words they retired, Lena to her room and Vorasho and Arvadis to the cellar. There they sat and spoke softly of the past as the shadows danced slowly along the wall. In his mind, Arvadis could see his younger son and his brave orc companion, off on some noble adventure winning the hearts of the people. In the days to come his father would need to do the same, for in the people lay Arvadis's only hope of regaining his kingdom.

Chapter 24

The younger son of Arvadis was not thinking of home or his father at that moment. He was attempting to urge onward a large mass of refugees to the mysterious Passage of Cronakarl, a destination about which he knew nothing. Diaga's fear of the place had sparked doubts in both he and Grimtooth, but they had no choice in the matter now. The knight rode up and down the line of wagons, urging the men and women driving them to hurry forward, "We must reach the entrance before dark, quickly now!"

Grimtooth trotted up beside him on Thunder and grunted, "Why ye be tellin' everyone ta get a movin' befo' dark?"

Logan slowed and met his gaze. "Do you remember what happened when night fell at the inn? Those strange shades came among us. Jovan is for all practical purposes unconscious since he, Trem, and the Napalian returned, and Diaga has been wielding magic all day. Neither is fit to fight. If we do not reach the caverns before those things catch us then we will be defenseless against them."

"What makes ye so sure they be wit' tha' army?"

"I am not sure, but can you think of anyone else they would be serving around here if they do have a master? And has there been a more opportune time to strike at us than as we are now?"

That quieted the orc, and he rode back down the line to check on the others. Trem had been laid in a cart along with Jovanaleth, who was receiving some medical attention from Diaga. The mage had used some minor spells to slow his bleeding and was now resorting to old-fashioned stitch work to finish the job. Jovan had been roused from his exhausted slumber and now leaned against the wagon wall as Diaga worked swiftly, grimacing in pain as the needle went deftly in and out of his skin. Grimtooth matched their pace beside the cart. "How are ye, Jovanaleth? Feelin' liveliah?"

Jovan managed a smile before replying, "A bit, Grimtooth, thanks."

The orc gave a huge and comical wink. "Ah'll see if Ah can find ye some watah."

He rode off, leaving the two younger men and Neep, who was never far from Diaga, in the cart. The firecat was curled up on Diaga's feet protectively, apparently sleeping, but every movement Jovan made brought her head up sharply and he strange paws stole to her weapons when she did so. Each time, the young wizard would stroke her ears and softly tell her all was well and she would return to semi-slumber. Battered but alive, Jovan looked down at Trem, who had fallen asleep suddenly during his return ride to join the others. "What made him come back, do you suppose?"

Before Diaga could answer, a gruff voice came from in front of their cart, "No mystery to that, boy. That madman of a half-elf seems to think he owes you his allegiance. Me, I was all for leaving these people behind and worrying about ourselves, but it seems he is more foolish than I thought him."

Diaga said softly, "Foolish enough to not abandon those in need you mean?"

Ghost shot the wizard a look of cold hatred and moved further forward. Jovan watched him go then asked, "Is it true Diaga? Ghost really betrayed his people?"

Diaga looked up from his stitching. "Ghost did not betray his people, but Greymane Squall certainly did. I spent a great deal of my time as an orphan in Napal City and I remember hearing stories of him. For a time of relative peace, Greymane Squall was a military legend, the greatest commander of his age. Yet when the invaders came he opened the gates to the city and let them in. He regrets his decision, I know, but such an act is difficult to forget and perhaps impossible to forgive. It has fueled his quest for revenge, but it seems he has not rediscovered his humanity along the way."

Jovanaleth took this in thoughtfully. "Do you think then that this item he seeks in Southron has something to do with the invaders of Napal? Or those Broken that attacked Delmore?"

"He claimed as much before we reached the town." Diaga went back to the stitching, "On that matter, I am fairly certain he speaks the truth."

"Neep!" The firecat growled.

Diaga smiled slightly and translated for Jovan. "Neep does not trust him."

"Nor do I, yet he did save my life and Trem's."

Diaga looked up once more. "Yes, but understand this. Ghost did so because he recognized Trem's potential in Gi'lakil and wants to keep him around. He will do only what is necessary to ensure Trem sticks with him, even if it means he has to pull him clear of a lost battlefield."

"But Ghost saved all of us, not just Trem. You really think he's beyond all redemption?"

"No, Jovanaleth, he is not. But he is a man who sees life and death as calculations to be made. Only one thing motivated the former thane of House Squall, and it is not the preservation of any of our lives."

Jovan could not think of how to respond. They rode in silence a while longer, with Diaga still working away on Jovan's leg. The spear had pierced deep, but Diaga had managed to repair some of the damage with his magic, at least slowing the flow of blood enough to keep Jovan clear of the danger of bleeding out. In the wagon behind them,

Joseph was not so lucky. His wounds were severe and Diaga feared he did not have the power to overcome them. Even Khaliandra had shaken her head sadly when she saw the old man. She had done her best to make him comfortable, but that was all she could do. Diaga and Jovanaleth sat back, the stitching complete, and watched Trem as he lay near them, still as death, but with moving lips.

Jovan looked at Diaga askance. "What is he doing?"

Diaga glanced at the ranger from Bladehome then leaned towards Trem. He paused, looking confused, then said, "He is arguing with someone."

As soon as he had left the sight of Delmore behind, Trem had been taken by a growing suspicion that gnawed deeper and deeper into his mind, until he became convinced that it was more than just paranoia that was causing him to wonder. The warning from Gerand Oakheart had seemed so contrary at the time, disparate from his first meeting when he had spoken of life without others as a life not worth living. Why then would such a man tell him to abandon those who would not simply pass Delmore and her plight by? Trem had sat behind Ghost on Carock and slowly become convinced of one thing: he had been deceived in some way.

Upon reaching the others he had insisted he needed rest and been placed in the same cart as Jovanaleth and Diaga. Almost immediately, he had lain down and begun concentrating on drifting away from the world about him, soon passing into an unnatural sleep that was brought on by his need. Instantly he sought the dreamscape, his need growing so rapidly that he drew on a great reserve of memory and emotion he had never found before. The world formed and deformed swiftly about him, but he ignored the immaterial nature of it and drove his will to find Gerand Oakheart, or whatever being had claimed to be him.

Trem felt the outside presence take him and did not fight it. He careened backward in time, flying to the battlefield of his past. This was not Delmore, though the images were hauntingly similar. Trem swept over the bodies, the blood and flame of the hateful combat, and took it all in calmly. This was gone, over and done with. Trem held onto reality, that he was no longer here and the past was beyond his control. The vision took him down to the field and slowed, reaching the body of one man in particular. Trem was released, felt his feet touch ground. He knelt slowly, studying the massive frame, the heavy armor. Bull the Warrior lay dead before him, a strange and unnatural smile on his face. Trem had been here when he passed on, remembered their final conversation vividly, and knew this was some foul caricature. Despite himself, he let the deep sadness creep in, the scene before him sharper and clearer than his own memories of the moment.

Trem was jerked from this place to another, similar memory. Now he was within the fortress, climbing the wall to the parapet. The wind throws back his cloak as he ascends the stairs to the curtain wall, revealing a full solid frame but one that moves with an eerie grace. The long dirty blonde hair is swept back, revealing a face as of marble; shorter, curling hairs flowing in the wind, slightly obscuring silvery-gray eyes. He pauses to shield his vision against the biting cold in the wind. An army waits below him, an enemy he knows the knights cannot hope to defeat.

The memory broke then and Trem was back in the field outside the fortress. Trem glanced about him and was slightly alarmed to see that there were no men near him, no castle, nothing. It was as though he stood in emptiness. Trem's senses suddenly came back to him and he refocused on the thing he sought. None of this was happening now. He had been in Delmore, with Jovan and the others, and was now on his way to Southron. He looked down at the sword in his hand; the sword of Vactan el Vac and it felt real, everything had been incredibly real. Find the one, he needed to seek out the imposter, for he was sure now he had been an imposter, that had worn the face and voice of Gerand Oakheart. In his need, he spoke, "Where are you? Show yourself."

"As you wish."

Trem turned slowly, recognizing the voice, knowing it far too well, for he had heard it, long ago at the Fortress of Aves. Standing a few feet behind him was a gaunt form in silken black robes. Pale, almost translucent skin covered a drawn face with burning eyes. A long head of jet-black hair seemed to meld with the robes covering the thin but substantial shoulders. A crown, steel and silver spiked with black iron thorns, rested atop the figure's head. Trem recognized him immediately in all his dark grandeur. "Neroth."

The god moved towards him slowly, stopping a respectful distance away. The God of Death took in the mortal before him with searching eyes. Then he spoke again and the voice was soft and almost soothing, "You have allowed yourself to come back to this place. How interesting."

Trem did not move. "It is but a dream."

Neroth shot him a stern look. "Is it?"

Trem shifted uncomfortably. "Why are you here?"

Neroth turned slightly and looked outward at the empty horizon. "I am here to check on the progress of Kurven's child. That, and to see what you have decided to do."

"What do you mean? Is it you that impersonated Gerand Oakheart and told me to abandon the others in Delmore?"

Neroth ignored Trem's demanding tone. "When you left the Fortress of Aves you went into seclusion, deep into Silverleaf Forest. That was over thirty years ago and you have not wielded a blade since. Why then did you go to Gi'lakil and on to Delmore?"

Trem kept his eyes locked on the god, probing for reasons behind the question. "I came out of my seclusion to help a young man who needed it."

Neroth crossed his arms and turned to face Trem. "But you yourself do not believe you can help people, you have said as much in whispers in the dark night. Something more selfish drives you out of your solitude and into my path yet again."

Trem regarded the god angrily. "You make it sound as though I have intentionally opposed you all my life."

Neroth chuckled darkly. "Perhaps not knowingly, but you certainly have been a thorn in my side several times. I could use you, Trem. Oh, I know the others you travel with want you to believe my army to the north is a threat to be destroyed, but they are too quick to trust the deceptions of my former wife. I had hoped you would be wise enough to see past the simplistic interpretation of such minor events."

"Events like the torching of villages and murder of innocents?"

"There are going to be casualties," Neroth held up a hand to stave off Trem's protestations. "You must recognize the greater purpose of my actions."

"Did you impersonate Gerand Oakheart to prevent my death in Delmore?"

Neroth became enraged then, moving towards Trem threateningly. "You do not understand, boy! Wasting my time with these matters that are not of consequence! Steps must be taken to bring the people of Teth-tenir back from the brink of their own self-destruction!" The god's face softened somewhat and he looked slightly haggard. "A price must be paid. Paid by all. It is not as if you possess the strictest creed when it comes to the sanctity of innocent life."

"Did you impersonate Gerand Oakheart?" Trem repeated.

Neroth looked as though he would strike the mortal, but then he relaxed. "I did not. And it matters not who, if anyone, did. You need to stop fretting over the minor events of your world. I wish to work with you, not against you."

"Perhaps you do." Trem's resolve seemed to waver, but then remained firm. "Nevertheless, I am not going to stand with you. No, in fact I deny you."

"Deny me?" Neroth laughed madly. "All of you mortals have denied the gods! Our world you have altered and tainted with your selfish desires, forgetting from whom the very gift of your existence came. You have grown proud and trusting in your own hands and crafts, fools!" The dread god reached out and grabbed Trem's collar pulling him in and the stench of death poured from his mouth. "You truly want to know who told you to pass Delmore by? Who tried to save you from almost certain death? It was not I, but the words could have as easily come from my lips. You, and those with you, waste your time dealing with small matters when the greater, unimaginable doom of us all sits on the thin edges of our worlds."

Trem could not feel the killing cold in the grasp of Neroth, only the burning hatred in his own heart for this deity before him. Reaching out, he grasped the corpse-like hand and wrenched it free of him. Neroth stepped back and his eyes widened in shock as the half-elf stretched outward and pulled the god in as close as he had the mortal. "Plan your charred future all you want, God of Death. Think up every devious punishment for me you can, because if you come for the survivors of Delmore and my friends, I will be waiting for you."

Trem released him and stepped back. Neroth was stock-still taking in the strength of his defiance, still unable to fathom the sheer gall of this lesser being before him. Trem gestured where the fortress of his dream had stood with the phantasm of the sword he had taken from Vactan el Vac. "I walked away from my duty once. I shall not do it again."

Saying this, he saluted Neroth, the salute of the Eagle Knights, sword tip to head then kissing the pommel and lowering the blade. Turning, he walked off into the nothingness, fading from sight with each step, but Neroth's furious words followed him like the frigid wind on the battlements of Aves. "Deny me then! But my servants are coming and they will show you and those you travel with no mercy!"

Trem's eyes opened into soft rain. He lay in the cart amid the hay, feeling the gentle rhythm of its motion as he was pulled down the road towards their destination. He could see Jovanaleth and Diaga talking softly near him, but he closed his eyes again and feigned sleep so as to avoid speaking to them right away. He found he was not comforted to know that the warning he had been given about Delmore had been a deception. Yes, it was a kindness to know Gernad Oakheart had not been a part of the lie, but it was not pleasant to dwell on how quickly after his departure from Silverleaf the God of Death or his agents had begun hounding Trem. He put from his mind the warning and threat of Neroth's broader message; the deity had let slip in his frustration that they were being hunted still and Trem knew he had to tell the others.

Before he could bring himself to do so, he first attempted to eavesdrop on Diaga and Jovan's conversation. Trem understood that they would welcome him back to the group for now, but there were misgivings that would need to be addressed. He would have to answer for his abandonment of the others, and while Jovanaleth might be willing to accept his change of heart, Trem very much doubted Logan would. Though they were once again together, as they had been in Gi'lakil, it was the same necessity of survival that bound them now as it had then. The fracturing of values and beliefs might be too much to overcome and Trem knew he would be faced with deciding between the practical satisfaction of Ghost's need for revenge and the nobler selflessness of Logan's sense of duty to the greater mortal world.

But for the moment there were more pressing issues at hand. Trem believed Neroth when he said that there were enemies after them all. It could be that the Broken had sent a small unit to chase them down, but Trem suspected something far more sinister. The shades that had struck at Gi'lakil had been deadly and single-minded, and he believed they were more apt to be chosen for a mission of extermination. The companions did not have the manpower to withstand them if they did indeed come. Diaga was likely weakened from the battle at Delmore and his magic, if present at all, would be limited. Trem was the only one in possession of an enchanted weapon strong enough to harm the creatures, but he could not hope to defeat more than one of them in combat, their numbers and unearthly, jolting movements would overwhelm him. He opened his eyes and glanced at the sky. It was dusk already and he needed to come up with a plan swiftly or they were all going to die.

Trem rose abruptly, and immediately Jovan was beside him, helping him up. Trem met the young man's eyes and said softly, "I should think I need to help you, not the other way around."

Jovan averted his gaze. "You have already done enough."

Trem shook his head emphatically. "No, I ran away. I fled your side when I should have stayed to protect you. I am sorry, Jovanaleth."

Jovan accepted this cautiously. "Joseph told me some things that might explain why you left, but maybe someday you can tell me yourself."

"Someday, yes, maybe," Trem said offhandedly. "But we need to get moving, I believe the dark-robed fiends from Gi'lakil are coming after us. We have to get into the caverns before they reach the caravan."

"How do you know they are after us?"

Trem shot him a warning look. "I just know."

Jovan said nothing. The two turned to stare behind them as hooves approached. Logan and Grimtooth rode up from the rear and hailed them. Logan slowed down to the cart's pace, glancing only briefly at Trem, and spoke, "The army has stopped its pursuit, apparently we frightened them off." He looked at Jovan. "How are you, Prince of the Blade?"

"I will live."

"Glad to hear it."

Trem spoke up, "We have a problem."

Logan looked at him and Jovan threw his support behind his fellow half-elf. "Trem believes the shades are after us again, the same ones that attacked us at the Inn of the Four Winds."

"Ach, 'ow does 'e know that?"

All three looked at Trem and he sighed in expectation of their disbelief. "I saw it in a dream." Logan's eyes widened quizzically. "I know how that sounds but you must believe me. They are coming, or something as deadly is on our heels."

Logan stroked his moustache thoughtfully. "I admit I had the same fear, though it was a danger I reasoned out, not brought to me in my sleep. No matter, if this is true then we are in grave danger and cannot chance ignoring the possibility they are indeed hunting us. Grimtooth, find Gend, ask him how far we are from these caves of his." The orc rode forward swiftly, and Logan turned to Trem. "Can you fight?"

"Yes, but I cannot hope to handle more than a few of them. At this point I do not even know that I could defeat one on my own."

"Perhaps you were mistaken in this dream of yours?"

Trem shook his head emphatically. Logan glanced back over his shoulder and rubbed his chin in frustration. "These things will catch up with this and the other wagons with the wounded first, since they are traveling the slowest. If we are near the caves, we might get half the people in before it becomes totally dark, but I do not know that we should count on that. We will have to make a stand somewhere."

"We do not need to do anything. I will delay them as long as I can."

Jovan looked at Trem reproachfully, but Logan spoke first, "As noble an offer as that may be you cannot hope to stop them for very long, as you yourself admitted, so you will need us with you."

Trem shook his head. "You do not have the weapons necessary to fight them. It would be a slaughter."

"Be that as it may, you are not going by yourself."

Jovan nodded emphatically, and Trem threw up his hands. "Fine, might as well die together rather than alone."

Diaga appeared suddenly, standing beside the wagon carrying Jovan and Trem. Keeping pace on foot easily he spoke quietly. "Trem, I am afraid I need you for a moment. Joseph is awake, but I do not think he will live much longer."

Trem looked at Diaga in shock then jumped down from the cart with surprising spryness. "Where is he?"

Without answering, Diaga began walking to the front of the caravan shadowed by Neep. Jovan eased himself down from the cart gingerly and Trem paused to assist him. Leaning on Trem, Jovanaleth hobbled along with him. Logan rode forward to find Ghost and the others and learn how far they were from the entrance to the passage. Trem kept his eyes ahead on the ragged robes of Diaga. The rain was slowing somewhat, but it was rapidly darkening about them. He hadn't much time, but he needed to see Joseph. If he indeed was dying, then Trem had little time to say things he should have said long ago.

Diaga hopped onto the end of one of the carts. Khaliandra was there with two children. The mage spoke softly to her and they shifted down to one end of the cart, as Neep climbed swiftly and silently up after the wizard and stationed herself on guard. Trem boosted Jovan into the wagon then hauled himself up. He almost missed Joseph entirely. He was lying at the end of the cart they had climbed onto, his head resting on some burlap sacks near Trem's soft deerskin boots. The old man looked terribly thin and small lying before him, and Trem choked back tears seeing the blood soaked blanket covering what was surely a broken body. Diaga leaned in and whispered, "I am sorry, Trem, but his wounds went far beyond my or Khaliandra's skill to heal. It simply is not my area of expertise, but I think we have made him comfortable."

Trem patted the youth's shoulder and managed a sad smile. "You did your best, I am sure, Diaga. Is he awake?"

"I'm awake, lad," Joseph gasped, or so it seemed. His voice had a terrible wheezing sound too it. "You came back, saved my home you did."

Trem knelt beside the old man and gently rolled his head to one side so he could look into his eyes. "I saved no one, Joseph, I left you behind. I am sorry."

Joseph smiled. "You remembered my name. I was afraid you had forgotten it. But then, I suppose you have forgotten very little about me."

Trem didn't answer. He simply swallowed with difficulty and nodded. Joseph took a shuddering breath and continued, "What happened so long ago, it was not your fault. You tried to help... do not... do not let failures of the past deter you from hope for the future. Do not give in to fear and doubt.

"You," Joseph lifted his head slightly with a last great effort, "you can do much for this world. I do not understand what you are or how you have remained the same for so long a time, but I have seen good in you. Do not abandon those in need. Use your strength to help them. I know I am dying. I have accepted this, and I hope that what I have done in my later years may absolve me from any sins of the past. I have done evil, Trem, evil through indifference to the suffering of others. Do not fall into the same trap I once did."

Trem wiped his eyes. "You stood by Jovanaleth when I would not. You saved his life many times this day. Consider your conscience clear."

Joseph seemed at ease then. "I am leaving soon, Trem. Please sit with me a while. I should like to stare at your eyes while I go. It seems I can see where I am going already."

Trem sat with Joseph, holding his hand until it was stiff and cold. Slowly, he reached out his free arm and closed the dead man's eyes, which still looked unseeingly into his own. It had not been long; Joseph had passed quickly and quietly. Trem kissed his forehead gently. "At least one of us has found peace."

Looking up, he saw Diaga watching him. The mage came over slowly and covered Joseph's face with the blanket. He said nothing, but sat quietly next to Trem and watched the stiff bundle for a while. Trem sat with his head in his hands, trying to cope with the pain and finding it far more overpowering than he would have expected. Diaga looked up when he felt a tug at his sleeve. Looking down, he saw Samuel, holding Coal, staring at him. "Is he dead?"

Diaga felt his heart sink to his knees. "Yes, Samuel, I am afraid he is."

Samuel looked at the blanket and nodded. "He was a nice man. He used to cook stew for me and Coal."

Trem looked up from his hands at this brown haired boy and smiled with real affection. "You are right child. He was a very nice man."

Diaga picked up Samuel and set him on his knee. "Trem, this is Samuel Jovian. Samuel, meet my friend Trem."

The boy said quietly, "Hello, mister Trem."

Trem laughed heartily at the boy's formality. "Hello, Samuel. You are a lovely child, do you know that?"

Both Diaga and Trem laughed when the boy nodded emphatically. Trem continued to talk to the youth a while and then noticed another boy next to him, watching the three talk. "And who is this?"

Diaga looked down and smiled. "Ah, this is Nawendel. He is a friend of Samuel's."

Trem nodded and waved. Nawendel did not respond, he simply looked at Trem with overly big brown eyes. The boy was about Samuel's age in size, but his stare seemed much older to Trem. He had shockingly dark black hair that hung to the middle of his back. His body was slim and his bones seemed more pronounced than usual for such a young boy. Then Trem caught sight of his ear tips protruding through the nest of his black hair, and said softly to Diaga, "He's elven."

Diaga nodded, he set Samuel down and the two boys moved back to the other end of the wagon where Khaliandra held both of them, talking quietly. "Yes. He was found in the woods by one of the men from the town. They do not know where he is from. All he has ever told them is his name."

Trem looked quizzically at Diaga. "And this priestess of Endoth, who is she?"

Diaga flushed despite himself as he stammered, "Oh, just a kind soul who took up her calling in Delmore. She adopted the both of them. Samuel's parents were killed during the earlier Broken attacks."

Trem pressed on mischievously. "Does she have a name? What else did you learn about her?"

Diaga caught his look and shifted uncomfortably. "Her name is Khaliandra. I spoke to her a bit... she's about my age." His mouth opened and shut, but he could not seem to find further purpose to his speech.

Trem laughed and patted the mage on the back. "Well, I wouldn't worry. The boys seem to like you. I am sure you will see more of her after today."

"Yes, if we make it through the day."

"I will think of something."

Diaga looked at him surprised. "You tell us these spectral, possibly undead or otherwise immortal, beings are following us because you saw it in a dream, and then point out we haven't the necessary skills to deal with them, and against those odds your solution is that you are going to think of something?"

Trem shrugged.

"Well I am glad you are suddenly so confident!"

"It is not that I am confident," Trem grew deathly serious again. "Joseph gave his life for that town. So did many other men I never even got to know, and he asked me to save them for him. Those children, the women, the others who survived, I am not going to let something happen to them. Joseph has already paid a high enough price."

Diaga nodded in support, "Nevertheless, we are in a precarious position."

"I've been in worse."

Jovan hobbled to their end of the wagon, glancing briefly at the body of Joseph under the blanket. He murmured, "It is getting dark. Where are the others?"

As he spoke, Grimtooth, Logan, Rath, and Ghost rode up to the wagon. They were all checking their weapons and shifting in their saddles as though itching for something to happen. Trem noticed Rath toying with what looked like a vicious crossbow that matched the black color of his robes and hood. He glanced at Logan, who said, "Gend has reached the entrance to the Passage of Cronakarl and says it will be open momentarily. He will lead the people inside along with their carts and animals. Apparently it is quite wide at the entrance and most of the way through, since it was once intended to be a trade road through the Sunteeth Mountains. Still, it is going to take almost an hour to get them all beyond the doorway, and we may be dealing with those shades by then."

Ghost snorted, "This is ridiculous. Why would they be here?"

Jovan shot him a look. "I thought you said they would be following you everywhere?"

Ghost did not have an answer and so remained silent. Logan cleared his throat before saying, "Given the situation, we do not stand much of a chance. We cannot harm them with simple steel, and only Trem possesses a blade capable of injuring them. However, it seems Rath may have an alternative."

They all turned in surprise to the dark cloaked man sitting silently in the shadows of his black cloth. Rath glanced at his audience and then removed a vial from the folds of his robe. It glowed with a strange aura as he held it up. "These beings, I know of their kind. You call them shades, and that is true, but your understanding of their nature is incomplete. This will allow us to fend off the creatures."

Diaga leaned forward. "What is it?"

Rath eyed him distrustfully. "A treasure from my homeland. It is not for outsiders."

"Where is your home, Rath?" Trem said with piercing calm.

The robed man caught his look and held it steadily but did not respond. Again Logan broke the awkward silence by clearing his throat. "It is, unfortunate though it might be, our only chance. There is no way we can kill these things, so we have to trust Rath's artifact will drive them off long enough for us to escape"

"I have to be close to them," Rath said softly, "you will need to distract them for a short time."

"The only way we can buy enough time is if we engage them." Logan made the pronouncement with reserved finality. "Some of us are wounded, if you do not think you have the strength to fight and run then you should help get the people inside the caves."

Jovan stood up straighter. "I am staying with you."

Diaga leaned on his staff and nodded emphatically. "As am I."

Logan nodded at both of them. "Then let us move north. No horses, we are going to catch them off guard."

Trem spoke up, rubbing his chin thoughtfully, "I think I may have a plan."

The others leaned in to listen.

Chapter 25

Valissa Ulfrunn stood atop the hill overlooking Delmore with cold eyes, her expressionless gaze taking in the scene below. Some distance from her, Frothgar Konunn stood as well. He was afraid to come closer, as he knew Valissa's stony, unmoving form hid her wrath, which was terrible. The attack had been a miserable failure. They had lost Goranath's ballista, more than a score of gnolls, and the casualties among the Broken regulars continued to mount, now reaching over three hundred men dead and as many again wounded. By the end of the day, Valissa expected to hear even more were dead from slow-killing injuries or infection. No matter how many survived, the fight for such a meager victory had cost a significant number of her forces, even if she had another ten thousand at her disposal. The loss of so many gnolls particularly irked her. She had intended to recruit more as she went south and east, hoping to reach numbers of over twenty thousand men and five hundred gnolls. After their setback here she would be lucky to convince the ones they had to stay.

Goranath was still down in the village somewhere, no doubt plundering the entire thing himself. She had seen the great gnoll chieftain, Gren, coming back from the main gate, his body pierced by several heavy arrows. She had demanded to know what had happened, having seen the explosion to the west, but the gnoll snarled at her and moved on without comment. Normally Valissa would have been infuriated with such insubordination, but the beast was clearly not going to stop for anyone and she did not need to infuriate him further.

A great cloud of smoke, black and hot, was rolling up and out of Delmore as the town burned. Valissa continued to watch with her arms crossed, waiting for Goranath to drag himself out of the chaos as her rage burned as hot as the flames. In normal circumstances she would have tried seduction on the hot-blooded Broken leader, but now her anger was so great that she was seriously considering gutting him before he got a word in. Valissa had made her way through life on her sharp mind, skill with a sword, and incredible beauty. This had required a unique mix of discipline and temptation to gather every scrap of recognition and authority she rightly deserved. Never before had she had the opportunity to command such a mighty army as this one and she was determined not to fail now. However, she had also never envisioned reigning over such a violent and honorless group of marauders. She had watched the public execution of

Goranath's rivals at Delmore's northern gate and understood what he was doing, but in his selfish, cutthroat desire to consolidate his power she believed he had sacrificed planning and reason in his approach to taking the town. Thus, many had been killed by the unexpected defenders within, who had been given time to organize a real defense and cost many more lives in Valissa's great army. That was why she wanted to kill Goranath, because his petty motivations as a Broken chieftain were subverting the greater goals of this campaign.

As Valissa stood impatiently awaiting the Broken leader, she felt a sudden chill come upon her and spun around with her hand on her swordhilt. Instantly, she recognized the form near her and her grip on the handle tightened in fear. She tried not to cower before the presence of the shade, the commander of Daerveron's elite unit of Night Cloaks. The hooded form came nearer to her and she resisted the urge to step back. Slowly, the monstrosity reached up and pulled back its heavy black hood to reveal a white face with black pools for eyes and strange, barely visible scars in symmetrical patterns on the perfectly bleached skin. Valissa could see the emptiness in those eyes, so she tried to focus her own elsewhere. The bald head, also replete with elaborately woven scars, tilted as the thing regarded her briefly. The creature looked skyward, then back at the Swordmistress. "We must leave soon. The one my master seeks is fleeing."

Valissa shrugged as nonchalantly as she could manage. "Then go, I do not need you here."

When it spoke, the thing's mouth opened to reveal a black, endless void, just like the eyes. "Yes, but you must follow us swiftly. Cut off their escape to the west if they evade us."

Valissa agreed. "I will move as soon as I am able."

The shade stared at her a moment or two longer then it replaced its hood, spun, and seemed to disappear and reappear in fits and starts, getting further away from Valissa until it was simply gone. Seconds later, she felt an icy wind rush by as the Night Cloaks swept silently past her on their dread mounts, down into Delmore. Shuddering, she glanced up to try to follow their progress and saw a haggard Goranath stumbling up the hill to her, leaning heavily on a great branch to support himself. Valissa tried to assume her intimidating stance once again and failed. The Broken warlord looked horrid, his body was covered in bandages across on his left side, and she could see innumerable cuts on his face and hands. Reaching her, he saluted as best he could, which was quite poorly, and then collapsed into a sitting position beside her. "Those damned fiends nearly ran me over."

Valissa looked down at him. "They are pursuing the strangers who led the defenders."

Goranath adjusted his sitting position and grimaced. "I hope they have better luck than we did."

The Swordmistress felt her anger rise again and she kicked the sitting commander. "What happened down there? How incompetent are your men?"

Goranath leaped up, much faster than Valissa would have bet he was capable of in his battered condition, and held his curved dagger to her chest. "We got attacked by an orc, a knight, and a mage. Would you like to explain what you sent me into?"

Valissa sniffed disdainfully at the dagger and pushed it away. "I told you they would be there."

"You never said they were trained combatants," Goranath snarled.

"I knew nothing of them. Your scout was responsible for finding out who was in Delmore."

"Well your ghastly friend did! That thing is looking for someone particular remember? I would wager it is one of them. The knight was a true Angladaic and I would swear the orc had an Angladaic tattoo!"

Valissa snapped at the Broken leader, "Excuses! I sent you to take the town, and you used the opportunity to execute potential rivals to your leadership. If you had been more cautious in planning your attack, or more urgent in reaching Delmore in the first place, this likely would have been far less costly a battle."

"Nevertheless," Goranath grunted, pointedly ignoring her observation and sitting once again, "they were there. The mage blew up their defenses as we were scaling them and nearly burnt me alive. The orc ruined my ballista, too! We are going to need to rest a few days before we can move on."

Valissa shook her head. "We have to move west and cut off the road to Gi'lakil, so that if the Night Cloaks miss whoever they are hunting they will not escape them by moving inland."

"My men are in no shape to go anywhere."

"Then move the ones who are, you have plenty of soldiers, just cut off the damned road!"

Goranath grimaced and stood. "Very well, but only because I do not think it would be in my best interests to cross those Night Cloaks. As we move west I will try to replenish our numbers, but we need to make a decisive strike somewhere soon, my men tire of the petty spoils from villages."

Valissa paused to consider this, but before she could speak Frothgar, who had been listening silently off to the side, walked up and said softly, "We could bypass the Dust Plains and strike the Fortress of Aves sooner. Our approach has been too methodical and the Eagle Knights will not expect us to ignore Gi'lakil and move against them so quickly. We will catch them unawares and more susceptible to our strike."

Valissa looked at Frothgar with renewed respect. "That is actually a rather intelligent plan Frothgar. I cannot believe it came out of your mouth."

Goranath nodded in agreement. "Attacking the fortress would give us the incentive my men need and likely draw us more soldiers as well. But we need to resupply, and Gi'lakil will be ripe with food stores."

"Then we take a tribute from them to leave the town be," Frothgar replied.

"The sooner we destroy Aves, the sooner the whole region falls. We've burnt enough of this wretched land." Valissa turned to Goranath again. "How many soldiers can you get for me by the time we reach the fortress?"

"Perhaps another six thousand men and double our number of gnolls, if we are lucky. That would give us enough to storm the walls, though we will need siege engines to make quicker work of it. I believe the gnolls can break the gate down once we wear out the defenders on the battlements, although I have never seen the fortress myself."

Frothgar tapped his bow confidently. "With my archers covering them we should be able to the get the gnolls to the gate unmolested."

"A few ballistae and other siege weapons would also make shorter work of the matter," Goranath rubbed his chin in thought. "Perhaps we can put the people of Gi'lakil to work constructing those as well?"

"We will sort out the details when we reach the town." Valissa waved her hand to indicate the discussion was over. "It is settled, we march to the Fortress of Aves with all speed. No more raids unless absolutely necessary. That should give us the decisive victory Wolfbane is looking for. When it is finished we will come back and occupy the towns and settlements we left behind."

Their impromptu meeting concluded, the three split off to their respective tents to rest. Within the town, the Broken army set fire to the homes and trees, burning everything that could be put to the torch. They let their dead rot where they fell as they ran through the roads demolishing everything before them in a terrible orgy of violence. Fights broke out among the pillagers, some ending in death. Yet even as they tore down the remnants of the town, they heard through rumor that bigger targets and greater spoils were coming soon. In the dark of the night and flickering flames of Delmore's destruction the tide of murder built to a boil in anticipation of the coming of an even vaster slaughter.

Lena Engrove had never envisioned herself as anything even remotely resembling a heroine, nor had she ever truly planned to engage in any activity one might mistake for an adventure, but she had always been a bold and brave woman. Perhaps it should come as no surprise that it was her family home that sheltered the king in exile. Lena had always been a bit of an outsider. She had cared for both her parents for many years before they passed away, managing the bakery while also maintaining the living quarters attached to it. Lena was only sixteen when both her father and mother died. Though Angladais was home to far less criminal activity than many nations, there was always the threat of a hostile takeover through aggressive would-be land barons or opportunistic merchants. Lena had fended them all off and refused the hands of a great many men whose families had hoped to wed to her and, through marriage, obtain her estate and business. She dismissed most of her suitors outright, entertained the few that interested her, and made it clear that she and she alone would be remaining in control of the bakery and its spacious living quarters.

Her encounter with Logan had been by chance, in his and her mind perhaps more the hand of fate, and that he had treated her as a person with whom he could argue, laugh, and wonder at the world was what set Logan apart. He had tried to hide and, when hiding soon failed, dismiss his noble heritage as immaterial when around her. Lena had chastised him for this foolishness, as she saw his denial of who he was to be wasteful. She had been able, from the first, to discern Logan's character and impressed upon him the importance of honesty: honesty with her, but moreover with himself. It had opened up a new world to him and been the root of their love, which had led to their separation upon Vorasho's discovery of the scandal. However, that had not prevented the birth of Lena and Logan's son, who she had in absence of her beloved named after his father. In motherhood, Lena had expected she might change or soften from her brash and outspoken ways, but it had only made her more sure of her convictions even as she prayed for Logan's safe return to meet the child he did not know existed.

For his part, this particular morning was, by far, the most exciting breakfast in young Logan Engrove's life. Not only had he learned that he could finally talk about his father openly, but it turned out his father was not just any knight, he was a prince! Moreover, that made the younger Logan something like a prince himself, or so he thought. He was still youthful enough to not truly understand how these things worked. He did know that now, most importantly, he was sitting at his mother's table with the heroes of his homeland. Giddy with excitement, the young boy was seated between Highlords Calavar and Irindein, kicking his heels against the bench and looking wide-eyed back and forth between the two of them. He liked Calavar the best. The Highlord was noisy, and therefore very amusing.

Calavar had nephews, grandnephews to be frank, but none of his own children. He was a little uncomfortable with this youth, who he had just learned was the grandson of his good friend and king Arvadis. Still, the boy amused him almost as much as he entertained the boy. The two were already well on the way to becoming fast friends. Irindein sat quietly on the right of the child, sipping his tea and thinking away. Despite being the youngest of the present High-lords, he knew it was his responsibility to come up with the plan and account for every possible impediment to their success. Even when he was a young man still deep in scholarly studies, the king had asked his opinion on everything. Irindein had a habit of reasoning things out completely and such a skill was being put to the test on a grand scale now.

Arvadis was at the head of the table, flanked by Vorasho and Lena. The matron of the house had her most important patient, Renon Ordlan, nearest to her, but spent more time chiding Calavar about restraining his temper lest he reopen his stitches in his face. The Highlord, who could strike fear in the proudest and most sea-soned of paladins, was perfectly contrite before the young woman. Women were not Calavar's strong suit, and frankly he was petrified of them. Renon, by contrast, was far more at ease and appeared to be feeling much better. He was now eating in great amounts and able to move about slowly on his own. All had agreed that the rescue was a rousing success, but their celebration had begun to recede as they considered the challenge of retaking of the throne.

"We ought to just storm the damned city and take that Vendile snake out by his forked tongue!"

Lena shot Calavar a warning glance as she chided him, "Mind your own tongue in my house, Highlord. My child is not to be ex-posed to such language."

Runiden was immediately apologetic. "Forgive me, my lady. Heat of the moment, you understand."

Irindein cleared his throat and said calmly, "Perhaps we ought to consider a course of action that does not involve assets we are lacking, like an army to storm the city."

Vorasho shrugged. "We have some house guards, and Renon may know others sympathetic to our cause."

The young knight, looking far better than he had when they'd arrived at Lena's home, shook his head in response. "For better or worse, my lord, a soldier is trained to follow orders. I disobeyed out of a devotion to my king. Most of my peers will continue to fight for Bwemor even if it goes against their beliefs. It is the way of the mili-tary."

Calavar nodded his grudging agreement with Renon's assess-ment. Arvadis sipped his tea and posed a question, "Perhaps we ought to consider entering the city by devious means once again?"

Graham, returning from behind the counter with some rolls for him and Derek grunted, "Sneaking around isn't much my style, m'lord. I would prefer a straight on fight."

"Even if we could get back in, where do we go if we are to go unseen? We are not exactly faces that can easily hide."

Arvadis nodded. "What my son says is truest of all. A king is hard enough to keep a secret, never mind two Highlords and a prince."

The boy spoke up, trying hard to get involved, "But Grandpa, if you are the real king can't you just parade into your palace like in the stories?"

Lena shushed him, "Logan, do not interrupt."

"No wait!" Irindein set his tea down suddenly and sat up, steepling his fingers as the idea crystallized in his mind. "He's right!"

All eyes turned to the young Highlord, and Arvadis said ruefully, "Really, Fremont, I would not expect you to fall into the romance of this whole thing. This is a serious business, staging a coup."

Irindein waved him silent. "First, it is not a coup if you are still the rightful king and second, the boy is right. Has not the word been spread throughout the kingdom of your death, Arvadis?"

Vorasho sat up and placed his palms on the table in disbelief. "You want us just to march into Alderlast and into the palace like we never left?"

"That is precisely what I want us to do."

They all sat in silence as they contemplated the words of the Highlord. Renon shook his head. "I am sorry, my lord, but I fail to see how getting ourselves captured in such a grandiose way will avail."

Irindein laughed. "We are not going to be captured. Look, the only difficulty will be getting through the gates, as they will have guards. Once we are in the city, we will be fine."

Vorasho's eyes widened as the plan dawned on him. "By Paladinis's sword, it could work!"

Arvadis looked at his son. "Please, someone explain to me how?"

Vorasho smiled at his father. "You said it yourself once, the people love you, they still do, and they assuredly do not love Vendile. They will flock to you! They will escort us to the very steps of the palace!"

"More so because they believe you to be dead, and your return will seem a miracle to many and disprove Vendile's lies that he is no doubt spreading as the reason for your demise. Once we reach the palace, you can reveal the dark machinations of Vendile and win back the kingdom," Irindein said decisively. "With the people behind us he will not stand a chance."

The king sat silently, considering the proposition, but in the end it was not he who made the decision. Graham snorted loudly, so loudly he brought the attention of the entire table upon himself. Recovering, he muttered, "Well, it is a daft plan, that much is certain, which is probably why it will work. Walk into the heart of enemy territory and hope we can rally a city behind us. I'm all for it."

Derek concurred with his elder, as did the rest of the table. Arvadis sat still a moment longer, and then he too gave his assent.

"Lena, please see if I can buy some horses off the good people of your village. We have a throne to recover."

Deep night had settled in the blink of an eye. A great horned owl sat in the branches of her tree, stretching luxurious wings as she prepared for a long evening of hunting. In the swiftly gathered darkness the hunter was queen, gazing out into the deep black, searching for prey. Suddenly, an unsettling calm came over the woods and the hunter froze. A black wind swept past the owl's roost and the creature that normally owned the night crept back into the hollow safety of her tree. Fear had more than wings this night, and there would be no hunting.

South from where the owl was cowering, a lone figure strolled down the road like he was in the midst of a fine summer day. Trem whistled an old tune, the name of which he had forgotten, and tapped his sword blade against his shoulder to the rhythm. For all his relaxed posturing, his eyes roved the black before him in earnest. For the others this darkness would have been impenetrable, but for him it was not so bleak. He could make out the moving creatures about him darting from tree to tree and cutting before him across the road. Trem ambled along carelessly, feeling unburdened as a dangerous relaxation had settled over him.

He heard the hooves, but they were so quiet he knew he had not been intended too. Nevertheless, Trem's senses were unspeakably strong and he stopped, knowing instinctively that these were the ones he sought. Raising his hand he made a sharp gesture to his right and left, praying the others could see him in the dark and would move as quietly as they could to the cover of the trees along the road. Trem continued to whistle and tap his sword as he stood in the center of the cart tracks, impatiently waiting for things to begin. The night about him was utterly silent and the dark clouds blotted out stars and moon. Trem stood straining his eyes before him, waiting for some glimpse of his enemy.

The riders slowed having heard him as well. They crept up painstakingly, materializing slowly and eerily from the gloom, but soon it was plain that he had already spotted them long ago and was unafraid. There were a great number of them, far more than Trem had anticipated. Their black shrouds hung about their eerie shifting limbs and the emaciated horses shook silent manes of wilting hair. Trem tried to pierce the folds of their cloaks with his eyes to see if they wore any armor, but he could not tell. A lack of armor would have been a nice, if likely irrelevant, advantage. He had thought he might slice through a few of them with less trouble, though it would not be his blade that did the damage. The leader moved his undead horse closer to the half-elf and turned so he could look down on him from the saddle, then to Trem's surprise it dismounted. In swift succession the rest followed suit. Trem made a rough count as they did so, and realized to his dismay there were twelve of the cloaked beings this time.

The lead shade paused a moment, then reached upward and removed its hood. Trem took in the white skin, shining in the faint moonlight and highlighted with many rasied scars in odd, symmetrical patterns. The others kept their faces hidden, but Trem found one was unnerving enough. Its eyes were bottomless black pools that seemed to bore through him. Determined to not show his fear, Trem spoke first, "Are you afraid I am going to injure your mount?"

The undead figure did not move but waited, then said slowly, methodically, "You have come alone. This is supposed to be noble? You wish to spare your friends?"

"You are just barely enough sport for me, I did not want them in the way."

The thing's mouth opened slightly, revealing another empty black hole, and an echoing laughter issued forth. "You may have the sword of el Vac, but we are many. You will die. Stand aside and be spared. You are not the one we seek."

"I have a different idea. You turn around, and I will let the rest of your filthy band go with you, heads and limbs still attached."

The figure shifted and Trem saw it draw its blade. "Enough! You bore me, die."

Trem lunged forward first, howling, *"El dath du hakin!"*

As he sprang towards them, the woods about the shades seemed to explode. From all around, the adventurers struck. Jovan came first, gamely hurtling at two of the creatures, his mighty swing hewing the gauntlet from one and taking the hand with it, though fortuitously sparing his blade. The blow exposed the stark white appendage that fell freely to the ground before melting away and quickly reforming. The second creature deflected Jovan's second attack and the battle was joined. Neep came streaking out of the trees to assail the shades closest to Trem, dagger in one paw and her sword clutched in the other. Logan and Grimtooth took one apiece from the back of their party, driving them into the rest. Ghost, recalling the damage striking one had caused his last sword, hurled a knife as he rushed forward and parried two swift strikes from a pair of shades. Rath held back, firing a bolt into the crowd that disarmed one of the creatures.

As they had in Gi'lakil, the shades moved most unnaturally. They seemed to teleport in short spurts from one place to the next, their forms so incorporeal and difficult to track that they were able to flank and put off-balance the ambushers fairly swiftly. They seemed also to move in concert with one another, appearing and reappearing in coordinated efforts to confuse their foes. The battle was even for the moment, but at every shift it seemed the fell beings would gain the upper hand.

Then from deep in the woods, the companions could hear chanting and suddenly a red-hot beam of energy shot out and burned through two of the cloaked devils. There was a deafening shriek and then the folds of the robes collapsed onto the ground. The destruction of the shades only seemed to strengthen their fellows as they redoubled their efforts against the ambush. Jovan was finding himself hard pressed against the onslaught of the two shades that had singled him out. His injured leg was on the verge of giving way and only his will was keeping it underneath him. Logan saw the young prince's plight and shouted to Grimtooth, "Help him!"

The orc was engaged with his own foe, but in his desperation to assist Jovan he launched himself into the shade assailing him and breezed past it. A long slash opened up across his arm as he passed, but he did not notice. Grimtooth arrived in time to distract one of the shades attacking Jovanaleth. Ghost appeared, as if out of nowhere, beside the young man and together they beat off his attacker just in time to turn and face the two still pursuing the Napalian. Trem was surrounded, swinging away at four of the monsters at once. His burning blade kept them at a distance, but with so many they were soon to overcome him. Neep arrived in time to provide a distraction, spinning away from her own foe to attack the rear of those flitting and moving about Trem, but soon the two were forced to retreat as the shadowy, nimble creatures honed in on the sound of Diaga's chanting and sought to kill the mage.

Trem shouted above the clash of blades, "Rally! Rally! Put the road to our backs, together now!"

Ghost hefted most of Jovanaleth's weight onto his shoulder and the two made a hopping dash to the half-elf. Logan, cut off from the rest, put his head down and rushed forward, his armor deflecting most of the blows, but when he reached the others he was cut in several places. The foul blades of the shades burned the skin about the wounds they inflicted and Grimtooth and Logan were placed behind the others while they tried to halt the spread of the damage. Diaga stepped forward to join the rest, his simple metal staff glowing spectacularly now as he held it towards their black-clad enemies. The beam of light pushed back the shades a moment, but they gathered to strike again. Trem braced himself when Jovan gasped, "Where is Rath?"

The same thought was in Trem's mind when the shades closed suddenly, but just before they reached the beleaguered defenders, the assassin appeared before them holding his strange vial aloft. The advance halted sharply and the monsters shrieked in dismay as Rath cast the vessel to the ground. The noise was deafening, and the light that exploded forth was blinding. The companions were thrown back several steps but kept their feet. The shades, on the other hand, seemed to expand and then rapidly dissolve. They could be heard howling in rage, but their now-vaporous forms were gone, streaking outward into the night, and then nothing remained.

Rath was hunched over his crossbow where he had been standing, his black cloak and robes smoking. Slowly, the dark figure stood and turned, stumbling, back towards the others. Logan stepped forward to aid him, but the assassin curtly pushed him away. "Leave me knight. It will pass."

Trem stepped forward then. "You could have warned us it was going to do that."

Rath's eyes leapt up to meet his and the assassin's voice was cold, "I told you what you needed to know, nothing more or less."

Trem didn't attempt to stop the strange man as he roughly shoved past him, but instead regarded Logan and Grimtooth. "Can you make it to the caves?"

Grimtooth shrugged nonchalantly. "Ah've 'ad far worse."

Logan simply nodded. Ghost was helping Jovan back and, much to the youth's surprise scolding him sternly like an annoyed father, "The next time you are too hurt to fight, stay out of the way! You are going to get yourself killed sometime when I am not there to save you."

Jovanaleth glanced at the Napalian. "So why bother saving me at all?"

The older man snorted loudly, "You're not half bad with a sword boy, do not flatter yourself by thinking I care." And to emphasize his point, Ghost released the prince and moved towards his massive horse. Jovan caught himself and watched him a moment before hobbling forward to his own smaller gelding.

Trem brought up the rear, practically carrying Diaga. The young mage's eyes were rolling in odd directions though he was still coherent. "I think I may have pushed my limits a bit today."

"You should be alright. We can strap you to the horse. Neep will lead it where we are going."

"I do not want to slow us down."

"It doesn't matter, the danger is gone for now."

Rath materialized from the darkness before them. "No, half-elf, the creatures are simply separated from our plane for a time. They will return and we should be going, now."

Trem paused to lock eyes with the assassin, attempting to assess how much of a threat there was in his words, then he helped Diaga into his saddle and the party began the ride south.

Edge awoke slowly. He could feel a strange numbness in his body, a sort of dead warmth. Opening his eyes, he was surprised to see only brightness, but nothing else. Then Edge realized the whiteness was snow and that he was buried in it. Moving slightly brought his head out from under the soft blanket, and he could see the fire had gone out and both Romund and Raymir were asleep in strange mounds like his own. The fire had not been dead long, as it was still sending small tendrils of smoke skyward. Edge glanced toward what he thought was Romund and saw the older man was sleeping upright, apparently, or otherwise had been completely still for several hours. As swiftly as he dared, Edge heaved himself upwards. The snow had kept him warm by holding in his body heat, but at the same time it had dampened his clothes. They would need more kindling.

Testing his leg in the snow, Edge began a painstaking march away from their camp to roughly where he though Romund had found wood earlier. Not far from the encampment he looked back and realized he could not see it in the gentle snowfall. In a slight panic he glanced down and was relieved to see he could still follow his footprints back, but not for long. He increased his pace as much he dared. Moving further forward, he nearly toppled over the edge of the cliff. Glancing down, he froze as stiff as the cold wind about him. Climbing the cliff wall like some kind of strange spider was a robed figure. It was far enough away that Edge could not be certain, but he had no doubt it was Saltilian. How that frail wizard had managed to get this far, the lost elf had no idea, but he was moving at a frightening pace. Edge forgot all about wood and spun round, willing himself to run back.

Edge shook Romund hard, knocking all the snow from him. The older man was awake instantly with his sword drawn, but Edge put a finger to his lips and whispered, "On the cliff."

Romund did not ask questions. He tossed some snow over the ashes of the fire and put his back to Raymir and Edge, watching the sheer rock face below for signs of the mad mage. Edge roused Raymir and softly whispered the same warning to her. Raymir's eyes widened and she stiffened in his arms, but Edge held her tighter and she relaxed. Raymir spoke quietly, "What do we do?"

Edge helped her up. "We climb."

Iceblade became more punishing as the travelers got higher and higher up its massive form. Romund brought up the rear, backpedaling occasionally. He could not have slept more than a few hours, but he was alert and taut with energy and anticipation. Edge was in the lead, his leg seemingly healed as he forged ahead with a newfound strength borne of necessity. Raymir trailed him, looking around in search of easier paths to the top as they moved onward and pointing them out when she could. Romund thought he saw a shadow come over the edge of the ledge they had occupied earlier, but he said nothing. Edge had set a blistering pace and they were surely increasing the distance between themselves and the crazed wizard.

Edge paused momentarily as they reached the end of the steep path he had found. They had run out of easy options. Romund came up beside him and craned his neck upward. The cliff had few handholds and it was at least a hundred feet of vertical rock to the next outcrop they could stand on. Romund looked at Edge and then Raymir. He and Edge wordlessly weighed their options and the older man shrugged. Edge pulled out his halberd and gripped it from the end of the haft and took a massive swing, aiming for one of the gaps in the rock. The balancing spike struck the heavy stone but did not remain. The sound echoed off the mountain and Romund flinched at the sound, but Edge steadied and swung again. Again the sound reverberated off the cliffs, but this time the spiked metal opposite the halberd's axeblade stuck. Edge took a deep breath and grabbed Raymir about the waist. "Hold onto me."

The lost elf began to climb. He heaved his weight and Raymir's up the cliff almost by will alone. Somehow the haft of his weapon did not snap, nor did it come free of the rock. Beside them Romund had pulled his dagger and in a similar fashion to Edge, though far more slowly, was battling his way up the cliff using the dagger to find purchase where hand and footholds were not present. Raymir was stunned by the sheer power of Edge as he went hand over hand up the wooden haft, driving with his legs when he was able. When he reached the axehead he grasped a small handhold firmly, planted his feet, and pulled the weapon loose. Gripping it closer to the blade, he drove it into the rock again and continued to climb, driving the spike deep to form a handhold whenever he needed one.

It went on for what seemed to Raymir an eternity. Edge kept dangling by one hand, often without resting his feet on anything and again and again he slammed his weapon into the mountainside. Finally, they reached the outcrop and Edge set Raymir down. Turning, he lowered his polearm to Romund, who sheathed his sword and gripped it gratefully. Edge seemed to pull him up effortlessly. They paused a moment to catch their breath, then Edge glanced up to the next supportable part of the cliff and picked up his weapon. "Come on, we cannot rest yet."

Neither argued with him. The unstoppable lost elf started his climb once again, Raymir clinging gamely to his shoulders. He heaved himself up hand over hand with a deathly calm. Romund kept up as best he could, his pursuit futile but valiant. They reached the second resting point a little slower than before, once again waiting for Romund, but eventually they all were safely standing against the snow and stone. Edge insisted they rest longer than before so Romund could recover. The entire time, he kept peering over the lip of the edge to see if they were being followed, but there was no pursuit in sight. Romund tapped him on the shoulder after a few more minutes and they both looked up. The final point they could bivouac at was the farthest yet, nearly twice as long a climb as the others had been. Edge looked at him. "Can you make it?"

Romund snorted and began to haul himself up the cliff. Edge waited until he had a significant start, then he hefted Raymir one last time and readied to swing. Before he could strike, she kissed him hard on the cheek. He looked at her in surprise.

"For luck," she said.

Edge shook his head. "You should not distract me like that." Then he grinned.

The moment was short lived. The rock face was more jagged than the one before it, offering more opportunities to grasp at the stone with their hands and not need the aid of their weapons, but the climb was farther and the strain constant. Romund seemed driven to stay ahead of the other two, though he was not supporting Raymir as Edge was. About halfway to the top, Raymir sensed Edge weakening and released her hold on him, grabbing the rock face herself with one hand and setting her feet. Despite his protests, she clenched his cloak tightly in her free hand and heaved upward, trying to propel him further. It seemed to inspire a new burst of energy in the lost elf, which allowed him to surge past her before taking her on his shoulders once again. As they neared the top, he lobbed his weapon over the edge and scrambled upward.

They caught Romund, breathing hard, at the edge of the outcrop. Edge allowed Raymir to clamber over him and grabbed his friend, heaving him up after her. Edge then pulled himself up and collapsed next to the others. Romund was still short of breath, and Raymir felt tired just from the strain of holding on to Edge. The three lay there in the now clear-sky and looked out on the Frozen Reach and beyond, to the part of the Wastes sometimes called the Empty Lands. The great expanse of frozen ground stretched on forever beneath them, occasionally interrupted with jutting rocks. Edge found himself surprised and not a little proud they had crossed so much treacherous terrain in so short a time. Raymir rested her head on his shoulder and Romund, unable to stay awake, began snoring loudly to his left. The lost elf glanced to both sides and allowed himself a small smile.

Had he made it here alone, it would not have been as sweet. With Raymir and now Romund he felt he had preserved something of the faith in mortal kind Wolfbane once had. Algathor had demanded of him that he protect his granddaughter, and Edge knew he would do so. Once this Twisted Spire had been found and they had braved the dangers of its secrets, Edge would take Raymir somewhere south, perhaps into the lands called Dragon's Watch he had heard so much about. There they could live in peace and harmony for as long as they wanted.

The Sword

Of Romund, Edge was not so certain. He was a spy from a town in the former Napalian Empire still dedicated to the resurrection of that former nation. Romund would need to return home before he could think about ending his heroic travels. Looking at him, Edge reconsidered his own motivation. He owed Algathor his promise, but he owed Romund his life many times over. He would have to help him get home at the very least. The thought of all of this, so far ahead, made Edge rub the haft of his halberd thoughtfully. When he had first met Wolfbane, the great warrior had showed him his axe and told him, "You look at this, Edge. This is a weapon, but before it ever struck a man it was made to cut wood to keep him warm. The weapon is not responsible for the death it causes, the wielder is. Eventually, we all want to put aside the killing weapon and pick up the useful tool."

Edge looked his own deadly instrument up and down. Today had been the most useful it had ever proven to him. Today it had saved the lives of those he cared about without taking the life of someone he did not know. Deep inside, Edge dreamed of a day when he would never need to harm another mortal for any reason. As sharply as that thought came so did another of Wolfbane's early teachings: "If you take this weapon, you sign your fate. To live a life in which you will kill, and will always kill more than you will work to preserve the living. Become a warrior, Edgewulf, and you will embrace what it means to be one. You will never be able to let go of the weapon all your life if you take it now."

Edge had considered what his master had said, then without hesitation had reached out and plucked the halberd from his hand. In his memory, he could vividly see Wolfbane's expression as he did so. His long black hair and neatly trimmed beard seemed to contort into an expression of sudden sadness, as though he had wanted Edge to refuse the fate he had consigned himself to. Then he placed a hand on the young student's shoulder and whispered, "Learn this thing well, Edgewulf el Vac, it is the only companion you will ever have for all of your days."

Atop the high cliffs of Iceblade, Edge began to rethink what Wolfbane had said. He was not alone now, and the halberd was not his only companion. He had friends and he had love, and he had fought and bled for them as they had for him. This was not the same fate Wolfbane had accepted. Edge would not allow his warrior side to overtake his entire soul. He would be a companion first, and a combatant second. In that moment, he chose to honor his new vision for his life by pulling Raymir a little bit closer.

Chapter 26

Vendile sat bent upon his new menacing throne in the Palace of Alderlast, holding his crownless head up with one bejeweled hand. Freyan stood before him as he awaited his lord's reaction to the latest news surrounding Arvadis's escape. Freyan had personally investigated the evasion of Vendile's guards and happened upon the truth of the matter. Beyond the betrayal of Renon, which Bwemor continued to insist could not have possibly have been true, their foes had managed to use secrets known only to them to escape the palace from the dungeons. Freyan, for his part, was little troubled by this, but Vendile had gone into a long period of furious, and possibly fearful, silence. The rumors that Vorasho Hawking had played a part in the escape had done nothing to absolve Bwemor's fault in all of this. In truth, the blame for Vendile's current predicament fell squarely on the shoulders of the Highlord, but Freyan was all too familiar with the reality that the messenger was often the one to receive the brunt of his new king's anger. Freyan twirled his fingers along his newly commissioned and unwanted purple robes, bracing himself for the unpredictable reaction.

Vendile picked his head up and glanced about his throne room as if in a daze. Then he stood and descended the dais on his soft velvet slippers, all the while rubbing his dark goatee thoughtfully. Freyan managed to avoid moving from his spot as he approached and the maniacal king began to pace before him. "So they escaped, all three, but not through my men?"

"Yes, my lord."

"But," Vendile murmured thoughtfully, "no one knows that they are out, they have not been seen, and they took a passage which you believe has not been used in over a thousand years?"

Freyan shifted. "We may expect, my lord, that they perished in the tunnel. The chamber it is rumored to lead to is perilous. At least according to the records I was able to access in the king's library."

"It is fortunate I have you around for such things, Freyan. Scholarly work is contrary to the role of the king, in my eyes. More important matters concern me of late." The king lifted his arm and slowly selected a chalice from the many gaudy vessels atop the table standing at the foot of his throne. Sipping carefully, he turned his eyes back on the former seer. "What should we do differently Freyan? My crowning by Hladic must be done, and swiftly, so as to cement my reign."

Freyan removed a small roll of paper from his sleeve. "This may aid you, my lord. By announcing the execution of Arvadis Angladais and the other Highlords for crimes against the state you may upset the populace, but you will put the nail in the coffin of any resistance that might arise. You will have justice on your side if they were dealt with for the reason of protecting the kingdom. Once our peace agreement with the invaders is announced, we will be responsible for stabilizing the nation of Angladais where your predecessor only cost the lives of her citizens. You will appear a true hero and none will see any reason to oppose you."

Vendile took another sip of his wine and smiled happily. "This plan, Freyan, is excellent. It will give me the power I desire and minimize the resistance. You can send in the incompetents now, we must find and eliminate Arvadis as fast as possible in order to complete this takeover. I cannot have him appearing suddenly at a later date and making me look like a fool."

Freyan bowed low. "As you wish, my lord. Take this. It outlines your speech, as you should read it this afternoon. I have already instructed Gelladan Bwemor to round up a sizeable crowd for your coronation ceremony, so that your support will appear strong and to encourage word to spread rapidly of Arvadis's execution among the people of Alderlast. Once enough of them know of his demise, it will not matter how many went of their own accord to your crowning, they will realize you are our rightful king." Freyan handed Vendile the slip of parchment from his robes and turned to leave.

The massive throne room doors swung open slowly as the guards heaved them apart. On the other side, Bwemor and Brusius Hladic were waiting in their ceremonial robes. Bwemor had a visible amount of sweat on his balding head and his already ruddy complexion seemed even worse than before as he walked nervously inside. Hladic appeared calm but wary as he approached Vendile. He would be there to crown him this afternoon, so any potential punishment of him would have to at least be delayed. At the time, however, both suspected Bwemor might have slipped up badly enough to not survive this latest error.

Vendile turned slowly toward them as they bowed low. Freyan gave a small bow to the would-be monarch from the doorway and swept out of the room in search of news from the ceremony. Bwemor shifted his crimson robes and adjusted his ruby hilted sword in an attempt to keep from making eye contact with Vendile. The king laughed loudly and sharply, causing the Highlord to jump. "Bwemor, do not fear, death would be too simple for you, and a messy beginning to a reign, particularly when I have already killed two Highlords and a king today."

The general looked confused but Hladic allowed himself a small smile as he caught wind of his king's plan. The obese priest leaned on his staff of white oak and chuckled as he tried to contain himself. "My lord, this is truly a brilliant solution."

"Of course it is, you ignorant fool. Stifle that despicable laugh of yours." Vendile sighed deeply. "I honestly do not know why I took you two in as my accomplices in this little coup. One of you let the former king get away from his guards after you sent a traitorous soldier to kill his son, and the other thinks my plan is clever, yet he has not offered up any of his own ideas to solve my problems."

The two Highlords remained silent as Vendile drained his glass and set it back down on the small end table with its bejeweled counterparts. He paused to dab at his mouth with a handkerchief then spun towards them, swirling his violet robes and eyeing them severely. "You have none to suggest still, I assume?"

Bwemor made as if to respond, but thought the better of it. Hladic cleared his throat awkwardly, but also said nothing. Vendile sighed and strode commandingly towards them, glaring darkly. "I should not have to rely solely on my own brilliance to overcome this problem. Hladic, while you may see the ease with which this solution solves our little quandary, brother Bwemor appears at a loss and I cannot debase myself by explaining, so you shall do it for me."

The sallow-faced priest turned towards his counterpart. "He is going to announce that Hawking was successfully executed, along with Irindein and Calavar, for treason and attempted escape from justice."

Bwemor furrowed his brow. "But they escaped. What if the people hear of that?"

Vendile placed a gloved hand on the Highlord's shoulder. "I have it on good authority that their escape route was impassable."

Bwemor was still skeptical as he fingered his signet ring, "But if they should emerge...."

"Silence!" Vendile delivered a brutal backhand to the puzzled Highlord's face. "They are deceased or as good as so by now! We will proceed with the coronation as planned. I trust you managed to fulfill the simple task you were assigned and gathered me a large crowd for the coronation?"

Bwemor wiped the blood from his mouth in a stunned silence. Even when Arvadis Hawking had disagreed vehemently with his profit-making war propositions, he had never struck his counterpart. Their disagreements had been volatile, but never violent, and Hawking had even seemed to treat Bwemor as an equal. His already slow brain now thoroughly fogged, Bwemor muttered his response, "Yes, your majesty. I had to pull away most of the guards to protect the ceremony. However, the main gates of the city are practically untended."

Vendile waved this away. "It matters not. There is no one coming from beyond my walls. I need the crowd controlled and quelled so that I can assume my reign without complaint or resistance."

Hladic stepped forward solemnly. "I have ordered the entire priesthood there to see you crowned, my lord. We will perform the largest High Chant seen in this kingdom since we began the crowning of kings. Your holy coronation will go down in history as the greatest ever."

Vendile nodded as he stroked his small beard. "Yes, and with Galden and Xarinth under house arrest, I can control the grain and the construction of the new Alderlast. Galden will begin by withholding much of his crop to drive up prices, enough to fund the grand rennovations I have planned for this city under Xarinth's master architects. But that will come in time. The first thing to do will be to appoint someone to Fremont Irindein's post who can record the executions as necessary actions undertaken to defend the sanctity of Angladais. Arvadis Hawking will go down in history as what he was, a handcuff on the rightful future of our kingdom. I will be this nation's savior."

Bwemor and Hladic were silent as Vendile stood there staring beyond them into a dark future only he could fathom. In the deepest recesses of their minds, they contemplated what might become of their home, but they would not allow those thoughts to creep to the surface where they might take vivid form and show the affronts to tradition and Angladaic values in all the horrible profanity they might express. The two shifted nervously, unwilling to depart until dismissed, but clearly uncomfortable at remaining before their fearful leader.

Vendile seemed to recover from his dread imaginings and his gaze fell down upon his co-conspirators. His blackened eyes, ringed in circles that told of many sleepless nights, took a moment to register their figures as the imaginings departed and the present rushed back to him. With a snarl and a shake of his head he cried, "Go! Prepare the people for my coming! This shall be the greatest moment of Angladaic history, at least until the dawn of the new realm under my bold guidance."

The two Highlords departed swiftly to carry out their respective duties. Vendile listened to the heavy doors slam behind them and paused to linger before his throne. That Angladais was his was difficult to process still, there seemed a piece somehow missing to his conquest and he could sense what it was. He wanted Arvadis's body before him. He wanted to spit on the face that had constrained his power for so long and laugh as he sat on the symbol of his victory with the prostrate form before him. And he could not, so the conquest of Angladais was incomplete and always would be. His rule was nothing without being able to see the destruction of his despised enemy. This kingdom was not entirely his so long as Arvadis lived on in the memory of the people.

"It will pass," Vendile whispered. "I shall destroy all memory and burn my own truth into the souls of all people. I will have dominion over hearts and minds. I will be lord over the greatest realm in all history."

The king sat heavily in his throne and rubbed at his temples, trying to push his thoughts through the strange fog that seemed to cloud them. He reached to his breast and grasped the pendant resting there in an attempt to steady himself with its comforting presence. Vendile struggled in his seat a moment longer, then he seemed to become aware of himself and rose. Straightening his robes, he turned and walked unsteadily out of the throne room to dress himself for the coronation.

At the gates of Alderlast, only a few guards, mostly young and newly raised to the responsibility of their appointment, were on duty. The majority had been pulled away for Vendile's ceremony and these few were considered too green and impressionable to understand the importance of containing the crowd at all costs. Most Angladaics did not agree with the coronation of Vendile, but the veterans knew what could happen if a succession was not carried out quickly and smoothly. The near civil wars of many years past were a testament to the importance of continuity. Highlords had orchestrated the rise and fall of their own many times, and in each instance the feuds had nearly spilled over into open conflict. No Angladaic intentionally mentioned the clandestine bloodletting that had accompanied those days when the nation stood at the edge of anarchy unless required, but the chaos of such periods lingered in every studious mind and had been carefully catalogued by Irindein's historians. This was a nation that should have stood for order and honor and it was difficult to defend those ideals when the past contained events that were such an obvious affront to the nation's values. Arvadis had emphasized to his sons that these tribulations had forged stronger men who knew their mortal flaws, though it had not made the evils of the past any easier to digest.

These young men now on guard were fearful of the future. They had grown up under Arvadis and had admired him, he was a fair and just ruler and widely regarded as the most personable king Angladais had ever had. They believed the older soldiers who spoke of his wisdom, and they were most afraid of what those veterans would not say. The experienced men would not offer any thoughts on Vendile or his character. They were simply mute on the subject. This unnerving fact kept the young guards on their toes, concerned that there was something coming they were not prepared for, and in this estimate they were correct.

The city of Alderlast is formed in a massive octogon with eight gates at the center of each segment of the curtain wall and, at each joint, further walls extend to the center of the city: the palace. Thus, should the city ever be under siege, it could be fought for in sections, limiting the ability of any foe to take all of Alderlast at once. During times of civil unrest, Alderlast had indeed broken into independent districts, allied in blocs against one another or used to contain uprisings among the people. The intent had always been that an ill-prepared invader would not understand the layout of the city and thus fail to strike for its heart, the palace, before attempting to secure the streets themselves. By the time they realized such an undertaking was nigh impossible, it would be too late. Each of the spokes of the great wheel that made up the walls separating the districts formed a raised defensive road, all eight leading to the elevated seat of the palace itself. The true trick to taking Alderlast, therefore, was not holding the districts, but the high roads forming the divisions between them and allowing access to the palace itself.

The unique layout of the city was therefore a problem, but only for the ignorant invader. Arvadis Angladais was not such a man, nor was his company. They rode straight to Alinormir's Cradle, the gate that opened to a long ramp leading to the height of the Zenith Road, and paused outside awaiting the hailing of the guards. Arvadis was in front in a grey cloak, his companions behind him similarly clad and looking particularly inconspicuous. Calavar and Irindein were immediately behind the king, Graham and Derek protectively at their sides. Vorasho and Renon were behind, keeping Lena between them. Young Logan had been left at home with promises of more visits from his grandfather and "uncle" Calavar.

The small company sat before the great gate, not making a sound. The young guards on duty were confused. They were accustomed to being greeted by travelers seeking entry and given the customary information about their origins and business in the city. These newcomers were behaving oddly as they simply sat beyond the gate, waiting. The discussion between the present watchmen was furtive and nervous. What to do? Should they send out a few men to detain the group in case they were there to disrupt the ceremony? Did they refuse to open the gates under any circumstances? No one on the wall was prepared to deal with even this apparently minor challenge to their authority.

Finally, one of the bolder men on the wall adjusted his armor and, clearing his throat, took up a position on the battlements where he could be plainly seen. "Good day to you, travelers. What business have you here?"

Arvadis kept his head low and covered. "We are here to witness this afternoon's ceremony. We heard of it as we rode toward the city."

There was a pause on the wall as orders were relayed to the guard and he conversed with his companions. Assuming what he believed was an authoritative stance, the young man called, "No one is permitted to enter until the crowning ceremony is complete."

"Under whose command do you oppose my entry?"

The guard was puzzled. "The word of Highlord Vendile, soon to be king of Angladais."

Arvadis tossed his hood back and pointed dramatically at the young man on the wall. "Then I overturn this order as the rightful king, and demand you open the gates to my city so that I may take back what was wrongly stolen from me."

The reaction on the wall was one of shock. Slowly, the others removed their hoods. What began as murmurs rose on the wall to general hubbub. The word that all below were deceased had spread like wildfire through Alderlast, and yet here they stood! The young guard tried to reason with himself. "We cannot allow you in, my lord, as you are no longer the king."

It was spoken in an apologetic, nearly pleading tone, and Arvadis responded calmly and sympathetically, "My title was wrested from me through deception and violence. I am here to correct that violation. I will use force if necessary, but I do not think you are an enemy of our nation, my son."

Calavar had his war hammer halfway out of his belt, but a remonstrating glare from Irindein halted him there. The guard on the wall seemed torn between law and loyalty, but he held fast. "I cannot go against the decree my lord, by our Code."

Vorasho trotted forward and pointed his staff at the man on the wall. "There are things higher than the Code, boy. Highlord Vendile has not yet been appointed king, and his predecessor stands before you. Moreover, the man being crowned has violated that which sustains the purity and righteousness of our nation to bar us from entry. He has conspired to commit murder against men falsely accused and unfairly tried. To which is your allegiance, the Code or what it stands to protect?"

There was brief pause then the guard made a sharp motion to his companions. There was no hesitation, they rushed to hurl open the gates. The company rode through as the guards bowed to either side of them. Arvadis drew his sword and held it aloft. "If you wish to aid your country, follow me, my brothers, before the soul of our people is defiled through treachery."

The guards filed in behind the riders and soon a company of twenty men was marching behind the slow walk of the horses. Arvadis did not rush onward; he cast his grey cloak aside and it fell to the street. With his newly won followers marching behind him he now proudly displayed the bronze and white colors of his house. Calavar and Irindein shone behind him, glowing in their resplendent tunics patched and cleaned with Lena's precise stitching. In their armor, Vorasho and Renon were grim, as were the two guards, Derek and Graham, before them. Lena was proud in the center with her dark velvet riding dress and long dark hair floating softly in the breeze. She turned to Vorasho. "I would never think to hear you denounce the Code for any reason."

The prince kept his eyes forward as he answered her, "There is much about me you have misread, my lady."

"That is good to hear."

The march remained unhurried as they went past the roofs of the houses below, cries of recognition coming up from the people in the districts. The sound of hooves on cobblestone attracted attention from the homes. Those not coerced into viewing the ceremony leaned out of windows, craning their heads upward, and responded with awe to the sight before them. A great roar began to rise behind the king's return. The rumor of his arrival spread faster than the return itself could, children clambered up the stairs to the raised road and ran before Arvadis, laughing and cheering the king. The old man could not restrain a smile. He felt as though he were reborn. In the past months, he had been crushed by helplessness and isolation in trying to rule his land. Now he realized that this new threat to his home had not been only his to face. The people were indeed with him, and they welcomed his apparent return from the grave.

Irindein came beside his friend to bathe in his enjoyment of the moment. "It is nice to be home, Arvadis."

The man before him turned calmly. "We are far from home. A great challenge awaits us at the end of this road."

"Well," the younger man sighed, "we certainly will not be facing it alone."

Arvadis glanced back at the sea of people following him. "Yes, that is something isn't it?"

Diaga fell asleep shortly into their ride south. Trem thought he might join the young mage, but he willed himself to stay awake. The night was dark and the road was winding before him, yet he could not say how much farther they had to go. Ghost led the way, unusually concerned about the others behind him. He often paused to retreat back to check on the rest of the party. For the moment, it seemed he had forgotten his rapid desertion of them and his single-mindedness of purpose. Grimtooth had bound his wounds and Logan's for the time being, and the flesh about the cuts seemed to have stopped burning, though the orc felt compelled to check on them from time to time. Neep was awake and aware, keeping a close eye over Diaga's slumped form. Rath had disappeared into the night and Trem did not wish to speculate the reason why.

Ghost materialized before him and spoke gruffly, "The people of Delmore are just ahead. They have opened the caverns and are waiting for us to go inside."

Trem nodded weakly. "Send them in, we will bring up the rear."

"I can have the halfling seal it behind us," Ghost said. "Hopefully that will buy us a little time."

As the Napalian started back towards the front of the line, Trem called out, "What have they done with Joseph, the old man, his body?"

Ghost paused and turned. "I told them we would build a cairn in the caverns. I thought you would want to be present."

Ghost trotted off before Trem could respond, leaving the half-elf confused at this rare kindness from the Napalian and feeling still more exhausted. His body seemed to want to collapse and only his will to reach relative safety held him in the saddle. Trem heard the approach of hooves and tilted his head to see Jovan riding slowly behind him. The youth overtook him eventually and matched his pace. They did not speak for some time, simply riding forward into the gloom. Jovan's face knotted in pain as his horse missed a step, and Trem reached out to steady the beast. Jovan's hand came down on his and gently moved it off the reins. "I think I should steer my own horse, Trem."

The former hermit brought his arm back and the deep silence continued a few moments longer. Jovanaleth finally straightened himself, as though preparing for a battle and spoke demandingly, "What are you?"

Trem reacted as though struck, flinching from Jovan's words but recovering quickly. Moments of quiet passed before he was able to talk. "I do not really know."

"Joseph told me he knew you over twenty years ago. He said you looked exactly the same."

Trem shifted uncomfortably. "He spoke the truth."

Jovanaleth scoffed. "How is this possible? You can not be much older than me!"

Trem halted his horse and stared coldly at his companion. "I am fifty-six winters young. I was at the battle of the Fortress of Aves where, as you deduced, I took the sword once belonging to Vactan el Vac."

"That's just not possible, Trem, it is...."

"Regardless of whether it should be possible, what other explanation could there be? And to what end would I wish to lie to you about something so fantastical?"

Jovanaleth knew it was the truth, but the confirmation he had waited for still stunned him into silence. Trem did not give him the opportunity to probe or respond further. "When I was eighteen years old, I entered into a trance for several days. When I came out of it, my parents told me they had adopted me mere days after my birth. They were instructed by my mother to raise me to the age of eighteen and then I would receive a powerful gift from the gods themselves. At that time they were to tell me the truth.

"When I learned they were not my real parents, I resolved to find my true relatives, particularly my mother, who had abandoned me to the kindly couple I had long thought were my actual family. I left them to search for my birth mother. I spent many years in various places before I stumbled upon the Fortress of Aves during the War of the Lion. I joined them as a scout when they were desperate for any volunteers, even me with my mixed blood. Through rash action and unhappy chance I was given the opportunity to become a knight. I was at the final battle between Goran the Painted Knight and Bull the Warrior. I watched Bull kill the general from the west, and then die himself. Afterwards, I walked away. I went to the woods and resolved never to leave."

Jovan was silent a moment, but managed to say, "And you met Joseph when?"

"As a child I read a great deal. I dreamt of being a hero, I even tried to join the Eagle Knights when I first left my foster parents. Their racial restrictions barred me, and soon I learned most men and elves despise those like you and I who are proof of a mingling of our species. I kept my hope of becoming a man stories would be written about alive in the Dust Plains for a long while. When I met Joseph, I had become known as the Warden of the Plains, a mysterious figure who wandered the hills protecting travelers." Trem's eye could not help lighting up as he spoke of his past, the times when he had believed in the ideal of absolute good and evil and worked in earnest to be a paragon of the former. "In failing Joseph, I lost my childish belief in mythical heroes for a time. In truth, it would have been better had I lost it completely, but hope is a terrible thing."

Jovanaleth looked up and down at Trem, as though seeing him for the first time. He was transfixed by this revelation. To think he was riding next to someone he had felt was his peer, only to learn he was more than twice his age and had seen and done things that likely no other person in all of Teth-tenir had, it was astounding. But more than that, his cold and despondent view of the world made somewhat more sense now. Jovanaleth could connect the dots of his companion's failed adventures, understand the hurt and sadness he had to have experienced several times over, and most of all he thought he understood what had made Trem venture forth on Jovan's account.

"Well?" Trem said softly, head down. "Anything else you would like to know?"

After a moment, Jovan cleared his throat. "Did you ever find your mother?"

"No," Trem said quietly. "I have given up searching."

"Is that why you helped me? Because I am looking for my father?"

Trem looked up, ashamed. "At first I intended to leave you to die in the woods. I still do not know why I took you to my home. After I healed you, I felt a degree of responsibility for you. Your similar ordeal regarding a parent did strike a nerve. I suppose."

Jovan sighed, "Until we reached Delmore."

"I told you that I eventually lost the misguided notion that noble and ignoble actions, right and wrong, heroism and villainy, are things that one can draw a clear line between. I did not want the people of Delmore, or you and the others, to die. However, I saw no reason for us to sacrifice ourselves in a futile attempt to save them.

And even now I wonder if you or Logan have considered what will become of these people? Where they will go and what their future will be?"

Jovan remained steadfast in his decision. "That will be figured out in time. Innocent people cannot just be left to suffer and die when we have the ability to help them." He did, however, recognize the truth in Trem's misgivings and chose to change the subject back to his odd ally. "What will you do now?"

Trem shrugged. "Continue south. Help Ghost. Help you. That is, if you still want my help?"

Jovan straightened himself and averted his eyes. "I do not even know who you are, Trem. For now we are traveling in the same direction, and I will not object to your company, but once we found whatever it is Ghost seeks, perhaps we should go our separate ways."

Trem was about to respond as Logan rode by with Ghost and Grimtooth on his heels. "Come on, the entrance is just ahead, and Rath says those things will be back before long."

"Where is he?" Jovan called.

A shadow flitted past them. "Right beside you, prince."

Jovanaleth spun and saw the tail of black cloth as it disappeared into the night. He shook his head and turned to say something to Trem, perhaps to reassure him, and there was no one there. Jovan sat in his saddle alone on the road, watching the long cloak of Trem Waterhound disappear before him. He adjusted his heavy broadsword and trotted his mount forward. The mass of humanity soon emerged ahead of him, crowded around a great thicket of trees of which one seemed to loom over the rest. Jovan could not see a cave from where he was, and in truth the mass of refugees drew his attention more than his other surroundings.

The crowd of people at the cavern was disheveled and exhausted. There were mournful but faint wails throughout the refugees, in some cases just realizing that a loved one was not coming back to them. Jovanaleth tried to remember the names of the men he had commanded, but not one came to him. Something in that realization pierced his heart and he sat there, drained of all his emotional fortitude, with eyes averted lest he begin weeping himself. He recovered his composure and rode forward, the crowd parting to allow his passage.

Ghost had dismounted and stood beside the entrance. The passageway was formed in a great tree that was wider than the road itself, its doors a curious dark rock with the living wood woven into the hinges. The portal itself was massive, and on the stone was carved scenes of elves, men, halflings, and dwarves all marching off into the distance, descending great stairs into caverns below. Gend came forward and opened them with a strange stone key inserted into the crevice between the great slabs. It slid in with a quiet scraping sound and, with a few jittery twists, he pulled it forth and the doors ground slowly outward, bent by the shifting of the great tree.

The halfling quickly pocketed his artifact and stepped aside. Gend remained outside, politely guiding people through the hollow alcove and downward along a steep ramp to a large cavern some distance within. He managed to find torches and a dry corner for everyone to get reasonably comfortable. Ghost had to gruffly acknowledge the halfling had not proven entirely useless. No one bothered to inquire how Gend had acquired his key.

As the last refugees made their way slowly through the door, Ghost ushered Jovan in ahead of him. "Make certain the rabble stay together and send me the halfling so we can seal these damn doors. No need to advertise our presence."

The young man made no response and Ghost considered hauling him back and boxing his ears, but then the knight and his orc bloodbrother appeared from within the caves. "Gend says we have to shove these doors back so he can reseal them."

Ghost grunted, "It's going to take a lot of muscle to even budge them, let alone get them back to where they were."

"Ah guess tha' means Ah'm the one ta do it."

Logan chuckled. "I do not know who else could do better."

"Even you will not be able to move these things," Ghost tapped the massive hunks of rock. "They are a foot thick and solid stone, not to mention the heavy wood of this strange tree. I doubt it is going to give simply because we wish to conceal our passing."

"Well, Ah'm not gonna jus' sit 'ere an' stare at um."

And with that Grimtooth braced himself, grasped the edge of one of the doors and gave a great heave. It flew inward and the orc nearly fell onto his back. Perplexed, Ghost gave the second door a light tug with one hand. It slid easily shut as though greased. The Napalian laughed. "Dwarven engineering, I suppose?"

Logan shook his head as the two closed the doors. The pitter-patter of small feet caused the knight to turn. Gend appeared, looking unusually strained. The knight spoke to him with gentle concern, "You alright, friend? You seem a bit distracted."

Gend's head snapped up. "Oh no, no, everything is quite alright, just a rather hectic day, don't you think?"

"Of course," Logan agreed. "All over now though, if you could seal the doors that is?"

"Yes, yes of course." The small figure rushed forward fumbling in his pack. He pulled out the odd key, shaped like a narrow pyramid, and slid it into the gap between the doors where, on the interior, the carvings actually depicted a round and rising sun. After a little jerking and twisting, there was a creaking sound and the walls seemed to shake. The small shaft of light from the narrow gap in the doors went out. Gend grumbled and scrambled a bit more and then the light of a torch appeared. The others filed in behind him as they turned and made their way to the rest of the group.

"Are all the refugees together into the cavern, Gend?" asked Logan. "We don't want anyone wandering off on their own."

"What? Oh, yes, yes, they are quite settled."

"Excellent, I could stand to get some rest."

"Well, we should be able to, nothing to bother us in here."

Ghost ran his hand along the stone. "I still do not feel comfortable without a watch for the night, even under all this thick rock."

Gend smiled back at him. "Well, naturally, famous soldier that you are, but here we should be just fine."

Ghost snarled, "Do not try to flatter me, halfling, I wouldn't care if we were under the protection of a hundred thousand warriors and the gods themselves, I would still set a watch. Tonight will be no different."

Logan's mailed hand came down none too gently on Ghost's shoulder. "I don't believe it is your decision to make anymore, Greymane."

Ghost flinched at the mention of his former name. Before he could respond, they rounded a corner to see the cavern erupt out of the low-ceilinged stone rampway they had been following deeper under the earth. A few improvised torches lit the darker corners of the expanse, but the high ceiling held a few small patches of glowing moss that gave the room an eerie, soft glow. Despite the strange surroundings, those within had done their best to make do. Straw and wood planks had been laid down as improvised bedding for the night, and most of the people had simply fallen onto them in exhaustion. Logan spotted Neep attending to Diaga in one of the corners. He pointed this out to the others and they walked over.

Khaliandra was aiding the firecat as the two tried to make Diaga comfortable. Neep spun as Logan approached and only barely relaxed when she recognized him. The knight knelt beside the mage and asked the priestess, "How is he?"

The young woman smiled. "Oh, I know very little about his condition, but his friend seems to think he is fine."

Logan smiled, "Neep would know best."

"Neep? Is that its name?"

Grimtooth chimed in, "'Er name actually lass. Turns out cats can be gels too."

The firecat cocked her head at the orc as though trying to determine if she should be insulted by his comment. Deciding it was not worth her time, the brightly colored feline nestled up against Diaga to keep him warm and curled her long tail protectively around Khaliandra as well. The gesture drew a smile from the young woman and Logan spoke up, "You are Khaliandra, correct? A priestess of Endoth and friend of Jospeh?"

"Yes. I am sorry I could not save him."

Logan gently patted her shoulders and stood. "I am sure you did all you could. Please keep an eye on my friend Diaga, we need him."

Another smile crossed her face. "I know, sir, I will. We need him too."

Ghost tapped the knight on the arm. "One of the men told me that Trem and Jovanaleth have headed that way," he pointed to a tunnel off of the main cavern. "They took Joseph's body with them."

Logan adjusted his armor. "We should go then. We all need to talk."

As they crossed the stone floor, a shadow detached itself from the wall and joined them. Grimtooth nodded at Rath as he fell in beside them. The assassin did not respond and the orc shrugged. Rath had saved their lives, which for Grimtooth was enough to warrant his respect and silence on the unnerving habits of the cloaked man. Logan glanced back disapprovingly, but he did not suggest the soft stepping figure leave. Ghost waved Gend to join them and the group disappeared into the small passage.

A few feet into the tunnel, Logan slowed to allow the others to catch up. They only walked for a few moments before opening out into another smaller cave where Trem and Jovan, stripped to the waist, were busily stacking stones about the body of the old man. Trem had placed Joseph's sword, hilt up, in his dead hands, the blade pointed down to his feet. Jovan was heaving a large boulder onto the fourth layer of the cairn. Without asking, Logan and Grimtooth shed their armor and started to help. Ghost casually pulled out his blade and sat sharpening it off to one side while Gend wandered around without purpose and Rath leaned silent and unmoving against the grey wall of the cave. The four workers kept at their duty for almost an hour until Trem laid the last stone on top. No one said a word as they stood around the cairn, then Trem simply turned and walked to the wall where he sat down.

The others gathered around him on the floor, passing a waterskin between them. Rath stayed somewhat out of the way as the rest avoided breaking the silence. Jovanaleth let Logan check his leg over until Trem finally broke the quiet. "How long do we have to travel underground?"

Gend piped up from outside the group, "Less than a week or so if we hurry!"

Ghost shook his head in doubt. "We cannot move very fast with all these people, and those wagons barely fit beneath the roof of the downward entrance to the first cavern. How can we know they will make it the whole way through?"

Gend jumped in again, "I think it is wide enough, if I remember right."

Grimtooth nodded. "'Ave ta leave um behind. Cannae take the chance of bein' slow an' runnin' out of food, but we best bring the 'orses."

Logan stood and gathered himself, meeting the eyes of everyone in the room before saying, "This is all well and good to think about our immediate future, but there are other issues we need to discuss. Now, Grimtooth and I joined this quest with the intent of fulfilling our duty to protect and serve the innocent people of Legocia, which we have done. Still, the motivations of everyone in this room must be made known, and before all present. No more secrets, no more hidden agendas. Why are we here?"

There was a moment of silence that Ghost would not allow to stand for long. Laying his blade on the stone he rubbed his hands together. "I assume, knight, that you are addressing me in particular. My intentions have seemed deceitful even when I claimed to tell you truly what I seek, but I have had reason to be untruthful. My purpose is as simple as it is unforgiving."

Ghost closed his eyes momentarily then continued in a steady voice, "The young mage caught onto my identity first, being a Napalian himself. I am indeed the infamous Greymane Squall, who betrayed his people to try to save his family and himself. As you can see, my plan did not work to my benefit. I had to stand in the presence of this Wolfbane and watch members of my family murdered before my very eyes. I was told that no turncoat could be trusted with their freedom and thrown in prison, where I heard the last gasps of my remaining family members curse my name. I intend to repay Wolfbane with every hurt he has brought upon my kin and me. I am continuing south to find this mysterious city I spoke of, Yulinar, where, supposedly, they can direct me to an ancient weapon of the gods that will give me the power to carry out my vengeance."

Gend spoke up, "Yulinar! That's the great city of the Melarrians."

Ghost shot him a baleful look. "Melarrians? Why did you not mention you knew of them before?"

The halfling looked as though he desperately wanted to take back what he had said, but he averted his eyes and muttered, "It must have slipped my mind."

"Even if you find this weapon," Jovan interrupted, "what makes you think the gods or whatever they have set to guard it would let you have it?"

Ghost glared at the young warrior. "If they will not give it to me, I will take it. What is your plan, boy? Still intend to hunt down your father?"

Jovan met his gaze. "Yes, and I will still help you if you help me."

"Then you had better hope we get what I want."

Logan interjected, "All well and good, Ghost, but I do not believe Grimtooth and I can in good conscience assist a man who would leave innocent people behind to die at the hands of murderous bandits."

"I did what I thought was best. Your sympathies for these people are understandable, but they represent a small portion of the suffering occurring in Legocia. Worse, they are only slowing us down and it will get harder as the days go by. Where exactly do you intend to take them? How will you feed so many? Did you even consider these things, knight?"

Logan scratched his chin in frustration. "It is not for me to determine what to do after saving them. We could not leave them behind when they were asking for our aid."

"Aye," Grimtooth added, "we 'elp people, always."

"Then can I assume you two will be leading these people to safety when we are clear of the caverns?"

"We," Logan answered steadily, "shall do our best to ensure their safety. If we can stay with you and the others, we will. Your quest, misguided though it might be, has great implications for Legocia and our homeland. We will not sit idly by."

Ghost seemed to accept this and turned his attention to Trem. "What about you half-elf? We have all heard strange, unbelievable things about you, and we have all seen what you can do with that magical sword of yours. What will you do?"

Trem looked away from the pile of stones before him and spoke softly, as though to no one. "I will not discuss my origins or past with anyone here. Those who need to know have already been told. I am no longer bound to Jovanaleth, since I broke that oath when I deserted him in Delmore. So, I will make my own way and do as I see fit."

"Not to argue with you, Trem," Logan remarked, "but you are one of us. You helped us save Ghost back at Gi'lakil and you rescued Jovan from the invaders at Delmore, even if you abandoned him at first. Your actions say you are bound to us whether you will admit it or not. And, even if those instances were not enough, you have nowhere else to turn to. If you had truly wanted to go, you should have done so before we came into the caverns."

"Perhaps you are right. I went back to make amends for my abandonment of Jovan, and I have fulfilled that duty. I want no part of weapons or gods."

Gend interjected quickly, "Nor do I! My adventures are the stuff of legend, of course, but this all seems to be a bit much!"

"Whether you like it or not, you are with us for a while longer, Trem. I will not let you go back through the entrance we used, opening it could alert any enemies who managed to follow us here and may be watching for our return."

"And if you are coming through the tunnels," Ghost added, "you may as well consider remaining with us all a while longer once we are clear of them."

Trem stood and hurled a rock at the wall in sudden rage. "What have I possibly done to make any of you want me around? Do you not see what has happened to those who put their faith in me?" He gestured furiously to the freshly made cairn. "Twice I failed Joseph, and the second time it killed him. I am more a danger to all of you than an asset."

"Trem," Jovan said softly, "you are basing that belief on your past. Show them the blade, and tell them all the truth."

There was a moment of silence as the two locked eyes. Trem's face went from a mask of anger and betrayal to gradual resignation as he gave in. Grimtooth and Logan exchanged a look. "What is he talking about Trem? What about your sword?"

"It is not his sword," Jovan said stepping towards Trem. "Show them."

Trem held the younger man's gaze for a long moment then withdrew the sword from its sheath and laid it held it out, hand shaking. Logan and Ghost stepped forward to examine it and even Rath seemed to perk up from his perch of disinterest. The blade shown forth clearly and interwoven in its steel were pulsing runes of an ancient language, one Diaga would have recognized as that of the gods themselves had, he been there. Logan's eyes widened in shock as he whispered, "I know those symbols. I've seen them in sketches and diagrams. This is the blade of Vactan el Vac. I should have recognized it before. The sword that killed Bull the Warrior, and then was used against Vactan himself."

"That shade in Gi'lakil," Ghost breathed, "it said the name el Vac, I could not figure out why until now."

"Ach!" Grimtooth cried. "Than that'd mean...."

Trem cut him off. "Yes, I took his blade from the battlefield. I was there when Bull the Warrior died. Joseph did know me before. I tried to aid him many years ago, and failed. I have lived a great deal longer than any of you would believe, an existence that was not of my choosing and has proven more punishment than blessing.

"I look as I do because I was cursed by the God of Time, Kurven. He froze me at my nai'valen. In my dreams I have spoken with him and he tells me that a great horror is bearing down on our world and, somehow, with a piece of him inside me, I am to play a part in what is to come. Except that I wanted nothing to do with any of it and still do not. Kurven made my true mother give me away to another family when I was born. All I have ever wanted was to find her, to learn why she would abandon me, and to become a name remembered in the grand stories of Teth-tenir as a hero, like Coldran Berron, Cran Broadaxe, Tovas Uratha, or any number of other legends I read about as a child. Instead, I have been shown the harsh truth of the world as it grows darker and bleaker each passing day."

There was a silence following Trem's declaration, as Logan lifted the blade and examined it further. Jovan broke in, speaking directly to Trem, "Perhaps I acted in haste when I told you I could no longer trust you, you came back for me after all. I do not see how any of us can survive alone, even you. And though you say you wish to retreat from this doom you believe is preordained, you are here, now, and I believe some small part of you still holds to that noble scrap of hope."

"Trem," added the knight, "Jovanaleth sees the truth of you better than you can see yourself. You say you want nothing to do with this coming dark time, yet you left your home with Jovan. You could have turned back at any moment, but the only time you have changed course was brief, and then you went back to Delmore. Who are you really lying to, if not yourself?"

Trem looked around at each one of them. "Even you?" he asked Ghost, "You would have me stay?"

The Napalian snorted. "I don't believe in any coming calamity or dire threat, and the gods have no hold on me. You have a gift for violence and a powerful weapon at your disposal. I suggest you shed this belief in your own futility and seize the chance to change your future. You think you have lost much, half-elf, but until you truly lose everything, you will be amazed how deep the suffering can take you. Maybe once you really reach the bottom you will stop lamenting your lot in life and embrace the opportunities given to you."

"But it is a choice," whispered Rath, "the half-elf must make it alone. Each of you gives him your reasons for staying on a course that is similar to your own. He must decide what to do with his gift."

Trem sighed. "I don't know what I am going to do yet. But you are correct, Logan. I have not turned back yet, and certainly cannot do so now. We remain together for the forseeable future."

"Good," Logan said with finality. "So, what do we do in the meantime?"

"We need to set our priorities," Ghost said. "You've brought a small village into the caves with us. Before we take them any further, there needs to be a decision made about how much is owed to them." He held up his hands to stave off the onslaught of criticsm. "I know you all believe I do not care about these people. That is not true. I simply care more about my own quest. They are with us now, we have to figure out what to do with them once we are clear of the caves."

"Ah think it be obvious." Grimtooth crossed his great arms as though daring Ghost to argue. "We find 'em a new 'ome."

"Easier said than done, orc."

"Ghost is right," Logan admitted. "Few of us know what is at the other end of this tunnel, and the time it will take to find Yulinar will likely exceed our supply limit. We have to determine what to do, where to lead these refugees, before we get above ground."

"There should still be dwarves here!" Gend piped up. "They used to be the caretakers of this road. And if they have moved on, there are the Unclaimed Lands to the west, near the town of Glimmerhold. That region is not unlike the fields found near Delmore."

Ghost shook his head. "I cannot and will not waste time marching these people to safety. It could take months."

"Then I guess that is where we will part ways," Jovan said matter of factly. "Some will choose to go to Yulinar and others to Glimmerhold."

"There is something else," Trem retrieved his sword from Logan. "As I see it, if that army in Gi'lakil has already moved this far south then much of Legocia is in danger. Angladais is pinned within their own homeland. We saw how meager the defenses of Gi'lakil and the Dust Plains are. This Nerothian-backed army could consume all of

The Sword

Legocia by the time we bring the people of Delmore to safety or recover information on the weapons Ghost wants."

"What are you saying?" Jovan asked.

"That we may already be too late in either case. I do not think this invasion will end with the Dust Plains, or even Legocia for that matter. First, the army will incinerate the lands east of the Dragonscales with the Broken, and then Aves, and your homeland will be next."

Jovan grew pale at the thought. "But we can't go back. Not now."

Ghost raised his voice in defiance of the idea, "We go forward and bring back what we need to fight the invaders! Do not be deceived by my urgency to go south, Jovanaleth, I intend to return and fight back."

"You are going to need a lot more men," Trem said.

Ghost rounded on him. "And where would you suggest I find them, half-elf? I can't even get this soft-hearted troop to recognize the necessity of my actions."

"We need to enlist the help of the Eagle Knights. They are the only military organization strong enough to aid us."

"Aye," Grimtooth said, "but Trem ya forget, they won't be likely tah 'elp us bein' strangers an' all."

"True, half-elf," Ghost added. "I doubt they would believe your story of the sword either. They would be more likely to accuse you of theft than help you."

"I can gain their trust."

The others turned to Jovan. The young man cleared his throat before saying, "My mother, she traveled to the Fortress of Aves as an ambassador for my father. Bladehome and my father represent people who were once part of the Eagle Knights, and recently there has been talk of patching up old differences. My mother was still in Aves when I left. There is no reason to think she would leave until her work was complete."

"And she could get them to listen to us?" asked Logan.

Trem cut Jovan off, saying, "We have to try. Reaching Bladehome would take too long, and we would leave the Eagle Knights in the wake of the Broken army. Besides, there are other allies near them we can call upon."

Jovan was puzzled. "Who could that be if not my people?"

Trem took a deep breath. "The Silverleaf Foresters."

Ghost laughed. "Come on, half-elf! Even you cannot be that foolish. Those elves despise the Eagle Knights. They've fought three bloody and hate-filled wars with them! Why would the elves of Silverleaf come to the aid of their greatest foes?"

"He is right, Trem," Logan added. "The two hate each other, you must know that."

"You are correct, the Eagle Knights despise all things elven, but I was once a servant to Aves and I have elven blood. Gerand

415

Oakheart and Coldran Berron united the two groups to oppose the God-Sorceror during the Arcane Wars. Why, Jovan's own mother is elven and she is there negotiating with them. Clearly, there are precedents for such cooperation."

"Coldran Berron also lost his position as commander of Aves because he sided with Gerand Oakheart," Ghost reminded Trem. "Even in the darkest of times, the Knights and Foresters have been unable to put aside their differences."

"You are suddenly talking as though you mean to take part in all of this, Trem." Logan said, ignoring Ghost. "Do you really think we can broker some kind of truce?"

"Those in Aves will have their backs against the wall. The Foresters will try to hide in Silverleaf, but Neroth and his army have shown a willingness to slaughter and burn anything necessary to cull the mortal people. Only together will they stand a chance. We have to convince them both that their doom is at hand, which it assuredly is if they do not do something about it."

"It's a risky gamble, Trem," Jovan warned, "you are asking them to forget years of feuding and band together. Something they have never considered, not even during the invasion of the Army of the Lion."

"We just have to convince them the danger is greater this time," Trem murmured.

"We?" Ghost chuckled, "You say you are unsure what you will do once we are free of these caverns, but as the knight pointed out, you talk as if you are one of us."

"Whether I remain with you or not I am simply assessing the realities of the present. You want a weapon to fight back against the people who took your home and family from you, Logan wants to ensure the safety of the people of Delmore. I am simply pointing out that neither is really possible until you solve the greater challenge of halting the invasion of Legocia." Trem closed his eyes and leaned against the wall of the cave. "But that is really a moot point, we must get out of here first."

"Yes," Logan agreed. "And what of the refugees?"

"We must guide them through the caverns. Perhaps if we can find this city, Yulinar, we can use that as a safe haven for them temporarily. But we need to find out where it is and if it is even possible to reach."

"Gend knows," Jovan said, the realization suddenly coming to him. "Didn't you say you had heard of this place?"

"What?" the halfling seemed caught off guard by being addressed directly. "Oh, well, yes. But it is not necessarily as easy as knowing where it is."

"Be clear, halfling," Ghost growled. "Why is it not so easy?"

"Well," Gend brushed his gaudy clothes nervously, "there's the issue of the land itself. You see, Southron is mostly desert and rock, and Yulinar is supposed to rest in the middle of one of the greatest expanses of desert they call the Endless Sands. It's very difficult to locate, even if you know where you are going. No roads or signs to speak of that would guide you on your way."

"But you can find it," Jovan said in a way that sounded more like a question than a statement.

"Yes," Gend said confidently before adding, "it just might take a while."

"So," Logan interjected, trying to keep the group focused on the moment, "we haul the wagons and supplies through this underground road. Once we are clear of the caves, we try to find this city and a place for these people to start over."

"Then somehow find news of this weapon, find a way to get the people to these Unclaimed Lands, and reach Aves and Silverleaf in time to broker a truce between two factions who have one of the bloodiest and longest standing feuds in the history of Teth-tenir." Jovan shook his head and laughed mirthlessly. "Doesn't seem possible."

"Well, I am damned well going to try," Ghost said defiantly.

"Wait," Logan looked over at the still shifting and nervous Sylrastor Gend, "I know you said you had been south before, but didn't you also meet Rath there?" Logan turned to the black-robed form. "Do you know this city, Yulinar?"

Rath stared him down. "I know of it."

Trem met the eyes of the dark figure. "Can you take us there?"

The assassin held his look a moment. "I can."

"Ach! That do be makin' things a bit easier, mebbe."

"And," Ghost said, "if we push these refugees hard and long enough we can give ourselves more time to reach Silverleaf and Aves, regardless of what any of us decide to do. I know you all have reasons to distrust me, but if Rath can take us to Yulinar, why not remain together until then? It will get your precious survivors to a place where they will be safe, at least for a time."

"Yes," Logan said slowly, rubbing his chin. "It seems to be the simplest solution. And by staying together, we'll have an easier time protecting these people."

"Ach, it is gonna be an unpleasant walk."

Trem cocked his head at the orc. "Do you have a better idea?"

Grimtooth grinned broadly. "Ah nae can say Ah do."

"It is settled then," Logan concluded with authority. "Now, we should all get some rest."

"You go on ahead," Trem waved them away. "I want a moment alone with Joseph."

The others nodded and filed solemnly out of the small cave. Jovanaleth left last, pausing as though he wanted to say something to Trem, but then he continued on. Trem took in the silence of the cavern and cast his mind back to the words that had been exchanged before, when the others were still there. Desperately, he wished Joseph would speak to him, both to advise and to forgive him once again. But of course he did not hear his voice, for the old man was dead and gone. The half-elf stood there in the flickering light from the torch Logan had left for him. He did not leave nor did his eyes waver from their vigil until at last it burned itself out some hours later.

Chapter 27

Vendile waited anxiously for the coronation ceremony to begin. He had outdone his first public appearance after Arvadis's death announcement, grandiose as that might have been, by clothing himself in the most brazenly decadent garb he could find. Vendile wore ten rings, one on each finger and thumb, each of the most resplendent silver and bedecked with jewels. His hair was shining black and slicked neatly with wax. Vendile's robes hung over two feet past his boots, dragging heavily behind him. They were trimmed in the snow colored fur of some strange creature from the north, brought in and carefully skinned at immense personal expense some years ago when he had dreamt of this day. His tunic was as shocking and deep a violet as his robes and over it he wore three heavy gold necklaces, each with a progressively larger stone, hung at varying depths over his chest. A thin metal chain held his prized pendant, given to him by Freyan, beneath his thin undershirt so it's simple design would not contrast with the finery of his ensemble. Though he knew it did not mesh with his opulent appearance, Vendile was loath to be apart from the item. His odd attachment to it mattered not, for Vendile was dressed as the mightiest of kings, and all that he awaited was the refurbished crown of the Angladaic kingdom to confirm his posturing.

That final piece of his triumph sat outside the palace on a dais before the steps, repaired from its earlier fall. The marble floor of the entrance had been covered in deep purple runners stretching over the entire hundred feet of stairs that was the entry to the palace. They matched the long, heavy wall hangings of Vendile's house that framed the entrance. Huge braziers had been erected on either side of the stairway to hold massive blazing fires, even though the sun had not yet dipped below the horizon. Guards were on hand, most of them Vendile's personal soldiers, and the crowd of his so-called supporters was hemmed in by many of them. Bwemor and Hladic knew that few would willingly attend the ceremony, so they had persuaded many nearby residents to be present with the ends of their soldiers' swords. Their willingness was of no concern. Both Highlords simply wanted a large enough crowd to satisfy their benefactor, and to distract him from the noticeable absence of Highlord Calavar's paladins.

Clad in their bright red robes with fine golden trim, the priests of Paladinis made their approach up the stairs singing the ancient chant of the kingdom. Hladic, dressed slightly finer than his subordinates in a gold weave robe and large bejeweled conical cap, led the procession. Bwemor stood next to the crown, his ruddy face nearly matching his burnished fiery armor highlighted with shining black tints. Several of his guards stood around the doors to the palace, awaiting Vendile's arrival. Hladic reached the dais just as the trumpeters at the base of the steps hit their crescendo. As silence fell, he straightened his robes and began his speech in a loud, clear voice: "People of Alderlast! Angladaics and countrymen! I am here to present to you your new king, one who shall move us beyond the dark days of his predecessor into a new era of supremacy and power. I give you the one man grand enough to lead this great people into the future through his wisdom. I give you, Highlord Karsyrus Vendile!"

There was little cheering, though the guards attempted to prod several onlookers into rejoicing. Vendile did not seem to notice as he slowly strode through the grand high doors of the palace and down the steps. He took his time, bathing in his victory at last. Vendile's eyes were glued to the crown before him, and he did not notice when the crowd stopped watching him and began to look down the road behind them. He only paused when he was a step above the dais and the trumpets went suddenly quiet. Vendile's head shot up as he heard the sound of hooves on stone and cheering voices coming nearer and nearer. The color flew away from his face when suddenly the leading rider became clear before him. Arvadis Hawking rode to meet the new king, and he had brought his city with him.

Hladic was still frozen with his arms spread wide, the Book of the Code held aloft in one hand for the ceremony. Bwemor was looking around rapidly for any exit. The men below the stairs did not seem clear on what to do, but Vendile reacted quickly. "Guards! Stop these usurpers and traitors to the people! Take their weapons from them! They threaten the safety of our grand kingdom!"

Vorasho, in his thin mail vest, rode to the edge of the guards brandishing their spears. "There is only one traitor here, he who drives the people into his service like beasts! We, on the other hand, come not against the people, but with them!"

Vorasho thrust his staff aloft and a great roar went up from the crowd behind him. Vendile could not see the end of the mass as it stretched out before him, along the Zenith Road and atop houses and in the windows of buildings below it. Looking about wildly he hissed at Bwemor, "You idiot! The gates were to be sealed against all travelers! How could they have gained entry?"

Bwemor did not answer, but instead motioned his guards to form a line of defense before himself and the would-be king. Vendile snorted at his unresponsiveness and grabbed the still frozen Hladic by the robe. "You! Have your priests disperse this rabble so I can kill the Hawking scum in peace!"

Hladic looked into the madman's eyes. "How, my lord? The people are too many and my priests are forbidden from doing violence to anyone."

"Fool!" Vendile hurled Hladic from him and down the steps, causing an immediate lull in the cheering of the people. Ripping a crossbow from one of the guards he cried out shrilly to Arvadis, "I am the rightful king, Hawking! You have lost the throne and your authority! This rabble of unwashed masses will not take it back for you! Die!"

Vendile aimed the crossbow hurriedly and fired. The shot went wide of Arvadis and Graham deflected it off of his shield. The riders and their guard allies from the wall drew steel and held their weapons aloft. "Surrender, Vendile!" cried Arvadis. "There is no need for further bloodshed!"

"Quite the contrary," Vendile laughed hysterically to himself, "it seems there has not been enough. Guards, fire on the crowd. Kill anyone who does not get out of the way. Leave none of these traitors alive."

There were over forty men stationed around the stairs and palace and each drew a crossbow and aimed it. A great panic went up among the crowd before the stairs as they tried to get clear. The additional forty men holding them in panicked as well, trying to move out of the way and contain the crowd at the same time. Vorasho shouted over the chaos, "Behind the walls! Get under cover!"

The grand steps leading from the raised base of the palace to its doors were flanked by low walls, which mimicked the eight elevated roads of the city. The two low walls nearest Arvadis and the others ran down either side of the walkway to the palace entrance. Calavar leapt from his horse and made for the one to his left, Graham and Derek grabbed Arvadis from his horse and pulled him with them to the right. Vorasho spun and shouted for the people to move back while Lena jumped down and tried to convince the guards to move away and let the people through.

There was a loud and sudden twang as the crossbows all fired at once. Graham and Derek had Arvadis between them, shields raised to protect him from bolts falling over the thick white marble of the wall. Calavar yelled for Lena, standing in the open directly before the bolts as they flew from the strings. Irindein came galloping past her and grabbed her cloak, propelling her toward the other Highlord as the bolts flew into the crowd. Vorasho turned in horror, deflecting the bolt aimed at him with his staff. The innocent people crammed before the stairs were hit hard, several guards on both sides also went down. One of the missiles hit Irindein in the arm with which he was holding Lena and he cried out before falling hard over the back of his horse. The people began fleeing in all directions as Vendile started screaming for another volley. Vorasho rode to Irindein and pulled him to Calavar, where he quickly dismounted, putting his back against the wall.

The people of Alderlast, who had turned out in droves to support Arvadis's return, now ran desperately for shelter. Another volley of bolts ripped through those not moving fast enough. More spectators went down screaming as blood began to run freely in the streets, and Arvadis was unable to tear his eyes from the carnage before him. Graham and Derek were calling over as many of the young guards as they could, but most were caught so unaware by the suddenness of the attack, and as new recruits were unprepared for such violence, they reacted slowly. Of the twenty or so loyal servants of Hawking House they had claimed from the gate, only fifteen were still left. The other five were either writhing on the cobblestones or worse, not moving at all. Six of the contingent managed to join the two bodyguards and the king. The others, with only spears and shields for protection, went to the prince.

Arvadis was stunned by the horror around him. Since entering the city, it had seemed their plan to march nobly into Alderlast and win back his home through the purity of their just and true mission was going to succeed in fairy tale fashion. But this was no storybook adventure, and Arvadis was not a mythical hero. There were real men and women dying in his streets, and Vendile was a true villain, so insane with his desire to rule that even in the face of failure he would not relinquish his rapidly dwindling grip on the kingdom. The shock of reality refused to fade, and Arvadis remained unable to act for a time.

Behind the opposite wall, Vorasho and Calavar propped Irindein against the barrier as Lena pressed the ripped fabric of his shirt onto the wound to staunch the bleeding from his arm. "It seems," the young Highlord smiled meekly, "I am not cut out for battle."

"You are going to be fine, my lord," Lena said, tearing the lower end of his sleeve free and wrapping the cloth tightly around the wound. "Just stay still and hold that cloth down for me will you?"

"You are alright, my lady?" the injured man asked her.

"She is fine, you oaf, look after yourself!" Calavar grunted, his gruffness doing little to hide his obvious concern for his fellow Highlord. Runiden tested the weight of his war hammer in one hand. "Not much we can do without bows of our own."

Renon appeared beside them, dragging a wounded soldier. "Miss, if you could look after him next," but then the wounded man's face froze and his body went stiff. Renon screamed in frustration, "Gods be damned! I will carve that foul beast's heart from his body!"

"You are going to do no such thing," Vorasho said gravely. "We have to move, flank them somehow, or we are done for. You and Lena stay with Irindein and protect him." Vorasho turned to the paladin commander. "Calavar?"

"Yes, my lord?"

"We need to move around them to the left. Any suggestions?"

The Highlord peeked over the lip of the wall from under his shield. "I do not rightly know, lad, there's a lot of those damned crossbows up there and I don't think they will be running out of bolts any time soon."

"We have shields, yes?"

"Aye, small ones though, and only nine men and myself to carry them."

"That is plenty. You men! Shields in front and get ready to leap the wall. We will get as far towards their position as we can before making the jump over to the steps. If we rush them we might be able to catch them off guard. Calavar, stay close to the rear and when I say, duck down with your shield over your head. You understand?"

The Highlord looked confused, but he nodded. Vorasho filed in behind his men. "Shields over your heads until I give the word. Move!"

Lena watched them go before turning back to Irindein. Renon examined the wound and looked at her. "He should be alright. It is not too deep."

The dark-haired woman met his gaze. "I think we are going to have worse to deal with before this day is over."

At the other side of the steps, Arvadis had just managed to tear his eyes away from the terrible death and destruction about him when Graham grabbed his shoulder and shook him. "M'lord, the prince appears to be making some sort of maneuver."

Arvadis watched his son round the corner with the few guards he had. The king glanced over his own wall at the imposing sight of Vendile and his crossbow wielding guards. "He is trying to catch them unaware. It's no good; Vendile can see them moving. We have to do something."

Derek suddenly rounded the corner and charged up the steps, sword drawn. Graham grabbed for him, but missed. "Derek! Derek what are you doing!"

Arvadis caught the older guard as he started to rise. "Wait! Graham, don't be a fool!"

"M'lord," Graham tried to shake Arvadis free as his voice caught in his throat, "there is no way he can make it!"

"I am your king and I am giving you an order! Stay here!"

The commanding nature of his king's voice caused Graham to turn, stunned, and to stare at Arvadis in disbelief. But such was his long-ingrained sense of deference to the man that he did not move, but his eyes did turn to follow Derek's progress up the steps. The young guard was howling something incoherent as he charged. He had timed the move well. The crossbowmen were all reloading as he started his rush. Derek reached the first plateau before the guards could adjust to his approach. He rammed his shield into the face of one foe and slashed the other's legs out from under him with his blade. The other two men drew their short swords and rushed him. Vorasho caught the movement out of the corner of his eye and yelled to his men, "Go, go now!"

The prince's contingent hopped the wall a few feet behind Derek and charged forward. The now readied crossbowmen were confused, but most were still trained on the young guard. Derek deflected one of the swords to the stone at his feet and bashed his shield into the other blade-bearing enemy. He did not see the three bolts that raced towards him and so was baffled when they landed in his chest, knocking him back and onto the stairs. Graham and Arvadis had just started up the steps when he went down, and the older guard cried out as though the bolts had hit him as well.

Arvadis and Graham made for their downed companion while the guards with them joined Vorasho's men. Calavar ducked and held his shield high as Vorasho rushed forward, leaping off the shield and spinning into the largest group of guards. Calavar raced around the platoon of men and began swinging his war hammer about, smashing heads and limbs left and right. The assault was brutal and the guards from Vendile's contingent began to fold quickly. Several ran for the palace, a few threw down their weapons and knelt in submission. Those still desperate enough to fight packed in around the dais and met the brunt of Vorasho's assault.

The prince was mowing through the unprepared soldiers and had nearly reached the tyrannical Highlord responsible for all this carnage. Vendile saw his men faltering and did not stay to see the outcome of the fight. He snatched the crown from the pedestal on which it was resting and bolted for the palace, leaving Bwemor to defend the entrance. The Highlord had not moved from his position since the fighting began. It was as if the repercussions of his actions had just been made clear to him. With a wave he spoke quietly to his men, "Lay down your arms. We are done here."

Vendile's guards kept fighting but Vorasho dropped the last resisting man, turning to address Bwemor. The eldest Hawking son prepared to berate the man for his cowardice, when Arvadis shouted from behind and despite the incoherence of his words Vorasho knew from their tone they were a warning. Suddenly a dagger flew past the prince's face, narrowly missing his cheek and striking a skulking Vendile loyalist about to jump Vorasho from behind. The dagger buried into the man's throat, killing him instantly. Vorasho looked towards the direction it had come from and saw Lena striding up the steps. "I told you to stay with Irindein."

Lena glared at him. "No need to thank me, prince. I am not sitting idly by while good men die for my country."

Only two of the guards from the gate had been killed in the assault, mostly due to the heroic effort of Derek. Graham knelt beside his friend cradling his head. Derek coughed and specks of blood flecked his chin, yet he smiled. "No crying old friend. Not over me."

Graham shook his head in frustration. "What possessed you? Why?"

Derek coughed again and forced a bloody smile. "Remember what you told me in the palace? You are too old for this."

Graham sobbed. "Of course, boy, of course, but you are too young for this, far too young."

"No, remember... my life for the king." Derek smiled once more as his eyes began to fade to glass, "It was an... honor."

The gasping and wheezing shakes of Derek's body did not last long. Graham held his stiffening form and sobbed uncontrollably on the steps. Arvadis stood behind him, watching but not interfering. In that moment, Derek's salute toward Arvadis as he had marched under unlawful arrest to the palace came clearly to the king's mind. The boy had fulfilled his promise, and all because Arvadis had allowed Derek to die in order to retake the steps of his palace. His conscience weighed heavily. Arvadis turned from the scene to see Brusius Hladic attempting to rise from the stone of the steps where Vendile had flung him. The returning king approached the struggling form and kicked him onto his back, pinning him with one foot. "Do not move, Highlord. You are not going anywhere."

Lena appeared beside Arvadis, her eyes wide with shock and despair as she spotted the body of Derek. The king was about to console her when Vorasho turned around and addressed them all, "My lord, we must capture Vendile now, before he can raise more men and do our home more harm than he has already done."

Arvadis stepped harder on Hladic. "Get your priests into the streets and help the injured. And do not even consider trying to flee or I promise you I will hunt you down with dogs and let them finish you when they catch up." The king released his pressure on the Highlord and went to join his son. "Let us end this, now."

Lena picked up a blade from the steps. "I am coming too."

Vorasho turned to admonish her and send her to wait with the others, but Arvadis spoke first, "Bring anyone who is willing. We must all face down this vile usurper if we are to cleanse the kingdom."

Arvadis strode past Vorasho, and Lena went to follow but the prince grabbed her arm. "Please, Lena, stay here. I do not want any harm to befall you."

The young woman pulled free of his hand. "That man in there is responsible for killing Derek, and all the pain and grief that Graham feels right now. They are my friends as much as yours. This is my battle as much as yours. I am going, and you cannot stop me."

She marched up the stairs and joined the few guards from Alinormir's Cradle who were waiting to storm the palace. Arvadis had paused on the steps beside Bwemor, who removed his signet ring and handed it to the king. "My lord, I have betrayed my people and you personally. I allowed myself to be blinded by the desire for wealth and status and have done grievous harm to too many people. I tied myself to a madman. I hereby abdicate my position as Highlord for that betrayal to this land and our Code."

Arvadis glanced down at the ring then at Bwemor. "What you say is correct," he retrieved the ring from the Highlord's hand, "I accept your abdication. These guards will take you and your men to my home and keep you there until I can decide what is to be done with you."

Bwemor nodded solemnly and departed with his watchful escort down the Zenith Road. Arvadis watched him go, and then turned to Calavar and Vorasho. "We shall have to do this deed ourselves. No time to raise more guards, and I cannot allow him to go on his own or he might try to escape justice."

Vorasho grabbed one of the surrendered Vendile soldiers by his hair and wrenched his head backward. "How many of you are within? What dogs does your master still keep kenneled?"

The man cried out in pain and blubbered, "None! None! We were all to be outside for the coronation! Only his bandit advisor is still inside."

Vorasho looked at Arvadis questioningly and the king grunted in understanding. "Freyan. He should not be a threat to us."

Arvadis turned to the doors and heaved them open. Calavar and Vorasho filed in behind him with Lena kept protectively in the rear. As they strode through the massive entryway, Lena glanced back to see Graham still cradling Derek's body on the steps. A quiet rage built inside her and she hefted her newfound sword as she passed into the dark halls of the palace. The doors slammed shut behind them as the priests hurried down the steps to aid the wounded.

A frigid wind still swirled around Mount Iceblade, and something in it jerked Romund out of his deathlike sleep. He glanced to either side and saw Edge and Raymir had also drifted off in deep slumbers, their minds and bodies consumed by exhaustion. Romund jumped up and looked over the brink of the outcrop. He saw no sign of the strange figure Edge had claimed to have seen and breathed a little easier. Romund did not really believe Saltilian had followed them this far, it was hard enough to fathom they had made it themselves, but the tiniest possibility still sent a shiver down his spine, not borne from the cold. Turning around, he gently shook both of the others awake. Edge was up almost immediately upon being touched, brandishing his weapon, but relaxed when he saw it was only Romund. Raymir came to more slowly, but was soon ready to move on. Romund glanced above them where he could see clearly the peak now in the empty, cloudless sky.

Edge stepped next to him and patted him on the back. "Not much farther."

Raymir called them over; "There is a path over here. It looks safe enough."

The three filed into a tight line, with Raymir between the two men and Edge in the lead. Edge found the going incredibly easy for so high up the mountain, especially after their previous ordeals along the rock face. The path was not so steep and they took their time as much as they could. Edge kept glancing back to make sure he did not outpace his companions, and Romund did the same but more to keep himself believing they were not being followed. The walk went on for some hours and finally they crested a last steep rise, sharper than the more established walkway they had taken.

Edge came over the top first and paused. He could see for what seemed to be hundreds of miles into the distance, massive planes of white snow interspersed with sharp teeth of rock. Raymir and Romund stood beside him taking in the sights. Edge began gesturing in wonder. "There, to the south and east. That is where we came from, from among all those mountains and the snows beyond. And over here, in the west, that is the sea out there, somewhere, that Wolfbane and I crossed to reach these shores."

Raymir pointed southward. "Look, the mountains extend even further, down into the warmer lands."

Romund chuckled. "All I see is snow and ice. I am not even sure there are warm lands anywhere anymore!"

Raymir laughed with him, but Edge silenced them with a sudden raising of his hand. "This tower or spire is not here. Do you have your spyglass still, Romund?"

"Yes," the older man pulled his carefully wrapped prize free and extended the collapsible lengths of metal. "I'll start scanning in the west? Or the north?"

"Compromise," Raymir said lightly, "start to the northwest."

"Alright," Romund smiled broadly and put the device to his left eye, closing the right. He held it upward and talked as he began to search the horizon, "It's fortunate the sky cleared just as we reached the top, I can see farther than I would if the clouds and snow were still...."

Concerned, Raymir brought her head up from where it had been resting in Edge's shoulder. "What is it Romund?"

Without a word, he held his device outward and stepped to the side, but did not take his eyes off of the direction he had been staring in. Raymir took the spyglass and stared through it. Edge heard her sharp intake of breath and came to join them, taking the lens from her as she too looked uncomfortably in the direction Romund had. As Edge took in the same sight as the other two, a great quiet fell over all of them. "That," he breathed, "must be what we are looking for."

Rising out of the pure white snow like an impaling blade was a massive tower, still a great distance from the mountaintop on which they stood. Even from that far off, with the spyglass they could see the sharp, cruel edges that made up its form. The tower seemed to bend and swirl upon itself as it rose into the sky, a massive height and width to be so clearly seen from so far away, even with the device's enhancement of their vision. The form was nightmarish, with no apparent rhyme or reason to its structure that would have made it accommodating to even the most eccentric master. It was as though it had grown independently, as a living thing, expanding wherever it found room to extend its sharp contours. Despite the clear sky of the early evening, a massive dark cloud hung over the area about the tower; the occasional crackle of strange color lancing out of the sky to strike its dark form. About its base a large grove of foreboding black trees grew, wavering in the distant breeze.

Romund took a deep breath. "So that is our destination. It does not look particularly inviting from here."

Edge did not respond but glanced at Raymir. She returned his look and said softly, "It has to be the place, what else would it be?"

"Oh, I a-a-assure you it i-is."

The three spun round to meet a horrific sight. Saltilian stood there, snow rising up above his ankles in his dark, tattered robes. He gripped his shimmering staff with bloodied fingers, nearly all the nails having all been ripped off in his delirious climb to the peak. The heavy cowl that hung loosely over the shoulders of his robe hid his face. All his finery had been worn down so that Saltilian now resembled some nightmarish caricature of a wizard having been harried and worked to the bone, degrading aggressively the cloth he had been wandering in. Edge reacted swiftly, and grabbing his halberd he started forward with one determined step.

It was the only step he would take, for Saltilian's eyes shot up and instantly the lost elf froze where he was. His otherworldly gaze passed over the other two, pausing on Raymir a moment before returning to Edge. All three found themselves immobilized, frozen as stiffly as the ice around them. Saltilian smiled, revealing cracked and red lips with blood oozing through his teeth. His eyes danced madly within the hood. "Oh n-no, my dear l-l-lieutenant, you are not g-going a-a-anywhere." Saltilian's lisp began to fade and his voice took on an otherworldly tone, "Y-you see, this j-journey has destroyed my physical body, b-but it has unleashed a power in me beyond my corporeal limitations. However, I will leave your mouths free to work so that the lady will hear every beautiful scream of pain as I rend you unmade before her eyes."

The madman began to approach Edge as Raymir strained to cry out at him in rage, "Leave him alone, you beast! Do not touch him!"

Saltilian paused and smiled at her. "Oh, do not worry, my dear, it will all be over soon."

Trem slept fitfully, dreamlessly, on the floor of the cavern. He had found it difficult to fall asleep and in the minutes or hours that passed, for he could not tell how long he struggled, he woke frequently as he shifted on the hard ground. Trem felt a strong sharp pain pull him at last to true wakefulness. He shot up from his bedroll and snapped back into reality. He glanced to the right where Neep and Diaga were both still slumbering. He was still in the cavern with the refugees and his companions. Trem relaxed a moment, understanding that in his broken bits of sleep he had lost his sense of place. He searched for the cause of the sudden pain that had awoken him expecting a rock beneath his roll, though he could not find one. He shook his head and rubbed his matted hair, trying to clear his mind from the fogginess of fatigue and limited rest. Realizing he could not return to bed, even if he needed to, he rose and made for the edge of the cave where the road, according to Gend, continued to the other side.

Trem found he was not the only one who couldn't sleep. Ghost stood by the exit to the cave, sharpening his blade once again near a small flame. The Napalian simply nodded in acknowledgement. Soon it became clear that almost everyone who had been thrown together since Gi'lakil was there. Jovanaleth and Logan were leaning against the rock wall talking quietly. Grimtooth sat tossing a throwing axe in one hand. Gend and Rath were standing quietly to the side, the halfling conspicuously avoiding eye contact with anyone while the assassin seemed determined to force it. Trem lifted his head questioningly at Logan. "Trouble sleeping?"

The knight nodded. "You too? All of us, except the mage, and he seems to be so spent an earthquake would not rouse him."

Jovan shook his head. "Something is not right here. I have a bad feeling in this place."

Ghost stopped sharpening his sword and shrugged resignedly. "We cannot change our course. There is only one way."

Trem agreed. "He is right." The half-elf reached into his travel pack, which he was holding by the straps and dangled at his side, pulling out his small container of teas. "Would anyone like something to warm their blood?"

"I'll take some," Jovan said coming forward. The two scrounged the area about them quietly for something to boil water in, which Ghost poured sparingly, as he insisted they not use too much of their limited supply. Logan turned down the opportunity for refreshment, but Grimtooth and, surprisingly to most, Rath, produced cups and accepted one of the darker-leafed varieties Trem had selected. They soon sat about the low fire cross-legged and sipping the bitter concoction, happy to have some small comfort.

"I don't like it down here," Ghost grumbled, leaning against the wall and looking down the long unlit path that was to take them south. "Too dark and disorienting. Those shafts of light near the doors tell you if the sun is out, but not the time of day. The road looks worse, no light at all. Impossible to tell how long we'll have traveled or slept."

"We'll just have to move when we can and rest when we tire," Trem said.

"Aye," Grimtooth said, sitting serenely beside Jovan, "it be as simple as trustin' ta body."

There was a longer silence then, but one broken by the arrival of an unexpected guest. Khaliandra came into the firelight with her hands holding a small wooden cup, the sight of which brought a smile to Trem's face. "Are you looking for some refreshment?"

"If you do not mind, my lord," the priestess said politely. "I have not had much tea since I moved to Delmore, and I miss it."

Trem poured some leaves and the remaining hot water into the cup as Jovan asked, "Where did you come to Delmore from, Khaliandra?"

The priestess set her cup on the ground to cool and tied her hair back as she set herself down, kneeling, on the floor, "I grew up far to the south actually, in the Haven Isles. When I became an adult, I chose to devote myself to Endoth and went in search of a village in need of a healer."

"The tales say no one leaves the Haven Isles," Logan said with a smile. "The land is too beautiful and life too peaceful. Supposedly even the pirates that go to raid their settlements end up simply taking up residence there."

Khaliandra laughed with genuine mirth at Logan's jest. "Yes, it is quite lovely and my people have turned many to our way of life. My parents chose to stay after trying to make a living as merchants and investigating the isles for items to sell in Legocia. It captivated them as it does many, but I found curiosity and devotion to others in need compelled me to leave, and they accepted my choice."

"A brave decision," Logan said.

"Perhaps," Khaliandra replied. "Or a natural one for those who wonder about the world beyond their front door."

Trem stood abruptly and swallowed the last of his cup. "If this journey is going to take several days, we should begin now. Get these people up and let's be on our way."

The end of pleasantries was sudden, but not uncalled for. The importance of haste was clear to all, adventurers and refugees alike. Though the people of Delmore took some time to wake and assemble, they recognized the necessity of marching on and did not complain. Diaga still would not come out of his deep sleep, so Neep hefted him herself, carrying his body like a child in her arms. Logan had all the people line up before the exit to the cave and addressed them; "People of Delmore, we are traveling to the other side of this cavern, which our guide Sylrastor Gend tells us was once called the Passage of Cronakarl. It will take us to the continent of Southron. There we will do our best to find you shelter and supplies. However, the journey may take a great while, at least several days, and we have limited food and water for everyone here. We have wounded, elderly, and the young with us who will need to be helped along. If you can, please leave behind anything that will slow us down."

There was some grumbling amid the people, but they complied. Most were happy just to be alive and on the move. Trem turned to Gend as they began to line up before the exit. "You and I will stay in the lead. The rest will mix in with the people. You are responsible for finding the path, and as swiftly as possible."

The halfling, perhaps affected by the stern and irritable tone Trem used, simply nodded his assent. They began the trek slowly but steadily. Gend walked just in front of Trem holding aloft a torch to light the way. Trem's stronger vision was helped greatly by this, and he was one of the few in the caravan that could see the remains of artwork and architecture adorning the walls as they marched. On several occasions he thought he spotted the remains of ancient writing on the stone, in places seemingly written over the carvings carefully etched into the walls. Trem felt the hairs on the back of his neck rise when he wondered whether someone in a violent fury had scratched some of the script over meaningful art. The hours of walking and the consistency of such strange sights eventually caused the concern to fade and, like the others, he concentrated on putting one foot in front of the other.

The line of refugees stretched far back down the road through the caverns. So far in fact, that messages had to be passed through the line and would take many minutes to reach one end from the other. Those behind eventually stopped trying to communicate with those in front, and continued to walk as long as whoever occupied the space in front of them was moving forward. As the hours passed, with only a very brief pause for the distribution of rations, the groan of wheels and snorting of horses were the only sounds in the tunnels.

In the middle of the line, Ghost walked beside Carock, keeping his ornery mount on the opposite side of himself and the people he was watching. Several in his pocket of the column had faltered or slipped as they grew tired, and he had begun paying particular attention to an older couple that was clinging to one another for support. As the man stumbled yet again, Ghost caught him and, with surprising delicacy, helped him atop Carock with kind words for the passenger and a stern, almost threatening tone, for the beast he was clambering onto. He turned and helped his wife up as well, cautioning them to remain vigilant and alert him if Carock proved a poor host. The great horse snorted in response, but plodded forward with markedly more care than he had while walking next to his master.

Ghost was watching them go when a voice came, quiet but biting, behind him, "Your occasional kindnesses do not erase everyone's memory of who you are, Napalian."

Caught somewhat unawares, Ghost turned to see Logan standing behind him with his arms crossed. Their contentious relationship had softened somewhat with the need for cooperation, but it seemed the younger man wished to rekindle the feud. At that moment, the exile from the north determined it was not worth his time to trade barbs with the Angladaic and simply answered, "It keeps the line moving, nothing more."

But Logan was not done, and he approached Ghost suddenly, leaning in to speak quietly but in a challenging tone, "I know you care nothing for them and perhaps even less so for us. Whatever it is you might think you can accomplish going south, it will not wipe away the foulness of your deeds. When we are clear of these tunnels I expect you to walk your own dark path as soon as you are able. We will not need people of your ilk in our midst."

"You seem especially intent on badgering me, knight." Normally, the mention of his past would have caused Ghost to recoil in pain at the memory, but he was not going to allow this high-minded man to admonish and judge him so. He leaned in as well, and through gritted teeth came sharp words that pierced Logan's thin armor of righteousness. "You can drop your façade around me, Angladaic. I'm not a fool. You are on no Rite to achieve the title of paladin with your people, and if I were you I would concoct a better lie to explain your presence here to the others. Some of them are more than clever enough to figure you out."

Logan recoiled sharply and stammered out, "I do not know what you are suggesting! I left my home two years ago to perform an act that would be honorable enough to draw the attention of the god Paladinis and am still acting in accordance with the Code of our people in my pursuit of his validation."

"I know I do not come across as a well-read man," Ghost said, "but my father was quite insistent on the depth and breadth of my studies as a young man. The Angladaic Rite calls for quests lasting any length necessary as deemed so by the participant, but few last longer than a year without the candidate admitting failure or dying in the attempt. You may claim you were looking for a cause noble enough to undertake, but had not my home fallen to the coils of that serpent Neroth around the time you left your own lands? Do you really expect me to believe you thought there was a more pressing endeavor to throw your sword behind than the hostile takeover of a neighboring nation by one of your own god's greatest rivals?"

Now Logan was truly off-balance, unable to form any sort of respone under the verbal onslaught of Ghost, spoken so calmly and matter-of-factly that he had to have put the pieces together some time ago. The Napalian straightened and stared down his crooked, angular nose at Logan. "I've no interest in revealing your lies, though I do wonder what really drove you out of Angladais. I also wonder how much you told your fanged friend. With his dog-like loyalty, I doubt you needed to say much to gain his assistance when you left."

"Leave Grimtooth out of this, you bastard," Logan hissed. "He is my bloodbrother, that was enough for him to come along."

"Convenient for you," Ghost said. "Now listen very carefully to me. I am not a man who goes about airing others' secrets or demanding they come clean. Keep your sins, whatever they are, to yourself, knight. But if you ever again dare to pass judgment on me or feel it your duty to remind me of my failures remember this: a man as foul as you deem me would have no qualms about killing someone like you."

Without another word, Ghost spun on his heel and rejoined the men and women walking steadily down the cavern road. Logan felt his head swimming in shock and frustration as he tried to calm himself after the unexpected turn his conversation with Ghost had taken. The knight had thought to assert some manner of control and authority over what he believed was the most poisonous element in their small, fracturing group. Instead he felt his own conscience tested and almost undone. He wiped sweat from his brow and tried to slow his racing heart. Logan nearly struck Grimtooth when the orc clapped him on the shoulder. Sensing his bloodbrother's disturbed mood, Grimtooth tried to find the root of it. "Ach, Logan. What be eatin' ye so?"

But, strangely, the knight brushed his hand away and his face became a mask of determination and focus once again. "Nothing, just a bit tired is all. Let's keep moving."

Without waiting for Grimtooth, Logan turned and walked onward at a rapid pace, surpassing the gait of many in the caravan as he sped into the darkness ahead of him. The orc watched him for a time, greatly confused and not a little concerned, before shrugging and helping a few struggling refugees keep their young children going next to a wobbling cart that seemed to be threatening collapse. Whatever was eating at Logan would surely not come to anything of dire importance before they reached the end of this lightless road.

The first two days of the journey were little more than a blur of marching, brief stops to eat and rotate the young and infirm through the limited spaces allocated them on the carts, and the rare extended periods of rest when Gend stopped to investigate the road signs carved in stone. Diaga had awoken midway through the first day of their trek and his strength and energy had returned rapidly. He soon joined Trem and Gend at the front of the line of survivors and watched every perusal of the wall markings with the curious eye of a scholar. Gend seemed extremely uncomfortable with Diaga's presence and even more so with his questions about the dwarven script he was interpreting, particularly those related to how he learned such an archaic language. The halfling always rambled on with some vague explanation and changed the subject, which Diaga feared might mean he was going largely off of memory rather than any actual ability to interpret the runes on the walls.

Trem was more supportive of their diminuitive guide, and tried to keep his confidence up through reassurance and gentle chiding of Diaga for his more incisive queries. The mage tried to voice his concerns about their becoming lost in the tunnels, which after the first day had begun to branch off from the main road with increasing frequency, but the half-elf continually reminded him they had little choice but to trust Gend. It was not as though there was another guide there with them and Diaga had admitted he was unable to read the dwarven runes here, which were older or of a different dialect than what little dwarven he had learned in his own studies. Though he did not like the circumstances they were traveling under, Diaga did have to admit Trem was right about them having little choice, and began to consciously limit his pestering of the halfling guide.

Instead, the young wizard tried to carry on conversations with his half-elf companion, which was difficult to do, as Trem seemed determined to keep his distance even when he was willing to talk. At times, Diaga was certain he would have had more productive and insightful discussions with Rath, whose shadow occasionally crept into the corners of his vision. Trem once told Diaga that he suspected the black-clad figure was keeping an eye on his unlikely halfling friend, but also admitted he too was sometimes unnerved by the stealth Rath exhibited flitting about the caves.

It was on the third day that Diaga finally worked up the courage to broach a topic with Trem that he had felt compelled to discuss for some time, but had not yet found the chance to mention. Trem was in a rarely conversational mood, explaining his earliest days away from his adoptive parents when he made for the town of Halden Bay in an effort to find some word of his birth mother. As he tried to pass, like a somber cloud, over the subject, Diaga brashly interrupted him, "You cannot hide forever behind the excuse of being an orphan, or cursed, or whatever woebegotten tale you tell yourself to validate your guilt and fear, Trem. Among the members of our unlikely company, such self-deceptions hold no water."

Trem halted and looked at him with such shock and borderline fury that Diaga almost immediately regretted what he had said, but rather than apologize he too ceased walking and plunged forward with his argument. "Maybe you have overlooked the fact that I, and Neep, and Grimtooth are all orphans as well. Or that Ghost has been through a loss possibly worse than ours: that of his children and wife caused by his own misguided actions. And what about Jovanaleth, whose pursuit of his missing father drove him to you? Even Logan told me his mother died giving birth to him and he holds a deep-seeded guilt for his part, however unintended, in her passing. Do you not see that you are not unique in your loss?"

Trem's initial anger softened as the insight of Diaga's words came through, but still he tried to deflect them. "It is not the same. You cannot understand...."

"Enough!" Diaga shouted, and his authoritative bellow brought the attention of Gend and those at the front of the caravan. "Cease your self-pity and excuse making and take accountability for your decisions, no matter their defensibility! Even Ghost does not try to deny his own reprehensible behavior, though he may wish to hide it to dull the pain it brings him when dragged into the revealing light.

Whether you have done good or ill you cannot use the excuse of the gods choosing you as a reason to feel more entitled to grief and mistakes than the rest of us. Was it not those same gods who allowed my parents to be killed, or Grimtooth's? In your loss, you are not unique. All of us who have taken to the aimless wanderings of the road have done so to fill a hole in who and what we are. Your pain and sense of emptiness is common. Did you not yourself say the world was a harsh and brutal place?"

Trem had gone quite still. "I did."

"Then accept it, and do not try to excuse your behavior because misfortune came knocking at your door once or twice or more. You say you gave up the dream of being a hero upon realizing the world is not made up of tales of good battling against evil, fine. I agree, this world and that of the gods is made up of flawed beings fighting over their own beliefs and ideologies. There is no external cause of absolute good or evil, we do either and the fault or praise for both lies at our own feet."

Trem did not speak for a time, as Diaga's words hung in the air and those close enough to have heard his admonishment of the half-elf filed, eyes averted, past them both. Then he gave Diaga a slight nodding of his head, as though acknowledging his words without really accepting them. "Someone once told me that, though perhaps phrased a bit differently. I thought him quite wise at the time."

Despite himself, Diaga was intrigued. "Who was that?"

"Vactan el Vac," Trem answered flatly, and then he bowed his head and rejoined the column walking southward through the caves. Diaga, caught unawares by the revelation, did not watch him go but stared blankly at the space before him where Trem had been for several moments. Then he felt Neep brush up against him reassuringly, and as though he was coming out of a trance, he stroked her fur and allowed her to lead him down the road with the rest of the column, deep in thought and unsure if he had made his point to Trem or had it utterly and unquestionably refuted by him.

The third day of travel seemed to bring them to the darkest stretch of the caverns. The shafts of light that sometimes pierced the roof were nowhere to be seen and the torches, which had been replenished with hay and pitch from the wagons, were a necessity. Moreover, the road itself had become uneven and in places was covered with debris ranging from shards of rock to items of wood and metal. Several times, the travelers stopped to examine what was left lying in the road, but all of it seemed aged and worn to the point of uselessness. Diaga had agreed with Gend, the make of everything they found was dwarven, but he insisted it was older than most crafts one would find among the dwarves of the present age. It went this way for three more days and the mood of all the members of the long line was foul. Even the normally kindly Grimtooth grew sullen and quiet.

By the sixth day, Gend was actively trying to cheer them all up, promising they were near the dwarven settlement of Sunhall and there would be rest and respite for them there, as well as the good news that they were within a single day's march of the exit. This word spread down the line and the mood brightened among everyone significantly. The passages became more clearly marked with directions for various smaller settlements, at least according to Gend, and even Trem noticed a distinct difference in the frequency and shape of the symbols. As they began to walk downward into the caves at the beginning of the sixth day, the number of carvings increased. Trem saw several that caught his attention.

In the first few there seemed to be words or directions along with markers suggesting they might have been road signs for underground travelers. Trem noted that Gend stopped to check these markings whenever he encountered a fork. The half-elf watched as the markings began to be accompanied by drawings of what he supposed were dwarves. The short squat figures were depicted brandishing axes or picks and usually hammering away at rocks or outcrops in stone walls. In a few cases, he thought he made out the figure of giant clawed creatures carrying the dwarves through heavy stone, but he could not be sure.

The walk went on for several hours. Gend's pace remained steady the entire way and he eventually started them up several stone ramps. Trem took this as an indication they were nearing the exit, since they were now climbing instead of descending or traveling on what he had perceived as flattened earth. At last, they seemed to find a final massive fork with two impressive stone archways carved above the tunnels. One had ivy leaves down to the smallest detail wrapping about it, with a large sun rising over the height of the arch. Another was decorated with small pieces of gold and silver along with other fine minerals. Trem assumed this led to a mining region of the caves, just as he expected the central one, wrapped in strange vines with the symbol of the rising sun, led to the surface.

But Gend turned to the right tunnel, which appeared to be descending once again. Trem paused and examined the arch, now noticing it too was wrapped in vines but much thicker and with small thorns. He also thought he could make out the shapes of strange humanoids, clearly not dwarves, among the weaving tendrils. Gend stopped a few feet into the tunnel. "Come on now, this way. We're going to make a stop in Sunhall"

Trem looked at the halfling then brushed the archway to his tunnel. It was smoother and more worn as though someone had tried to sand away the carvings or portions of them. Trem looked back towards the central path where the column of refugees was waiting. "Are you sure, Gend? I can practically smell the wind from this direction."

The halfling smiled disarmingly. "Oh, to be certain that leads to the surface, but the dwarves down here can resupply us all. It will make the journey beyond the passage more bearable and it's a very short walk from here."

Trem hesitated a moment longer, then shrugged. "Well, I suppose you would know best."

The archway opened up into a wide, spiraling ramp that, like a screw, spun down into the earth. The caravan continued downward for a short time, just as Gend had promised. The walls in this part of the caves were not dry as they had been before. Moisture clung to the rock and dripped from the ceiling, and though it had been cool beneath the earth during most of the journey, Trem now felt a distinct chill in the air. Gend forged ahead at the same pace as always and the half-elf matched his speed, though he kept an eye on those behind him to make sure they did not falter. The spiral finally flattened out a few moments later and Trem could see they were in another massive cavern, this one dripping water from the walls and, improbably, growing strange plants in the gloom. Far above and in the distance, he could see a vast opening in the ceiling that, had it been daytime, would have revealed a great deal of light. Gend stepped towards the center and turned. "This is the dwarven settlement of Sunhall. We can rest here, as I said, it is not much farther now."

Trem nodded and made room for the rest of the procession. The refugees gratefully laid down their wounded and few remaining belongings for a break they had not expected. The wagons and horses were left above the spiraling ramp, tethered to stone hooks that Gend had helpfully pointed out to the people of Delmore as they entered the long rampway. Standing in the great cavern, Trem was joined by Logan and Jovan, while Neep and Diaga wandered off to a nearby alcove to examine the odd things growing about the walls. Logan glanced around and rubbed his thickening facial scruff quizzically. "Strange cavern we have here. I dare say I have never heard of such a thing."

Grimtooth plucked one of the leaves from a nearby plant. "Ach, they do be smellin' somethin' terrible, Logan."

The knight wrinkled his nose in agreement as Ghost grunted, "If the mage could be bothered I bet he could tell us more about what this place is. He seems to know about these sorts of things."

"This is Sunhall," Gend piped up, "the youngest of the Hulduvarn dwarven settlements, founded by Wyldan Cronakarl to serve as a trade town connecting Southron and Legocia."

Diaga rejoined them, several samples of the plantlife in his possession now. "And the dwarves here have not been heard from in centuries. Most believe them to be dead."

"It certainly doesn't look occupied," Ghost agreed.

A sudden crash whirled the company around. Across the cavern, they heard stone strike the floor and then the distinct soft whisper of leather on rock. Trem waved at the people of Delmore to be quiet and began sneaking around the foliage and boulders to get a look at the far side of the cave. Trem had his sword drawn and the knight and Napalian were slowly following suit, covering his flanks while trying to remain quiet. Jovan glanced back behind them and whispered to Diaga, "Where have Gend and Rath gone to?"

The Napalian waved him into silence as Trem reached his vantage point. The half-elf paused as he studied the odd sight, and then he motioned the others to join him. He pointed around the corner and they all leaned out to see what he had spotted. The scene beyond the large rocks that had obscured their view of the main portion of the cavern was astounding. Great stalks of strange, brilliantly colored fungi and lichen were clinging to the walls, but also sprouting in all directions from the floor. Amid the growths were a number of ramshackle buildings, seemingly on the verge of collapsing, made of stone and some sparse bits of wood or perhaps hunks of the alien plantlife of the cavern. They were of a design and form that was impossible to place and perhaps not meant to be reflective of any one culture or society, for it seemed that the lowest structures had been carefully assembled from professionally cut stone, the work of true artisans. Yet, the gaps amid those fine works were filled with hunks of unmatched rock and debris, simply meant to do the job of sealing up holes in the original design. The windows of the low, squat buildings looked to have metal bars in them, not for imprisonment but the support of glass, but there were no panes in any of the portals and it gave the whole settlement an uninviting and rather bleak look.

Trem and the others could hear, though not see, the dripping and bubbling of flowing water, and it seemed there must be a stream beyond the settlement, which was lit not by torches but by several transparent sacks of indeterminate material holding writhing swarms of fireflies. Among the faint light that shimmered and shook across the faces of the buildings were shadows of the worn homes and shops, though the purpose of each structure was unclear from design and they bore no signs or symbols to denote their intended use. The scenery itself would have been astounding, but it was enhanced further by a large number of moving forms amid the mushrooms and structures. Several short stocky figures were wandering around the section nearest the travelers' end of the cave, apparently listening intently. Trem looked back towards the refugees. The somewhat stifled noise of their chatter was drawing the group towards them. Logan hefted his sword in preparation to fight, but Jovan stayed his hand whispering, "Look!"

As the figures came closer, Trem could make out the distinct beards and thick hair of dwarves. They came slowly and tentatively in the direction of the milling people. They were clad in heavy leather armor and carried spears and axes, though very crude ones. To Trem they looked rather out of place, like a race of dwarves from long past. Their weapons were of metal, but a roughly forged kind and their leather armor looked poorly cured. Still, he knew of no dwarves that would wish to bring harm on the refugees of Delmore or his friends, and Trem sheathed his weapon turning to his party. "There are dwarves here, as Gend claimed. I doubt they are a danger to us. We should at least greet them instead of hiding behind these rocks."

The company made its way slowly out from their hiding spot and approached carefully so as not to startle the mass of dwarves. As soon as they were spotted, the apparent leader, judging by his slightly taller stature and finery, held up his hand and halted his own troops while watching the newcomers patiently.

Trem went a few extra steps forward and he could see there were nearly fifty of them there. The half-elf waved in greeting. "Underdwellers," he addressed them in common with their formal name, "I am Trem Waterhound, and these are my companions. We are merely passing through your realm on our way to the southern lands. We were told we might find you here and would be grateful of any assistance you can offer."

The leader of the group, the same slightly larger dwarf with a graying beard with gold circlets banded round several thicker braids responded in a halting, choppy pattern of speech, "Friends are you to us. We not enemies. We bring food."

And with a wave of his hand the leader sent twenty or so dwarves scurrying away into the settlement behind them where they began rummaging about loudly and calling to one another in a language none of the adventurers recognized. Trem led the rest of the odd dwarves to the refugees who, though initially frightened by the strangers, were happy when they learned food was to be brought to them. The dwarves also hauled in large tables, crude ones but certainly sturdy enough, along with benches to match. The people of Delmore began to talk excitedly when they realized a real feast was being prepared.

Trem stood off to one side with the leader of the dwarves. The strange and slow speech of their kind surprised him, but he presumed they had been living far from outsiders for so long they probably barely kept any knowledge of the common tongue. The dwarves, at least now that they appeared organized, hardly spoke among themselves and only in strange, haltingly guttural, voices. Some of the Delmore refugees tried to engage them, but found they either could not or would not respond. This oddity was forgotten as more and more strange food began to arrive to decorate the table.

The leader of the dwarves addressed Trem, "We have king. You, leader of people outside, come meet king."

Trem looked at Logan as though seeking permission or perhaps hoping the knight would lay claim to the responsibility, but the Angladaic waved him off. "You took up the task of speaking to them, Trem, go and meet their king. I'm tired of acting as the diplomat. We will be sure to save you something to eat."

Trem waved to the knight in acceptance, and strode off to the far side of the cavern with his guide and two other dwarves. Jovanaleth sat at the bench and watched the food being slowly piled onto the massive table before him. Ghost plopped down next to him and snorted, "Doesn't smell like much, but I will eat anything at this point."

Jovan smiled and glanced around. Then he turned to Ghost. "Where is Trem going?"

The Napalian waved disinterestedly. "Oh, to meet their king or some such nonsense."

Jovan took another, harder look around. "And where are Gend and Rath? They have been missing since the dwarves arrived."

Ghost slapped the young man hard on the back. "Stop fretting, boy, I am sure they will turn up. Try and enjoy a little respite once in a while."

Trem followed the older dwarf back to the end of the cave, through the strange and ruined settlement. He tried to engage his companion in conversation, particularly with questions about the disheveled and seemingly unsafe conditions of Sunhall, if that was indeed the area he was being led through, but received only curt and vague answers. As he walked through the town, he noticed many eyes watching him from the open windows and around the dark corners. The whole place seemed to have turned out to see him pass through, which seemed odd but not threatening. They passed the edge of town and a tunnel appeared before them, well lit and finely carved like those above the spiraling ramp that had led to Sunhall. The leader gestured with one hand. "You go there. Meet king."

Trem paused and looked at the walls. A clearly human figure with a well trimmed goatee and slick dark hair of obsidian stone rested over the entrance to the tunnel. The carving looked newer than those he had seen elsewhere, and at the same time also oddly familiar. Trem turned to his guide. "Who is he? I mean, what should I call him?"

The dwarf shrugged and did not answer, but gestured more earnestly towards the tunnel. Trem looked at the carving once again, but was still unable to place its origin and so he nodded in thanks and proceeded through the entrance. The tunnel curved gently and at a gradual angle, but the perfect placement and order of wall torches gave it an almost never ending feel, though Trem guessed he only walked for several minutes. He came to the end with another arch and the same strange figure astride it. Trem paused once again, an odd feeling of forboding coming over him, and then stepped into the room.

The room was a perfect dome with a fine mosaic-tiled floor. Everything about it suggested it was much more recent and better maintained than the other areas the dwarves appeared to inhabit. Trem stepped onto the mosaic and examined it. A large plain with woods and mountains in the background made up the majority of it. The image was well crafted and captivating, and Trem felt he could not tear his eyes away. He could see humans, elves, dwarves, all with incredibly minute details in appearance and dress cleverly composed of glasslike colored tiles, all a wide variety of sizes and used to increase the degree of clarity to stunning effect. They were depicted hunting, farming, trading, and wandering the various scenes of towns, hills, and forests. To Trem, it seemed like the artwork itself was alive.

The lights about Trem seemed to dim and he glanced up. The wall torches in the hall began to go out one by one. Then, in a circular pattern about the chamber, several sconces dimmed slowly before ultimately being snuffed out and the room darkened considerably. Only two of the largest wall torches remained burning across from where Trem stood on the edge of the tiled floor, framing a great black iron throne he had failed to notice upon entering, in its seat a pile of oddly yellow roses. He expected the trick of the light to bring the arrival of the king he was expected to meet, but a few moments of quiet where nothing stirred told him he was mistaken.

Waiting, Trem glanced back down at the mosaic and was horrified to see the sudden changes that had taken place. A thick, dark cloud had settled over the pastoral image, and streaks of red and white bolts lanced from the sky. The once-peaceful mortal inhabitants were being struck by fire and lightning or were under attack from strange black robed creatures and other, shadowy monsters appearing from all about them. Before Trem's eyes, the mosaic seemed to move, and he thought he could hear cries of fear and confusion from it, though he knew that must have been impossible.

"Trem Waterhound, at last we meet."

Trem did not recognize the voice, but the visage was the same he had seen over the archway entering the throne room. It was a smiling, handsome face, not of a dwarf but a human man, with an immaculately maintained and oiled goatee beneath smooth, well-kept hair. The figure sighed and sat languidly in the throne, tossing the roses to the ground. "You almost made it out, you know. All you had to do was stay in the forest with your nice little hut and your sad little life. Then you could have lived through all this. For a time at least."

"You're no dwarf," Trem straightened defensively. "Who are you?"

"Ahh," the man said, throwing one leg over the arm of the throne, "I am someone you know well, though maybe you do not realize it. Perhaps a shift in appearance?"

Trem watched agog as the figure reformed and, sitting in the same position was a man with elven features but far more advanced in age. Though he had not seen him clearly in his dreams, Trem recognized this as Gerand Oakheart and this was driven home when the man spoke in his voice, "You really do not take advice well, do you know that? You went back to Delmore, and now the fates of so many are irreparably altered for the worse."

Trem glanced down to find he had drawn his blade unconsciously. He twirled it restlessly and said, "You impersonated Grandfather Forest and tried to lead me here alone, without the others. Why? What sort of man are you, who rules over dwarves and can enter another's dreams in disguise?"

A loud spurt of laughter followed Trem's impassioned questions. "Oh truly, Trem, you are too much. You really think I am some petty lord over a load of unwashed dwarves? Can you not see the truth before you?"

Trem was baffled and slow to respond, so, now rather annoyed at the delay in Trem's understanding, the man continued, swinging his velvet robes forward majestically as he stood. "I am Balthazain, the God of Betrayers, and you are in my temple. Indeed, all of these caverns are mine to hold sway over. I sent one of my most loyal servants to join your little band of adventurers and steer you here, just as I sent my slyths to kill and impersonate the dwarves of Sunhall so many eons ago."

Trem snarled in sudden understanding and anger. "You are planning on killing my friends, and the people of Delmore! For what, simply traveling with me?"

"They would have been spared if you had listened to me, or Gerand Oakheart, if you prefer to think of it that way. I was tasked only with ensnaring you and one other, the rest are an unfortunate addition, but one that will please my loyal slyth disciples. They have been without fresh victims for so long."

The half-elf spun to leave and warn his companions, but found his path blocked by the robed form of his enemy, having appeared before him without apparent effort. Balthazain smiled unkindly at him. Trem raised his sword to strike. "Get out of my way, fiend. I am not one of your victims or servants."

"Ah, Trem," Balthazain laughed, "what are you thinking of doing? Rushing out there to save your 'friends' as you call them? Or perhaps you want to run me through with your sword. Well, that won't do. It is time to stop pretending you have lived life more honorably than is true."

Trem felt the blade quivering in his hands. The shaking grew more and more violent as he held it, and Balthazain's eyes bore down on the steel. The blade shimmered and fire lanced across it. Trem grasped it with both hands and tried to steady his command over the weapon. Balthazain's laughter echoed around him. "This is my realm you stand in now, Trem Waterhound, and anything taken in betrayal is mine to rule. And if I want to," Balthazain's mirth ceased and he grew impossibly immense, overtaking the room itself, "I can break that which is mine."

The sword exploded in Trem's grip. Shards of metal flew from it and embedded in his head, hands, chest, and arms. Trem howled in pain and fell to one knee. Balthazain's laugh returned to rebound off the walls. "Now what will you do, Trem Waterhound? You are not even worth my time. I will leave you to someone else, the same one who led you here in the first place, and you do not even know whom, do you? A shame, because you will not be able to see them in the dark."

And as Balthazain spoke, the last torches went out and Trem was plunged into complete blackness.

Chapter 28

Arvadis led the way back into his palace. The large doors of the throne room closed slowly behind the small group as they stalked cautiously down the carpeted hall. Arvadis halted them and waved Calavar to one side, sending Vorasho to the other. He continued up the center towards the throne with Lena positioned protectively behind him. Vorasho swept back the nearest wall hanging, ensuring no one was lurking behind it, and moved on to the next one. Calavar continued the same process on the other side, pushing back the heavy woven cloth with his war hammer. As Arvadis neared the throne, he thought he caught movement to his right. He paused just as Lena cried out, "Above us!"

Vendile appeared on the balcony with a crossbow tucked under one arm and fired. Arvadis turned at the same moment as Lena shouted. The bolt struck him in the shoulder and knocked him back a step. He grunted and pointed his blade to the twin curving stairs beyond the throne. "After him!"

But Vendile was just a distraction. From behind the throne itself, two of his guards appeared, swinging aggressively for the returning king. Arvadis deflected the blade of the first and Lena managed to deter the second by feigning a jab with her sword. Calavar turned to come to their aid, but down the stairs rushed five more men, one in the rear with another crossbow. Calavar made a snap decision and sprang into action, intercepting the new arrivals before they could help the other two guards. Vorasho careened into the men who had charged down the stairs as well, thrusting his staff forward like a spear and catching the first guard in the face, breaking his nose. Vorasho spun around another guard and rushed the crossbowman in an attempt to stop him before he could fire.

Lena put her back to Arvadis's and the two struggled to fend off the guards attacking them. Arvadis slammed his fist into the chest of his opponent. "Duck!"

Lena dove for the floor and Arvadis' blade cut over her head with shocking speed for such an old fighter. The wild swing forced the second guard back and Lena was granted an opening. Arvadis set his feet and adopted a defensive stance calling, "Go after Vendile! Stop him if you can!"

Lena rolled away from their assailants, pausing to consider helping Arvadis, but Vorasho had carved a clear path up the stairs for her so she flew past the enemy, following the wake of the prince's barrage. Calavar flattened the foot of one of the guards with his hammer, and he fell screaming to the floor. The Highlord raised his shield to block the swing of the other two men attacking him and backed towards the throne. Lena sprinted past them, but on her way thrust her sword into the back of the guard with the ruined nose. The crossbowman saw her intent and trained his weapon on her, but Vorasho dove, tackling him on the steps and sending them both rolling to the bottom in a fearsome grapple. Lena dodged as one of the soldiers on the stairs gave her a half-hearted swing and began looking around for his best chance of escape. She was now clear of the fighting and on her way up the stairs, taking them two at a time.

Arvadis thrust at the guard he had driven backward and felt his blade bite through his armor and into his chest. Unprepared, he threw up his metal gauntlet, deflected the second guard's blade off of its steel, and pulled his weapon free. With incredible ferocity, he slashed at his foe's shoulder, hewing his arm nearly off. The guard shrieked and fell writhing to the ground. Arvadis did not stop to finish him, but instead rushed to aid Calavar. Vorasho had the archer on the ground and delivered an overhead smash with his staff that split his head in two. He leapt up, tripping the guard that had swiped at Lena, and started up the stairs. As he glanced back his father yelled, "Go, my son! We can handle these!"

Vorasho made haste, taking the stairs in leaps and bounds, shouting Lena's name as he went. Arvadis went back to back with Calavar, the two older men catching their breath and sizing up the remaining opposition. Calavar was wheezing slightly but his ruddy face was split in a mad grin. "Can't recall why I gave this up, Arvadis, I feel young again!"

Vorasho glanced back one last time, seeing the two older men ready to strike at their uncertain enemies. Confident they would be able to handle themselves, he redoubled his efforts to find Lena. He heard her calling as he crested the stairs. Reaching the landing of the main balcony, he paused and then broke into a sprint in the direction of Lena's voice as she called out to him, "Here! I am over here!"

Vorasho sped after her, staff raised, looking for any threat that might be lying in wait. It seemed most people, from servants to Vendile's remaining thugs, had abandoned the hallways as he raced along, trying to train in on the sound of Lena's footsteps and cries. She had not slowed her pace as Vendile's purple robe flitted around a corner and up some stairs. She followed him doggedly. Lena paused briefly, looking back to see that Vorasho was some distance behind her but coming on as fast as he could. Afraid of losing the usurper, she did not slow her gait, instead counting on him to keep up. She spun round a corner and into another long hallway off the main throne hall and skidded to a sharp halt. Vendile had frozen suddenly before her and was looking wildly about him as though he had lost his way. Lena relaxed slightly and gestured at him commandingly. "Vendile! You have nowhere to go!"

Karsyrus snarled and ripped off his heavy robe, tossing it to the ground. It had slowed his escape, but he had been loath to leave it behind as it symbolized his waning authority. Seeing his plans were coming down around him, he looked to his right and saw the hallway turn out of sight of his pursuer, who was still some distance away. Running around the corner, he recognized the door to the alcoves above the council chamber. He threw himself into them and rocketed forward, but as he stood against the railing he hesitated, now seeing the floor was a fair distance below him. In desperation he put one foot up on the railing and almost threw himself off of it, but then his cowardice took over and he raced back into the hallway and, without considering his destination, burst into another room.

Vendile paused inside. This was the study he had formerly occupied as a Highlord, and he briefly thought about how odd it was he had not recognized it when he rushed madly into the room. Without much pause for reflection, he slammed the heavy oak door shut and heaved a large bureau in front of it. He leaned against the obstruction, breathing hard. Vendile had discarded his crossbow and was left with no more elaborate schemes for his escape or victory. In his brief moment of respite, he simply wanted to find a way out of the palace.

Vendile glanced around and nearly fell over when he saw Freyan sitting calmly at his former desk as though it were any normal afternoon. The former Broken raider was perusing some manual with which Vendile was, intentionally, unfamiliar. As if reading his mind, the former advisor to the false king spoke, not bothering to bring his head up from his reading, "Such a waste of valuable texts in this room. Truly your family must be proud of your lack of knowledge. One would almost suspect you worked harder to maintain your ignorance than some do to overcome it."

Freyan slammed the heavy cover shut and turned in the chair, smiling pleasantly. Vendile was livid, but he was too stunned, and admittedly a bit unnerved, by Freyan's behavior to answer. Never had Freyan been anything but subservient; it was as though a different man sat before him. The slight figure rose from the chair, brushed his smooth, simple robes and reached out to grab a thin wooden staff. He smiled again at Vendile, framed around his nondescript face were his long, shining black strands of hair. "You were almost good enough, Karsyrus. I thought your obvious madness might be tamed through my careful interference, particularly if I remained embarrassingly cowed and at your beck and call. Still, your family history, which I have been perusing for some time while the ruckus outside has escalated, should have been enough for me to realize you were not capable of ruling. It is probably for the best. I'd have had to remove you before you held the title for very long."

Vendile straightened himself, wiping the sweat from his brow. "I gave you a life when you were but a beggar, Freyan! How dare you stand here and tell me you have pulled my puppet strings!"

"But I do, even now." Freyan's eyes fell on the strange metal pendant with its three dark stones that Vendile was unconsciously clutching in his free hand, the thin chain pressed tightly against the skin about his neck as he pulled on it in anger. The Highlord looked down at his hand and yelled in fury, snapping the chain, but as he held the item outward, ready to discard it, he hesitated. His former advisor smiled unnervingly at him. "Still you cannot rid yourself of it. Your family has a history of insanity and sadistic behavior, but that item enhanced it and made you easier to manipulate. Though I fear I allowed it to go too far."

"It's just a piece of metal," Vendile insisted, but still he could not release his grasp.

Freyan shook his head, apparently ashamed at Vendile's ignorance. "I have, from the first day we met, merely played the role of your servant. I am indeed a servant, but it is not to you. Nor will it ever be. This experiment of mine was doomed from the beginning. I will allow my hands to be wasted on such foolish projects no more."

Vendile laughed then. "They will not let you live, Freyan. Arvadis knows well the role you have played."

"I will not be here to receive his judgment. At least not today."

Vendile snarled and slammed his fist holding the pendant into the wall. "You have nowhere to go. No exit other than out that window and onto the hard ground below, and I doubt you have the stomach for that."

"Ah, and you do?"

"I will not have to," the madman chuckled. "The Code, old Hawking loves it and his pathetic laws. He cannot execute a man of the Highlord rank. We can only be imprisoned. If he can escape those dungeons than so might I."

Freyan tapped his staff on the floor and pulled his hood over his head. "You will do no such thing, Highlord Vendile. The wind tells me you will not outlive this coup, nor will your branch of the family line. Your name dies today."

Vendile sputtered in fury then began to laugh, high-pitched and cackling. "And now my former ragged advisor is a true clairvoyant! A speaker of real fortunes and not some charlatan worming his way into my good graces! What a travesty you are, Freyan, a disgrace even to your vile people!"

Freyan turned and paused for a final parting shot over his shoulder, "The Broken are not my people. Goodbye, Karsyrus."

Vendile continued to laugh as Freyan walked slowly to the window and pushed the shutters wide. Strapping his staff to his belt he climbed into the opening. "You best grow wings quickly, Freyan," Vendile shrieked hysterically, "lest you end as a grease mark on the stones of my kingdom!"

But Freyan leapt from the high window and Vendile could not resist rushing to it to watch his former servant's demise. But as he fell, Freyan's shape changed, his black robes pulled in and collapsed his limbs, as his feet seemed to spread across his body. Then a raven flew like a bolt up past the window with a last cry as it zipped away, heading south towards the tall, imposing woods of Silverleaf Forest. Vendile stood stunned with his hands upon the windowframe, unable to comprehend what had happened. Then he heard a snapping of wood and spun to see a blade appear in the doorjamb. It shot up and down, trying to snap the thin wood block as someone slammed against the heavy door. Vendile's eyes flitted back and forth. He held up his hands before his face and tried to will a similar change to Freyan's own in them.

Lena threw her weight into the door again. She had dashed around the corner after Vendile, finding an empty hall with closed doors and no sign of her quarry. She had directed Vorasho to cover their enemy's escape, in case he had hidden and was waiting for her to enter the wrong room so he could slip past her. Vorasho had called from behind her, pleading with Lena to wait as he sped towards her position, but Lena could see only the face of Graham contorted in unending sorrow as he clutched Derek's body. She was determined to reach Vendile first. She had recognized the finery of the doors to the council chamber, but even more importantly the bat shaped seal on the knob of Vendile's study. Guessing correctly, she had tried to enter Vendile's quarters and been rebuffed, but heard the voices beyond. Her slight body slammed into the heavy door again, and the bureau, filled at its top with fine jewelry of extraordinary weight, tipped and fell inward, its base cracking the door as it ground against it. Lena hacked at the door with her sword to finish the job and then she was within the chamber.

Vendile was at the desk, his back turned to her with his left hand, a thin metal chain running through a strange medallion beneath it, resting on the pages of some old volume. The page that was to the right was blank, but Lena did not pause to consider why Vendile would be looking in an unfinished book. She crept towards him and he looked up almost immediately. She stopped and raised her sword, for his eyes were wild with madness. Lena steadied the blade. "Do not move, snake. You are staying right here until my friends come."

Lena thought she could hear Vorasho's footsteps in the hall and his voice calling loudly for her, but she was fixated on her target. Vendile's fingers slid slowly off the page and the bauble and chain fell to the floor. "Of course, my dear," he took a step towards her, "no need to threaten me. I am done for."

Lena thrust the blade forward, stopping his advance. "Not another move or I will carve out your eyes."

Vendile curled his lip in a half snarl, but he took half a step back. A cry came loudly down the hall and Lena recognized Vorasho's voice. She called out, "Here! I have him in here!"

Vendile relaxed in front of her and Lena heard Vorasho's voice calling to her again, now closer but unsure. She looked over her shoulder and shouted, "In here! I am in...."

Lena's hand released the sword and she slumped. Her body seemed to fold and she had trouble looking up. Vendile's rough facial hair brushed against her forehead as he slowly pulled free the dagger he had driven under her ribs. Lena felt the blood rise in her mouth and coughed. Bright red flecks spattered onto his cheek as Vendile lowered her to the floor. Lena continued to cough, struggling to breathe. Vendile straightened and stepped over her prostrate form and into the doorway. He caught sight of Vorasho coming around the corner as he paused, looking desperately from side to side. Vendile sprang from the doorway and took off back towards the observation platform above the council hall. Vorasho reached the open door and immediately saw the crumpled form of Lena. He stopped short and fell to his knees, crying, "Lena!"

The young woman coughed a few times and more blood foamed and ran down the side of her mouth. Vorasho cradled her head, letting his staff fall to the floor. "Lena, oh gods, Lena! Hold on, I will get you to Calavar or the priests!"

But as he began to straighten and pull her up with him a terrible grip seized his arm and held him back. She mouthed a few words, but Lena Engrove's mouth was full of blood and she could not speak. Vorasho tried again to raise her from the ground, but she held him fast and coughed again, red flecks spattering across Vorasho's armor. The eldest Hawking son was openly crying now. "Lena, please do not make me do this."

Lena's eyes bored into him, even as they looked beyond his face, and then her body slumped hard into dead weight and the blue orbs glazed over. Vorasho watched his tears hit her face as it relaxed and she seemed to reach a peaceful, yet inhuman, state. Vorasho cradled her as her blood continued to spread across the floor in a bright crimson pool. Lena felt heavy in his arms and he had to place her head on the ground. He went to reach for his staff, just to have something to lean on, and a smooth soft velvet boot pinned it to the ground. Vorasho looked up to see Vendile, whom, having seen the weakness in Vorasho's grief had once again abandoned his risky attempt at escape, looming above him. He held a bloody knife in his hand and smiled madly. "A shame, really, she was lovely enough to be a future concubine. But you see, I will have plenty when I go to the invaders and get my own army. Something I should have done before, instead of playing games with your foolish father!"

Vendile kicked Vorasho in the face, sending him sprawling. He bent and tossed the staff behind him and walked forward. "Freyan flew the coop," his laughter was hysterical and his speech rapid and broken, "and now I have to get out on my own. I think I might just ask your father how he did it through those dungeons. But I will be sure to bring him with me so I can leave a trail of blood for his loyal subjects to follow."

Vorasho rolled to his side and up on one knee. "You are insane. I will not be letting you anywhere near my father."

Vendile laughed even louder. "Oh, do not fret little Hawking, I intend to kill you first."

The mad Highlord lunged, but Vorasho was too quick, rolling away from him. The crazed nobleman recovered swiftly and slashed Vorasho across the arm. Gritting his teeth, the prince hurled himself through the air, backward after his staff. Vendile rushed him but Vorasho got hold of his weapon and swung it at almost the same moment. The heavy metal staff slammed into Vendile's kneecap just as he neared Vorasho. Howling in pain, the Highlord went down. The prince hopped, catlike, to his feet and swung again, knocking the knife free and backing the now limping Vendile up against the wall. He fell onto his back and scrabbled away from Vorasho in fear. The Highlord attempted to rise but Vorasho kicked him onto his back. Vendile raised his hands defensively. "Please! You cannot kill me! I invoke the Code! I invoke the law! You cannot kill a man without proper trial and justice."

Vorasho slowed, lowering his staff. Vendile's smile was sickly sweet. "And I know you, young Hawking, the Code is your life. You will not betray it like your foolish brother. You have morals and rules to guide you. I know you, I know your family."

Vorasho looked downward at Lena's prone form lying peacefully on the tiles of his kingdom's palace. He hefted his staff and glared sidelong at Vendile. "My family," he whispered, "will understand if I overlook the law, this one time."

Vendile screamed as the heavy staff smashed into his face, again and again, until he could scream no longer. And even then, Vorasho continued the beating until a hand caught the bloodied end of his staff raised for another blow. Spattered in blood and tissue, he turned to see his father with tears in his eyes. Vorasho released the staff and heard its steel crash on the marble floor as though it were miles away. "Justice is done. You are king again, sire."

Arvadis was left staring at the bloody massacre before him. Calavar, over his shoulder, did not stay to speak, but gathered Lena's body gently and left with it as quietly as he could. Arvadis did not cry, in that moment he resolved to hold back his tears for his family and nation, broken as they were. He knelt and picked up his son's heavy staff, feeling the slippery grip of blood-drenched scales beneath his worn fingers. He could not raise it, but tossed it to the ground again and sat on the floor, his head slumped. The cost of his victory fell upon him, the pain settled deep and irremovable within him, and worst of all the knowledge that for all this death he had gained only the right to command a country trapped in its own borders, with no idea still how to save them. The battle had changed nothing, for Arvadis Hawking was still alone.

Chapter 29

Saltilian's eyes remained locked on Edge as he lurched closer, his body moving in a halting, jerking mimickry of walking. Raymir was screaming and her every muscle was stretched taut, yet she could not move to assist him. Edge's eyes remained focused on the mage as he slid close to him, looking his victim up and down as he relished his victory. Edge snarled through barely moving lips at Saltilian, but he could not manage to work his tongue. The mad wizard grasped his face with clawed and bleeding fingers. "No talking yet, no, the pain I will cause will make you strong enough to speak; though I do doubt we will understand your words."

Edge strained his arms, but could not move them against the power of Saltilian's spell. His lisp was gone, his voice changed, something had possessed the wizard, though Edge could not say what. The mage had given himself over to some strange power and nothing the lost elf did was enough to stop his horrific triumph. Saltilian pulled a thin, curved knife from his robes and held it to Edge's face. "We should begin I think, with those magnificent eyes of yours."

Romund had been next to Edge, held as he and Raymir were, but the focus of Saltilian was lessened on him as the wizard began to gloat. The others were the prizes, Romund was just a witness, but as the shell of former humanity before him reached out to torture Edge in front of Raymir, the man from Hethegar could contain himself no longer. Romund wrenched at his invisible bonds and found them loose. With a desperate lunge, he hurled himself awkwardly towards Saltilian and the power holding him broke. The mage's reaction was swifter than the stumbling assault. He whirled to face the desperate older man and extended his hand. A beam of white heat lanced from the wand he held, smashing into Romund's body and hurling him to the snowy ground. Saltilian turned back to his other prisoners and froze.

Edge's fearsome axe-blade protruded from Saltilian's skull. He had been freed by Romund's distraction, and with his one chance he struck true, as Wolfbane had trained him. The maddened eyes rolled back in Saltilian's broken head and he slumped into the snow. Raymir rushed past Edge to Romund's huddled form, now looking so small and frail in the cold snow. The older man raised his hand in warning and slung his cloak over his chest. "No closer child, nothing for you to see here."

Raymir tried to move forward but Edge held her shoulder. "No," was all he said.

Romund propped himself onto his right arm, away from where Saltilian had struck him. His breathing was labored, and his skin white as the carpet of flakes about him, but still he smiled. "Are you both wearing those long faces for me? Come now, I am well past nine lives." He coughed and grimaced. "This was bound to happen."

"Let me see the wound, Romund, I can try to heal...."

A sharp shake of his head cut Raymir off and his voice, now ragged, came sternly towards her, "There is nothing left of me there to heal. Look at him, he knows."

Raymir followed Edge's eyes, which stared stoically at the unnatural dip in Romund's cloak that seemed to envelop his entire left side. She fell to her knees in the agony of her frustration. "Romund! Romund, please, let me try!"

"No," Romund smiled again. "This is the end of the road for me. You must go on, together. Find that tower and stop whatever madness is going on within." Romund sucked in a labored breath, wheezing and gasping. "Promise me something, when you are done I must beg a task of you."

Edge took a step closer and knelt to hold his hand. "Anything, I will do whatever you ask of me."

Romund smiled again, more forced this time. "I know you wish to be done with this violent world we have inherited. I know it. I see it in your eyes every time you look at her. But I must beg this of you, this one thing."

"It is granted, I owe you as much."

Romund nodded and paused to gather some breath. "I am not who I led you to believe. I claimed to be a servant of Hethegar and the Napalian resistance... but I am not." He gasped again, and Edge now knelt at his side and tried to support his slumping head. "I am the king of the Order of the Blade. My true name is Jonathan Blade... and... and I have a son and wife who must be missing me. Please when you are done here go south. Find them... tell them what is coming. Tell them... I did my best to warn them... through you."

Edge nodded, "I will do this Romund, I swear."

"Good," Romund gathered strength from nowhere and sat up a little more to look Edge in the eye. "You are a good man Edge el Vac... never let your past tell you otherwise." The man they had known as Romund slumped slightly and Edge caught him. The old man's hand snapped upward and grasped Edge's cloak with impossible strength as he gasped out one last time, never taking his eyes from Edge's face.

A last wheezing exhalation came from him as Jonathan Blade struggled to get his dying breaths in and out. Edge sat with the man who had been his friend, a true friend, as he slowly faded into death. The wind swirled about them as he held his head and gripped his hand, squeezing the palm. Jonathan Blade stayed alive for some time, though he did not speak. Raymir cried silently to Edge's side, but the lost elf shed not a tear as his friend slowly passed away before him. Even as his hand went cold and limp Edge knelt there in silence, staring at his stiff form. He only moved when the snow began to hide his friend's face, and he was beyond recognition. Then Edge stood, helping Raymir to her feet, and retrieved his halberd. The two turned silently, and aligned themselves with the dark spire. Edge looked down at her and squeezed her shoulder, pulling her in tightly. Wiping her tears, Raymir gathered herself before kneeling to carefully remove the Mirage necklace from around their dead friend's throat. Gently tucking it into her robe, she turned back to Edge and they began to descend the mountain. In their grief, they did not notice amid the swirling snow the torn and tattered pages in an unrecogizeable language fluttering around them, carrying their madness off to the emptiness of the Frozen Reach.

Diaga had been in a dreamless sleep for nearly twenty hours before he had woken in the caverns, a situation he had not experienced since he was deep in training in Ozmandias. The feeling of coming out of such a state was always slow and broken, like scattered thoughts flashing through his mind. In the days since that first awakening, the fogginess had come upon him a few times once again. When rising from the brief respites the group took on their long, dark journey, Diaga would not even open his eyes at first, but simply clutch his wizard's staff, running his fingers over the intricately etched runes. The staff was the one gift he had accepted during his training, an ornate and delicate wood encased in thin metal with strange symbols. Only about a quarter of them did he know or understand, but those he did had proven useful in time. One helped to dispel illusions, and in turn, remove the foggy feeling in his head brought on from arcane exertion if he only used a small amount of magic to power it. Now, amid the strange dwarves of Sunhall, he stroked this same rune with his thumb. Something about this place and the odd plants he had found had made him feel foggy. The soft glow cleared his head and his eyes began to see the world around him more vividly.

Diaga sat beside Ghost at the long table, now laden with strange food, and felt his senses come through more sharply than before. The dwarves had been oddly insistent that the famished travelers wait until all was prepared before dining, perhaps a custom that was native to their kind. Ghost seemed to be increasingly impatient and about to break protocol, gripping the wooden fork he had been given as tightly as he was. The Napalian was not paying him any mind, so Diaga reached within himself and scanned the scene about him, hoping to obtain greater understanding of what made him so uncomfortable about this place. The rest were nearby, seated and talking or laughing with one another and the survivors from Delmore. Diaga could clearly see his friends and allies, but the shapes that were continuing to haul food to them were oddly blurred as though they were underwater. Diaga shook his head and looked down at his staff, thinking he might be touching the wrong rune. It was not, and it glowed and filled him with its familiar warmth, but the blurriness was still there as he looked at the dwarves about them. Sitting up, suddenly concerned, he dug deeper and projected his strength inward to enhance the spell. The images sharpened and at once Diaga saw the horror all around them. He shoved himself up from the bench, knocking much of the food to the ground and startling those near him as he shouted, "Do not eat the food! Get away from them! Get away!"

The entire multitude turned and looked at him in confusion. Neep rushed over in bewilderment with weapons drawn as Jovan strained up from his seat on the other side of Ghost and limped quickly towards his suddenly distraught friend. The young man tried to calm the mage. "It is alright, Diaga. Trem spoke to the dwarves already, they mean us no harm."

But Diaga shoved him away and swept the rest of the food nearest him clear of the table. "They are no dwarves! They are slyths, lizardkin shape-shifters! Get clear of them! They are sworn to Balthazain the Betrayer, and mean us harm!"

The crowd of villagers was perplexed, and Ghost snorted in disbelief, but he halted the forkful of food before his grizzled face. Logan stood atop one of the benches, his arms held high, intending to try and calm everyone down when he spotted one of the dwarves hand's stealing into his armor. He glanced about and saw they were closing in, all reaching for knives or swords kept hidden in their clothes. Logan pulled his own blade free and smashed the table before him in two, dashing the food atop it to the ground. "Ambush! We are deceived!"

Chaos ensued almost immediately. The people of Delmore grabbed the children and backed towards the cave wall in a mad rush. Logan and Grimtooth hurled the pieces of the table towards the now revealed slyths. They were disgusting creatures, large moistened monsters with dark skin and bright stripes or spots all across their hideous bodies, which were some cross of reptile and amphibian. They had lidless eyes of white and mouths of thousands of tiny sharp teeth. They hissed like snakes as they approached, clad in loincloths and bearing the crude weapons they had held as dwarves. The panic among the refugees was escalating quickly and threatened to doom them all if a plan was not formulated swiftly. Jovanaleth and Diaga rushed to Logan's side to be joined by Ghost. "We have to get the people to the surface if we can."

"I know!" Logan shouted, "How would you propose we do that Napalian? We do not have our guide!"

"Rath is gone too, we haven't seen him since Trem went to meet their king!" Jovan chimed in.

Ghost swiped at one of the creatures that had gotten too daring for his liking and drove it back. The thing hissed more loudly than before and gathered itself as if to spring at him. "There has to be at least a hundred of them. They must have killed the dwarves that lived here and taken over."

Diaga gripped his staff. "Some time ago no doubt. There are too many of them here. They have had time to spawn more of their kind." The mage looked upward instinctively and cursed loudly. "There are far more than a hundred."

The others followed his eyes and unthinkingly stepped backward. The roof and walls of the cavern writhed with soft, fleshy bodies as they moved to close in on them. Grimtooth hurled an axe into the crowd of lizardkin before him and was rewarded with a screech of pain. "Ah think we need ta stop worryin' 'bout 'ow they got 'ere and figger out 'ow we be leavin'!"

Logan nodded in agreement, but it was Jovan who spoke up, "There was a shaft, left of the one we came through to get here. Trem said he smelled the outdoors but Gend told him we should stop here first." Realization dawned on the young man from Bladehome, "Do you think Gend...?"

"Not important now," Logan snapped. "If that is a way out we need to get there before they cut us off." Logan shoved Diaga back towards the corkscrew ramp. "Take them, mage! Get the people clear and we will follow as soon as we can!"

Diaga hesitated. "But I can help, you could use...."

"Now!" Logan shouted furiously, "take them now! We will buy you some time, as much as we can!"

Diaga still did not move, seeing the increasingly larger horde of slyths now crawling out of holes in the floor and walls of the cave. There had to be thousands of them massing to strike. Ghost grabbed him, warning Neep off with a glare. "You might be the only one of us that gets out of here boy, move!"

Diaga turned and ran, calling to the crowd behind him, "With me! We are leaving! Forget the horses and wagons! Cut the beasts loose and let them run behind or ahead of us, but we must go now!"

In a great mass of terror, the people followed as Diaga ducked into the tunnel they had come from. He urged them on once he reached a few hundred feet into the winding ramp. As the others passed he repeated instructions, "Go to the place where the paths fork, take the center tunnel. It leads outside, hurry!"

The great rush of humanity was horrible to behold. Families carrying their children rushed upward and pressed against the old and infirm. Many fell and were trampled, though some tried to help the fallen rise. Amid the rush, Neep protected Diaga from the swarm of fleeing bodies as he tried to calm the mad flight from the cavern. Through the storm of men and women, Diaga spotted Samuel, Nawendel, and Khaliandra, who spared him a fleeting and frightened glance before being swept along with the rest of the crowd. Diaga nearly went after them, but resolved to stay and wait until all had passed him. Once the last few moved towards the fork, he followed and cut loose the reins of the horses and oxen behind them, slapping the beasts' hindquarters to urge them out of the caves. The animals belonging to his companions below he led on himself, shouting to those in front of him, "Do not stop! Not until you are under the sky! Keep going!"

Diaga's voice faded as it passed down the tunnel into the deadly cavern. His friends within were now quite surrounded. At first, they had tried to leave themselves some way out, but they had been forced to cut off the slyths trying to pursue the fleeing refugees. Pushing back the lizardkin stretched their line, and once the last person had made it to the tunnel they had quickly compacted to avoid being overrun, but it had allowed the slyths to move between them and the exit. They could not even see the tunnel opening now. Logan kicked the body of a slyth he had slain towards the milling crowd. They had not yet tried a concerted assault, but he did not see how the defenders would survive it once they did. Ghost had his shoulder pressed against that of the knight and grunted, "If we charge for the tunnel, we might break through, but we will be leaving our backs open and leading them right to the refugees."

Jovan swung his torch towards the creeping shapes nearest him. "They do not like the light of the fire, maybe sunlight will be too much for them."

Grimtooth chuckled humorlessly, "We 'ave no idea what time o' day it be, lad, might be runnin' into dead o' night."

"No chance to run, we have to fight, maybe kill enough and we will look like too much of a chore to be worth trying to bring down."

Ghost scoffed, "Nonsense, knight, put the pieces together."

"What pieces are you talking about, Napalian?"

Ghost finally spun to lock eyes with Logan. "Driven into the caves by those shades, sealed in the tunnels, and our only deviation from our egress led through this cavern. The boy figured it out. We were being set up all along. Those two we picked up on the road meant for us to come here, and these foul creatures were waiting for us, waiting with the perfect trap for people on the run: food and shelter. They are not retreating until they have killed us. And you can be certain these lizardkin did not set up this ruse on their own."

Logan's eyes widened as the truth of Ghost's words dawned on him. The Napalian smiled mirthlessly and turned to face the coming attack. "We were betrayed, knight, and this time you cannot blame me."

Trem was lost in utter darkness; so impenetrable he knew it could not be natural. There were not even embers from the torches to give off a faint light he might have magnified with his powerful, elven eyes. Moreover, his senses seemed dulled by the sharp pain of the metal shards in his face, hands, chest, and arms. He straightened and tried to move cautiously towards the edge of the room, seeking the walls of the chamber. A soft footstep somewhere behind him caused him to spin, his hands outstretched. Trem was ceratin he had heard something, but the room went silent again. Then another soft pitter-patter came to his left. Trem whirled again. "Who is there?"

A great rush of soft steps came so suddenly he could not react, and he felt a searing pain as a blade bit and cut deeply across the back of his right leg. His hamstring snapped and he fell to one knee, screaming in agony. Trem could feel the blood pour down his leg as he howled, "Where are you? Show yourself! Fight me, you coward! Balthazain, face me!"

The steps sped past him again and his other leg gave out. The screaming pain tore through him once more, now in his other limb, and Trem fell onto his side shrieking in rage and frustration. He thrashed wildly on the floor, trying to stand, trying to do anything to fight back. He heard the steps coming towards him, slowly this time, and contorted his body to face the approaching attacker. Trem still could not see. His desperation peaked and he laughed a laugh that broke into a sob. "I see, I see. Rath, I know you are here. I know. Come, at least show yourself, have the courage to face me when you murder me!"

A voice he recognized as Balthazain's came echoing off the walls of the chamber, "Surrender, Trem. Join my father, Neroth, and help us bind the mortal world in purpose."

"And let you kill the others? You think I will let that happen?"

"Please," Balthazain's voice was condescending, "you did not return to Delmore to do the right thing. You went back out of guilt. Embrace your true self and forget the others. Begin fighting for something greater and discover the depths of your potential."

Trem did not respond, his mind racing for possible solutions and weakened as he was from the loss of blood. Then a light appeared suddenly from the entrance to the chamber, its power blinding Trem for a brief instant, as he lay prone and helpless on the floor. Blinking to clear his vision, he saw Rath in the doorway of the circular room. To his shock he also could see, standing over him, brandishing a vicious blood-soaked knife, was Gend, his face contorted in a strange ecstasy that rapidly turned to fear. Trem blinked again, thinking his mind was playing tricks on him, but there Gend stood, poised to end his life. The halfling looked down at him in surprise, realizing he had been caught in the act.

Rath's voice called out firmly from the entrance, "Enough, Gend, I will not allow you to kill him."

Gend's face warped from confusion to madness. "We had a deal! He has to die! You know whom I serve!"

"Your master is misguided," Rath said, more softly this time, his voice tinged with what Trem's pain-warped mind thought might be compassion. "You know this. Leave the half-elf. Do not make me kill you."

Gend glanced at the shrouded figure, seeing his deadly crossbow notched with a bolt, but pointed downwards. Gend seemed to consider surrender, and then he shrieked and whirled back towards the helpless Trem with his knife raised to deliver the killing blow. The bolt smashed through his back and burst out of his chest. Gend's knife clattered to the ground harmlessly as he fell to the floor. He sputtered and gasped, eyes inches from Trem's own.

"Fool," Rath whispered, walking softly into the room to stand over the halfling. "You know the children of Neroth keep few promises, his son Balthazain particularly." Rath knelt beside the dying halfling and turned his head up, shining the light from his strange orb above them. "I convinced you I could protect you, Gend, when I met you on the road. We were walking the same path then, but I did not know what I do now."

Gend gasped, but could not speak. Rath knelt and held his head gently. "I will make this swift and painless for you."

Rath pulled a short blade from his long black cloak and dipped it into one of his pouches. He nicked the halfling's arm and the wheezing soon stopped. Rath then turned to Trem and pulled free another strange flask, biting off the cork top and pulling the half-elf's head back. "This will slow your bleeding, drink."

Trem had no chance to resist, and he nearly coughed up the ice-cold liquid, but his pain seemed to lessen and the rush of blood slowed to a mere ooze. Rath tossed the vial aside and placed his light orb gently on the ground as he helped Trem up, though he was holding the majority of Trem's weight, given the severity of his injuries. They looked at one another for a moment, Rath's face still covered in black cloth, Trem's battered and blood-flecked with jagged bits of metal lodged in his skin. Rath spoke in his soft voice. "I did not trust you, Trem Waterhound, I was here to do much the same thing that one was, but I have seen in you things I did not expect. I am sorry I was not swift enough to stop this, the blackness of the tunnel caused me some delay even with my light orb."

Trem could not summon the words to respond. Rath bent down and hefted him in his arms. "I will carry you from here, as a penance for my error. And I will take you to the city of Yulinar that the traitor seeks."

"You will be doing no such thing, Rath ib Athor ain Elman."

Trem turned his head to follow Rath's eyes. Balthazain had re-appeared by his throne. The dark god grimaced as he stepped down to the floor covered in Trem and Gend's blood. He kicked the carcass of the halfling with a look of disappointment, and paused to stamp on the orb Rath had set down. The torchlights had been relit, eerily illuminating Balthazain's return. "Did you think I would just let you heroically retrieve him from my intricate little trap? There are thousands upon thousands of my servants outside killing your friends, Waterhound, though that damned mage managed to warn them of my delectable feast before they could partake. A pity; I had promised the slyths a bloodless victory."

Trem coughed and spoke with great effort, "You cannot touch us here, even in your own temple. You are not permitted."

Balthazain stepped towards them both, pausing less than an inch from Trem's face and appearing to ignore Rath entirely. "So good of you to keep up with our rules, half-elf. You are correct. However, I can affect the very stones of my domain, and with the fall of Sun-hall to my servants this entire cavern is now my temple. I hope you have not gotten too accustomed to daylight, because this will be your grave one way or another," his attention shifted to Rath. "And yours as well, assassin. You are such a disappointment, Rath, so much hatred and violence to be controlled by some vestige of false morality within you. Have you not learned? Morality is for the weak."

Rath stared back at the immortal before him, apparently un-fazed, "You have no right to invoke my family name, Betrayer."

The god recoiled in anger, unhappy to have his threats be so obviously ineffectual, and turned sharply, putting his back to them. "My father wished for me to turn you to his cause Trem, though in truth this is the outcome I much prefer. Welcome to your tomb."

As he spoke, Balthazain disappeared and the ground and walls began to shake and crack. Rath hefted Trem and spun for the door. Trem grabbed his sleeve. "Leave me! You can make it clear without me holding you back!"

Rath glanced at him, as though considering this alternative, then gripped his weak form tighter and rushed forward, propel-ling them into the hallway as stones began to fall around them. The torches were cracked and collapsing out of the walls and the dust and dirt had nearly filled the chamber already. Rath was hard pressed to stay ahead of the falling debris. They flew around the corner and into the main chamber, just as a massive chunk of rock came crashing down directly above them.

Jovan spun and narrowly avoided the falling rock to his left. Dust flew into his face and he hacked, choking on the tiny pieces of grit filling the air. As he opened his eyes, he sliced the arm from a lurking slyth and lurched backward, away from another collapsing chunk of debris that drove the lizardkin clear of the exit to the spiraling ramp leading upward. This time, through the cloud of stone chips all around him, he caught sight of a swirling black cloak across the cavern. Jovan strained his eyes and thought he made out a streak of forest green cloth in the distance as well, and then the ceiling collapsed upon the figures and he lost them. He began to lunge forward, but something caught him by the arm and yanked him back. Jovanaleth struggled but received a hard smack to the face, and Ghost's grey beard obscured his vision. "You fool! We have a chance to flee, now run!"

Jovan roared unintelligibly at him and struggled to get free, but Logan was dragging him out of the cavern along with Grimtooth. "Let me go! I saw something across the cave! Let me go, curse you!"

Logan heaved him forward and through the door. "We go back and we are as good as dead. If you won't flee on your own then Grim and I shall do it for you."

They dragged him further even as Jovan battled to get loose. Ghost rushed past them, not stopping to see if they were able to dodge the falling rock of the caves, somewhat lessened in the tunnels beyond the great cavern. Jovan's struggles slowed their progress and the roof continued to rain down upon the three like some hellish storm. The shaking finally loosened the floor and tossed all three of them down as they reached the intersecting passages. Grimtooth hopped to his feet and grabbed Logan and Jovanaleth in his massive hands, charging forward into the central path, just steps ahead of the tunnel quaking apart behind them.

Diaga stood at the opening of the cavern, his feet upon an overgrown but still visible road of dirt cart tracks. The realization that he and his friends had been deceived, that this was in fact the exit they had been seeking all along and it had been so close to the trap they had walked willingly into, had struck him like a physical blow. Once the others had passed him by and gathered themselves and the horses at a safe distance, he returned to the cavern entrance. The already suffering people of Delmore had lost more of their number in the caves, some struck by falling stone and others knocked down in their flight and unable to rise. It was unclear how many had made it out, but Diaga was certain he had seen none of his companions amid the crowd.

Thus he waited and watched the mouth of the cave, internally debating the wisdom of trying to forge inward and find his friends. Neep was beside him, following his line of sight, and he could sense she would intervene if he tried to move much closer. Diaga could still feel the hemorrhaging earth beneath him, and could also sense the incredible amount of power causing the terrible heaving and roiling underground. Unable to do anything, Diaga stood there leaning on his staff and praying, something he was not accustomed to, for he had little faith in anything except his magic and his newfound friends. Now, he felt certain he was in real danger of losing them and it brought him to a desperate reach for belief in something else.

A soft hand slid into his and Diaga opened his eyes to see the caretaker of the child Samuel. Khaliandra smiled shyly and squeezed his hand. Diaga opened his mouth to say something, flush with joy that the priestess had escaped the chaos of the escape, but had no words he could use at that moment. She turned her eyes downward and whispered, "You fear for your friends."

Diaga opened and closed his mouth a few times before saying, "Yes, I do."

They stood there and watched as the tremors began to slow and grow less powerful. A final, massive aftershock cracked the cavern exit and the gaping maw caved inward with a deafening groan. Diaga swept his robe up to shield them both from the flying rock and dust. As the slight shaking and final vibrations began to slow and weaken, Diaga tried to will movement in the now sealed stone rubble before him. But when the rollicking and rolling earth finally settled and he could no longer feel the magical power raging in the air, there was no sign of his friends or any movement in the once vast cavern opening. His shoulders slumped and he fought back tears while his silent companion squeezed his hand tighter and tried to comfort him.

A massive crunch of grinding stone brought Diaga's eyes up. A huge boulder crashed down and, coughing and sputtering, Ghost emerged, falling more than stumbling down the debris. Carrying his bloodbrother, Grimtooth came rolling downward after him. The three collapsed at the bottom of the stone blockade, only to be disturbed by the disheveled and limping form of Jovanaleth, who Logan managed to catch before he landed face first on the long forgotten road. Diaga reached them then, kneeling to make sure they were really there, really the people he had come into the tunnels with. Ghost roughly shoved him away and continued to cough dust and wipe tiny rock particles from his great beard. Logan tried to smile, but he was too busy grimacing in pain and stiffness. Jovan slumped on the ground, a vacant look in his eyes as he lay there staring up at the setting sun. Grimtooth seemed to be the only one capable of movement, heaving himself to his feet and trying to steady his stance.

But before any of the survivors could drag themselves upward, help arrived. Khaliandra was there to aid the orc with the same shy smile and little calming touches of her healing hands. Yet she was not alone, the rest of the people who had lived through the assault on Delmore were also there, offering shoulders to lean on and carrying water to their saviors. Even Ghost could not refuse the kindness of the refugees as they helped him towards their makeshift camp. Jovanaleth leaned on an assisting farmer, but halted as they were crossing into sight of the horses and safety. Jovan looked back at the blocked cavern, the fingers of dawn receding behind it as twilight came on. Jovanaleth smiled sadly at his aide and pulled his arm free. "Thank you, but I am not ready to turn back yet."

Logan exchanged a look with Diaga and the young mage peeled himself away from his companion. "Bring us some water if you could, I do not want him to be alone."

Jovan limped painfully back to the cavern entrance and settled himself on a chunk of broken rock facing the imposing maw, now choked with dirt and stone. Diaga arrived a moment later and sat silently next to him. The two stared at the obstruction for a time without speaking, but Diaga could not contain himself, "You know, if there were one person who could survive that...."

"It would be Trem," Jovan finished for him. "He went back for me, even if I could not forgive him for leaving us in the first place. I should have been allowed to do the same for him."

Diaga shook his head. "You would have died too, what would that have accomplished?"

Jovan shrugged and brushed dirt from his leather breeches aimlessly. "We are all of us bound together somehow. I can feel it when we are together, and I believe the glue that unites us is, for better or worse, Trem. I know Ghost brought us here, but only one of our number seems to matter."

Diaga nodded. "You discussed what he is, did you not?"

Jovanaleth glanced sideways at the younger man,. "He told us much. Are you saying you knew everything before we entered the caverns?"

Diaga laughed softly. "I am a mage, Jovanaleth. We are supposed to study magic in all of its forms. I knew that there was something about Trem that was unusual. Encountering Joseph merely confirmed my suspicions."

"Do you think there is a reason he left his cottage for me? A reason he left his self-imposed exile to help me find my father?"

Diaga shrugged. "There is true danger in thinking that you are, in some way, more important to him than anyone else. I fear for you, Jovanaleth, for I believe that your sense of loyalty, even love, for Trem will only bring you disappointment." He gestured with his staff towards the cavern. "If he does, by some miracle, come out of that devastation you would be wise to remain distant. Though I agree that we are all in some way bound to him through his unique existence."

"And what about fate?" Jovan asked. "You wish me to stay away from him, but what if I, maybe even we, are meant to walk with him for good or ill?"

"Fate," Diaga said softly. "I do believe in fate, but I would like to think it can be altered if the individual is determined enough."

Jovan said nothing, but sat there in quiet contemplation. Khaliandra arrived with water and food, which the two watchers both took wordlessly. She and Diaga were curled up against the rock a few moments later, fast asleep. Jovan never even glanced at them, but sat methodically eating his ration of food and watching for movement in front of him. The darkness began to set in, deeper and deeper around him, but he remained still as a statue. His eyes drifted west of the mountainous caverns to the fringes of Silverleaf Forest. Jovan's memory searched back for that first encounter with Trem in the woods, waking up in a strange home healed by a strange man who seemed to offer nothing but concern and kindness for him. It seemed ages ago.

Jovanaleth of Bladehome, far from his family and city, closed his eyes and lowered himself to the ground so he could use the rock to keep his head up. He looked upward then at the night sky now bedecked with stars and whispered to himself, "My oh my, how far we have come."

Chapter 30

Arvadis Angladais was once again ruler of the Angladaic Kingdom, the most glorious nation in all of Legocia. As it should be, he was the king of a grand society, the pinnacle of its neighbors' monumental aspirations, and a shining example to the world of Teth-tenir. That same Arvadis Angladais was also lord of a decimated, broken, and totally shattered home, a monarch ruling over a trapped and terrified populace, leader of a justified march to regain his rightful throne. It was a march that had killed innocent people in its effort to make right what his nemesis had done wrong. Arvadis Angladais, the father of one broken son, with another son in exile, and grandfather to a boy who had just lost his mother. In that moment he was everything and nothing all at once.

That same man sat bent under the weight of his crown in the palace throne room, holding the second day of open audiences with his people. The idea had been Highlord Irindein's. He encouraged Arvadis to allow the voices of the population of Alderlast and beyond to come before their king and speak their mind about the events of late. Some came with advice for the king, others with requests or pleas for help, and many came with tears and fury over lost family members. Arvadis heard every one of them in turn with respect and diligent attention for their words, but in the listening he felt his majesty was gone. He was just an old man in an overly large chair wearing a crown too heavy for his ancient head. The last visitor of the day concluded his request for more water to be sent to the southern farmlands, currently experiencing an unusual drought. Right behind him came Highlord Irindein in considerably cleaner robes than he had worn a few days ago, his injured arm fully healed by the holy magic of the nation's priests. Beside him walked a contrite Gelladan Bwemor with a bowed head and wearing the clothes of a peasant.

Arvadis glanced at Irindein for some sort of prompt to this unusual visit, but he received none. Bwemor brought his eyes upward and cleared his throat before speaking slowly and with heavy concentration on his words, "My lord Arvadis, I have committed a dire crime against my kingdom and my people. I cannot excuse what I have done, nor am I going to ask that you forgive me. What I am asking, my lord, is the right to join the ranks of your army. I wish to begin again as a common soldier, preferably directly under your command."

Arvadis's eyebrows climbed up his forehead as he considered the proposition before him. He looked at Irindein, who shrugged and said, "He asked for this opportunity to speak and nothing else. I believe him to be serious."

Arvadis examined the overweight and aging man before him. "You are physically unfit for combat and will be targeted by every member of what is now Renon Ordlan's army. You are certain this is not a clever attempt to avoid public execution or a lifetime of imprisonment by committing indirect suicide as an unready warrior on the field of battle?"

Bwemor shook his head. "I am aiming to atone for the sins I have committed against our nation by serving it. I have the determination to see my re-entry into the army through, if you will grant me the opportunity."

This seemed to satisfy the king and Arvadis nodded. "Then it is so ordered. You will be under Renon's personal supervision. I believe he might find you useful in maintaining the organization of the army as you have it in place now. At least you can familiarize him with the finer points. In your free time I suggest you get yourself fit to fight."

Bwemor bowed graciously and turned to leave. At the massive doors, he paused with his hand holding one open and turned. "If I may ask my lord, what happened to Highlord Hladic?"

Arvadis paused as his eyes drifted to the gilded arms of his chair. "Brusius Hladic was found dead this morning. He slit his own throat with a letter opener while under house arrest. We will be putting the Archbishop in charge of the priests and rituals of our nation until a better solution can be found."

Bwemor's reaction was merely to nod and depart through the massive doors. Irindein and Arvadis were left alone in the massive chamber. Fremont cleared his throat and said, "Brusius's wife is already making inroads to retain her husbands title and become Highlady Hladic in his stead, as well as appoint one of Vendile's cousins, a younger woman who maintains the trade policies of Trinalith Port, to his open position. While Bwemor willingly passed his title on, I suspect you will be hard-pressed to keep those two from claiming the other vacancies."

Arvadis did not respond and Irindein could not be certain he had even heard him. The younger Highlord made no attempt to spark further conversation with his king, instead strolling among the pillars and hanging tapestries depicting the history of Angladais, finally restored after the removal of Vendile's personal banners that had dominated the hall in his brief reign. As he walked he spoke loud enough for Arvadis to hear, but it sounded as though he were talking to himself, "In all of our glorious history we seem to be perpetually ignorant of the dark times that caused us to rise up in such vigorous defense of the virtues we built this kingdom upon. For every noble act, there was a villainous deed that prompted it. Even the stones of this palace seem to rest upon the very foundations of a most nefarious race come before us."

Arvadis sighed. "Do you mean to imply that in our darkest hours we have always risen to our greatest heights?"

Irindein paused in his examination to glance at his world-weary friend. "I was just making a casual observation."

The silence lingered a few moments longer as Irindein left the tapestries and walked over to Arvadis. He laid a gentle hand on his back and remained there, unspeaking, in the hall. Arvadis straightened a few moments later and rose stiffly. The king wore none of the gaudy robes his foe had, but his back bent as though he carried a long train made of lead. Arvadis rubbed his hands over his simple grey tunic and stepped down from the small dais to the carpeted floor. Irindein fell in next to him. "A good thing that Vendile did not have the gall to destroy these fine works, the hall would not be the same without them."

Arvadis said nothing as they crossed the hall and exited through the massive main doors. He still did not speak as they made their way through the foyer to the outer stairs and the cool night air. Arvadis paused once they were outside, as the horrors of those same steps came back to haunt him. Irindein moved to comfort his friend, but Arvadis started down the stairs before he could. "Are Xarinth and Galden prepared to take on the responsibilities of the Highlords we have lost?"

"I believe their youth can be compensated for with their enthusiasm and faith in you. As I said, Hladic's wife intends to lay claim to her deceased husband's title. I do not think we have strong enough evidence to refute her, nothing indicates she was involved in his alliance with Vendile."

"She has every right to the position. I will hear her out, though I know nothing of this supposed cousin of Vendile's in Trinalith Port. Still, we must have a council, and any with relation to Vendile have the most deserving claim. Appointing Renon to a Highlord position was a stretch itself, given he is not highborn. This may be a concession that must be made to appease the established nobility."

Arvadis continued down the steps and into the street, striding purposefully along the Zenith Road. Irindein continued his assessment unprompted, "We still cannot find Freyan. It is believed he escaped during the commotion. Renon and Calavar have managed to gather all the able-bodied soldiers and paladins they could. They seem to think that if we assemble our strength, we will come up with a solution for the fortress currently sealing our egress through the Pillars of Light. Personally, I think it is going to take more brains than brawn, but they are the military men and it is a wartime operation."

There was no response from his friend, and as they reached one of the stairwells leading down to the main district of the city Irindein knew he needed to leave the Zenith Road and descend to the streets or he would be facing a long walk to his own home. The Highlord stopped and waited, expecting Arvadis to speak with him again before they parted ways, but the king continued to walk onward as though Irindein was not there. The Highlord watched him go, his hands slipping into his robes and finding a thin chain and odd pendant. He pulled them both free and examined them in the faint torchlight of the streets. Irindein had discovered the item when searching Vendile's quarters in the palace, and something had compelled him to take it for himself. His eyes lingered on the metal and strange dark stones a moment longer, and then he returned the medallion and chain to his pocket, went to the steps, and descended to the streets below.

Arvadis walked in silence for some time, watching the light of the moon reflect off of the cobblestones beneath his boots. When he too took one of the stairs nearest his home, he found the houses, finely made and well kept by the people, his people, loomed above him like judging hosts. Arvadis moved determinedly forward, trying to ignore the pressing demand he felt them heaping upon him, but they were not really the ones piling the weight on his shoulders, and there was no way he knew to shed a demon he could not see nor sink a blade into. His guilt was a monster that he could not slay.

Arvadis arrived at his door to see Graham standing guard, alone. Arvadis received a formal salute, something Graham had not done for decades, and a curt nod. Arvadis made no move to the door, but stood in front of the old guard. "You were not needed tonight, Graham. Derek's funeral was this evening."

Graham snorted. "You did not deign to abandon your duty for Lena's burial and I saw no reason to ignore mine."

Arvadis sighed. "Old friend, I am sorry for what pain I have caused you."

Graham slammed his spear onto the ground and stepped so close he was practically on top of Arvadis. He addressed him sternly, "That is precisely the problem, m'lord! Your sorrow is what causes the bile to rise in my throat. It is what keeps the mourning clothes on your people! It keeps your son within that house drinking himself to death! You are a king, m'lord. You make decisions as a king that cost people their lives. These people know that and they accept it, but not when they see you doubting your own conclusions. One would almost think you wish you had left Vendile on the throne!"

Arvadis met the old guard's glare with his own stony eyes, but that did not halt his tirade. "Derek was like a son to me. He is the only person I ever grew close to, outside of your family, and his sacrifice was his choice. Through his unwavering sense of duty, he won you back your kingdom. That is our job, our lives for yours and your causes. We accept the price we are to pay. Why can you not do the same?"

"I did not ask anyone to die for me."

"And yet Derek did, because he believed you will be the one to see us through this dark time," Graham laid his hand on Arvadis' shoulder. "You carry the weight of our people, I know, but you must not show how heavy it has become. You lost a potential child in this conflict, do not lose the son who stood by you throughout."

Arvadis met Graham's eyes again and saw the plea, and the hope, resting within them. He nodded with all the determination he could muster and went to his door. Arvadis swept inside and surveyed the scene before him. Maps were still spread about the central table and a compass and quill pot lay near them. The table chairs were all leaning against the wall to his right and in the massive armchairs before a raging fire, he could see his son, back to the stairs leading to the second floor, sitting shirtless with his staff propped between his legs and a massive bottle of black rum in one hand. He took a hard pull from the bottle and set it down on the arm of his chair, his eyes never leaving the raging fire that had turned the room into a sauna. Arvadis walked over and threw on some dirt to quell the flames a bit before sitting in the chair next to his eldest. He extended his arm and Vorasho handed him the bottle. Arvadis took a long sip and coughed. "This is as awful as I remember it."

Vorasho did not move. "It begins to taste better after you sit here long enough."

Arvadis took another drink and coughed again. "Seems to me it must take quite a while."

"Yes, I have sat here most of the day."

Arvadis handed the jug back and turned to his son. "You could not have saved her, Vorasho."

The younger man snorted and drank again. When he put the bottle down he turned his tearstained eyes to his father. "Oh, but I could have. I could have stopped her so many times."

"I am the one who allowed her to go inside, Vorasho."

"And I was the one who tried, and failed, to protect her, father." Vorasho shook his head and his hair, soaked with sweat from the heat of the fire, stuck to his brow. He brushed it back and gazed into the licking flames. "I sent my brother away from his home and I failed to protect the woman he loved. His son will grow up without a mother because of me."

Arvadis leaned forward and grabbed his forearm. "You went by the Code! You did what our ancestors taught us was right!"

Vorasho hurled the bottle into the flames and the fire shot outward before roaring furiously back into the stone fireplace. "I forsake the Code! I beat that bastard's head into the marble until it was nothing more than a bloody smear and I enjoyed it! I wish that I could do it again a thousand times over, but I also know, I know, that it was my own head I was bludgeoning in that senseless rage, for all the harm I have caused. No amount of devotion to the order I believed in so strongly could ever erase the guilt from my soul, nor wash the blood from my hands."

"Vorasho, for the Code or not, you did what you thought was right."

The prince slumped in his chair and bowed his head. Arvadis rose and leaned over the chair to hug his son. "My boy, you have done more for me and our people than you can imagine. For whatever mistakes you think you have made, you have more than atoned, even if you refuse to believe so."

Vorasho patted his father on the head gently. "Be quiet when you go upstairs, Logan is asleep in his father's room. It took some time to get him to bed."

Arvadis released his embrace and walked slowly up the stairs. He passed those same beaten shields of his forebears that he had examined over a week ago. Arvadis again lingered to consider the men who had borne them for their kingdom. Was Irindein right? Did the greatest heroes of the Angladaics rise from the ashes of such misfortune as this? He prayed they did. He paused at Logan's room to check on his grandson, fast asleep in his father's bed. Arvadis watched him doze a few moments and then closed the door slowly, making his way to his own room at the end of the hall.

Once inside he undid his tunic and slipped on a thin night-shirt. He sat at the edge of his bed and considered the fate of his people for one last moment before turning his thoughts to his immediate family. Somewhere, Logan was wandering the world with his erstwhile companion Grimtooth, unaware of the terrible things that had befallen those he loved. At that moment, his father envied him on his adventures, sleeping under the stars and watching out only for himself. He hoped his son was well and without care for that evening at least, for he dreaded what his return home would bring.

Arvadis glanced at the head of his bed, to his wife's portrait. She had died when Vorasho was very young, as young as his grandson Logan was now, giving birth to her second child. Her death had left him with only his two children and the adopted orc to keep him whole, and with their love, Arvadis had survived. That his own son would have to deal with that same pain did not please him. How he had wished for better days for his offspring. His door creaked open and he saw Logan standing there in the faint candlelight, rubbing sleepy eyes. Arvadis rose and went to him, kneeling to rub his hair gently. "Can't sleep, little one?"

The child sniffed. "I miss mommy."

Arvadis picked him up and carried him to the bed. "I do too, child. She is still watching you, you know, and I think she would want you to be happy. She loved you, Logan."

"Grandpa, will my father ever come home?"

Arvadis pulled the covers of his bed up to nestle Logan's shoulders before lying down atop them, beside his grandson. "If I know your father, Logan, he is on his way home right now."

Logan nodded, then said sleepily, "Please tell uncle Vorasho not to cry again, grandpa, I don't think mother would want him crying."

Arvadis watched as Logan slipped off and whispered quietly, "No, Logan, I do not think she would."

On the first floor Vorasho was still slumped in his chair, now with a fresh bottle of black rum to work on. He was having trouble focusing on the dancing flames in front of him, there seemed to be images in them he could not quite make out. At times he thought he wavered between sleep and wakefulness, but it was impossible to tell. Even in his dreams he saw only the fire before him. He took a big swig from his newest jug to dull his senses further, and looked to his right at the empty chair, only to see Lena sitting there in a white dress. Vorasho did not move or cry out, but simply stared and then laughed. "You are not Lena Engrove. I must be too deep in my cups."

The figure did not say anything, but simply stared back at him. Vorasho scratched his chin and shook his head in an attempt to clear it. She was still sitting there. The prince reconsidered. Maybe he had not drunk enough. He closed his eyes and took another long, painful drink and when he opened them, Lena was standing in front of him. Tears welled up in his eyes and he cried, "What? I am sorry! I am sorry I failed you! Are you to haunt me now for the rest of my years? Do you not think my own shame will be enough of a burden, that the betrayal of my brother will not sting me as deeply as I deserve?"

Still the specter said nothing, but she bent down and kissed Vorasho gently on the forehead and brushed her hand across his cheek. Vorasho woke suddenly, in the same position he had been when Lena had kissed him. His hand stole to his forehead. The touch had felt so real. As he held his fingers to his face, a feeling of total calm came over him. Vorasho set his bottle down and stood; the haze of drunkenness seemed to have vanished from his body. He brushed his forehead once more in disbelief and then threw down dirt from the sack by the fire to quench it entirely. Turning slowly, he walked up the stairs and found his father and Logan sleeping peacefully in his parents' room. Shutting the door, he turned and walked into his brother's bedroom. Holding onto the bedpost, with his fingers running over the initials of his brother, himself, and Lena in the fine wood, he broke down and sobbed fiercely at last, no longer fighting to hold back. Vorasho sank to the floor slowly, and eventually, when his sorrow could sustain him no longer, he slept.

The massive stone cavern remained silent, despite the staring protestations of Jovanaleth. Night had completely fallen at last, the western edge of Silverleaf climbed up onto the edges of the cave, thinning as the trees went higher. The woods were quiet; as were the mountains they were rubbing up against in timeless contention. The incredible lack of sound was lulling Jovan to sleep, but he fought against rest viciously. Even though he could not will Trem to come out undaunted from beyond the wall of stone he refused to turn his back on him and believe that all was lost. For the others, it might be easier to accept the death of the half-elf and move on, but for Jovanaleth it was not so simple. He did not understand Trem, did not think he ever could, really, but he felt a duty to him he could not explain.

It was not that Trem was unique. His heritage was incredible to be sure, but that had not been what initially made Jovan feel a kinship with him. For all of Diaga's warnings, to abandon him now would be betraying that first moment of empathy between them. Jovan did not think he would ever feel the same trust he had when he first met Trem, but he might be able to resurrect some of that companionship. Thus, he sat and waited for any sign of hope, anything to give him the fleetest chance to rekindle their bond.

Dust fell from the blockaded entrance. Jovan's eyes followed the movement, but the sudden feeling of elation was no longer rising in his chest. He had seen small rivulets of sand and stone coming down from the wall before and it had meant nothing. A larger chunk fell and broke on the remnants of the road, then another. Jovanaleth sat up and strained his eyes. More rock fell, and he thought he could hear the sound of clanging steel on stone. Jovan lifted himself to his feet and limped forward. A black-gloved hand suddenly protruded from the earthen wall and he spun to shake Diaga. "Get up! Get up! Someone is coming through the rubble!"

Diaga took a moment to rouse and Jovan did not wait for him. The mage rose and helped Khaliandra stand before trotting after the young man from Bladehome. Jovan had reached the wall and was tearing at the rock and loose stone near the extended arm in an attempt to widen the hole. He was yelling for Trem, but there was no response coming from the other side. The hole opened up quickly and the arm disappeared. As Diaga reached the digging Jovanaleth, a form was shoved through the gap in the pile of stone and dirt. Jovan gasped and pulled it out. Diaga drew a sharp breath and helped him lower the bloody and mangled form of Trem. Jovan knelt by him and shook his head in disbelief, horrified at the sight. "What did this to him?"

Rath emerged from the hole and rolled to the base of the obstruction. The young woman rushed to help him, but the mysterious outsider waved her off. "The god Balthazain did that, young prince. He broke Waterhound's blade and had Gend rend his flesh so he could not stand."

"You saved him," Diaga said, looking wide-eyed at the black clad assassin, now brushing dust from his clothes. "You rescued Trem from Gend?"

Rath made no comment, but sat leaning his head against the rock in exhaustion. Jovan peeled back the torn cloth wrapped around Trem's arms. "Diaga," he said softly, "he has steel embedded in his arms as well as his face. Rath, how much blood has he lost?"

The dark-clad man shook his head in uncertainty. "I gave him one of my potions to slow the bleeding and covered his wounds as best I could, but I am sorry, it took a long time to dig our way free and I had twice the weight to carry."

Jovan awkwardly extended his hand and patted Rath on the shoulder awkwardly. "You did well Rath. Thank you."

The assassin seemed taken aback, but recovered his composure quickly. He looked at the young mage. "Can you not heal him, wizard?"

Diaga shook his head. "I can mend some of his injuries if we remove the metal from his flesh, but he will not walk again without powerful magical aid and it will have to come soon."

Jovan knelt by Trem's head and grabbed his shoulders. "Help me, Rath, we have to carry him back to the camp. If we cauterize the wounds then they will not bleed after the steel is pulled out. That way Diaga and Khaliandra can focus on healing his legs."

The two hefted Trem's limp form and began carrying him towards the encampment as fast as they dared. Diaga stood and watched a moment before a soft hand slid onto his arm. "Do you think we can heal him?"

Diaga looked at Khaliandra and shook his head doubtfully. "Healing is not my specialty. My studies were always focused on Ruination magic, as it was my strength as a student of the arcane. I can do some good to the outer skin and halt the bleeding in the worst spots, but to repair the massive damage to the deeper parts of his legs... it is just beyond me."

Her dark eyes searched his. "I believe that together, we can do more than just patch him up."

Diaga smiled. "Your faith is appreciated." He paused and considered her. "You have been so welcoming and friendly towards me and I must admit, I do not understand why. The others played a great role in saving you and the people of Delmore. I was only responsible for some rather theatrical explosions."

She turned her eyes down and said softly, "I have watched you with the others. They are aware of their strength and prowess, indeed they identify with it as a measure of their worth. You, unlike them, are wary of your own gifts. I admire humility and vigilance in people, and in you especially."

Diaga finally dared to put his arm around her and was delighted to have her accept such closeness willingly. They started after the others together. "Your words are very flattering, Khaliandra."

They reached the camp where the others had already awoken. Neep joined Diaga and Khaliandra as they passed the border of the camp. The firecat had been resting and watching over Diaga from afar all evening. Logan helped move Trem near the fire and knelt beside Jovanaleth as he tried to make him comfortable. Grimtooth was turning a hot iron in the flames while Ghost grimaced just outside the light. "Someone will have to hold him down, he is going to thrash once the poker touches his skin."

Khaliandra brought a bowl and a skin of fresh water with a cloth. Jovan glanced up at Logan. "Have you done this before?"

"I've seen it done but never actually been a part of it. This sort of procedure is rare in the Angladaic armies. We usually have priests nearby during battles."

"Ah can do it."

Logan looked up at Grimtooth. "When did you ever cauterize a wounded man?"

The orc shrugged, remarking, "It dinnae seem ta be so much 'bout experience as bein' determined. Ah'll pull the metal free if yon lass will clean the wounds."

Khaliandra nodded, and Grimtooth gestured for Logan and Jovan to hold Trem's limbs down. The orc reached out and pulled a large piece of steel free from Trem's forehead, dropping it into the bowl. Khaliandra wiped the blood free then Grimtooth took the hot iron from Ghost and pressed it to the wound. Trem's eyes snapped open and he screamed in pain, but Jovan and Logan held him down. Grimtooth wasted no time, pulling the other large piece of metal from his cheek and searing the wound shut. He then moved on to the metal pieces in Trem's arms, pulling the dozens of shards out and burning the flesh to prevent bleeding. About halfway through the first arm, Trem stopped struggling, passing out in shock from the pain. Once all the chunks of metal were out of his skin, Khaliandra wiped the burned flesh again with cool water and chanted softly, praying to Endoth for the power to heal the injuries and alleviate his pain. The others watched, astounded, as the angry, raised red marks of burned skin faded and white scars began to form in their place. Jovanaleth grimaced as he looked at Trem's broken form. Logan patted him on the shoulder as Diaga laid his hands on Trem's head and added his own magical contribution to the efforts to undo the horrible damage that had been wrought.

Soft chanting could barely be heard, but as the priestess and the mage wove their individual spells, a faint glow surrounded the wounds on Trem's legs and the blood oozing down his torn breeches receded. The effect lasted only a few moments, but when Diaga was done, he slumped against Neep, and Trem was resting more comfortably. Neep and Khaliandra, less weakened than Diaga from their efforts, led the young mage over to his bedroll and Grimtooth took the bloody bowl of metal and tossed it into the fire with a scornful look. Ghost shook his grizzled head and walked away from the scene quietly. Jovan sat next to Trem and said with some hope to Logan, "He seems better, he will live won't he?"

The knight glanced down and rubbed his haggard chin. "I should think so, the wounds in his legs were the most serious and Grimtooth did well cleaning the other injuries. If he has not died by now then we may hope he will make it a few more days, barring infection. Perhaps by then we can find someone to help us who is more gifted in the art of healing than Khaliandra or Diaga."

Rath materialized out of the gloom. "Knight, I can take you where you need to go."

Logan looked distrustfully at the assassin before saying, "I think before we follow your lead, you owe us an explanation for what happened back there. It seems clear that Gend did this to Trem, but how did you meet him and why were you traveling with him before we met at that inn? And for that matter, were you lying in wait for us in that village on the road to Delmore?"

Jovan expected Rath to balk at the interrogation and waited for his curt response and subsequent withdrawal from the conversation. The intrigue of the moment brought Ghost and Grimtooth back to within range of the flames, the Napalian's arms crossed as he awaited the shadowy figure's response. To Jovan's surprise, Rath sighed in resignation, and reached up to his cowl. Undoing the tie at the base of his head that had kept his face almost entirely covered in black cloth he slowly wound it free, revealing a dark black face that was hardly a shade lighter than his clothing. Jovan gasped, and Ghost pointed at the assassin in disbelief. "You! You are one of the Sun People, the legendary reclusives of Southron!"

"Sun People?" asked Logan, now thoroughly confused.

Ghost turned to him. "The creation legends tell us that the humans of Southron were placed in the burning heat of the deserts there. It was a people under a sun so unforgiving that it burned their skin black. Only the strongest survived.

"And," Ghost continued stepping forward in excitement, "they are the people who rule Yulinar! That same city I seek!"

Rath met the eyes of the Napalian and spoke, "Yes, I am a man of the Sun People, as you call us, though we prefer to be known as Melarrians, and I do hail from Yulinar. I am what my people call a Watcher, responsible for defending the borders of our lands. As to how I met the halfling, his home lies just east of this cavern. He begged me to help him find you and kill a man named Trem Waterhound. He was a loyal servant to Balthazain and had information on where we could find his target. At the time it was a convenient alliance, since ensuring the demise of the half-elf touched by immortal power was why I was sent from the Endless Sands in the first place. I did await you in the inn with Gend and allowed him to bargain for our inclusion in your party. It was my intent to permit him to spring his trap, but at the last moment I chose to end the halfling's life instead."

A stunned silence followed. Jovan spoke first, his voice heavy with confusion, "You rescued Trem and killed Gend. Why?"

Rath met the young man's eyes. "My people have taken great pains to gather knowledge of all that has been, is, and will be. The Speakers, Keepers, and Tellers of all Melarria, not only the great city you seek, convened and through their investigations concluded a great threat loomed. Trem Waterhound will, if he lives long enough, bring about the complete and total destruction of Yulinar and possibly our people as a whole. His existence threatened everyone in out nation, and that is why I was chosen to find and kill him."

"That does not answer the question," Logan said, "because you did not kill Trem. Why?"

"To be truthful, Angladaic, I still am not sure." Rath shook his head and sat slowly on the ground rubbing his brow. "I was committed to the plan when Gend first told it to me. Lead Trem to the caverns and trap him there, but after he returned to Delmore to rescue you," Rath looked at Jovanaleth, "he displayed devotion to another the likes of which I have rarely seen in people other than my own. It gave me pause. And then the whole of that doomed town was coming through those caverns, and their deaths were not mine to bring about. Moreover, while I was sent to kill Trem Waterhound to save Yulinar, there were many in the city that believed such an action was too much interference in the flow of time and fate. I must admit that I was perhaps not as devoted to the act of execution as I should have been when I left the Endless Sands."

Ghost snorted. "Yet you still allowed Gend to lead us to the slyth cave and nearly got all of us killed."

Rath glared at the older man. "I did not know the nature of his trap, nor the road out. We came to Legocia another way, despite what Gend told you, through the twists and turns of the Silverleaf Forest. Gend only informed me we would be near the exit when the trap was sprung. He never told me how he meant to escape." Rath paused reflectively. "Gend was doing this to gain great power and stature in the eyes of Balthazain the Betrayer. I do not think he considered anything beyond how to accomplish the deed."

Logan bowed his head towards Rath. "I believe we do owe you a degree of gratitude for saving Trem, Rath. If you can lead us to the city we are seeking we will be in true debt for your services."

Rath nodded in compliance. "This I will do for you, knight, and more. My people possess magic even greater than the trinkets I carried with me. They will be able to heal the half-elf if we bring him to them. The city is not far from here."

Jovan held up his hand. "But you said your people want him dead, to save their city no less. Why would they heal him?"

"My people have rarely taken any action that would bring change, much less harm, to another mortal or nation. The decision to send me was one that was furiously debated in Yulinar. We do not believe ourselves above other civilizations or peoples. I suspect that

Trem, with you as his allies and his conscience, can be a great power that may save Teth-tenir from a calamity that many in Yulinar fear is coming, whether he dies or not." Rath looked up from where he had been staring at his hands in contemplation. "Trem will not be safe in Yulinar, but he will be protected by those who value the greater fate of mortality over their own. And it is the only place where he can be truly healed."

Logan stood and extended his hand. "We do owe you a large debt Rath. Thank you."

The dark-skinned man stood and bowed slightly before receiving the arm clasp of the knight firmly. Then he turned and stalked off into the night without further remark. Logan looked down at Trem's prostrate form and ran his hand through his already graying hair. He glanced over his shoulder and locked eyes with Jovan. "You should get some rest. We have a lot to do tomorrow."

Jovanaleth nodded and wandered off to find a place to sleep for the last few hours of the night. Ghost stuck around a moment to check Trem's condition and then, nodding as though to reassure himself, he saluted Logan mockingly and stomped away. Grimtooth and his bloodbrother remained, watching the slow breathing of their companion. Logan sat pensively, rubbing his hand against his face. He slumped near the fire. Grimtooth cocked his head, examining Logan's tired frame. He stepped a bit closer and crouched to head level asking, "Ya alright there, Logan?"

The knight picked his eyes up slowly and sighed. "Oh, yes, I think so, Grim. It is just... a weird feeling came over me the last few hours. It feels like I lost something important, but Trem is back and alive and all appears to be well, relatively speaking, so what could it possibly be?"

The orc shrugged and patted him on his back. "Jus' the stress Ah reckon, been through a bunch lately, eh?"

"Yes," Logan forced a smile, "You are probably right. Go get some rest, brother."

"Aye," Grimtooth smiled back, "g'night, Logan."

The knight sat there alone in the dark with a dying fire behind him. He flexed his hands, feeling the pain and cracking of knuckles stiff from holding a blade for so many hours. He looked down at Trem and shook his head. To have taken that much abuse and lived, what resolve he must have had. The scars though, Logan traced a finger just above the marks on Trem's arms, so many it looked like a hellish spider web. His cloak and tunic were torn and bloody, even the carefully placed bandages on his legs, despite the healing touch of Khaliandra, were bled through in a few spots. Logan reached to his right and hefted his sword, checking the balance instinctively. He was still feeling uneasy and there was no one else on watch, so he decided it might as well be him.

Logan laid the blade down and turned his attention back to Trem. The half-elf was writhing slightly, moaning in his sleep. Logan pulled his cloak about him and tried to cover him as best he could. When that failed, he took his own blanket from his pack and tossed it over Trem. That seemed to calm him down a bit. The knight watched him a while longer as he settled down and finally returned to a seemingly undisturbed sleep. Perhaps Grimtooth was right. The stress was merely weighing down on Logan. After all, what else could have gone wrong? Trem was back and alive and Rath was taking them where they needed to go. The knight kept telling himself things were as well as could be expected, but he never totally relaxed the tight grip on his sword hilt.

Trem was home. He wandered up the old path, seeing his mother's roses lining the finely raked dirt his father maintained. Massive spruce trees rose out of the ground around it, but they grew slightly apart from the green grass, as though showing some unspoken respect for the pastoral beauty of that place and the quaintness of the scene. Trem wanted to skip to his home, but he restrained himself. He was a boy no longer, though his bright blue tunic trimmed in silver and soft deerskin moccasins were the trappings of a youth. He twirled his hunting bow instead and whistled a soft tune as his house came into view.

It was not a large house, but a ramshackle cottage, a single story structure with a tilted fireplace, with smoke rising from it at that moment. This told Trem it would be warm and welcoming inside. The carefully stacked logs of the walls had been worn down to reveal a homely, weathered grey he found endearing even if they looked a bit neglected. The door was painted a bright gaudy red that made Trem smile. Such an outlandish color would be his father's idea of an impressive looking bit of flash, though no one in town would be caught dead with such a bizarre contrast to the natural wood about it. His mother's garden was ripe with carrots, tomatoes, and all sorts of delicious plants. Trem could hear the brook babbling behind the house and longed to run to it, but he restrained himself. They would be waiting inside.

He felt no reason to keep them in suspense. Trem called out, "I am home!" and picked up his pace slightly. He tried to match his whistling to the tune of the birds in the trees around him, but found it too difficult. As he reached the door, he extended his hand towards the knob, surprised neither of his parents had come out to greet him yet. "Mother? Father?"

They are not there, Trem.

The spell broke almost as abruptly. The paint on the door before Trem suddenly cracked and peeled and the knob came off in his hand. He looked to see the shutters fallen or partially hanging onto the window frames, the smoke from the chimney no longer rising and holes with nesting birds now overrunning the roof of his home. Turning he saw his mother's garden choked with weeds, and watched the tall grass appear to crawl into the path, squeezing it until it was barely able to be seen. His shirt faded to a filthy white with tears, his back weighed down by a ripped cloak and his light hunting bow replaced by a battered soldier's longbow. His hip carried a sheath, but bore no blade, and he felt a strange burning sensation in his arms and face. He stumbled, falling to one knee and his combed hair grew disheveled and matted with dirt, dropping in front of his eyes. Trem tied to brush it back but he felt weak and lowered his hand to steady himself.

Do not strain, Trem. Even here, your body is somewhat broken.

Trem forced his head up. Kurven hovered before him like some strange specter, bright, fiery blue eyes amidst a brilliant blue cloud. Trem nearly collapsed as memory washed over him. The sword exploding, the pain in his arms and face, the slashing tears in his legs, Rath carrying him. All the memories flooded back and he gasped in realization. He was alive, but not awake.

"Kurven," he managed, "where am I? Are we beyond the caverns?"

Yes, the god spoke calmly, *Rath carried you out safely. You are now in Southron, making your way to his home city, Yulinar, the same one that Ghost seeks. There you will also be healed of your wounds, for while Diaga and the servant of Endoth were able to save your life, they cannot completely repair the damage Gend did to you.*

Trem digested the flood of information. "The others, they are alive?"

All are well. Your determination and defiance of Balthazain cost you your weapon, a powerful tool, but spared you your life and that of your friends. Had you given in at any point, succumbed to weakness of mind or body, you would have been consumed, and they along with you.

Trem considered Kurven's words as he stood, with great effort, "But to what end? Balthazain was meant to kill me? Break me? Then why steer me away from Delmore by imitating Gerand Oakheart?" Trem steadied himself and focused his gaze on Kurven before him, seeing the dissonance on the edge of his form and the wavering in the clarity of his presence. "Stop hiding behind the masks of others, Betrayer."

As though he were stepping through a doorway, the finely garbed form of the God of Betrayal stepped out of the illusion of Kurven and it faded behind him. Trem stood there, the broken memory of his home around him becoming amplified. The trees drooped, and he could hear the crack of rotting wood as his home began to crumble. Trem closed his eyes and gritted his teeth. This was one of his few fond memories of life; his home before he learned it was not his home. The being before him was trying to break it. He exhaled slowly, purposefully, and tried to suppress the pain and confusion in his battleworn mind. Trem opened his eyes. Balthazain still stood there before him, a smug smile on his face. Yet the half-elf could sense he was not as self-assured as he presented himself.

"Tell me." Trem said firmly.

"Well," Balthazain said smoothly, "you certainly have grown more perceptive, or perhaps less trusting. I would consider both an improvement." The god folded his hands inside the arms of his robe. "But you also nearly fell to a desperate and inept servant of mine, if not for the interference of the Melarrian assassin."

A smooth chuckle escaped the oily goatee as Balthazain stepped off the path, breaking a rotting branch from one of the trees that now oozed with termites black as coal and with carapaces as slick as oil. Balthazain plucked one free and crushed it in his hand. "You see, Trem? You are just like these here, easily dispatched when one wants to, but we did not want you dead just yet."

Trem smirked. "You tried awfully hard to kill me for someone who wanted me alive."

Balthazain thrust his chin forward. "I merely wanted to see the kind of determination you possessed, and leave you with a sign of our encounter."

Trem looked down at his arms then and the burning made sense. Long hot bulging scars on his arms and he could feel the same on his face. Trem ran his hands along the facial swells above his eye and along his cheek. He felt his heart grow fiery, and rage boil over. "You think a few scars on my skin matter to me after what all of you immortals have done to me? You think I care about how I look on the outside? This is how I ought to look, I welcome it."

"Good," Balthazain howled back, his composure broken at last, "it is only the beginning after all. Do you even understand what is at stake here? You are traipsing about with this band of misfits, worrying over petty matters, while my father and his loyal servants work to save your miserable lives."

Trem spat at Balthazain. "You truly live up to your title. You expect me to believe this was some form of test to turn me to your cause and that of Neroth? By rending my body and allowing Gend to dispatch me piece by piece?"

Balthazain ripped another branch down and hurled it at Trem. "Wise once again! No, I did want you to die. My father believes you are a being of great potential, a demigod that can rise with us to face the danger threatening your world. But I see through you. I know your past." The rage receded and Balthazain became oddly calm and somber. "I was not always the God of Betrayal, I was once the God of Faith. But you," his finger jutted accusingly at Trem, "you and all your kind twisted the gift of mortal life and found dark corners of yourselves to bring forth in such quantities that they changed not just you, but us as well. Do you think I relish my duties? I despise them, but they are necessary. You, you are unwilling to embrace what you are and to do what must be done. Yes, I would have been pleased to have you die, but in this realm perhaps I can do what Gend could not."

The dreamscape spun and Trem remembered the cautionary words of Kurven, understood the threat Balthazain posed to him, but even in his weakened state he felt a surge of immense determination. He was done running and being bullied. Trem smiled cruelly. "This is my home. You are not welcome."

The dreaming world shifted, spiraling and bending as Trem unmade it. Balthazain stumbled, trying to regain his footing and failing, feeling off balance and incredibly confused. He reached out, tried to step towards the half-elf, but he faltered and nearly collapsed. Balthazain found purchase for a moment and cried out, "You will learn, Trem Waterhound! One way or another, you will come to understand the futility of your efforts and the depths of true woe!"

Cursing the defiance of his foe, Balthazain relented and pulled himself out of the dream and back to his own realm. Trem relaxed his hold over the dreamscape, the effort sending him into deeper and fleeting unconsciousness. He clung to thoughts and images that moved him as he fell out of the dream. This was his memory, not Balthazain's, not anyone's, just his. Trem would lose control of most things in his life it seemed, but not this place, not ever. Closing his eyes, Trem stopped fighting the descent out and away from the dream, released his memory, and floated off into a deep slumber. He was embraced in a total oblivion that was difficult to reach, unless one knew the way.

Epilogue

The teeth worked: gnawing, ripping, rending. The rat and his brood tore at what was left of their rare and sumptuous meal. It had been a long time now with no fresh meat for the writhing rodents. The screaming had made the first few hours of feasting so pleasurable and exhilarating, the rats had worked too quickly and gorged themselves. Now, days later, they worked hard for little results, grinding their incisors against bone hoping to reach the marrow within. The rat turned away, letting his brethren continue the futile effort and wandered down to the entrance of the cell. A light flared down the hall and the rat froze as the illumination rolled forward, rapidly lighting and extinguishing torches bursting to life and winking out almost as quickly as a massive, dark figure came by.

Daerveron strode purposefully forward down his long hallway. He stopped at the cell door to examine the gruesomely dismembered body for a moment, and then moved on into his laboratory. Once within, he scanned the room, moving across it to a large object covered in a great sheet. He pulled back the thin shroud to reveal a great opening shaped like a perfect ring of stone, the circle devoid of any carvings. It was a wonderfully symmetrical piece, but looked like little more than a meager decoration. Daerveron removed his gauntlet and waved his spectral, undead hand before it. The vacuous doorway shimmered and a portal of swirling dark water emerged, held within the frame of stone. After a few moments, one of the Night Cloaks appeared, standing in a rippling watery mirror held within the circle. The being bowed before him and Daerveron settled onto a beaten stool before the strange opening. "Where are they now?"

The shade's otherworldly voice poured through the portal, "They have passed through the caves."

Daerveron snarled, "Alive? All of them?"

"Yes."

Daerveron shot up from his seat and slammed his mortal hand onto the table. "All of them! How is that possible?"

He did not wait for a response but swept his undead hand across the portal frame and whirled to depart the room in a rage as the watery gateway fell in solid chunks and shattered like thin ice across the floor. Daerveron stormed down the hallway and paused at the door to his summoning chamber. Gathering himself, he pushed the door open and stepped inside. Crawling behind him in hopes of finding more food, the rat narrowly squeezed past the closing door. Without any other place to hide in the featureless room the rat hugged the wall of the chamber. Daerveron entered his small circle and tossed a handful of bone dust to the floor, the wall sconces alighting with blue flame as he reached the circle.

The chant took a short time, and the cloud of black smoke dissipated swiftly. Neroth made no pretense of a dramatic entrance as he materialized out of the smoke suddenly and stood before his servant. "Tell me, Daerveron, why did your Night Cloaks fail to kill any of the party before they reached the caverns?"

Daerveron bowed. "My lord, I cannot say. It seems they had the assistance of a being possessing items powered by the essence of light. He disbanded my servants before they could complete their work." The mage paused. "And if I may say, my lord, another was to arrange their demise once I drove them to the caverns. I am not the only one who failed to achieve your goals."

"Oh, quite the contrary."

Daerveron looked to his right and was shocked to see Balthazain standing there. "This is impossible, I did not summon your presence!"

Neroth waved his hand in a sign of peace. "I brought him here. You have done well in your work to bridge the mortal and immortal worlds, Daerveron. Now when I am in your chamber I can manipulate much of it to my liking, and as my power grows here I will be able to affect more and more around me. But for now I merely wish to inform you of how damaging your incompetence has been."

"I had put failsafes in place, should your gambit with the Night Cloaks and Broken fail," Balthazain said mildly, "but my servant and his ally were less reliable than I expected." Balthazain took a step forward and held out his palm, an empty vial hovering above it where Daerveron could see it clearly. "The Melarrian knew much of your servants and how to defeat them, but nonetheless, you did not fail completely. The party did enter the caves and I met this mortal, Trem Waterhound, at last. But I was unable to turn or slay him."

"You were the other waiting for them in the caves? And the second target of my investigation, Waterhound, was with Greymane Squall all along?" Daerveron shook his head in confusion. "How long have you known Trem was among them? Why threaten and cajole me to kill this party if you wanted to try turning Waterhound instead of ending his life?"

Balthazain sighed. "I wanted Waterhound dead." He eyed his dread father askance. "Others thought he might make a useful ally if properly taught through force."

Daerveron was having difficulty containing his anger. "Why keep the truth of the mission from me? Do you doubt my abilities?"

"The demise of the traitorous Napalian was your goal." Neroth waved his hand, preventing Daerveron's protests before they began. "It was important that the rest felt truly threatened and the death of any of their number would have been fruitful."

Balthazain sighed and rubbed his goatee. "Yes, Greymane Squall was the only one you truly needed to eliminate. He has learned much of Yulinar and ancient weapons that he does not need to know. His death, and that of the assassin, would have been useful in preventing them from seeking the Melarrians at all."

Daerveron grew angrier still. "Perhaps if I were privy to more details of my tasks, I might be able to carry out those missions more effectively."

Neroth stepped forward, dangerously close to Daerveron. "You will not forget your place. I gave you life, and I may take it away. What power you have you have through me alone."

Daerveron did not flinch, but he also was wise enough not to respond. The God of Death could not stretch beyond the confines of the circle, but the air in the room crackled as both he and his servant stared threateningly at one another across the invisible wall between them. Balthazain stepped to his father's side. "This is not necessary. The half-elf is broken, and even if they reach Yulinar, the Melarrians are as likely to kill them as they are to offer aid."

Neroth did not break his stare, nor did he draw back from Daerveron. The foul wizard held one hand to his ruined face, covered in its silken wrap, and said quietly, "I will serve you in whatever capacity you ask of me. Tell me what I should do next, and it will be done."

There was no apology or subservience in the voice, but it seemed to satisfy Neroth for the moment. He pulled back from the barrier between him and his summoner and spoke, "The Night Cloaks are no longer needed to the south. What is done is done, and those striving to reach Yulinar are not your concern anymore. Even if they receive help, they are far away and weakened. By the time they discover a means to oppose my conquest it will be too late. You, Daerveron, will see to the defense of Marlpaz and assist Valissa Ulfrunn and Frothgar Konunn with the war in Legocia. As for the particulars of your mission, it is simple enough: crush all resistance remaining on the continent and deliver it to me. I trust that is not too elusive a task for you to grasp?"

Daerveron resisted the urge to bite back and simply bowed. "It shall be done, my lord Neroth."

Without further comment Neroth faded before Daerveron, taking his son with him. For a time, Daerveron stood staring at the space where Neroth had been. He was enraged and would have relished destroying the entire chamber, putting an end to the usage of the portal and his service to Neroth, had he not understood it would have led to his demise. The furious wizard snorted in derision at his own weakness and turned to leave the room. He placed his hands on the great door and heaved it open with unnatural strength.

The rat had waited patiently by the door to flee. The strange presences in the room had made it desperate to return to the brood. As the door opened, it made a break for the laboratory. A raven swept down and ripped the rat from the stone floor, carrying it into the chamber and impaling it on its beak at the center of the circle. The rat died instantly, writhing in death throes on the stone of the summoning chamber. Daerveron let the door go and spun towards the bird, yelling in disgust, "Damn it, Freyan, I told you not to practice that foul habit in my presence!"

The raven shifted and grew into the Broken advisor who wiped blood from his mouth with a sly smile. "I apologize, Daerveron, it is my nature."

Daerveron regained his composure, but shook his head in irritation. "Your nature aside, please refrain from doing that in my chamber."

Freyan smiled. "As you wish." the strange visitor cocked his head at the mage. "Did your meeting not go so well?"

Daerveron crossed his arms. "I am not a mere apprentice, nor am I a fool. I should know the implications of what I am doing."

Freyan approached him slowly. "And you do. Our true master has been clear with us. You must continue to serve the ignorant fool in his war to cow these mortals, and when the time is right we will have all that should be ours. And unlike your other master who gives you only harsh words and accusations of failure, I bring you a gift."

Freyan pulled forth a tome from his robes. It was a massive book, black leather sheets stitched together at broken seams over the covers. The spine was stiffened by long bones bound together with a strange sinew of grey. On its cover, there was only a deep imprint of a smiling skull surrounded by a ring of ice. Daerveron could not believe his eyes, he reached out slowly with both hands and Freyan laid it carefully into them. The undead mage looked at his cohort. "Is this the book?"

Freyan smiled deviously. "Would I give it to you if it was not?"

Daerveron ran his mortal hand over the cover reverently. "Am I to use this?"

Freyan stepped backward, leaving Daerveron with his prize, and nodded. "Our master says it will take time to study, but once you have the knowledge within, your power will be nearly limitless."

Daerveron met the eyes of his counterpart and smiled victoriously. "I will begin reading it immediately."

The nondescript man in plain robes stepped back. "Very good. If you could open the door for me, I have places to be."

Daerveron moved to the door, but paused with his grip on the large handle. "Tell me, Freyan, where was the book?"

The strange man smiled. "Within the secret royal library of the Angladaics, of course."

The undead mage digested this strange revelation. "Of course."

Daerveron heaved the massive door open, and Freyan's raven form flew through it and down the hall. The wizard stood at the entrance to his casting chamber and ran his hand over the book once more. He glanced back into the summoning room and sighed when he saw the corpse of the rat. Daerveron strode over and picked up the broken form, holding it in his palm he examined it. A strange thought went through his mind. Balancing the heavy book in his spectral hand, he set the corpse back on the ground. He opened the tome, flipping though the pages slowly until he reached what he sought.

The language was strange and archaic, but Daerveron could read it with some care. He ran a finger underneath the writing slowly, hearing the words in his mind as he went. Once he found the part he was looking for, he stopped and read it over several times. Then he balanced the book before his eyes and held his hand over the corpse, reciting the words in a chant that grew louder and louder. The body of the rat began to glow with a strange green light and rose off the floor. Daerveron increased the speed of his chanting and the glow grew stronger, until it was so bright he could hardly see the rat's body. Then, it winked out.

Two unearthly red orbs glowed out from the floor by Daerveron's feet. They moved side to side about the chamber, taking in the sights around them. Daerveron smiled and snapped the book shut. He strode to the entrance and opened it, letting the torn and bloody body of the rat precede him. Daerveron followed it out into the hallway and then to the laboratory. He swept the scrolls and books on his reading desk to the floor and slammed the new tome down in their place. Opening it to the first page he waved a hand to light the nearest wall torch as brightly as possible and sat down to read.

The rat skittered back to the brood. His world had gone strangely black and then returned, but was somehow different than it was before. Through a dim, red haze, the rat watched the large figure before it, feeling a strange kinship to the form it had never shared before. The rat smelled the brood down the hallway and quickened its run towards it. They were still there in the cell, writhing over the corpse of the dead prisoner. The rat crept in quietly, but the others smelled him, smelled the change in him. They stopped the feast and a few slowly crawled down to investigate.

The first one came near the strange new rat and sniffed him. There was the unmistakable odor of death on him, yet the rat seemed to move. The brood knew dead things did not move; yet this member of their clan was acting as though he was still alive. A more curious rat crawled closer and sniffed the face of his companion. The rat, through the red haze of his new eyes, saw his family before him, but there was no sense of unity or kinship between them. Instead, the rat was overtaken with a sudden raging hunger. The jaws of the rat opened and snapped forward, closing on the face of his curious brethren.

Daerveron smiled at his desk as he heard the shrieks of pain and horror from the rats in the cell. He stroked the pages of his book lovingly, and continued to study the dark secrets within.

Appendices

I. The Godly Realms, Dreamscape, and Teth-tenir

The connection between mortals and immortals is complicated and begins with the construction of the Godly Planes, Teth-tenir, and the strange intersection of those two worlds that is found in the realm of dreams. One can think of the Godly Realms as a series of rooms, connected by various hallways, which all lead back to one chamber where the Archway Temple sits. This central room is neutral in origin, the place where the First Gods all emerged and worked together to craft the mortal realm of Teth-tenir and its features. The Archway Temple, and the area around it, is a construction that allows for the gods to meet in a place where no harm can be brought to one another, advantageous for the sorting out of differences between them.

The "hallways" and "rooms" of the Godly Realms exist only in the metaphorical sense. There are no actual physical boundaries in the immortal world except as composed by the builders. Each god has total control over their individual realm, and the size of their home is mostly an illusion, as there is no physical confinement. There are also varying degrees of power as it relates to the realms. The level of power is determined by two factors: the age and strength of the god and the faithfulness and following of mortals who worship them. Thus, Neroth, the God of Death, is always one of the most powerful gods and his realm is quite expansive, while Pavaron, the God of History, is less powerful, and always will be regardless of how strong his following among mortals is, because of his lesser status.

For mortals to make sense of the godly hierarchy the image of hallways and rooms is useful, if technically inaccurate. From the realm holding the Archway Temple extend fourteen hallways to the respective realms of the fourteen sitters. From those fourteen extend further hallways to their "children." It is useful to think of the relative power of each god by the distance they are from the central realm, though many illustrations of the Godly Realms also use the relative size of the realm's representation to show the strength of each deity. Further "hallways" also extend to the realms of deceased mortals who have been welcomed by a deity to whom they were particularly faithful in life, and the immortal allows the deceased to visit their god or goddess in their own "home" when they desire. For those who die and are brought to the afterlife by Neroth so that they do not wander forever in emptiness, their realm is connected to the site of the Archway Temple, but they rarely journey from it. For most, the Dead Realms act as a strange eternity of near-life, often with few companions even among the other residents of that strange place. Those who find themselves in the Dead Realms are often tied to their mortal existence so strongly that they cannot perceive the immortal planes clearly, and thus do not totally understand what has happened to them. Neroth often compares this existence to a form of perpetual dreaming.

All of the Godly Realms are constructions of the immortals within them. Any physical limitations to a space, such as a closed door, narrow walls, or low ceilings, are merely constructs used to create the illusion of order. This is comforting to some deities and especially natural for most mortals. Still, it is important to remember that the entire physical limitation of the Godly Realms is pure illusion. There is no limit to what a god can create within their sphere of influence except their own power and belief in what they can accomplish. Thus, a god can form a great castle or tower from nothing, but they could just as easily exist in floating emptiness and without a physical body. For most, this is too akin to the emptiness, fear, and isolation of the worlds beyond their own and thus physical barriers such as homes and natural spaces are a calming presence.

The mortal realm of Teth-tenir is described in great detail in the histories and geographies of that world, which will not be discussed here. The most important aspects of Teth-tenir as they apply to the other realms are the interrelationship between mortals and gods, the constructed and self-enforcing laws of physics that apply to the mortal world, and the limited but expandable capacity by which mortals can use the powers of the immortals in the form of magic. The co-dependence of god and mortal is important. The strength of mortal belief in a god empowers the deity, and the most faithful of mortals receive the most attention of their patron and greater powers for their devout service. The true priests of a god become capable of greater feats within that god's dominion the longer and more ardently they study what the god represents. In contrast, wizards or mages and mortals who have studied the ancient language of the immortals and learned to work some small degree of their creative power through invoking it. This does not require faith in a deity, but diligent study of the language and dexterous motions of hand required to will the existence of arcane power. In these two ways, mortals are able to call upon the powers of those who created them and, in some ways, bend the laws that dictate what is possible in the mortal world.

These laws of physics were composed to keep the world of Teth-tenir self-maintaining and are identical to the laws of physics present on our own terrestrial earth. This is an important limitation when comparing the world of mortals with that of gods or even the dreamscape. The only limitation a god has is his or her imagination and raw power. As mentioned before, the physical constraints of the godly realms are illusions or constructs. They help keep the world of the immortals neatly organized and comprehensible. This varies depending on the deity; for example Kurven is notorious for forgoing almost all semblance of physical space and, unlike his peers, does not bother with any but the most rudimentary of physical forms.

Between the two realms of gods and mortals is the dream world, which is only loosely understood by mortal and immortal alike. This realm is one that overlaps the other two and maintains some of the laws and aspects of both. The person or god within the dream can manipulate it, though their understanding of the fact that they are in the dreamscape and have control over it greatly influences that ability. Most gods are fairly adept at this manipulation, having the ability to perceive the existence of all three realms more clearly than most mortals. Some mortals spend a great deal of time in the practice of dream control, especially those who worship Morphus. Those who do are often able to command extensive power within the world of dreams and can communicate with gods there directly. Mortals without training are still able to take command of a dream and alter it in significant ways, but they lack the control to truly command the realm and bend all aspects of it to their will. When confronted with a god, most mortals are inferior in power and unable to resist alterations of the dream world brought forth by the deity, though they can escape the god's influence merely by traveling away from them or shutting off their awareness of the deity's presence. In other words, by convincing him or herself that interactions are not real, a mortal is shielded from the effects. The more one believes in the power of the dream world, the stronger their influence, but also the greater their vulnerability.

This brings up the issue of movement between the three planes. The dreamscape is largely considered a kind of "bridge" realm, where both gods and mortals can interact. However, in both cases it is not a full extension of the entire being. The gods can send a projection of themselves, with a limited degree of their power, into dreams. Similarly, mortals can project a part of themselves into the dream world and the more they actively seek out the dreamscape the more powerful the projection becomes. This act is dangerous, especially for mortals, as harm done to the projection is reflected on their physical bodies. This is also true for gods, but given the immense power of immortals and the relatively lesser demand required for them to enter the dreamscape the danger is usually minor. The exception is when confronted with another deity bent on harming them, which could theoretically result in the destruction of an immortal. This is the primary reason why, while considered a powerful tool for interaction between mortal and immortal, the wisest of both fear the dream world.

The methods by which communication and movement can occur between the plane of the gods and the plane of Teth-tenir are many and varied. The most common movement is that of deceased mortals to the Dead Realms, guided by Neroth, as is his duty as the

God of Death. Once, it was possible for the gods to come to Teth-tenir as avatars of their greater, true forms, and bestow powers and wisdom on their subjects, but this ceased to be possible during a period of immortal conflict little understood and referred to only as the Immorbellum. Now, the gods are only able to communicate with mortals in their hallowed temples or in the dreamscape, and only then if they can locate the particular mortal in question, a task made much more difficult since the Immorbellum. For their part, mortals have some particular uses for the fluidity of movement between the realms that are commonly practiced. The most common is mortals attempting to seek out the dead in dreams and communicate with them there, as those who are aware of their death become cognizant of the ability to enter the dreamscape and interact with the living. Usually this amounts to nothing more than reassurance for a love one left behind, but it can also be used by dead or living alike to impart information.

II. The Napalian Empire: A Brief Overview

Outsiders often regard the Napalians, as a people, to be one culture. While they did undergo a bonding during the famed Unification of Napal, no one country in all of Teth-tenir boasts more unique orders and sub-cultures within its larger holdings. The many houses that rule over the vast lands of the region somewhat explain this diversity, but there are many aspects of the Napalians that may be considered shared traits: toughness, familial and regional pride, and complex social constructs defined by loyalty and cultural or tangible debts of various types.

The northern region of Legocia is an especially hard and unforgiving place. The Evenlar and Auvandaran elves, in the northern stretches of Westia, deal with the presence of cold and storms on a significant scale, but their cultural link to magic and its applications to everyday life mitigate much of the hardship. Additionally, their regions, while snow-covered much of the year, are significantly less dangerous. The northerners of the Legocian continent contend with terrible storms and rending winds that blow off the jagged rocks of the Dragonscale Mountains as well as trolls, orogs, and all manner of deadly creatures wandering the cold lands and as equally desperate to survive as their human counterparts. The people of the north also have an internalized fear of arcane magic, which prevents them from discovering methods that might help them resist or alleviate some of the brutality of living in their region. However, for the Napalians at least, all of these challenges double as advantages. The people of the Napalian Empire are rarely targeted by outside forces and use their environment to their advantage in war, making them a difficult people to conquer in their own lands. It is precisely because of the danger their homeland poses to those who live there that they chose to make it their own, and for a time no one else in Teth-tenir seemed too interested in laying claim to the northern region of Legocia.

That inherent toughness, ground into the people of Napal by their long years there in the cold and dark, is also what binds them together in fierce loyalty to one another. Familial ties are of incredible importance to Napalians. Most recognize this in the sixteen major houses that make up the Napalian's most powerful thanes, but even the lowliest of families value loyalty to their kin above almost everything else. Secondary to blood ties; there are the connections between Napalians based on the regions they reside in. People from Hethegar or Tianis may be loyal to the High Thane in Napal City and have good relationships with those in Glaciar, but they identify and regard themselves as men and women of Hethegar or Tianis above all else. These regional identities are what keep the many distant settlements of Napal strong. In the cold and dead of winter, the tightly packed homes, small islands of civilization in the wastes of the north, band together to ensure everyone contributes to their survival. While it is true each of the houses and their followers may handle law and order within their domains slightly differently, the unifying concept of their ability to persist is their reliance on one another.

The complexity of Napalian loyalty, by blood or by oath, is difficult for outsiders to understand. A man who seeks shelter from another family incurs a debt that is taken very seriously. Moreover, it is the responsibility of his family to not only to repay that debt when called upon, but also to record and pass down both the debt and the record of exchange between him and his benefactor. These exchanges, often appearing to be minor to outsiders, are of the utmost importance to a Napalian. If a member of one family feeds that of another and the act is not returned in kind when requested, it can lead to violence that escalates rapidly. This is due to the central philosophy of the Napalians, which is that resources are scarce and the world is deadly, but caring for others in equal exchange ensures the continual survival of most. This is why orphanages exist in the major settlements, the authority of the nation regards the raising and education of the orphaned to be a debt they owe to them that will be returned in kind. This is also why theft and other crimes are punished so harshly in Napal, often with death or the amputation of limbs. In the north a debt has to be paid, one way or another.

The easiest representation of loyalty to understand, for outsiders at least, is that of the housekarls. Each thane of the major houses gives those who will swear loyalty and military service to them the title of housekarl. Along with that title comes land, annual payment in the form of necessary supplies or precious materials, and the support of both the thane and the housekarl's fellows. Housekarls are usually bound to a house for life, thus one who swore to follow House Kaldegar in the earliest days of the Napalian Empire has bequeathed that duty to his or her descendants forever, barring some significant violation of trust by the thane of Kaldegar or their family. Because of this, there are often feuds between housekarls of major houses, though these are usually minor and more boasting or bravado than violent, but occasionally things boil over to true fighting that, if unchecked, can border on outright war.

Religion in Napal is also treated rather differently than it is in most of Teth-tenir. In the nations and cities of the rest of the world, temples are commonplace and the idea of designated times for worship is a normalized practice. In Napal, there are no structures that could truly be considered temples, but rather areas of the nation that contain shrines to the various gods. Due to the connection that the Napalians have to nature and cold, they worship a collection of deities they refer to as the Gods of Winter: Venna, Ryst, and Shotima. In addition, many who make their living on the cold waves of the Longwater or Frostsea pray to Liridon for safety on the oceans. The most telling example of the difference in religious observance among the Napalians is in their worship of Shayatha, who is known to most of Teth-tenir as the Goddess of the Moon and Darkness. In the north however, they regard Shayatha as the Goddess of the Hunt, and she is especially revered in Hethegar, where forays into the Whitewood are common and often necessary to supply enough sustenance to make it through the winter months. This interpretation of the goddess, almost completely unique to the Napalians, is but one example of how they see and interpret the world a bit differently than their fellow mortals.

Most of the Napalian houses share dominion over a settlement, though some of the more isolated towns have only one thane acting as head of the local government. Most of these have been loosely connected to the other towns of the north, the exceptions being the three most independent families. The only settlement west of the Dragonscale Mountains, Sheerwater Cove along the coast, belongs to House Erefoss, whose descendants were cast out of Glaciar by House Squall and harbor a long-simmering distaste for the greater Napalian Empire. To the northeast, House Jarth and House Uratha reign over their respective holdings in the Everwinter Isles, largely removed from the affairs of the mainland. The other houses are considered the true members of the Napalian Empire, though House Erefoss has been incorporated into the realm at various points, often against their will.

The founding of Napal, as a region and culture if not necessarily a united nation, began with the feud over the City of the Four Hills, later renamed Napal City. In this conflict, several minor houses, including the Squalls, who founded Glaciar; Varnns, who founded Winter's Folly; and Ulfrunns, who founded Tianis; would leave the region to establish their own independent settlements. The remaining families of Kaldegar, Holt, Dolg, and Konunn would become the ruling powers of Napal City and, some time later, Thane Vladar Konunn would lead a campaign to unite the north as one nation. The effort was successful, but not in the way that Vladar had intended, as it was not he who would be named the first High Thane of the Napalian Empire.

In addition to the houses whose origins can be traced back to the City of the Four Hills, there are those who took greater initiative in the earliest days of the nation and moved beyond the relatively temperate, for Napal at least, region where the capital was established and founded their own towns. There is Lowinter to the east and near the Pillars of Light, which is overseen by House Furegar and House Hlunn. House Hethegar rules over the city that bears their name alongside House Fang, north of the eastern edge of the Whitewood. Finally, House Gale and House Tempest maintain the town of Crestwind, north of the Dragonscales and next to the Gulf of Thunder. Each of these houses, after the Unification, became a part of the greater Napalian government and has a say in the appointment of the High Thane as well as the laws of their land. Moreover, the Napalian Empire tends to support the independence of her disparate parts and is sometimes seen as more of a loosely bound nation of city-states rather than a truly singular entity. This interpretation is supported by the history of independent rule maintained by some families, like Uratha and Jarth.

The fall of the Naplian Empire to the Nerothian invaders led by Wolfbane, and aided by traitorous factions within their own ranks, most notably House Konunn and House Erefoss, was a great blow to the proud nation and her people's sense of honor and independence. Despite the history of disagreements and resistance to true cooperation among the houses, the Napalians have always believed themselves to be united by their culture and values. The betrayal of Greymane Squall and the orchestration of Wolfbane's conquest of their nation was a shock to all and left deep scars, both physical and political, on the people of the north.

III. The Kingdom of Angladais: A Brief Overview

Angladais is a nation built on the people's powerful faith in the gods, specifically Paladinis, the God of Honor. In the earliest days of the nation, the majority of people lived on rural farms or in small cabins near the thick and dangerous woods of Silverleaf Forest. Over time, they began to experience dark dreams and visions, connections to the Forgotten imprisoned beneath the ruins that would later be reformed into the city of Alderlast. The citizens' prayers for aid brought the sympathy of Paladinis, who handed down a divine set of laws for the people to follow that would protect them from the influence of the Forgotten. The adoption of those laws sparked a lengthy civil war in the Cloud Peak Basin ending in the victory of Cerestus Angladais, the chosen servant to Paladinis. His name became synonymous with the nation, and though he produced no heir of his own his powerful allies, and some of his foes, during the war assumed the roles of the Highlords. These families formed the eight noble houses of the capitol city of Alderlast and from their ranks a new king or queen is chosen to rule for the entirety of their life.

Despite its reputation as bastion of good and righteousness, the true fabric of Angladaic society is marked by strict and often brutal adherence to their faith as well as clear divisions between social class and rank. One of the more subtle markers of this contrast is the naming of families and individuals. The Highlords, or Highladies when the position is filled by a woman, all have ostentatious and dramatic names that go back to the founding of the nation, while the common people are expected to be named more humbly. Indeed, it is a common point of conversation between Angladaics as to whether or not parents have given their son or daughter a name that is too grand for their station and place within the kingdom and might be a sign of hubris or overreaching of station.

The Angladaics established the Angladaic Code, bound and collected as The Book of the Code, an extensive collection of laws and dictations handed down from Paladinis himself to Cerestus and his followers. In Alderlast in particular, the Code is incredibly important to the daily life of every person, providing expectations and social standards for every citizen from peasant to ruler. The major cities and towns outside of Alderlast are also adherent to the code, but more independent in their management of daily life and enforcement of it. The Code is enforced and adapted as necessary by the Highlord of Hawking House with input from his or her peers. The Hawkings are just one of the eight Highlord Houses, each responsible for some significant aspect of Angladaic life. The Highlords each maintain control over one of the eight districts of Alderlast and from their ranks the king or queen of the nation is selected and advised by the others. Through this organization the nation is maintained and balance of power between the Highlords is supposed to be preserved, but some Highlords possess greater influence than others due to the aspect of Angladaic civilization they oversee.

Since the worship of Paladinis is so central to the nation, priests play an especially dominant role in the country's politics. Highlords of Hladic have traditionally held a great deal of sway over events in Angladais, though they rarely ascend to the throne. Most Hladic Highlords use their influence within the church to dictate the actions of their peers, and no king or queen of the nation has ever done well that has crossed the reigning Highlord or Highlady Hladic. Similarly, Highlords from Bwemor command the army and therefore the maintenance of peace within the realm and often use this as leverage to get what they want, though their power is often offset by Highlords from Calavar who command the paladins, holy soldiers in service to Paladinis that are nigh unstoppable in battle. Even the less militant or legislative Highlord families play the political game with their influence over important facets of daily life such as agriculture, commerce, history, and city planning. Alderlast, despite its popular reputation as a beacon of Angladaic greatness, is more accurately the seat of political intrigue and machination.

The Sword

As mentioned, the lands of the kingdom outside Alderlast experience her influence less frequently. Near the Pillars of Light, the twin towns of Beroh and Dunagen function as mining and trade centers, with the administrative offices of Beroh having the closest connection to the Highlords, as overseers from Xarinth issue edicts on the growth and progress of farmlands in the Cloud Peak Basin. Dunagen, being the only mining town in the entire nation, has something of its own independence and influence within Angladais handed down by Cerestus during the unification of the kingdom. Supplying the metal for armor and weapons as well as more practical construction work, the lesser houses of Dunagen are both powerful and wealthy and largely resented by their neighbors in the more working-class town of Beroh.

But both of those towns are consider fairly backwater compared to Trinalith Port, a town constructed in the cliffs of the eastern edge of the kingdom that serves as both a fishing village and customs port for importing precious items from afar. The Angladaics are, as a nation, isolationist and self-sufficient. However, they do import rare items or materials that cannot be found in the Cloud Peak Basin. As such, there is a great deal of money to be made in Trinalith Port and it is from this small city that the Highlords of Vendile and Xarinth emerged and still hold a small enclave of distant cousins that reign there. The rest of the nation is primarily farmland, and the fertile valley of Cloud Peak Basin is more than able to supply every Angladaic with ample food. Throughout most of Angladais' history, the kingdom has been a peaceful and pleasant place to live.

Much of the prosperity and peace found in Angladais comes from her aggressively isolationist approach to the rest of the world. Angladaic forces have campaigned in regions immediately surrounding her borders to bring order and safety to those living there, but those campaigns are often brief and limited. The Angladaics value the preservation of their pious society over all else, including expansion and dominion of lesser kingdoms. This has led to them representing a mysterious, but usually benevolent, presence in Legocia, welcomed by their neighbors though rarely seen. Yet, while the Angladaics have been known to venture into other nation's territories uninvited, they will not allow any incursion into their own lands even by traders and travelers without express permission granted through the Highlords themselves. This is almost impossible to obtain and very limited even if one is granted admission to the kingdom, with most only being allowed to journey to Trinalith Port or, under rare circumstances, to Beroh and Dunagen.

The Angladaics have been able to enforce their borders effectively because of the natural defenses present. The Pillars of Light, immense and sheer cliffs that tower over the northern edge of their lands, provide only a narrow road into the kingdom that is monitored by paladins and soldiers on its southern side. The mountains extending around the western border give way to Silverleaf Forest, but the trees and undergrowth in that part of the wood are so thick and dark that few dare to walk among them and most become lost. Great vertical cliffs ranging from four hundred to seven hundred feet in height and almost impossible to climb even with advanced tools or arcane magic dominate the eastern edge of the nation. In short, the country is tightly sealed and entry is available only to those who are invited. Even those who manage to slip into Angladais rarely go more than a day before being apprehended and exiled. It is through this harsh maintenance of their lands that the Angladaics have been able to preserve their way of life and remain steadfast in their service to Paladinis and his allies among the gods.

A last note about Angladais, particular to the Code and Paladinis's watchful eye over his chosen people: arcane magic is strictly outlawed. Where most crimes in the nation will result in imprisonment or exile, the practice of arcane magic is met with swift and decisive judgment and execution. Paladinis was well aware of the danger the Forgotten beneath Alderlast presented to the people of Angladais, and it was made very clear in the Code that the powers of the arcane were to be feared and hunted if possible. To that end, there have been a few trials of those in Angladais who showed arcane affinity, most of which ended in quiet executions away from the public eye. However, many suspect that there are some with an attunement towards arcane magic within the kingdom that remain in hiding. This would fit with the general undertone of the incredibly pious nation, for other "crimes" such as infidelity, adultery, homosexuality, and pre-marital sex are considered an affront to Paladinis himself and cause for exile or, on rare occasions, harsher punishments.

About the Author

T.H. (Trevor Howard) Paul is a private secondary school literature teacher at Hebron Academy in Hebron, Maine. T.H. has lived most of his life in Maine, though he did attend Wheaton College in Massachusetts and spent time living in Germany and the People's Republic of China.

T.H. started working on the Legacy Chronicle when he was a freshman in high school, tasked with writing a serial story by his freshman English teacher, Ross Markonish. That story blossomed into a lengthier book, a deepening mythology, and even spawned his own variation on popular tabletop role-playing games, which was dubbed *Ascension* by one of his good friends and players in Tianjin, PRC.

T.H. lives on the campus of Hebron Academy with his wife, Molly, and their dog, Zoe. When not writing he enjoys playing ice hockey, board and video games, drinking tea, and hoarding Legos he swears are for that aforementioned tabletop RPG he runs sometimes.

This is his first novel and series; built from over fifteen years of tinkering, rewriting, frustration, and hope.

Made in the USA
Middletown, DE
04 May 2016